Frazetta

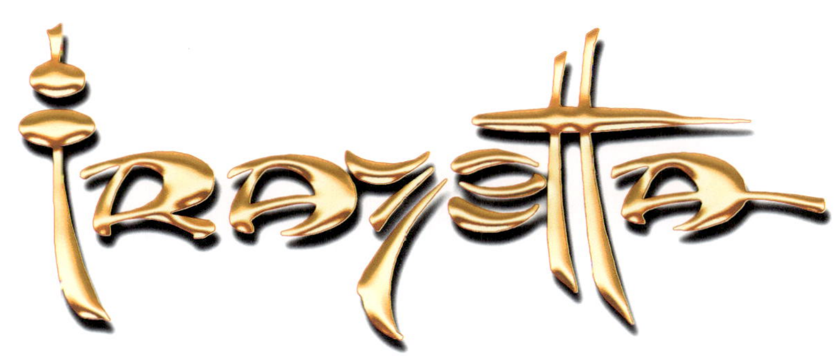
Frazetta

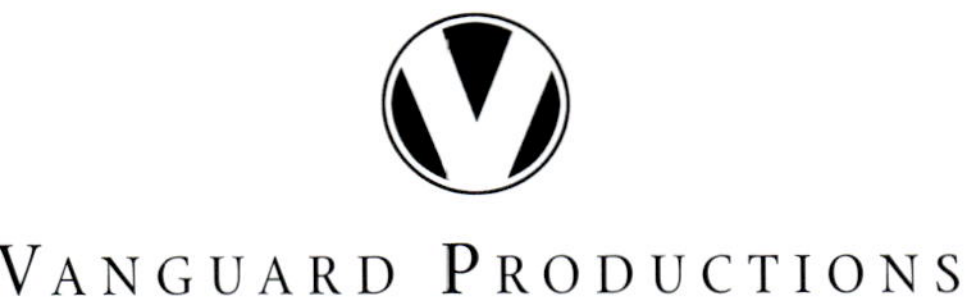
Vanguard Productions

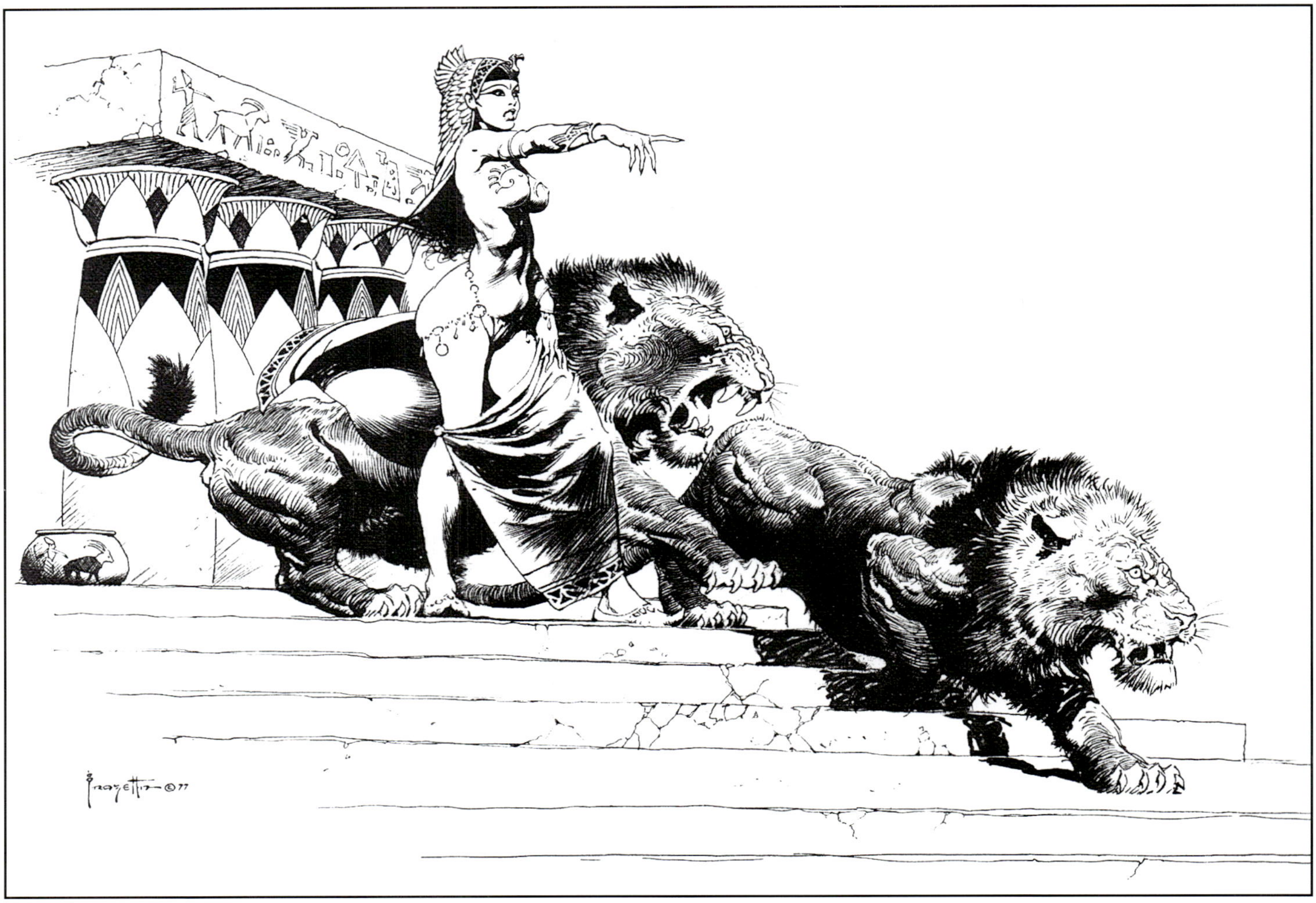

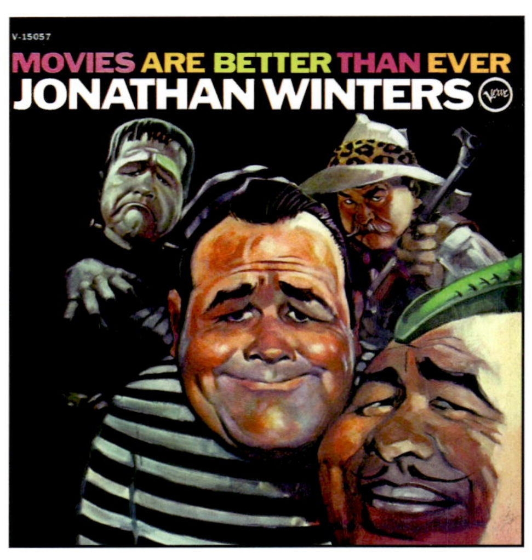
V-15057
MOVIES ARE BETTER THAN EVER
JONATHAN WINTERS
Verve

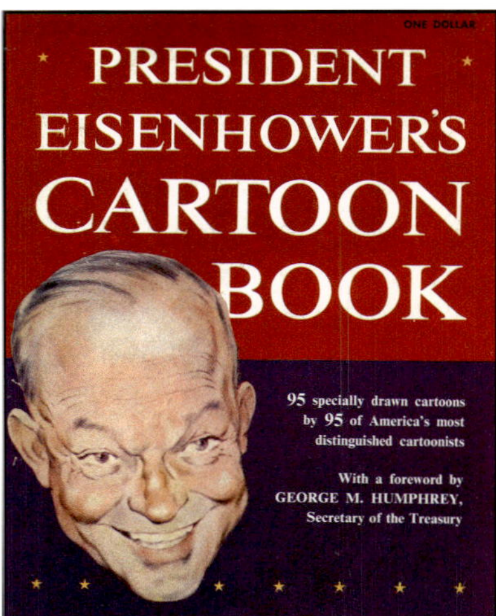
ONE DOLLAR
PRESIDENT
EISENHOWER'S
CARTOON
BOOK
95 specially drawn cartoons
by 95 of America's most
distinguished cartoonists
With a foreword by
GEORGE M. HUMPHREY,
Secretary of the Treasury

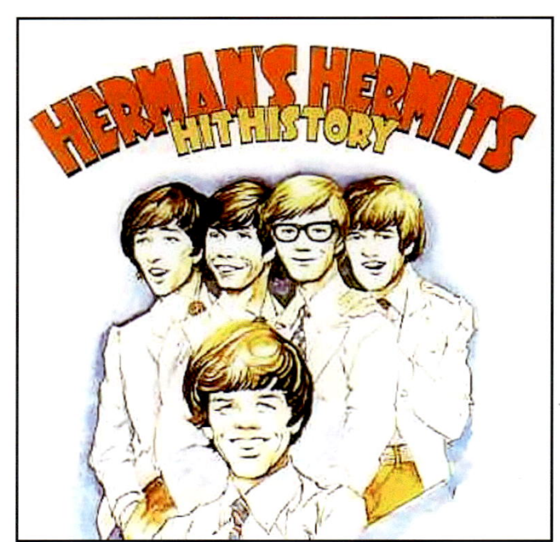
HERMAN'S HERMITS
HIT HISTORY

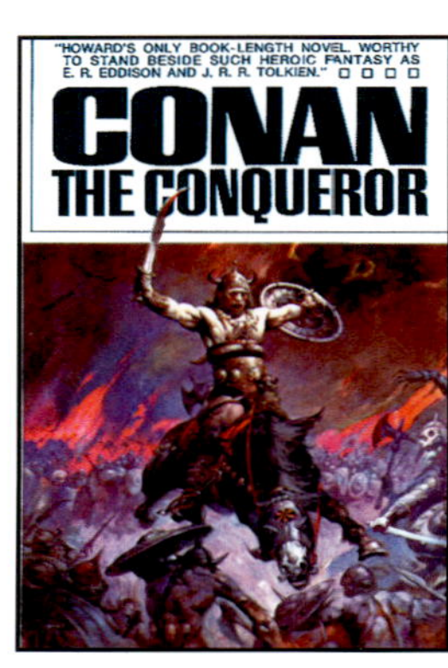
"HOWARD'S ONLY BOOK-LENGTH NOVEL. WORTHY
TO STAND BESIDE SUCH HEROIC FANTASY AS
E. R. EDDISON AND J. R. R. TOLKIEN."
CONAN
THE CONQUEROR

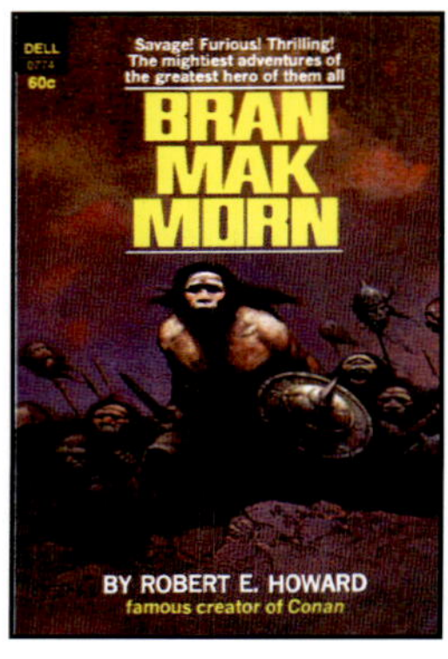
DELL
60c
Savage! Furious! Thrilling!
The mightiest adventures of
the greatest hero of them all
BRAN
MAK
MORN
BY ROBERT E. HOWARD
famous creator of Conan

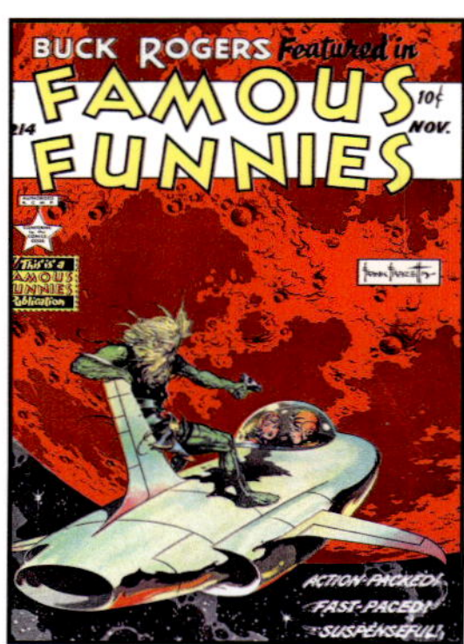
BUCK ROGERS Featured in
FAMOUS
FUNNIES
10¢
214
NOV.
ACTION-PACKED!
FAST-PACED!
SUSPENSEFUL!

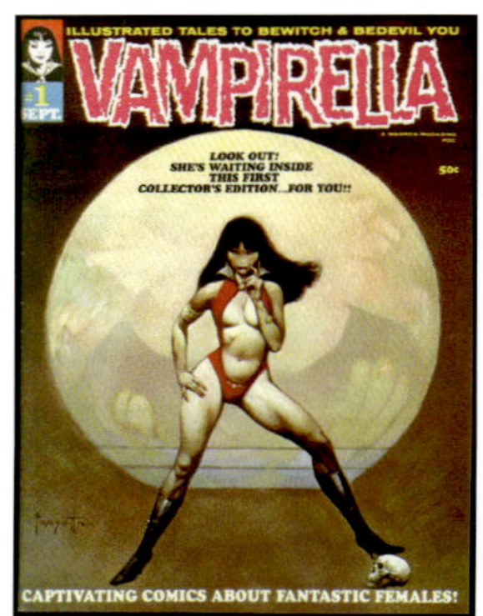
ILLUSTRATED TALES TO BEWITCH & BEDEVIL YOU
VAMPIRELLA
1
SEPT.
LOOK OUT!
SHE'S WAITING INSIDE
THIS FIRST
COLLECTOR'S EDITION...FOR YOU!!
CAPTIVATING COMICS ABOUT FANTASTIC FEMALES!

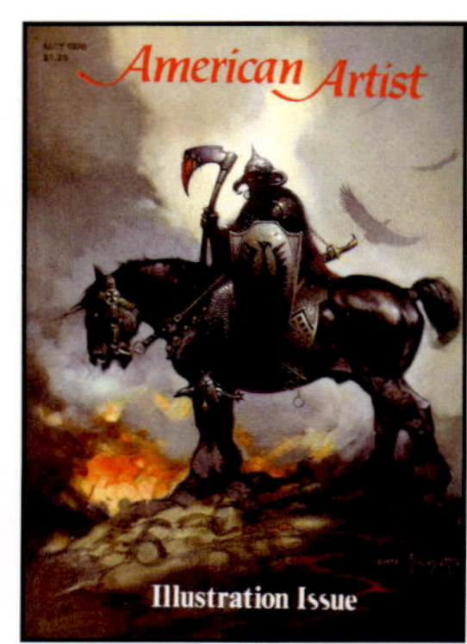
American Artist
Illustration Issue

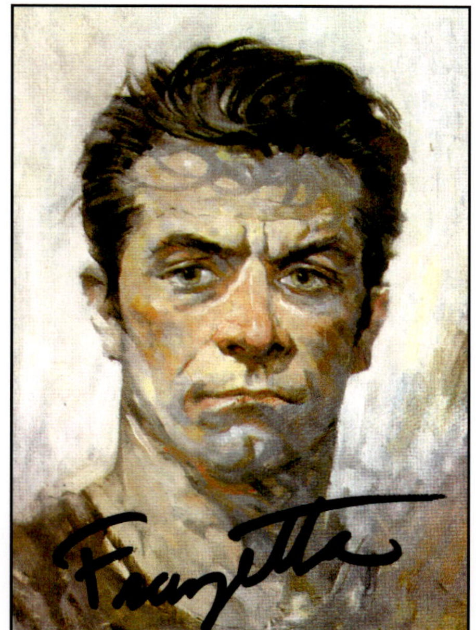

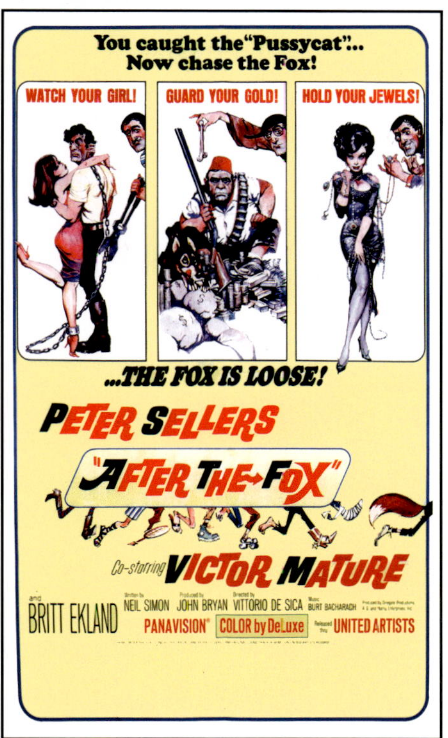

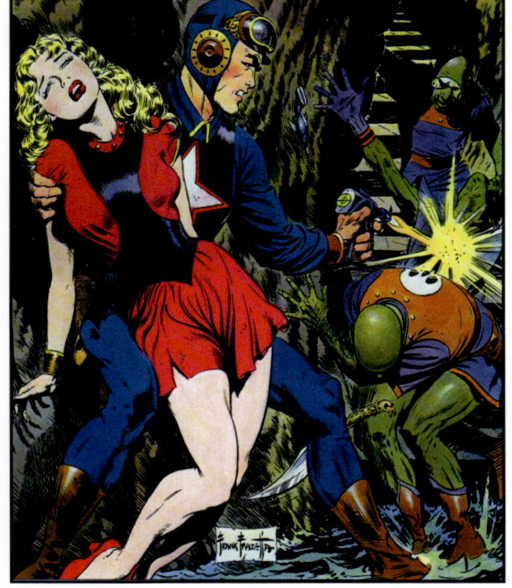

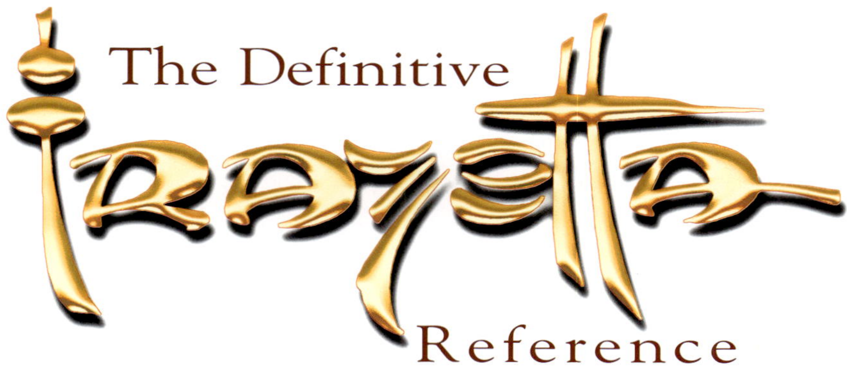

The Definitive Frazetta Reference

JAMES A. BOND

DR. DAVID WINIEWICZ

ANDREW STEVEN

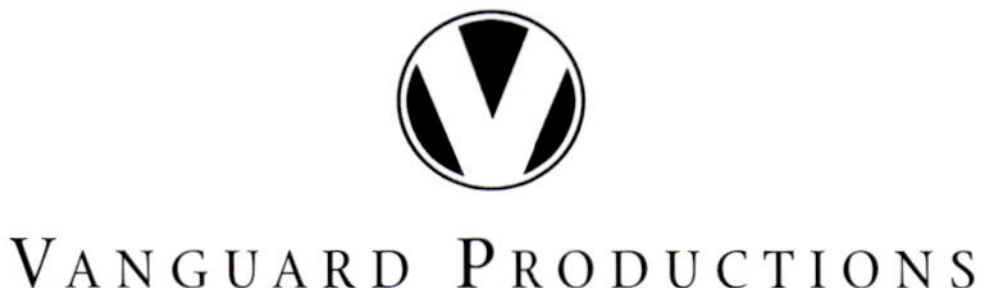

VANGUARD PRODUCTIONS

THE DEFINITIVE FRAZETTA REFERENCE

Compiled by James A. Bond

Contributing editors
Dr. David Winiewicz, Andrew Steven, Dean Motter and J. David Spurlock

Dean Motter – Book design and layout
Andrew E. C. Gaska – Additional production
J. David Spurlock – Art & Design direction

"This book is dedicated to the legions of Frank Frazetta's loyal fans.

Frank's works are indeed great.
But remember, his legendary status cannot exist without the enormous following of those who love his work."

– Ellie Frazetta

The Definitive Frazetta Reference is published, in association with James A. Bond and Dr. David Winiewicz, by Vanguard Productions, with offices in Lakewood New Jersey and Miami Florida. Northeast office and distribution center: 575 Prospect Street, Lakewood NJ 08701.

The majority of the images in this book are courtesy of The Andrew Steven Collection.

OPPOSITE: "*Fang Mail*" illustration for the letters page of *Monster World* magazine (Warren, 1964)

—

Deluxe Slipcased Hardcover ISBN-13: 978-1-934331-10-1 $59.95 (1st printing only)

Regular Hardcover ISBN-13:1 978-1-934331-09-5 $39.95

Trade Paperback: ISBN-13: 978-1-934331-08-8 • ISBN-10: 1-934331-08-2 $29.95

First Printing Halloween, 2008 • 2nd Edition (revised), August, 2010

www.VanguardProductions.net

Printed in China

CONTENTS

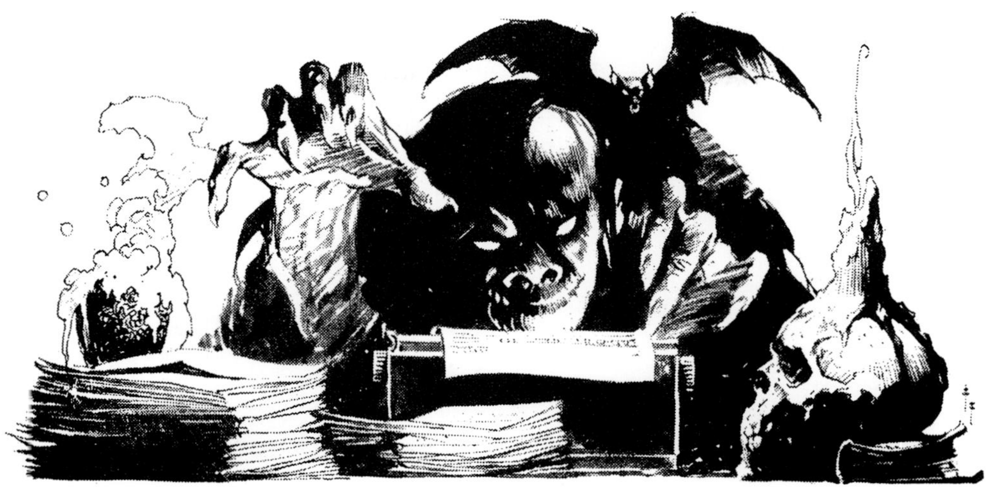

INTRODUCTION

BY *DR. DAVID WINIEWICZ*

DAVID WINIEWICZ is a creative consultant, doctor of Mediaeval Philosophy and a close personal friend to Frank Frazetta. His essays and information grace numerous volumes of work pertaining to the artist. David also boasts a large collection of original Frazetta art including a number of legendary pieces for Canaveral Press.

The Frazetta volume in your hands is a genuine labor-of-love. It started as an idea in the mind of James Bond (Yes, that is his real name). James is a longtime fan and collector of Frazetta's work and he had the dream to assemble a comprehensive and definitive index to the voluminous published works of Frank Frazetta.

He worked quietly for many years, compiling mountains of data for inclusion in the book. He went to several fantasy and science-fiction fan conventions and "talked up" the project. As fate would have it, I had also been keeping a growing index devoted to Frazetta. James and I met and decided to merge our efforts. James and I met with Ellie Frazetta at the Frazetta Museum and presented her a rough copy of the index. Ellie immediately understood the importance and value of such a thorough reference work documenting her husband's great legacy.

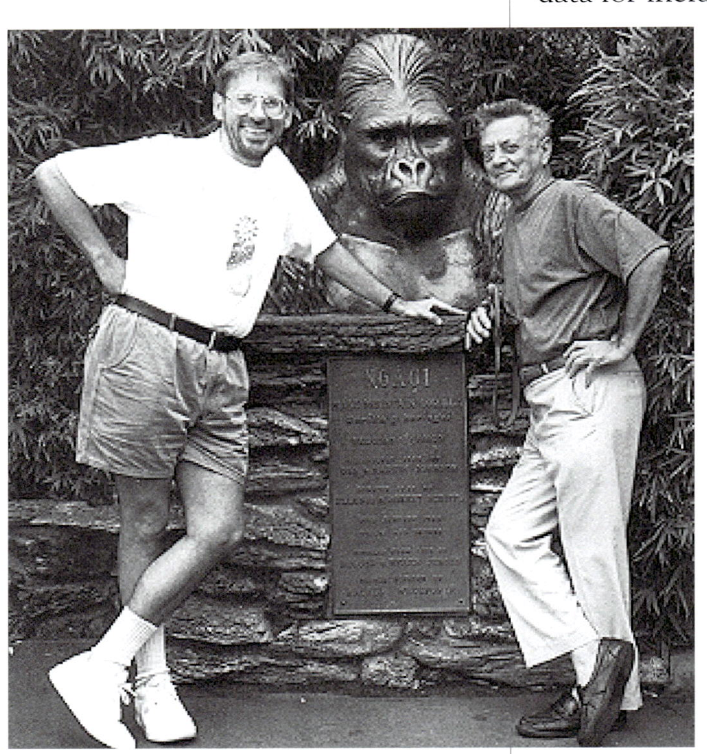

David Winiewicz and Frank Frazetta stand alongside a bust of the mountain gorilla, Ngagi at the San Diego Zoo.

We struck a deal, signed a contract, and then proceeded to bring this book into existence. Ellie introduced James Bond to David Spurlock, the owner/publisher of Vanguard Publishing. Ellie suggested that David would be a great choice to handle the publication. David has a long resume of fine publications including work by Wally Wood, Hal Foster, Al Williamson, and many other notables. As a lifelong Frazetta fan David had the right expertise and proper sensitivities to handle this project properly. Ultimately, David Spurlock was selected to bring this important work into existence. One final piece to the puzzle was solved by bringing in noted collector, Andrew Steven, who owns a vast collection of Frazetta materials spanning Frank's entire career.

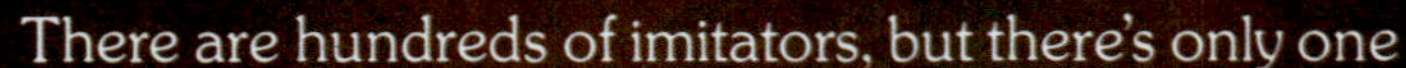

There are hundreds of imitators, but there's only one

FRANK FRAZETTA

You know what his covers have done for DELL, BALLANTINE, WARNER, and the great CONAN series. Now Frazetta has done his first cover for ZEBRA. Match added sales power of a Frazetta cover to a collection featuring the most popular names in science fiction and fantasy in

SWORDS AGAINST DARKNESS

edited by andrew j. offutt

(239, $1.95)

Featuring Novelets
and Stories by
POUL ANDERSON
MANLY WADE WELLMAN
RAMSEY CAMPBELL and the
Last Unpublished Story by
ROBERT E. HOWARD!
Creator of CONAN
(partial list)

Every Frazetta is a collector's item, and the fans have been hollering for more. This painting is one of two done by Frazetta in 1976, and the first Frazetta cover to be published in 1977. Display with Peacock's best seller... *THE FABULOUS WORLD OF FRANK FRAZETTA!* *SWORDS AGAINST DARKNESS* is a double-bladed collection for the millions of book buyers and fans who have made Zebra's fantasy line the most talked about line in science fiction!

BIG NAMES +
GREATEST ARTISTS +
TREMENDOUS
$$$$$$$$$$$$$$$$

Distributed by Kable News Company, Inc.,
777 Third Avenue, New York, NY 10017

Printed in U.S.A.

Zebra ad slick, $8^1/_2$" x 11"

Andrew agreed to fact-check the index and make sure all the references and numbers were accurate and in the process adding many undocumented items to the book. The majority of the images in this book were scanned from Andrew's massive reference collection. We owe a big debt to Andrew for his persistence in getting everything "just right." Finally, James Bond devoted countless hours to the actual writing of the index and even more hours inputting the data, an exhausting and time-consuming task made easier by his passion for Frazetta's art and his vision of the importance of such a work for the legion of Frazetta fans worldwide. Of course, James Bond was supremely correct. Frazetta is arguably one of the two most influential artists of the latter part of the twentieth century (the other being Norman Rockwell.) Frazetta's career has spanned over 60 years. He has innovated an art style whose influence is so vast that it cannot be calculated. An entire volume could be written detailing Frazetta's impact on the world of comic books, comic strip art, paperback covers, movie posters, tattoo art, van and motorcycle painting, set design, jewelry, fashion, video games, and other categories too numerous to list. For decades artists have been heavily influenced by Frazetta's approach to color, to design, to the portrayal of the human figure in motion. Many artists have fashioned careers by using his ideas and adopting his visual language to solve artistic problems. Others have used Frazetta simply as a constant source of inspiration, as a standard of excellence to approach. This volume pays homage to that great corpus of influential work. One cannot help but be in a bit of awe at the sheer amount of significant work Frazetta has contributed to art history. Countless unforgettable images have burned Frazetta into the visual fabric of modern culture. Genius is, of course, one of the most overused words in our vocabulary. However, this term can be applied to Frazetta with complete accuracy. Frazetta is pure creative power.

> *"For decades artists have been heavily influenced by Frazetta's approach to color, to design, to the portrayal of the human figure in motion.*
>
> *"Others have used him simply as a constant source of inspiration, as a standard of excellence to approach."*

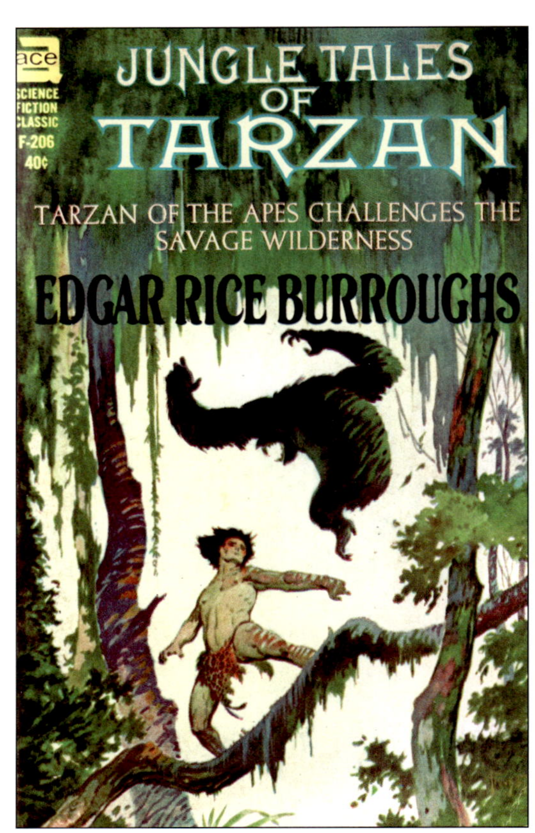

This index documents the growth of his abilities from humble comic book artist to his ultimate achievements as world class painter and supreme draughtsman. In the coming years Frazetta's fame is certain to grow. Quality has a way of persevering and affecting each succeeding generation. Quality endures; it is timeless. There will be more books, more essays, more academic studies, more projects inspired by the output from this creative master.

OPPOSITE:
Jungle Tales of Tarzan
Ace Books (1963)

LEFT:
Conan the Usurper
Lancer Books (1977)

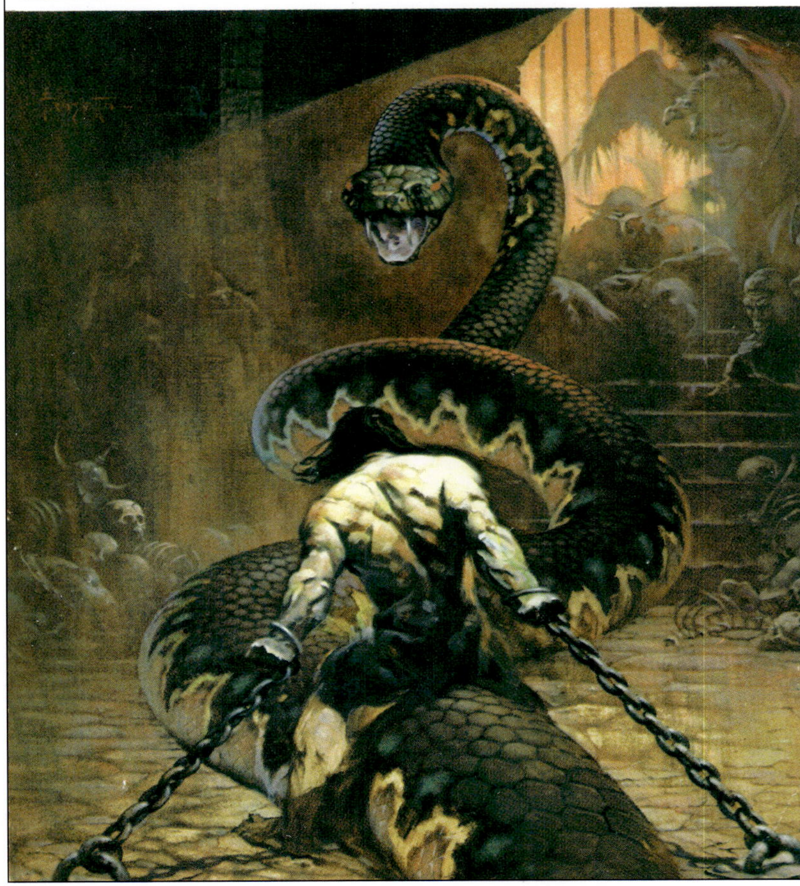

All in all, this book has been a quintessential labor-of-love fueled by our mutual passion for Frazetta's art and our firm belief in his ongoing importance to art history. Frazetta's great art is fine art in the truest sense of the term. His work transcends all categories and all efforts to segregate him. This book is just a first step. Hopefully, in the near future a catalog raissonne will be assembled, detailing all the extant originals sitting in collections throughout the world. In the meantime, browse this volume, take in all the rare imagery that has been assembled, and sit back and enjoy the world of Frazetta that is in your hands.

Dr. Dave Winiewicz
Las Vegas, NV

FOUR COLOR FRITZ

The Comic Book Years

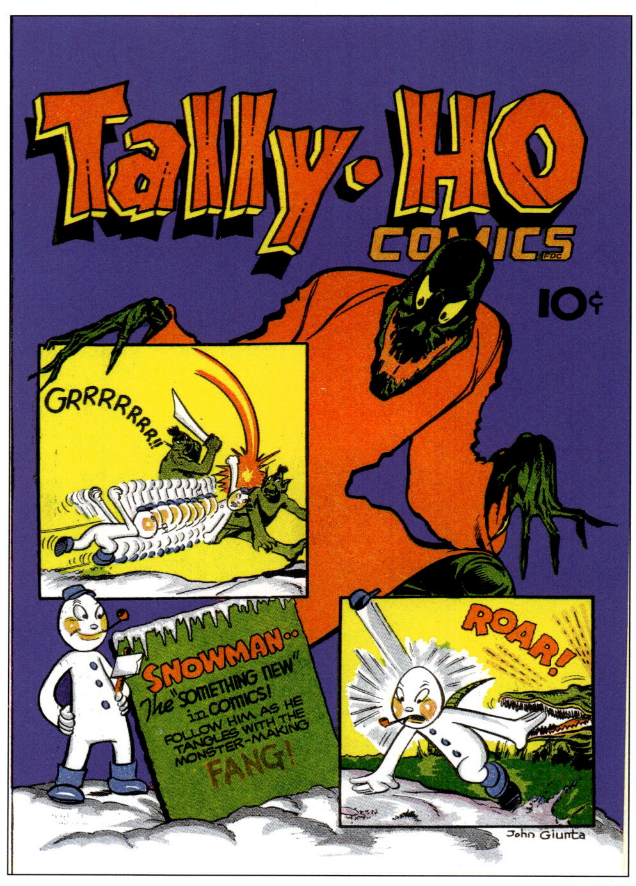

ABOVE: Tally Ho
December, 1944
Within the pages of this historic comic lies Frazetta's first published work, Snowman. *This seven page story was a collaborative project with Baily Publishing artist, John Giunta.*

OPPOSITE: Capt. Kidd Jr.
Treasure Comics #7, 1946
This little known single comic book page is Frank Frazetta's very first solo comic book work. It appeared in Treasure Comics *#7, a Prize Publications book, and is reprinted here for the very first time since its original release. Frank was asked if that was him in the bathtub. Laughingly, he replied "No."*

At age 15, after his studies at the Brooklyn Academy of Art, Frazetta landed a meager job in Bernard Baily's studio doing pencil cleanups for the house artists. While there, he was befriended by artist John Giunta. John, impressed with Frank's ability, decided to collaborate with the young artist on a story showcasing one of Frazetta's characters.

Frank recalls, "All I did was one story. I was the kid who had created the character, and I did the pencils. Giunta proceeded to really go over (the pencils) big time, and he did the inking. I was only a kid. I didn't even know how it was done." The 7-page story simply titled "*Snowman*" appeared in TALLY HO. Because of Frazetta's limited participation and the book's lack of followers due to its one-shot printing, the story didn't give Frank the recognition he had hoped for. Nevertheless this comic-magazine boasts Frazetta's first published work and is a valued addition to the die-hard collector. The first and only issue of TALLY HO was released December, 1944. Two months later Frank Frazetta turned sixteen years old.

CAREER BEGINNINGS

He was finally able to stretch his creative legs in 1946 when Prize Publications gave him a chance to contribute a solo story to TREASURE COMICS. This was definitely a far cry from TALLY HO and Frank

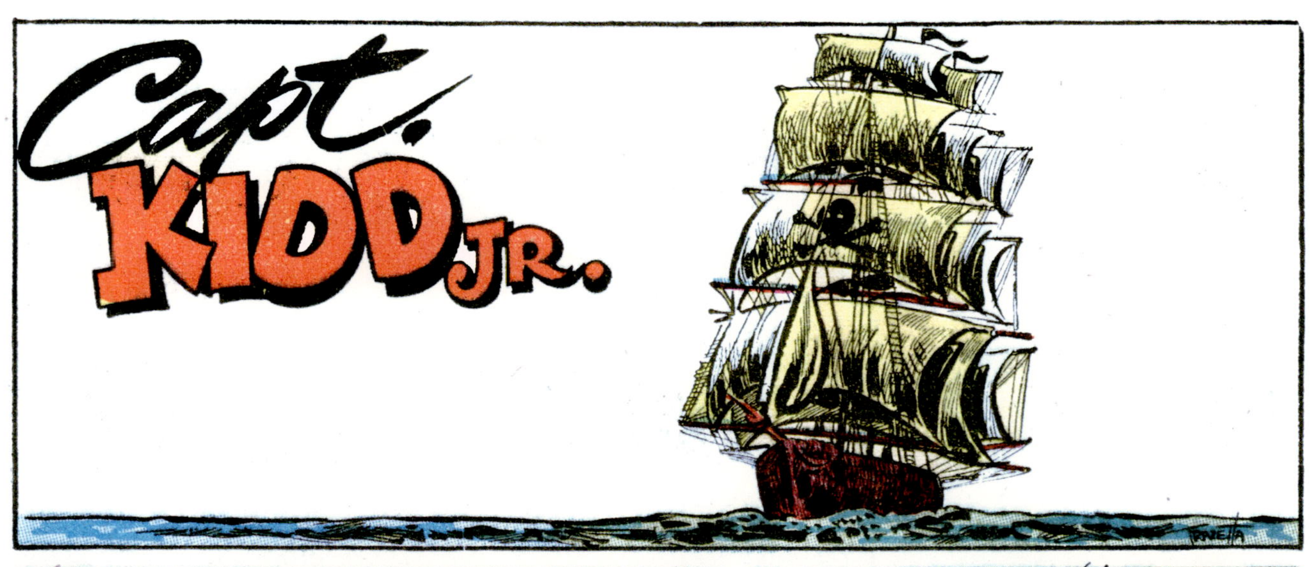

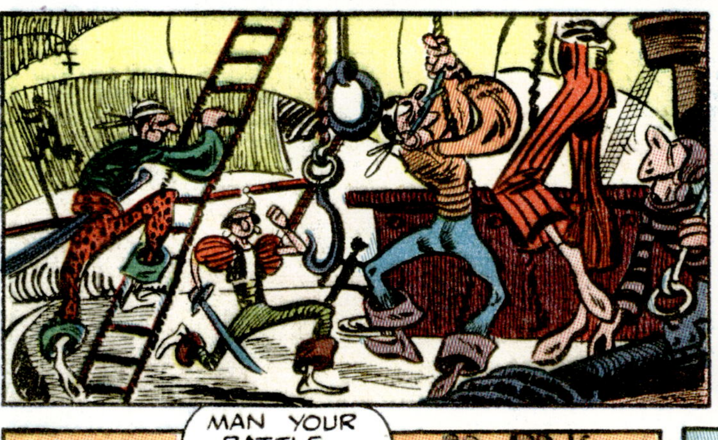

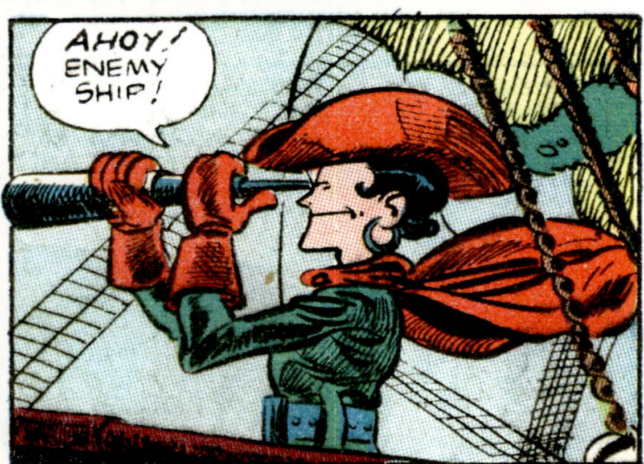

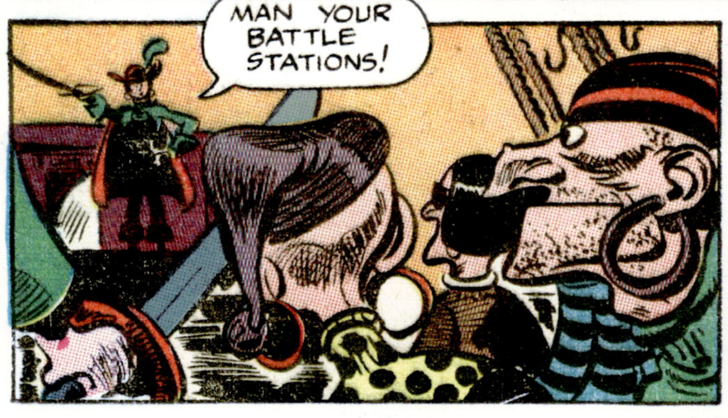

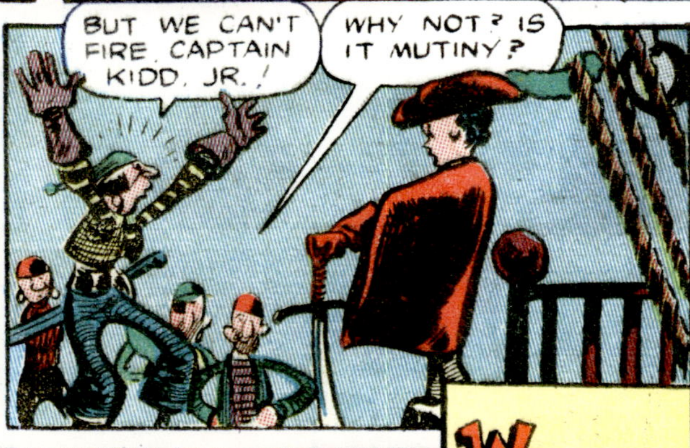

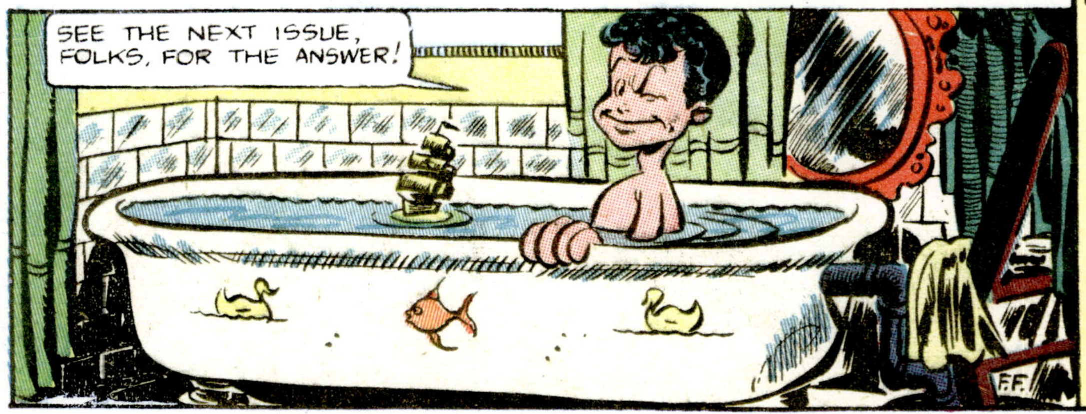

WATCH FOR BETTER AND BIGGER STORIES... STARRING... Capt. KIDD JR.

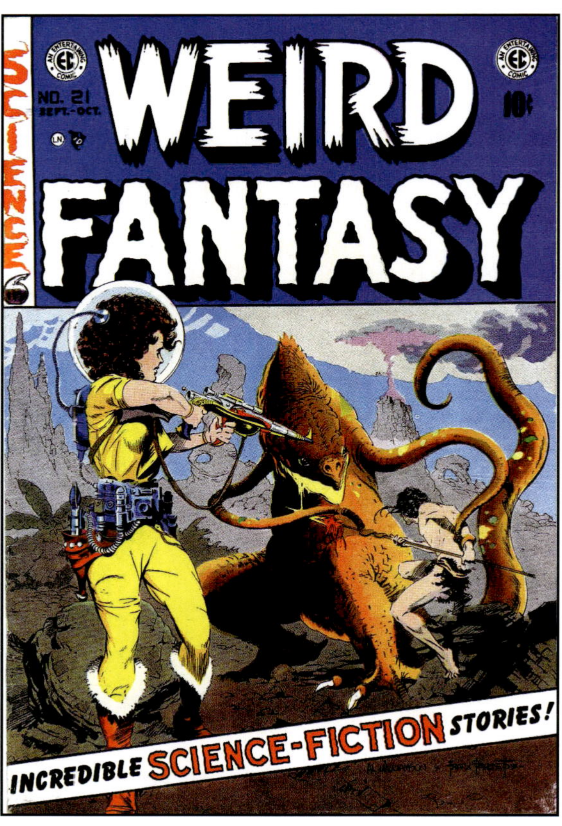

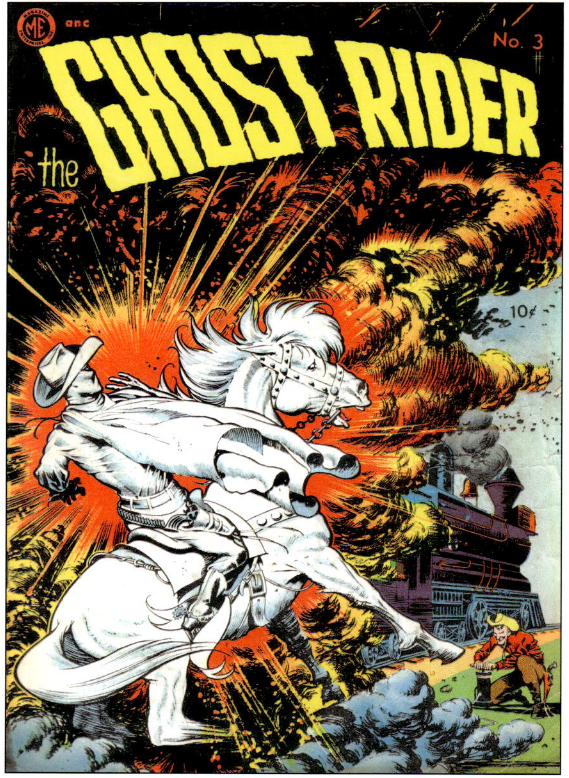

TOP: Weird Fantasy #21, *with Al Williamson, EC Comics (1953)*
ABOVE: Cover to A-1 Comics #1 (GHOST RIDER #3).
OPPOSITE: "The White Wolf" *from* DURANGO KID #15 *(1952)*
Never before reprinted.

felt pressure to prove himself with a story that could earn him some merit. The historical value of this item is commonly overlooked, as it was this author who first discovered the real treasure of TREASURE COMICS. The story; *"Know Your America"* is Frazetta's first solo published work and the issue also contained the single page funny-adventure serial, *"Capt. Kidd Jr."* which is his first credited work; signed simply, F.F.

After his work for two issues of TREASURE COMICS, Standard Publications hired him to help illustrate their funny animal books. Between the years 1947 through 1950 he worked diligently with Standard on 15 different titles. He began illustrating books like BARNYARD, COO COO, HAPPY and SUPERMOUSE to name a few. But when Frazetta's talent really began to bloom (about 1948) he was offered a nine page story for EXCITING COMICS, one of Standard's action-adventure titles. He was also asked to provide a quarter page illustration for a *"Looie Lazybones"* story about the same time. The fan response of Looie Lazybones persuaded Standard to create an ongoing series, and of course, they gave Frazetta the job to draw them. The stories in the EXCITING comic books are credited as the ones that caught Al Capp's attention and resulted in Frazetta eventually ghosting the LI'L ABNER newspaper strip for nine years.

HITTING HIS STRIDE

The period of 1948 through 1951 was undoubtedly the most productive in the young artist's comic career as other companies were introduced to his work. Not only did he continue working for Standard's humor and adventure titles, D.S. Publishing offered him a seven page story in OUTLAW #9. This was the first of many western stories Frazetta would eventually do. The publishing company, Magazine Entertainment contacted Frank to help on their A-1 line of books. The popularity of TRAIL COLT, Frazetta's first work for A-1, quickly led to the production of another A-1 western title, THE DURANGO KID. This book introduced Dan Brand, *"The White Indian"* and Tipi, his Indian sidekick. It continued well into 1952 with sixteen issues. This particular run of stories well illustrates the span of development during Frazetta's early drawing style.

By early 1950 Frank was doing stuff for such companies as D.C.'s ADVENTURE COMICS, Toby Press'

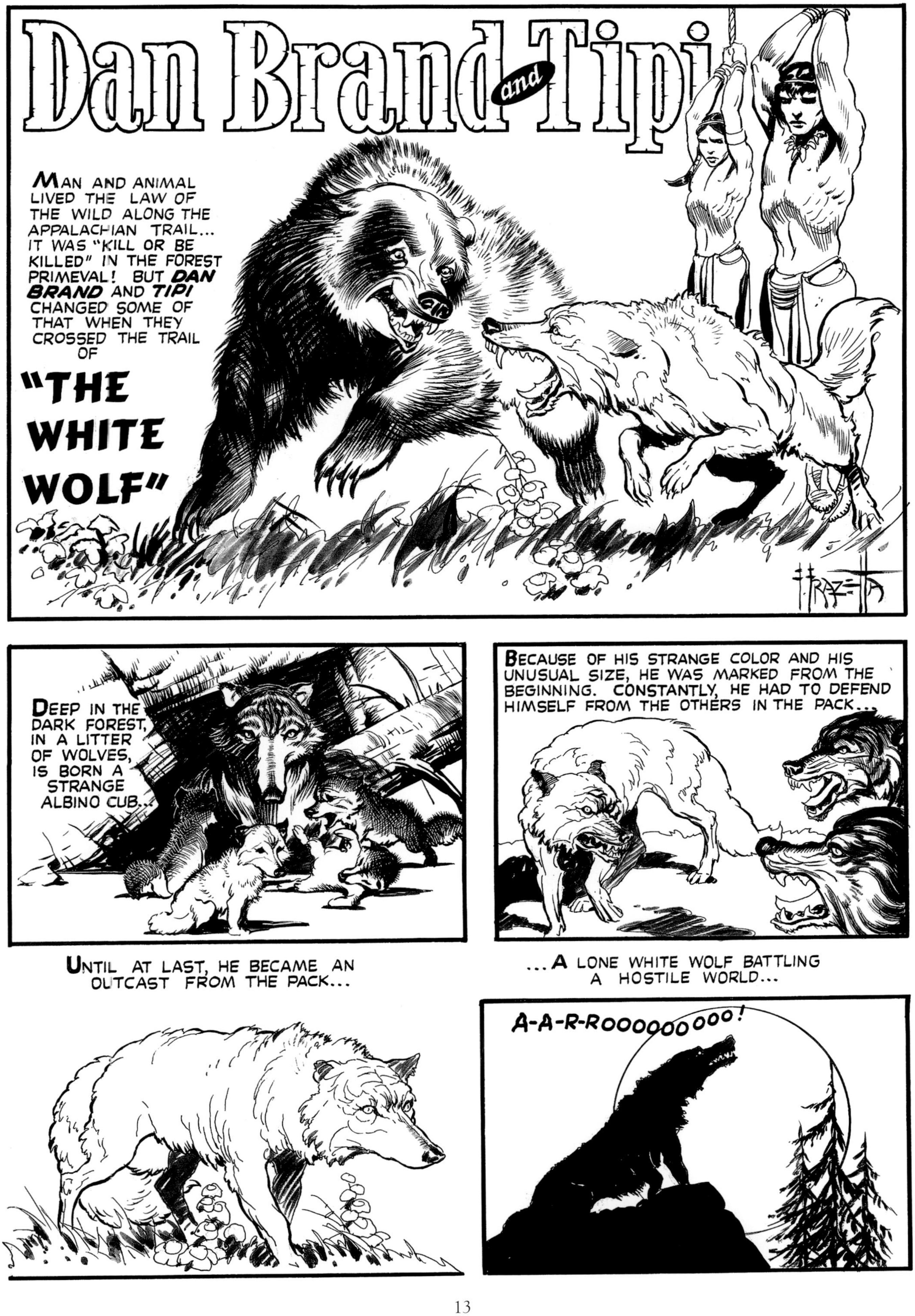

Dan Brand and Tipi

MAN AND ANIMAL LIVED THE LAW OF THE WILD ALONG THE APPALACHIAN TRAIL... IT WAS "KILL OR BE KILLED" IN THE FOREST PRIMEVAL! BUT ***DAN BRAND*** AND ***TIPI*** CHANGED SOME OF THAT WHEN THEY CROSSED THE TRAIL OF

"THE WHITE WOLF"

FRAZETTA

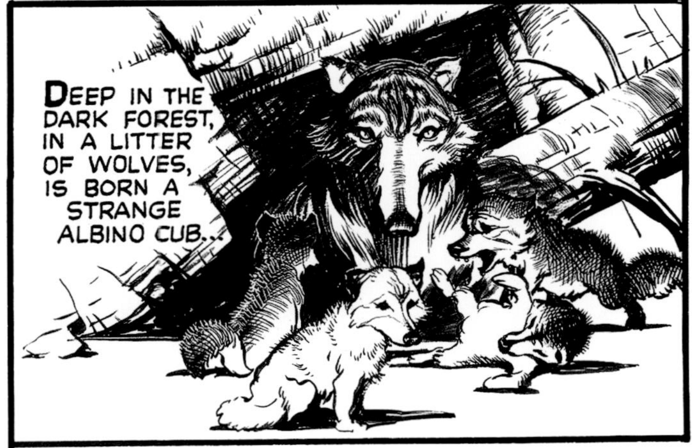

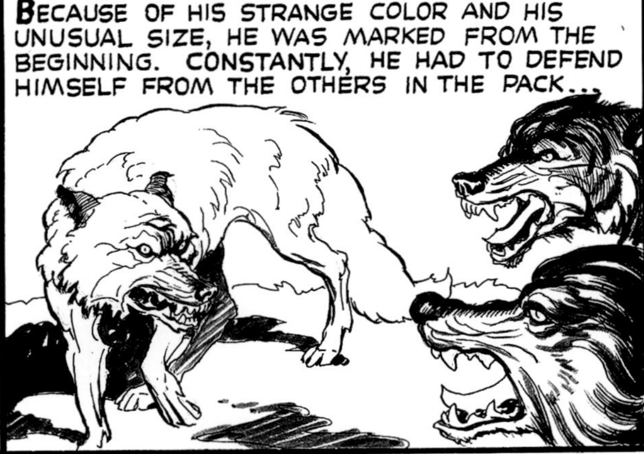

UNTIL AT LAST, HE BECAME AN OUTCAST FROM THE PACK...

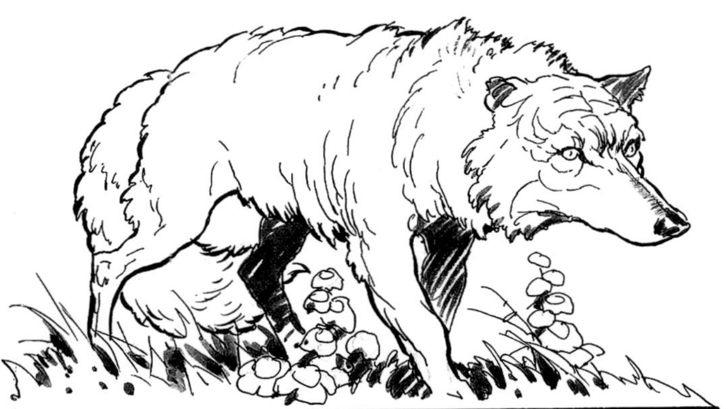

...A LONE WHITE WOLF BATTLING A HOSTILE WORLD...

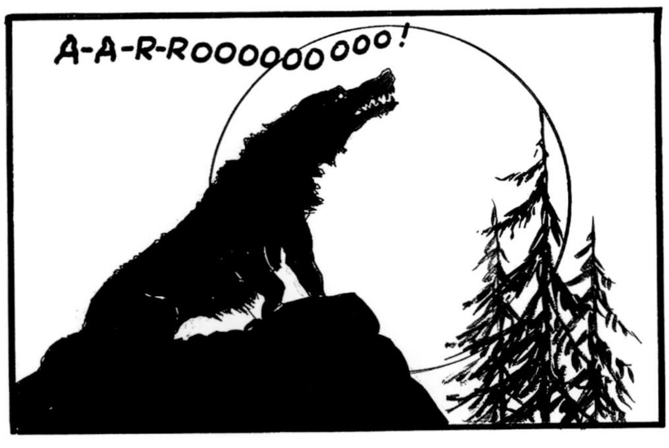

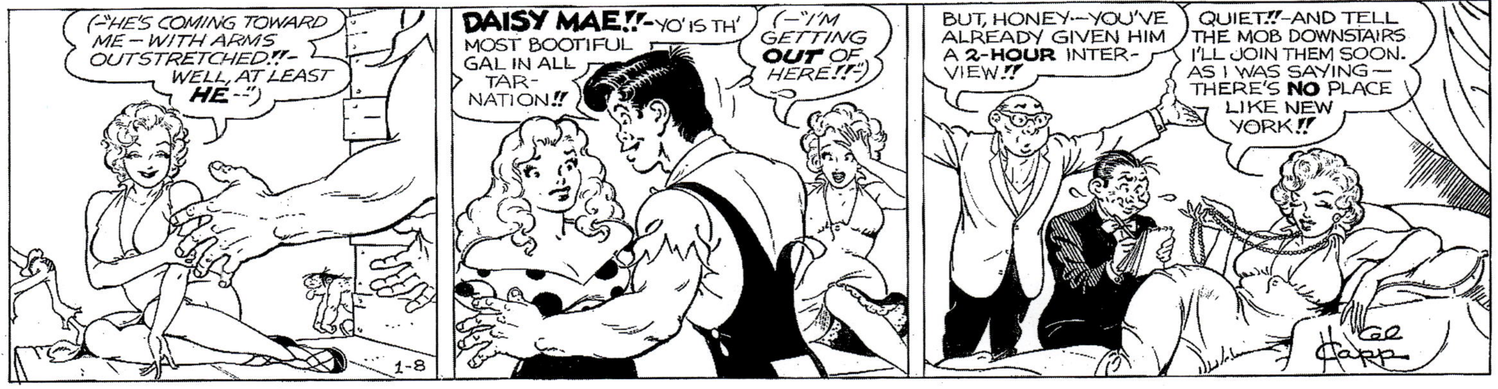

ABOVE:
Li'l Abner *Sunday strip Jan. 8, 1956.*
OPPOSITE:
Famous Funnies *covers.*

JOHN WAYNE ADVENTURE (with Al Williamson), and E.C.'s sci-fi title WEIRD FANTASY (also with Williamson). 1950 was the first year that showcased Frazetta's finer art style. his work within the more serious titles grew while his funny animal illustrations dramatically fell. By 1951 the anthropomorphic work had completely disappeared from his schedule. Still, his production output in 1951 easily matched that of 1950 because he continued to supply art for some of the industry's leading publications.

QUALITY TIME

Nineteen fifty-two was the year Frazetta's popularity really exploded. It seemed every publisher in the industry wanted what Frazetta had to offer. For the first time Frank was able to pick his projects. He had always wanted to do a Tarzan feature, so when THUN'DA, KING OF THE CONGO was pitched his way he immediately grabbed it. It's a watershed period in the history of Frazetta's career. It's the only book entirely penciled and inked by Frazetta. The only other book that comes close is a LI'L ABNER giveaway where Frazetta penciled and inked the interior. Thun'da allowed Frank the chance to do a Tarzan-esque feature, finally fulfilling his lingering dreams to do so.

Nineteen fifty-two also marked a time where Frazetta decided to branch out from the comic book medium and try his hand at newspaper strips.

JOHNNY COMET first appeared in the papers Monday, January 28 1952, written by Earl Baldwin and illustrated by Frank Frazetta. It was an adventure yarn about a young racecar driver living fast and driving hard while dealing with smugglers and the other usual bad guys found within the strips back then. Originally, writing credits were given to Peter DePaolo, the winner of the 1925 Indianapolis 500. This was probably done to help sell the strip and lend credence to the stories. JOHNNY COMET (which later became ACE McCOY) eventually ran out of gas and, in early 1954, the strip folded. It was at this time Al Capp popped in to ask Frazetta to work with him on LI'L ABNER. Capp's offer was readily accepted.

It was due to his work on LI'L ABNER that created a drop in his comic book output for the next few years. A drop in quantity yes, but the quality of Frank's comic book work was unrivaled. Basically his work for LI'L ABNER allowed Frazetta the opportunity to draw a week's worth of strips in a couple of days and that left him the rest of the week to do what he wished. Usually he played baseball or hung around with his friends AKA "The Fleegle Gang" (Angelo Torres, Al Williamson, Nick Meglin, Roy Krenkel, and George Woodbridge). But sometimes he'd get the creative urge to sit down and draw. Usually he'd draw something just for the sake of creating but once in a while he'd take on a stray comic book project. Relaxed with the knowledge that there was no rush to complete it, Frazetta created some truly beautiful comic stories. For instance, his work for PERSONAL LOVE immediately springs to mind.

Frank Frazetta's work for the comic PERSONAL LOVE started in late 1953. Only 5 stories were illustrated by the artist. Each one appearing within a dif-

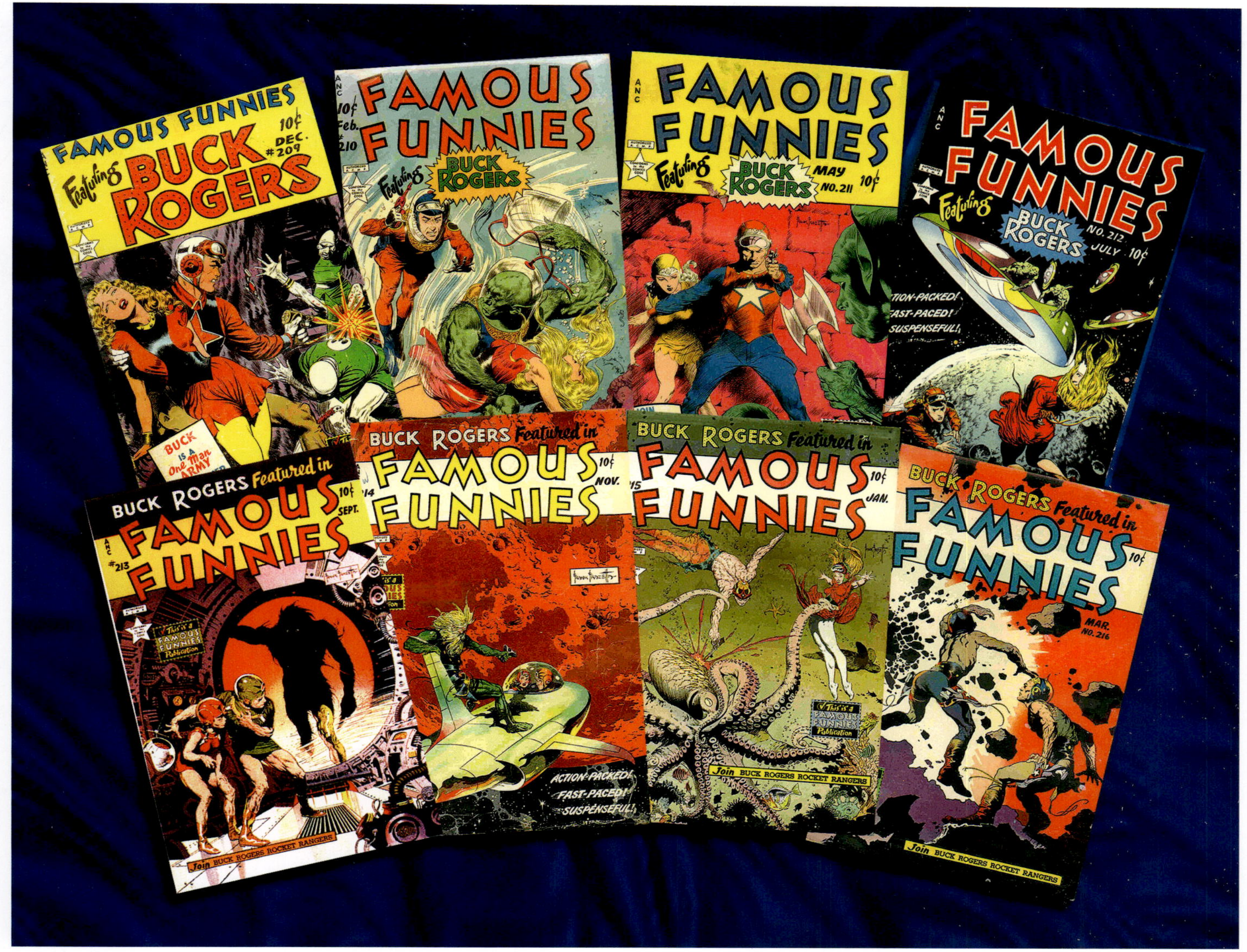

ferent issue. The fifth story, entitled *"Untamed Love"* has been unanimously decreed by Frazetta collectors as the greatest story illustration done for comics. His cover art for eight issues of FAMOUS FUNNIES, also created around this time, is yet another testament to Frazetta's illustration prowess.

The years 1954 and 55 show a generous handful of well-crafted covers and stories for E.C. Comics. This includes *"Squeeze Play"*, Frank's only solo story for the publisher. Another E.C. publication, WEIRD SCIENCE-FANTASY #29 appeared on the racks. For one dime you could purchase what is now considered by many to be the finest piece of comic book cover art ever produced.

A NEW DIRECTION

Frazetta's work on comic books between the years 1956-1962 is virtually non-existent. He credits this to mere laziness, after all, Capp continued to pay well and there was no end to the work. After his stint with Capp was over in 1962, times became a bit lean for a couple of years. Frank had to resort to doing odd jobs for various men's magazines like the few *"Little Annie Fanny"* strips for PLAYBOY or the beautiful ink-wash pieces done for the MIDWOOD paperbacks. His comic book work restarted in 1964 when Jim Warren acted on an idea for a magazine that mirrored the old E.C. format. CREEPY #1 debuted on the stands boasting a Jack Davis cover and seven stories inside. The story, *"Werewolf"* is Frazetta's first of many contributions to the magazine. While "Werewolf" has been cited as the last comic story done by the artist, technically this isn't true. Issues #2 and 7 each contain a one page feature illustrated by Frazetta. It can be said, by definition, they are stories and, in May, 1966, he drew an anti-

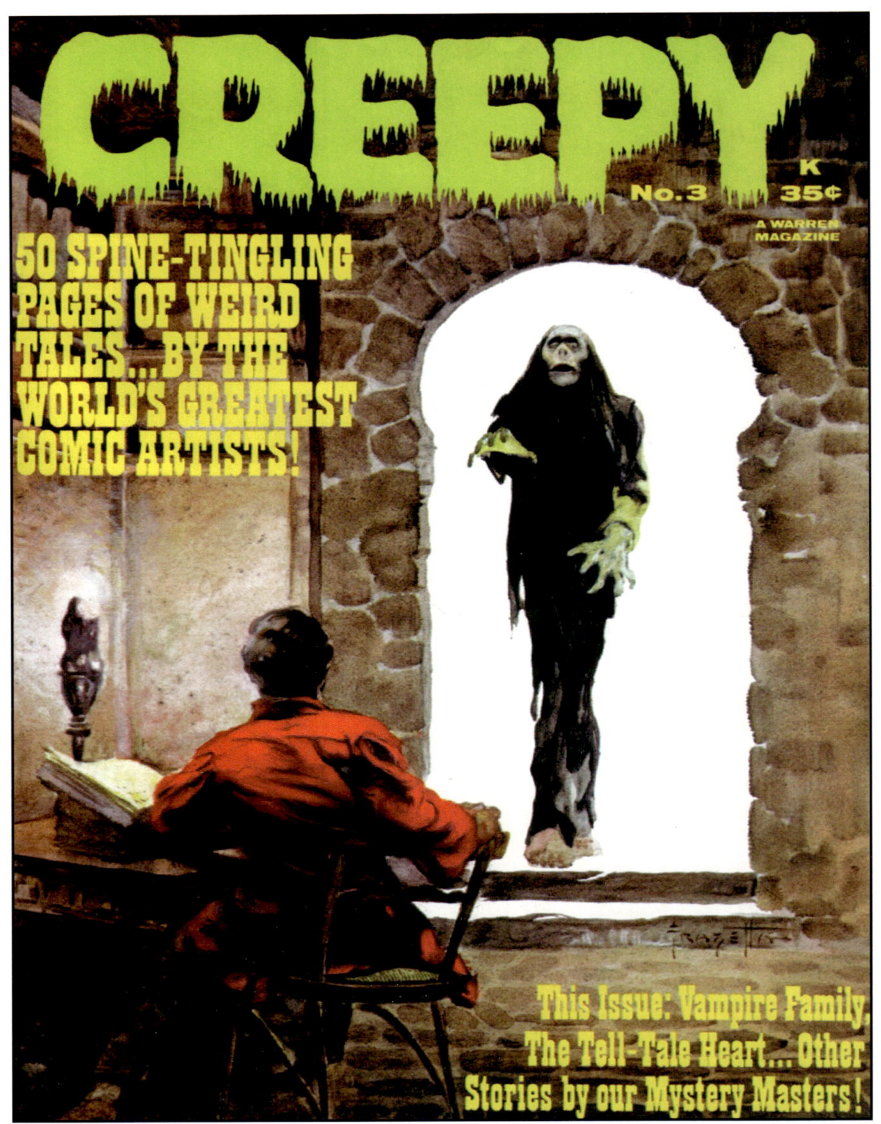

smoking advertisement in the form of a six-panel strip for Eerie #3.

Thirty-two covers were painted for Warren's magazines (BLAZING COMBAT, CREEPY, EERIE and VAMPIRELLA). Frazetta fondly remembers this period as one of the happiest. Not only was he given the freedom to create with almost no restriction, he was also allowed to keep the original art. Having fun was the only reason he continued work for the lower-paying magazines as his career took off through the sixties. He could have easily done paperback covers or movie posters but that wouldn't have been half as fun, or creative.

AND NOW

Because of the greener pastures of movie posters and paperback covers coupled with the marketability of his painted art, Frank put his comic book work behind him. He couldn't completely forsake the medium though and did return once in a while to prove he could still do it. His first return to comic work is within the pages of NATIONAL LAMPOON (1971). It's a parody of a comic cover entitled *"Dragula."*

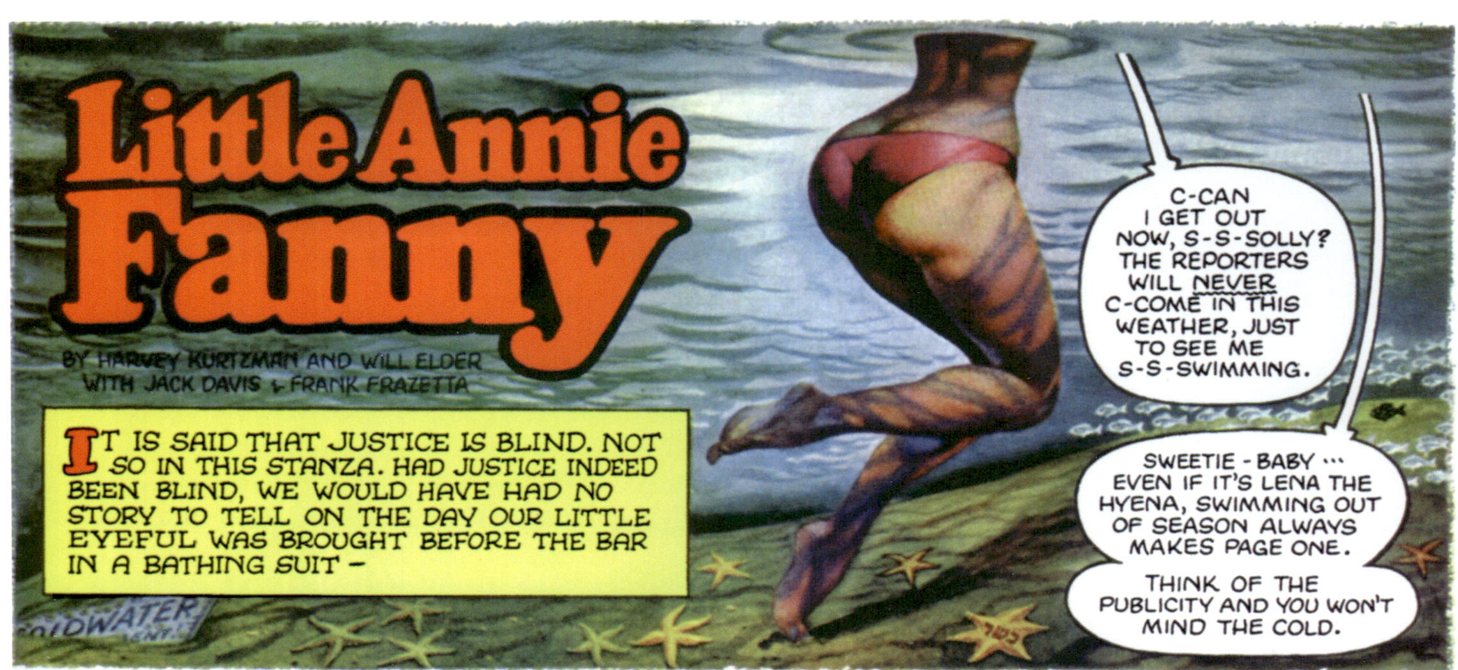

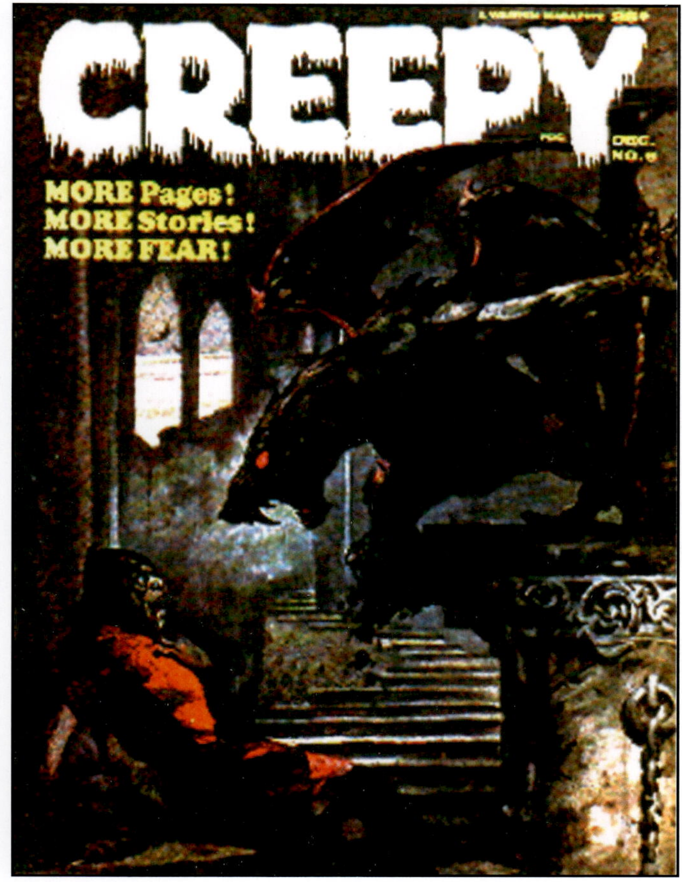

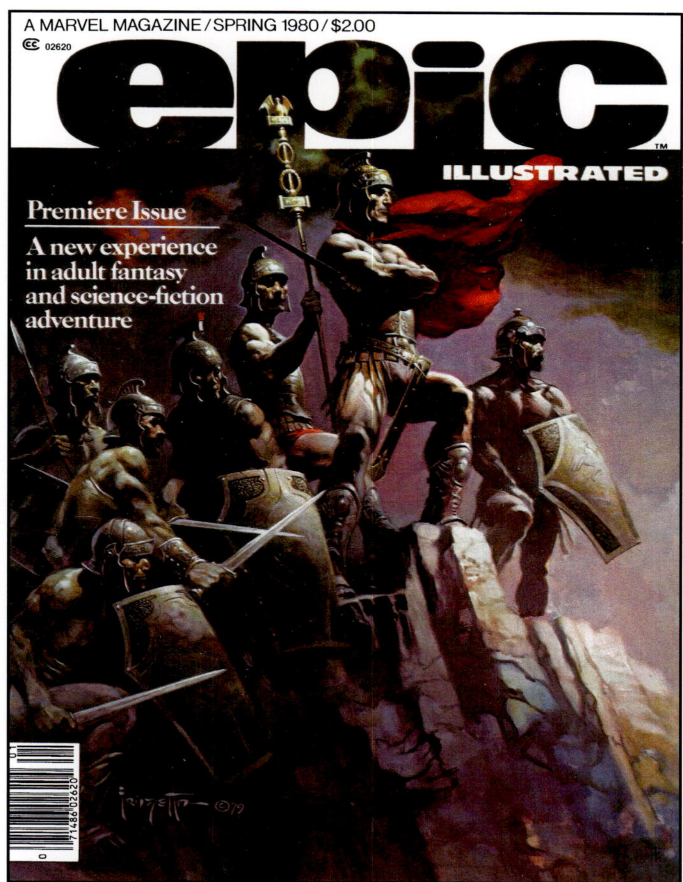

ABOVE LEFT:
Creepy #3 *Warren Publications. (1965)*
Based on a Roy Krenkel preliminary drawing.

ABOVE: Epic Illustrated #1 *Marvel Comics. (Spring 1980)*

Nine years passed before Frank would again produce work for comics. Marvel Comics' magazine EPIC ILLUSTRATED #1 (1980), had a beautifully painted cover. In 1988 a little known comic titled LAST OF THE VIKING HEROES was published. Even though the Frazetta cover looked like a convention sketch it was his first new work to actually appear in the traditional comic-book format since WEIRD SCIENCE-FANTASY in 1955.

Musician Glenn Danzig is a long time fan of Frazetta and the founder of Verotik, a hard edged comic publishing company, now defunct. The company's flagship title, DEATH DEALER featured the Frazetta character from the famous 1973 painting. The book's popularity was quickly followed by another comic, JAGUAR GOD. The Jaguar God character design was based on that of Dark Wolf, a figure from the Bakshi / Frazetta movie, FIRE & ICE. Both DEATH DEALER and JAGUAR GOD showcased Frazetta covers. The first issue of JAGUAR GOD had a beautifully painted cover which was later discovered to be a repainted version of the JONGOR OF LOST LAND paperback cover.

BELOW:
from National Lampoon *(November 1971)*

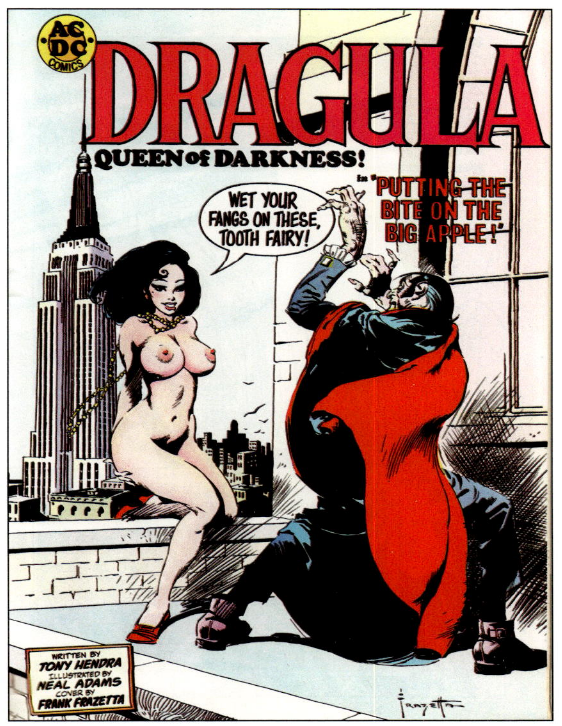

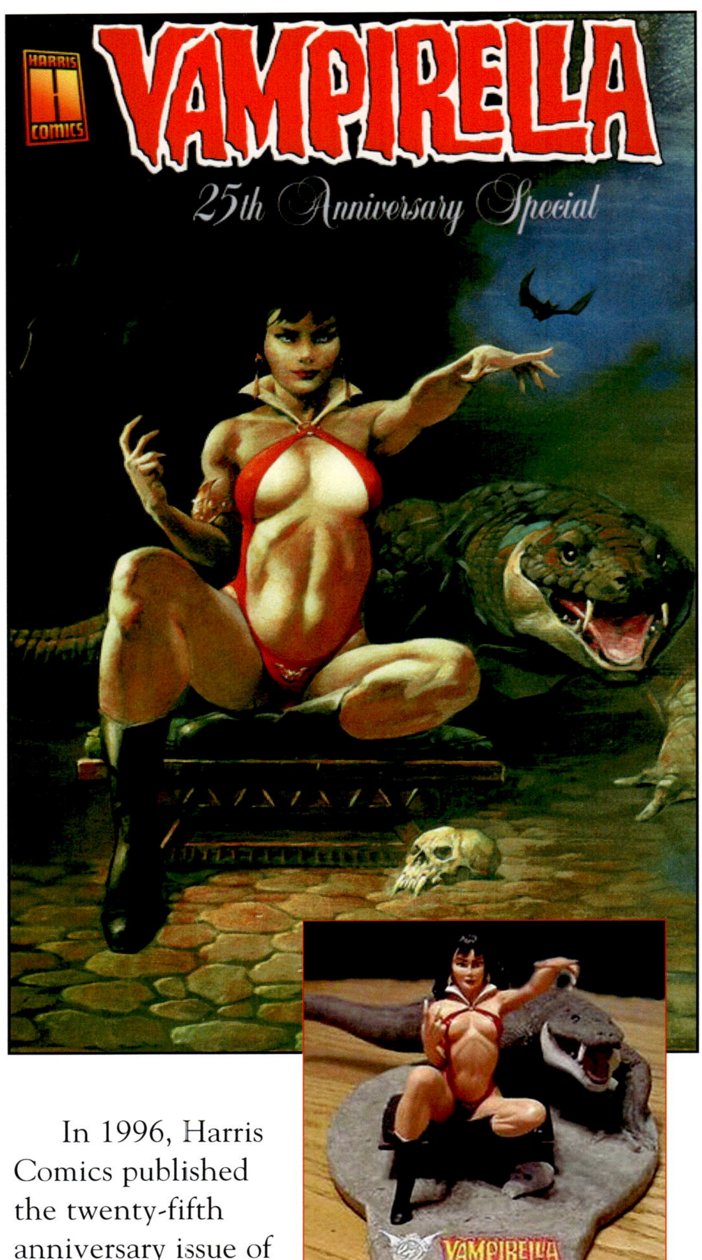

In 1996, Harris Comics published the twenty-fifth anniversary issue of VAMPIRELLA.

A nice Frazetta painting graced the cover and was soon afterward sculpted and made available as a porcelain figurine.

So as one can see, Frank's comic work, though not as prolific as some, is nevertheless considered by some collectors to be the finest. There are over 100 different titles listed in the following section, not including reprints. The genre of comic boasting Frazetta's largest contribution is undoubtedly the funny animal comics. They consisted mainly of his quarter page text illustrations with a few 3 to 7 page stories. This group is followed closely by the action-adventure titles which are, for the most part, the most desirable Frazetta collectibles. Westerns come in closely in third place due mainly to his work on books such as JOHN WAYNE ADVENTURE COMICS and DURANGO KID. In fourth place the numbers drop considerably to a handful of well produced sci-fi and fantasy titles. Frank also had a hand in a few of the short lived crime comics of the 1950's bringing this genre in at fifth place. The romance stories he did were not numerous (hence the sixth place slot) but they were beautiful.

A HERO'S RETURN

But now a question arises; what about the superhero genre? Why did Frank Frazetta's work never appear in a superhero comic book? I'll try to answer that here. A dramatic decrease in the number of published superhero books started around 1947, about the time Frazetta began his career. The hole left by the superhero departure was filled instantly by a demand for funny animals and westerns. To put it simply: Frank went where the popularity was. The heroes slowly returned during the late 50's through mid 60's but by this time Frank had moved on to greener pastures. Can you imagine though, Frank Frazetta penciling a 1940's CAPTAIN AMERICA or SUPERMAN? Or, imagine if you can, teaming him up with Stan Lee on the early FANTASTIC FOUR? Think of what he could have done with CONAN THE BARBARIAN.

Frazetta's comic book work has helped to lift comics as a whole out of the mire as "tabloid entertainment". His attention to detail and consistently polished form has helped raise the standard of comics to be accepted as "fine art". When available, original Frazetta comic pages bring extraordinary prices in auction houses. They are hung on gallery walls and looked at with as much awe as an original Rembrandt. More often than not his comic illustration is found to be more sought after by collectors than his original paintings. That desire stems from the incredible talent displayed on the page and the enduring quality the Frazetta name has always invoked.

ABOVE:
Vampirella 25th Anniversary Special;
Harris Comics (1999) and statue.
OPPOSITE:
Various covers for Warren Publishing. (1970s)

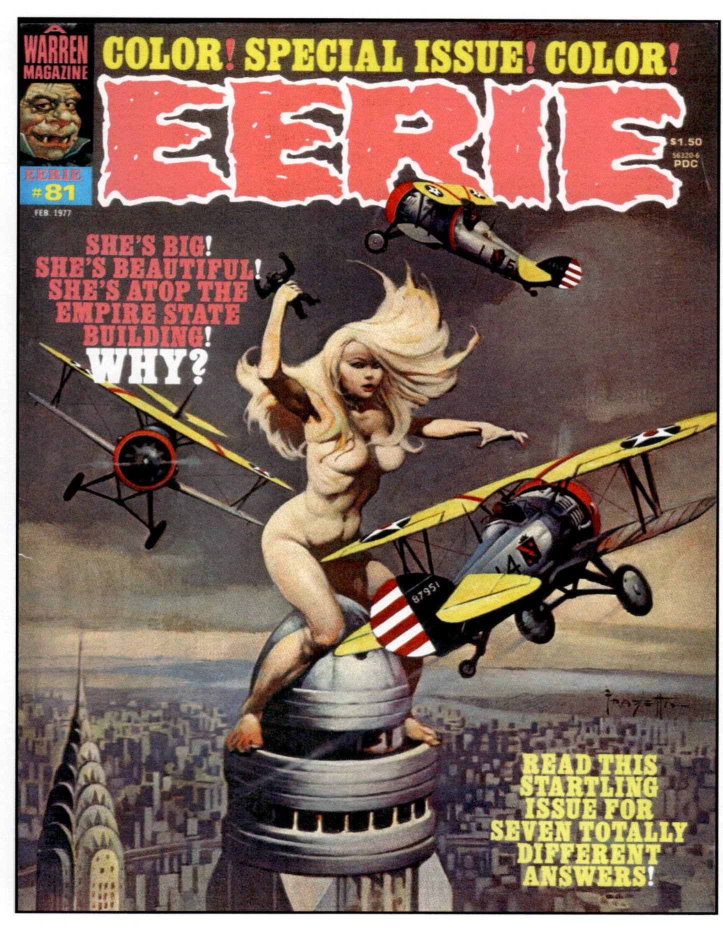
A WARREN MAGAZINE
COLOR! SPECIAL ISSUE! COLOR!
EERIE
$1.50
PDC
EERIE #81
FEB. 1977
SHE'S BIG! SHE'S BEAUTIFUL! SHE'S ATOP THE EMPIRE STATE BUILDING! WHY?
READ THIS STARTLING ISSUE FOR SEVEN TOTALLY DIFFERENT ANSWERS!

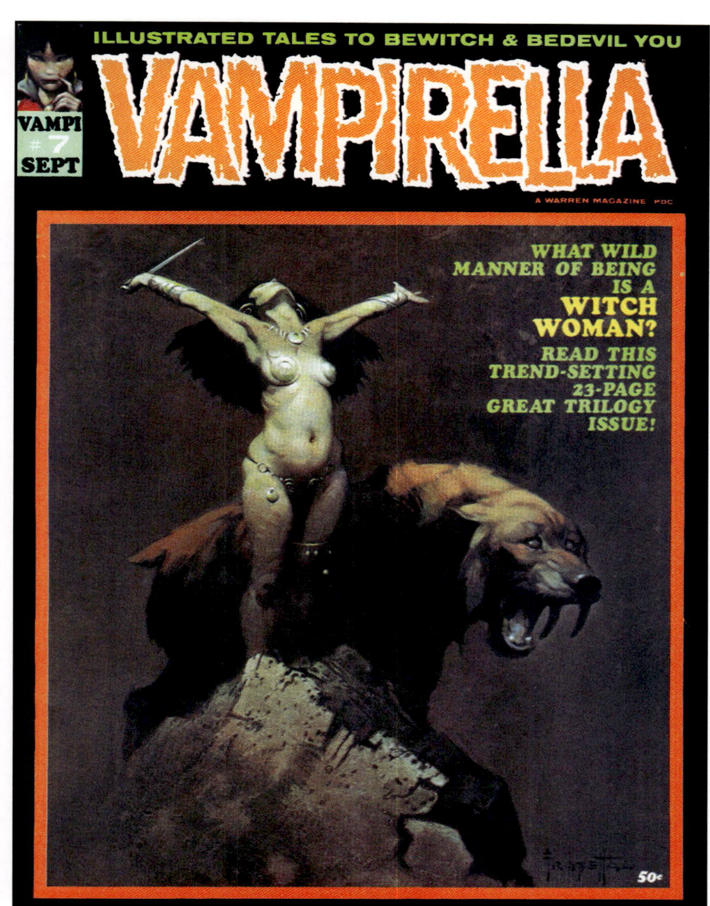
ILLUSTRATED TALES TO BEWITCH & BEDEVIL YOU
VAMPIRELLA
VAMPI #7 SEPT
A WARREN MAGAZINE PDC
WHAT WILD MANNER OF BEING IS A WITCH WOMAN?
READ THIS TREND-SETTING 23-PAGE GREAT TRILOGY ISSUE!
50¢

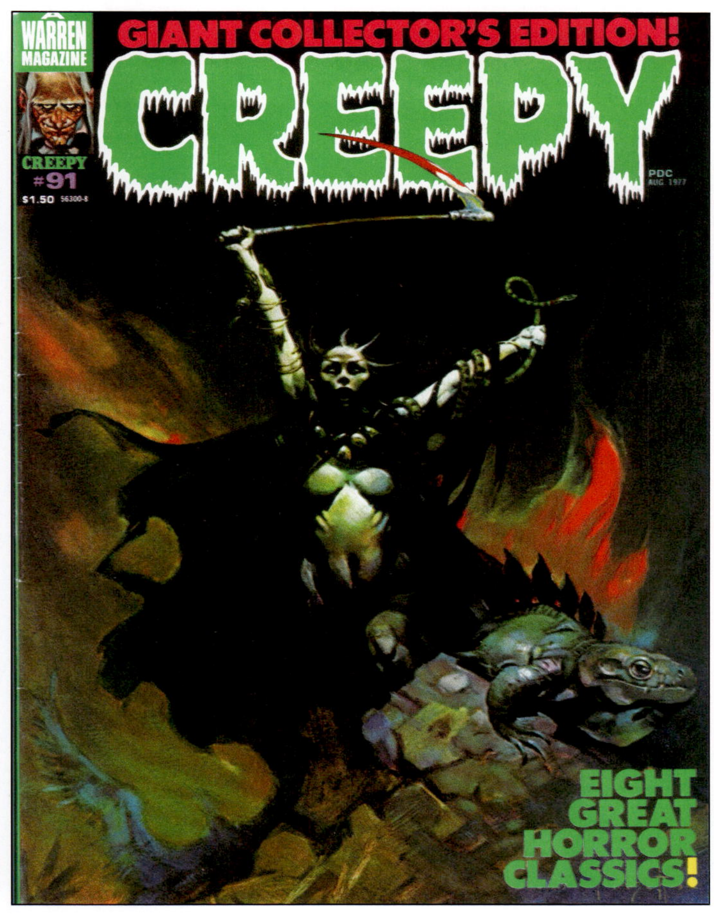
A WARREN MAGAZINE
GIANT COLLECTOR'S EDITION!
CREEPY
CREEPY #91
$1.50
PDC
AUG 1977
EIGHT GREAT HORROR CLASSICS!

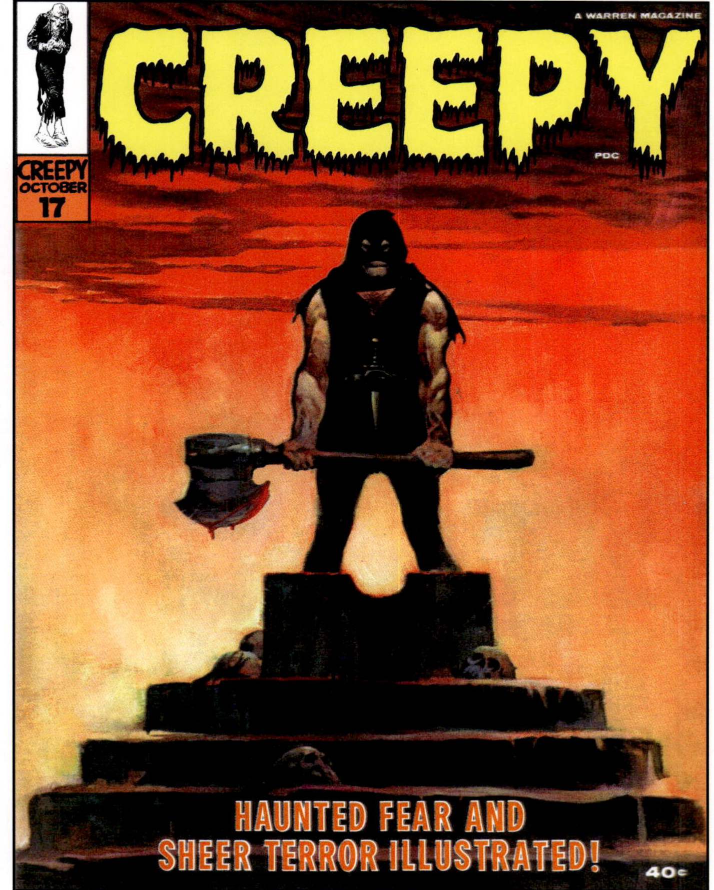
A WARREN MAGAZINE
CREEPY
PDC
CREEPY OCTOBER 17
HAUNTED FEAR AND SHEER TERROR ILLUSTRATED!
40¢

A-1 COMICS

1944 - #139, Sept-Oct 1955
Life's Romance Publications / Comix / Magazine Enterprises

Every issue has two different titles and two different issue numbers. A-1 COMICS is the title located in each book's indicia. The covers show a different title and number of the book featured that month. They are first listed according to what appears in the indicia and secondly according to the cover title / issue number.

- 24 (AKA.- TRAIL COLT #1) 1949
  - *"The Rodeo Robbers"* 7 pp.
    - **reprinted in** A-1 COMICS #63 (AKA. MANHUNT #13)
- 29 (AKA.- GHOST RIDER #2) 1950
  - COVER
    - **reprinted in** RETROSPECTIVE (art book), b/w
    - **reprinted in** COMIC BOOK MARKETPLACE #41
- 31 (AKA.- GHOST RIDER #3) 1951
  - COVER
    - **reprinted in** RETROSPECTIVE (art book), b/w
    - **reprinted in** ICON (art book)
- 34 (AKA.- GHOST RIDER #4) 1951
  - COVER
    - **reprinted in** LEGACY (art book)
    - **reprinted in** FRAZETTA TREASURY (fanzine)
    - **reprinted in** SPA-FON #2 (fanzine)
- 37 (AKA.- GHOST RIDER #5) 1951
  - COVER
    - **reprinted in** RETROSPECTIVE (art book), b/w
    - **reprinted in** SPA-FON #2 (fanzine)
    - **reprinted in** COMIC BOOK MARKETPLACE #41
    - **reprinted in** THE COMICS JOURNAL (magazine)
- 47 (AKA.- THUN'DA #1) 1952

A-1 COMICS #47 is one of the most sought after Frazetta collectibles. It's the only book entirely penciled, inked and colored by the artist. Writing credit belongs to Gardner Fox. It was done as a vehicle to show Frazetta's talent in a Tarzan-esque feature. It is recommended to find an original copy because the reprint editions are re-colored untrue to the original.

  - COVER
    - **reprinted in** FRANK FRAZETTA: THE LIVING LEGEND
    - **reprinted in** KING OF THE CONGO (movie poster)
    - **reprinted in** CD ROM COMICS - FRAZETTA SPECIAL EDITION
    - **reprinted in** THUN'DA
    - **reprinted in** LEGACY (art book)
  - *"King of the Lost Lands"* 10 pp.
    - **reprinted in** FRAZETTA #1 (fanzine)
    - **reprinted in** FRANK FRAZETTA: THE LIVING LEGEND
    - **reprinted in** FANTASTIC EXPLOITS #20 (fanzine)
    - **reprinted in** THUN'DA
    - **reprinted in** FRANK FRAZETTA'S THUN'DA TALES
    - **reprinted in** CD ROM COMICS - FRAZETTA SPECIAL EDITION
    - 3 pages **reprinted in** COMICS INTERVIEW - FRAZETTA SPECIAL)
    - first page **reprinted in** ICON (art book)
    - Page 2 **reprinted in** THE DINOSAUR SCRAPBOOK
    - 6 consecutive panels **reprinted in** ARIEL VOL. 1 (art book)
  - *"The Monsters From the Mists"* 7 pp.
    - **reprinted in** FRAZETTA #2 (fanzine)
    - **reprinted in** THUN'DA
    - **reprinted in** FRANK FRAZETTA'S THUN'DA TALES
    - **reprinted in** CD ROM COMICS - FRAZETTA SPECIAL EDITION
    - **reprinted in** FANTASTIC EXPLOITS #20 (fanzine)
    - 1 panel **reprinted in** ARIEL VOL. 1 (art book) b&w
    - 6 consecutive panels **reprinted in** ARIEL VOL. 1 (art book)
  - *"When the Earth Shook"* 6 pp.
    - **reprinted in** THUN'DA
    - **reprinted in** FRANK FRAZETTA'S THUN'DA TALES
    - **reprinted in** CD ROM COMICS - FRAZETTA SPECIAL EDITION
    - **reprinted in** FANTASTIC EXPLOITS #20 (fanzine)
  - *"Gods of the Jungle"* 8 pp.
    - **reprinted in** COMIC AND CRYPT #7 (fanzine)
    - **reprinted in** THUN'DA
    - **reprinted in** FRANK FRAZETTA'S THUN'DA TALES
    - **reprinted in** FANTASTIC EXPLOITS #20 (fanzine)
    - **reprinted in** CD ROM COMICS - FRAZETTA SPECIAL EDITION
    - 1 page **reprinted in** THE COMICS JOURNAL #174
    - 1 panel **reprinted in** ARIEL VOL. 1 (art book) b&w
- 63 (AKA.- MANHUNT #13) 1953
  - *"The Rodeo Robbers"* 7 pp.
    - **first printed in** A-1 COMICS #24
- 94 (AKA.- WHITE INDIAN #11) 1953
  - untitled first White Indian story 7 pp.
    - **first printed in** DURANGO KID #1
  - *"Blood on the Frontier"* 7 pp.
    - **first printed in** DURANGO KID #2
  - *"The War on the River"* 7 pp.
    - **first printed in** DURANGO KID #3
  - *"Brothers of the Wilderness"* 7 pp
    - **first printed in** DURANGO KID #4
- 101 (AKA.- WHITE INDIAN #12) 1954
  - *"Trees of Doom"* 7 pp.
    - **first printed in** DURANGO KID #5
  - *"Tory Treachery"* 7 pp.
    - **first printed in** DURANGO KID #9
  - *"Sleep of Death"* 8 pp.
    - **first printed in** DURANGO KID #10
  - *"The Blood of Valley Forge"* 7 pp.
    - **first printed in** DURANGO KID #11
- 104 (AKA.- WHITE INDIAN #13) 1954
  - *"River Gauntlet"* 7 pp.
    - **first printed in** DURANGO KID #12
  - *"The Trail of the Traitor"* 7 pp.
    - **first printed in** DURANGO KID #13
  - *"The Voyage into Danger"* 8 pp.
    - **first printed in** DURANGO KID #14
  - *"Underworld of the Wilderness"* 7 pp.
    - **first printed in** DURANGO KID #16

ACE McCOY

Avalon Communications

- 1 2000 Reprints ACE McCOY newspaper comic strips
- 2 2000 Reprints ACE McCOY newspaper comic strips
- 3 2000 Reprints ACE McCOY newspaper comic strips

ACG SPECIAL COLLECTION

ACG Comics

- 10 2001
  - Binds together Johnny Comet #1-5 and Ace McCoy #1-3
    - Limited to 300 copies

ADVENTURE COMICS

#32, November 1938 - #491, September 1982 - #503, September 1983
National Periodical Publications / D.C. Comics
(All stories feature the Shining Knight)

- 150 March 1950
  - *"The Ten Century Lie"* 6 pp.
    - **reprinted in** MASTERWORKS SERIES #1
- 151 April 1950
  - *"Sir Justin, Bronco Buster"* 6 pp.
    - **reprinted in** MASTERWORKS SERIES #1
- 153 June 1950
  - *"The Duel of the Flying Knights"* 6 pp.
    - **reprinted in** MASTERWORKS SERIES #1
    - **reprinted in** WORLDS FINEST COMICS #205

STOPPING THE ENEMIES OF YOUTH

Frank Frazetta's Public Service Announcements

BY PAUL D. SHIPLE

By 1950, what would later be known as a "public service announcements (PSAs)" were regularly being shown in classrooms across America. Perfected during the Second World War with home front campaigns urging car pools and victory gardens, this process to teach moral responsibility was now being used as a tool to fight anti-social behavior. Such mental hygiene films as *"Duck and Cover"*, *"Subject: Narcotics"* and *"Street Safety is Your Problem"* were being viewed by millions of school children. Proponents hoped to encourage, if not to indoctrinate, acceptable social behavior. Between Dr. Spock's "proper ways" of child rearing and Betty Crocker Bake-Offs, conformity and being accepted was the key towards obtaining happiness during the 1950's.

What does any of this have to do with Frank Frazetta? By 1951 Famous Funnies Publications, in conjunction with various children associations, were running like-minded in-house ads. They spoke out against such things as dope peddling and the like as well as promoting such civic duties as first aid. Frazetta, working mostly as a free-lance artist at the time, was drafted into designing several public service announcements.

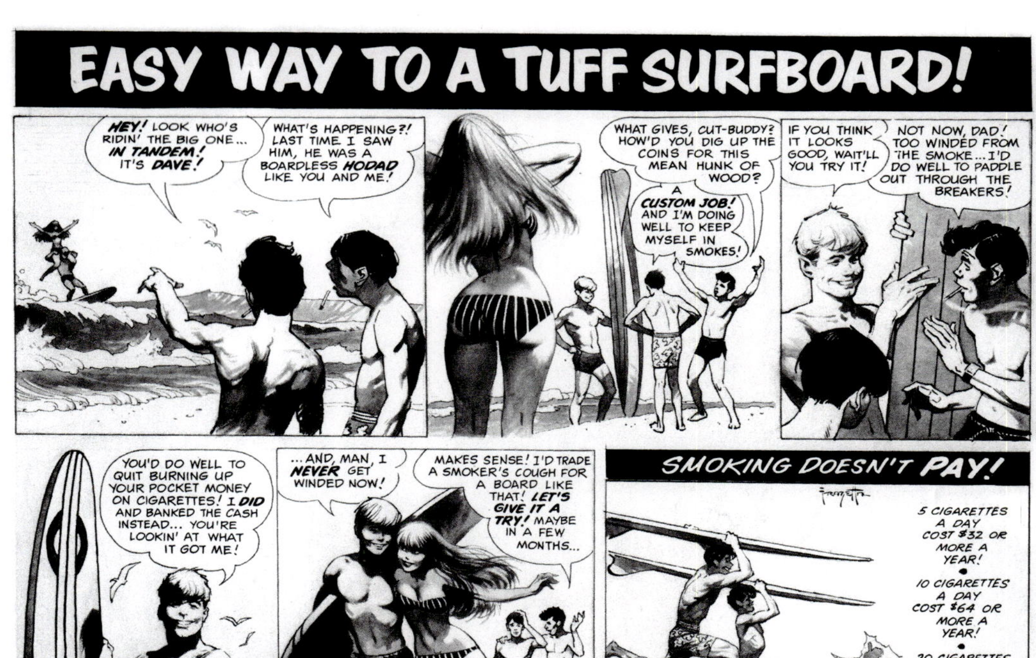

TOP: The back pages of Eerie presented this little half page ad. It's reminiscent of the "We Can Stop the Enemies of Youth" *P.S.A. created twelve years prior.*

The first of the Frazetta drawn ads was the anti-drug campaign entitled *"We Can Stop the Enemies of Youth"*. First to appear in the pages of BUSTER CRABBE #1, this full page ad was done in cooperation with The New York City Children's Board and The Association of Comic Publishers. Of all these ad spots that Frazetta illustrated, this one is by far the most often reprinted.

Next to appear was *"Prayer Works Wonders"*. This in-house ad expounded on the power of faith. It's curious to ponder the real impact such an ad could have had upon the readers of a "lurid crime comic".

The third PSA to appear with Frazetta's artistic touch was entitled *"Boy Scout Jamboree"*. This advertisement was directed towards encouraging all of America's Scouts to attend that year's National Camp in Irvine Ranch, California.

Another rarely used ad entitled *"Red Cross - New Method of Artificial Respiration"* was published to demonstrate to kids the newly developed methods to help a choking victim. All of these PSAs were intended to distract teenagers from straying down the wrong path as many had done before them. And, like the Red Cross Advertisement, occasionally taught important life saving skills.

(Continues on page 16)

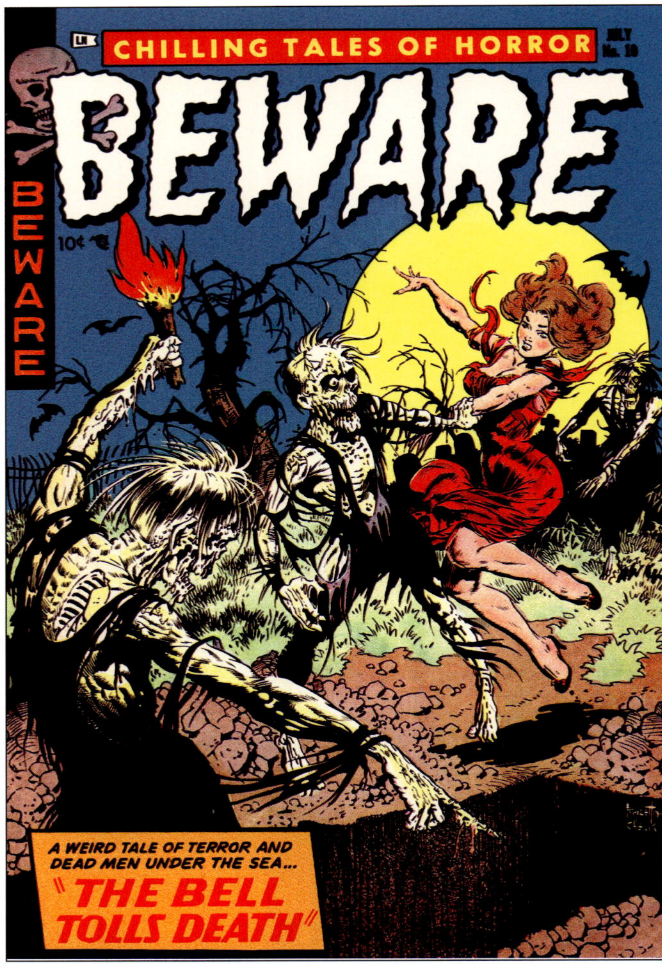

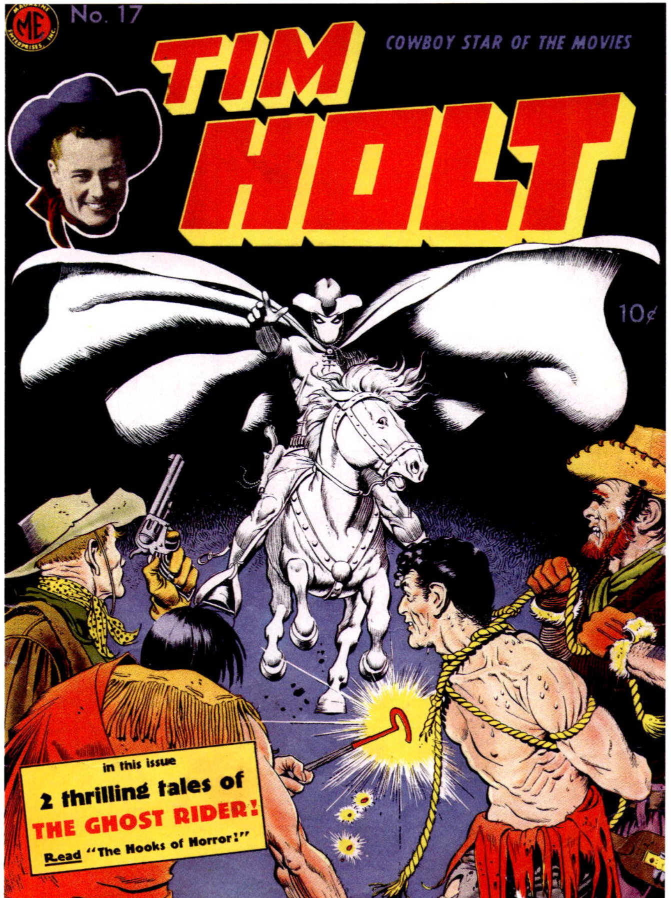

ADVENTURE COMICS cont'd

- 155 August 1950
  "The Imitation Knight" 6 pp.
  reprinted in MASTERWORKS SERIES #1
- 157 October 1950
  "Camelot U.S.A." 6 pp.
  reprinted in MASTERWORKS SERIES #1
- 159 December 1950
  "Knight of the Future" 6 pp.
  reprinted in MASTERWORKS SERIES #2
- 161 February 1951
  "The Flying Horse Swindle" 6 pp.
  reprinted in MASTERWORKS SERIES #2
  reprinted in ADVENTURE COMICS #417
- 163 April 1951
  "The Knight in Rusty Armor" 6 pp.
  reprinted in MASTERWORKS SERIES #2
- 417
  "The Flying Horse Swindle" 6 pp.
  first printed in ADVENTURE COMICS #161

ADVENTURES INTO THE UNKNOWN
1990
Sword in Stone Publications
- 1 1990 COVER - **Fire Demon**
- 2 1990 COVER - **Stranded**

AIRBOY COMICS
Vol. 2 #11 December 1945 - Vol. 10 #4 May 1953
Hillman Periodicals
- Vol. 9 #7 August 1952 1 pg. ad

ALL STAR COMICS (ALL STAR WESTERN #58 on)
Summer 1940 - #57 Feb-Mar 1951; #58 Jan-Feb 1976 - #74 Sept-Oct 1978
National Periodical Publications / All American / D.C. Comics
- 50 Dec-Jan 1950 *"The 37 Terrible Days"* 3 pp.

ALL STAR WESTERN (formerly ALL STAR COMICS #1-57)
#58 Apr-May 1951 - #119 June-July 1961
National Periodical Publications
- 99 Feb-Mar 1958
  "Botalye-Immortal Indian Warrior" 3 pp.
  first printed in JIMMY WAKELY #7

ALL STAR WESTERN
Aug-Sept 1970 - #11 Apr-May 1972
National Periodical Publications
- 9 Dec-Jan 1972
  "The Town Jesse James Couldn't Rob" 3 pp.
  first printed in JIMMY WAKELY #4

AMERICA'S BEST COMICS
Feb 1942 - #31 July 1949
Nedor / Better / Standard Publications
- 26 May 1948
  "Miss Masque" text illustration & some panel work

- BABY, YOU'RE REALLY SOMETHING! (one shot)

1990
Eros Comics
Reprints interior illustrations from the rare Midwood paperbacks and men's magazine illos.

TOP: Beware #103 (July 1954)

RIGHT: Tim Holt #17 Eastern Colo (Jun. 1954)

OPPOSITE: One of many Public Service Ads drawn by Frazetta in the 1950's

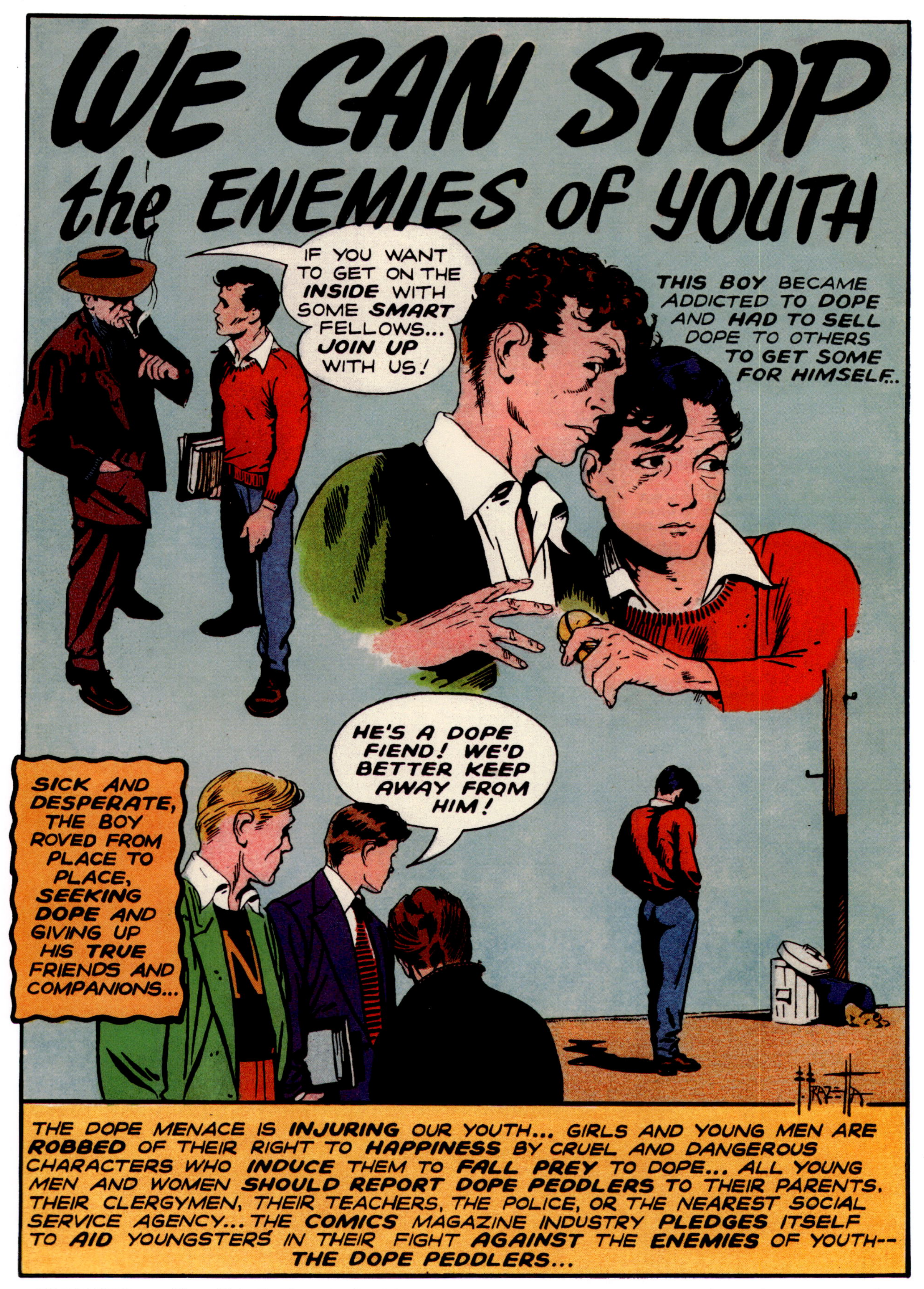
WE CAN STOP the ENEMIES of YOUTH
IF YOU WANT TO GET ON THE INSIDE WITH SOME SMART FELLOWS... JOIN UP WITH US!
THIS BOY BECAME ADDICTED TO DOPE AND HAD TO SELL DOPE TO OTHERS TO GET SOME FOR HIMSELF...
SICK AND DESPERATE, THE BOY ROVED FROM PLACE TO PLACE, SEEKING DOPE AND GIVING UP HIS TRUE FRIENDS AND COMPANIONS...
HE'S A DOPE FIEND! WE'D BETTER KEEP AWAY FROM HIM!
THE DOPE MENACE IS INJURING OUR YOUTH... GIRLS AND YOUNG MEN ARE ROBBED OF THEIR RIGHT TO HAPPINESS BY CRUEL AND DANGEROUS CHARACTERS WHO INDUCE THEM TO FALL PREY TO DOPE... ALL YOUNG MEN AND WOMEN SHOULD REPORT DOPE PEDDLERS TO THEIR PARENTS, THEIR CLERGYMEN, THEIR TEACHERS, THE POLICE, OR THE NEAREST SOCIAL SERVICE AGENCY... THE COMICS MAGAZINE INDUSTRY PLEDGES ITSELF TO AID YOUNGSTERS IN THEIR FIGHT AGAINST THE ENEMIES OF YOUTH-- THE DOPE PEDDLERS...
PREPARED THROUGH THE COOPERATION OF NEW YORK CITY YOUTH BOARD AND THE ASSOCIATION OF COMICS MAGAZINE PUBLISHERS...

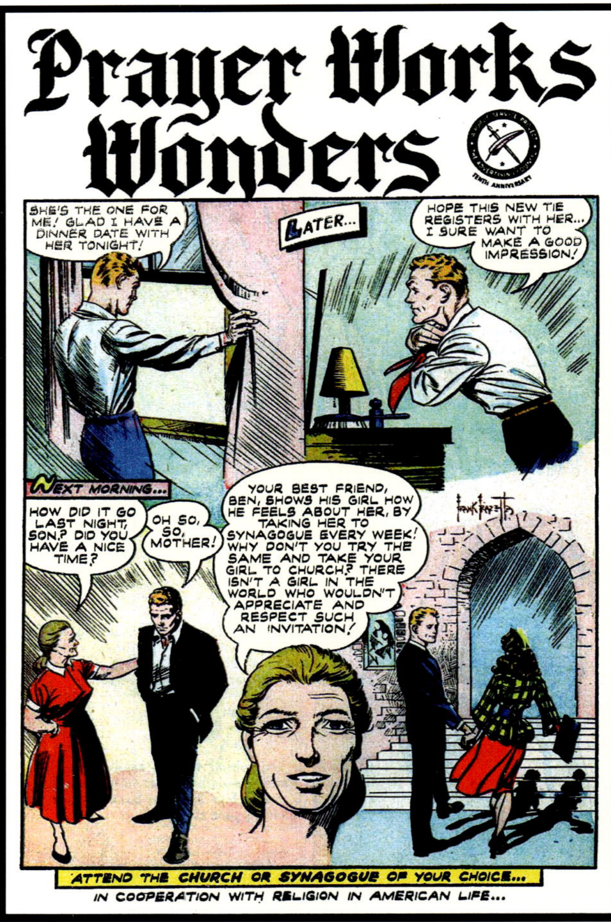

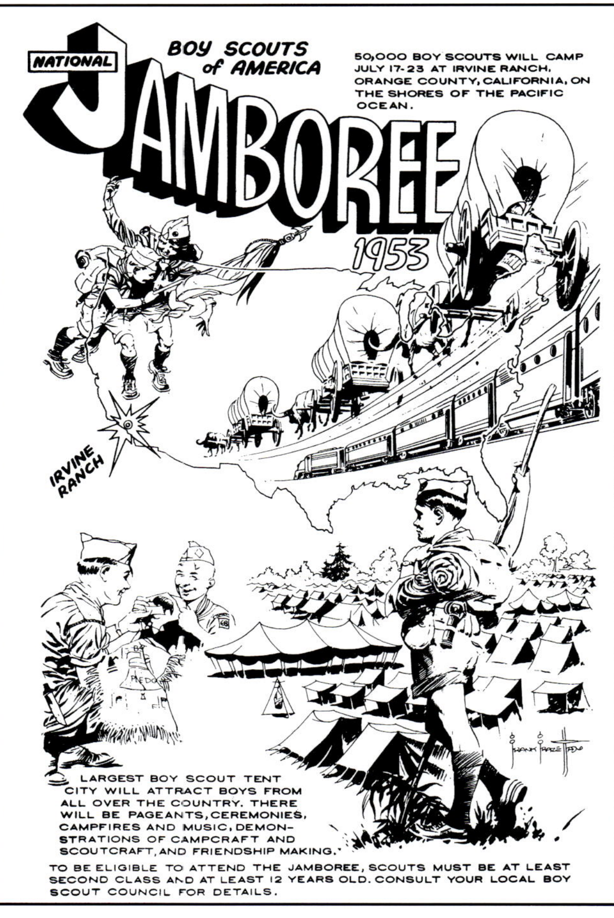

(Continued from page 14)

Frazetta wouldn't create his last PSA till he joined forces with Warren Publishing in the early sixties to work on the fledgling issues of CREEPY and EERIE magazine. This time it was to speak out against the hazards of smoking with the in-house ad, *"Easy Way to a Tuff Surfboard"*. It wasn't one of those lung cancerous, growth stunting, fetus damaging advertisements that we're all used to seeing today. Instead it spoke of the only hazard that could really be proven back then; smoking was a huge waste of money.

As it is obvious, PSAs are here to stay; with such current pitches as anti-smoking billboards and "buckle-up" television spots. Such PSAs as, *"This is your brain on drugs."* have become so ingrained within the American psyche as to have become part of modern pop culture. Considering how much Mr. Frazetta has already contributed to the breadth and width of this culture, it's rather interesting to note that he had an impact very early on with something as mundane as PSAs.

Paul Dennis Shiple graduated from the University of Toledo in 1993 with a BA in both Sociology and Political Science. He is currently living under the poverty line but is constantly amazed by "really good comics".

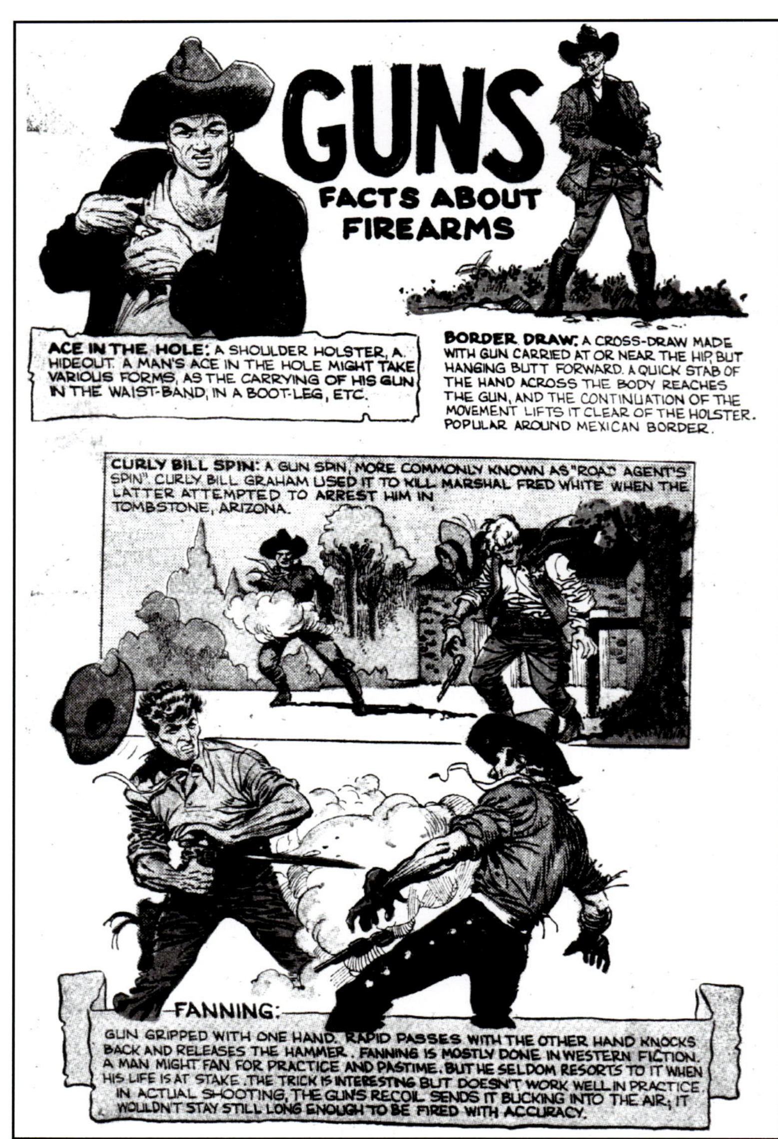

OPPOSITE: Artificial Respiration PSA 1950s.
Here, Buster Crabbe, drawn by Frazetta, is shown giving artificial respiration.

THIS PAGE: Various PSAs from the 1950s drawn by Frazetta.

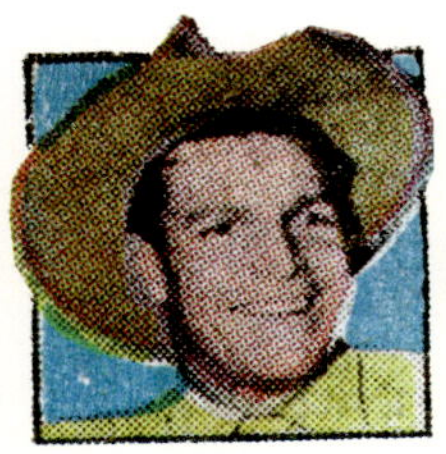

RED CROSS NEW METHOD OF ARTIFICIAL RESPIRATION

Washington, D.C.: correct positions for the back pressure--arm lift method of artificial respiration, recently adopted by the American National Red Cross upon recommendation of the National Research Council, are here illustrated by Buster Crabbe. In this method the victim is placed prone with the elbows bent and with one hand upon the other. The cheek is placed on the hand with the face turned slightly to one side. The operator kneels on one knee at the head of the victim.

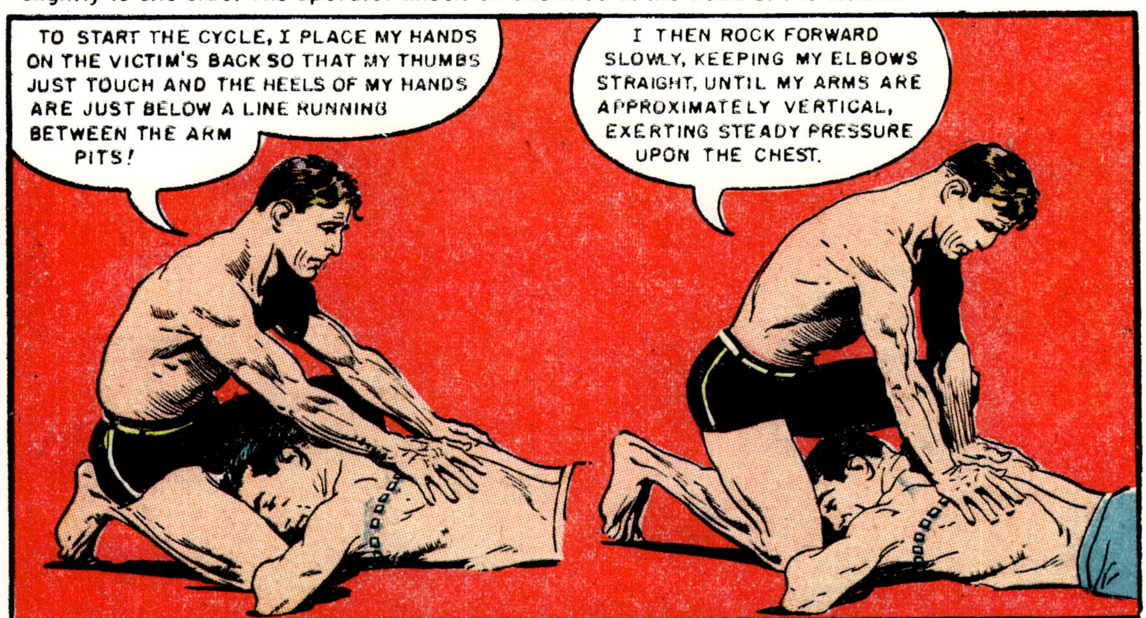

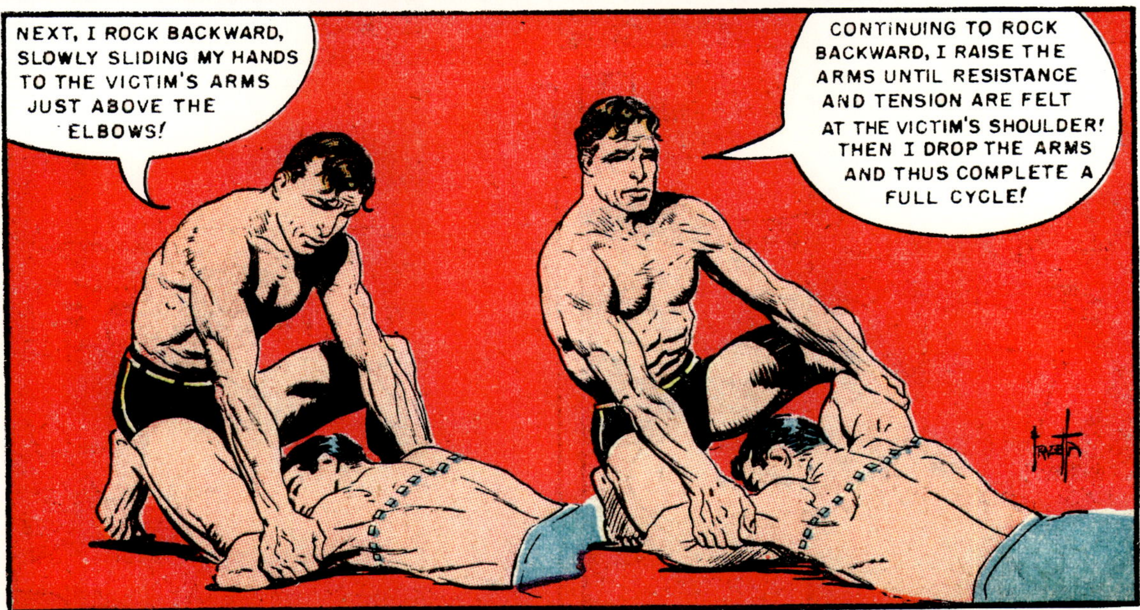

The cycles are repeated twelve times per minute, the expansion and compression phases being of equal length, and the release periods of minimum duration.

BARNYARD COMICS (DIZZY DUCK #32 on)
June 1944 - #31 September 1950
Nedor / Polo Magazines / Standard (Animated Cartoons)

The following issues, unless otherwise noted with page counts, contain quarter page text illustrations.

- 12 June 1947
  - *"Little Brother"*
  - *"Lazy Opposum"*
- 13 August 1947
  - *"Goldfish and the Sparrow"*
  - *"Flying Pig"*
  - *"Grateful Bear"*
- 14 October 1947
  - *"Jimpy Jumps"*
  - *"Jungle Prince"*
- 15 December 1947
  - *"Homeless Cat"*
    - **reprinted in** SMALL WONDERS (art book) b&w
  - *"The Walking Stick"*
    - **reprinted in** SMALL WONDERS (art book) b&w
- 16 February 1948
  - *"The Heroes of Duck Lake"*
  - *"The Hermit Frog"*
  - *"Baby Bunny"*
- 17 April 1948
  - *"Talking Giraffe"*
  - *"Bold Brave Moose"*
  - *"Kitten Who Wanted to Swim"*
- 18 June 1948
  - *"Circus Tickets"* 6 pp.
  - *"Beppo the Monk"*
  - *"Mouse and the Moose"*
  - *"Greedy Mole"*
- 19 August 1948
  - *"Barney Rooster"* 7 pp.
    - **reprinted in** FRANK FRAZETTA SPECIAL (fanzine)
    - **reprinted in** SMALL WONDERS (art book) b&w
  - *"Hucky Duck"* 2 pp.
    - **reprinted in** FRANK FRAZETTA SPECIAL (fanzine)
    - **reprinted in** BURIED TREASURE #1
    - First page **reprinted in** FRAZETTA TREASURY (fanzine)
  - *"Cats With Beautiful Tails"*
    - **reprinted in** FRANK FRAZETTA SPECIAL (fanzine)
  - *"The Cleverest One"*
    - **reprinted in** FRANK FRAZETTA SPECIAL (fanzine)
    - **reprinted in** SMALL WONDERS (art book) b&w
- 20 October 1948
  - *"Barney Rooster"* 7 pp.
    - first page **reprinted in** ICON (art book)
  - *"Big Ears and Little Ears"*
    - **reprinted in** SMALL WONDERS (art book) b&w
  - *"Ollie the Ostrich"*
  - *"The Forest Concert"*
    - **reprinted in** SMALL WONDERS (art book) b&w
- 21 December 1948
  - *"Let's Always Be Friends"*
  - *"Stubbornest Mule"*
  - *"The Lazy Beaver"*
- 22 February 1949
  - *"The Peculiar Duck"*
  - *"Freddy Bear to the Rescue"*
    - **reprinted in** SMALL WONDERS (art book) b&w
  - *"Hucky Duck"* 7 pp.
  - *"Mike and Jerry"*
    - **reprinted in** SMALL WONDERS (art book) b&w
- 23 April 1949
  - *"Miggles and Bojo"*
    - **reprinted in** SMALL WONDERS (art book) b&w
  - *"Scaredy Cat"*
    - **reprinted in** SMALL WONDERS (art book) b&w
  - *"Firefly's Light"*
- 24 June 1949
  - *"Barney's Little Helper" 7 pp.*
    - **reprinted in** SMALL WONDERS (art book) b&w
  - *"The Wonderful Machine" 3 pp.*
  - *"The Big Race"*
    - **reprinted in** SMALL WONDERS (art book) b&w
  - *"The Colt Who Was Too Good"*
    - **reprinted in** SMALL WONDERS (art book) b&w
- 25 August 1949
  - *"Circus Ticket" (Hucky Duck)* 6 pp.
    - **reprinted in** SMALL WONDERS (art book) b&w
  - *"Bashful Cricket"*
    - **reprinted in** FRANK FRAZETTA SPECIAL (fanzine)
  - *"The Talented Bear"*
    - **reprinted in** FRANK FRAZETTA SPECIAL (fanzine)
- 26 October 1949
  - *"Ollie the Ostrich"*
  - *"The Jitterbug"*
- 29 April 1950
  - *"The Gossip"*

• BEST OF HORROR AND SCIENCE FICTION COMICS
(one shot)
1987
Bruce Webster
  - *"Gave Life to Save Lives"* 2 pp.
    - **first printed in** HEROIC COMICS #72
  - *"We Can Stop the Enemies of Youth"* 1 pg. anti-drug ad
    - **first printed in** BUSTER CRABBE #1

• BEST OF LI'L ABNER
1978
Holt Paperbacks
Reprints LI'L ABNER newspaper strip

BEST OF THE WEST
AC Comics
- 25 2002
  - COVER - cover to Ghost Rider comic book
    - Ghost Rider text head illustration.

BEWARE
#13 January 1953 - #16 July 1953; #5 September 1953 - #15 May 1955
Trojan Magazines / Merit Publications
- 10 July 1954
  - COVER with Sid Check

BILLY THE KID ADVENTURE MAGAZINE
October 1950 - #30 1955
Toby Press
- 1 October 1950
  - *"Guns"* 2 pp. with Al Williamson
    - **first printed in** JOHN WAYNE ADV. COMICS #2
  - *"Draw"* 2 pp. with Al Williamson
- 3 February 1951
  - *"The Claws of Death"* 4 pp. with Al Williamson
    - **first printed in** JOHN WAYNE ADV. COMICS #3
- 6 August 1951
  - *"Nightmare"* 7 pp with Al Williamson
- 14 1952
  - *"Guns"* 2 pp. With Al Williamson
    - **first printed in** JOHN WAYNE ADV. COMICS #2
- 22 1953
  - *"Guns"* 1 pg. with Al Williamson
    - **first printed in** JOHN WAYNE ADV. COMICS #2

BLACK DIAMOND WESTERN
#9 1949 - #60 February 1956
Lev Gleason Publications
- 31 1954
  "*We Can Stop the Enemies of Youth*" 1 pg. anti-drug ad
  first printed in BUSTER CRABBE #1

BLACKHAWK (formerly UNCLE SAM #1-8)
#9 Winter 1944 - #243 Oct-Nov 1968 - #244 Jan-Feb 1976 - #250 Jan-Feb 1977 - #251 October 1982 - #273 December 1984
Comic Magazines (Quality) #9-107 (December 1956) National Periodical Publications #108-250 D.C. Comics #251 on
- 118 November 1957
  "*The Town Jesse James Couldn't Rob*" 3 pp.
  first printed in JIMMY WAKELY #4

BLACK TERROR
Winter 1942-43 - #27 June 1949
Better Publications / Standard
- 22 April 1948
  "*Violins for Villainy*" 11 pp. (certain panels)
- 24 October 1948
  "*From the Black Terror Scrap Book*" (lower left panel of the splash page)
  first printed in BLACK TERROR #22 single panel

BLAZING COMBAT b&w magazine
October 1965 - #4 July 1966
Warren Publishing Company
- 1 October 1965
  COVER - **Combat**
- 2 January 1966
  COVER - **Blazing Combat II**
- 3 April 1966
  COVER - **Blazing Combat III**
- 4 July 1966
  COVER - **Blazing Combat IV**
  "*Easy Way to a Tuff Surfboard!*" 1/2 pg. anti-smoking ad
  first printed in EERIE #3

BLAZING COMBAT comic format
1993
Apple
Contents of all issues reprinted from Warren Magazine series.
Korean War and Viet Nam
- 1 August 1993 COVER - **Blazing Combat III**
- 2 September 1993 COVER - **Combat**

WW I and WW II
- 2 June 1994 COVER - **Blazing Combat IV**
- 3 July 1994 COVER - **Blazing Combat II**

- **BLAZING COMBAT** graphic novel
  COVER - **Combat**

BOBBY BENSON'S B-BAR-B RIDERS
May-June 1950 - #20 May-June 1953
Magazine Enterprises
- 9 Jan-Feb 1951
  COVER
  reprinted in LEGACY (art book)
- 11 May-June 1951
  COVER
- 13 Sept-Oct 1951
  COVER featuring Ghost Rider

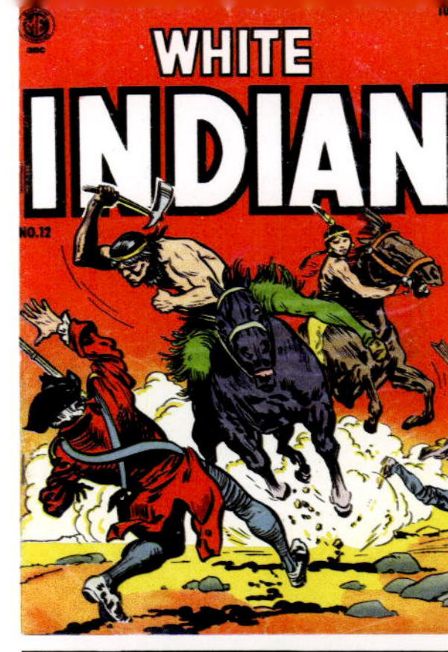

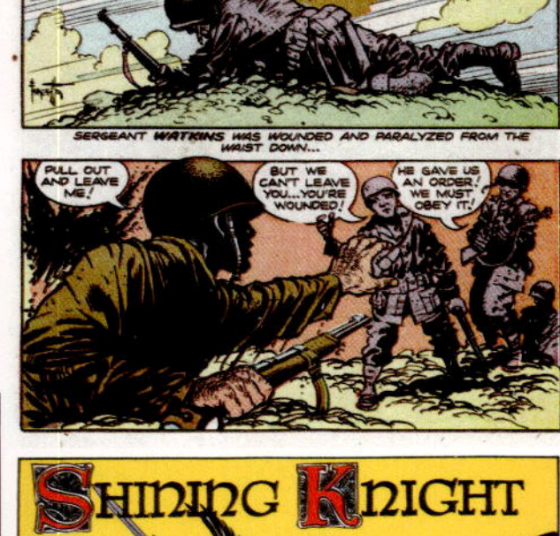

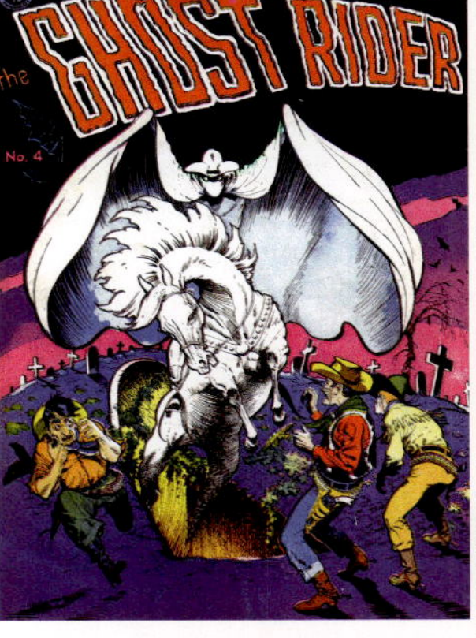

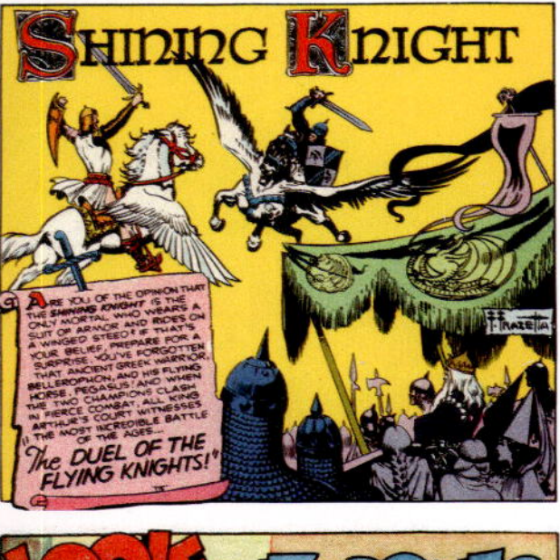

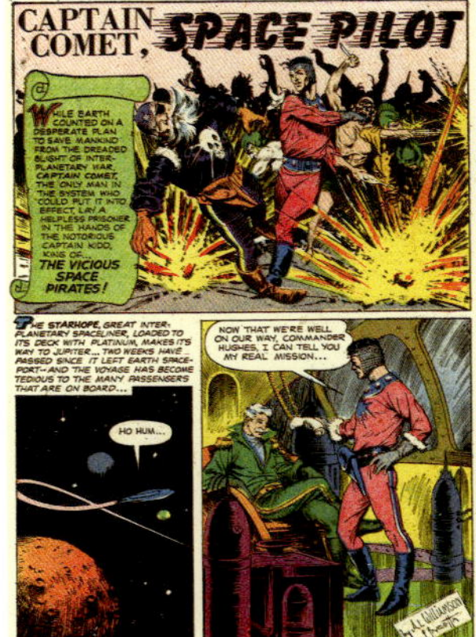

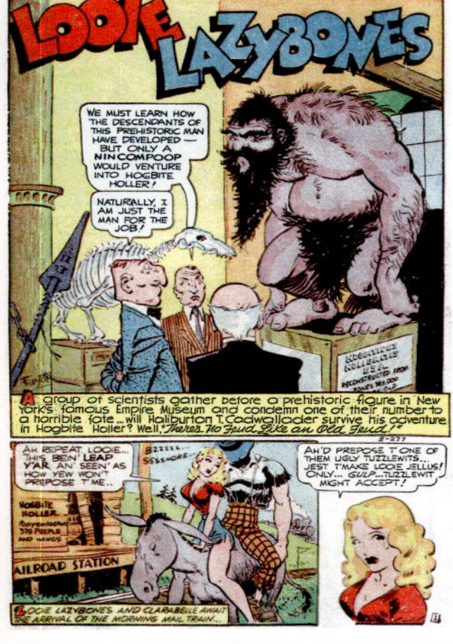

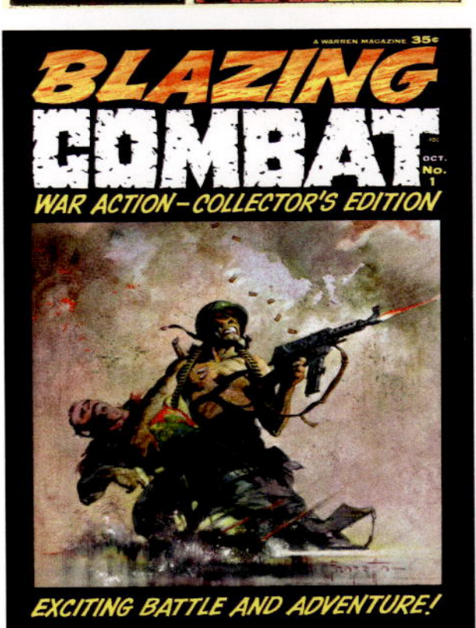

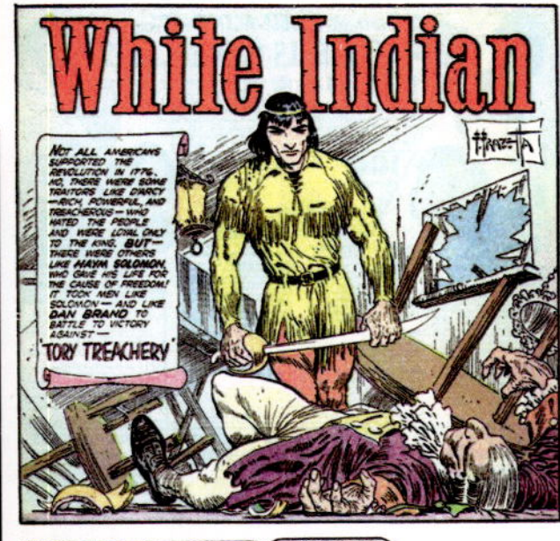

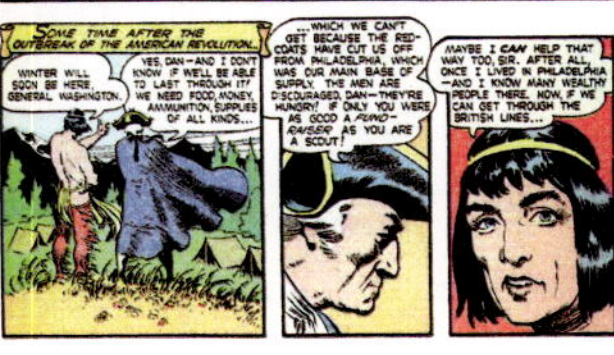

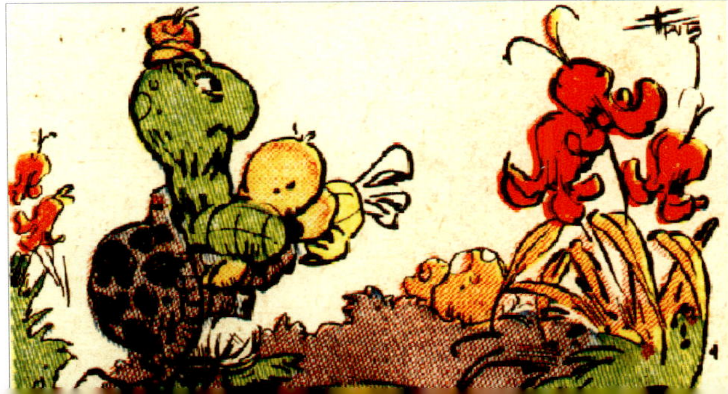

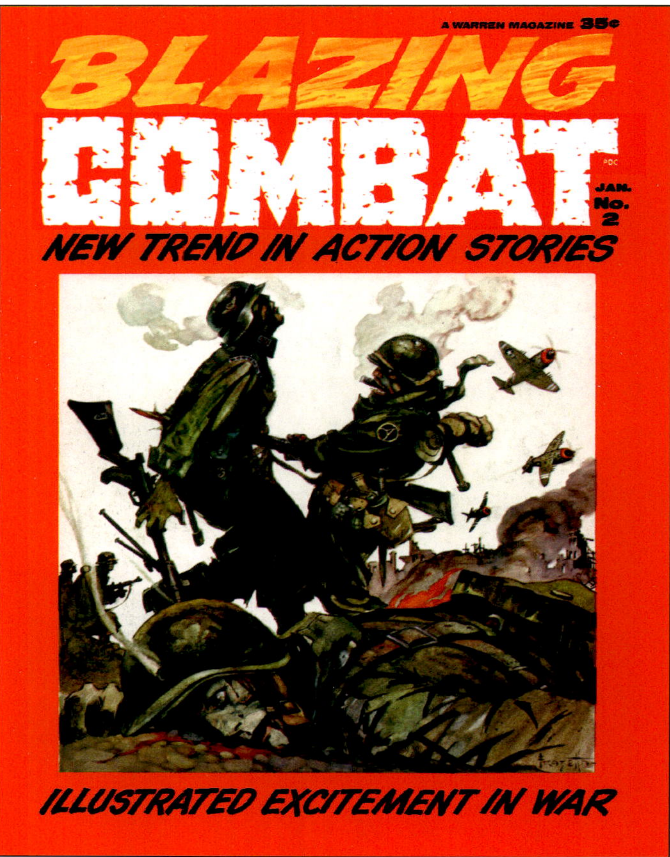

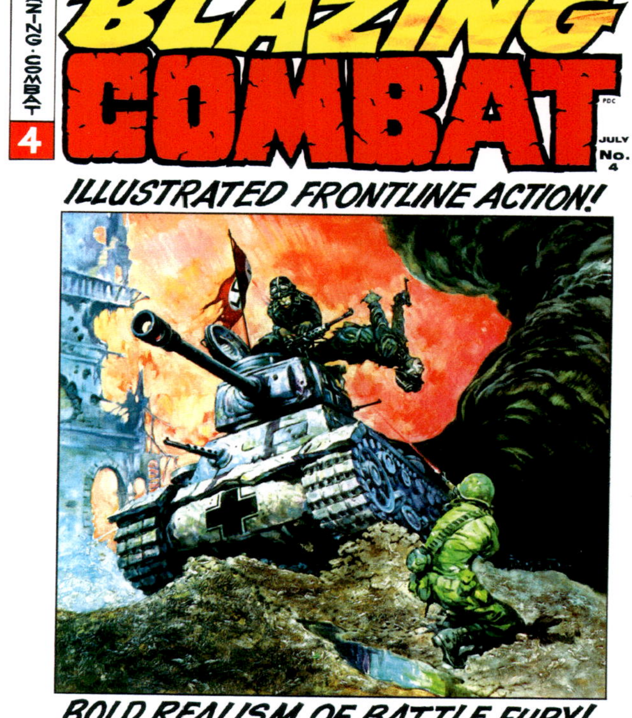

TOP: Blazing Combat # 2.
Warren Publications (Jan 1966)

ABOVE: Blazing Combat #4
Warren Publications (July 1966)

- **BOBBY BENSON'S B-BAR-B RIDERS** REPRINT one shot

AC Comics

COVER

first printed in BOBBY BENSON'S B-BAR-B RIDERS #11

BOOTS AND HER BUDDIES

#5 September 1948 - #9 September 1949

Standard Comics / Visual Editions / Argo (NEA Service)

- 9 September 1949 "*Toppsy Twins*" strips 2 pp.

BOY COMICS

Lev Gleason Publications / Comic House / Golfing

- 73

"*We Can Stop the Enemies of Youth*" 1 pg. ad

first printed in BUSTER CRABBE #1

BURIED TREASURE

1991

Caliber Press

- 1 April 1990

"*Hucky Duck*" 2 pp.

first printed in BARNYARD COMICS #19

- 2 1990 Frazetta nude illo (for a Harlan Ellison story)
- 3 August 1990

"A Love of My Own" 8 pp.

first printed in PERSONAL LOVE #24

- 4 1991

"*Always Around When Needed*" 2 pp.

first printed in HEROIC COMICS #70

"*Memorable Memorial Day*" 3 pp.

first printed in HEROIC COMICS #69

"*Brought Back to Life*" 1 pg.

first printed in HEROIC COMICS #75

"*Bivouac*" 2 pp.

first printed in HEROIC COMICS #73

"*Beyond the Call of Duty*" 3 pp.

first printed in HEROIC COMICS #69

"*He Stayed Behind*" 1 pg.

first printed in HEROIC COMICS #71

"*Heroism on the Korean Front*" 2 pp.

first printed in HEROIC COMICS #73

"*He Chose to Fight*" 2 pp.

first printed in HEROIC COMICS #72

"*With Only a Shovel*" 2 pp.

first printed in HEROIC COMICS #72

"*Stranded in a Mine Field*" 3 pp.

first printed in HEROIC COMICS #87

"*Only Doing His Job*" 2 pp.

first printed in HEROIC COMICS #86

untitled 3 pp.

first printed in HEROIC COMICS #72

BUSTER BUNNY

November 1949 - #16 October 1953

Standard Comics (Animated Cartoons) / Pines

- 1 November 1949

"*Davey*" 1/4 pg. text illustration

"*The Busy Bear*" 1/4 pg. text illustration

- 2 December 1949

1/4 pg. text illustration

BUSTER CRABBE

November 1951 - #12 1953

Famous Funnies Publications

- 1 November 1951

"*We Can Stop the Enemies of Youth*" 1 pg. anti-drug ad

reprinted in THE BEST OF HORROR AND SCIENCE FICTION COMICS
reprinted in BLACK DIAMOND WESTERN #31
reprinted in WHITE INDIAN (fanzine)
reprinted in COMICS INTERVIEW - FRAZETTA SPECIAL
reprinted in THE COMIC STRIP FRAZETTA (fanzine)
reprinted in CRIME DOES NOT PAY #106

reprinted in DAREDEVIL COMICS #82
reprinted in MURDER TALES #10
reprinted in TALES OF THE KILLERS #10

- 4 May 1952
  COVER
  reprinted in LEGACY (art book)
  reprinted in COMIC AND FANTASY ART APA #6 (fanzine)
  reprinted in LEGACY (art book)
  "*Red Cross Method of Artificial Respiration*" 1 pg.
  reprinted in HEROIC COMICS #72
  reprinted in PERSONAL LOVE #72
  reprinted in COMICS INTERVIEW - FRAZETTA SPECIAL
- 5 July 1952
  COVER
  reprinted in RETROSPECTIVE (art book), b/w
  reprinted in COMIC AND FANTASY ART APA #6 (fanzine)
  reprinted in FRAZETTA TREASURY (fanzine)
  reprinted in cover to BUSTER CRABBE #5 (b&w print)
  reprinted in THE GOLDEN AGE OF COMICS (trading cards)
  "*Maid of Mars*" 11 pp. with Al Williamson, Roy Krenkel and Joe Orlando
- 7 November 1952
  "*Prayer Works Wonders*" 1 pg. ad
  first printed in REAL CLUE CRIME STORIES Vol.7 #6
- 9 March 1953
  "*Boy Scout's Jamboree*" 1 pg.
  first printed in HEROIC COMICS #81

• CHIEF VICTORIO'S APACHE MASSACRE (one shot)
1951
Avon Periodicals
"*Chief Victorio's Apache Massacre*" 7 pp. with Al Williamson
reprinted in JESSE JAMES #20

CIRCUS COMICS
Winter 1948-49
D.S. Publications
- 1 1948-49
  "*Riddle in the Sawdust*" 2 pp.

COO COO COMICS (...THE BIRD BRAIN #57 on)
October 1942 - #62 April 1952
Nedor Publishing Company / Standard (Animated Cartoons)
The following issues, unless otherwise noted with page counts contain quarter page text illustrations.

- 34 July 1947
  "*Busy Billy Beaver*"
  "*Turtle and The Pelican*"
  reprinted in SMALL WONDERS (art book) b&w
  "*Percy The Puffer-fish*"
- 35 September 1947
  "*The Lonely Turtle*"
  "*Word to the Wise*"
  reprinted in SMALL WONDERS (art book) b&w
  "*Kitty on the Keys*"
- 36 November 1947
  "*Ferdinand and his Friends*"
  "*Pat Pony Heads the West*"
- 37 January 1948
  "*Maggie the Magpie*"
- 38 March 1948
  "*Elephant Who Never Remembered*"
  "*Playful Bear*"
- 39 May 1948
  "*Ferocious Lamb*"
  reprinted in SMALL WONDERS (art book) b&w
  "*Barnyard Hero*"
  reprinted in SMALL WONDERS (art book) b&w
  "*Flying Possum*"

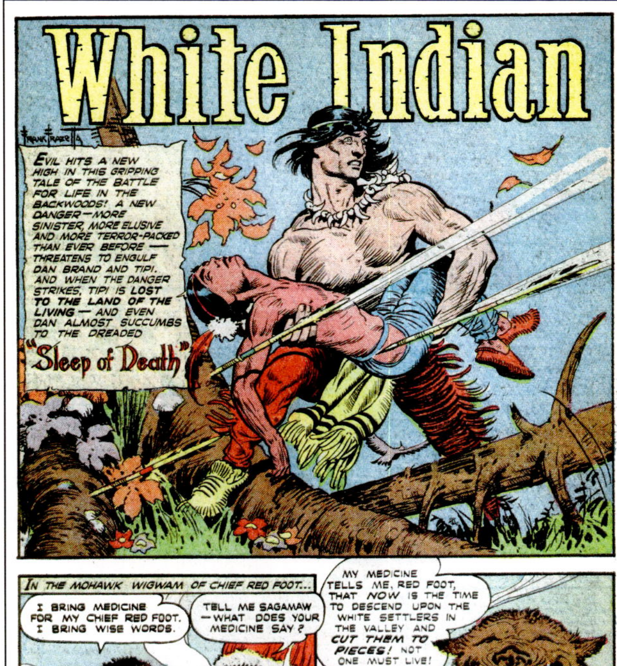

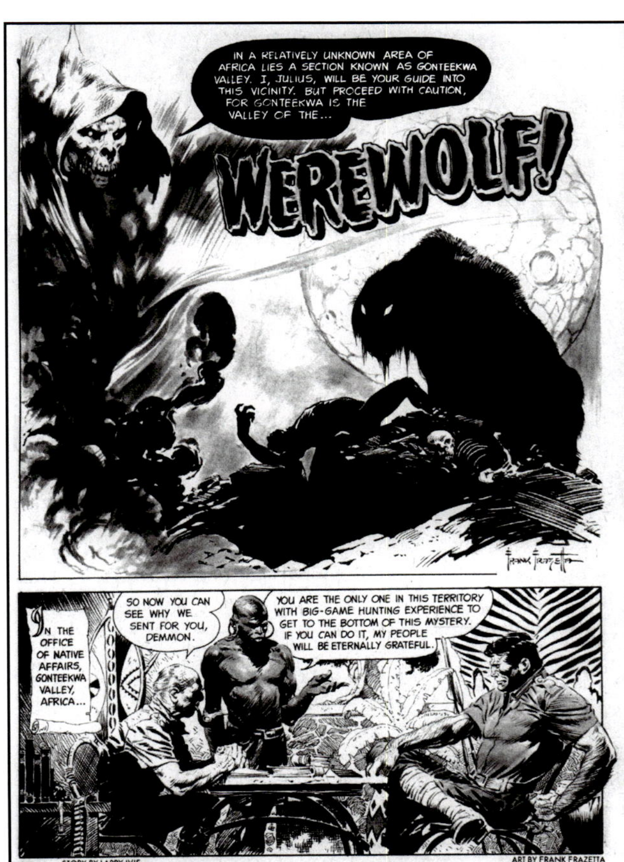

TOP: White Indian *from* The Durango Kid *#10*
Magazine Enterprises (April/May 1951)

ABOVE: "Werewolf" *from* Creepy *#1*
Warren Publishing (1964)

COO COO COMICS *cont'd*

- 40 July 1948
  - *"Wingtown Drummer"*
  - *"Ambitious Fox"*
  - *"Lion and the Hyena"* 2 pp.
- 41 September 1948
  - *"Supermouse"* 9 pp.
  - *"Dodger"* 6 pp.
  - *"Clunky the Elephant"*
  - *"The Lamb Who Wanted to be Somebody"*
  - *"The Showoff"*
- 42 November 1948
  - *"Dodger the Squoil"* 5 pp.
  - *"The First to Crow"*
  - *"The Strange Little Creature"* 2 illustrations
    - **reprinted in** SMALL WONDERS (art book) b&w
- 43 January 1949
  - *"Small Fry"*
    - **reprinted in** SMALL WONDERS (art book) b&w
  - *"Johnny Sheds His Pride"* 2 illustrations
- 44 March 1949
  - *"Supermouse"* 9 pp.
  - *"Butch and Buttercup"* 5 pp.
  - *"Wishful Willy"*
  - *"Chauncy the Chick"*
  - *"A Cure for Chubby Chipmunk"*
- 45 May 1949
  - *"Butch and Buttercup"* 5 pp.
  - *"Bunny who Wanted to Know"*
  - *"Fisty"* 7 pp.
  - *"Hardback Softheart"*
- 46 July 1949
  - *"The Busy Bear"*
  - *"Trouble Twins"*
- 47 September 1949
  - *"The Unsociable Turtle"* 2 text illustrations
    - **reprinted in** SMALL WONDERS (art book) b&w
  - *"Spare That Tree"* 5 pp.
    - **reprinted in** SMALL WONDERS (art book) b&w
    - 3 panels **reprinted in** THE COMICS JOURNAL (magazine)
  - *"Kitten and the Mitten"*
- 48 November 1949
  - *"Foolish Spider"*
  - *"The Head of the School"*
- 49 January 1950
  - *"Forest Hero"*
  - *"Nothing At All"*
    - **reprinted in** SMALL WONDERS (art book) b&w
- 50 March 1950
  - *"Willy the Willing Whale"*

CREEPY b&w magazine
1964 - #145 February 1983 - #146 1985
Warren Publishing Company / Harris Publications #146

- 1 1964
  - *"Werewolf"* 6 pp.
    - **reprinted in** CREEPY YEARBOOK 1968
    - **reprinted in** CREEPY, THE CLASSIC YEARS
    - 3 panels **reprinted in** COMICS INTERVIEW - FRAZETTA SPECIAL
    - first page **reprinted in** ICON (art book)
  - Uncle Creepy with Gremlin appears in subscription ad.
- 2 April 1965 COVER - **Circle of Terror**
  - *"Creepy's Loathsome Lore"* 1 pg. (werewolves)
    - **reprinted in** TESTAMENT (art book)
- 3 June 1965
  - COVER - **Dead of Night**
- 4 August 1965
  - COVER - **Wolfman**
- 5 October 1965
  - COVER - **Count Dracula**
- 6 December 1965
  - COVER - **Gargoyle** (with Roy Krenkel)
- 7 February 1966
  - COVER - **Dracula Meets the Wolfman** (with Roy Krenkel)
  - *"Creepy's Loathsome Lore"* 1 pg. (werebeasts)
    - **reprinted in** ICON (art book)
- 9 June 1966
  - COVER - **Winged Terror**
    - **reprinted in** TESTAMENT (art book)
  - *"Easy Way to a Tuff Surfboard!"* 1/2 pg. anti-smoking strip
    - **first printed in** EERIE #3
- 10 August 1966
  - COVER - **Beyond the Grave**
- 11 October 1966
  - COVER - **King Kong** (original version)
- 15 June 1967
  - COVER - **Neanderthal**
- 16 August 1967
  - COVER - **Cat Girl** (original version)
- 17 October 1967
  - COVER - **Executioner**
  - *"Creepy's Loathsome Lore"* 1 pg. (subject: werewolves)
    - **first printed in** CREEPY #2
- 27 June 1969
  - COVER - **Mongol Tyrant**
- 29 September 1969
  - VAMPIRELLA teaser advertisement
- 30 December 1969
  - *"Easy Way to a Tuff Surfboard!"* 1/2 pg. anti smoking ad
    - **first printed in** EERIE #3
- 32 April 1970
  - COVER - **Nightstalker**
- 34 August 1970
  - *"Easy Way to a Tuff Surfboard!"* 1/2 pg. anti smoking ad
    - **first printed in** EERIE #3
- 55 August 1973
  - COVER - includes collage of artwork from earlier covers
  - *"The Creepy Crawly Castle Game"* pull-out game contains pieces of artwork from earlier covers
- 83 October 1976
  - COVER - **Neanderthal**
    - **first printed in** CREEPY #15
- 89 June 1977
  - COVER - **Combat**
    - **first printed in** BLAZING COMBAT #1
- 91 August 1977
  - COVER - **Woman With a Scythe**
    - **first printed in** VAMPIRELLA #11
- 92 October 1977
  - COVER - **Egyptian Queen**
    - **first printed in** EERIE #23
- 97 May 1978
  - COVER - **Sea Monster**
    - **first printed in** EERIE #3
- 128 June 1981
  - COVER - **Beyond the Grave**
    - **first printed in** CREEPY #10
- 131 September 1981
  - COVER - **Wolfmoon**
    - **first printed in** CREEPY #4
- 144 January 1983
  - COVER - **Dracula**
    - **first printed in** CREEPY #5
- 1968 yearbook
  - COVER - reprints cover #s 4, 5, 7
  - *"Werewolf"* 6 pp.
    - **first printed in** CREEPY #1
  - Inside Front Cover - Uncle Creepy with Gremlin
    - **first printed in** CREEPY #1

- 1969 yearbook
  "*Creepy's Loathsome Lore*" (Werebeasts) 1 pg.
  first printed in CREEPY #7
- 1970 yearbook
  COVER - reprints cover #s 11, 15, 16, 17

- **CREEPY: THE CLASSIC YEARS** (one shot)

1997
Harris Comics
"*Werewolf*" 6 pp.
first printed in CREEPY #1
also contains reprinted covers from various issues

CREEPY ARCHIVES
2008-present
Dark Horse Comics
- Vol. 1 Reprints Creepy #s 1-5
  COVER **Count Dracula**
- Vol. 2 Reprints Creepy #s 6-10
  COVER **Gargoyle**
- Vol. 3 Reprints Creepy #s 11-15
  COVER **King Kong** (1st version)
- Vol. 4 Reprints Creepy #s 16-20
  COVER **Cat Girl** (1st version)
- Vol. 5 Reprints Creepy #s 21-25
- Vol. 6 Reprints Creepy #s 26-30
  COVER **Mongol Tyrant**
- Vol. 7 Reprints Creepy #s 33-36
  COVER **Night Stalker**

CRIME AND PUNISHMENT
Lev Gleason Publications / Comic House / Golfing
- 46
  "*We Can Stop the Enemies of Youth*" 1 pg. ad
  first printed in BUSTER CRABBE #1

CRIME DOES NOT PAY Formerly SILVER STREAK COMICS No. 1-21
#22 June, 1942 - #47 July, 1955
Lev Gleason Publications / Comic House / Golfing
- 106 January 1952
  "*We Can Stop the Enemies of Youth*" 1 pg. ad
  first printed in BUSTER CRABBE #1
- 114
  "*We Can Stop the Enemies of Youth*" 1 pg. ad
  first printed in BUSTER CRABBE #1

CRIME MYSTERIES
May 1952 - #15 September 1954
Ribage Publishing Corporation
- 3 September 1952 1 pg. ad
- 4 November 1952 1 pg. ad

CRIME SMASHERS
October 1950 - #15 March 1953
Ribage Publishing Corporation
- 12 September 1952
  "*Prayer Works Wonders*" 1 pg. ad
  first printed in REAL CLUE CRIME STORIES Vol.7 #6
- 13 November 1952
  "*Prayer Works Wonders*" 1 pg. ad
  first printed in REAL CLUE CRIME STORIES Vol.7 #6

CRIME SUSPENSTORIES (formerly VAULT OF HORROR)
#15 Oct-Nov 1950 - #27 Feb-Mar 1955
E.C. Comics
- 17 June-July 1953
  "*Fired*" 6 pp. with Al Williamson
  reprinted in THE COMPLETE E.C. LIBRARY (art book)

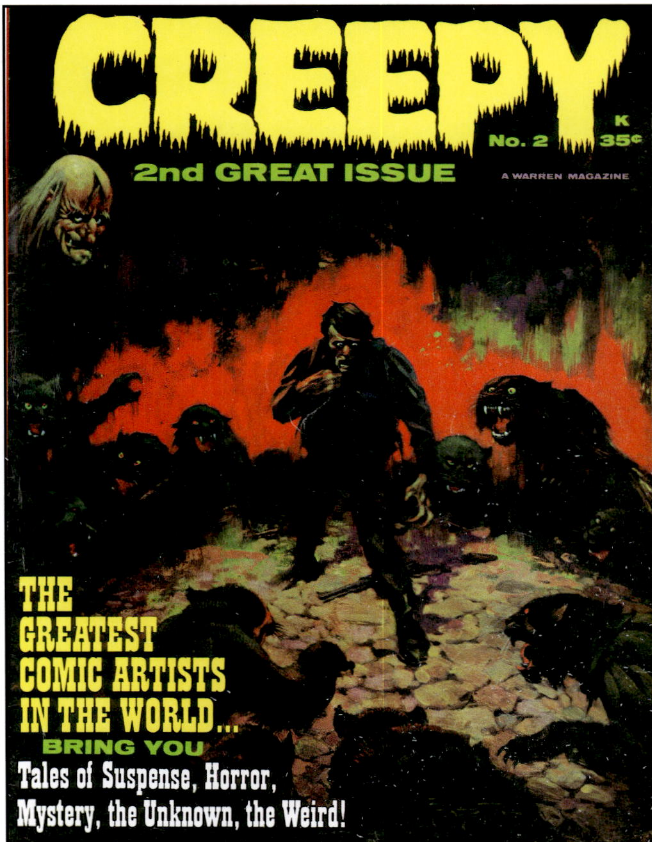

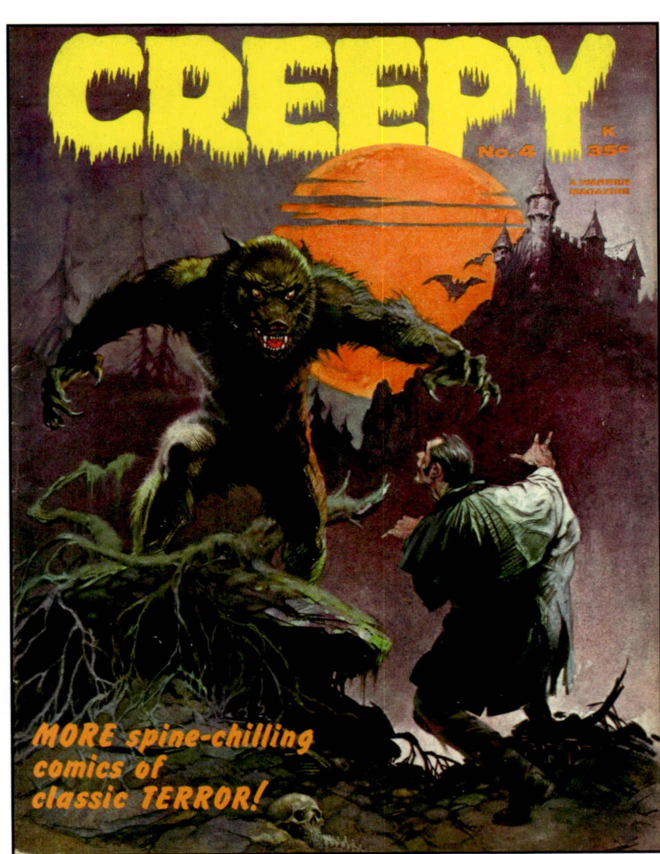

TOP: Creepy #2
Warren Publications (April 1965)

ABOVE: Creepy #4
Warren Publications (Aug. 1966)

DANGER IS OUR BUSINESS
December 1953 - #10 June 1955
Toby Press
- 1 1953
  "*The Vicious Space Pirates*" 6 pp. with Al Williamson
  reprinted in #9
  reprinted in THE ART OF AL WILLIAMSON (Art Books)
  4 pages **reprinted in** RUSS COCHRAN COMIC ART #4 (auction catalog)
- 9 1964
  "*The Vicious Space Pirates*" 6 pp. with Al Williamson
  first printed in #1

DAREDEVIL COMICS
July 1941 - #134 Sept. 1956
Lev Gleason Publications
- 82
  "*We Can Stop the Enemies of Youth*" one pg. ad
  first printed in BUSTER CRABBE #1
- 90 one pg. ad

DEAD EYE WESTERN COMICS
Nov.- Dec, 1948 - vol.3 #1, Apr.- May, 1953
Hillman Periodicals
- 9
  "*Prayer Works Wonders*" one pg. ad
  first printed in REAL CLUE CRIME STORIES Vol.7 #6

DEATH DEALER
July 1995 - 1997
Verotik
- 1 July 1995 COVER – **Death Dealer II**
- 2 May 1996 COVER – **Death Dealer VI**
  1 pg. text by Frazetta w/ **Self Portrait**
- 3 April 1997 COVER – **Death Dealer**
  1 pg ad for Frazetta Museum w/ **Conan**
- 4 July 1997 COVER – **Death Dealer IV**

DEATH RATTLE
Vol. 2 #1 October 1985 - #18 1988
Kitchen Sink
- 10 April 1987
  "*Savage World*" 8 pp. with Al Williamson, Torres and Roy Krenkel
  first printed in WITZEND #1 (fanzine)

• DOC WEIRD'S THRILL BOOK
1986
Pure Imagination
"*Demons of Destruction*" 10 pp. with Al Williamson
first printed in FORBIDDEN WORLDS #1

DREAM OF LOVE
1958
I.W. Enterprises
- 9 1958
  single illustration from "*Guns*"
  first printed in JOHN WAYNE ADV. COMICS #2

DURANGO KID, THE
Oct-Nov 1949 - #41 Oct-Nov 1955
Magazine Enterprises
ALL STORIES FEATURE WHITE INDIAN
- 1 Oct-Nov 1949
  untitled first White Indian story 7 pp.
  reprinted in A-1 COMICS #94
  reprinted in WHITE INDIAN (fanzine)
  reprinted in L'INDIAN BLANC (international publication)
  reprinted in FANTASTIC EXPLOITS #17 (fanzine)
- 2 Dec-Jan 1950
  "*Blood on the Frontier*" 7 pp.
  reprinted in A-1 COMICS #94
  reprinted in WHITE INDIAN (fanzine)
  reprinted in L'INDIAN BLANC (international publication)
- 3 Feb-Mar 1950
  "*War on the River*" 7 pp.
  reprinted in A-1 COMICS #94
  reprinted in WHITE INDIAN (fanzine)
  reprinted in L'INDIAN BLANC (international publication)
  reprinted in CD ROM COMICS (miscellaneous)
- 4 Apr-May 1950
  "*Brothers of the Wilderness*" 7 pp.
  reprinted in A-1 COMICS #94
  reprinted in WHITE INDIAN (fanzine)
  reprinted in L'INDIAN BLANC (international publication)
  Splash page **reprinted in** LEGACY (art book)
- 5 June-July 1950
  "*Trees of Doom*" 7 pp.
  reprinted in A-1 COMICS #101
  reprinted in WHITE INDIAN (fanzine)
  reprinted in L'INDIAN BLANC (international publication)
  reprinted in CD ROM COMICS (miscellaneous)
- 6 Aug-Sept 1950 "*Pirates Fury*" 7 pp.
- 7 Oct-Nov 1950
  "*The Battle of the Dungeons*" 7 pp.
  reprinted in THE COMIC STRIP FRAZETTA (fanzine)
- 8 Dec-Jan 1951
  "*Massacre*" 7 pp. with Al Williamson
  reprinted in THE COMIC STRIP FRAZETTA (fanzine)
- 9 Feb-Mar 1951
  "*Tory Treachery*" 7 pp.
  reprinted in A-1 COMICS #101
  reprinted in WHITE INDIAN (fanzine)
  reprinted in L'INDIAN BLANC (international publication)
  reprinted in CD ROM COMICS (miscellaneous)
- 10 Apr-May 1951
  "*Sleep of Death*" 8 pp.
  reprinted in A-1 COMICS #101
  reprinted in WHITE INDIAN (fanzine)
  reprinted in COMIC AND CRYPT #7 (fanzine)
  reprinted in L'INDIAN BLANC (international publication)
  reprinted in CD ROM COMICS (miscellaneous)
- 11 June-July 1951
  "*The Blood of Valley Forge*" 7 pp.
  reprinted in A-1 COMICS #101
  reprinted in WHITE INDIAN (fanzine)
  reprinted in L'INDIAN BLANC (international publication)
  reprinted in CD ROM COMICS (miscellaneous)
- 12 Aug-Sept 1951
  "*River Gauntlet*" 7 pp.
  reprinted in A-1 COMICS #104
  reprinted in L'INDIAN BLANC (international publication)
  reprinted in CD ROM COMICS (miscellaneous)
- 13 Oct-Nov 1951
  "*Trial of the Traitor*" 7 pp.
  reprinted in A-1 COMICS #104
  reprinted in RUSS COCHRAN COMIC ART #59 (auction catalog)
  reprinted in L'INDIAN BLANC (international publication)
  reprinted in CD ROM COMICS (miscellaneous)
- 14 Dec-Jan 1952
  "*Voyage Into Danger*" 8 pp.
  reprinted in A-1 COMICS #104
  reprinted in L'INDIAN BLANC (international publication)
  reprinted in CD ROM COMICS (miscellaneous)
- 15 Feb-Mar 1952
  "*The White Wolf*" 6 pp.
  reprinted in RUSS COCHRAN COMIC ART #60 (auction catalog)
- 16 Apr-May 1952
  "*Underworld of the Wilderness*" 7 pp.
  reprinted in A-1 COMICS #104
  reprinted in THE COMIC STRIP FRAZETTA (fanzine)
  reprinted in L'INDIAN BLANC (international publication)
  reprinted in CD ROM COMICS (miscellaneous)

DURANGO KID, THE

1990 - #2 1990
AC Comics
- 2 1990
  reprints of White Indian stories
  first printed in DURANGO KID (first series)

EERIE

September 1965 - #2 March 1966 - #139 February 1983
Warren Publishing Company
- 2 March 1966 COVER - **Sorcerer**
- 3 May 1966
  COVER - **Sea Monster** (original version)
  "Easy way to a tuff surfboard!" 1/2 pg. anti-smoking ad
  reprinted in BLAZING COMBAT #4
  reprinted in CREEPY #s 9, 30, 34
  reprinted in EERIE #s 3, 4, 23, 35, 1970 yearbook
  reprinted in FAMOUS MONSTERS #s 39, 67, 69, 80, 81, 1971 annual
  reprinted in VAMPIRELLA #s 8, 13
- 4 July 1966
  "Easy way to a Tuff Surfboard!" 1/2 pg. anti-smoking ad
  first printed in EERIE #3
- 5 September 1966
  COVER - **Swamp God**
  reprinted in ICON (art book)
- 7 January 1967
  COVER - **Sea Witch**
- 8 March 1967
  COVER - **The Brain**
- 23 September 1969
  COVER - **Egyptian Queen**
  "Easy way to a Tuff Surfboard!" 1/2 pg. anti-smoking ad
  first printed in EERIE #3
- 24 November 1969
  VAMPIRELLA advertisement with Frazetta illustration
- 35 September 1971
  "Easy way to a Tuff Surfboard!" 1/2 pg. anti-smoking ad
  first printed in EERIE #3
- 81 February 1977
  COVER - **Queen Kong**
- 84 June 1977
  COVER - **The Brain**
  first printed in EERIE #8
- 87 October 1977
  COVER - **Sun Goddess**
  first printed in VAMPIRELLA #7
- 124 September 1981
  COVER - **Dracula Meets the Wolfman** (with Roy Krenkel)
  first printed in CREEPY #7
- 1970 yearbook
  COVER - a collage of earlier covers
  "Easy way to a Tuff Surfboard!" 1/2 pg. anti-smoking ad
  first printed in EERIE #3
- 1971 annual
  COVER - shows **Egyptian Queen**
  first printed in EERIE #23

EERIE ARCHIVES

2008-present
Dark Horse Comics
- Vol. 1 Reprints Eerie #s 1-5
  COVER **Sorcerer**
- Vol. 2 Reprints Eerie #s 6-10
  COVER **The Brain**
- Vol. 3 Reprints Eerie #s 11-15
  COVER **Sea Monster**
- Vol. 4 Reprints Eerie #s 16-20
  COVER **Sea Witch**

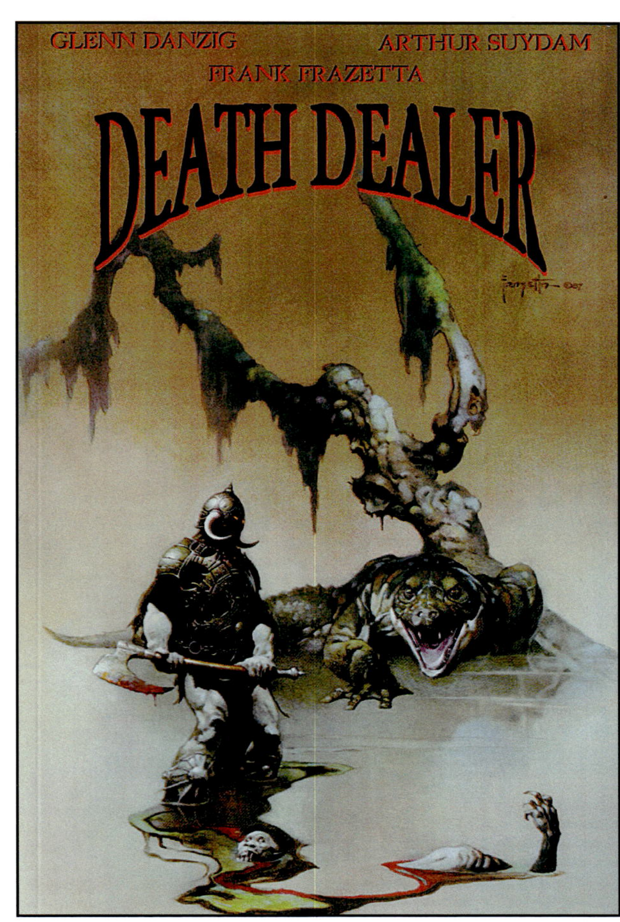

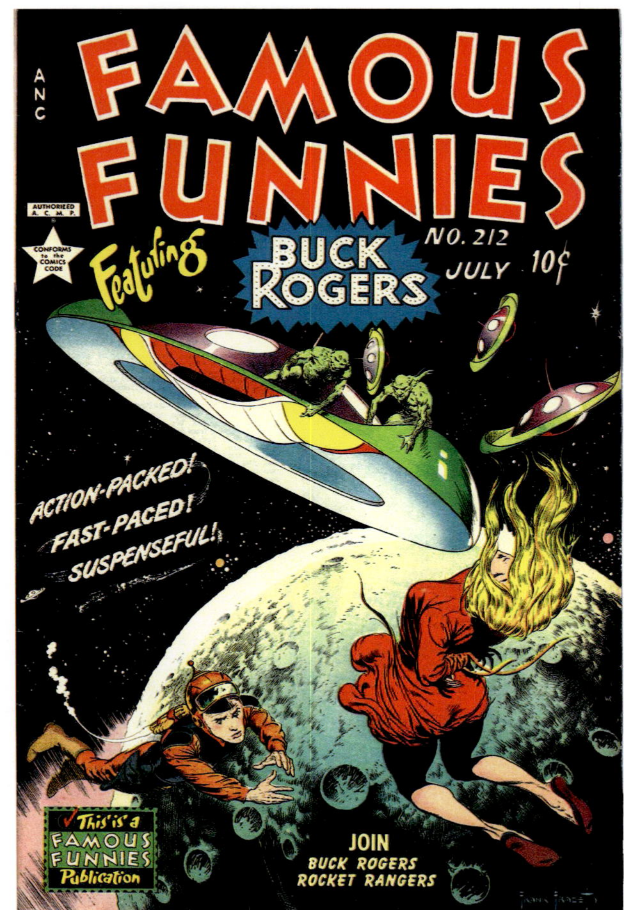

TOP: Death Dealer #2 *Verotik* *(July 1995)*

RIGHT: *Famous Funnies* #212 Eastern Color *(Jun. 1954)*

"Frazetta is a remarkably versatile artist. At a time when comics allowed many more genres, he could draw any one of them, and seemed to have a unique style for each one."

Mort Weisinger

Mr. Weisinger is a retired editor for D.C. Comics having worked there since the company's fledgling years. At the time, he was responsible for many of the giant titles published by D.C. This included Adventure Comics *during the time Frazetta was submitting his Shining Knight stories to the book.*

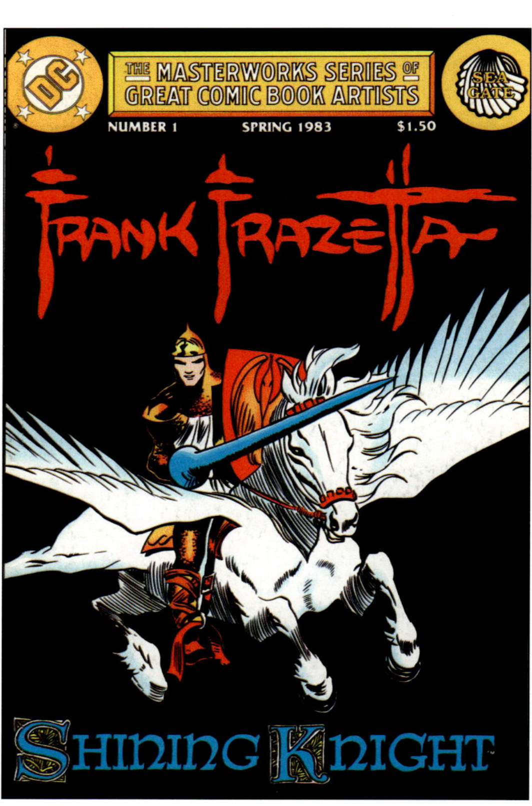

ABOVE: The Masterworks Series of Great Comic Book Artists #1 *DC Comics, (Spring 1983)*

EPIC ILLUSTRATED
Spring 1980 - #36 February 1986
Marvel Comics Group
- 1 Spring 1980 COVER - **Seven Romans**

EXCITING COMICS
April 1940 - #69 September 1949
Standard Comics
- 59 January 1948 *"The Deadly Quest"* 9 pp.

FAMOUS FUNNIES
1933 - #218 July 1955
Eastern Color
- 198 February 1952 1 pg. ad
- 200 June 1952 1 pg. ad
- 202 October 1952
  "Prayer Works Wonders" 1 pg.
  first printed in REAL CLUE CRIME STORIES Vol.7 #6
- 205 April 1953 1 pg. ad
- 209 December 1953
  COVER featuring Buck Rogers
  reprinted in FRANK FRAZETTA - THE LIVING LEGEND (art book)
  reprinted in LEGACY (art book)
  reprinted in GLAMOUR INTERNATIONAL (art book)
  reprinted in FRANK FRAZETTA: BOOK FIVE (titled "On The Stairs")
  reprinted in TESTAMENT (art book) (recolored version)
- 210 February 1954
  COVER featuring Buck Rogers
  reprinted in FRANK FRAZETTA - THE LIVING LEGEND (art book)
  reprinted in SPA-FON #2 (fanzine)
  reprinted in FROM AARGH! TO ZAP! (art book)
  reprinted in FRANK FRAZETTA: BOOK FIVE (art book)
  reprinted in TESTAMENT (art book)(recolored version)
- 211 April 1954
  COVER featuring Buck Rogers
  reprinted in ICON (art book)
  reprinted in TESTAMENT (art book)(recolored version)
- 212 June 1954
  COVER featuring Buck Rogers
  reprinted in FRANK FRAZETTA - THE LIVING LEGEND (art book)
  reprinted in RETROSPECTIVE (art book), b/w
  reprinted in COMICS INTERVIEW (magazine)
  reprinted in FRANK FRAZETTA: BOOK FIVE (art book)
  reprinted in THE BEST OF FRAZETTA (card set - subset)
  reprinted in TESTAMENT (art book)(recolored version)
- 213 Aug 1954
  COVER featuring Buck Rogers
  reprinted in SQUA TRONT #1 (fanzine)
  reprinted in THE COMICS JOURNAL #174 (magazine)
  reprinted in LEGACY (art book)
  reprinted in FROM AARGH! TO ZAP! (art book)
  reprinted in FRANK FRAZETTA: BOOK THREE
  (titled "Monster Entering Space Vehicle")
- 214 October 1954
  COVER featuring Buck Rogers
  reprinted in ICON (art book)
  reprinted in THE GOLDEN AGE OF COMICS (card set)
  reprinted in FROM AARGH! TO ZAP! (art book)
  reprinted in FRANK FRAZETTA: BOOK THREE (titled"Attack")
- 215 December 1954
  COVER featuring Buck Rogers
  reprinted in FRANK FRAZETTA - THE LIVING LEGEND (art book)
  reprinted in RETROSPECTIVE (art book), b/w
  reprinted in SPA-FON #3 (fanzine)
  reprinted in LEGACY (art book)
  reprinted in FROM AARGH! TO ZAP! (art book)
  reprinted in FRANK FRAZETTA: BOOK FIVE (art book)
  reprinted in THE BEST OF FRAZETTA (card set - subset)
- 216 February 1955
  COVER featuring Buck Rogers
  reprinted in FRANK FRAZETTA - THE LIVING LEGEND (art book)
  reprinted in FRANK FRAZETTA: BOOK FIVE (art book)
  (titled "Asteroid Explosion")

Covers for issues 209 – 216 are reprinted as a portfolio, re-colored by Frazetta see PORTFOLIOS, PRINTS AND POSTERS

FANTASTIC WORLDS OF FRANK FRAZETTA, THE
2009
Image
• VOL. 1 COVER - Swamp Demon
Reprints the following one shot comic books:
Frank Frazetta's Swamp Demon
Frank Frazetta's Creatures
Frank Frazetta's Dark Kingdom
Frank Frazetta's Dracula Meets the Wolfman

• VOL. 2 COVER - Moon Maid
Reprints the following one shot comic books:
Frank Frazetta's Sorcerer
Frank Frazetta's Moon Maid
Frank Frazetta's Neanderthal
Frank Frazetta's Freedom

FIGHT AGAINST CRIME
May 1951 - #21 September 1954
Story Comics
• 5 January 1952 1 pg. ad.

FORBIDDEN WORLDS
July-Aug 1951 - #34 Oct-Nov 1954 - #35 August 1955 - #145 August 1967
American Comics Group
• 1 July-Aug 1951
"Demons of Destruction" 10 pp. with Al Williamson
reprinted in DOC WEIRD'S THRILL BOOK
• 3 Nov-Dec 1951
"Skull of the Sorcerer" 7 pp. single panel contribution.

Frank Frazetta's Death Dealer Deluxe HC by Joshua Ortega, Nat Jones, and Jay Fotos (Hardcover - May 8, 2008)

FRANK FRAZETTA'S CREATURES (one shot)
Image
2008
• COVER - Strange Creatures
• Alternate cover by Peter Bergting
• Alternate cover by Nat Jones

FRANK FRAZETTA'S DARK KINGDOM
2008
Image
Frank Frazetta's Dark Kingdom
• 1 COVER - **Dark Kingdom**
This issue was originally intended as a one shot but developed into a four issue mini-series

• 2a COVER - **Carson of Venus** (2nd version)
• 2b Alternate cover by Tim Vigil
• 2c Alternate cover by Nat Jones

• 3a COVER - **Bloodstone**
• 3a Alternate cover by Tim Vigil
• 3a Alternate cover by Nat Jones

• 4a COVER - **Kane on the Golden Sea**
• 4b Alternate cover by Tim Vigil
• 4c Alternate cover by Nat Jones

• HARDCOVER COLLECTION (2010)
COVER - **Dark Kingdom**

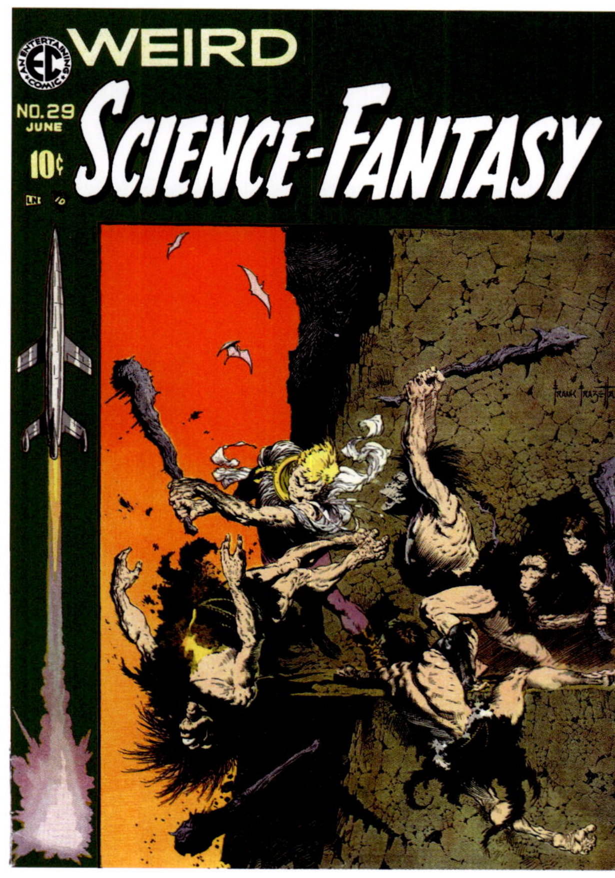

Cover to Weird Science-Fantasy *# 29. (1955)*

The cover to this ten cent comic book is arguably the best comic work ever created by Frank Frazetta. Some will even say it is the best piece of comic art ever done by ANYONE.

Originally intended to be the ninth Buck Rogers cover for Standard's Famous Funnies, *it was deemed "too graphic" in a time when paranoia ran rampant among comic book publishers. E.C. Publisher Bill Gaines , famous for his rebellious nature, jumped at the chance to publish what he knew was something special. He even included a story, drawn by Al Williamson, based on the cover.*

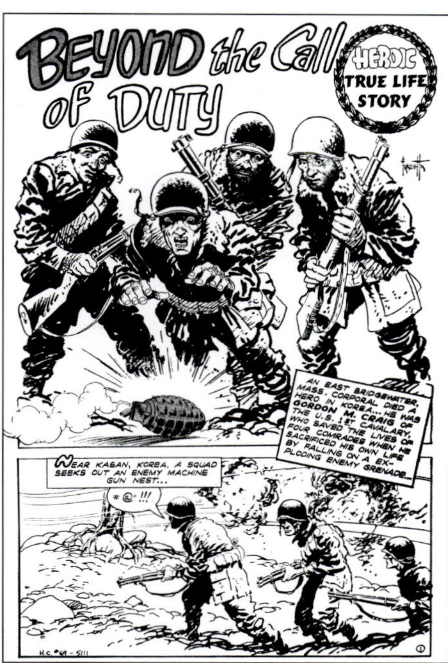

From Heroic Comics *#69 (1951)*

FRANK FRAZETTA'S DEATH DEALER

2008

Image

- 1a COVER - **Death Dealer** (1:2)
- 1b Alternate cover by Nat Jones (1:2)
- 1c Alternate sketch cover by Nat Jones (1:15) limited to 1000 copies
- 1d Alternate B/W version. COVER - Death Dealer

- 2a COVER - **Death Dealer II** (1:2)
- 2b Alternate cover by Nat Jones (1:2)
- 2c Alternate sketch cover by Nat Jones (1:25) limited to 1000 copies

- 3a COVER - **Death Dealer III** preliminary (1:2)
- 3b Alternate cover by Nat Jones (1:2)
- 3c Alternate sketch cover by Nat Jones (1:25) limited to 1000 copies

- 4a COVER - **Death Dealer IV** (1:2)
- 4b Alternate cover by Nat Jones (1:2)
- 4c Alternate sketch cover by Nat Jones (1:25) limited to 500 copies

- 5a COVER - **Death Dealer V** (1:2)
- 5b Alternate cover by Nat Jones (1:2)
- 5c Alternate sketch cover by Nat Jones (1:25) limited to 500 copies

- 6a COVER - **Death Dealer VI** (1:2)
- 6b Alternate cover by Nat Jones (1:2)
- 6c Alternate sketch cover by Nat Jones (1:25) limited to 500 copies

- HARDCOVER COLLECTION
  Reprints all six issues of the series.

FRANK FRAZETTA'S DRACULA MEETS THE WOLFMAN

(one shot)

Image

2008

- COVER - **Dracula Meets the Wolfman**
- Alternate cover by Francesco Francavilla

- FRANK FRAZETTA'S FREEDOM (one shot)

Image

2009

COVER - **Flash for Freedom**

FRANK FRAZETTA'S SILVER WARRIOR

Image

2009

- 1a COVER - **Silver Warrior**
- 1b Alternate cover by Nat Jones
- 1c Alternate sketch cover by Nat Jones
- 2a COVER - **Wolf Pack**
- 2b Alternate cover by Nat Jones
- 2c Alternate sketch cover by Nat Jones
- 3a COVER - **Fire Demon**
- 3b Alternate cover by Nat Jones
- 3c Alternate sketch cover by Nat Jones

FRANK FRAZETTA'S Moon Maid one shot

Image

2009

- 1a COVER - **The Moon Maid**
- 1b Alternate cover by Tim Vigil
- 1c Alternate sketch cover by Nat Jones

FRANK FRAZETTA'S NEANDERTHAL one shot

Image

2009

- 1a COVER - Neanderthal
- 1b Alternate cover by Jay Fotos
- 1c Alternate sketch cover by Nat Jones

FRANK FRAZETTA'S SORCERER one shot

Image

2009

- 1a COVER - Sorcerer
- 1b Alternate cover by Josh Medors
- 1c Alternate sketch cover by Nat Jones

FRANK FRAZETTA'S SWAMP DEMON one shot

Image

2009

- 1a COVER - Swamp Demon
- 1b Alternate cover by Josh Medors
- 1c Alternate sketch cover by Nat Jones

FRANK FRAZETTA FANTASY ILLUSTRATED magazine

Spring 1998 - present

Quantum Cat Entertainment

A magazine devoted to the influence Frazetta has had on other artists.

- 1 Spring 1998
  COVER - **Silver Warrior**
  page 2 intro by Frazetta with photo
- 2 Summer 1998
  COVER - **Kane on the Golden Sea**
  pg. 6 commentary on "Kane on the Golden Sea" by Winiewicz
- 3 Fall 1998
  COVER - **The Huntress**
  pg. 6 commentary on "The Huntress" by Winiewicz
- 4 Winter 1998
  COVER - **Death Dealer**
  pg. 6 commentary on "Death Dealer" by Winiewicz
  pg. 40 "*The Graphic Genius of Frazetta*" 10 pp. by Winiewicz
  article contains the following:
  "*The Spell of the Mahar*"
  AKA - "*A Mahar casts her sinister spell*"
  first printed in E.R.B. - MASTER OF ADVENTURE
  "*The Savage Attack of the Sagoths*"
  AKA - "*My shaft pierced the sagoth's savage heart…*"
  first printed in AT THE EARTH'S CORE and PELLUCIDAR PORTFOLIO
  "*Tooth and Claw*"
  AKA - "*They buried their talons in his back.*"
  first printed in AT THE EARTH'S CORE and PELLUCIDAR PORTFOLIO
  "*Lord of the Savage Jungle*"
  AKA - "*He had me captured by an African Chief.*"
  first printed in TARZAN AND THE CASTAWAYS
  cover to TARZAN AND THE CASTAWAYS
  first printed in TARZAN AND THE CASTAWAYS
  "*The Kingdom of the Mahar*"
  AKA - "*I caught my first sight of the dominant race of the inner world.*"
  first printed in AT THE EARTH'S CORE and PELLUCIDAR PORTFOLIO
- 5 March 1999
  COVER - **Snow Giants**
  pg. 8 commentary on "Snow Giants" by Winiewicz
- 6 May 1999
  COVER - **Egyptian Queen**
  pg. 8 commentary on "Egyptian Queen" by Winiewicz
  pg. 96 "Day of Wrath" ink sketch (not the Jaguar God painting with the same name)
- 7 July 1999
  COVER - **Indomitable**
  pg. 8 commentary on "Indomitable" by Winiewicz

Early One Morning In The Jungle

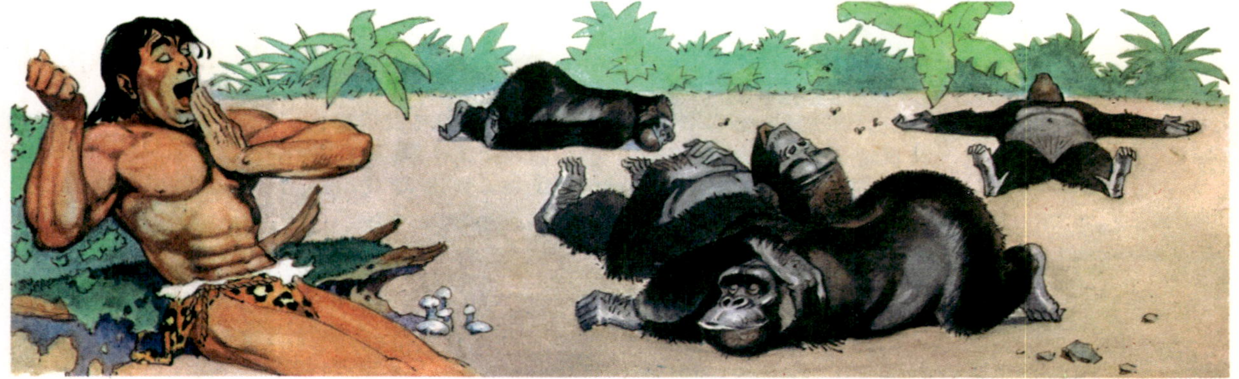

ARTIST: FRANK FRAZETTA WRITER: DON EDWING

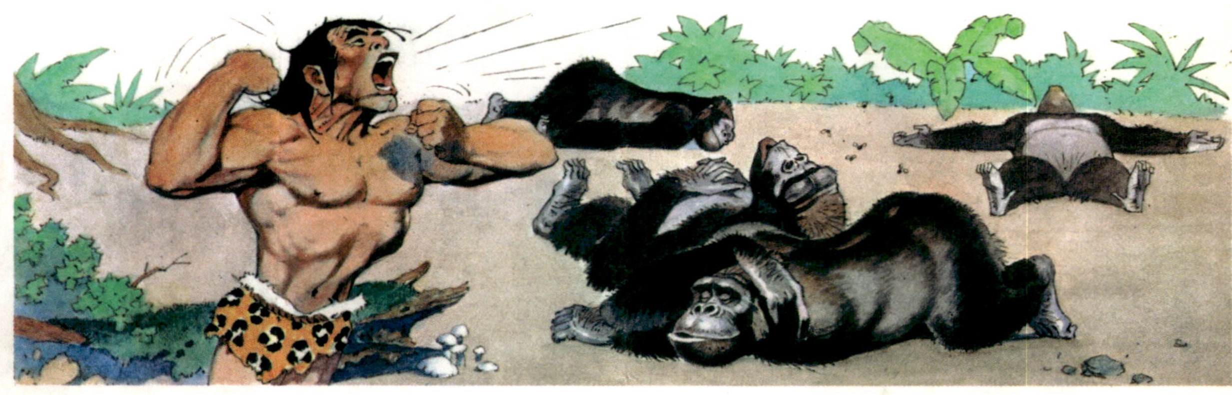

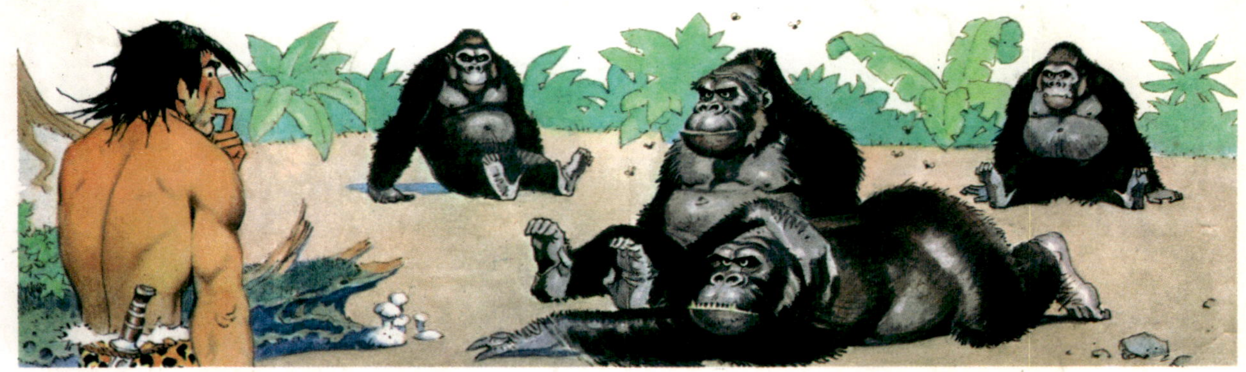

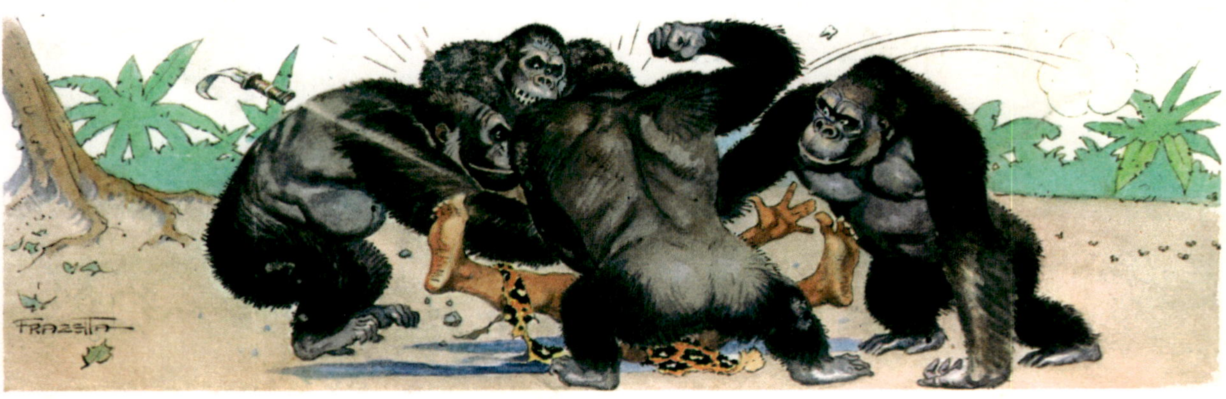

Back cover of Mad magazine #106

- 8 September 1999
  COVER - **Spiderman**
  pg. 8 commentary on "Spiderman" by Winiewicz

- **FRANK FRAZETTA'S THUN'DA TALES** (one shot)

1987
Fantagraphics Books
"King of the Lost Lands" 10 pp.
"The Monsters From the Mists" 7 pp.
"When the Earth Shook" 6 pp.
"Gods of the Jungle" 8 pp.

Note: The entire contents were first printed in A-1 COMICS #47. The cover was reprinted from a panel in the book.

- **FRANK FRAZETTA'S UNTAMED LOVE** (one shot)

November 1987
Fantagraphics Books
"Too Late For Love" 7 pp.
first printed in PERSONAL LOVE #25
"The Wrong Road" 8 pp.
first printed in PERSONAL LOVE #27
"Empty Heart" 6 pp.
first printed in PERSONAL LOVE #28
"Untamed Love" 8 pp.
first printed in PERSONAL LOVE #32

FROGMEN, THE

No. 1258, Feb-Apr, 1962 - No. 11, Nov-Jan, 1964-65
Dell Publishing Co.

- 1258(#1) Feb-Apr 1962
  Possible Frazetta pencils assisting George Evans.
- 2 May-July 1962
  Frazetta inks assisting George Evans. Especially evident on pp. 23, 25 and 26.
- 3 September 1962
  Frazetta inks assisting George Evans.

GANG BUSTERS

Dec-Jan 1947 - #67 Dec-Jan 1958-59
National Periodical Publications

- 14 Feb-Mar 1950
  "I Gallop With Danger" 8 pp.
- 17 Aug-Sept 1950
  "I Wrecked the Cattle Rustlers" 8 pp.

GHOST RIDER (see A-1 COMICS)

GOLDEN AGE GREATS

AC Comics

- 7 1996
  Frontis art from RED MASK and STRAIGHT ARROW
  "The Rodeo Robbers" 7 pp.
  first printed in A-1 COMICS #24
  "Voyage into Danger" 8 pp.
  first printed in DURANGO KID #14
  Frank Frazetta checklist of Magazine Enterprises work
  cover to BOBBY BENSON'S B-BAR-B RIDERS #9 (color)
  cover to STRAIGHT ARROW #22
- 14 1999
  quarter page insert from *"King of the Lost Lands"*
  first printed in A-1 COMICS #47
  "Judy of the Jungle" 9 pp.
  first printed in EXCITING COMICS #59

GOLDEN AGE MEN OF MYSTERY

AC Comics

- 5 1997
  "Miss Masque" some panel work
  first printed in AMERICA'S BEST COMICS #27

GOLDEN AGE OF COMICS

- Summer 1982 reproductions of Frazetta strips

GOOD GIRL ART QUARTERLY

AC Comics

- 1 Summer 1990
  "Holiday in Hogbite Hollar" 7 pp
  first printed in THRILLING COMICS #70
- 4 Spring 1991
  "There's No Feud Like an Old Feud" 6 pp
  first printed in THRILLING COMICS #67
- 5 Summer 1991
  "A Bride Fer Kissin' Jim" 7 pp
  first printed in THRILLING COMICS #71

GOOFY COMICS

June 1943 - #48 1953
Nedor Publishing Company / Standard (Animated Cartoons)
The following issues all contain quarter page text illustrations.

- 20 June 1947
  "The Cowardly Cat"
  "Lucky Bird"
  reprinted in SMALL WONDERS (art book) b&w
  "Blinkys Bones"
- 21 August 1947
  "The Poor Little Woodpecker"
  reprinted in THE COMICS JOURNAL (magazine)
  reprinted in SMALL WONDERS (art book) b&w
  "The Bugland Mail Goes Through"
- 22 October 1947
  "Clumsy Bear"
  "Freddy Goes Golfing"
- 23 December 1947
  "Randy Racoon's Problem"
- 24 February 1948
  "The Bold Little Antelope"
  reprinted in SMALL WONDERS (art book) b&w
  "The Wanderers"
- 25 April 1948
  "The Eagle who Wouldn't Fly"
  "Ernie the Elephant"
- 26 June 1948
  "The Rabbit who Wouldn't Run"
  "The Wingless Wonder" 2 illustrations
- 27 August 1948
  "The Reckless Horse"
  reprinted in SMALL WONDERS (art book) b&w
  "Lonnie the Lone Wolf"
- 28 October 1948
  "Roaring Cat" 2 illustrations
  reprinted in SMALL WONDERS (art book) b&w
  "Come to the Pup"
- 29 December 1948
  "Forest Hero"
  "The Timid Pup"
  "The Adventurous Elephant"
- 30 February 1949
  "The Ghost"
  reprinted in SMALL WONDERS (art book) b&w
  "Worried Owl"
  "The Bully and the Blowfish"
  reprinted in SMALL WONDERS (art book) b&w

• 31 April 1949
"The Colt Who Wanted to Sing"
"Spotted Snob"
"Little Brown Dog"

• 32 June 1949
"The Beautiful Swan"
"Lazy Bear"
"Strong Little Elephant"

• 33 August 1949
"Butch the Bully"
reprinted in SMALL WONDERS (art book) b&w
"Wally the Whale"
reprinted in SMALL WONDERS (art book) b&w

• 34 October 1949
"In the Glass Bowl"
"Animal Act"

• 35 December 1949
"Silly Wish"
"Very Sad Bird"

• 42 February 1951
"The Surprise Shark"

HAPPY COMICS (Happy Rabbit #41 on)

August 1943 - #40 December 1950
Nedor Publishing Company / Standard Comics (Animated Cartoons)

The following issues, unless otherwise noted with page counts, contain quarter page text illustrations.

• 20 July 1947
"Crooner Cat" 2 illustrations
reprinted in SMALL WONDERS (art book) b&w
"The Big Badger Hunt"
reprinted in SMALL WONDERS (art book) b&w

• 21 September 1947
"High Flying Squirrel"
reprinted in SMALL WONDERS (art book) b&w
"The Friendly Spider"
"Sharpy and the Salmon"

• 22 November 1947
"Robin Redface"
"Wandering Kitten"
"The Conceited Squirrel"

• 23 January 1948
"Beautiful But Not Dumb"
"Silky and the Wren"
"Ernie the Earthworm"

• 24 March 1948
"Clean Little Pig"
"Golden Horse"
reprinted in SMALL WONDERS (art book) b&w

• 25 May 1948
"The Friendly Lion"
"Dan Uses His Head"
"Willy the Weasel"

• 26 July 1948
"Dobo the Dog'
"The Silent Monkey"
reprinted in SMALL WONDERS (art book) b&w
"The Silly Eagle"

• 27 September 1948
"Chocolate and Vanilla"
reprinted in SMALL WONDERS (art book) b&w
"The Just-The-Same Mouse"
reprinted in SMALL WONDERS (art book) b&w
"The Eating Contest"

• 28 November 1948
"The Boastful Mouse"
"Abbott the Rabbit"
reprinted in SMALL WONDERS (art book) b&w
"Elephant Who Wouldn't Help"
reprinted in SMALL WONDERS (art book) b&w

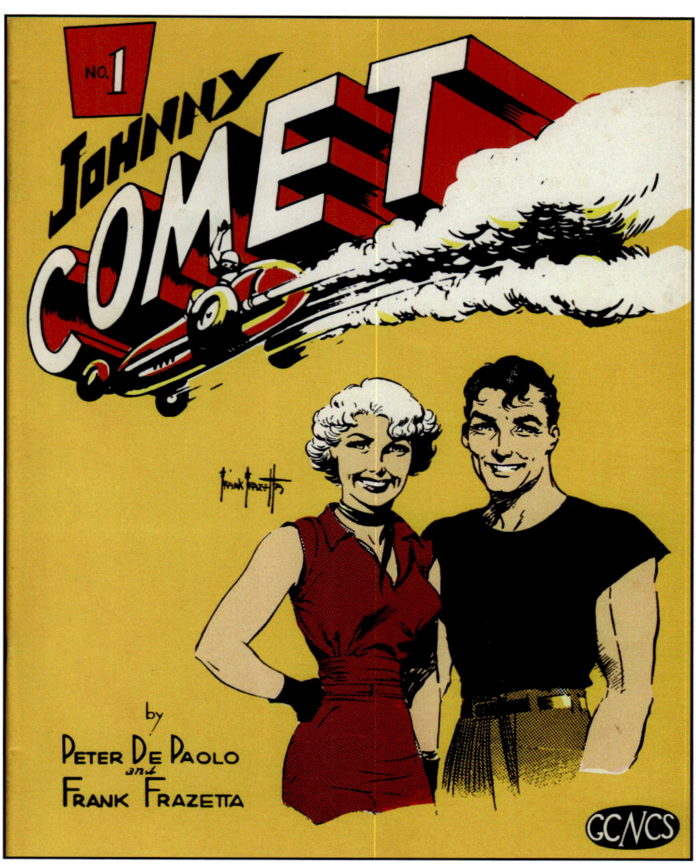

Johnny Comet *(reprint series) #1*
Avalon Communications (1999)

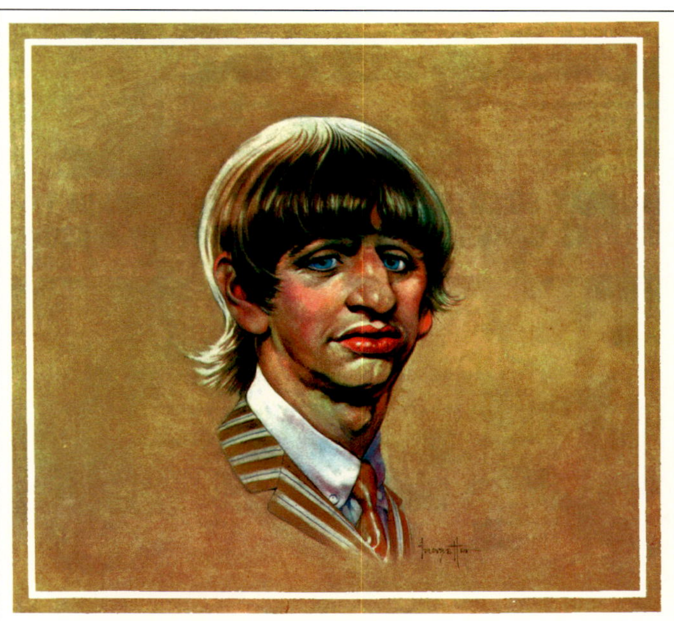

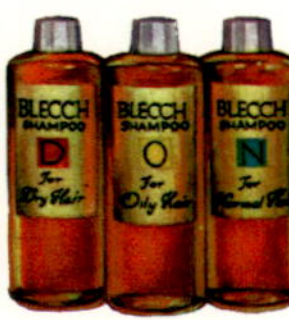

The famous Blecch Ad. Mad Magazine *#90 (1964)*

HAPPY COMICS cont'd

- 29 January 1949
  - *"Flippy the Monk"*
    - **reprinted in** SMALL WONDERS (art book) b&w
  - *"The Talkative Mouse"*
    - **reprinted in** SMALL WONDERS (art book) b&w
  - *"Eager Beaver"*
    - **reprinted in** SMALL WONDERS (art book) b&w
- 30 March 1949
  - *"The Wistful Bear"*
  - *"President Mouse"*
    - **reprinted in** SMALL WONDERS (art book) b&w
  - *"Coalie the Lamb"*
    - **reprinted in** SMALL WONDERS (art book) b&w
- 31 May 1949
  - *"Woodland Olympics"*
  - *"Jerry for President"*
  - *"Nibby"*
- 32 July 1949
  - *"The No-hound" 7 pp.*
  - *"Herbie"*
    - **reprinted in** SMALL WONDERS (art book) b&w
  - *"Miserable Mouse"*
- 33 September 1949
  - *"All at Sea"* 6 pp.
  - *"Diamonds and Pebbles"*
  - *"Bobby & the Cheetah"*
  - *"Timid Caterpillar"*
    - **reprinted in** SMALL WONDERS (art book) b&w
- 34 November 1949
  - *"A Job For Jimmy Grasshopper"*
  - *"City Cousin"*
- 35 January 1950
  - *"The Paleface"*
  - *"Smart as a Fox"*
- 36 March 1950
  - *"The Nightingale Who Couldn't Sing"*
    - **reprinted in** SMALL WONDERS (art book) b&w
- 37 May 1950
  - *"The Brave Pup"*

HEAVY METAL

HM Communications

- August 1985 Frazetta interview
- November 1990
  - COVER - **Princess and the Panther**
  - pg. 4article *"Interview With Frank Frazetta"* 6 pp.
    - contains a still life painting by an eight year old Frazetta

HEROIC COMICS

August 1940 - #97 June 1955

Eastern Color Printing Company / Famous Funnies (Funnies Inc.#1)

- 65 March 1951
  - *"Sunny's Sunday"* 2 pp. with Al Williamson
- 66 May 1951
  - *"Adrift in a Rowboat"* 2 pp.
    - **reprinted in** THE COMIC STRIP FRAZETTA (fanzine)
    - **reprinted in** THE RARE FRAZETTA (fanzine)
- 67 July 1951
  - *"Three-Year-Old Hero"* 2 pp.
  - *"The Scared Life-Saver"* 2 pp.
    - page 1 **reprinted in** TESTAMENT (art book)
- 69 November 1951
  - *"Beyond the Call of Duty"* 3 pp.
    - **reprinted in** BURIED TREASURE #2
  - *"Memorable Memorial Day"* 3 pp.
    - **reprinted in** BURIED TREASURE #2
- 70 January 1952
  - " *Always Around When Needed"* 2 pp.
    - **reprinted in** BURIED TREASURE #2
- 71 March 1952
  - *"Gave Life to Save Lives"* 2 pp.
    - **reprinted in** BURIED TREASURE#2
    - **reprinted in** BEST OF HORROR AND SCIENCE FICTION COMICS
  - *"He Stayed Behind"* 1 pg.
    - **reprinted in** BURIED TREASURE #2
- 72 May 1952
  - untitled 3 pp.
    - **reprinted in** BURIED TREASURE #2
  - *"With Only a Shovel"* 2 pp.
    - **reprinted in** BURIED TREASURE #2
    - **reprinted in** THE COMIC STRIP FRAZETTA (fanzine)
    - **reprinted in** THE RARE FRAZETTA (fanzine)
    - page 1 detail **reprinted in** TESTAMENT (art book)
  - *"He Chose to Fight"* 2 pp.
    - **reprinted in** BURIED TREASURE #2
    - **reprinted in** THE COMIC STRIP FRAZETTA (fanzine)
    - **reprinted in** THE RARE FRAZETTA (fanzine)
  - *"Red Cross New Method of Artificial Respiration"* 1 pg.
    - **reprinted from** BUSTER CRABBE #4
- 73 July 1952
  - *"Heroism on the Korean Front"* 2 pp.
    - **reprinted in** BURIED TREASURE #2
  - *"Bivouac"* 2 pp.
    - **reprinted in** BURIED TREASURE #2
- 75 September 1952
  - *"Brought Back to Life"* 1 pg.
    - **reprinted in** BURIED TREASURE #2
  - *"Prayer Works Wonders"* 1 pg.
    - **first printed in** REAL CLUE CRIME STORIES Vol.7 #6
- 81 March 1953
  - *"Boy Scout's Jamboree"* 1 pg
    - **reprinted in** BUSTER CRABBE #9
    - **reprinted in** HEROIC COMICS #82
- 82 April 1953
  - *"Boy Scout's Jamboree"* 1 pg
    - **first printed in** HEROIC COMICS #81
- 83 May 1953
  - one pg. ad
- 86 August 1953
  - *"Only Doing His Job"* 3 pp.
    - **reprinted in** BURIED TREASURE #2
- 87 September 1953
  - *"Stranded in a Mine Field"* 3 pp.
    - **reprinted in** BURIED TREASURE #2
- 94 December 1954
  - *"Cindy is Saved"* 2 pp.
    - **reprinted in** THE FANTASTIC ART OF FRANK FRAZETTA vol.1

JAGUAR GOD

March 1995 - present

Verotik

- 0 February 1996
  - COVER - **Day of Wrath**
- 1 March 1995
  - COVER - **Jaguar God I**
    - cover is a repainted version of JONGOR OF LOST LAND
- 2 October 1995
  - COVER - **Jaguar God II**
- 7 June 1997
  - COVER
    - Cover is a digitally colored pencil sketch and appears in its original form inside the front cover.

JESSE JAMES

August 1950 - #29 Aug-Sept 1956

Avon Periodicals

- 20 November 1955
  - *"Chief Victorio's Apache Massacre"* 7 pp. with Al Williamson
    - **first printed in** CHIEF VICTORIO'S APACHE MASSACRE

JIMMY WAKELY

Sept Oct 1949 - #18 July-Aug 1952
National Periodical Publications

- 3 Jan-Feb 1950
  - *"The White Indian Chief"* 3 pp.
    - **reprinted in** TOMAHAWK #29
- 4 Mar-Apr 1950
  - *"The Town Jesse James Couldn't Rob"* 3 pp.
    - **reprinted in** BLACKHAWK #118
    - **reprinted in** ALL STAR WESTERN #9
- 6 July-Aug 1950
  - *"The Million Dollar Tombstone"* 3 pp.
    - **reprinted in** TOMAHAWK #57
- 7 Sep-Oct 1950
  - *"Botalye-Immortal Indian Warrior"* 3 pp.
    - **reprinted in** ALL STAR WESTERN #99
    - **reprinted in** TOMAHAWK #131
    - **reprinted in** THE COMIC STRIP FRAZETTA (fanzine)
    - **reprinted in** MASTERWORKS SERIES #2
    - **reprinted in** THE RARE FRAZETTA (fanzine)

JOE COLLEGE

Fall 1949 - #2 Winter, 1950
Hillman Periodicals

- 1 Fall 1949 *"Boola Boola Jones"* (certain panels)

JOHNNY COMET

Avalon Communications

- 1 1999 Reprints JOHNNY COMET newspaper comic strips
- 2 1999 Reprints JOHNNY COMET newspaper comic strips
- 3 1999 Reprints JOHNNY COMET newspaper comic strips
- 4 2000 Reprints JOHNNY COMET newspaper comic strips
- 5 2000 Reprints JOHNNY COMET newspaper comic strips

JOHN WAYNE ADVENTURE COMICS

Winter 1949-50 - #31 May 1955
Toby Press

- 2 Spring 1950
  - *"Guns"* 2 pp. with Al Williamson
    - **reprinted in** BILLY THE KID ADVENTURE MAGAZINE #s 1, 14 and 22
    - **reprinted in** TRUE MOVIE AND TELEVISION #2
  - *"The Blue Lightnin' Twins"* 6 pp. with Al Williamson
- 3 Summer 1950
  - *"The Claws of Death"* 4 pp. with Williamson
    - **reprinted in** BILLY THE KID ADV. MAGAZINE #3
    - **reprinted in** JOHN WAYNE ADV. COMICS #25
    - **reprinted in** THE FRAZETTA TREASURY (fanzine)
    - **reprinted in** COMIC ART SHOWCASE #4 (auction catalog)
    - 2 pages **reprinted in** GRAPHIC GALLERY #9 (auction catalog)
    - 4 panels **reprinted in** COMICS INTERVIEW (magazine)
    - Splash page **reprinted in** ICON (art book)
- 4 Fall 1950
  - *"Black Gold"* 6 pp. with Al Williamson.
    - **reprinted in** JOHN WAYNE ADVENTURE COMICS #29
  - *"The Panther Man"* 10 pp. with Al Williamson
- 6 Spring 1951
  - *"Murder Will Out"* 10 pp. with Al Williamson
- 7 Summer 1951
  - *"An Invitation to Murder"* 10 pp. with Al Williamson
- 8 Fall 1951
  - *"The Weeping Walloper"* 12 pp. with Al Williamson
    - **reprinted in** COMIC AND CRYPT #7 (fanzine)
    - Splash page **reprinted in** THE COMICS JOURNAL #174 (magazine)
  - "The Ugly Duckling Bandit" 9 pp. with Al Williamson
- 18 Spring 1953
  - *"The Ugly Duckling Bandit"* 9 pp. with Al Williamson
    - **first printed in** JOHN WAYNE ADV. COMICS #8
- 25 Winter 1954-55
  - *"The Claws of Death"* 4 pp. with Al Williamson
    - **first printed in** JOHN WAYNE ADV. COMICS #3

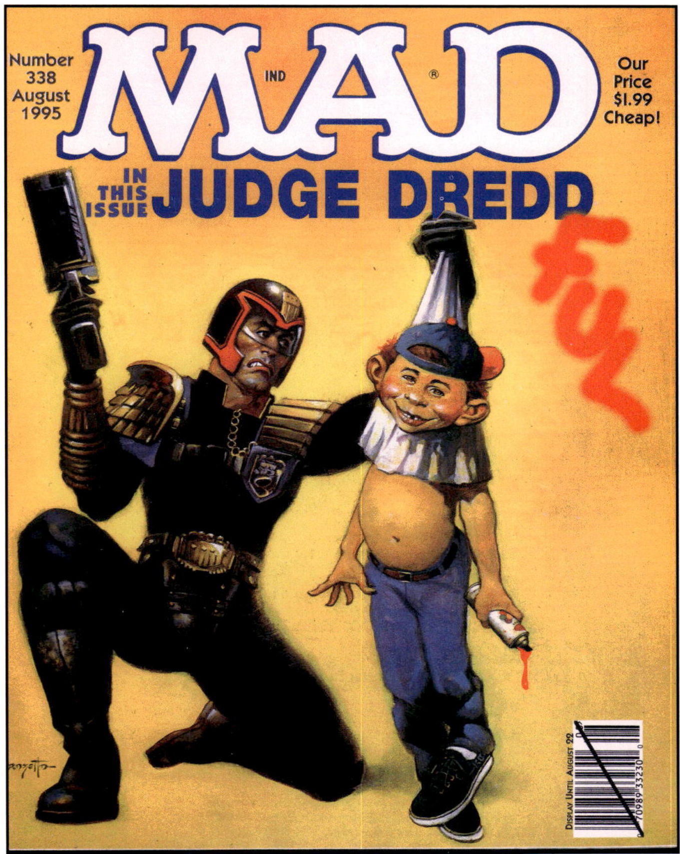

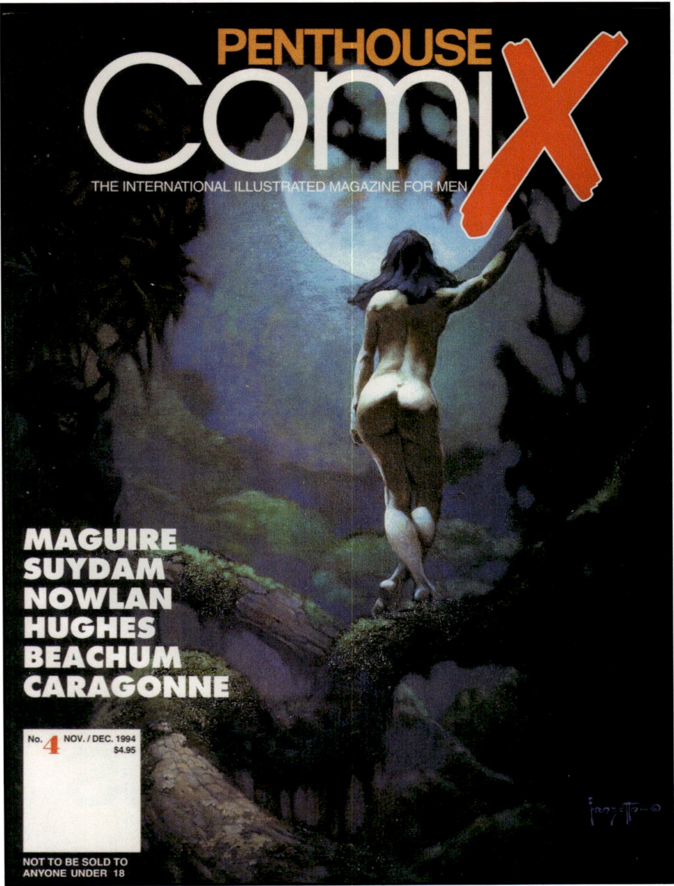

TOP: Mad Magazine #338 *(Aug. 1995)*

ABOVE: Penthouse Comix #4 *(Nov.-Dec.1994)*

Of course I'd seen Frank Frazetta's stunning work most of my life. My older brother, Lee, was a HUGE sci-fi fan and in addition to influencing my tastes in comics, his vast collection of paperbacks were an ever-present beacon of inspiration as well. I'm sure that had to be my first exposure to Frazetta, those KILLER paperback covers. I then remember seeing his art gracing a CLINT EASTWOOD movie poster. Again—KILLER.

Still, when something's ever present you tend to take it for granted. This is made clear when, as an aspiring artist, you start to understand working with colors like Frazetta can. This was something I found IMPOSSIBLE to ASPIRE to. My excuse? I'm color blind.

> *"I continue to study Frazetta's work, inked or painted, as masterpieces of composition peopled with powerful figures and amazing creatures."*

Then, as an adult, the comic book world beckoned me through newly aware eyes. Here was a place I could tell stories and work at illustration with black ink and a brush. My new passion sent me on a crash course of comics history where I rediscovered my childhood icon in wonderful works of sequential art. I've picked up everything I could find from JOHNNY COMET collections to the entire EC comics library. I was on an obsessive quest to collect his first five hard-to-find artbooks for over three years and stumbled across countless other rare treasures in the process. I continue to study Frazetta's work, inked or painted, as masterpieces of composition peopled with powerful figures and amazing creatures.

My greatest coup came when I first met Frank at the San Diego Comic Con a few years ago. He'd just released a new book of drawings after his most prolific period in years. I asked if he'd be willing to draw his version of my character MADMAN. And like my dad always said, "It never hurts to ask". Frank said yes! But it would only be a pencil drawing. Of course a DOODLE would have been more than I could ever have hoped for, but a few weeks later I got a phone call. He liked the drawing so much, he was inspired to go ahead and ink it. I've collected over a hundred drawings from most of my favorite artists including Alex Toth and Jack Kirby and with Frank's piece I don't argue when I'm told it's probably one of the greatest collections of artists on one project EVER. Thanks Frank!

Michael Allred

Michael 'Doc' Allred grew up in the '60s and '70s and was surrounded with the best in pop culture and a steady diet of music, movies and comic books. He is best known for Madman, the Atomics *and* Red Rocket 7.

- 29 February 1955
  "Black Gold" 6 pp. with Al Williamson
  first printed in JOHN WAYNE ADV. COMICS #4
- 31 May 1955
  "Guns" 2 pp. with Al Williamson
  first printed in JOHN WAYNE ADV. COMICS #2

LAST OF THE VIKING HEROES, THE

1988
Genesis West Comics

- Summer Special #1 May 1988
  COVER
  pg. 28 article *"The Meeting of the Masters"* 5 pp. contains:
  photo of Jack Kirby and Frank Frazetta
  Kirby and Frazetta artwork

LEROY

November 1949 - #6 November 1950
Standard Comics

- 2 January 1950
  "Beautiful But Sad" 1/4 pg. text illustration

• LI'L ABNER AND THE CREATURES FROM DROP-OUTER SPACE (one shot)

1950's Job Corp giveaway
Toby Press

penciled entire story (28 pages)
reprinted in RUSS COCHRAN COMIC ART #51 (auction catalog)

LOVERS (formerly Blonde Phantom)

#23 May 1949 - #86 August? 1957
Marvel Comics #23-24 / Atlas #25-86

- 43 1 pg. ad

LOVERS' LANE

October 1949 - #41 June 1954
Lev Gleason Publishing

- 20 June 1953
  1 pg. ad

MAD

Oct-Nov 1952 - present
E.C. Comics

- 90 October 1964
  back cover - *"Blecch Shampoo Ad"* - **Ringo Starr** 1 pg.
  reprinted in THE COMICS JOURNAL #174 (magazine)
  reprinted in COMPLETELY MAD (art book)
- 106 October 1966
  back cover - *"Early One Morning in the Jungle"* 1 pg. (Tarzan Parody)
  reprinted in CHRISTIE'S EAST 12/18/1992 (auction catalog)
  reprinted in TESTAMENT (art book)
- 338 August 1995
  COVER - **Judge Dredd with Alfred E. Neuman**
  reprinted in CHRISTIE'S AUCTION 11/17/1995 (auction catalog)
  reprinted in GUERNSEY'S ART OF POPULAR CULTURE 1/28/1998
  reprinted in ICON (art book)

MAD FOLLIES

E.C. Comics

- 4
  "Blecch Shampoo Ad" - **Ringo Starr** 1 pg.
  first printed in MAD #90
- 6 1968
  "Early One Morning in the Jungle" 1 pg. (Tarzan Parody)
  first printed in MAD #106

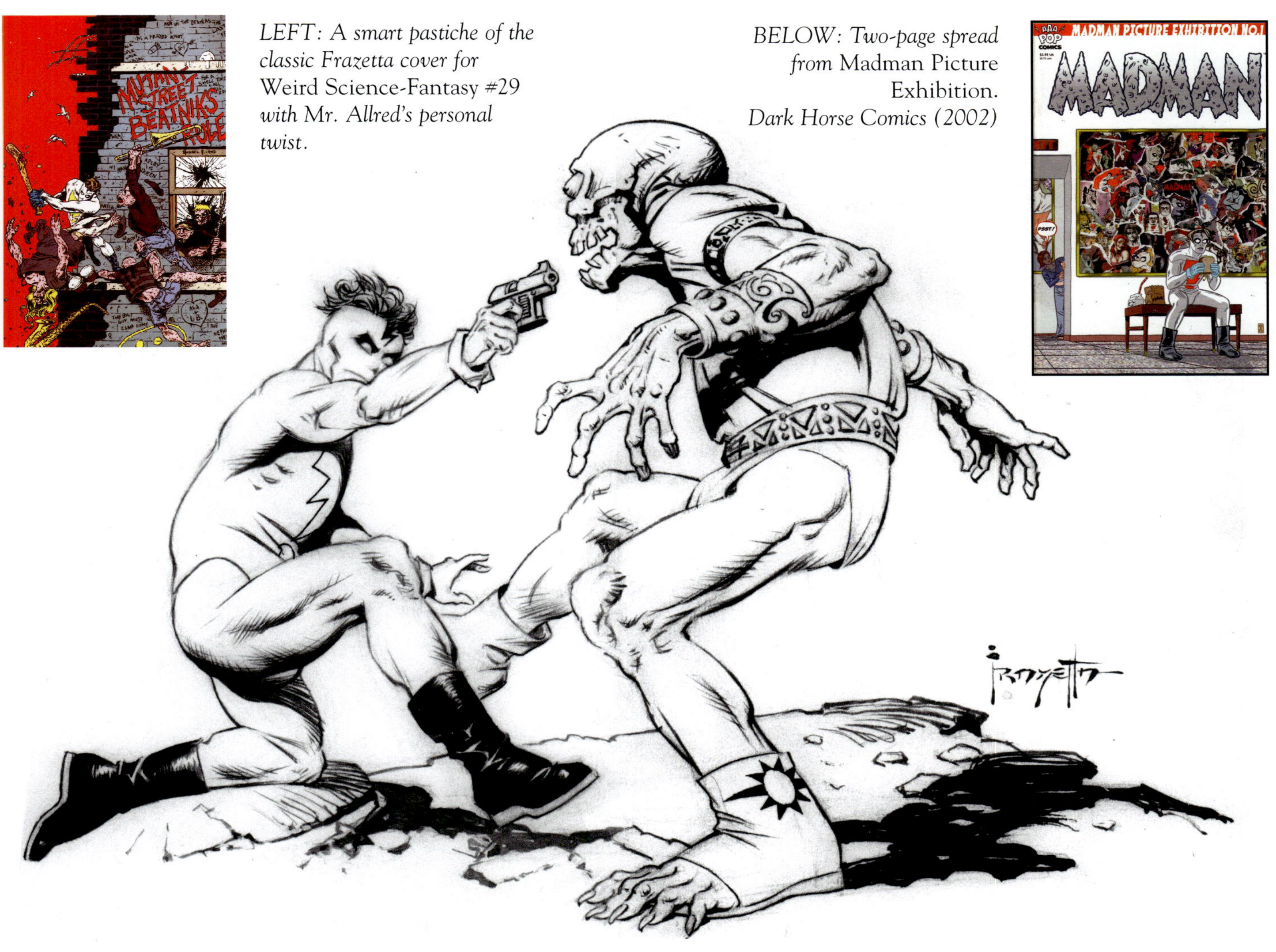

LEFT: A smart pastiche of the classic Frazetta cover for Weird Science-Fantasy #29 *with Mr. Allred's personal twist.*

BELOW: Two-page spread from Madman Picture Exhibition. *Dark Horse Comics (2002)*

MADMAN COMICS

April 1994 - present
Dark Horse Comics
- 11 October 1996
  back cover - Madman Vs. Demon
  reprinted in MADMAN CARD SET
  reprinted in MADMAN PICTURE EXHIBITION

MADMAN PICTURE EXHIBITION

AAA Pop Comics
- 1 April 2002
  Reprints Madman VS. Demon
  first printed in MADMAN COMICS #11
  Image is also reprinted as b/w line art for two page spread.

MANHUNT (see A-1 COMICS for #13)

October 1947 - #14 1953
Magazine Enterprises
Photo Journal #1202
- 11 August 1948
  "The Robber of Rainbow Buttes" 7 pp.

MASKED RANGER

April 1954 – #9 August 1955
Premier Magazines
- 1 April 1954
  story (with Sid Check)

MASTERWORKS SERIES OF GREAT COMIC BOOK ARTISTS, THE

May 1983 - #3 December 1983
Sea Gate Distributors / D.C. Comics
- 1 May 1983
  COVER
  "The Ten Century Lie" 6 pp.
  first printed in ADVENTURE COMICS #150
  "Sir Justin, Bronco Buster" 6 pp.
  first printed in ADVENTURE COMICS #151
  "The Duel of the Flying Knights" 6 pp.
  first printed in ADVENTURE COMICS #153
  "The Imitation Knight" 6 pp.
  first printed in ADVENTURE COMICS #155
  "Camelot U.S.A." 6 pp.
  first printed in ADVENTURE COMICS #157
- 2 July 1983
  COVER
  "Knight of the Future" 6 pp.
  first printed in ADVENTURE COMICS #159
  "The Flying Horse Swindle" 6 pp.
  first printed in ADVENTURE COMICS #161
  "The Knight in Rusty Armor" 6 pp.
  first printed in ADVENTURE COMICS #163
  "Botalye-Immortal Indian Warrior" 3 pp.
  first printed in JIMMY WAKELY #7
  "Spores From Space" 8 pp.
  first printed in MYSTERY IN SPACE #1

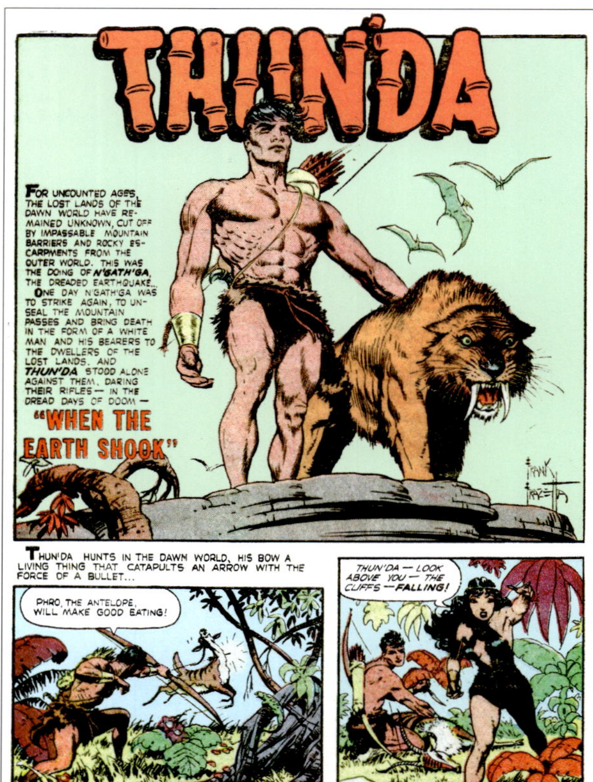

Thun'da *from* A-1 Comics # *47 (1952)*

"I first became aware of Frank Frazetta in the early 1960s through his illustrations for Edgar Rice Burroughs appearing in Canaveral Press and on the covers of Ace paperbacks. Also during that time he was occasionally doing covers for CREEPY and EERIE magazines. It is difficult to explain the appeal of Frazetta's art. His paintings and drawings seem to be filled with an energy. He has a magical ability to breathe life into these works of art."

Russ Cochran

Mr. Cochran is a publisher and comics historian best known for his work in bringing the E.C. Comics of the fifties back to life in reprint form.

MONKEYSHINES COMICS
Summer 1944 - #27 July 1949
Ace Periodicals / Publishers Specialists / Current Books / Unity Publ.
- 19 March 1948
  "Pete the Pike" 5 pp.

MOVIE LOVE
February 1950 - #22 August 1953
Famous Funnies
- 8 April 1951
  "William Holden" 6 pp. with Al Williamson
- 10 August 1951
  "Burt Lancaster" 6 pp.
- 17 October 1952
  1 pg. ad

MURDER TALES
Vol. 1 #10 November 1970
World Famous Publications
- 10 November 1970
  "We Can Stop the Enemies of Youth" 1 pg. ad
  first printed in BUSTER CRABBE #1

MY FRIEND IRMA
No. 3 June 1950 - No.47 Dec. 1954
Marvel / Atlas Comics
- 23 October 1953
  "Prayer Works Wonders" 1 pg. ad.
  first printed in REAL CLUE CRIME STORIES Vol.7 #6

MYSTERY COMICS DIGEST
March 1972 - #26 October 1975
Gold Key
- 3 May 1972
  "Perilous Journey" 10 pp. with Reed Crandall
  first printed in TWILIGHT ZONE #1
  "Voyage to Nowhere" 11 pp. with Reed Crandall
  first printed in TWILIGHT ZONE #1

MYSTERY IN SPACE
Apr-May 1951 - #110 September 1966 -
#111 September 1980 - #117 March 1981
National Periodical Publications
- 1 Apr-May 1951
  "Spores From Space" 8 pp.
  reprinted in MASTERWORKS SERIES #2

MYSTERY IN SPACE Trade Paperback
1999
D.C. Comics
Reprints science fiction story by Frazetta

OUTLAWS
Feb-Mar 1948 - #9 June-July 1949
D.S. Publishing Company
- 9 June-July 1949
  "Prairie Jinx" 7 pp.
- 3 (canadian)
  "Prairie Jinx" 7 pp.

OXYDOL-DREFT
1950 (set of 6 pocket-sized giveaways distributed through the mail as a set – 3" x 8 1/2")
Oxydol-Dreft
- 4 1950
  COVER -*"The Cowboy Trouble Shooter"*
  first printed in the first page of *"The Blue Lightnin' Twins"* as seen in JOHN WAYNE ADVENTURE COMICS #2

PENTHOUSE COMIX

Penthouse International Limited

- 4 Nov-Dec 1994
  - COVER - **Catwalk**
  - pg. 94 article "*Frazetta*" 1 pg.
  - pg. 95 **Catwalk**

PERSONAL LOVE

Jan 1950 - #33 June 1955

Famous Funnies

- 12 November 1951 1 pg. ad
- 16 July 1952
  - "*Red Cross Method of Artificial Respiration*" 1 pg.
    - **reprinted from** BUSTER CRABBE #4
- 17 September 1952 1 pg. ad
- 24 November 1953
  - "*A Love of my Own*" 8 pp.
    - **reprinted in** LEGACY (art book)
- 25 January 1954
  - "*Too Late For Love*" 7 pp.
    - **reprinted in** FRANK FRAZETTA'S UNTAMED LOVE
    - **reprinted in** UNTAMED LOVE (bound / reprint)
    - Splash page **reprinted in** THE COMICS JOURNAL #174 (magazine)
- 27 June 1954
  - "*The Wrong Road*" 8 pp.
    - **reprinted in** FRANK FRAZETTA'S UNTAMED LOVE
    - **reprinted in** UNTAMED LOVE
    - 1 panel **reprinted in** GLAMOUR INTERNATIONAL (art book)
- 28 August 1954
  - "*Empty Heart*" 6 pp.
    - **reprinted in** FRANK FRAZETTA'S UNTAMED LOVE
    - **reprinted in** UNTAMED LOVE (bound / reprint)
    - **reprinted in** ARIEL VOL. 1 (art book) b&w
    - 1 panel **reprinted in** SEX IN THE COMICS (art book)
- 32 April 1955
  - "*Untamed Love*" 8 pp. drawn and colored by Frazetta
    - **reprinted in** FRANK FRAZETTA'S UNTAMED LOVE
    - **reprinted in** UNTAMED LOVE (bound / reprint)
    - **reprinted in** CD ROM COMICS (miscellaneous)
    - Splash panel **reprinted in** FRAZETTA TREASURY (fanzine)
    - Splash page **reprinted in** FROM AARGH! TO ZAP! (art book)
    - 3 panels **reprinted in** COMIC BOOK MARKETPLACE #41 (magazine)
    - Last page **reprinted in** ARIEL VOL. 1 (art book) b&w

REAL CLUE CRIME STORIES

Vol. 2 #4 June 1947 - Vol. 8 #3 May 1953

Hillman Periodicals

- Vol. 7 #6 August 1952
  - "*Prayer Works Wonders*" 1 pg.
    - **reprinted in** ROMANTIC CONFESSIONS vol. 2 #9
    - **reprinted in** BUSTER CRABBE #7
    - **reprinted in** FAMOUS FUNNIES #202
    - **reprinted in** DEAD EYE WESTERN #9
    - **reprinted in** HEROIC COMICS #75
    - **reprinted in** MY FRIEND IRMA #23

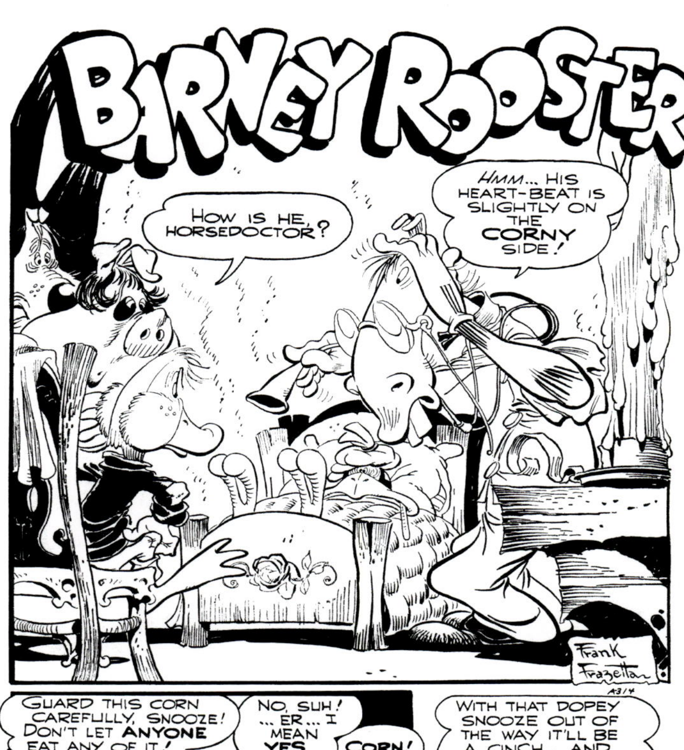

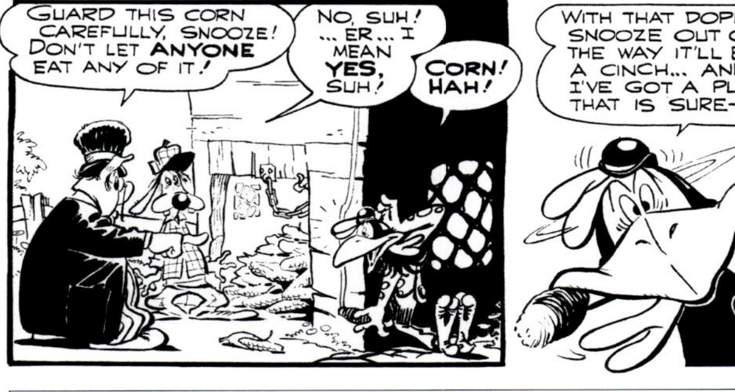

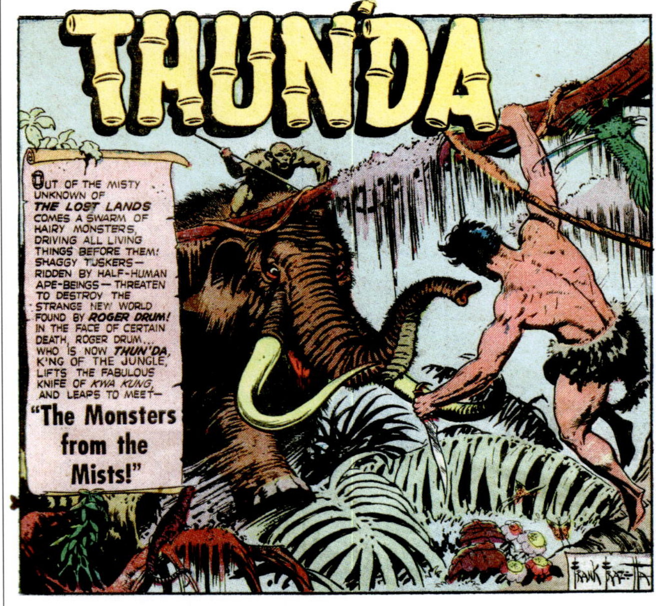

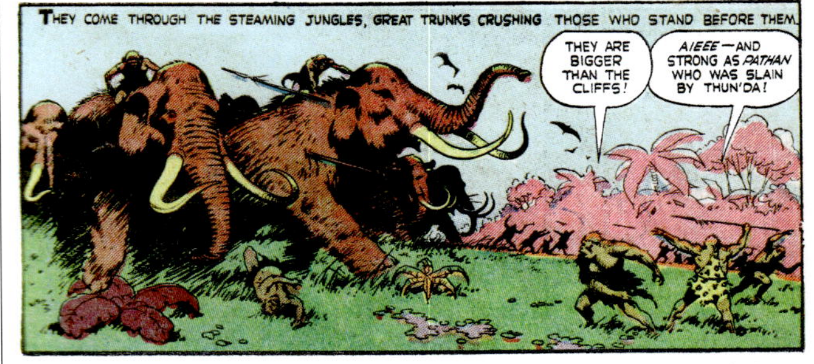

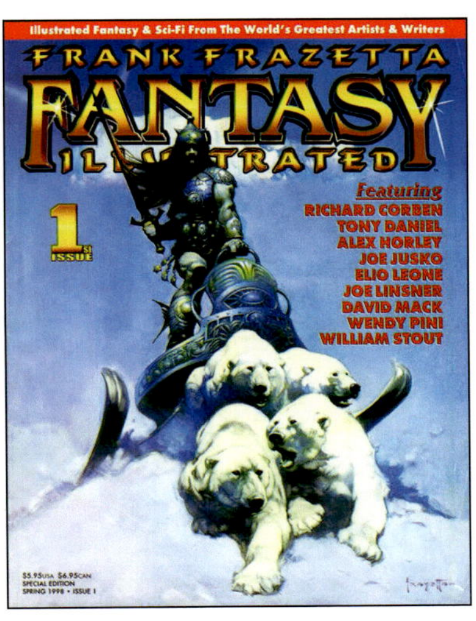

TOP: Barney Rooster *from* Barnyard Comics *#419 (July 1948)*

RIGHT: Thun'da *from* A-1 Comics #47 *(1952)*

LEFT: Frank Frazetta Fantasy Illustrated #1 *Quantum Cat (Spring 1998)*

REAL LIFE COMICS
September 1941 - # 59 September 1952
Nedor / Better / Standard Publications / Pictorial Magazines #13
- 50 October 1949
  "*War of the Gladiators*" 5 pp.
- 52 April 1950
  "*Leif the Lucky*" 4 pp.
- 59 September 1952
  1 pg. ad

ROBERT E. HOWARD'S CONAN: FRAZETTA COVER SERIES
2007-present
Dark Horse Comics
This is a proposed 8 issue series
- 1 2007 COVER **Snow Giants**
  "The Frost Giant's Daughter"
- 2 2008 COVER **Chained**
  "The God in the Bowl"
- 3 2009 COVER **The Barbarian**
  "The Tower of the Elephant"
- 4 2010 COVER **Destroyer**
  "The Hall of the Dead"

ROMANTIC CONFESSIONS
October 1949 - Vol.3 #1 Apr-May 1953
Hillman Periodicals
- Vol. 2 #9 June-July 1950
  "*Prayer Works Wonders*" 1 pg.
  first printed in REAL CLUE CRIME STORIES Vol. 7 #6

SATANIKA
January 1995 - present
Verotik
- 0 March 1995
  COVER

SHI - SENRYAKU COLLECTED EDITION
1995
Crusade Comics
- softcover edition
  COVER - **Shi**
- hardcover edition
  COVER - **Shi**

SHOCK SUSPENSTORIES
Feb-Mar 1952 - #18 Dec-Jan 1954-55
- 13 March 1954
  "*Squeeze Play*" 7 pp. (Frazetta's only solo story for E.C.)
  reprinted in BEST OF WEIRD SCIENCE FANTASY (fanzine)
  reprinted in RUSS COCHRAN COMIC ART #19 (auction catalog)
  reprinted in THE COMPLETE E.C. LIBRARY (art book) b&w
  reprinted in E.C. HORROR LIBRARY OF THE 1950'S (art book)
  reprinted in E.C. PORTFOLIO #2 b&w
  Some panels **reprinted in** COMICS INTERVIEW - FRAZETTA SPECIAL
  Splash page **reprinted in** FROM AARGH! TO ZAP! (art book)
  1 panel **reprinted in** THE GREAT COMIC BOOK ARTISTS (art book)

SNIFFY THE PUP
#5 November 1949 - #18 September 1953
Standard Publications (Animated Cartoons)
- 5 November 1949
  "*Ferdinand the Bullfrog*" (1/4 page text illustration)
  reprinted in SMALL WONDERS (art book) b&w
  "*Monkey Business*" (1/4 page text illustration)
  reprinted in SMALL WONDERS (art book) b&w

SON OF TOMAHAWK
See TOMAHAWK

SPACE COWBOY (one shot)
Vanguard Productions
2001
- Fall 2001
  INSIDE BACK COVER
  first printed in FAMOUS FUNNIES #214 (cover)
- Fall 2001 (alternate cover edition)
  COVER - Buster Crabbe sketch
  first printed in WITZEND #1 (fanzine)
  INSIDE BACK COVER
  first printed in FAMOUS FUNNIES #214 (cover)
- Fall 2003
  COVER
  first printed in FAMOUS FUNNIES #214 (cover)
  INSIDE BACK COVER
  first printed in FAMOUS FUNNIES #214 (cover)

SPUNKY (...JUNIOR COWBOY) (...COMICS #2 on)
April 1949 - #7 November 1951
Standard Comics
- 1 April 1949
  "*Ornery Critter*" 1/4 pg. text illustration
  "*Rescue of Cora Sue*" 1/4 pg. text illustration
- 2 May 1949
  "*The Winner*" two 1/4 pg. text illustrations

STAR SPANGLED COMICS
October 1941 - #130 July 1952
National Periodical Publications
- 113 February 1951
  "*The Black Cougar*" 10 pp.
  reprinted in TOMAHAWK #139
  Splash page repainted much later as **The Rider**

STRAIGHT ARROW
Feb-Mar 1950 - #55 March 1956
Magazine Entertainment
- 3 June-July 1950COVER
- 22 February 1952 COVER
  reprinted in LEGACY (art book)

STRANGE WORLDS
November 1950 - #22 Sept-Oct 1955
Avon Periodicals
- 3 May 1951
  "*The Invasion From the Abyss*" 7 pp. with Williamson, Wood, Krenkel, and Torres
  reprinted in THRILLING SCIENCE TALES #1

SUPERMOUSE (...THE BIG CHEESE)
December 1948 - #45 Fall 1958
Standard Comics / Pines (Literary Entertainment)
(The following issues contain quarter page text illustrations.)
- 1 December 1949
  "*Gnicky the Gnu*"
  "*Bobby Bunny Runs Away*"
  "*The Sad Crow*"
- 2 February 1950
  "*The Quiet Pup*"
  reprinted in SMALL WONDERS (art book) b&w
  "*The Lost Chipmunk*"
  reprinted in SMALL WONDERS (art book) b&w
  "*Willie the Weasel*"
- 3 April 1950
  "*Kimi*"
  "*Unhappy Animal*"

- 4 June 1950
  "Weasel Who Wouldn't"
  "Brave Explorer"
- 5 August 1950
  "The Foolish Fawn"
  "The Armor-Plated Softies"

RIGHT: Shi-Senryaku Collected Edition *(1995)*

BELOW: Space Cowboy *Vanguard Productions* *(2003)*

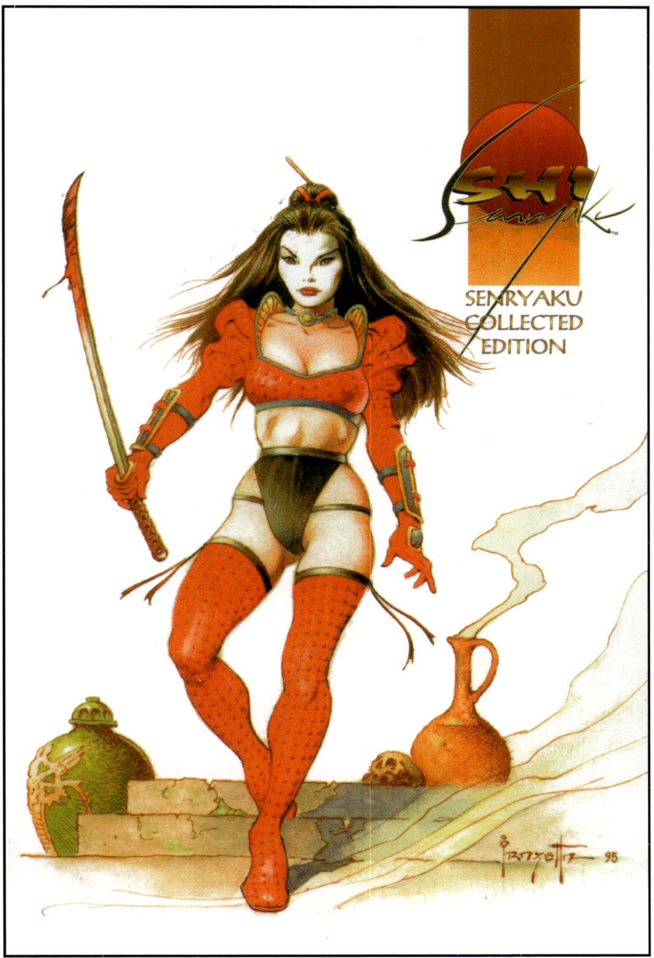

SWORDS OF VALOR
1990
Sword in Stone Productions
- 1 1990
  COVER - **Dark Kingdom**
- 2 1990
  COVER - **The Norseman**

TALES OF THE KILLERS
World Famous Publishing
- 10 December 1970
  "We Can Stop the Enemies of Youth" 1 pg. ad
  first printed in BUSTER CRABBE #1

- TALLY HO (one shot)

December 1944
Swappers Quarterly (Baily Publishing Company)
December 1944
COVER with John Giunta
"Snowman" 8 pp. with John Giunta
(Frazetta's first published work as assistant to John Giunta.)
reprinted in THE RARE FRAZETTA (fanzine), b/w
reprinted in SMALL WONDERS (art book), b/w

This is the first published work of Frank Frazetta. It was done as a collaboration with co-worker John Giunta when Frazetta was only fifteen years old.

TEEN LOVE STORIES
September 1969 - #3 January 1970
Warren Publishing Co.
- 1 September 1969 Frazetta art

THRILLING COMICS
February 1940 - #80 April 1951
Better Publications / Nedor / Standard Comics
- 66 June 1948
  "Don't Argue With a Gun" text illustration
- 67 August 1948
  "There's no Feud Like an Old Feud" 6 pp.
  reprinted in FRANK FRAZETTA SPECIAL (fanzine)
- 68 October 1948
  "Shutterbugs" 9 pp. with Mayo
  reprinted in FRANK FRAZETTA SPECIAL (fanzine)
  "Everything's Vine" 7 pp.
  reprinted in FRANK FRAZETTA SPECIAL (fanzine)
- 69 December 1948
  "Cake Fake" 8 pp.
  reprinted in COMIC AND CRYPT #7 (fanzine)
  "A Package Fer Pappy" 6 pp.
  reprinted in THE COMIC STRIP FRAZETTA (fanzine)
- 70 February 1949
  "Holiday in Hogbite Holler" 7 pp.
- 71 April 1949
  "A Bride for Kissin' Jim" 7 pp.
- 72 June 1949
  "Weddin' for the Widder" 5 pp.
- 73 August 1949
  "Lotions of Love" 6 pp.
  reprinted in COMIC AND CRYPT #7 (fanzine)

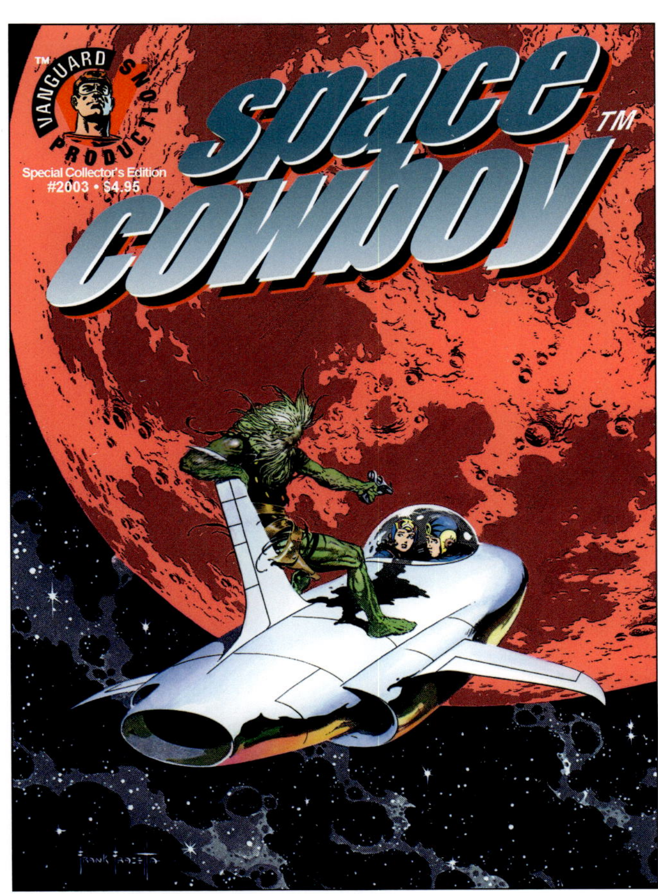

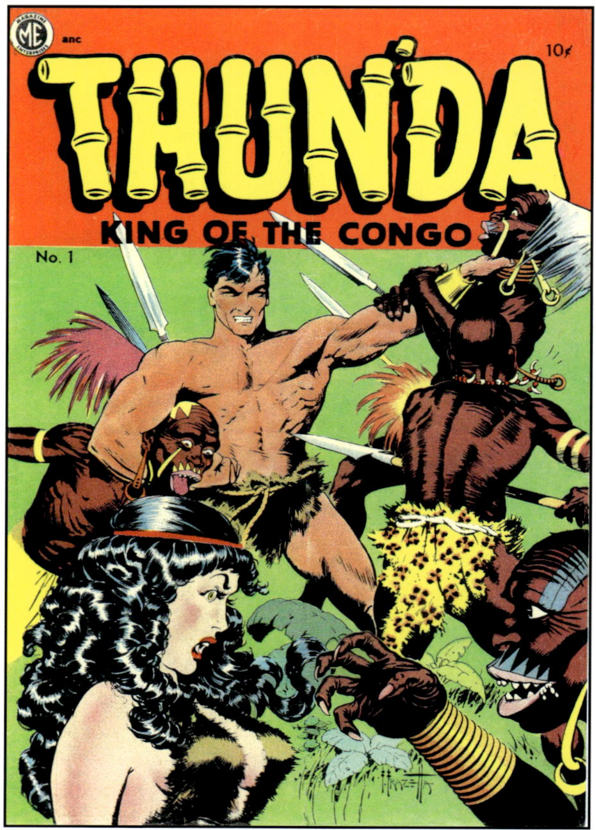

ABOVE: Thund'a *#1*
Magazine Entertainment (1952)

BELOW: Tim Holt *#23*
Magazine Entertainment (May 1951)

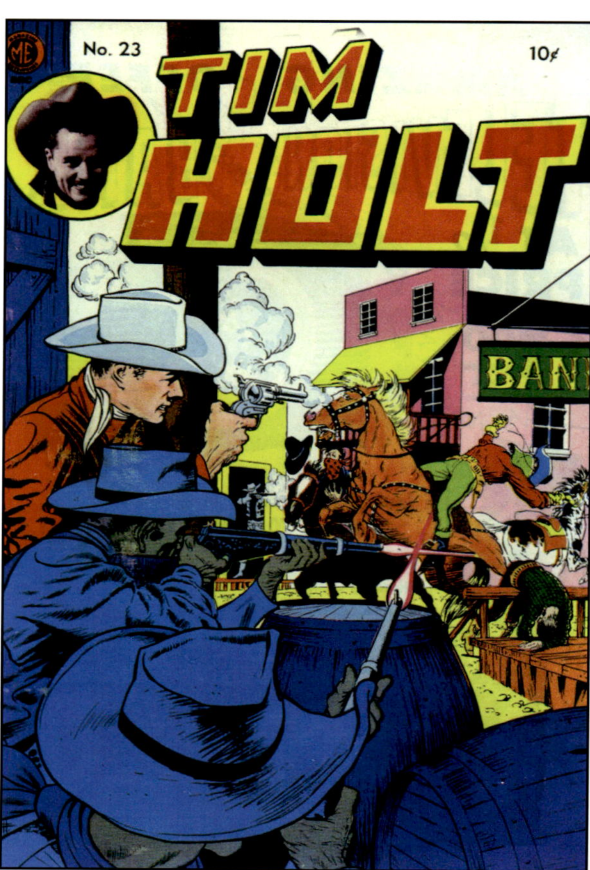

THRILLING LOVE 3-D
1989
Ray Zone
• 17 1989
"Untamed Love" 8 pp.
first printed in PERSONAL LOVE #32

THRILLING SCIENCE TALES
1989
AC Comics
• 1 1989
"The Invasion From the Abyss" 7 pp. with Williamson, Wood, Krenkel and Orlando
first printed in STRANGE WORLDS #3

THUN'DA
1973
Russ Cochran
COVER
first printed in A-1 COMICS #47
"King of the Lost Lands" 10 pp.
first printed in A-1 COMICS #47
"The Monsters From the Mists" 7 pp.
first printed in A-1 COMICS #47
"When the Earth Shook" 6 pp.
first printed in A-1 COMICS #47
"Gods of the Jungle" 8 pp.
first printed in A-1 COMICS #47

THUN'DA KING OF THE CONGO
(see A-1 COMICS)

THUN'DA TALES (see Frank Frazetta's Thun'da Tales)

TIM HOLT
1948 - #41 Apr-May 1954
Magazine Enterprises
• 17 May 1950
COVER (Ghost Rider)
(man being branded is based on Victor Mature)
reprinted in RETROSPECTIVE (art book), b/w
reprinted in SPA-FON #5 (fanzine)
• 21 January 1951
COVER (Ghost Rider / Red Mask)
reprinted in RETROSPECTIVE (art book), b/w
• 23 May 1951
COVER
reprinted in RETROSPECTIVE (art book), b/w

TOMAHAWK (Son of...on cover of #131-140)
Sept-Oct 1950 - #140 May-Jun 1972
National Periodical Publications
Photo Journal #1955
• 2 Nov-Dec 1950
"Texas Trailblazer" 4 pp. with Al Williamson"
• 29 January 1955
"The White Indian Chief" 3 pp.
first printed in JIMMY WAKELY #3
• 57
"The Million Dollar Tombstone" 3 pp.
first printed in JIMMY WAKELY #6
• 131 Nov-Dec 1970
"Botalye-Immortal Indian Warrior" 3 pp.
first printed in JIMMY WAKELY #7
• 139 Mar-Apr 1972
"The Black Cougar" 10 pp.
first printed in STAR SPANGLED COMICS #113
Splash page repainted much later as **The Rider**

TRAIL COLT (see A-1 COMICS)

TREASURE COMICS
June-July 1945 - #12 Fall 1947
Prize Publications (American Boys' Comics)
Issue 7 is an historical addition to any Frazetta collection. It contains the first published solo work by the artist.

- 7 June-July 1946
  "Know Your America" (featuring William Penn) 4 pp.
  "Capt. Kidd" 1 pg.
- 8 Aug-Sept 1946
  "Know Your America" (featuring Ben Church) 5 pp.

TRUE MOVIE AND TELEVISION
August 1950 - #3 November 1951
Toby Press

- 2 September 1950
  1 illustration
  first printed in JOHN WAYNE ADV. COMICS #2.

TWILIGHT ZONE, THE
#1173 Mar-May 1961 - #91 April 1979 - #92 May 1982
Dell Publishing Company / Gold Key / Whitman (#92)

- 1 November 1962
  "Perilous Journey" 10 pp. with Reed Crandall
  reprinted in MYSTERY COMICS DIGEST #3
  "Voyage to Nowhere" 11 pp. with Reed Crandall
  reprinted in MYSTERY COMICS DIGEST #3

UNKNOWN WORLDS OF SCIENCE FICTION
Marvel Comics Group
Jan 1975 - #6 Nov 1975-76

- 1 Jan 1975
  "Savage World" 8 pp. with Al Williamson, Torres and Krenkel
  first printed in WITZEND #1(fanzine)

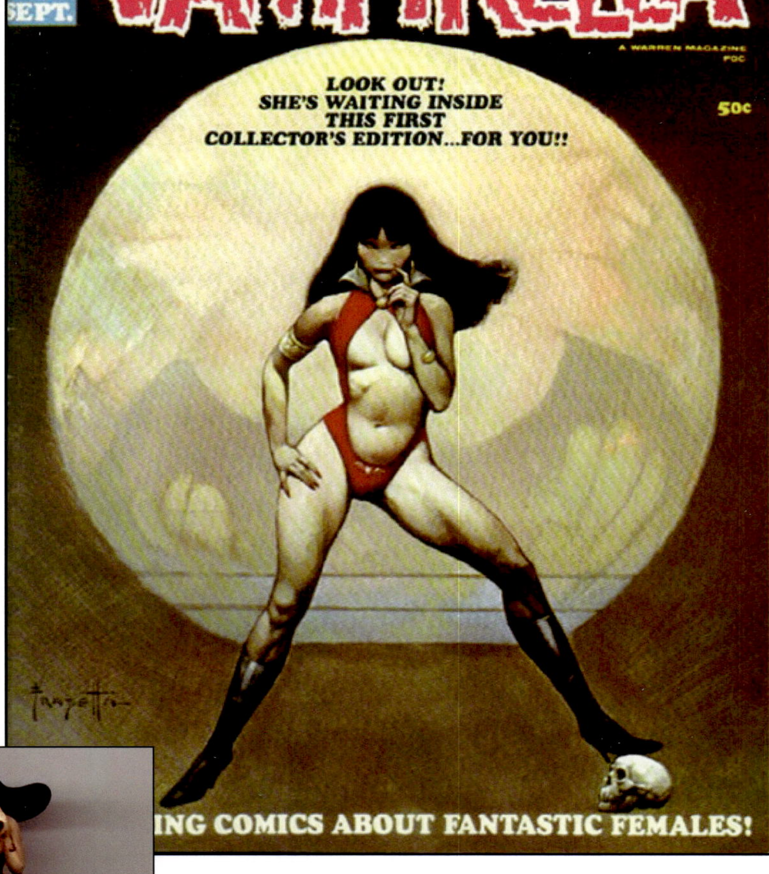

ABOVE :Vampirella *#1 Warren Publishing (Sept. 1969)*

LEFT: Vampirella *Resin Model kit (bootleg) (2003)*

BELOW: *Frazetta pencil sketch digitally painted by J. David Spurlock*

- UNTAMED LOVE

1973
Russ Cochran
COVER
1 panel **first printed in** PERSONAL LOVE #32
"Too Late for Love" 7 pp.
first printed in PERSONAL LOVE #25
"The Wrong Road" 8 pp.
first printed in PERSONAL LOVE #27
"Empty Heart" 6 pp.
first printed in PERSONAL LOVE #28
"Untamed Love" 8 pp.
first printed in PERSONAL LOVE #32

UNTAMED LOVE (see Frank Frazetta's Untamed Love).

VAMPIRELLA
September 1969 - #112 February 1983
Warren Publishing Company

- 1 September 1969
  COVER - **Vampirella**
  Vampirella illustration appears in inside front cover and also a subscription ad.
- 5 June 1970
  COVER - **Cornered**
  Vampirella illustration used as a subscription ad. It's different from the first issue.
- 6 July 1970
  Ken Kelly cover with partial Frazetta layout and touch-ups.
- 7 September 1970
  COVER - **Sun Goddess**
  Vampirella illustration used as a subscription ad. Different from issues 1 and 5.

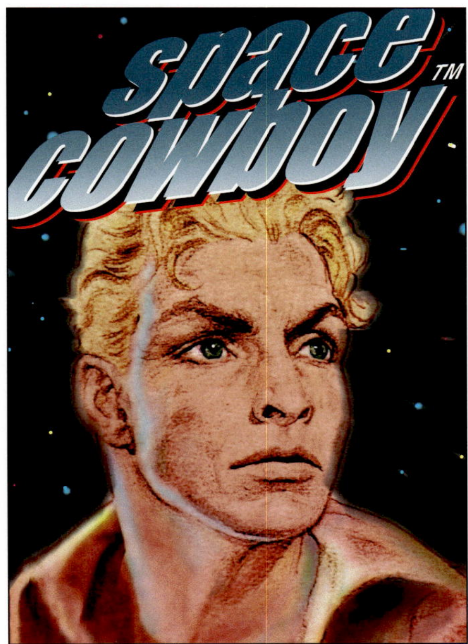

- 8 November 1970
  "Easy Way to a Tuff Surfboard" 1/2 pg. ad first **printed in** EERIE #3
- 11 May 1971
  COVER - **Woman With a Scythe**
  Vampirella illustration used as a subscription ad. Different from issues 1,5 and 7.
- 13 September 1971
  "Easy Way to a Tuff Surfboard" 1/2 pg. ad
  first printed in EERIE #3
- 31 March 1974
  COVER **Luana** (A sheet design)
  Originally used as movie poster image for LUANA.
- 94 March 1981
  1/2 COVER **Luana** (A sheet design)

VAMPIRELLA (25th Anniversary Special)
Oct 1996
Harris Publications
- nn October 1996
  COVER - **Vampirella 1996**
- nn October 1996
  special edition cover (same as above but without title header)
- nn October 1996
  silver edition w/ silver seal on cover - limited to 5000 copies

VAMPIRELLA CLASSICS
Feb 1995 - #5 Nov 1995
Harris Publications
- 1 February 1995
  COVER - **Vampirella**

- **VAMPIRELLA HALLOWEEN HORROR SPECIAL** (one shot)

Harris Comics
1 pg. - **Vampirella 1996**

- **VAMPIRELLA PINUP SPECIAL** (one shot)

October 1995
Harris Comics
1 pg. - **Vampirella**

VEROTIKA
December 1994 - present
Verotik
- 3 May 1995
  COVER - **Sorceress**

WEIRD FANTASY (formerly A MOON, A GIRL, ROMANCE; becomes WEIRD SCIENCE-FANTASY #23 on)
#13 May-June 1950 - #22 Nov-Dec 1953
E.C. Comics
Photo Journal #2108
- 14 July-Aug 1950
  "Mad Journey" 7 pp. provided some inks with Al Williamson and Roy Krenkel
  1 panel **reprinted in** COMICS INTERVIEW (magazine)
  reprinted in THE COMPLETE E.C. LIBRARY (art book) b&w
- 20 July-Aug 1953
  "I Rocket" 7 pp. provided some inks with Al Williamson and Roy Krenkel
  reprinted in THE COMPLETE E.C. LIBRARY (art book)
- 21 Sept-Oct 1953
  COVER with Al Williamson
  reprinted in BEST OF WEIRD SCIENCE FANTASY (fanzine)
  reprinted in THE COMPLETE E.C. LIBRARY (art book)
  reprinted in E.C. PORTFOLIO #3 b&w

WEIRD SCIENCE (formerly SADDLE ROMANCES; becomes WEIRD SCIENCE-FANTASY #23 on)
#12 May- June 1950 - #22 Nov-Dec 1953
E.C. Comics
- 19 May-June 1953
  "The One Who Waits" 7 pp. with Al Williamson
  reprinted in THE COMPLETE E.C. LIBRARY (art book)
- 20 July-Aug 1953
  "50 Girls 50" 7 pp. with Al Williamson and Roy Krenkel
  reprinted in TALES OF THE INCREDIBLE (paperback)
  reprinted in THE COMPLETE E.C. LIBRARY (art book)
  reprinted in E.C. PORTFOLIO #3 b&w
  Page 5 **reprinted in** FROM AARGH! TO ZAP! (art book)
- 21 Sept-Oct 1953
  "Two's Company" 6 pp. with Al Williamson
  reprinted in THE COMPLETE E.C. LIBRARY (art book)
  Partial page **reprinted in** FROM AARGH! TO ZAP! (art book)
- 22 Nov-Dec 1953
  "A New Beginning" 8 pp. with Williamson and Krenkel
  reprinted in THE COMPLETE E.C. LIBRARY (art book)

WEIRD SCIENCE-FANTASY (formerly WEIRD SCIENCE and WEIRD FANTASY; becomes INCREDIBLE SCIENCE FICTION #30 on)
#23 March 1954 - #29 May-June 1955
E.C. Comics
- 29 May-June 1955
  COVER (originally intended for Famous Funnies #217)
  reprinted in SQUA TRONT #1 (fanzine)
  reprinted in COMICS INTERVIEW - FRAZETTA SPECIAL (magazine)
  reprinted in THE COMICS JOURNAL #174 (magazine)
  reprinted in THE BEST OF FRAZETTA (card set - subset)
  reprinted in THE COMPLETE E.C. LIBRARY (art book)
  reprinted in FROM AARGH! TO ZAP! (art book)
  reprinted in E.C. PORTFOLIO #2
  reprinted in TALES FROM THE CRYPT (art book)

The above cover was altered slightly to remove any indication that the character is Buck Rogers. Among other things, his helmet was removed.

WESTERN FIGHTERS
Apr-May 1948 - Vol.4 3 7 Mar-Apr 1953
Hillman Periodicals / Star Publications
Photo Journal #2126
- 11 October 1949
  "Why They Call Themselves Mavericks" 6 pp. with Williamson

WESTERN HEARTS
December 1949 - #10 March 1952
Standard Comics
- 2 March 1950
  2 pp. (with Al Williamson)

WONDER COMICS
May 1944 - #20 October 1948
Great / Nedor / Better Publications
- 17 April 1948
  "The March of the Dinosaurs" (certain panels)
  "The Freezer Gas" 9 pp. (Frazetta inks)
- 19 August 1948
  "The Silver Knight" (certain panels)
- 20 October 1948
  "Curse on the Camelots" (mostly Frazetta)

WORLD'S FINEST COMICS (formerly world's best comics #1)
National Periodical Publications / DC Comics: No. 2, Sum, 1941 - N0. 323, Jan. 1986
- 205
  "The Duel of the Flying Knights" 6 pp.
  first printed in ADVENTURE COMICS #153

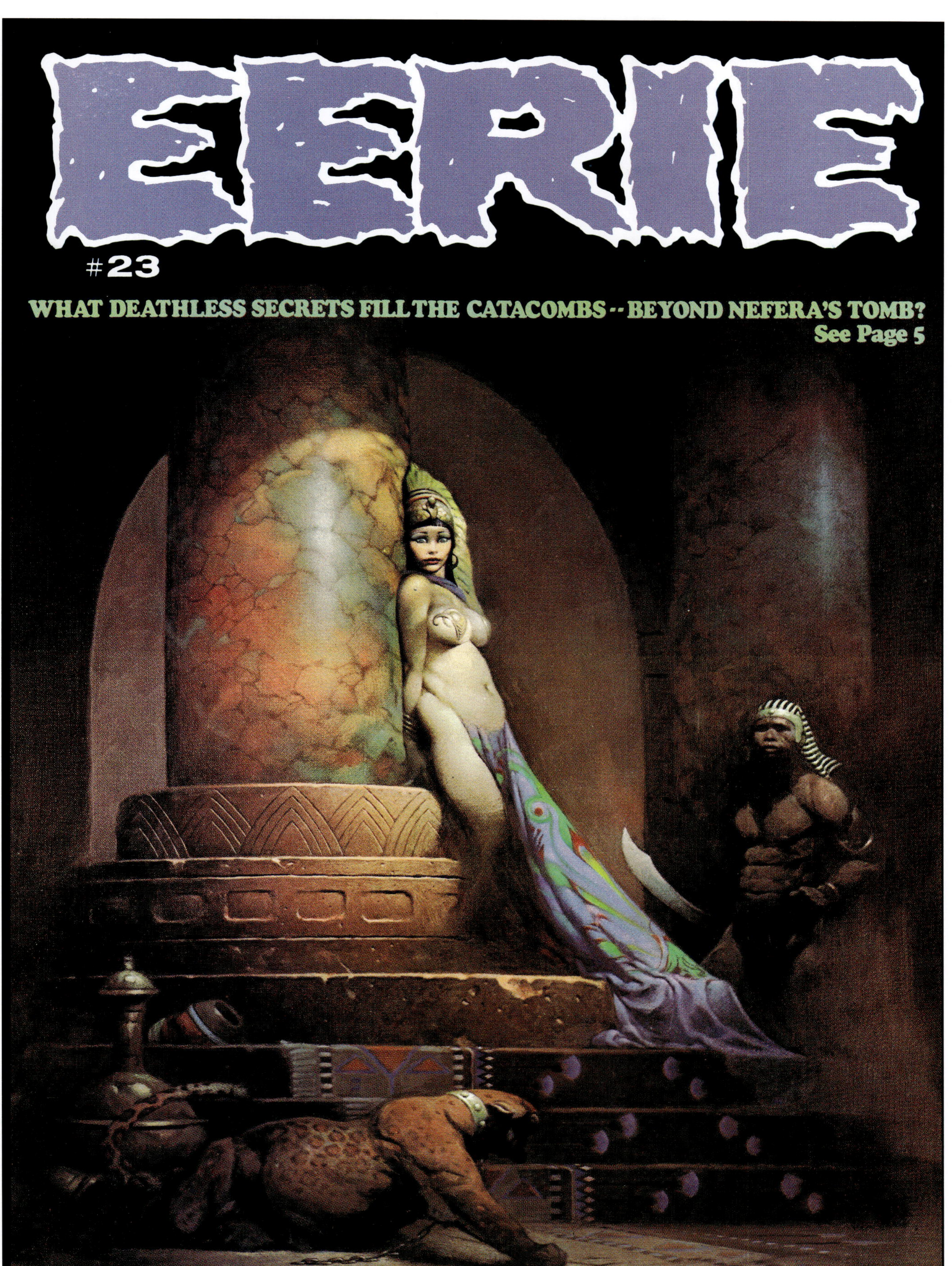

ABOVE: This poster from Warren Publishing is not identical to the EERIE *#23 magazine cover (Sept. 1969). It lacks various magazine markings including the 50¢ price (bottom-right) and Cousin Eerie portrait insignia (top-left). Note: this original version varies slightly from all other reproductions as Frazetta modified the piece after publication by Warren.*

DEVOTEES & AFFICIONADOS

Fan Publications

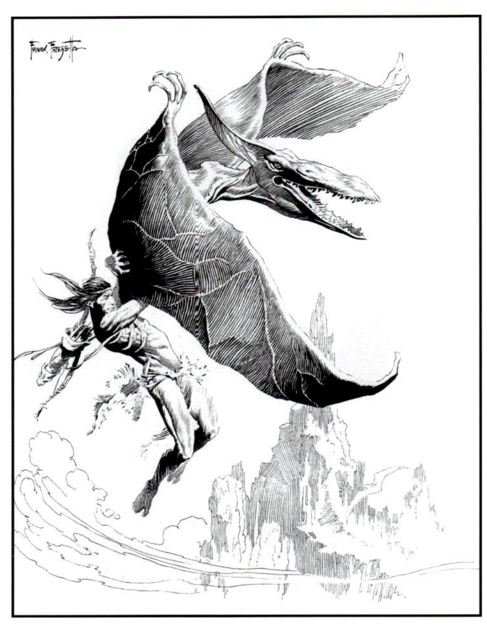

As fanzines caught on in the 1960s, they drew the attention of pros as well as fans. Frazetta's friend, legendary EC comics and MAD cartoonist, Wally Wood believed fanzines could become a valid outlet for professionals to express themselves through art-for-art-sake creations unencumbered by the threat and overbearing hands of mainstream comics editors and publishers. His vision manifested itself as witzend *(purposely not capitalized) which featured top creators including Wood, Ditko, Williamson, Goodwin, Frazetta and more. It came to be known as the first "pro-zine" and predated similarly-minded underground comics by at least a year.*

ABOVE:
Frazetta's back cover for witzend *#4 (1968)*

OPPOSITE:
Back cover of Witzend *#1 (1966)*

Fanzines (magazines by or for fandom), have been around for many decades. Most are completely black and white from cover to cover but sometimes, with time and budget allowing, the publisher may occasionally add color. The articles and stories inside these magazines can vary greatly from issue to issue. On many occasions the readers contribute to the fanzines they subscribe to, creating a very diverse publication. Usually, they're printed in low runs—frequently under 500 copies. Prior to the advent of comics specialty shops, fanzine distribution was limited to mail-order and comics conventions. While many last only a single issue, others, like some of the EC and ERB zines, grow to be highly professional and last decades.

Fanzines are targeted toward a specific audience. Sometimes, they're centered around a single author or artist but can grow to encompass an entire genre, like the heroic-fantasy fanzine AMRA. Many of today's artists and writers have honed their skills within the pages of fan publications. While personal computers have improved production quality, the development of the internet, is helping to make fanzines a thing of the past, as they are being replaced by their digital counterpart, the web site.

Though some Frazetta fanzines are of the low quality standards mentioned above, there are quite a few that rise above the common fare. They challenge the notion that such short-run publications equate to shoddy merchandise. For example, Frazetta's own fanzine simply titled FRAZETTA. This zine boasts high-quality paper, amazing black and white reproductions of color art, and a well rounded collection of rare Frazetta items. The cover price of $2.50 per copy, in 1969, was a lot to

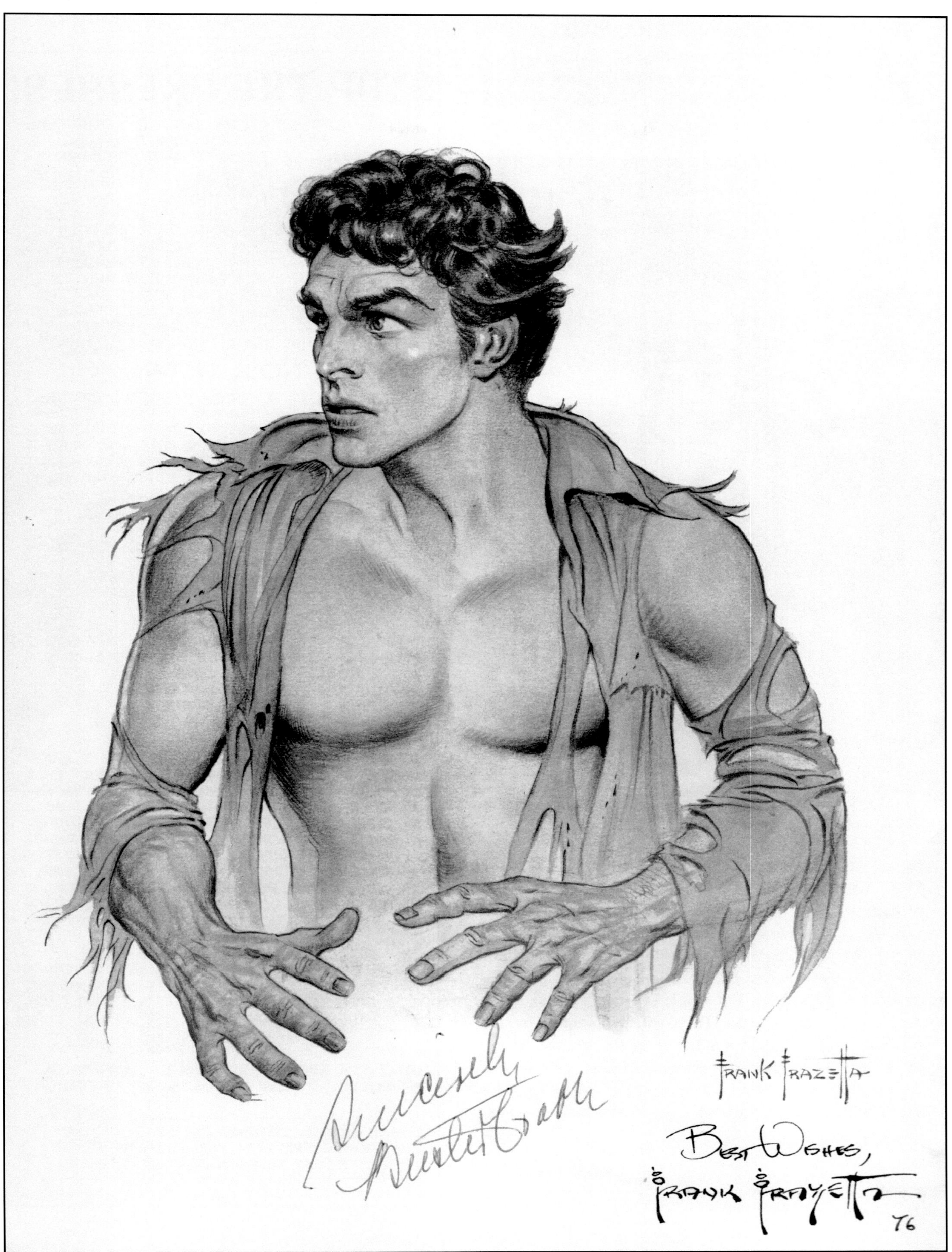
FRANK FRAZETTA
BEST WISHES,
FRANK FRAZETTA
76

pay for a black and white magazine for fans, but you know where that money went as soon as you peeked within it's brilliant white pages.

The fanzines listed within this index comprise the entire spectrum of quality. From the extremely cheap, poorly xeroxed, often unauthorized, non-informational rags that give the term "fanzine" a bad name, up to the supreme quality mags produced by up-and-comers or even professionals.

This section is compiled to enlighten die-hard collectors who are looking to venture into the broadest horizons, beyond mainstream Frazetta merchandise, and to open up a more rarely-viewed perspective available only to those who are willing to dig and search.

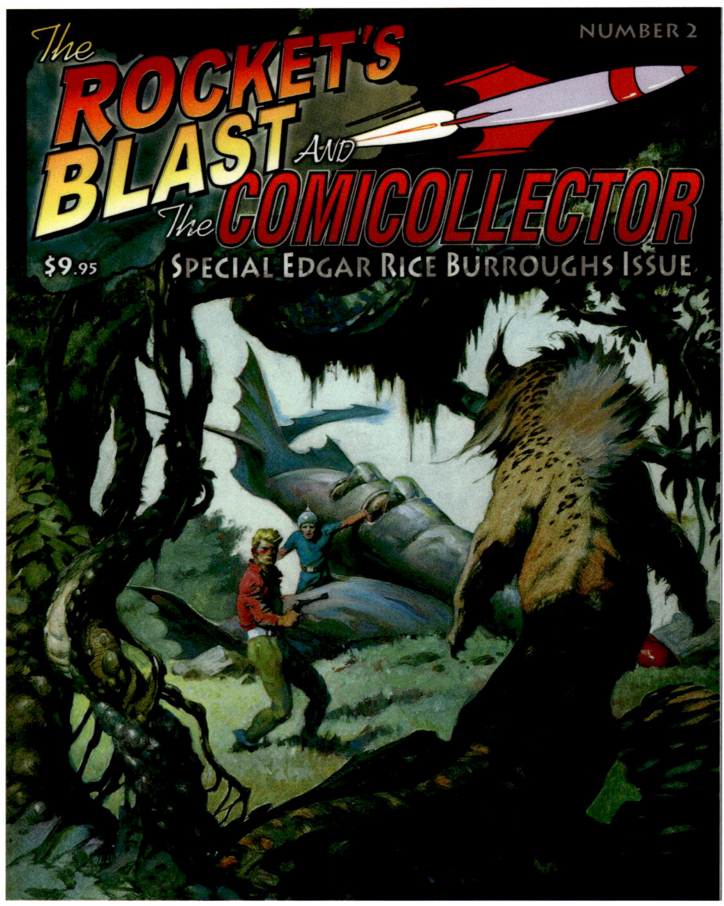

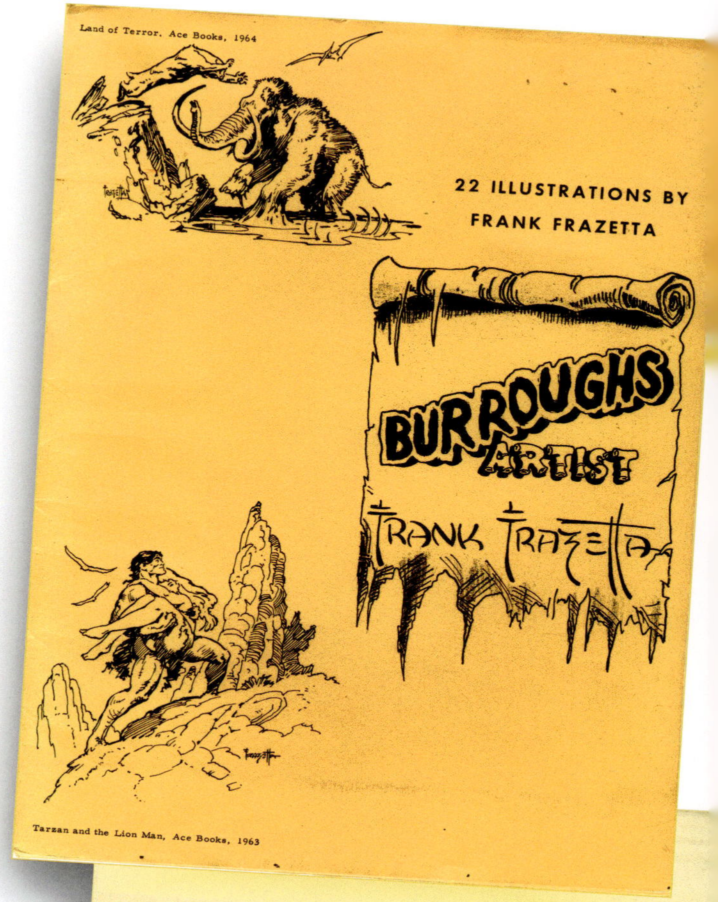

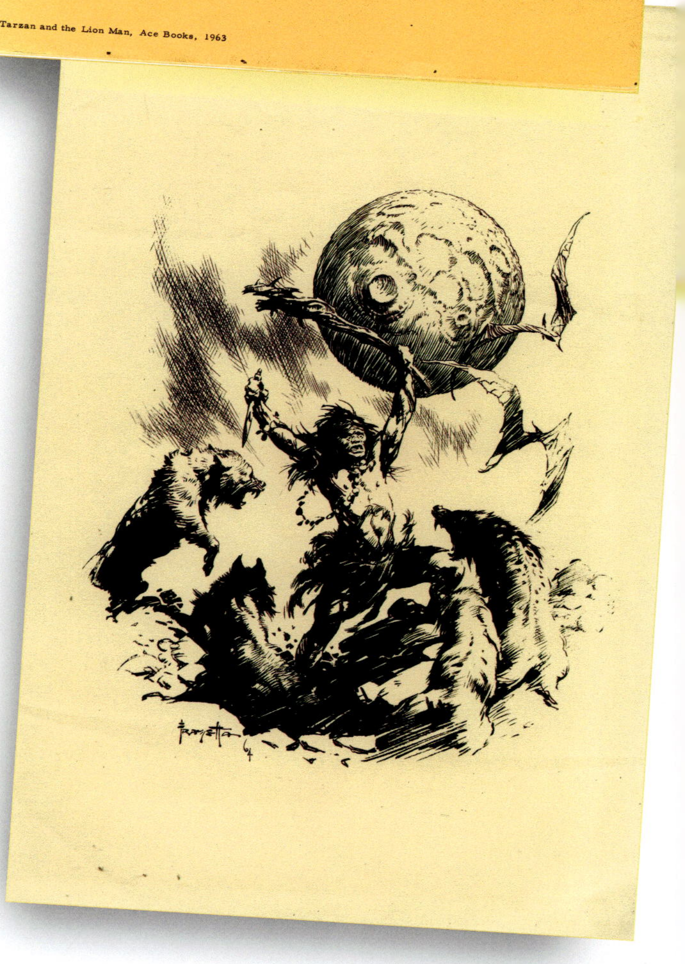

ABOVE:
Rocket's Blast and The Comic Collector *#2.*

RIGHT TOP:
Burroughs Artist Portfolio *cover (1974 reprint)*

RIGHT:
Unused Canaveral Illustration issued as a rare 11" x 17" print

OPPOSITE: Special plate from the Burroughs Artist Portfolio *exclusive to the 1974 reprint.*

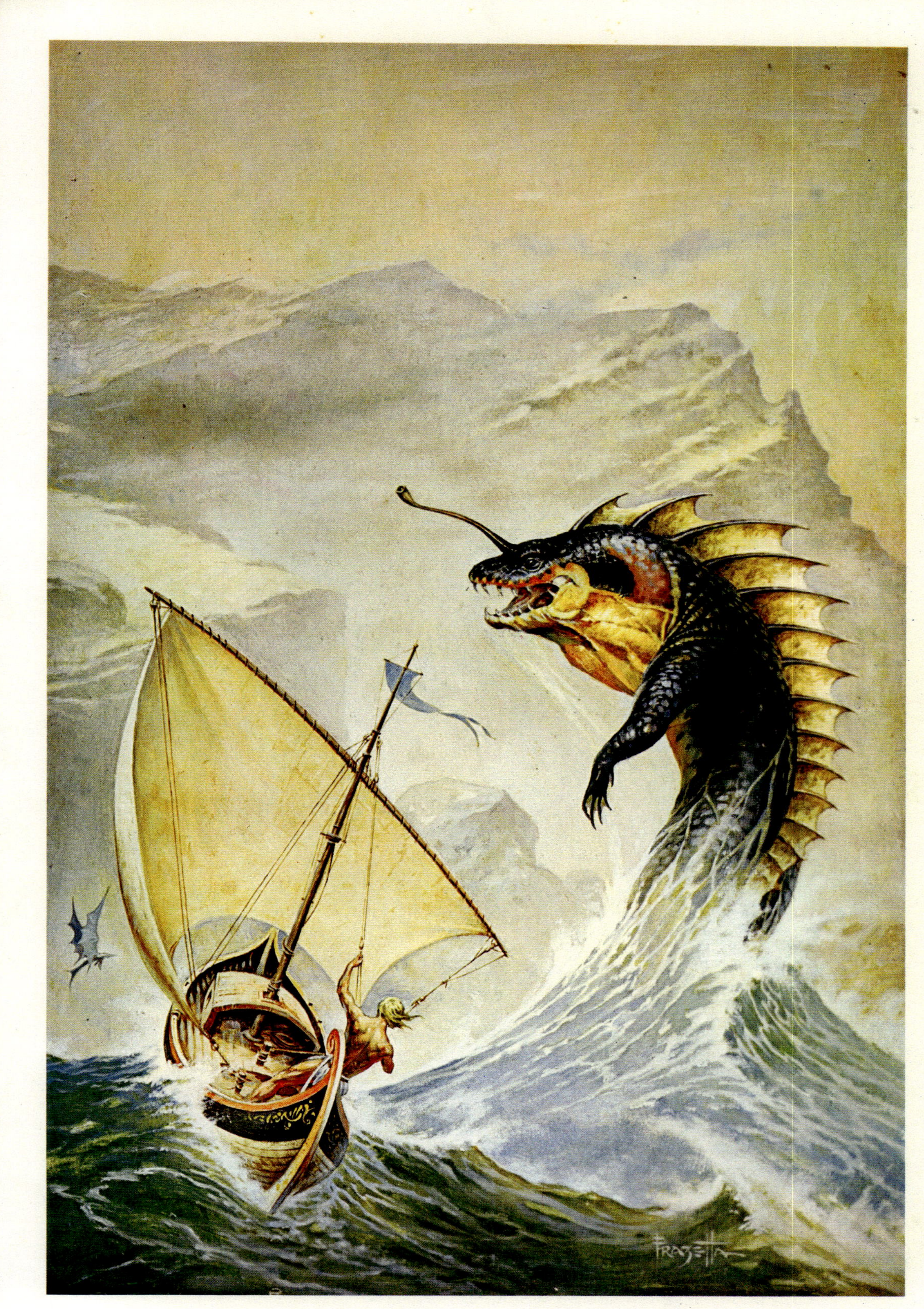

1. CARSON OF VENUS / "I saw monstrous creatures of the deep."

FAN PUBLICATIONS

AMRA

Terminus, Owlswick, & Ft. Mudge Electrick Street Railway Gazette

- vol. 1 #22
  pg. 5 Tarzan illustration
- vol. 1 #24
  pg. 20 Tarzan illustration
- vol. 1 #25
  pg. 6 Tarzan illustration
- vol. 1 #28
  single illustration
- vol. 1 #66
  single illustration

ART FANTASTIQUE

Trek Publications

- 2

COVER - Flash Gordon and Dale by Williamson and Frazetta

Canaveral, Tarzan illustration

AKA - *"The silent creature drove a long knife again and again into his tawny hide"*

first printed in TARZAN AND THE CASTAWAYS brochure advertisement

Dust jacket illo to TARZAN AND THE CASTAWAYS

AKA - *"Itzl Cha saw in one terrifying glance that the god who bore her was flying through the air."*

first printed in TARZAN AND THE CASTAWAYS

untitled illo of a man with spear killing a serpent

AKA - *"David Innes, A hydrophidian, Ja the Messop"*

first printed in E.R. BURROUGHS - MASTER OF ADVENTURE

Cover illustration from WEIRD SCIENCE-FANTASY #29

untitled Tarzan illo from TARZAN AND THE CASTAWAYS

AKA - *"Tarzan in perfect calm, raised his short, heavy spear above his right shoulder and waited"*

first printed in TARZAN AND THE CASTAWAYS

Cover illustration from WEIRD SCIENCE-FANTASY #29 (used a second time)

Midwood paperback illustration

Two women defending a space ship against two attacking men

Midwood paperback illustration

"A Mahar casts her sinister spell."

first printed in E.R. BURROUGHS - MASTER OF ADVENTURE

cover illustration from THE EFFICIENCY EXPERT

The Giantess illustration

untitled Canaveral Press illo

AKA - *"I saw three mighty thipdars"*

first printed in AT THE EARTH'S CORE AND PELLUCIDAR PORTFOLIO

untitled Canaveral Press illo

AKA - *"David Innes, Hyenadons, and man-apes of Pellucidar"*

first printed in EDGAR RICE BURROUGHS - MASTER OF ADVENTURE

untitled Canaveral Press illo

AKA - *"David Innes faces a labrithodon in Pellucidar"*

first printed in E.R. BURROUGHS - MASTER OF ADVENTURE

Cover to FAMOUS FUNNIES #216

BARSOOMIAN BAZAAR (bootleg)

- 4 pg. 1 Pellucidar and Tarzan illustration

- BEST OF WEIRD SCIENCE-FANTASY (bootleg)

Robert Brosch

"Squeeze Play"

first printed in SHOCK SUSPENSTORIES #13 (comic)

cover to WEIRD FANTASY #21 with Al Williamson

BURROUGH'S BULLETIN, THE

publisher - Vern Corriel

- 16 pg. 27 Tarzan illustration
- 19 1970
  pg. 25 Pellucidar illustration
- 20
  pp. 13,14 Pellucidar illustrations
- 21
  pg. 21 Tarzan illustration
- 22
  spot illustration
- 29 see FRAZETTA #2 (fan publication) for contents
- 30 Uncensored version of LUANA movie poster (b/w)
  LUANA teaser card

CAPT. GEORGE'S COMIC WORLD

- 15
  "The Frazetta You Didn't Know"
  Reprints 22 MIDWOOD illustrations
  Reprints 1 CANAVERAL PRESS illustration.
- 21
  "Boy Scout's Jamboree" 1pg. ad
  first printed in HEROIC COMICS #81

CARTOON ART QUARTERLY

- 2
  watercolor rough for cover to NATIONAL LAMPOON April 1971 issue

CARTOONISTS AND ILLUSTRATORS PORTFOLIO

- 2 1978
  JOHNNY COMET strip
  first printed in 12-7-52 Sunday strip
  LI'L ABNER strip
  first printed in 11-22-54 daily strip

CHACAL

1976

Nemedian Chronicles

- 1 Full page convention sketch - Nude with wolf

COLLAGE Limited to 250 copies

1972

SFCA

- White Indian story by Frazetta

COLLECTORS CHOICE

- 1 JOHNNY COMET strip
  first printed in 11-11-52 daily strip

COLLECTORS SHOWCASE

- 2 JOHNNY COMET strip
  first printed in 4-9-52 daily strip

- CREATION CON program

1971 2 sketches

- DEEPER THAN YOU THINK A literary glimpse of R.E.H.

January 1968

Joel Frieman

insert pen & ink sketch of Conan

• DEEP SOUTH CON program
August 23 - 25, 1968
New Orleans
single illustration

• DETROIT CON program
1971 single illustration

DETROIT TRIPLE FAN FAIR PROGRESS REPORT
• 2 1970 COVER

DREAMS
• 1 single illustration

• EC FAN ADDICT very limited print run 5 1/2" x 8 1/2"
2000
AACC
Given exclusively to those in attendance at the 2000 San Diego Comic-Con E.C. Reunion. Front and back covers by Frazetta.
front cover **Tales From the Crypt**
back cover **first printed in** TALES OF THE INCREDIBLE

• EC LIVES Fan Addict program
1972
article about Frazetta (1 pg.)
article includes *"Fired"* (6 pp. with Al Williamson)
first printed in CRIME SUSPENSTORIES #17

ERBANIA
• 39 1976 single illustration

• 45
article *"Frank Frazetta and ERB"* by Bob Barrett
article includes the following:
rough for BEYOND THE FARTHEST STAR book cover
many interior illustrations

ERB-DOM
C. Cazzeduceus
• 10 pg. 8
ink illustration
first printed in AT THE EARTH'S CORE and
PELLUCIDAR PORTFOLIO
• 14
pp. 15, 17 Tarzan illustrations
first printed in TARZAN AND THE CASTAWAYS interior book illo.
• 17 pg. 8 ink illustration
first printed in AT THE EARTH'S CORE and
PELLUCIDAR PORTFOLIO
b. cover ink illustration
first printed in AT THE EARTH'S CORE and
PELLUCIDAR PORTFOLIO
• 80 February 1975
AT THE EARTH'S CORE interior illos.
first printed in AT THE EARTH'S CORE and
PELLUCIDAR PORTFOLIO
• 86 April 1976
COVER - untitled Canaveral Press illustration
AKA- *"I saw three mighty thipdars."*
first printed in AT THE EARTH'S CORE and
PELLUCIDAR PORTFOLIO
inside cover - untitled illustration
• 88 COVER
first printed in NATIONAL LAMPOON ENCYCLOPEDIA OF HUMOR

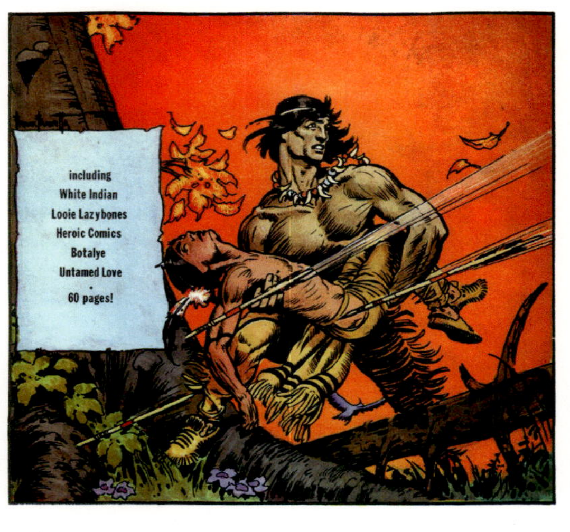

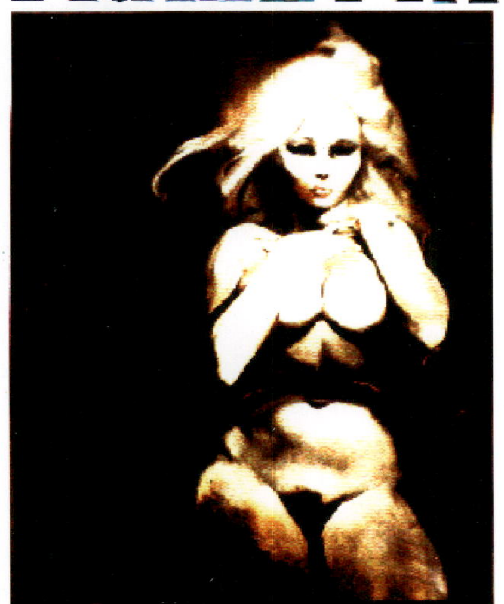

TOP: The Comic Strip Frazetta
(unauthorized)

ABOVE: The Rare Frazetta
(unauthorized)

FANTASTIC EXPLOITS (bootleg)
E.B. Love
- 15 "*Massacre*" first 3 pp
  first printed in DURANGO KID #8 (comic)
- 16 "*Massacre*" final 4 pp
  first printed in DURANGO KID #8 (comic)
- 17 1970
  untitled first "White Indian" story 7 pp.
  first printed in DURANGO KID #1 (comic)
- 20 1971
  THUN'DA, KING OF THE CONGO #1
  first printed in A-1 COMICS #47
  White Indian story
- 22 "*The Invasion from the Abyss*" 7 pp
  first printed in STRANGE WORLDS #3 (comic)

FANTASY CROSSROADS
1977
Stygian Isle Press
- 10/11 1977 back cover Frazetta sketch
- 15 Interior illo of a man running with a spear"

• FRANK FRAZETTA - BURROUGHS' TARZAN
FANZINE
Reproduces much of Frazetta's Burroughs illustrations

• FRANK FRAZETTA INDEX (bootleg, 28 pages)
1975 fairly comprehensive checklist includes the following:
Elements magazine illustrations
centerfold HOTEL PARADISO movie poster

• FRANK FRAZETTA BOOTLEG
CFA-APA
1970's Nice index that covers Frazetta bootleg items produced through the years
40 pp. Limited to 100 numbered copies.
Cover Color preliminary to **The Gauntlet**

• FRANK FRAZETTA - MASTER OF PEN & INK
FANZINE
Reproduces many of Frazetta's ink illustrations

• FRANK FRAZETTA PORTFOLIO (b&w, bootleg)
1979
52 pages of reprinted material including:
Entire LORD OF THE RINGS portfolio
Entire WOMEN OF THE AGES portfolio
Entire KUBLA KHAN portfolio
All eight covers reprinted from FAMOUS FUNNIES
4 **Battlestar Galactica** paintings

• FRANK FRAZETTA SPECIAL (bootleg)
Captain George Presents
38, 39 illustration from "*Baby, you're really something*"
pg. 2 "*Barney Rooster*" 7 pp.
first printed in BARNYARD COMICS #19
pg. 9 "*There's no Feud Like an Old Feud*" 6 pp.
first printed in THRILLING COMICS #67
pg. 15 "*Shutterbugs*" 9 pp.
first printed in THRILLING COMICS #68
pg. 24 "*Everything's Vine*" 7 pp.
first printed in THRILLING COMICS #68
pg. 31 "*Talented Bear*" illustration
first printed in BARNYARD COMICS #25
pg. 32 "*Hucky Duck*" 2 pp.
first printed in BARNYARD COMICS #19
pg. 34 "*Bashful Cricket*" illustration
first printed in BARNYARD COMICS #25
pg. 35 "*The Battle of the Dungeons*" 7 pp.
first printed in DURANGO KID #7
pg. 42 "*The Blood of Valley Forge*" 7 pp.
first printed in DURANGO KID #11
pg. 49 "*Massacre*" 7 pp.
first printed in DURANGO KID #8
pg. 56 "*The Scared Life Saver*" 2 pp.
first printed in HEROIC COMICS #67
pg. 58 "*3 Year old Hero*" 2 pp.
first printed in HEROIC COMICS #67
pg. 60 "*Cats with Beautiful Tails*" illustration
first printed in BARNYARD COMICS #19
pg. 61 "*Cleverest One*" illustration
first printed in BARNYARD COMICS #19

• FRANK FRAZETTA WOMEN (bootleg)
Reprints sketches and finished art of women by Frazetta.
Color covers, b&w interior.

FRAZETTA (b/w)
1969
Attezarf
Robert R. Barrett - publisher
- 1 COVER
  pg. 2 **Self Portrait**
  pg. 3 **Nude Bathing**
  pg. 4 **Girl Observed by Undressed Man with Hat**
  pg. 5 **Bear Watching Caveman Threaten Cub**
  pg. 6 cover to A-1 COMICS #47
  pg. 7 Sheba
  pg. 8 "*King of the Lost Lands*" 10pp.
  first printed in A-1 COMICS #47
  pg. 11 **La of Opar** centerfold.
  Color version in ARIEL (art book)
  pg. 20 **The Tempters**
  pg. 21 **Golden Girl**
  back cover **Eve**

• 2 (AKA THE BURROUGHS BULLETIN #29)
Spring 1973
collaboration with Vernell Coriell
This issue has two titles. The Burroughs Bulletin collaborated with the Frazetta fan publication to produce this well-crafted cross collectible.
COVER untitled (design resembles **Masai Warrior**)
pg. 4 article "*Frazetta - The History of a Burroughs Artist*" 2 pp.
small Tarzan sketch
pg. 6 cover to BUSTER CRABBE #4
pg. 7 JOHNNY COMET Sunday page
2 ACE McCOY dailies (JOHNNY COMET)
1 LI'L ABNER daily
pg. 8 article *Frazetta - The History of a Burroughs Artist*" 1 pg.
sketchbook drawings
pg. 9 personal work (Tyrannosaurus Rex)
sketchbook drawing
pg. 10 frontis illustrations from Ace TARZAN books 2 pp.
pg. 12 article "*The Case of the Miscaptioned Illo*" 1 pg.
ink illustration "*He had me captured by an African Chief.*"
first printed in TARZAN AND THE CASTAWAYS interior book illo.
pg. 13 ink illustration "*Tarzan took in the picture at a glance.*"
first printed in TARZAN AND THE CASTAWAYS interior book illo.
ink illustration "*A great tiger emerged from the underbrush.*"
first printed in TARZAN AT THE EARTH'S CORE interior book illo.
ink illustration "*The ape-man dealt him a terrific blow on the side of the head with his open palm.*"
first printed in TARZAN AND THE CASTAWAYS interior book illo.
ink illustration "*Tarzan in perfect calm, raised his short, heavy spear above his right shoulder and waited.*"
first printed in TARZAN AND THE CASTAWAYS interior book illo.

pg. 14 ink illustration
first printed in TARZAN AND THE CASTAWAYS cover
pg. 15 ink illustration *"He caught them on his tusks and tossed them high into the air."*
first printed in TARZAN AT THE EARTH'S CORE interior book illo.
"He struck suddenly upward with his blade."
first printed in TARZAN AT THE EARTH'S CORE interior book illo.
ink illustration *"The bear whirled about on the narrow ledge."*
first printed in TARZAN AT THE EARTH'S CORE interior book illo.
ink illustration *"Tarzan swung the body over his head."*
first printed in TARZAN AT THE EARTH'S CORE interior book illo.
pg. 16 article *"The Imaginative Years"* by Frazetta 2 pp.
header illustration used for NINA tryout strip
pg. 20 checklist of Burroughs material illustrated by Frazetta 1 pg.
pg. 22 Jana illustration
Dejah Thoris illustration
first printed in A PRINCESS OF MARS interior dust jacket illo.
pg. 23 b/w pencil sketch
AKA - Tarzan and Bolgani
pg. 24 *"The Monsters From the Mists"* 7 pp.
first printed in A-1 COMICS #47
Robert R. Barrett's letterhead containing:
Tarzan illustration
Lord Grandrith illustration
John Gribardsun illustration
back cover **Tarzan and the Ant-Men**

• FRAZETTA 100 DRAWINGS (bootleg)
1975 34 pages of poorly reproduced b/w art

• FRAZETTA INDEX BONANZA
2001
Milton Courter
COVER **A Requiem for Sharks** (revised version)
title page b/w **A Requiem for Sharks** (revised version)

• FRAZETTA TREASURY, THE (bootleg)
Frank Frazetta
1975
COVER **Conan of Aquilonia**
i,f cover **Snake bit** b/w
title page sketchbook drawing
pg. 2 *"Biography"* 1 pg.
Self Portrait
pg. 3 *"Interview"* 8 pp. contains the following:
"Burrough's Bibliophiles" letter-head
"The City in the Sea" panel
originally from NINA tryout page
2 sketchbook drawings (previously unpublished)
PRESIDENT EISENHOWER'S CARTOON BOOK
"Untamed Love" splash panel
first printed in PERSONAL LOVE #32
Doubleday Sci-Fi Book Club
AKA - **Fantasy World**
2 sketchbook drawings (previously unpublished)
cover to GHOST RIDER #4
sketchbook drawing
Tarzan drawing
first printed in FRAZETTA #2
panel from JOHNNY COMET strip

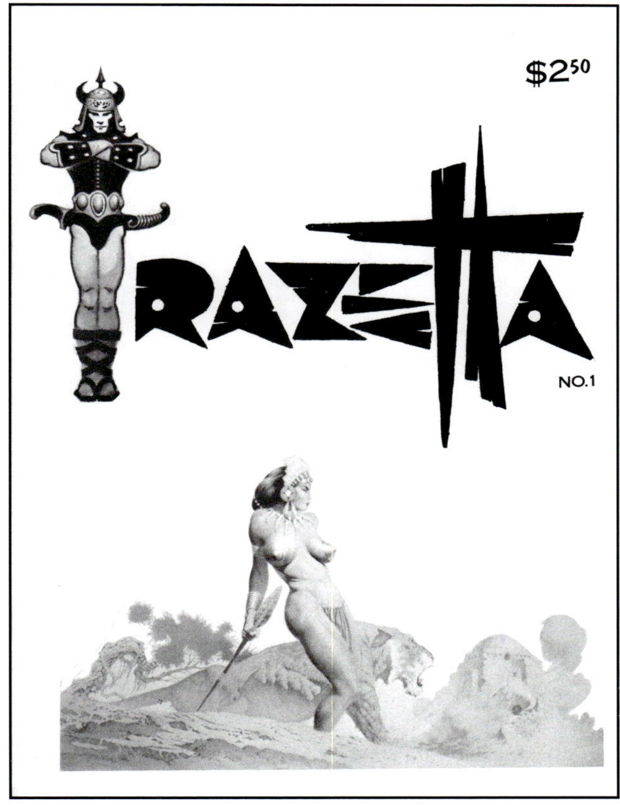

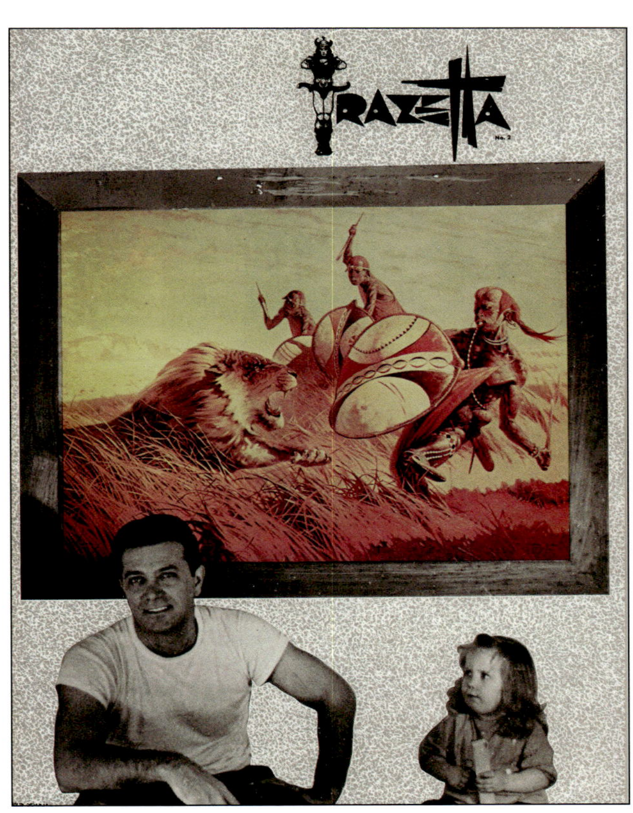

TOP: Frazetta Official Fanzine #*1*

ABOVE: Frazetta Official Fanzine #*2*

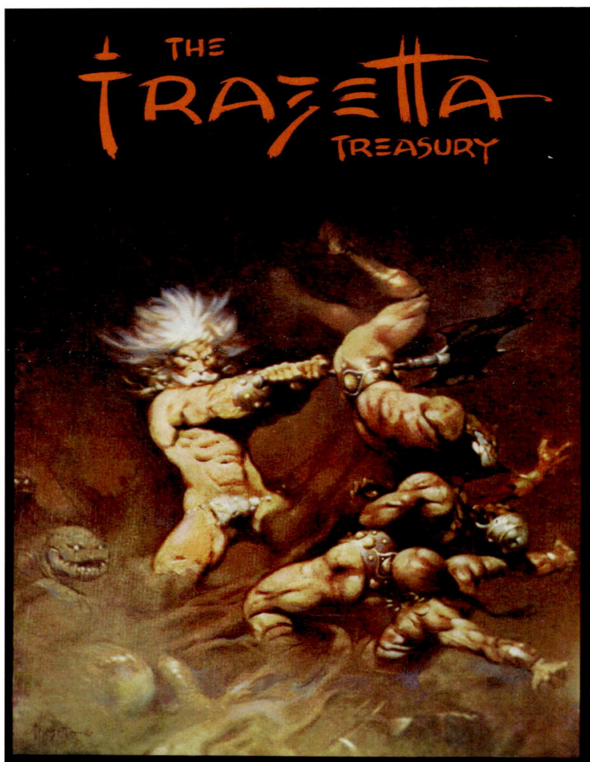

The Frazetta Treasury.

THE FRAZETTA TREASURY cont'd

pg. 11 "*Portfolio*" 17 pp. contains the following:
"*Sex in the Afternoon*" men's magazine illo
Doubleday Book Club pamphlet illustration
The True Memoirs of Charley Blankenship
AKA - **Bucking Bronco**
ink illustration
first printed in WITZEND #4 back cover
two men's magazine illustrations
Summer of the Drums detail
AKA - **Indian Brave**
previously unpublished sketchbook drawing
sketchbook drawing
"*Give us Barrabas*"
first printed in New York Times ad.
Madame Derringer
"*She raised her slim blade above the heart of Dar Tarus.*"
first printed in MASTERMIND OF MARS interior book illo.
The Trial of Judas Wiley
cover to THUVIA, MAID OF MARS & CHESSMEN OF MARS
1972 Infinity Convention program sketch
The Giantess ink illustration

pg. 28 "*Checklist*" 14 pp. contains the following:
ten previously unpublished sketches
Frogs on the Moon?
b/w illustration from Doubleday Book Club
Winter of the Coup
Are There Frogs on the Moon?
D.T.F.F progress report sketch
Luana (A sheet design)
After the Fox (A sheet design)
A Requiem for Sharks

pg. 42 "*Comics*" 7 pp. contains the following:
cover to BUSTER CRABBE COMICS #5
"*Hucky Duck*" 1 pg. (partial story)
cover to WILD BILL HICKOCK
Not a Frazetta cover, painted by Howard Winfield
"*The Claws of Death*" 4 pp. with Al Williamson
first printed in JOHN WAYNE ADV. COMICS #3

i,b cover cover to CONAN THE BUCCANEER (revised version)

back cover **Devil Rider**

GOLDEN AGE
S.F.C.A.
1969
- 4 "*The Frazetta Portfolio*"

GRIDLEY WAVE, THE
- 15 pg. 7 Tarzan illustration
- 18 pg. 4 Tarzan illustration
- 20 center fold
six illustrations from Canaveral Press editions of AT THE EARTH'S CORE and PELLUCIDAR
- 27 pg. 3 Dejah Thoris illustration
first printed in A PRINCESS OF MARS interior d.j. illo.
- 29 pg. 1 cover and frontispiece for GODS OF MARS
pg. 3 cover and frontispiece for WARLORD OF MARS
- 35 pg. 1 cover to Ace editions AT THE EARTH'S CORE and PELLUCIDAR
- 36 pg. 1 cover to Doubleday edition of THUVIA, MAID OF MARS and CHESSMEN OF MARS

HERITAGE
- Vol.1 #1 1972b-cover pencil sketch

HOWARD REVIEW
- 3 Burroughs Bibliophiles letterhead (chimp sitting at typewriter)

I'LL BE DAMNED numbered/limited to 1,000 copies
- 1 Cover
interior illustration

INFINITY
- 2 1970
interview with Frazetta
single illustration
- 4 1972 reprints sci-fi tryout page (with Williamson)

- **INFINITY CONVENTION PROGRAM**

1972 nice pencil sketch

JASOOMIAN
- 10 4 illustrations

- **JOHNNY COMET**

1967
Ed April jr. publishing
reprints dailies 1/28/52 - 4/26/52

- **MAGIC OF FRAZETTA** (bootleg)

1970s 26 pages of poor b/w reproductions

- **MIRKWOOD TIMES, THE** (bootleg)

1973 32 pp. Reprints 1 pg. P.S.A. by Frazetta

- **MORE MAGIC OF FRAZETTA** (bootleg)

1970s 29 pages of poor b/w reproductions

ON THE DRAWING BOARD (bootleg)
• Vol.3 #4

OUTLOOKS digest size (bootleg)
• 2 cover

PHANTASMAGORIA (bootleg)
Kenneth Smith
• 4 John Carter illustration colored by Kenneth Smith

PORKPIE (bootleg)
1976
Stephen R. Bynum
• 1 article - "*The Complete Frazetta Addict*" by Steve Ringgenberg
includes 6 illustrations, one unpublished

QUA BROT
• 1 1985 watercolor rough to **Into the Aether**
watercolor rough to **Pellucidar**
b/w illustrations
illustration (with Williamson)
Frazetta/Krenkel paperback checklist.

• RARE FRAZETTA, THE (bootleg)
circa 1975
Griffin Books
COVER **Temptation**
pg. 3 album cover THE FASTEST GUITAR ALIVE
pg. 4 album cover WELCOME TO THE L.B.J. RANCH
pg. 5 album cover (front)BOTH SIDES OF HERMAN'S HERMITS
pg. 6 album cover MOVIES ARE BETTER THAN EVER
pg. 7 album cover THE NIGHT THEY RAIDED MINSKY'S
pg. 8 movie poster THE BUSY BODY
pg. 9 movie poster MRS. POLIFAX, SPY
pg. 10 movie poster WHAT'S NEW PUSSYCAT? A sheet
pg. 11 movie poster WHAT'S NEW PUSSYCAT? B sheet
pg. 12 movie poster YOURS, MINE, AND OURS
pg. 13 movie poster AFTER THE FOX A sheet
pg. 14 **Alien Crucifixion**
pg. 15 **A Fighting Man of Mars**
pg. 16 title plate from LORD OF THE RINGS PORTFOLIO
pg. 17 plate one from LORD OF THE RINGS PORTFOLIO
pg. 18 plate two from LORD OF THE RINGS PORTFOLIO
pg. 19 plate three from LORD OF THE RINGS PORTFOLIO
pg. 20 plate four from LORD OF THE RINGS PORTFOLIO
pg. 21 plate five from LORD OF THE RINGS PORTFOLIO
pg. 22 plate six from LORD OF THE RINGS PORTFOLIO
pg. 23 sketchbook page
pg. 24 artwork from the movie poster THE FEARLESS VAMPIRE KILLERS
pg. 26 two pages of convention sketches (seven pieces)
pg. 28 sketchbook portrait
pg. 29 convention pencil sketch
pg. 30 cover to THE DANCER FROM ATLANTIS
pg. 31 **New World**
pg. 32 "*Botalye – Immortal Indian Warrior*" 3 pp.
first printed in JIMMY WAKELY #7
pg. 35 "*Adrift in a Rowboat*" 2 pp.
first printed in HEROIC COMICS #66
pg. 37 "*He Chose to Fight*" 2 pp.
first printed in HEROIC COMICS #72
pg. 39 "*With Only a Shovel*" 2 pp.
first printed in HEROIC COMICS #72
pg. 41 "*Snowman*" 8 pp.
first printed in TALLY HO (comic book)
back cover **Sunset**

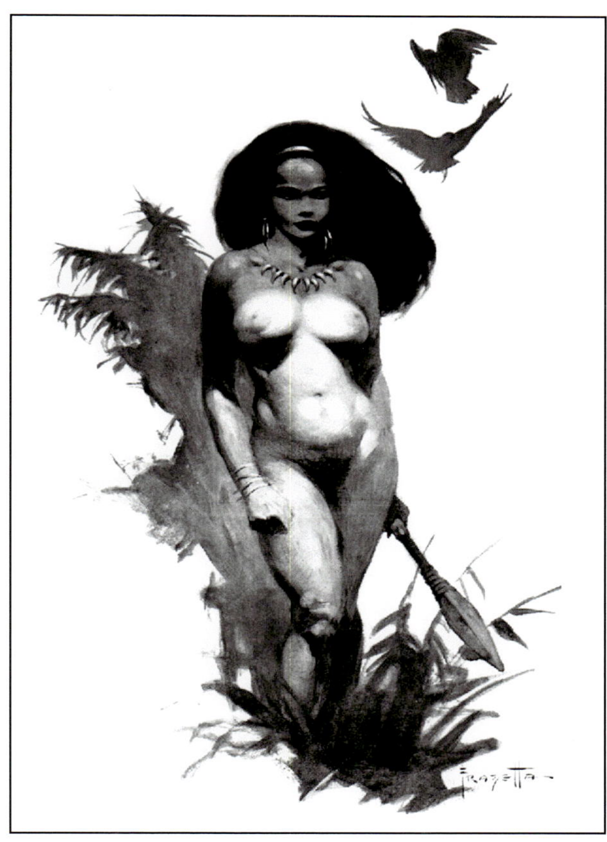

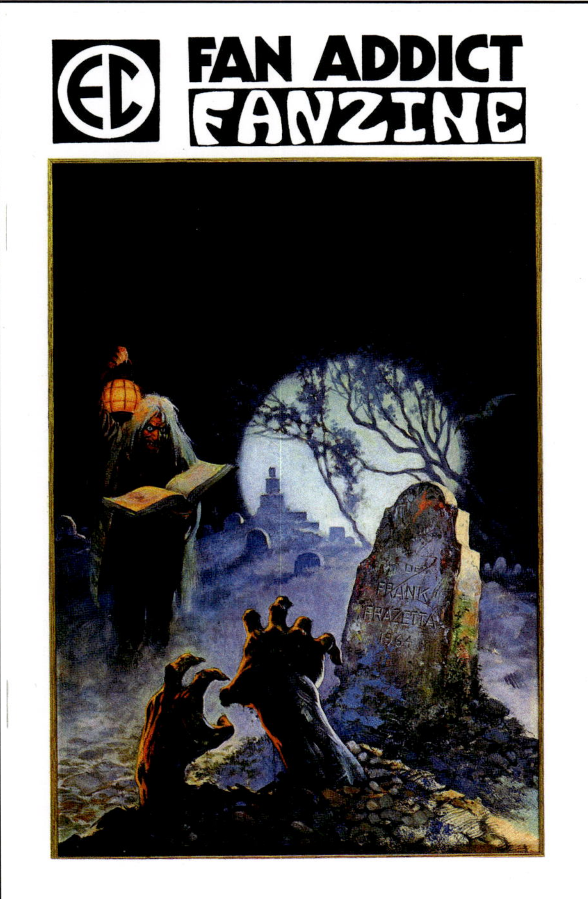

TOP: Centerfold from Frazetta Official Fanzine *#1*

ABOVE: The EC Fan Addict magazine.

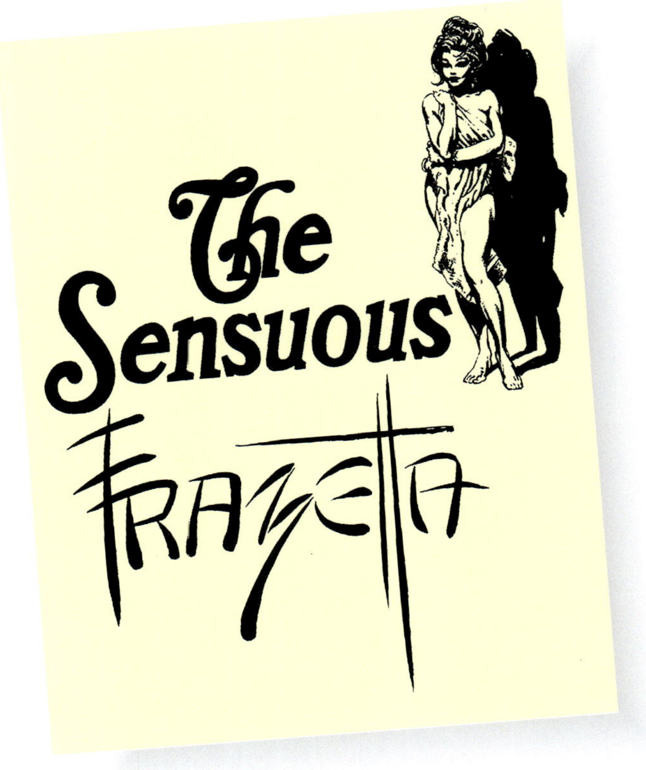

ABOVE: The Sensuous Frazetta *(1970)*

BELOW: Spa Fon #5 *(1969)*

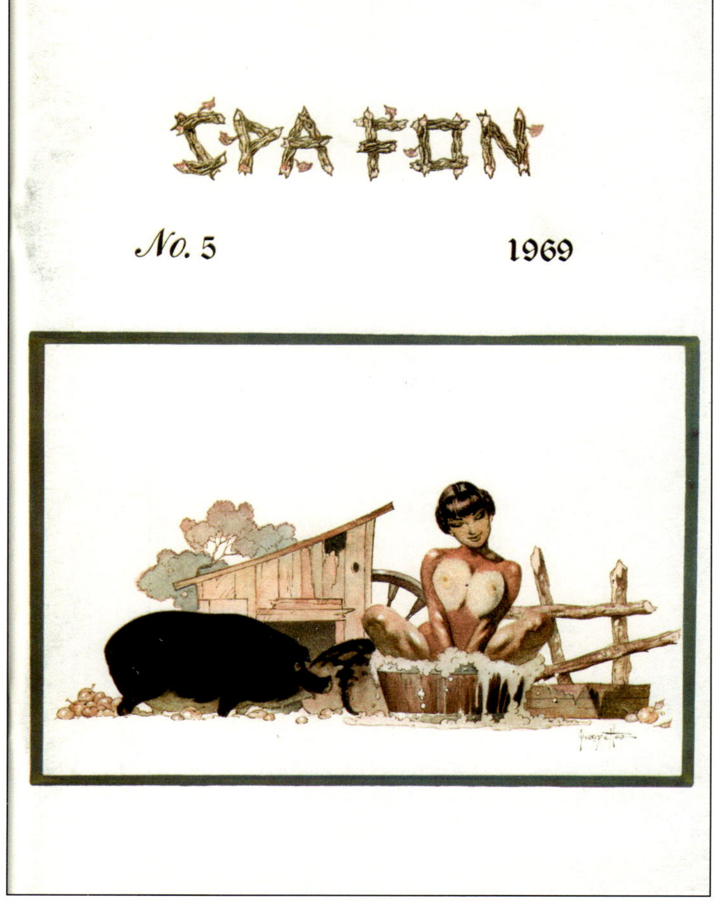

REALMS
Everyman Studios
- 5 19762 b/w sketches

R.E.H. LONE STAR FICTIONEER
- 4 b-cover pen & ink illustration

- SAN DIEGO 1972 WEST COAST COMIC CONVENTION
single contribution by Frazetta

SENSE OF WONDER (bootleg)
- 11 SWEET ADELINE Daily

- SENSUOUS FRAZETTA, THE
1970s reprints 21 illustrations from the MIDWOOD paperbacks

- SHAYOL
November 1977
Arnie Fenner
frontispiece from an Ace paperback (girl on elephant)

SPA-FON
Richard Hauser
- 2 September 1966
  Cover
  article (2 pp.)
  cover to GHOST RIDER #4 (comic book)
  cover to BUSTER CRABBE #5 (comic book)
  cover to FAMOUS FUNNIES #210 (comic book)
- 3 June 1967
  article (2 pp.)
  cover to FAMOUS FUNNIES #215 (comic book)
- 4 June 1968
  Three Spot Illos, article (2pp.)
  2 comic cover reprints
- 5 September 1969
  Cover
  checklist
  cover to TIM HOLT #17 (comic book)
  funny animal comic book reprints

SQUA TRONT
Jerry Weist
- 1 Sept. 1967
  pg. 35 article - "*The Frazetta Collector*" 5 pp.
  THUN'DA collage
  pg. 38 cover to FAMOUS FUNNIES #213
- 2 Sept. 1968
  pg. 1 illustration with Al Williamson
  pg. 23 article - "*The Frazetta Collector*" 6 pp.
  TIGA illustration
  pg. 24 TIGA strip 3 pp. (12 dailies)
  pg. 27 article on Frazetta's newspaper strips
  pg. 28 JOHNNY COMET (two strips)
  pg. 29 advertisement for FRAZETTA fanzine w/ illustrations
  pg. 46 cover to WEIRD SCIENCE-FANTASY #29
- 3 1969
  pg. 25 article - "*Frazetta Collector*" 13 pp.
  pg. 26 illustration
  pg. 28 pencil sketch
  pg. 29 illustration
  pg. 30 2 illustrations
  pg. 32 sketch
  pg. 33 2 portrait sketches Frank Jr. / Billy
  pg. 34 Flash Gordon dailies 4 pp. (10 dailies)
  pg. 38 Dodger De Squoil illustration
  pg. 49 pencil sketch

- 4 1970
  - pg. 77 article - "*Frazetta Collector*" 8 pp.
  - pg. 78 detail from **The Barbarian**
  - pg. 79 **The Barbarian**
  - pg. 80 **A Princess of Mars**
    Downward to the Earth
  - pg. 81 John Carter illustrations - 4 illos, 1 per page

THIS IS LEGEND (bootleg)
- 1 [Conan] head sketch

TRUMPET (bootleg)
Ken Keller
- 12 Summer 1981 Nude woman sitting on a log.

VOICE OF COMICDOM
- 16 Frazetta article with Tarzan illustration

- **WHITE INDIAN** (bootleg)

1981
Pure Imagination
- pg. 3 untitled White Indian story 7 pp.
  first printed in DURANGO KID #1 (comic book)
- pg. 10 "*The War of the Rivers*" 7 pp.
  first printed in DURANGO KID #3 (comic book)
- pg. 17 "*Brothers of the Wilderness*" 7 pp.
  first printed in DURANGO KID #4 (comic book)
- pg. 24 "*Trees of Doom*" 7 pp.
  first printed in DURANGO KID #5 (comic book)
- pg. 31 "*Tory Treachery*" 7 pp.
  first printed in DURANGO KID #9 (comic book)
- pg. 38 "*Sleep of Death*" 8 pp.
  first printed in DURANGO KID #10(comic book)
- pg. 46 "*The Blood of Valley Forge*" 7 pp.
  first printed in DURANGO KID #11(comic book)
- b cover "*We Can Stop the Enemies of Youth*" 1 pg. ad
  first printed in BUSTER CRABBE COMICS #1

- **WHITE SAVAGE** (bootleg) 5 1/4" x 7 1/4"

1970
White Savage Publications
Cover
"*Sleep of Death*" 8 pp.
first printed in DURANGO KID #10 (comic book)

WITZEND
Wonderful Publishing Empire
- 1 1966
  "*Savage World*" 8 pp. with Al Williamson, Angelo Torres and Roy Krenkel
  reprinted in DEATH RATTLE #10 (comic book)
  reprinted in UNKNOWN WORLDS OF SCIENCE FICTION #1
  b-cover illustration of Buster Crabbe
- 2 1967 b/w illustration
- 3 1967 "*Last Chance*" 9 pp.
  reformatted, unsold newspaper strip
- 4 1968
  b-cover "*He struck suddenly upward with his blade*."early version
  A later version was used in TARZAN AT THE EARTH'S CORE interior book illustration
- 8 "*The City in the Sea*" poem by Edgar Allen Poe (9 pp.)
  This poem was illustrated with NINA tryout page

- 13 1985 Jungle Girl illustration
  first printed in CANAVERAL PRESS PORTFOLIO

- **WT50 A TRIBUTE TO WEIRD TALES**

1974
Robert Weinberg single illustration of man with sword

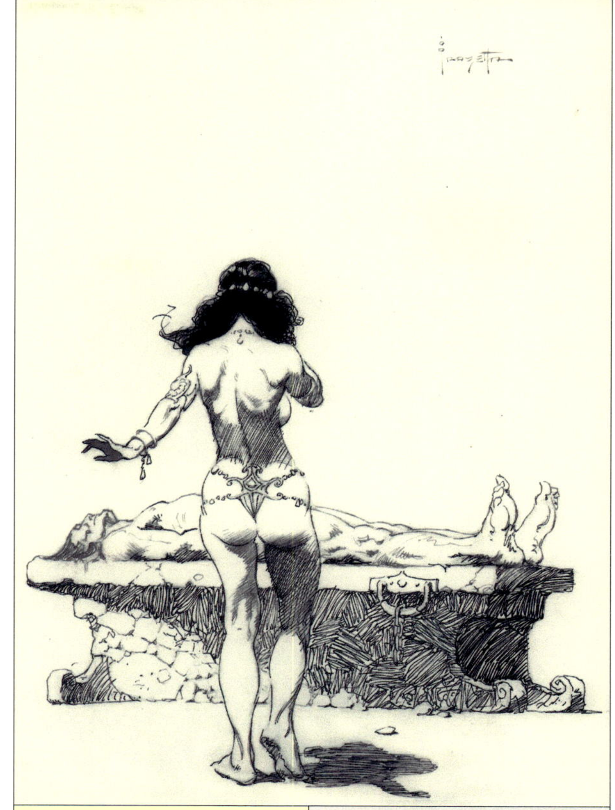

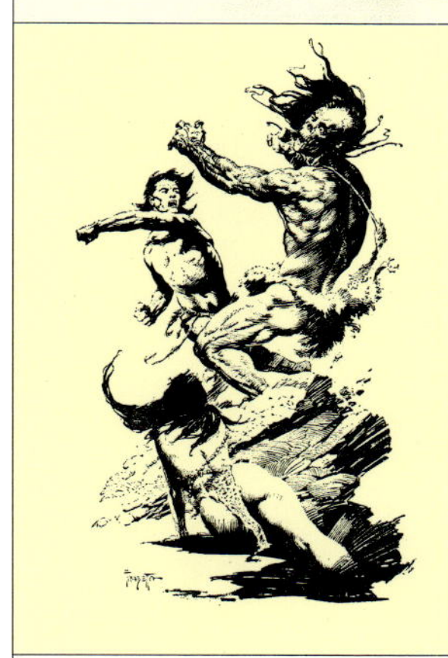

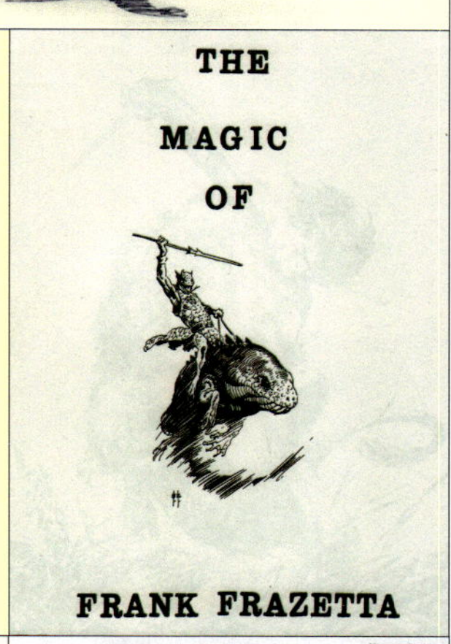

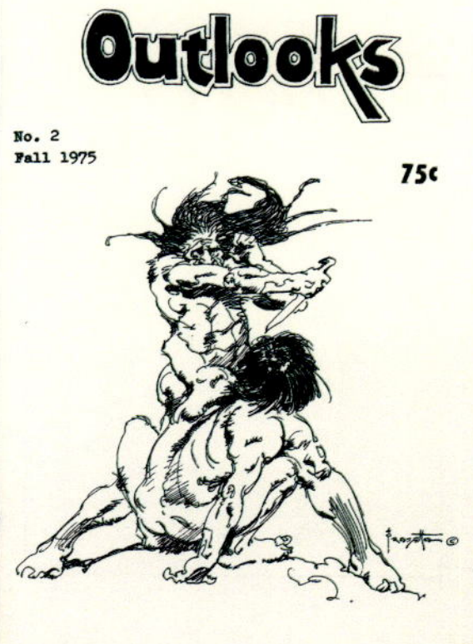

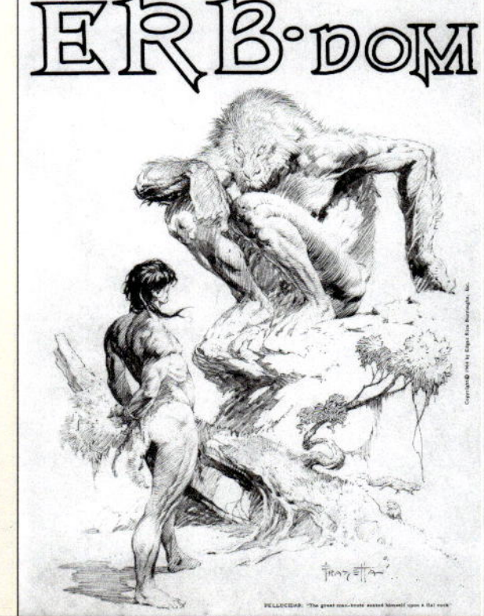

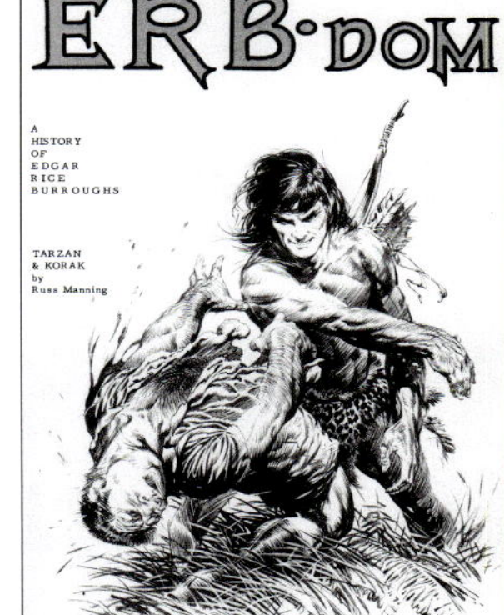

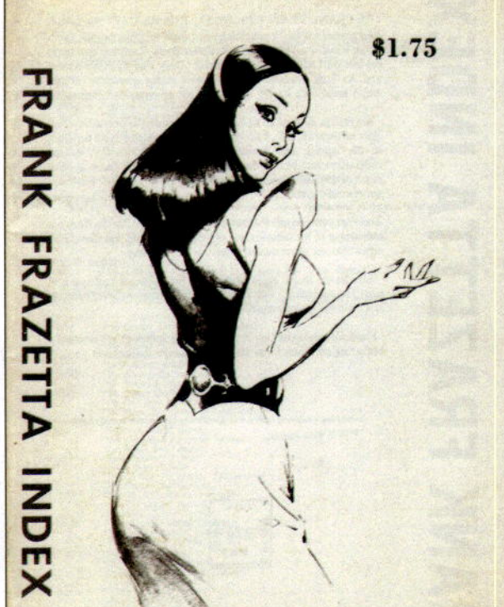

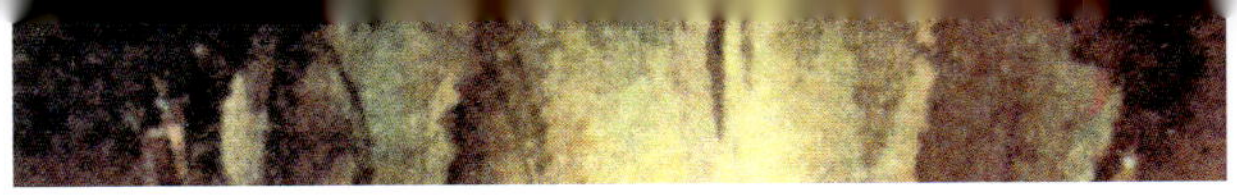

OFF THE RACK

The Magazine Years

By J. David Spurlock

This prolific, award-winning author, editor and illustrator, J. DAVID SPURLOCK, is a pop-culture historian and advocate for artists' rights who, has served as President of the Society of Illustrators in Dallas, in addition to teaching at the School of Visual Arts in New York. Spurlock's career also includes work for Disney, Sony, Dark Horse, Vanguard and MTV. Works by Spurlock include, *Wally's World: the Life & Death of Wally Wood, RGK: Art of Roy G. Krenkel, The Space Cowboy, The Paintings of J. Allen St. John* and *Steranko Art Noir*.

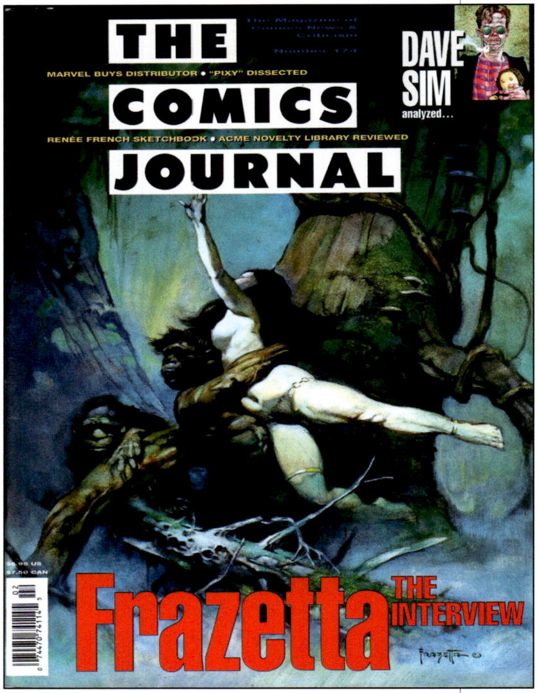

ABOVE: The Comics Journal *Fantagraphics Books* *(Feb. 1995)*

OPPOSITE: National Lampoon *21st Century Publications, Inc.* *(August 1973)*

Mention magazines to most Frazetta collectors and their mind goes to the Warren magazines—oversized horror comics—of the 1960s and '70s: *Creepy, Eerie* and *Vampirella*. Those magazines are listed in the comics section of this book despite the fact that, with only a few exceptions (including Frank's last-ever multi-page comics story in *Creepy* #1), Frazetta's contributions to those publications were almost exclusively oil paintings for the covers. The Warren magazines are not to be missed, as they are central to Frazetta's rise as a fan-favorite, gave him unprecedented freedom to follow his artistic muse, and they are filled with fabulous work by a wealth of other notables.

Still, frequently, the rarer, harder to find Frazetta magazine items are actually illustrations he produced for non-comics magazines and magazines with features on the artist and his work. These items are not only often hard to find, but nearly as often feature rare works and/or the best reproductions of some works. It is hard to say what is more surprising; to find Frazetta in such stalwart and iconic publications as *Newsweek, Esquire, American Artist*, and the *Chicago Tribune* magazine, or in counter-culture publications like *Circus, National Lampoon*, and *High Times*, or yet in risqué men's magazines like *Cavalcade, Gent, Dude, Game*, and *Playboy*.

What may be surprising—especially as Frank has discussed having trouble finding work in the early-'60s after leaving Al Capp—is that

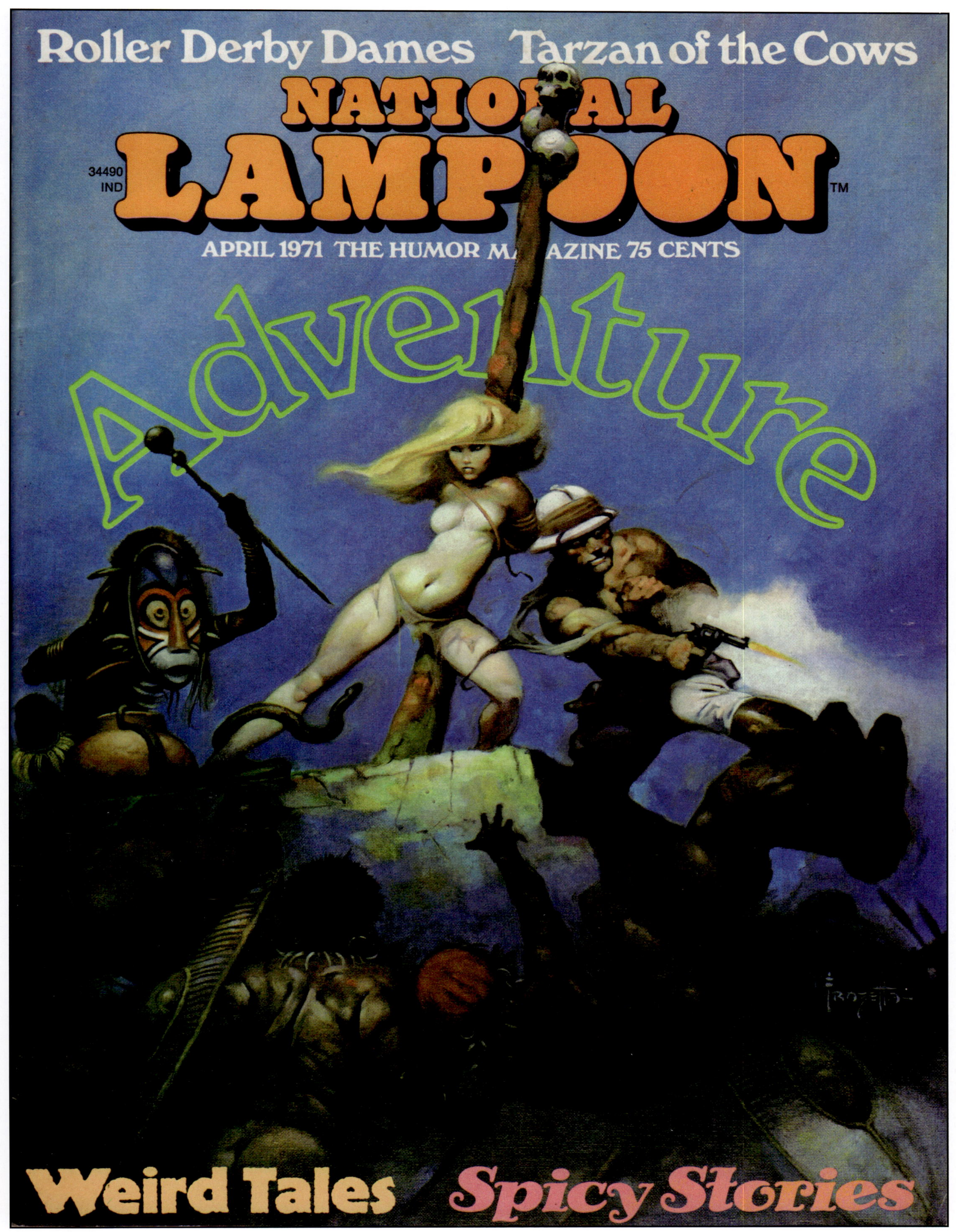
Roller Derby Dames
Tarzan of the Cows
NATIONAL
LAMPOON
34490
IND
TM
APRIL 1971 THE HUMOR MAGAZINE 75 CENTS
Adventure
FRAZETTA
Weird Tales
Spicy Stories

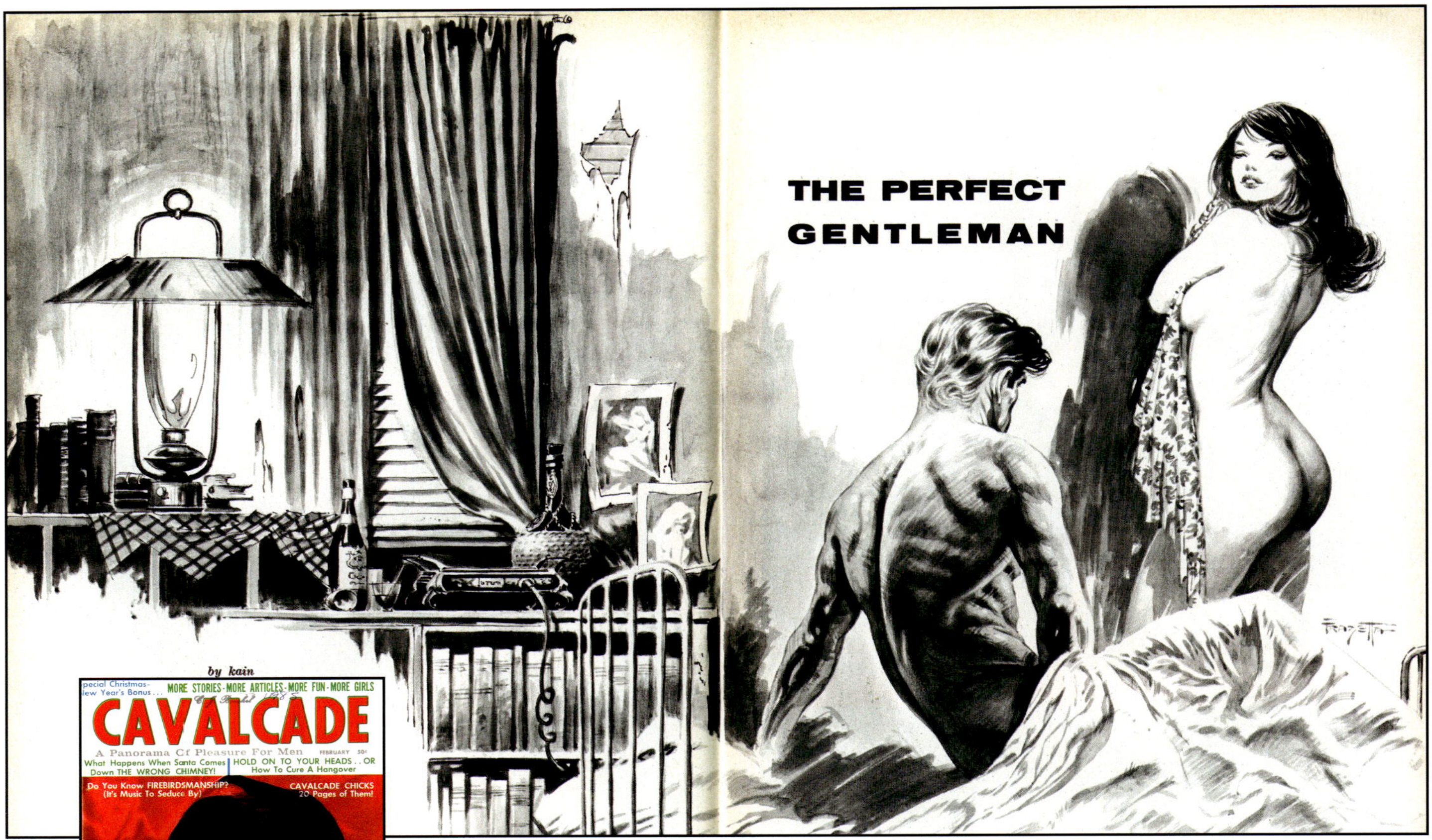

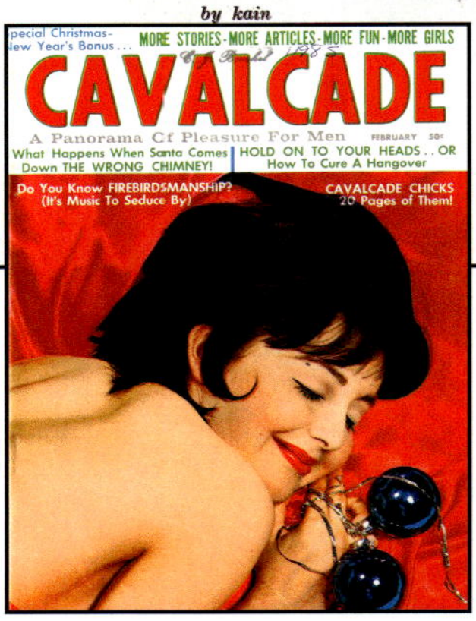

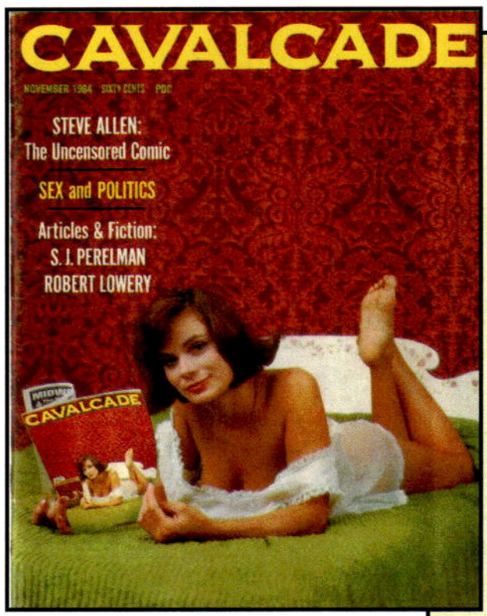

ABOVE: Cavalcade
Vol. 4 #15 Feb. 1964

RIGHT: Cavalcade
Vol. 4 #18 Nov. 1964

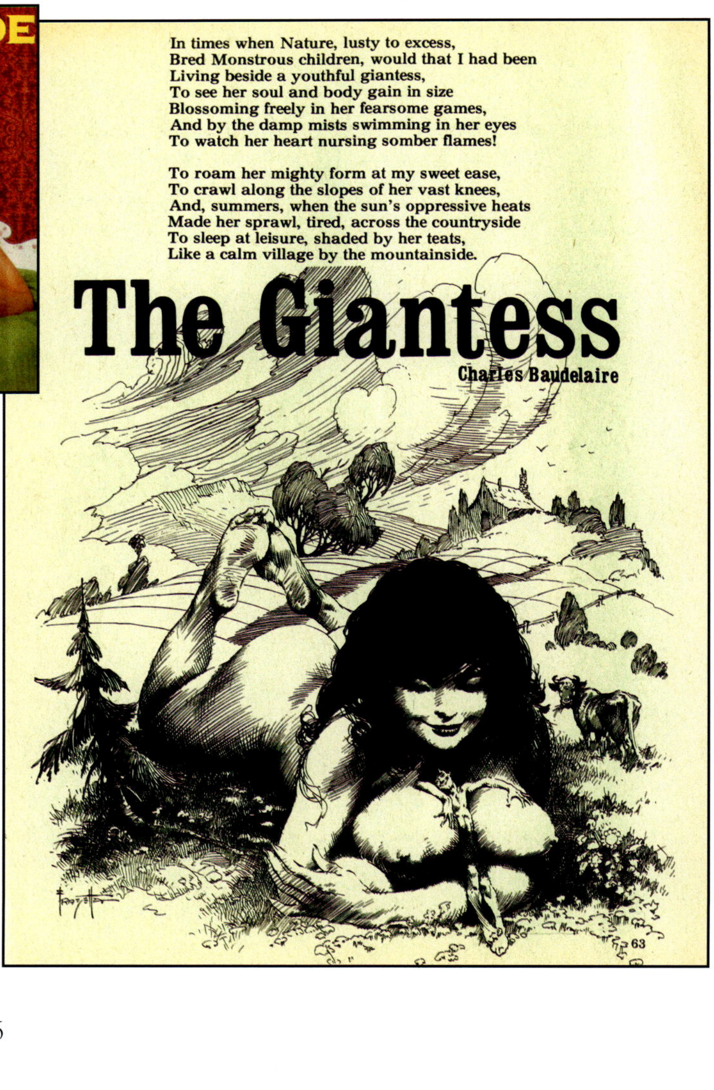

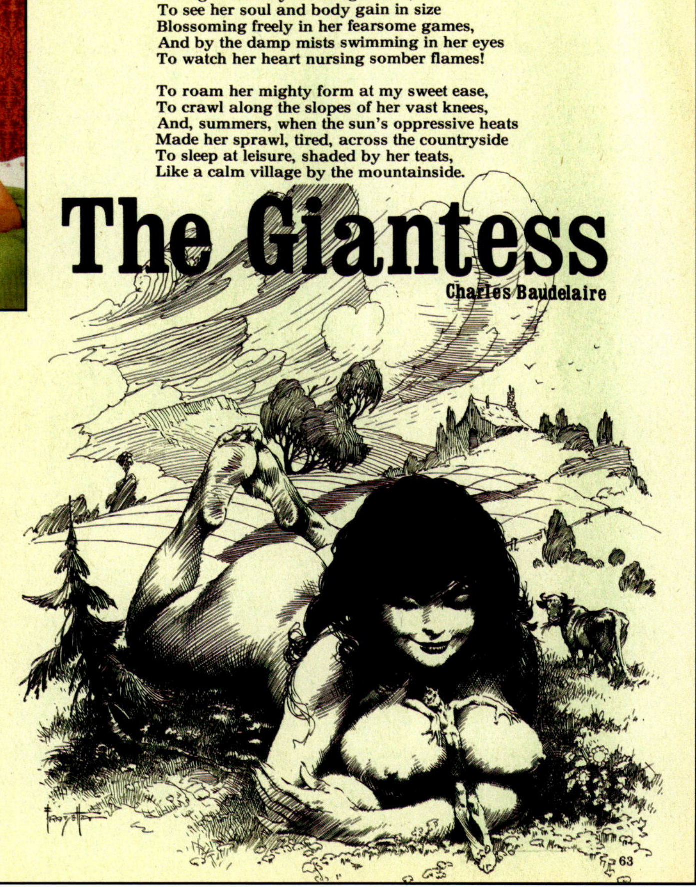
In times when Nature, lusty to excess,
Bred Monstrous children, would that I had been
Living beside a youthful giantess,
To see her soul and body gain in size
Blossoming freely in her fearsome games,
And by the damp mists swimming in her eyes
To watch her heart nursing somber flames!

To roam her mighty form at my sweet ease,
To crawl along the slopes of her vast knees,
And, summers, when the sun's oppressive heats
Made her sprawl, tired, across the countryside
To sleep at leisure, shaded by her teats,
Like a calm village by the mountainside.

The Giantess

Charles Baudelaire

63

he never worked (as did Norman Saunders, Mort Kunstler and Basil Gogos) for the many men's adventure magazines that proliferated at the time with titles like, *For Men Only*, *Men's Adventure*, *Men's Action*, and *Real Men*.

In this chapter we will explore and catalog these hard to find Frazetta magazine collectibles including a wealth of pro-zines like *Funny World*, *Prevue*, *SPFX*, *Fanfare*, *The Comics Journal*, and more. Particularly rare are specialty publications that were never distributed to newsstands including *Animal Kingdom* and, the Dow Chemical trade magazine, *Elements*.

It was a lazy, languid day in

Indian Summer

and the boys were swimming ... then a girl came down to the river bank — and nothing was really ever the same again.

by Erskine Caldwell

The water was up again. It had been raining for almost two whole days, and the creek was full to the banks. Dawn had broken gray that morning, and for the first time that week the sky was blue and warm.

Les pulled off his shirt and unbuckled his pants. Les never had to bother with underwear, because as soon as it was warm enough in the spring to go barefooted he hid his union suit in a closet and left it there until fall. His mother was not alive, and his father never bothered about the underclothes.

"I wish we had a shovel to dig out some of this muck," he said. "Every time it rains this hole fills up with this stuff. I'd go home and get a shovel, but if they saw me they'd make me stay there and do something."

While Les was hanging his shirt and pants on a bush, I waded out into the yellow water. The muck on the bottom was ankle deep, and there were hundreds of dead limbs stuck in it. I pulled out some of the largest and threw them on the other bank out of the way.

I waded out to the middle of the creek where the current was the strongest. The yellow water came almost up to my shoulders.

"Nearly neck deep," I said. "But there's about a million dead limbs stuck in the bottom. Hurry up and help me throw them out."

Les came splashing in. The muddy water gurgled and sucked

...body comes down here every day and pitches ...s in here," Les said, making a face. "I don't see ...uld get here. Dead tree limbs don't fall into a ... Somebody is throwing them in, and I'll bet a ... live a million miles away, either."

...wes does it, Les."

... it, He's the one I'm talking about. I'll bet any-

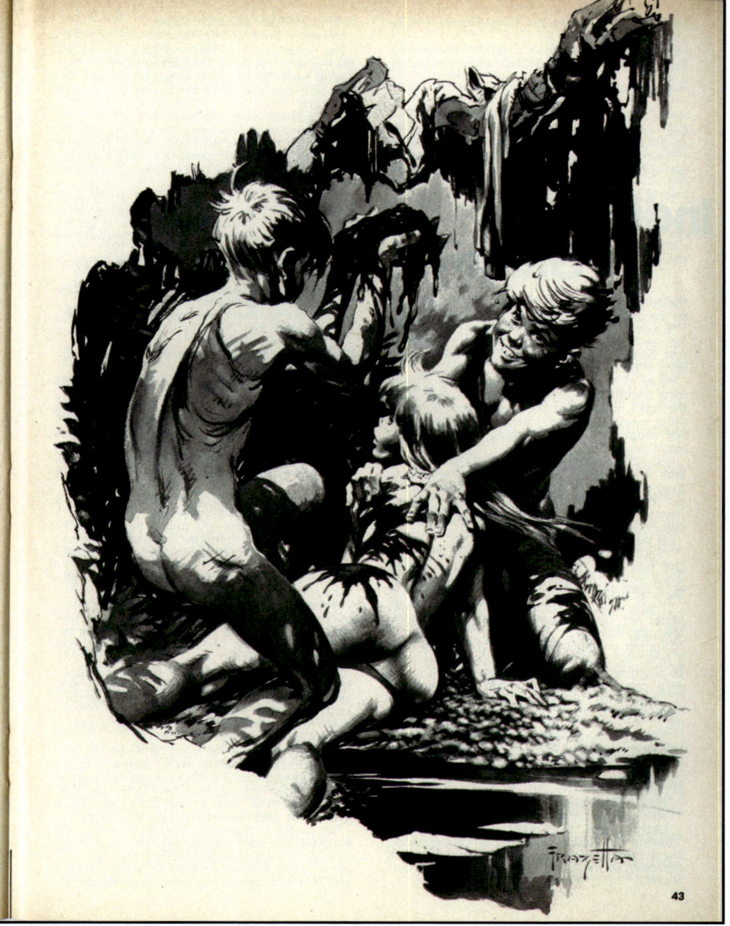

CAVALCADE

Original Story by ALBERTO MORAVIA

ERSKINE CALDWELL
PHILIP WYLIE
NELSON ALGREN

An Intimate Interview CLAUDIA CARDINALE

A Shocking Bonus Story JEROME WEIDMAN

ABOVE: Cavalcade *Vol. 4 #17 July 1964*

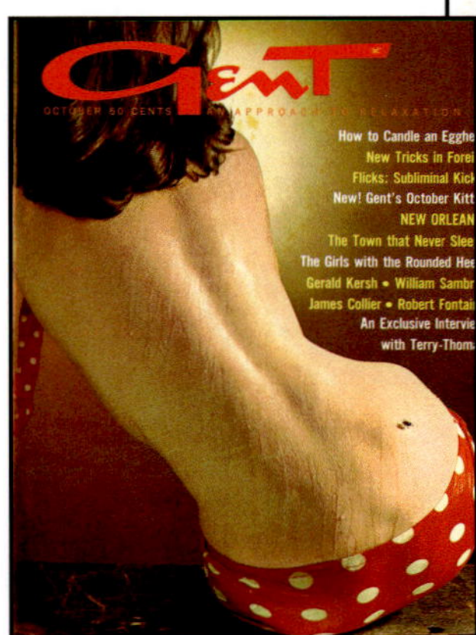

RIGHT: Gent *Vol. 7 #1 Oct. 1962*

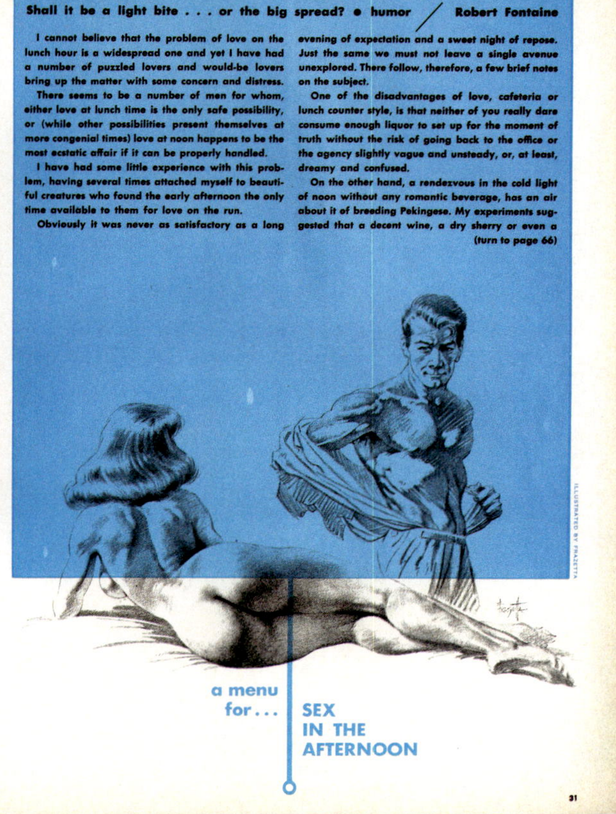

Shall it be a light bite . . . or the big spread? • humor / Robert Fontaine

I cannot believe that the problem of love on the lunch hour is a widespread one and yet I have had a number of puzzled lovers and would-be lovers bring up the matter with some concern and distress.

There seems to be a number of men for whom, either love at lunch time is the only safe possibility, or (while other possibilities present themselves at more congenial times) love at noon happens to be the most ecstatic affair if it can be properly handled.

I have had some little experience with this problem, having several times attached myself to beautiful creatures who found the early afternoon the only time available to them for love on the run.

Obviously it was never as satisfactory as a long evening of expectation and a sweet night of repose. Just the same we must not leave a single avenue unexplored. There follow, therefore, a few brief notes on the subject.

One of the disadvantages of love, cafeteria or lunch counter style, is that neither of you really dare consume enough liquor to set up for the moment of truth without the risk of going back to the office or the agency slightly vague and unsteady, or, at least, dreamy and confused.

On the other hand, a rendezvous in the cold light of noon without any romantic beverage, has an air about it of breeding Pekingese. My experiments suggested that a decent wine, a dry sherry or even a

(turn to page 66)

ILLUSTRATED BY FRAZETTA

a menu for . . . SEX IN THE AFTERNOON

31

MAGAZINES

AFTER DARK
Danad Publishing
- Vol.11 No.8 December 1978
  Swords of Mars

AIR BRUSH ACTION
Air Brush Action, Inc.
- August 2004
  Contents pg **Berserker**
  pg. 14 article - "Vargas Awards"
  Berserker
  pg. 18 **Escape on Venus**
  Berserker
  Night Winds
  pg. 19 Tarzan and Bolgani
  The Night They Raided Minsky's

AMERICAN ARTIST MAGAZINE
- 405 May 1976
  COVER **Death Dealer**
  article - Contains the following:
  pg. 39 **The Silver Warrior**
  pg. 40 **The Mammoth**
  pg. 41 **Neanderthal**
  pg. 42 **Wolfpack**
  pg. 43 TARZAN AND THE CASTAWAYS cover
  pg. 44 illustration - Beauty and the Beast (2 pp.)
  pg. 45 sketchbook illustration

ANIMAL KINGDOM not available through newsstands
NY Zoological Society
- Dec. 80-Jan.81
  article "*Nessie's African Cousin*" by Roy P. Mackel
  article contains the following:
  The Amali Legend

ASI MAGAZINE
- Vol 1 #3 1998
  interview with Frazetta w/photos and illustrations

BETTY PAGES
Pure Imagination Publishing
- 3 Fall, 1988 article w/illustrations

CASTLE OF FRANKENSTEIN
Gothic Castle
- 5 1964
  article "*Monsters of Edgar Rice Burroughs*"
  article contains the following:
  illustration for AT THE EARTH'S CORE
  illustration for PELLUCIDAR

CAVALCADE men's magazine
Sky Publishing Company
- volume 4, number 15 Feb. 1964
  "*The Perfect Gentleman*" by Kain 2 pp.
- volume 4, number 17 July, 1964
  "*Indian Summer*" by Erskine Caldwell 1 pg.
- volume 4, number 18 Nov. 1964
  "*The Giantess*" by Charles Baudelaire1 pg.
- volume 5, number 10 Oct, 1966
  "*The Giantess*" by Charles Baudelaire 1 pg.
  first printed in volume 4, number 18

CIRCUS music news magazine
- 198 Nov. 1978
  1 pg, article about Frazetta with photo
  centerfold **Space103 - Attack**

COMIC BOOK ARTIST
TwoMorrows Publishing
- 4 Spring 1999
  This Warren dedication issue reproduces Frazetta illos. and mentions Frazetta occasionally.

COMIC BOOK MARKETPLACE
Gemstone Publishing Incorporated
- 41 Nov. 1996
  COVER - **Tales From the Crypt**
  pg. 54 cover to A-1 COMICS #37
  cover to A-1 COMICS #29
  pg. 56 "*Untamed Love*" 3 illustrations
  first printed in PERSONAL LOVE #32 (comic book)

COMICS BUYERS GUIDE
Krause Publications
- 1249 Oct 24, 1997
  COVER- **Silver Warrior**
  used to promote FANTASY ILLUSTRATED (magazine).
- 1318 Feb 19, 1999
  COVER - The Princess sculpture, The Barbarian sculpture
  pg. 40 Article "*Frazetta Fantasia*" 2 pp.

COMICS INTERVIEW
Fictioneer Books Ltd.
- special edition 1987

This entire publication is an interview with Frank Frazetta. Originally appeared in COMICS INTERVIEW #42. Special edition contains the following:

COVER **Catgirl** detail
pg. 4 "*Give Us Barrabus*" NEW YORK TIMES illustration
pg. 5 two illustrations from GENT (magazine)
pg. 7 Krenkel panel from E.C. book inked by Frazetta
first printed in WEIRD FANTASY #14
pg. 8 three sequential JOHNNY COMET newspaper strips
pg. 9 cover to FAMOUS FUNNIES #212
pg. 10 one of the intro illustrations for the movie FIRE & ICE
pg. 11 untitled illustration
AKA - Sheba
first printed in FANTASTIC ART OF FRANK FRAZETTA, Vol. 1
pg. 13 John Wayne comic book panels
first printed in JOHN WAYNE ADVENTURE COMICS #3
pg. 14 **Madame Derringer**
pg. 15 WILD BILL HICKOCK pulp (magazine)
This painting has been commonly identified for years as being the first published painting by Frazetta. The fact is, Howard Winfield is the artist.
pg. 16 advertisement for the Frazetta museum using the plate "*Kubla's anguish*"
first printed in KUBLA KHAN portfolio
pg. 17 three Conan illos
Miscaptioned as designs for the Conan movie.
pg. 18 plate one from the LORD OF THE RINGS portfolio.

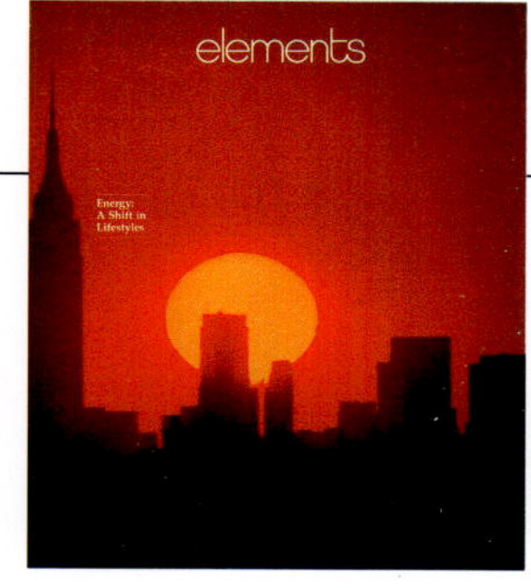

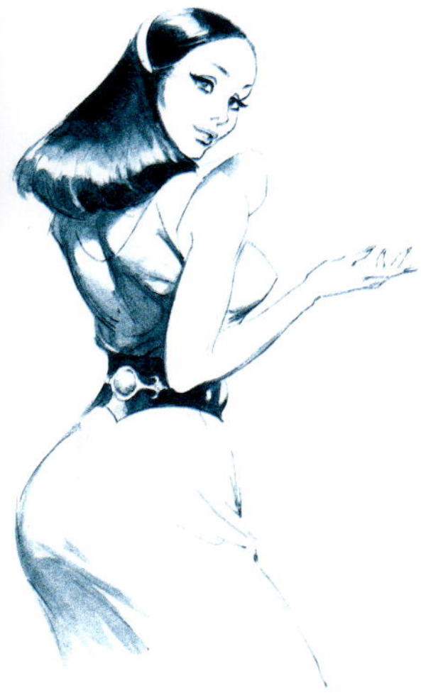

"Accommodation, Mr. Parkman. Accommodation. You'll find that given its head, technology has a rare penchant for pulling man out of the little traps he sets for himself. After all, nuclear energy was originally tapped to rid the world of a pernicious madness. Later, it was accused of being madness itself. But in one giant leap, the atom extended man's prospects for survival thousands of years beyond the limits of the fossil age."

"Yes, but I thought you said—"

"Today we enjoy the benefits of *thermonuclear* power, Mr. Parkman. It's clean, safe, dependable, and the 'waste' product is innocuous helium gas. But like most things, fusion didn't just happen. It evolved. Without the practical knowledge gained from splitting the atom, we might never have learned to put it together again. Now we're perfecting the direct conversion reactors where high-energy charged particles from the reactor core are trapped to produce electricity at about 400 kilovolts. It appears to be ideal for long-distance cryogenic power transmission."

"Uh-huh."

"But the majority of our reactors operate on a multipurpose deuterium-tritium cycle," Deina continued. "Imagine the heat of fusion being used first to generate steam, Mr. Parkman, some of which is diverted to industrial use while the remainder drives turbines to produce electricity—"

"I'm with you so far," I said.

"Some of the electricity goes out over super-conductive transmission lines using fusion's by-product helium as coolant, but the rest is used to hydrolize sea water."

"Hydrolize?"

"We break down the water by electrolysis into hydrogen and oxygen. The hydrogen is then siphoned off and used where it's needed.

"Hydrogen as a fuel?"

"Indeed," said Deina, "The *perfect* fuel. Its only product of combustion is water! None of the traditional fossil fuel pollutants. And it can be burned to produce heat, mechanical energy—even more electricity. We use it all the time. Directly like natural gas—and in fuel cells.

"But that's not the end of it, Mr. Parkman," said Deina with a smile. "Some of our reactors are being equipped to tap ultrahigh temperature plasmas from the fusion core. These plasmas are so hot they can vaporize, dissociate, and ionize any known substance, liquid or solid." Deina paused. "Does that suggest anything to you?"

"No."

"You're not thinking, Mr. Parkman," Deina chided me. "If we can reduce *any* kind of material to its constituent atoms for separation—"

"Of course!" I cried. "Recycling! You can recycle everything you make, everything you use. No more

16

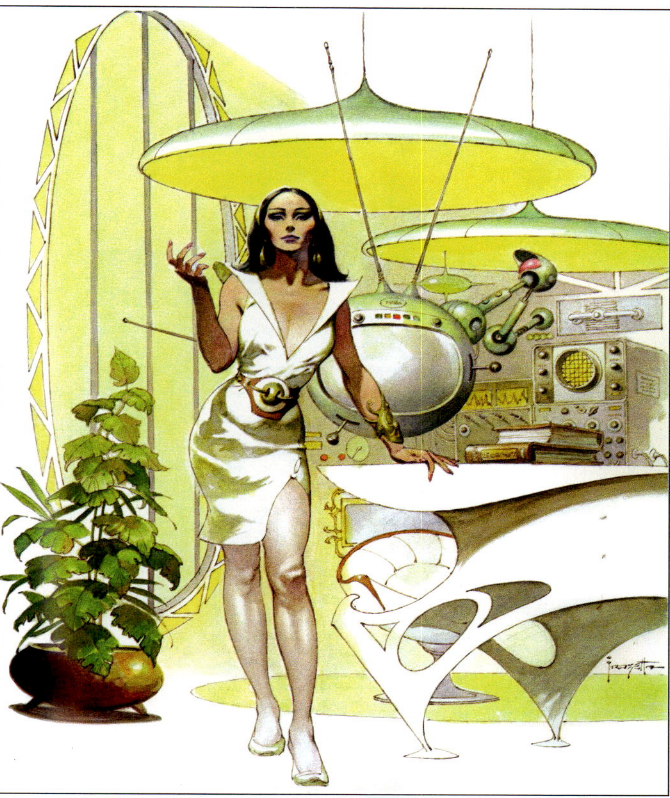

ABOVE: Elements *(Dow Chemicals in house magazine)*
Chemical Trade Magazine Vol.1, #3 (1973)

BELOW: Circus *music news magazine*
#198 (Nov. 1978)

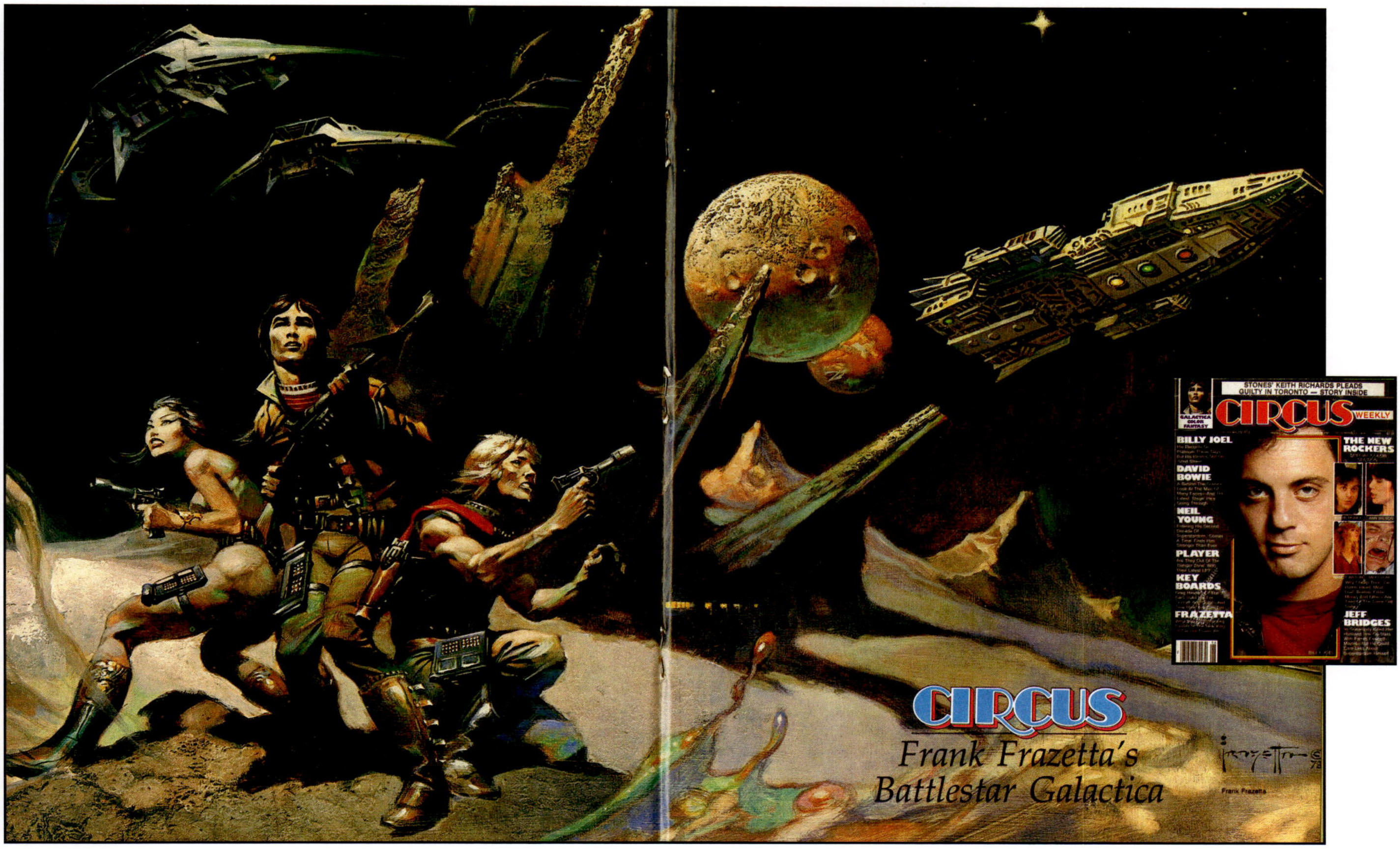

CIRCUS
Frank Frazetta's
Battlestar Galactica

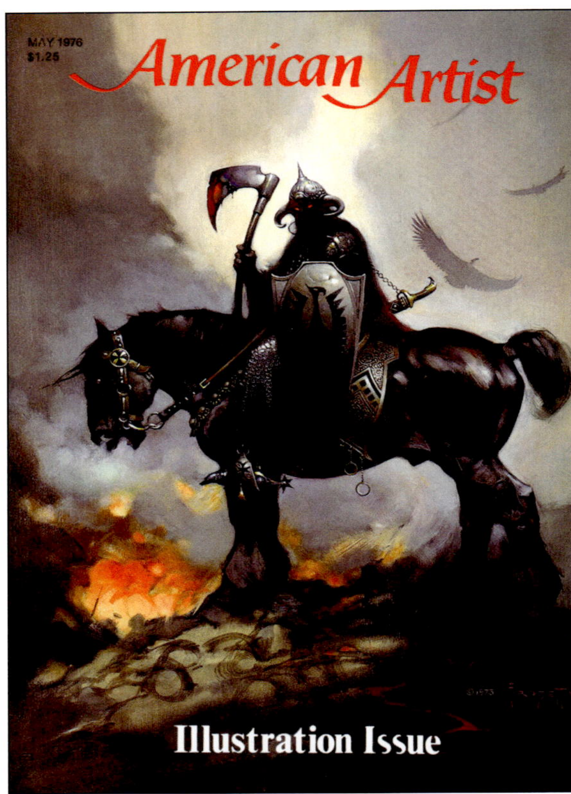

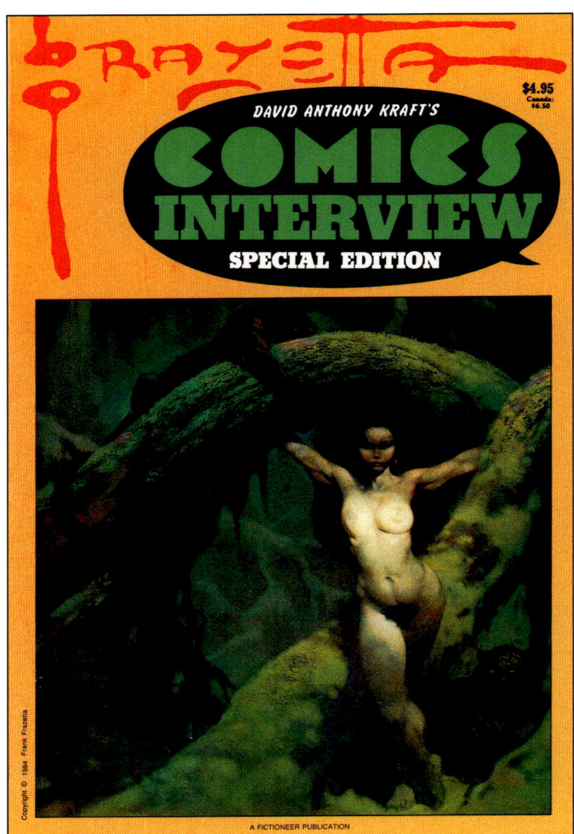

TOP: American Artist Magazine #405 *(May 1976)*

ABOVE: Comics Interview special edition *(1987)*

OPPOSITE: ASI magazine
Vol 1 # 3 (1998)
Interview with Frazetta with photos & illustrations

COMICS INTERVIEW *cont'd*

pg. 19 proposed dust jacket design for AT THE EARTH'S CORE
pg. 20 panels from *"Squeeze Play"*
first printed in SHOCK SUSPENSTORIES #13
pg. 22 panels from JOHNNY COMET strip
pg. 25 Four illustrations of Buster Crabbe.
The upper left is from BUSTER CRABBE COMICS #4
pg. 26 3 pages from *"King of the Lost Lands"*
first printed in A-1 COMICS #47
pg. 29 ink illustration
AKA - *"David Innes, hyaenodons, and man-apes of Pellucidar"*
first printed in E.R. BURROUGHS - MASTER OF ADVENTURE interior book illo.
pg. 31 text illustrations appearing in BARNYARD COMICS
pg. 33 LI'L ABNER strip
"We Can Stop the Enemies of Youth" anti-drug ad
pg. 34 cover to WEIRD SCIENCE-FANTASY #29 (comic book)
pg. 35 un-retouched art intended for FAMOUS FUNNIES #217
pg. 37 untitled watercolor
AKA - **Bear Watching Caveman Threaten Cub**
first printed in FRANK FRAZETTA: BOOK THREE (art book)
pg. 38 three panels from *"Werewolf"* story
first printed in CREEPY #1 (comic book)
pg. 40 two sketchbook drawings

• 42 In-depth interview with Frazetta.

COMICS JOURNAL, THE b/w
Fantagraphics Books
• 174 Feb. 1995
COVER - **Captive Princess**
pg. 52 *"Frank Frazetta"* interview 39 pp.
article includes the following:
sketchbook drawing
pg. 55 pencil illustration
first printed in ILLUSTRATIONS ARCANUM
pg. 56 pencil illustration
first printed in ILLUSTRATIONS ARCANUM
pg. 58 sketchbook drawing
two JOHNNY COMET strips
pg. 60 sketchbook roughs
good girl art
first printed in Midwood paperback
pg. 62 page from *"Red Devil and Goldy vs. the Monster"*
first printed in RETROSPECTIVE (art book)
pg. 63 artwork from *"Snowman"* - 2 illustrations
first printed in RETROSPECTIVE (art book)
pg. 64 *"The Poor Little Woodpecker"* (text illustration)
first printed in GOOFY COMICS #21
pg. 65 cover to A-1 COMICS #37
three panels from *"Munchy the Squirrel - Spare That Tree"*
first printed in COO COO COMICS #47
pg. 66 cover to WEIRD SCIENCE-FANTASY #29 (comic book)
pg. 67 page from *"Gods of the Jungle"*
first printed in A-1 COMICS #47
pg. 68 splash panel from *"Too Late For Love"*
first printed in PERSONAL LOVE #25 (comic book)
pg. 69 Moonbeam McSwine greeting card design
pg. 71 splash panel from *"The Weeping Walloper"*
first printed in JOHN WAYNE ADV. COMICS #8
pg. 72 illustration from A FIGHTING MAN OF MARS
AKA - *"Behind us came the fighting men of Ugor."*
first printed in THE MASTERMIND OF MARS and A FIGHTING MAN OF MARS interior book illo.
pg. 73 **Ringo Starr**
first printed in MAD #90 (comic book)
sketchbook drawing
first printed in FRANK FRAZETTA: BOOK THREE (art book)
pg. 74 **Egyptian Queen**

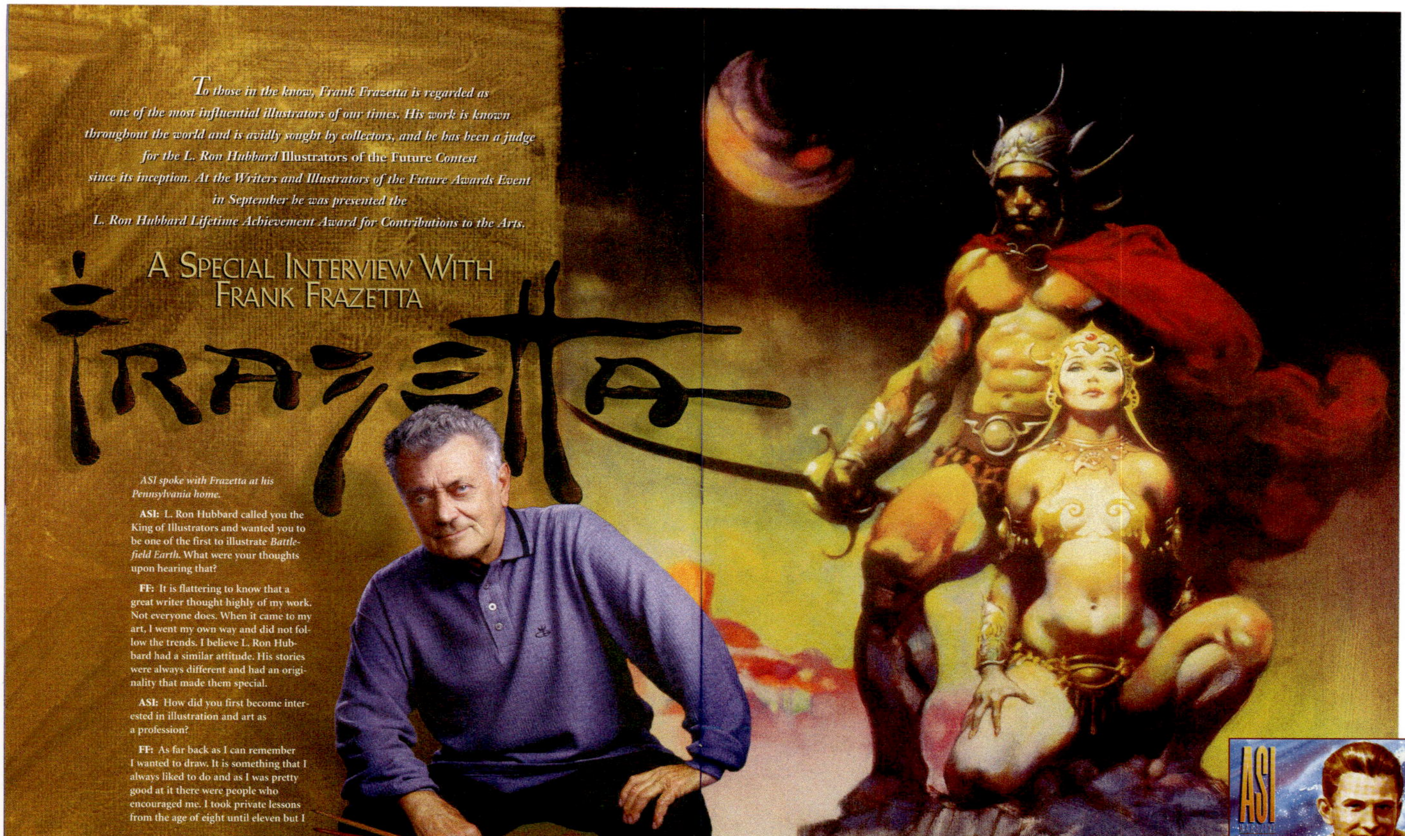

To those in the know, Frank Frazetta is regarded as one of the most influential illustrators of our times. His work is known throughout the world and is avidly sought by collectors, and he has been a judge for the L. Ron Hubbard Illustrators of the Future Contest *since its inception. At the Writers and Illustrators of the Future Awards Event in September he was presented the L. Ron Hubbard Lifetime Achievement Award for Contributions to the Arts.*

A Special Interview With Frank Frazetta

Frazetta

ASI spoke with Frazetta at his Pennsylvania home.

ASI: L. Ron Hubbard called you the King of Illustrators and wanted you to be one of the first to illustrate *Battlefield Earth*. What were your thoughts upon hearing that?

FF: It is flattering to know that a great writer thought highly of my work. Not everyone does. When it came to my art, I went my own way and did not follow the trends. I believe L. Ron Hubbard had a similar attitude. His stories were always different and had an originality that made them special.

ASI: How did you first become interested in illustration and art as a profession?

FF: As far back as I can remember I wanted to draw. It is something that I always liked to do and as I was pretty good at it there were people who encouraged me. I took private lessons from the age of eight until eleven but I didn't go to a special art school. I taught myself a lot and learned from others as I went along. By the time I was a teenager, I knew I wanted to be an artist. I was a born draftsman and liked all forms of art, so I just knew that's what I wanted to do.

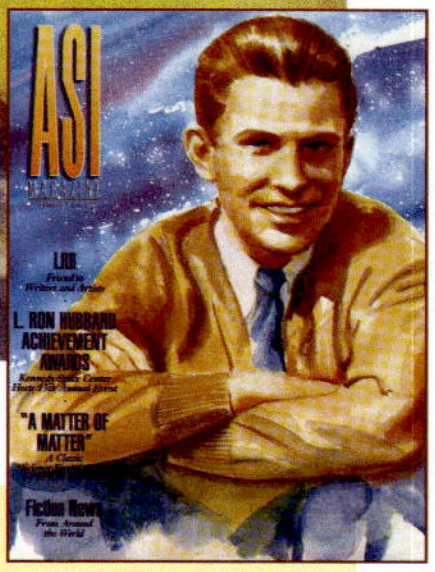

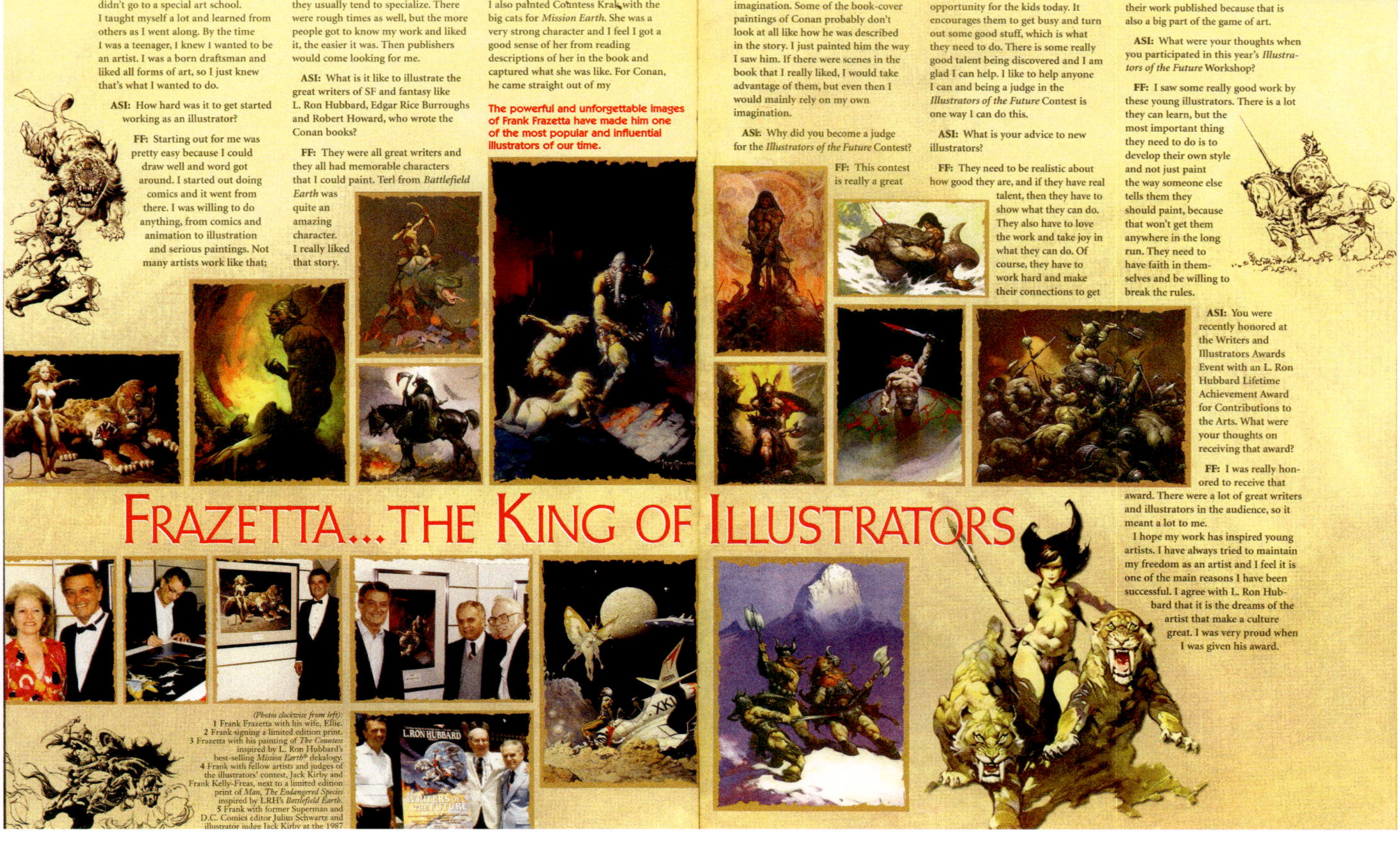

ASI: How hard was it to get started working as an illustrator?

FF: Starting out for me was pretty easy because I could draw well and word got around. I started out doing comics and it went from there. I was willing to do anything, from comics and animation to illustration and serious paintings. Not many artists work like that; they usually tend to specialize. There were rough times as well, but the more people got to know my work and liked it, the easier it was. Then publishers would come looking for me.

ASI: What is it like to illustrate the great writers of SF and fantasy like L. Ron Hubbard, Edgar Rice Burroughs and Robert Howard, who wrote the Conan books?

FF: They were all great writers and they all had memorable characters that I could paint. Terl from *Battlefield Earth* was quite an amazing character. I really liked that story.

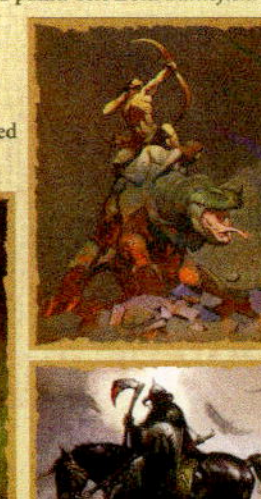

I also painted Countess Krak with the big cats for *Mission Earth*. She was a very strong character and I feel I got a good sense of her from reading descriptions of her in the book and captured what she was like. For Conan, he came straight out of my imagination. Some of the book-cover paintings of Conan probably don't look at all like how he was described in the story. I just painted him the way I saw him. If there were scenes in the book that I really liked, I would take advantage of them, but even then I would mainly rely on my own imagination.

The powerful and unforgettable images of Frank Frazetta have made him one of the most popular and influential illustrators of our time.

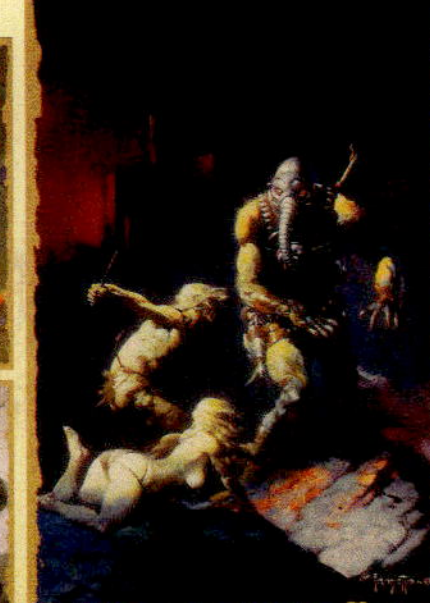

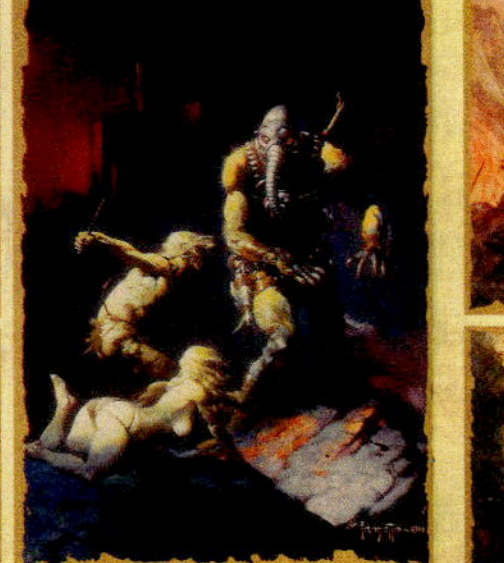

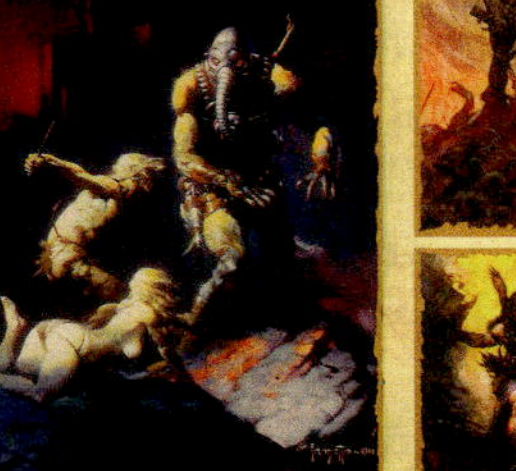

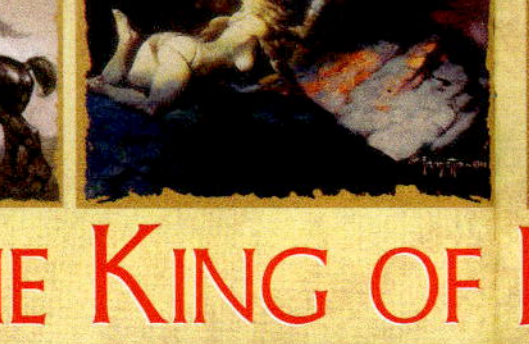

ASI: Why did you become a judge for the *Illustrators of the Future* Contest?

FF: This contest is really a great opportunity for the kids today. It encourages them to get busy and turn out some good stuff, which is what they need to do. There is some really good talent being discovered and I am glad I can help. I like to help anyone I can and being a judge in the *Illustrators of the Future* Contest is one way I can do this.

ASI: What is your advice to new illustrators?

FF: They need to be realistic about how good they are, and if they have real talent, then they have to show what they can do. They also have to love the work and take joy in what they can do. Of course, they have to work hard and make their connections to get their work published because that is also a big part of the game of art.

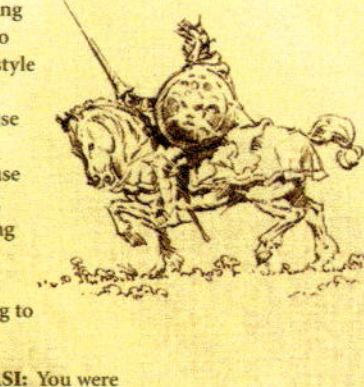

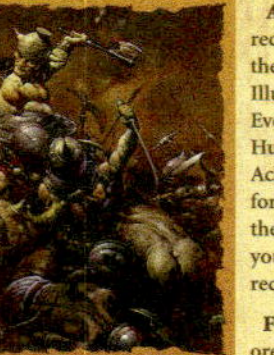

ASI: What were your thoughts when you participated in this year's *Illustrators of the Future* Workshop?

FF: I saw some really good work by these young illustrators. There is a lot they can learn, but the most important thing they need to do is to develop their own style and not just paint the way someone else tells them they should paint, because that won't get them anywhere in the long run. They need to have faith in themselves and be willing to break the rules.

ASI: You were recently honored at the Writers and Illustrators Awards Event with an L. Ron Hubbard Lifetime Achievement Award for Contributions to the Arts. What were your thoughts on receiving that award?

FF: I was really honored to receive that award. There were a lot of great writers and illustrators in the audience, so it meant a lot to me.

I hope my work has inspired young artists. I have always tried to maintain my freedom as an artist and I feel it is one of the main reasons I have been successful. I agree with L. Ron Hubbard that it is the dreams of the artist that make a culture great. I was very proud when I was given his award.

Frazetta...the King of Illustrators

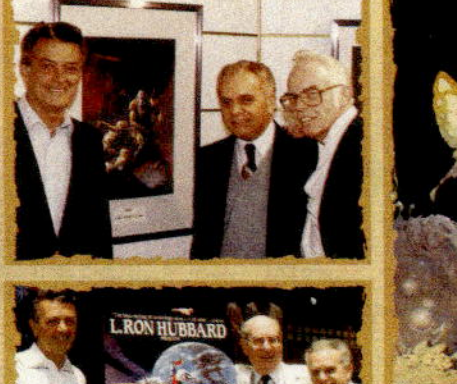

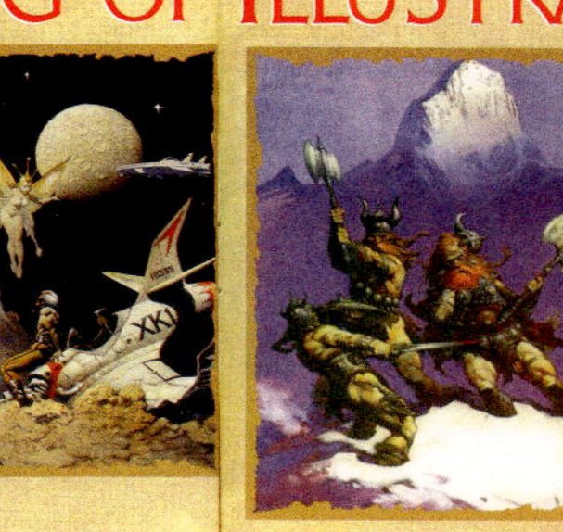

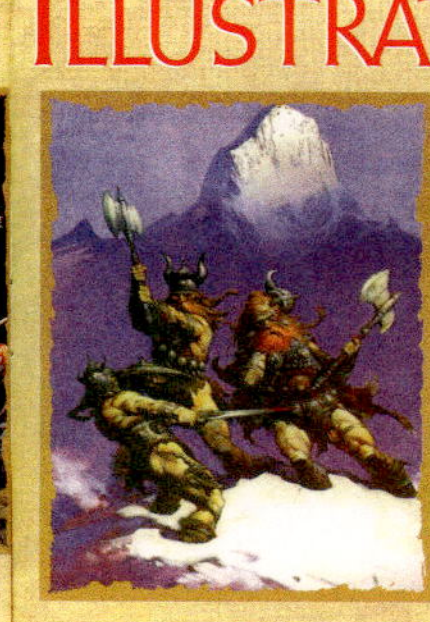

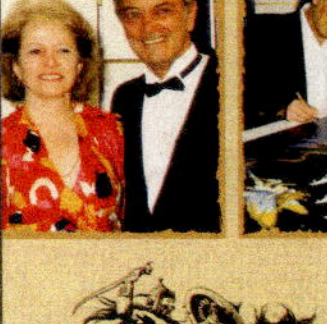

(Photos clockwise from left):
1 Frank Frazetta with his wife, Ellie.
2 Frank signing a limited edition print.
3 Frazetta with his painting of *The Countess* inspired by L. Ron Hubbard's best-selling *Mission Earth*® dekalogy.
4 Frank with fellow artists and judges of the illustrators' contest, Jack Kirby and Frank Kelly-Freas, next to a limited edition print of *Man, The Endangered Species* inspired by LRH's *Battlefield Earth*.
5 Frank with former Superman and D.C. Comics editor Julius Schwartz and illustrator judge Jack Kirby at the 1987

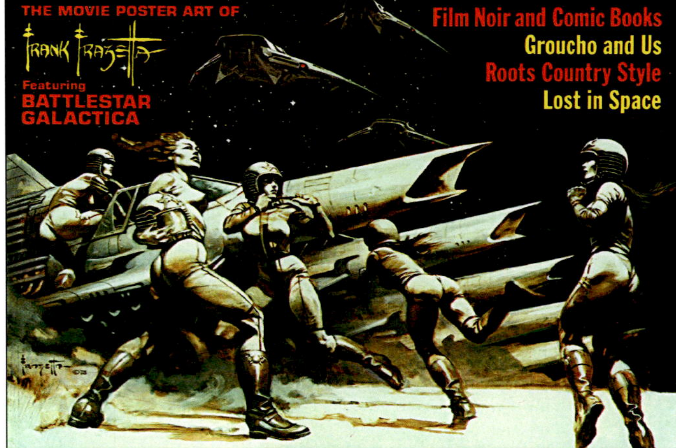

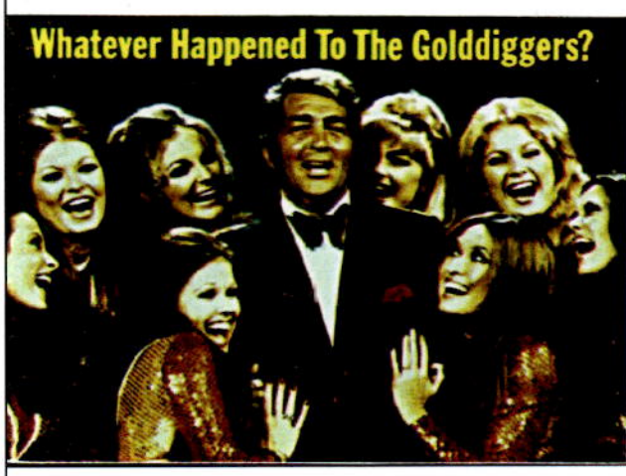

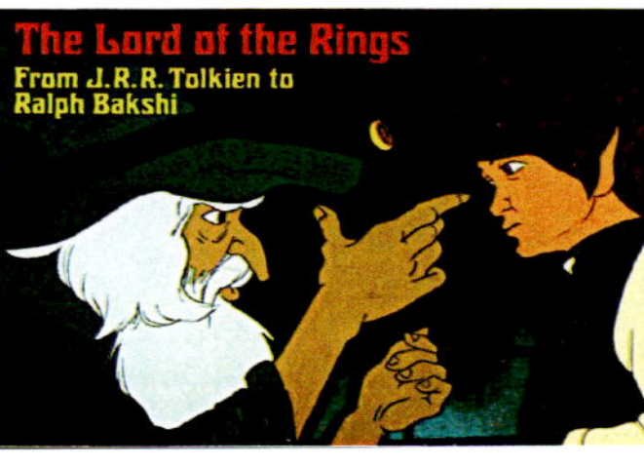

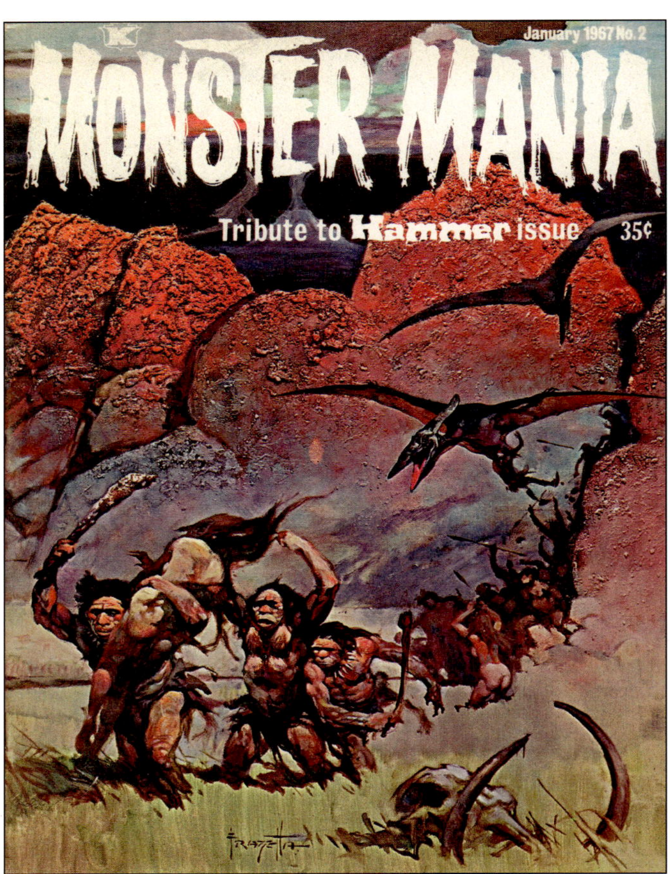

TOP: Fanfare #*2 (Winter 1978)*

ABOVE: Monster Mania #*2 (January 1967)*

COMICS JOURNAL *cont'd*

pg. 76 **Neanderthal**
pencil illustration
first printed in ILLUSTRATIONS ARCANUM
pg. 77 Vampirella illustration
first printed in FRANK FRAZETTA - THE LIVING LEGEND (art book)
pg. 78 pencil illustration
first printed in ILLUSTRATIONS ARCANUM
pg. 79 illustration
AKA - Jungle Woman
first printed in AT THE EARTH'S CORE AND PELLUCIDAR PORTFOLIO
pg. 80 **Flashman on the Charge**
pg. 81 sketchbook drawing
pg. 82 pencil illustration
first printed in ILLUSTRATIONS ARCANUM
pg. 83 sketchbook drawing
pg. 84 detail of **Death Dealer**
pg. 85 sketchbook drawings
pg. 86 good girl art
first printed in a MIDWOOD interior book illustration
pg. 87 cover to LUANA paperback
cover to THE MUCKER paperback
pg. 89 detail from **"Catgirl"**
pg. 90 sketchbook drawing
pg. 91 **Savage Pellucidar**
pg. 92 Monster Entering Space Vehicle
first printed as cover to FAMOUS FUNNIES #213
pg. 93 cover to CONAN THE ADVENTURER
cover to WITCH OF THE DARK GATE
pg. 94 **Snow Giants**
pg. 95 plate from WOMEN OF THE AGES portfolio

COMICS SCENE
1983
Comics World Corp.
- 9 May 1983
article *"Frank Frazetta"* 4 pp.
interview with Frazetta about FIRE & ICE
article *"A Comic Book Comes Alive"* 5 pp.
interview with Bakshi about FIRE & ICE

DIAMOND DIALOGUE
1998
Diamond Distribution
- June 1998
pp. 52,53, and 68
article *"Frank-ly Speaking"* 3 pp. by Dave Winiewicz
Contains photos of Frank and many originals.

DIFFERENT WORLDS gaming magazine not available through newsstands
- 41 Jan-Feb 1986
Cover **Charging Huns**
pg. 36 Frazetta interview 3 pp.

DUDE men's magazine
Sky Publishing Company
- vol.6, #6 July 1962
inside back cover - advertisement for GENT MAGAZINE
uses one of the 12 *"Gent Zodiac"* illos.
- vol.7, #1 Sept. 1962
"Cattin' on the Couch" by Fredric Brown 1 pg. illustration

The Incredible Paintings Of Frank Frazetta

by Donald Newlove

The artist as hero

"Her oval face was beautiful in the extreme, her every feature finely chiseled and exquisite, her eyes large and lustrous and her head surmounted by a mass of coal black, waving hair, caught loosely into a strange yet becoming coiffure. Her skin was of a light reddish copper color, against which the crimson glow of her cheeks and the ruby of her beautifully molded lips shone with a strangely enhancing effect. She was as destitute of clothes as the green Martians who accompanied her; indeed, save for her highly wrought ornaments, she was entirely naked, nor could any apparel have enhanced the beauty of her perfect and symmetrical figure. Similar in face and feature to the women of Earth, she was nevertheless a true Martian—and prisoner of the fierce green giants who held me captive, as well!"

—*A Princess of Mars*, Edgar Rice Burroughs

Who remembers Thuvia, Maid of Mars? Dejah Thoris, Princess of Helium? Ayesha—*She-who-must-be-obeyed*?

Or Dale Arden—and Princess Aura, lustful daughter of Ming the Merciless? *Jane*! (Lady Greystoke)? Princess Aleta (now mother of four little Valiants)? The Dragon-Lady? And Burma, temptress of *Male Call*? Moonbeam McSwine's cliff-like massif, which strongly abused a boy's imagination, to say nothing of the great milky groin under Daisy Mae's falling polka-dot blouse? Surely a history of adolescent sex aids must somehow include jelly-breasted Barbarella? Zaftig, *so* zaftig, Little Annie Fanny? And ravenous Vampirella, a gold bat twittering on her G-stringed pelvis (detail not to be missed!).

We are not exhausted (what a great assignment). . . . The inner eye floats off, magnetized to the skimpy halter of Taia, the four-thousand-year-old lovethrob of Ibis the Invincible. To Sunday mornings on the living-room rug with plump-busted Boots (*and Her Buddies*), her long rounded legs so blissfully marriage-able—mine forever, I'd never tire. Flirty French doll Betty Boop with the Mae West figure and come-hither eyelashes. Or back to Esquire's own Petty Girl from the Thirties and Forties, those buoyant boobs, lyric slabs of leg, her hosiery, her flesh color, her. . . . But enough; I thought I was over all that. Over Malory's mistily lecherous sorceress Morgan le Fey? King Kong's river-wet Fay? Electric-eyed Elsa's fantastically perverse, goose-hissing Bride of Frankenstein (even her totally bandaged body was head-spinning). And what of Homer's musky Helen "shaped by heaven," "the smoky sweetness and desire" infused in Helen's heart by Homer, her "Unearthliness. A goddess the woman is to look at"?

And now, out of the land that time forgot, from the earth's core and the mists of Pellucidar, from scarred landscapes ravaged by Cimmerian hordes, comes, clothed in sea spume and spidery breastplates (if clothed at all), attended by gigantic lizards, immense serpents, fat leopards and saber-toothed tigers, and defended by large-knuckled superheroes with whipcord arteries and wielding sledge-like swords, her doll's eyes dumb-brained with longing, desperate for bed play . . . comes, yes, yes . . . the Egyptian Princess . . . The Moonmaid with the Pearl-white Gluteus Maximus (at its maximal!) . . . the *Frazetta Woman.*

And come she truly has. To every college dorm and sci-fi collector's file across the land, throughout England, Italy, France and Germany, and even into Japan—wherever the name of Tarzan is known, wherever Conan the Conqueror may raid the paperback racks, wherever a grown man's heart still lusts for the impossible pleasures forever withheld (seemingly) by dull daylight. Oh, no human hand is without God-given livingness and light. B... hand lifts the foreb... erotic contemplation ... served for Rodin statu...

Donald Newlove's recent two-volume novel Leo & Theodore and The Drunks is about Siamese twins and alcoholism. His novel Eternal Life will appear this year.

Frank Frazetta

The Death Dealer, ...

Photographed ...

86 ESQUIRE: JUNE

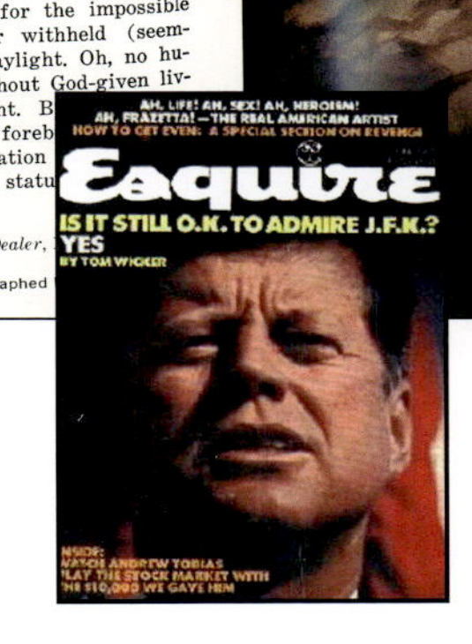

Esquire Magazine,
(June 1977)

ELEMENTS (Dow Chemicals in house magazine)
Chemical Trade Magazine
- vol.1, #3 1973
  - **Deina**
  - two spot illustrations

ESQUIRE
- vol.87 no.6 June 1977
  - pg. 86 article "*The Incredible Paintings of Frank Frazetta*" 8 pp.
  - article includes the following:
    - **Death Dealer**
    - **Moon Maid**
    - Banth b&w
    - **Silver Warrior**
    - **Sea Witch**
    - **Golden Girl**
    - **Swamp Demon**
    - **John Carter and the Savage Apes of Mars**
    - Study b&w
    - **The Destroyer**

FAMOUS MONSTERS OF FILMLAND
1 Feb. 1958 - #191 Mar. 1983
Warren Publishing
The following issues contain "*Easy Way to a Tuff Surfboard*" 1/2 pg. anti-smoking ad
first printed in EERIE #3 (comic book)
- 39 June 1966 •67 July 1970
- 69 September 1970 •80 October 1970
- 81 December 1970 •1971 ann.

FANFARE
1977
Bill Spicer
- 2 Winter 1978
  - COVER - **Battlestar Galactica: Scramble**
  - pg. 32 article "*The Movie Poster Art of Frank Frazetta*" (by Stout)
  - article includes the following movie posters:
    - WHAT'S NEW PUSSYCAT? (both versions)
    - THE SECRET OF MY SUCCESS (both Versions)
    - AFTER THE FOX (both versions)
    - HOTEL PARADISO
    - THE BUSY BODY
    - THE FEARLESS VAMPIRE KILLERS
    - FITZWILLY (both versions)
    - THE NIGHT THEY RAIDED MINSKY'S (both versions)
    - THE FASTEST GUITAR ALIVE (both versions)
    - YOURS, MINE, AND OURS
    - LUANA (all 3 versions)
    - MRS. POLIFAX, SPY
    - MIXED COMPANY
    - BATTLESTAR GALACTICA
    - KING OF THE CONGO
    - WATERHOLE #3
  - back cover MAD MONSTER PARTY

FANTASTIC FILMS
• 38 FIRE & ICE article

• FILM SWORDS MAGAZINE
2003
Albion Armorers
Frank Frazetta Special Issue
Cover - The Barbarian
Featuring:
Interview Frank Frazetta
A tour of the Frazetta Museum by Frank Frazetta, Jr.
A preview of the exclusive licensed Frazetta products coming soon from Albion/Film Swords

FORBES MAGAZINE
• Nov 24, 2003
ARTICLE - Schwarzenegger's Sargent by Christopher Helman

FUNNY WORLD
• 19 Fall 1978
COVER - Animation cell based on the painting **"Against the Gods"**.
Contains article about Jovan commercial based upon the painting **"Against the Gods"**.

GAME men's magazine
• Vol. 2 #10 Oct. 1975
Article"*Frazetta's Erotic Fantasia*" 6 pp. Contains art and photos.

GENT men's magazine
Sky Publishing Company
• Vol. 6 #6 Aug. 1962
pg. 13 "*The Gent Zodiac*"
12 illustrations of females representing the twelve zodiacal signs
reprinted in THE BEST OF GENT
"*A Free Fall Free For All*" by Robert Malcolm 1 pg. illo.
• Vol. 7 #1 Oct. 1962
"*Sex in the Afternoon*" by Robert Fontaine 1 pg. illustration.

• GENT, THE BEST OF men's magazine
1978
Sky Publishing Company
"*The Gent Zodiac*"
12 illustrations of females representing the twelve zodiacal signs
first printed in GENT Vol.6 #6

HEROIC FANTASY
Heroic Fantasy Publications
• 2 Feb. 1985
article about the movie FIRE & ICE 10 pp.
preliminary sketches from movie, photo, and interview with Frank

HERO ILLUSTRATED
• 19 Jan. 1995
pg. 62 interview "*Illustrator Arcanum*" 6 pp.
contains the following:
Death Dealer II
Jaguar God
photos and 2 illustrations from ILLUSTRATIONS ARCANUM
Packaged with promotional sticker for Death Dealer #1 comic book
(See Promotional Collectibles).

HIGH TIMES
Trans-High Corp.
• 57 May 1980
COVER **The Mothman**
pg. 42 article: "*UFOs, Mothman and Me*"
The Mothman

HORROR BIZ MAGAZINE
1998
Horror Biz Enterprises
• 4 Spring-Summer 1999
Jim Warren interview
Contains Frazetta art and brief discussion of Frank.

ILLUSTRATION MAGAZINE
2002
Dan Zimmer
• 2 January 2002
Article: "*Frank Frazetta's Little Miracles*" *8 pp*. by Winiewicz
Article includes the following:
pg. 26 Cover - Tarzan and the Castaways
pg. 28 Photo of Frazetta with Cat Girl painting
pg. 29 Tooth and Claw ink illustration
AKA - *"They Buried their talons in his back."*
first printed in AT THE EARTH'S CORE AND PELLUCIDAR PORTFOLIO
pg. 30 Lord of the Savage Jungle ink illustration
AKA - *"He had me captured by an African Chief."*
first printed in TARZAN AND THE CASTAWAYS
pg. 32 Photo of Frazetta with Weird Science-Fantasy #29 cover
Caricature of Dr. Dave Winiewicz by Frazetta
pg. 33 The Spell of the Mahar ink illustration
AKA - *"A Mahar casts its sinister spell."*
first printed in E.R. BURROUGHS: MASTER OF ADVENTURE
Article: "*An Interview with Russ Cochran*" *8 pp* by Hignite
Article includes the following:
pg. 44 Portrait of Russ Cochran by Frazetta
pg. 46 Cover to Cochran Auction catalog #45 (pencil)
Cover to GRAPHIC GALLERY #5 (**New World**)
• Vol.2 #5 January 2003
Cover Watercolor preliminary for **Encounter**
pg. 52 Watercolor preliminary for **Encounter**
pg. 53 Photo of Frank creating watercolor preliminary for **Encounter**
pg. 54 Oil and Watercolor preliminary for **Darkness Weaves**
AKA **Kane on the Golden Sea**
pg. 55 Pencil layout for **Dreamflight**
pg. 56 Pencil and Watercolor preliminary for **The Lost Continent**
pg. 57 Watercolor preliminary for **Death Dealer VI**
Pencil and Watercolor preliminary for **Massai Warrior**
pg. 58 Pencil and Watercolor preliminary for **Pellucidar**
pg. 59 Pencil and Watercolor preliminary for **Tarzan and the Lost Empire**
pg. 60 Watercolor preliminary for **Cat Girl**

INSIDE COLLECTOR, THE
Victoria Publishing, Inc.
• Vol.1 No.4 October 1990
Contains an article by Russ Cochran
Article includes the following:
A Princess of Mars
Tales From the Crypt

LIFE MAGAZINE
- December 7, 1959

  Li'l Abner Article *"Famous Cartoonists Share a Silver Jubilee"* Article includes illustration of L'il Abner with all the prominent women in the strip.

LOCUS
- 315 April 1987 photo of Frazetta
- 324 January 1988 photo of Frazetta with Karen Black

MEDIASCENE
Prevue Entertainment Incorporated
- 17 Jan.-Feb. 1976

  pg. 21 *"Edgar Rice Burroughs Centennial Portfolio"* 4 pp.
  first printed in CANAVERAL PRESS books.
- 25 May-June 1977

  "The Funny Animal Frazetta" 2 pp. Funny animal reprints

MONSTER MANIA
Renaissance Productions
- 2 Jan. 1967

  wrap-around COVER - **Young World**

MONSTER WORLD
Following issues contain *"Fang Mail"* Letterhead
Warren Publishing
1964

•1 •2 •3 •4 •5

•6 •7 •8 •9 •10

MOVIEGOER free distribution through movie theaters, not a newsstand item
1983
- Vol. 2 No. 11 November 1983

  Article *"Frazetta, The Barbarian"* by James Burns
  back cover - Photo of Frank, Heidi and painting, **Fire & Ice**.

MOVIES INTERNATIONAL - Special Edition
Sari Publications
- 6 Nov. 1968 pg. 22 *"A Mahar casts it's sinister spell."*
- 7 Jan. 1969 **The Night They Raided Minsky's** (uncensored version)

NATIONAL LAMPOON
- April, 1971 COVER **Desperation**
- November, 1971 comic book parody *"Dragula"* 1 pg.
- June, 1972 COVER **Alien Crucifixion**
- August, 1973 COVER **Ghoul Queen**

- NATIONAL LAMPOON'S ENCYCLOPEDIA OF HUMOR

1973

back cover ink illustration
first printed in ERB-DOM #88

This book was quickly removed from the store racks because of unauthorized Volkswagen parody ad.

NEMO: CLASSIC COMICS LIBRARY
1983
Fantagraphics
- 4

  Flash Gordon daily strips (12-30-52 to 4-20-53) (with Dan Barry)

NEWSWEEK
- July 11, 1977

  Article on fantasy art mentions Frazetta and reproduces **A Princess of Mars**.

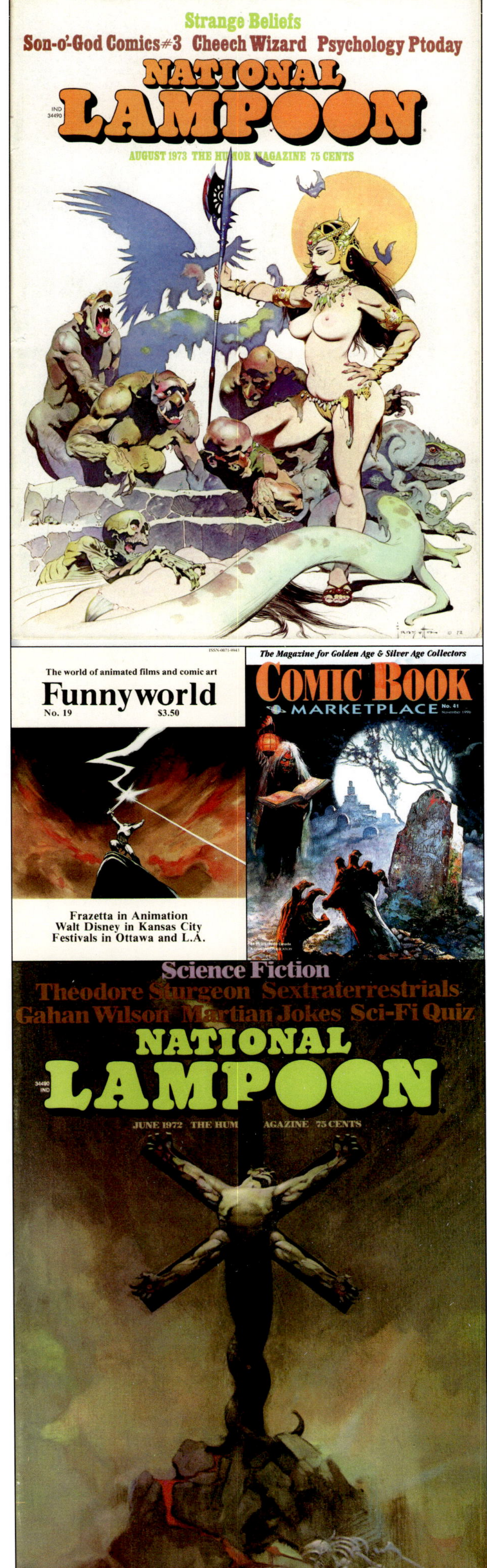

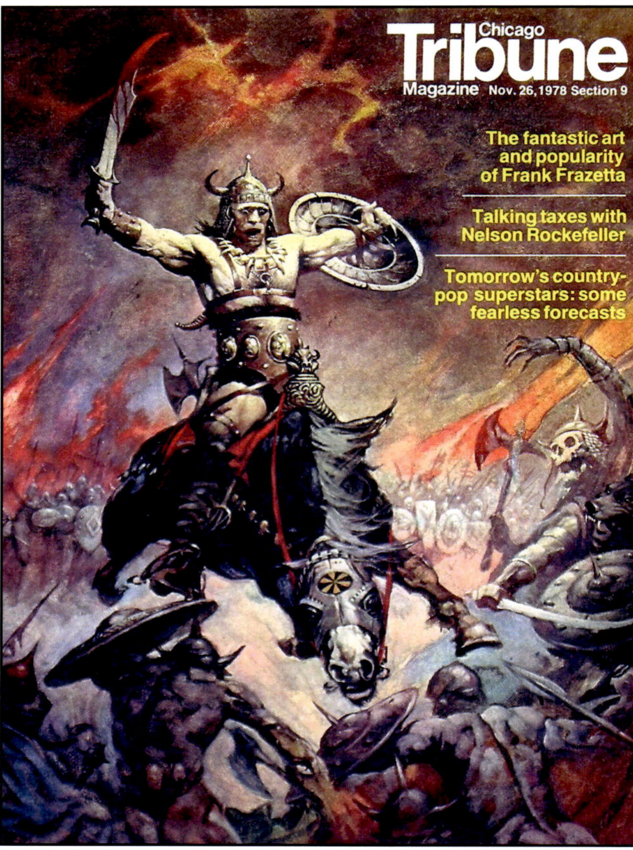

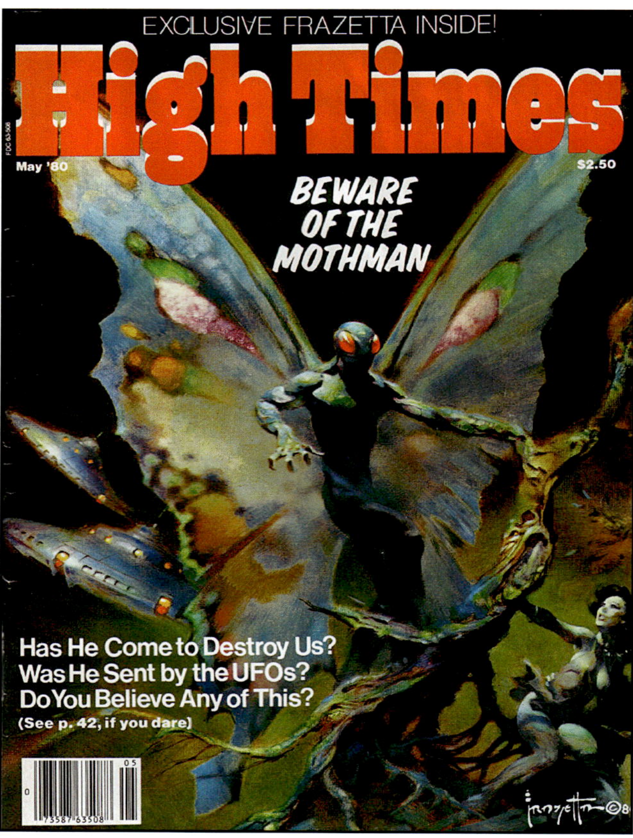

TOP: Chicago Tribune Magazine
The Chicago Tribune *(Nov. 26, 1978)*

ABOVE: High Times *(May 1980)*

NOSTALGIA JOURNAL, THE
Fantagraphics Inc.
- 27 July 1976 COVER

OMNI
- Sept. 1980 **Sea Witch** (cropped)

OVERSTREET'S GOLDEN AGE QUARTERLY
July, 1993 - present
Robert M. Overstreet
- 2 Oct-Dec 1993 COVER **A Princess of Mars**

- PACIFIC COMICS CATALOG

1977
Pacific Comics COVER **Ghoul Queen**

PLAYBOY
- February 1965
  Little Annie Fannie "*James Bomb in Russia*" part two 3 pp.
  with Russ Heath
- May 1965
  Little Annie Fannie "*Topless Bathing Suit Trial*" 5 pp.
  with Jack Davis
- July 1965
  Little Annie Fannie "*Surf Party*" 5 pp. with Jack Davis
- September 1978
  "*Arthur Rex*" short story by Thomas Berger. Frazetta painting:
  Arthur Rex (double-page spread)
- June 1986
  "*The Playboy Gallery*" **Arthur Rex** (double-page spread)

PREVUE
Prevue Entertainment Incorporated
- 50 Dec-Jan 1983
  pg. 54 article "*Fire & Ice*" by Steranko 7 pp.
  two pg. title illustration used during the movie
  see FIRE & ICE PORTFOLIO
- 54 Dec.- Jan. 1984
  article"*Fire & Ice*" interview
  FIRE & ICE movie poster (first color printing)
  various sketches for movie

QUESTAR
- vol. 3 no. 1 Oct. 1980
  COVER **Sound**
  pg. 33 **The Barbarian**
  pg. 36 **Kane on the Golden Sea**
  pg. 37 **Witherwing**
  pg. 38 **Stranded**
  pg. 39 **The Destroyer**

ROCKET'S BLAST and the COMICOLLECTOR, THE
- 2 Summer-Fall 2001
  COVER **Beyond the Farthest Star** (1st version)
  back cover **Tarzan and the Lost Empire**

ROLLING STONE East Coast Edition
- 478-479 (double issue) July 17, 1986
  Carlsberg Beer advertisement (**The Dispute**)
- 481 Aug. 28, 1986
  Carlsberg Beer advertisement (**The Dispute**)

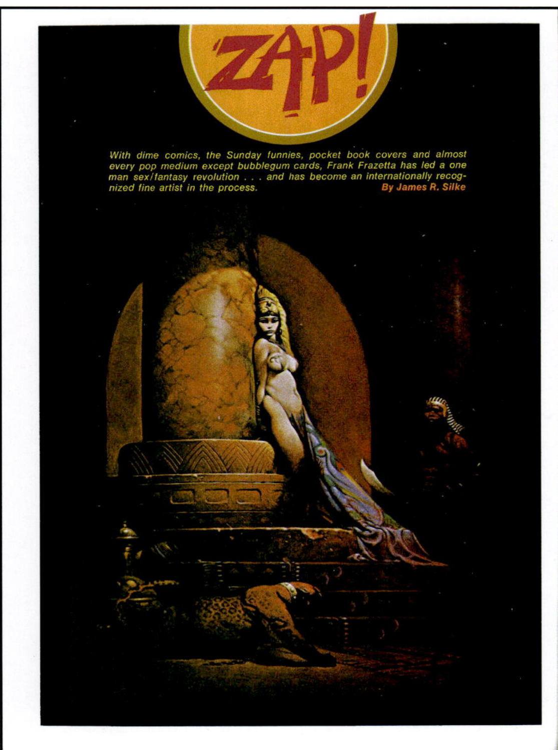

'ZAP!

With dime comics, the Sunday funnies, pocket book covers and almost every pop medium except bubblegum cards, Frank Frazetta has led a one man sex/fantasy revolution . . . and has become an internationally recognized fine artist in the process. **By James R. Silke**

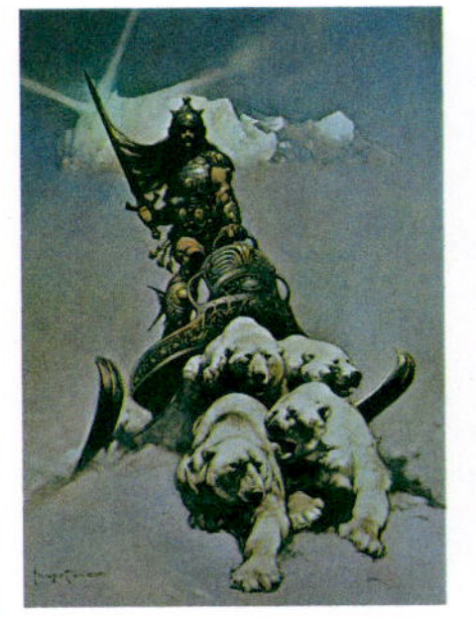

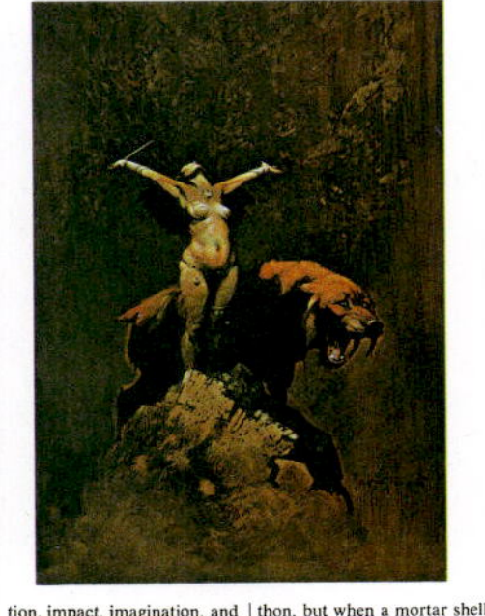

ZAP IS AN ARRESTING word. Zap describes that precise moment when a comic book character's guts are smashed to bits. Whap! and Splat! mean the same thing, but Zap! describes a whole life philosophy.

Comics thrive on wild, blood curdling, vulgarly obvious action. When an artist fails to spill enough guts with his drawings the editors resort to onomatopoeic word sounds followed by a frantic series of exclamation points all of which are rendered in large "balloons." When someone's had it in the comics you're not only supposed to know it, but to feel it. It's almost like real life!

Comic writers work overtime to devise word sounds that will convey the necessary sense of vitality required by their medium. They supply a Ka-Voom! when a man is destroyed by a howitzer, or a Ka-Blam! Blam! Blam! if he's wiped out by a T-47 Semiautomatic Rifle. For the love story fan there is Smack! and Slurp!, and for the blood sucking lurch-and-crawl crowd the standard Arrgggg!.

Zap, however, is an all purpose expletive, and now part of the language. It's lucid, clean, packed with brutal fun, and genuinely American. Technically it's a verb, but no one cares that it's used as a noun, adverb and even an adjective. Zap is also probably the only word that can define the drawings and paintings of Frank Frazetta. No other word adequately expresses his action, impact, imagination, and bone crushing vitality. There are Dada artists, Op artists and Pop artists, but Frazetta is a Zap artist.

G--GOOD NIGHT! ANYTHING SPECIAL-- FOR TOMORROW?

Drawing done in 1951 for "Personal Love"— Frazetta's girls were already going braless . . . were already liberated.

It's appropriate that the only word that can classify his work is derived from the comics, the field in which he started. His comic art, however, seldom had to rely on expressive word sounds. All the movement, heavy breathing and gasping delights of the flesh were more than apparent in his drawings. In his early work there was an occasional Rrrrr! for a menacing tiger cat or a Hiss! for an approaching python, but when a mortar shell tore off a shoulder blade, the Kaumph! was all in his brush work.

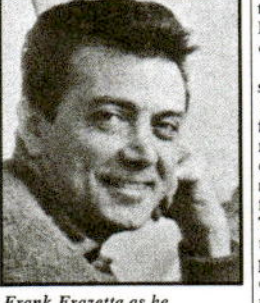

Frank Frazetta as he appears today on his spread of mountain land in East Stroudsburg, Pennsylvania.

His work was crude and obvious in his early days, and appeared to be going in exactly the opposite direction from the fine arts. "I was just drawin' 'em as I saw 'em." Occasionally he'd draw a girl for which there were no adequate word sounds to express the impact they had upon his young readers. He could make a pair of firm young breasts feel visually as if you had medicine balls in your hands. His audience was grateful. In the up tight Fifties all that they had to appreciate were Brigitte Bardot and a dime comic by Frazetta.

Frank started his professional career at fifteen, in 1944. He began by drawing funny little animals that romped among pretty flowers, butterflies and dripping moss, and stayed in the comic field until the mid-Sixties. To most people in the Fifties there was no great importance to comics. They contributed nothing to the understanding of ourselves, and there was no attempt whatsoever in them to improve our society, as the

41

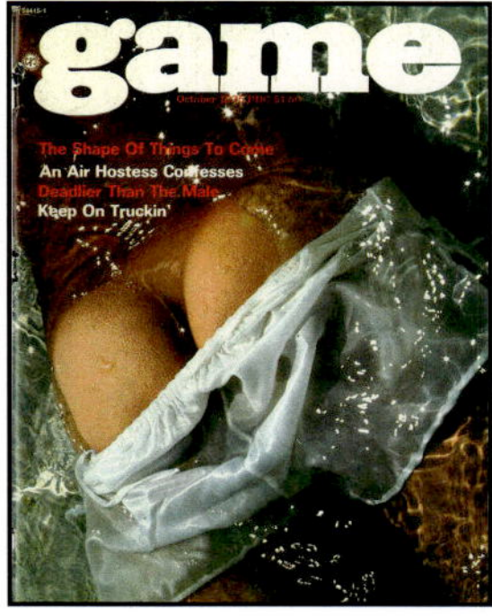

Game *men's magazine*
Vol. 2 #10 (Oct. 1975)

SCARLET STREET
• 18 Spring 1995
Color Insert - SON OF TARZAN paperback cover
SON OF TARZAN frontis illustration
John Carter of Mars line drawing

SPECTRUM
1998
• 22 April 2000 article on THE ULTIMATE TRIUMPH

SPFX
Ted A. Bohus
1999
• 8 1999
pg. 26 "*Frank Frazetta's motion picture and TV art*"
by William Stout 6 pp.
This is an updated version of an already existing article.

STARLOG (Japanese)
SEE INTERNATIONAL PUBLICATIONS

TEASE
• 4
article "*Mr. Frazetta Goes to Dogpatch*" 4 pp.

WEIRD WORLDS children's magazine
Scholastic Magazines
1978
• 1 1978
COVER **Space 103 - Attack**
4 full page, full color painting reproductions

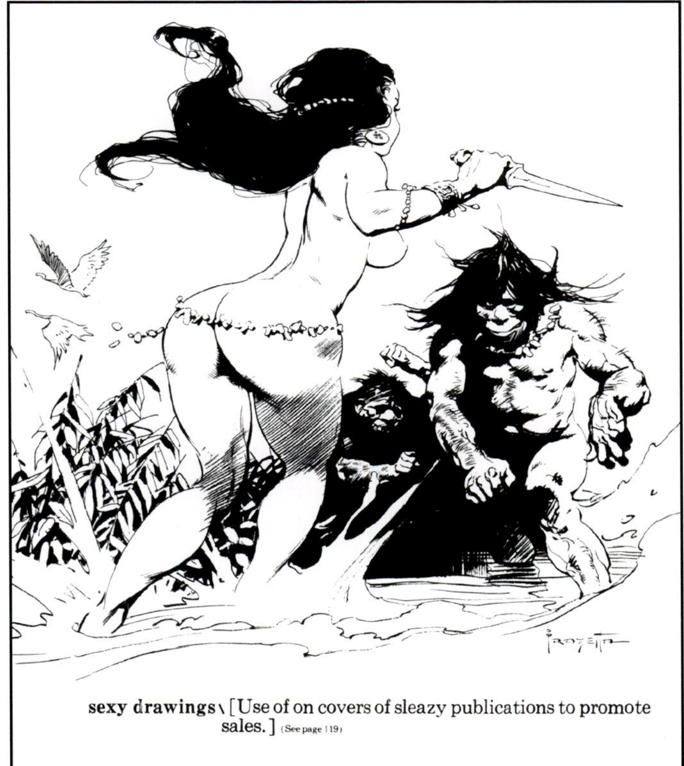

Back cover National Lampoon's Encyclopedia of Humor
21st Century Publications (1973)

FRAME BY FRAME

Entertainment & Advertising

By William Stout

WILLIAM STOUT has worked on the ad campaigns for over 120 films. Eventually he fell into the film business itself, working as a production designer and conceptual designer for over 35 feature films. His work on Pan's Labyrinth helped that film to win two of its three Academy Awards. Despite his extensive film work, Stout is primarily known for his reconstructions of prehistoric life. His murals are on permanent display at the Houston Museum of Natural Science, Walt Disney's Animal Kingdom and the San Diego Natural History Museum.

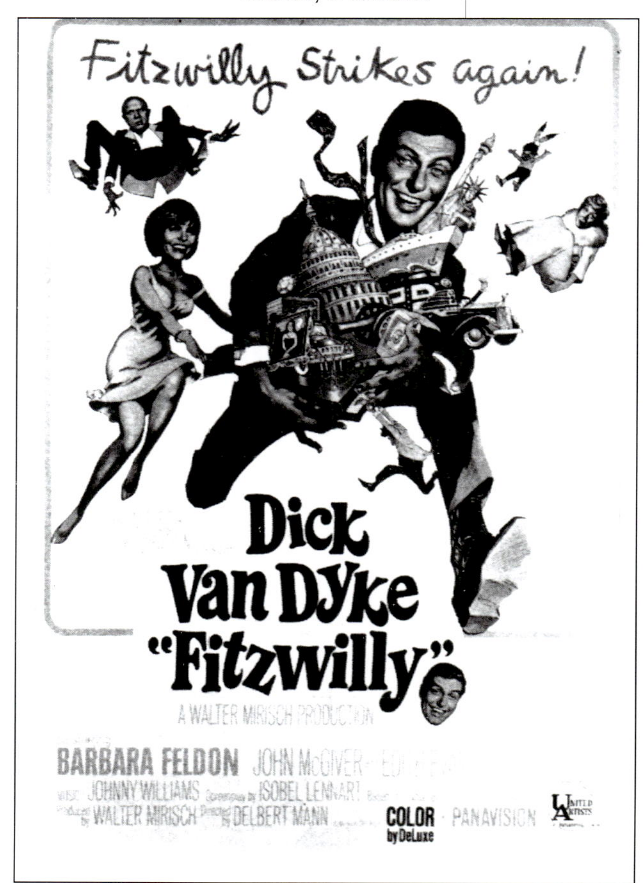

In his post-comics art career Frank Frazetta frequently ventured past the stylistic boundaries and subject matter limitations of science fiction and fantasy. One genre exposed his work to more people than any other graphic medium: motion picture and television advertising. Reproduced in nearly every newspaper in the country, Frazetta's entertainment promotions encompass a diverse variety of visual approaches. Especially interesting in this genre is the chance to glimpse the rarely seen but important humorous side of Frank.

Technically, the first Frazetta art ever to grace a movie poster was for King of the Congo (1952). The cover to Frank's comic book, Thun'da #1, is reproduced in a corner of the poster.

Frazetta's first real one sheets were for *What's New Pussycat?* (1965). He received the assignment after an art director saw Frank's Ringo Starr caricature on a MAD back cover. Frank was paid $5000 for the art --- "a whole year's pay," he remarked, "earned in one afternoon."

Although a third of Frazetta's movie art (for over thirty films, with many more that number in paintings as Frank was often hired to create variant art for each project) was produced from 1965 to 1968 (with his work for *After The Fox*, *Hotel Paradiso*, *The Busy Body*, *The Fearless Vampire Killers* and *The Night They Raided Minsky's* high quality standouts), he continued to regularly create work for that field up until 1987 (*The Barbarians* and *Salomé's Last Dance*). After a nine year gap, Frazetta painted one last

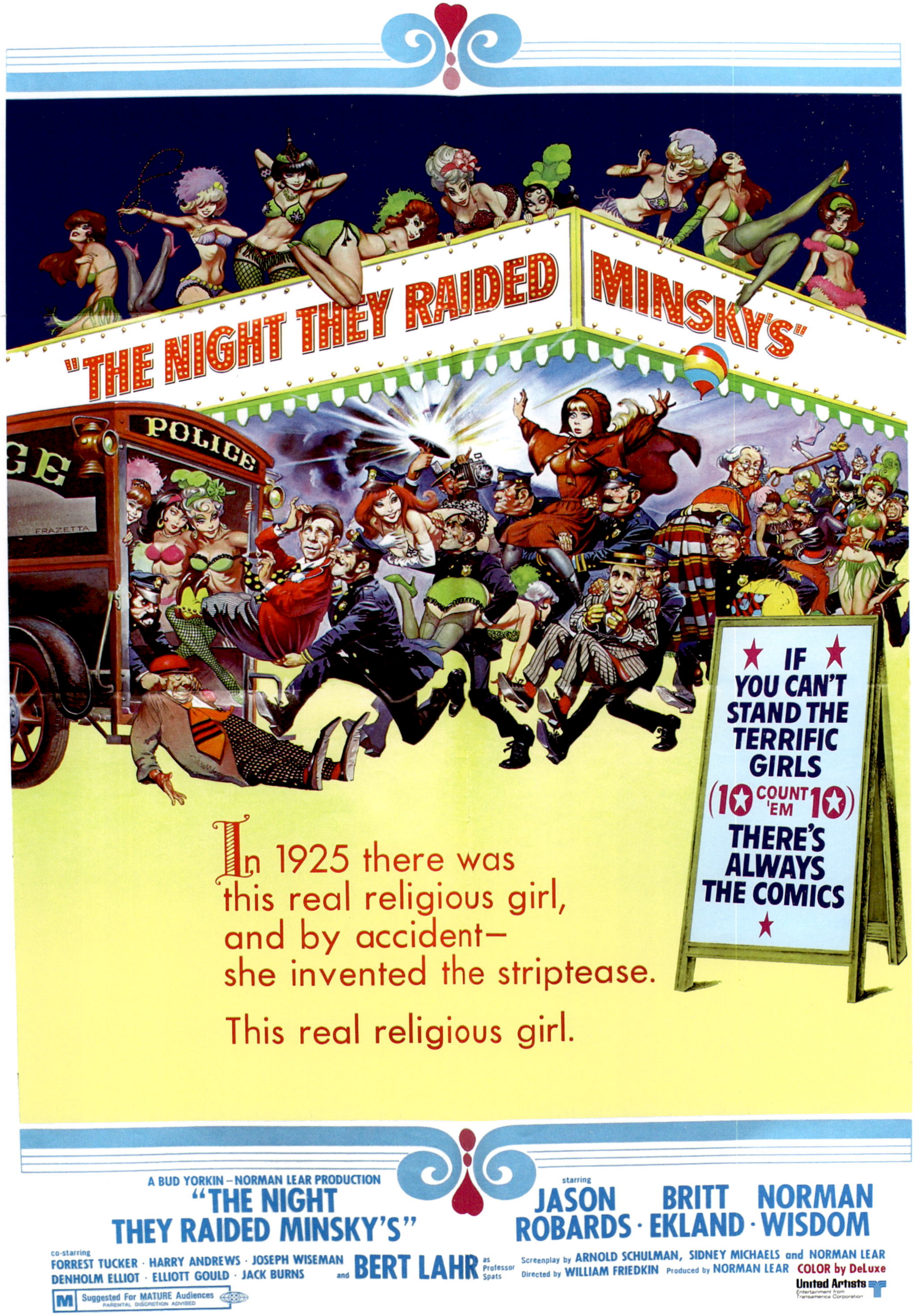

"THE NIGHT THEY RAIDED MINSKY'S"

POLICE

FRAZETTA

IF YOU CAN'T STAND THE TERRIFIC GIRLS (10 COUNT 'EM 10) THERE'S ALWAYS THE COMICS

In 1925 there was
this real religious girl,
and by accident—
she invented the striptease.

This real religious girl.

A BUD YORKIN – NORMAN LEAR PRODUCTION

"THE NIGHT THEY RAIDED MINSKY'S"

starring
JASON ROBARDS · BRITT EKLAND · NORMAN WISDOM

co-starring
FORREST TUCKER · HARRY ANDREWS · JOSEPH WISEMAN
DENHOLM ELLIOT · ELLIOTT GOULD · JACK BURNS
and **BERT LAHR** as Professor Spats

Screenplay by ARNOLD SCHULMAN, SIDNEY MICHAELS and NORMAN LEAR
Directed by WILLIAM FRIEDKIN Produced by NORMAN LEAR COLOR by DeLuxe

M Suggested For MATURE Audiences
PARENTAL DISCRETION ADVISED

United Artists
Entertainment from Transamerica Corporation

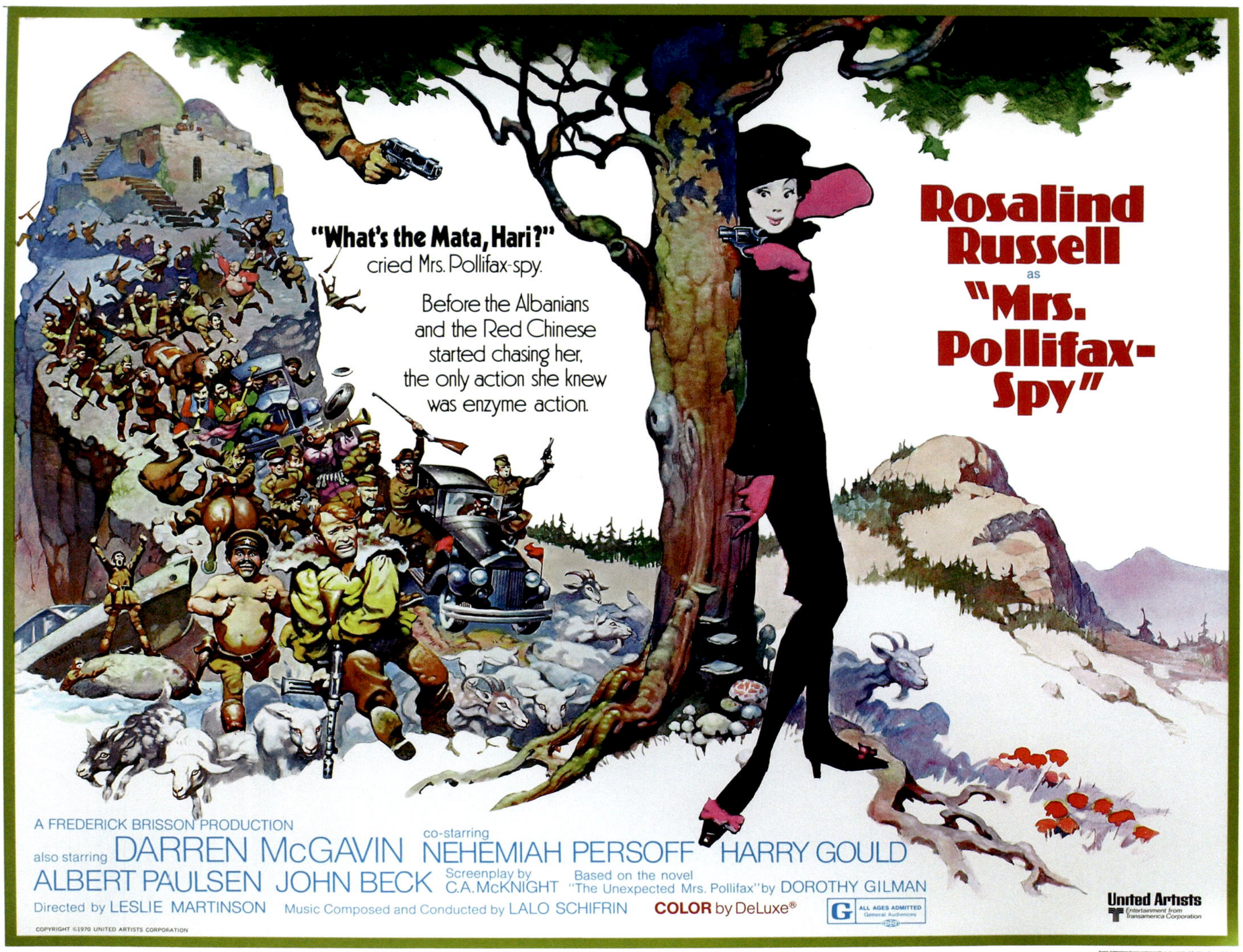

"What's the Mata, Hari?"
cried Mrs. Pollifax-spy.
Before the Albanians
and the Red Chinese
started chasing her,
the only action she knew
was enzyme action.

Rosalind
Russell
as
"Mrs.
Pollifax-
Spy"

A FREDERICK BRISSON PRODUCTION
also starring DARREN McGAVIN co-starring NEHEMIAH PERSOFF HARRY GOULD
ALBERT PAULSEN JOHN BECK Screenplay by C.A. McKNIGHT Based on the novel "The Unexpected Mrs. Pollifax" by DOROTHY GILMAN
Directed by LESLIE MARTINSON Music Composed and Conducted by LALO SCHIFRIN COLOR by DeLuxe®
G ALL AGES ADMITTED General Audiences
United Artists Entertainment from Transamerica Corporation
COPYRIGHT ©1970 UNITED ARTISTS CORPORATION

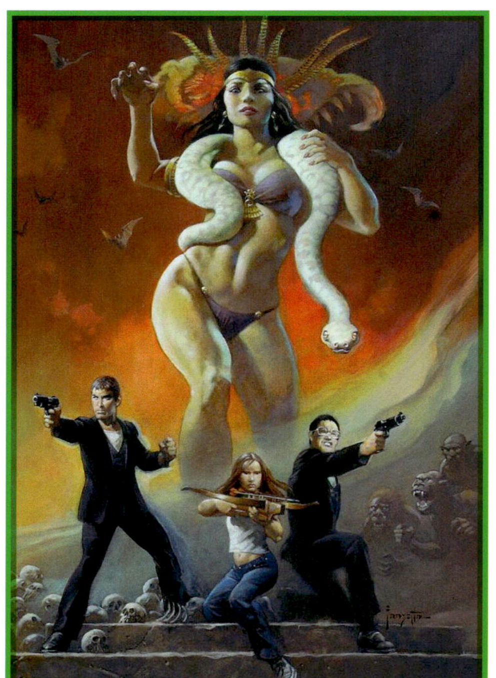

Unused art- From Dusk 'Til Dawn *(1996)*

poster, promoting the over-the-top horror thriller *From Dusk 'Til Dawn* (1996.)

Although some may feel it unfortunate that Frank's off-and-on thirty two year association with entertainment advertising has perhaps ended, we nevertheless have his graphic legacy in this field to enjoy. His subsequent efforts to create masterpieces that are "pure Frazetta" have provided the art-hungry public with an impressive body of work matched in its power and influence by no other living artist.

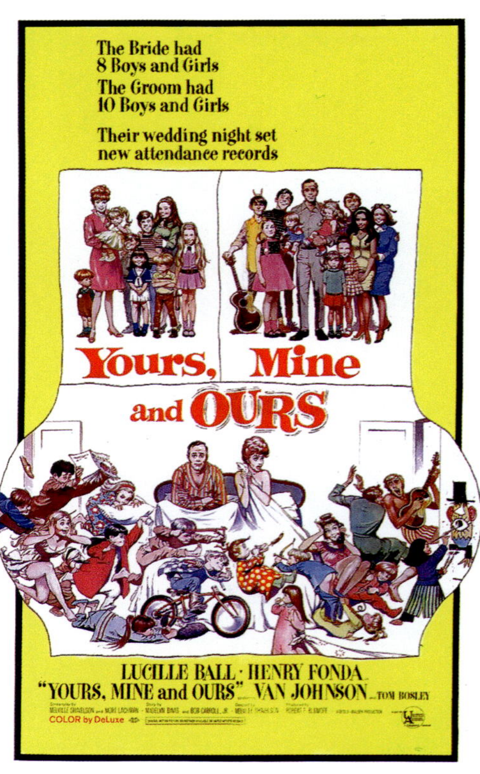

You caught the "Pussycat"... Now chase the Fox!

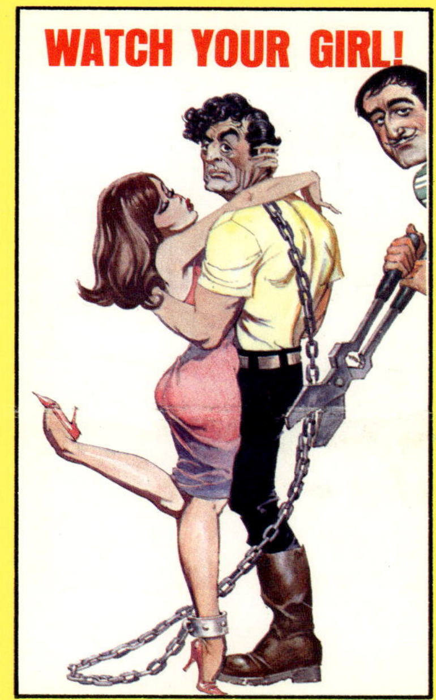

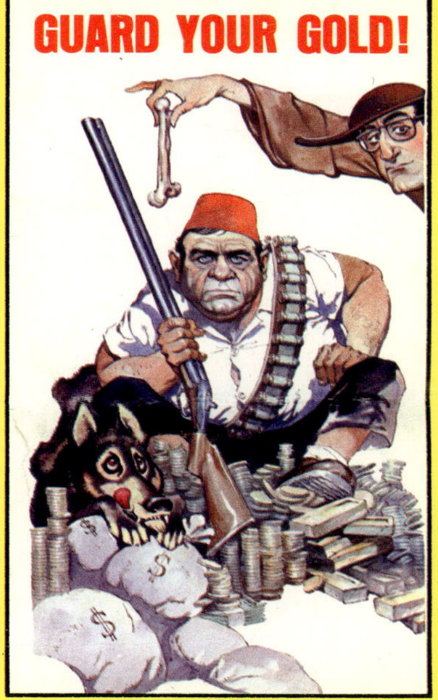

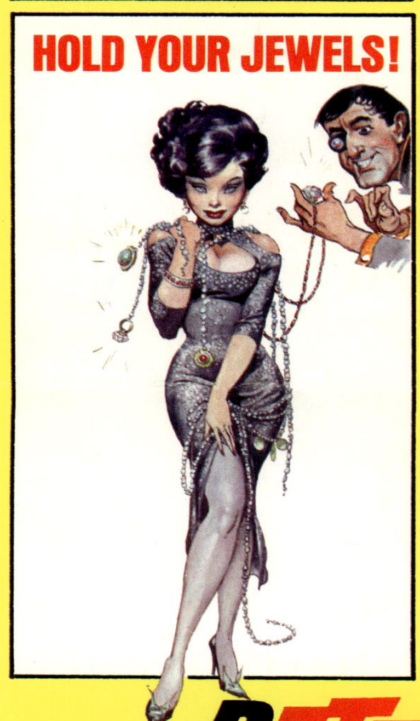

...THE FOX IS LOOSE!

PETER SELLERS

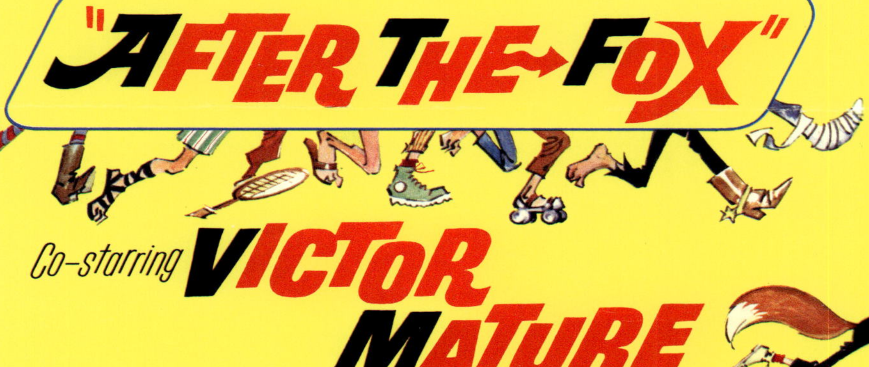

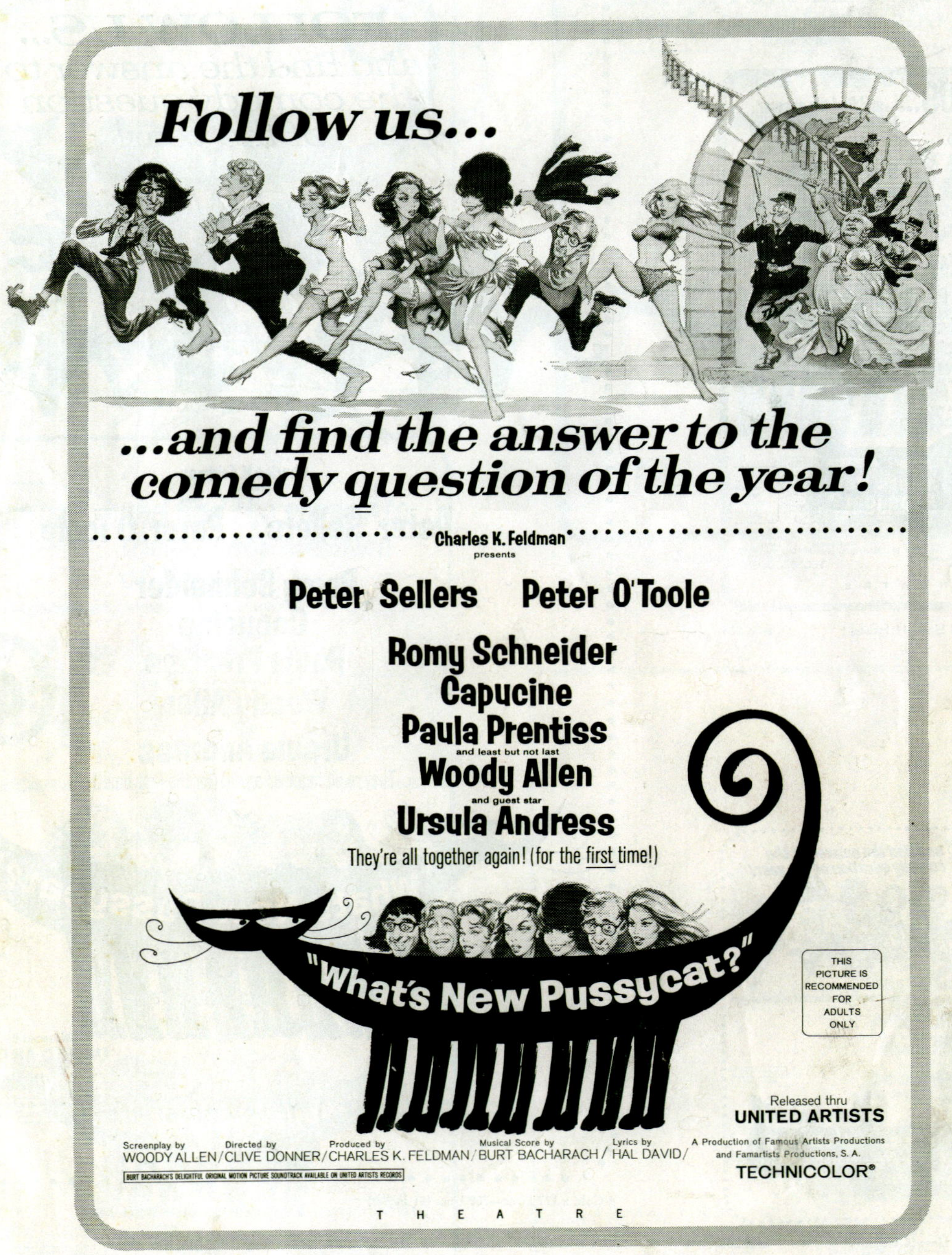

5 Cols. x 175 Lines—875 Lines (63 Inches)

Mat 502

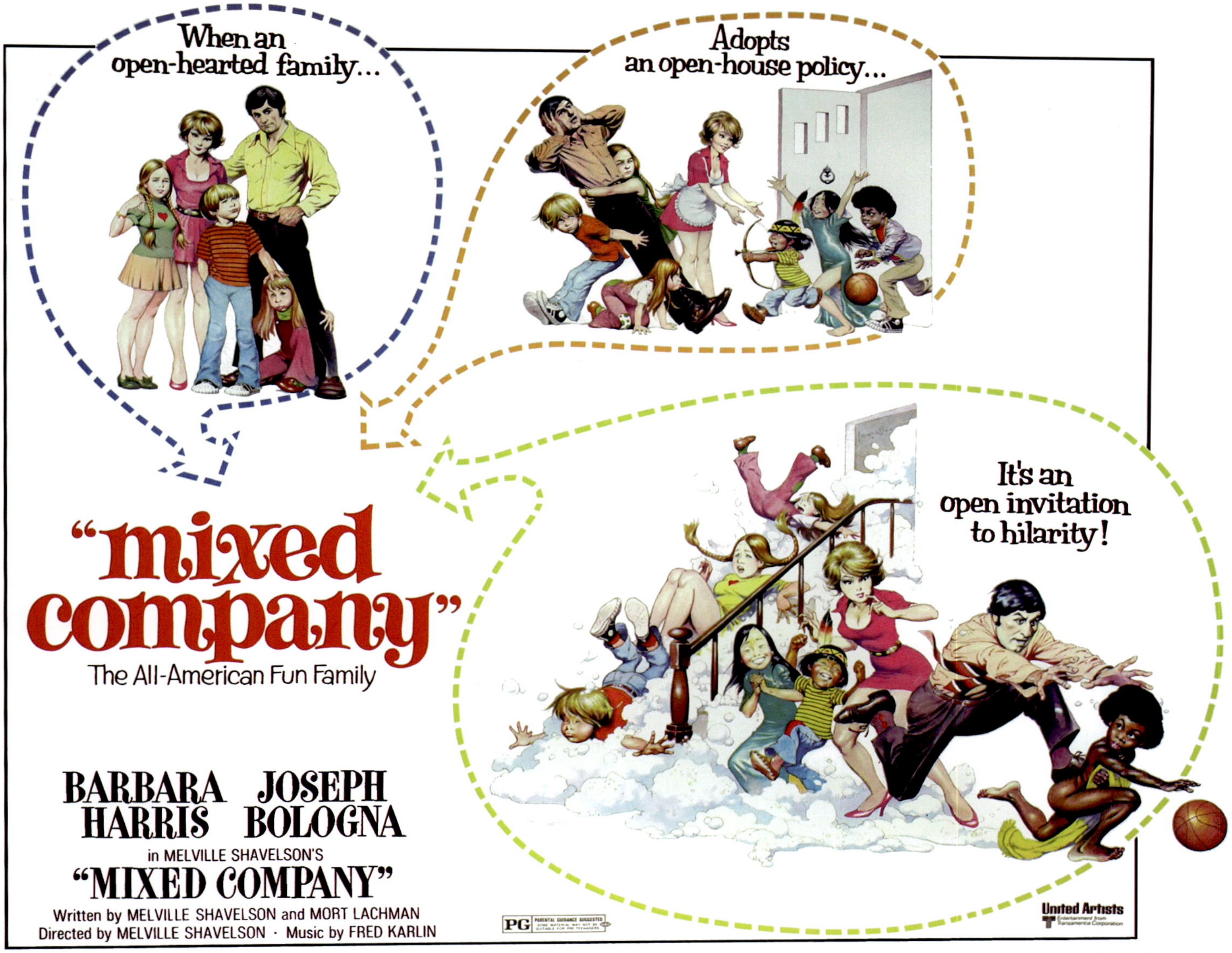

When an
open-hearted family...

Adopts
an open-house policy...

It's an
open invitation
to hilarity!

"mixed
company"

The All-American Fun Family

BARBARA HARRIS JOSEPH BOLOGNA

in MELVILLE SHAVELSON'S

"MIXED COMPANY"

Written by MELVILLE SHAVELSON and MORT LACHMAN
Directed by MELVILLE SHAVELSON · Music by FRED KARLIN

PG PARENTAL GUIDANCE SUGGESTED

United Artists

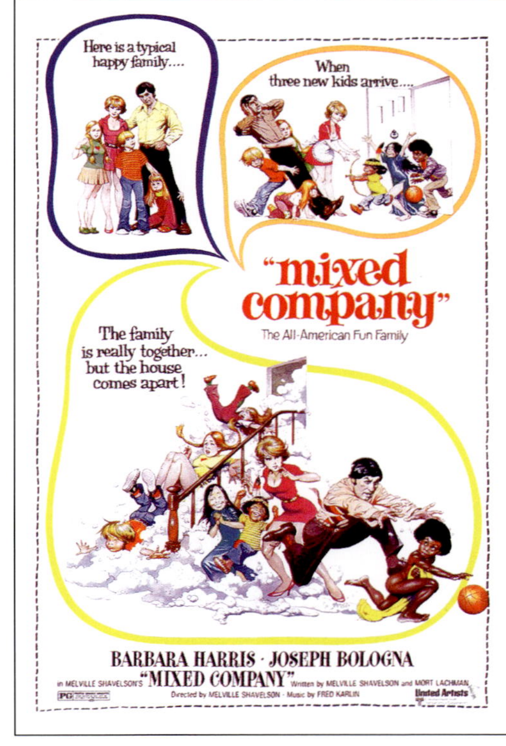

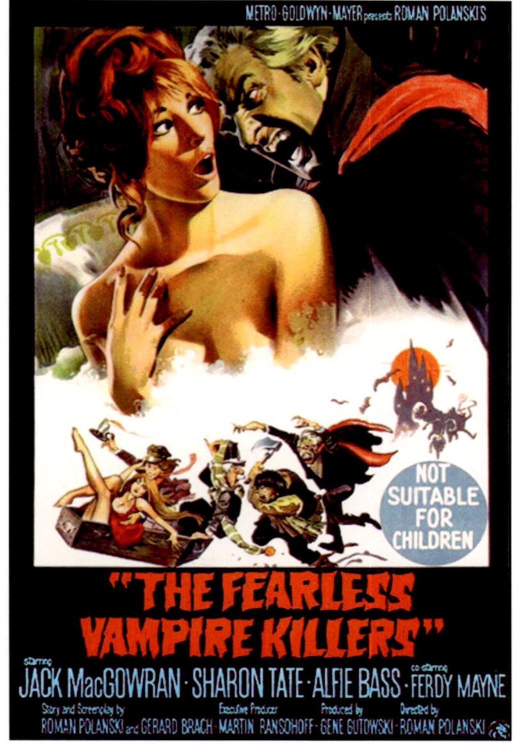

MOVIES & TELEVISION

AFRICAN ELEPHANT, THE documentary

1972 Promotional one sheet (unused)

first printed in FRANK FRAZETTA: BOOK FIVE (art book).

AFTER THE FOX

United Artists

1966

- 66-354 A sheet 66-354
- B sheet
- Pressbook – contains both poster images

SEE RECORD ALBUMS FOR SOUNDTRACK

BATTLESTAR GALACTICA television movie

1978

These were done exclusively as ads within newspapers and T.V. listings.

- Sept. 16 - 22, 1978 **Space 103 - Attack** (b/w)
- Sept. 23 - 29, 1978 **Space 104 - Scramble** (b/w)
- Sept. 30 - Oct. 6, 1978 **Pharaoh's Tomb** (b/w)
- Jan. 13 - 19, 1979 **Darkness at Time's Edge** (b/w)
- Jan. 20 - 26, 1979 **Darkness at Time's Edge** (b/w) (cropped)

BILLIE

Paramount Pictures

1965

Pattie Duke The Patty Duke portrait was intended for the movie but never used.

BUSY BODY, THE

Paramount Pictures

1967 • 67-41 one sheet

CONAN THE BARBARIAN UK Release teaser poster

Universal Pictures

1979

The Barbarian

Also used in American magazines as a pre-production promotion.

- 20" x 35"
- 22" x 27"
- French 17" x 25"

DRACULA proposed animated film project

Orsatti Production

1975

Provided production art. Most of this art went unpublished. See LEGACY (art book) for first published appearance.

FASTEST GUITAR ALIVE, THE

MGM

1968

- 67-202 One sheet, Jack Davis did main image. Frazetta image is a detail of a larger work.

Full Frazetta image appears on cover to soundtrack.

SEE RECORD ALBUMS FOR SOUNDTRACK

FEARLESS VAMPIRE KILLERS, THE

or: Pardon me, but your teeth are in my neck.

MGM

1967

- B67-26 One sheet, two artists
  Frazetta provides group shot at bottom.
- three sheet
- pressbook

FIRE & ICE (animated feature)

Producers Sales Organization

1983

Frazetta designed the look throughout this full length Ralph Bakshi film. He also sculpted head models of his key leads (see BRONZE BUST SET) and co-wrote the basic story. Many of his production drawings and paintings saw print at the time of the film's release in magazine articles. He painted two different posters for the movie. One was for the U.S. release and one was for German release. His U.S. design was not accepted and therefore went unpublished. The German release became the international artwork.

- one sheet
- German Lobby Card Set

A set of fourteen, full color lobby cards released only in Germany. No other versions of lobby cards exist.

FITZWILLY

United Artists

1969

- one sheet An alternate version of the artwork was used as soundtrack LP cover.

SEE RECORD ALBUMS FOR SOUNDTRACK

FRAZETTA - PAINTING WITH FIRE Documentary

April 2003

Cinemachine

- VHS 96 minutes
- DVD 2 disk set

- **FRAZETTA - PAINTING WITH FIRE** Movie Poster 13 " x 19 "

April 2003

Cinemachine

Printed on Archival Matte Paper

FRAZETTA - The Documentary

Cinemachine

2002 Documentary based on the artist.

- 11"x17" teaser poster shows **Self Portrait**

FROM DUSK TILL DAWN

1996

unused B version one sheet.

first printed in FRANK FRAZETTA (art book)

GAUNTLET, THE

Warner Brothers

1977

- 770162one sheet

SEE RECORD ALBUMS FOR SOUNDTRACK

The day the mob muffed!

Muff number one: purple suede shoes.
Muff number two: three stiffs in one coffin.
Muff number three: a stripper whose body had a wicked twist.
Muff number four: the million dollar muff.

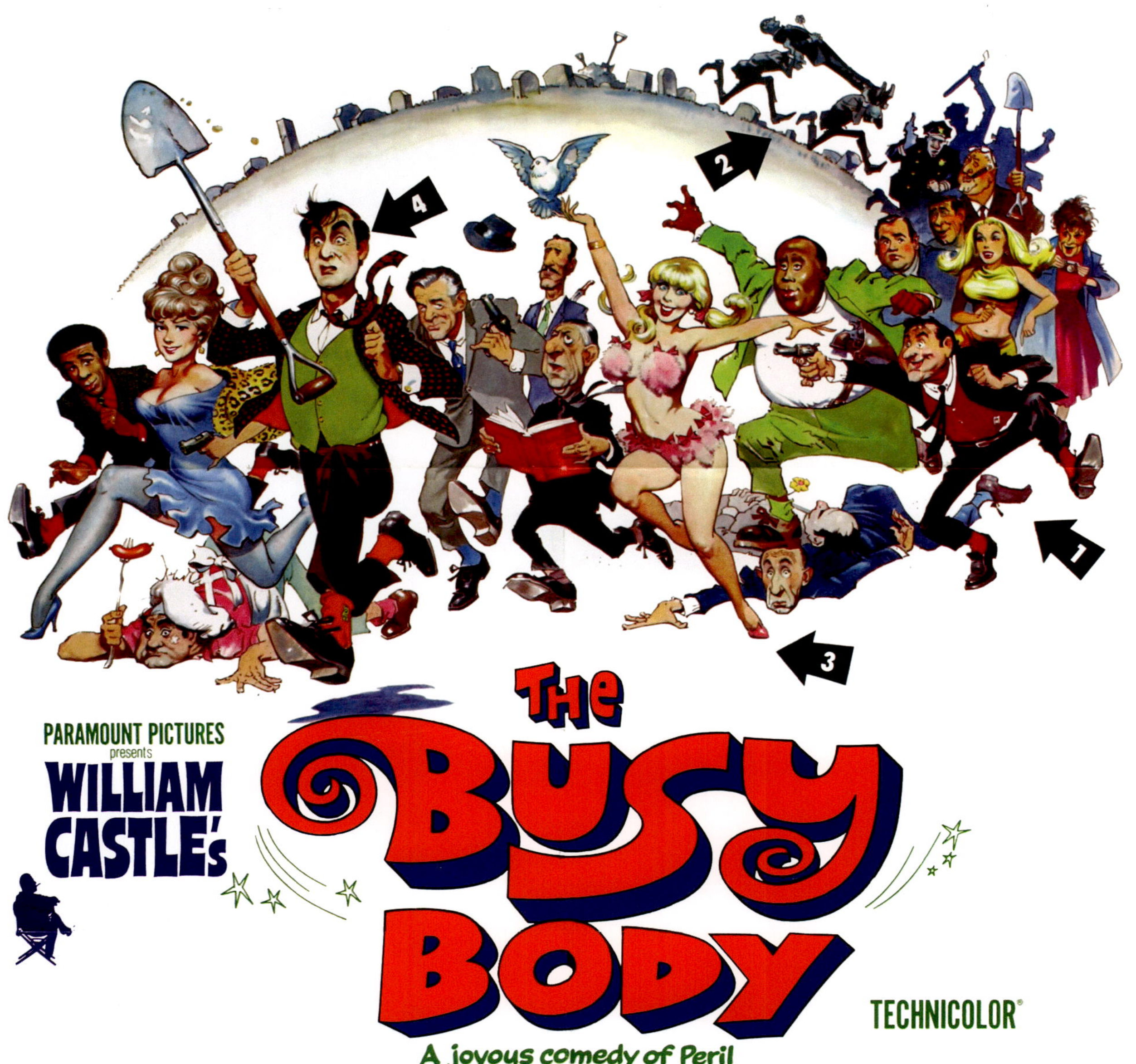

STARRING
SID CAESAR · ROBERT RYAN · ANNE BAXTER · KAY MEDFORD
JAN MURRAY · RICHARD PRYOR · ARLENE GOLONKA GUEST BODIES BEN BLUE
DOM DeLUISE · BILL DANA · GODFREY CAMBRIDGE · MARTY INGELS and GEORGE JESSEL
Screenplay by BEN STARR · From the Novel by DONALD E. WESTLAKE · Produced and Directed by WILLIAM CASTLE · Music by VIC MIZZY · TECHNISCOPE® A PARAMOUNT PICTURE

GIVE US BARRABAS newspaper advertisement

T.V. movie advertisement placed consecutively within three newspapers on March 28, 1969. The newspapers are as follows:
- Washington Post
- New York Times
- Chicago Sun Times

- GROUP, THE

MGM

1966 Frazetta painted the key portrait that appears throughout the film. Although not used as part of the formal advertising, the painting, which by that time had been heavily retouched by a studio hack, appears in the background during the movie.

1985 The video release is available through Key Video. Stock #4678.

HOTEL PARADISO

MGM

1966
- 66-271 one sheet

SEE RECORD ALBUMS FOR SOUNDTRACK

- JOVAN SEX APPEAL animated commercial

1978

Richard Williams (director)

This 30 second spot was based on Frazetta's **Against the Gods**. Frazetta had no other involvement in the making of the spot.

see FUNNY WORLD #19 (magazine) for details

KING OF THE CONGO (serialization based on the comic book "THUN'DA, KING OF THE CONGO")

Columbia Pictures

1952
- one sheet

  Frazetta did not paint poster image. Cover to A-1 COMICS #47 is featured in lower right hand corner of poster.

LUANA

Capital Productions

1973
- teaser card (color rough)
- 73-337 A sheet

  This design was reused as the cover to VAMPIRELLA #31
- B sheet
- 14" x 36" insert card

  uses cropped version of "A sheet" design

MAD MONSTER PARTY

Embassy Pictures

1967
- 68-239 A sheet (b/w with spot red) (monsters on a chandelier)
- B sheet (monsters and car)
- modern reprint of A Sheet design

  Identical to original except for minor quality reproduction.
  Released in 2001 by Blackboard Entertainment

MIXED COMPANY

United Artists

1974
- 74-256 one sheet
- 74-256 22" x 28" half sheet made of card stock
- teaser 14" x 36"

MOTORCYCLE MANIA 3 - Jesse James Rides Again - DVD

Discovery Channel, Original Productions

2004
- DVD First few minutes features Jesse James riding his Death Dealer bike. Bike features **Death Dealer** on tank and **Death Dealer IV** on rear fender.

MRS. POLLIFAX, SPY

United Artists

1971
- 71-50 one sheet
- 71-50 22" x 28" half sheet made of card stock

NIGHT THEY RAIDED MINSKY'S, THE

United Artists

1968

The original version was too risque and therefore toned down. It only appears in FRANK FRAZETTA: BOOK THREE (art book)
- 69-40 one sheet (revised version)
- press book (contains b/w alternate illustration) 9 pp.

SEE RECORD ALBUMS FOR SOUNDTRACK

ORCA

1977

Rejected poster art, eventually published in FRANK FRAZETTA: BOOK FIVE (art book)

PAINT YOUR WAGON

1969 Unpublished commissioned work consisting of line drawn watercolor portraits of Clint Eastwood, Lee Marvin, and Jean Seberg surrounded by loads of funny little western figures.

PAPA'S DELICATE CONDITION
- teaser 14" x 36"

SALOME'S LAST DANCE

1987

Movie poster art for an unreleased film

SECRET OF MY SUCCESS, THE

(How three beautiful girls love for fun and murder for profit!)

MGM

1965
- one sheet 65-253
- press book (contains b/w alternate illustration)

WHAT'S NEW PUSSYCAT?

United Artists

1965
- A sheet
- B sheet
- Teaser 14" x 36"
- Pressbook featuring artwork not on either poster. Artwork is caricatures of Peter Sellers, Peter O'Toole, Romy Schneider, Capucine, Paula Prentiss, Woody Allen and Ursula Andress.

SEE RECORD ALBUMS FOR SOUNDTRACK

YOURS, MINE AND OURS

United Artists

1968
- one sheet

SEE RECORD ALBUMS FOR SOUNDTRACK

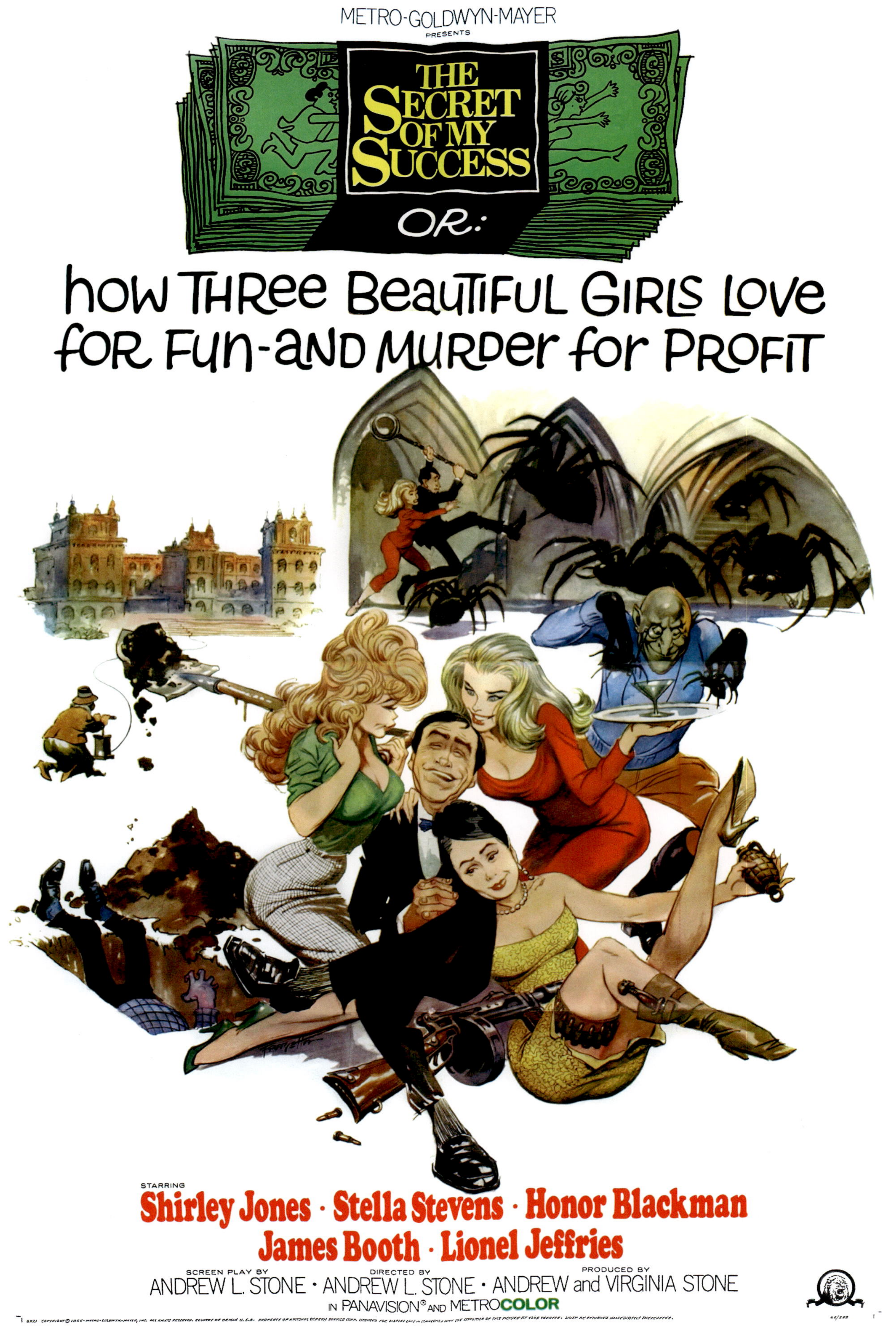

METRO-GOLDWYN-MAYER

PRESENTS

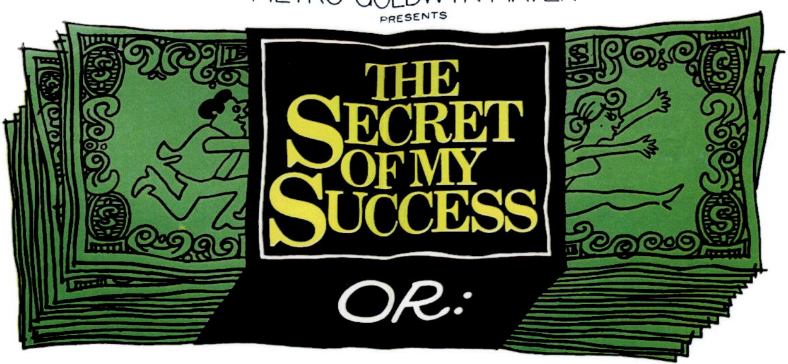

how THREE BEAUTIFUL GIRLS LOVE
FOR FUN-AND MURDER FOR PROFIT

STARRING

Shirley Jones · Stella Stevens · Honor Blackman

James Booth · Lionel Jeffries

SCREEN PLAY BY ANDREW L. STONE · DIRECTED BY ANDREW L. STONE · PRODUCED BY ANDREW and VIRGINIA STONE

IN PANAVISION® AND METROCOLOR

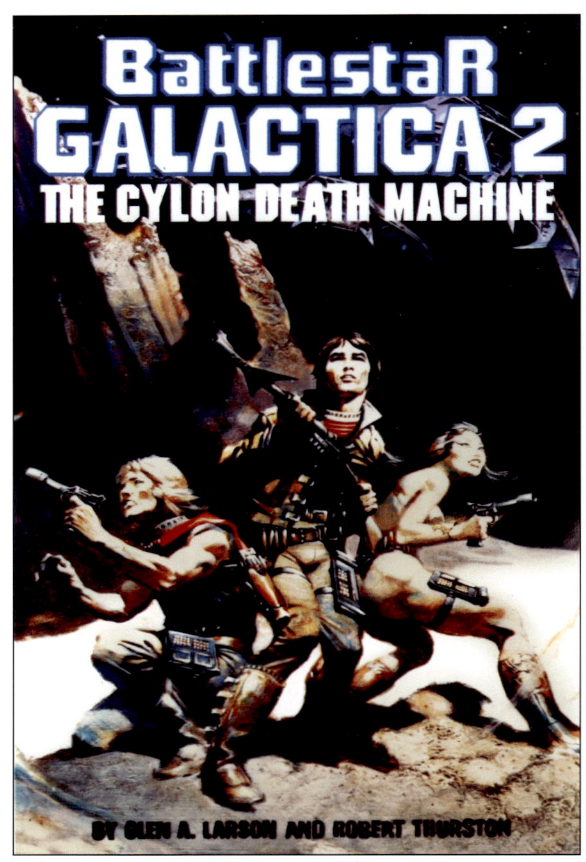

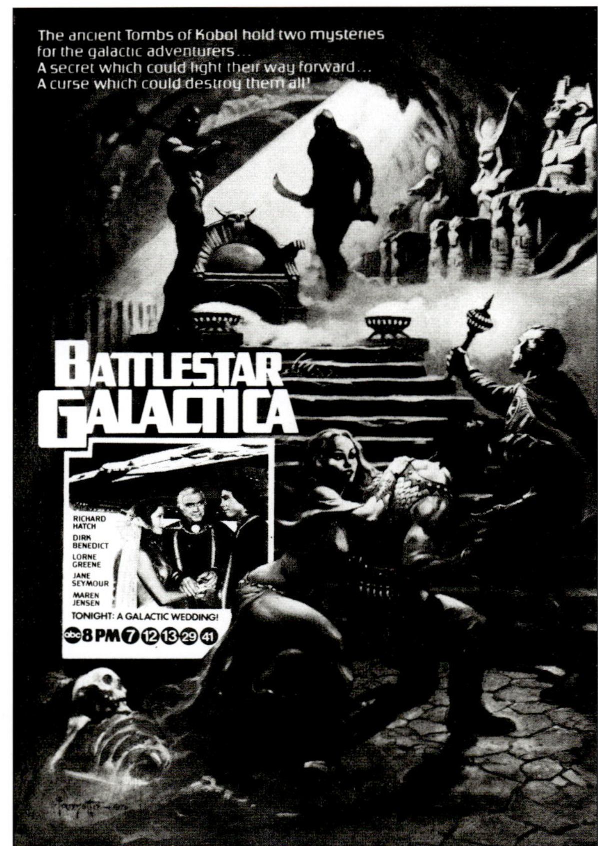

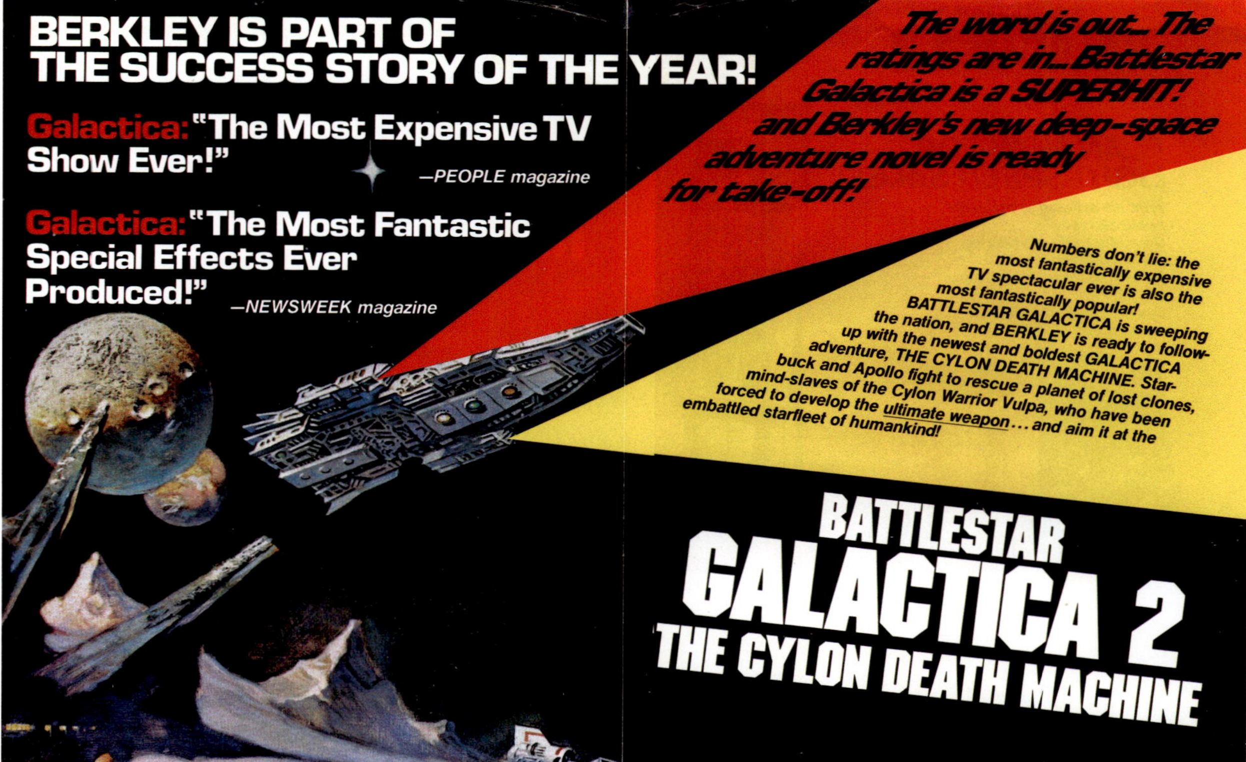

TOP LEFT: Uncensored version of promotional brochure (notice female' hip-covering—or lack thereof)

TOP RIGHT: Advertisement in TV Guide.

ABOVE: Interior of of promotional brochure.

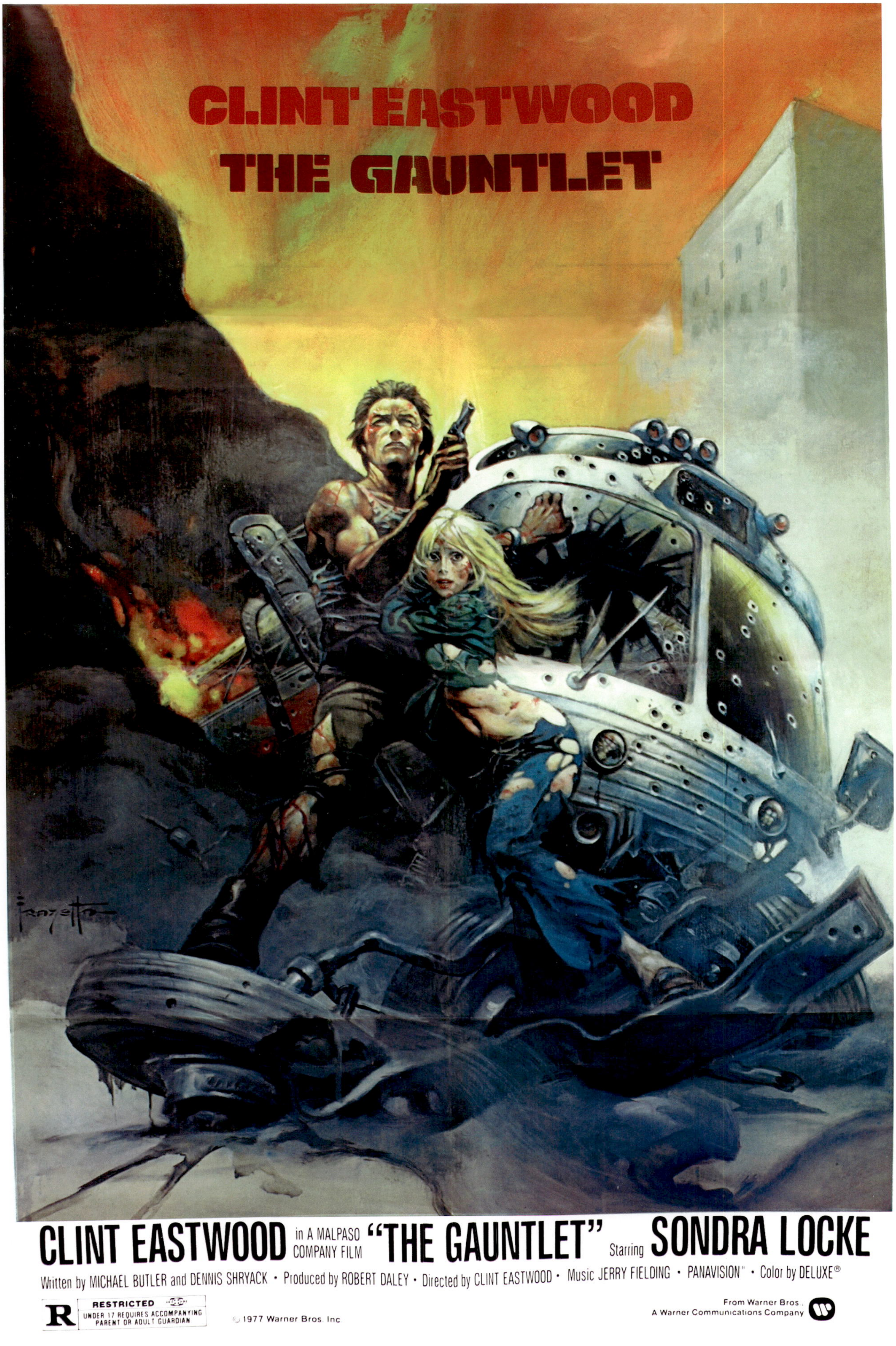

CLINT EASTWOOD

THE GAUNTLET

CLINT EASTWOOD in A MALPASO COMPANY FILM "THE GAUNTLET" Starring SONDRA LOCKE

Written by MICHAEL BUTLER and DENNIS SHRYACK • Produced by ROBERT DALEY • Directed by CLINT EASTWOOD • Music JERRY FIELDING • PANAVISION® • Color by DELUXE®

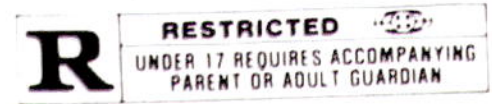

From Warner Bros.,
A Warner Communications Company

One-sheet

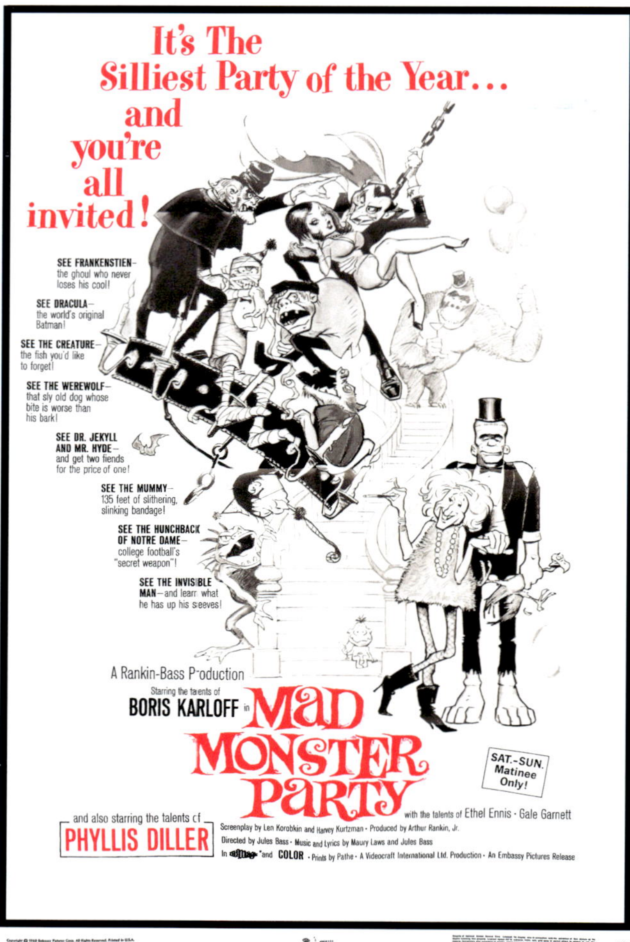

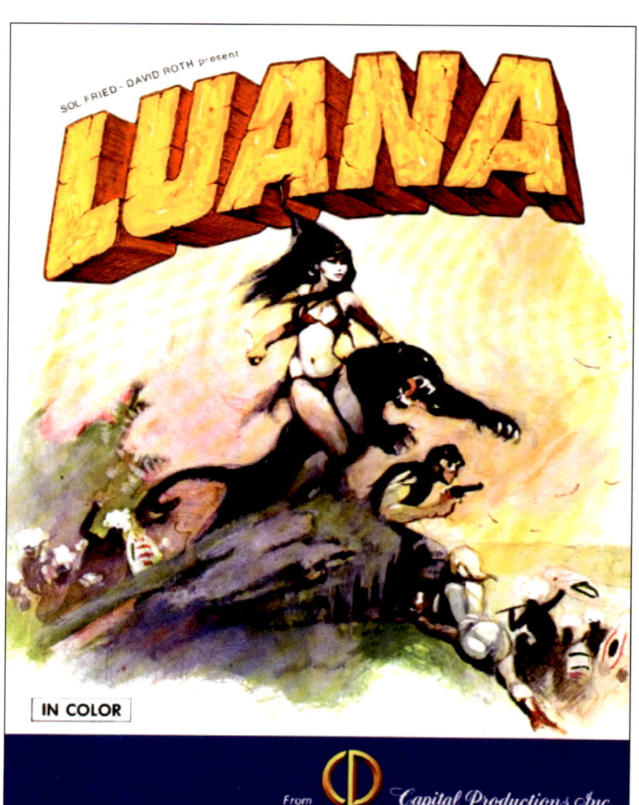

Teaser card

Insert

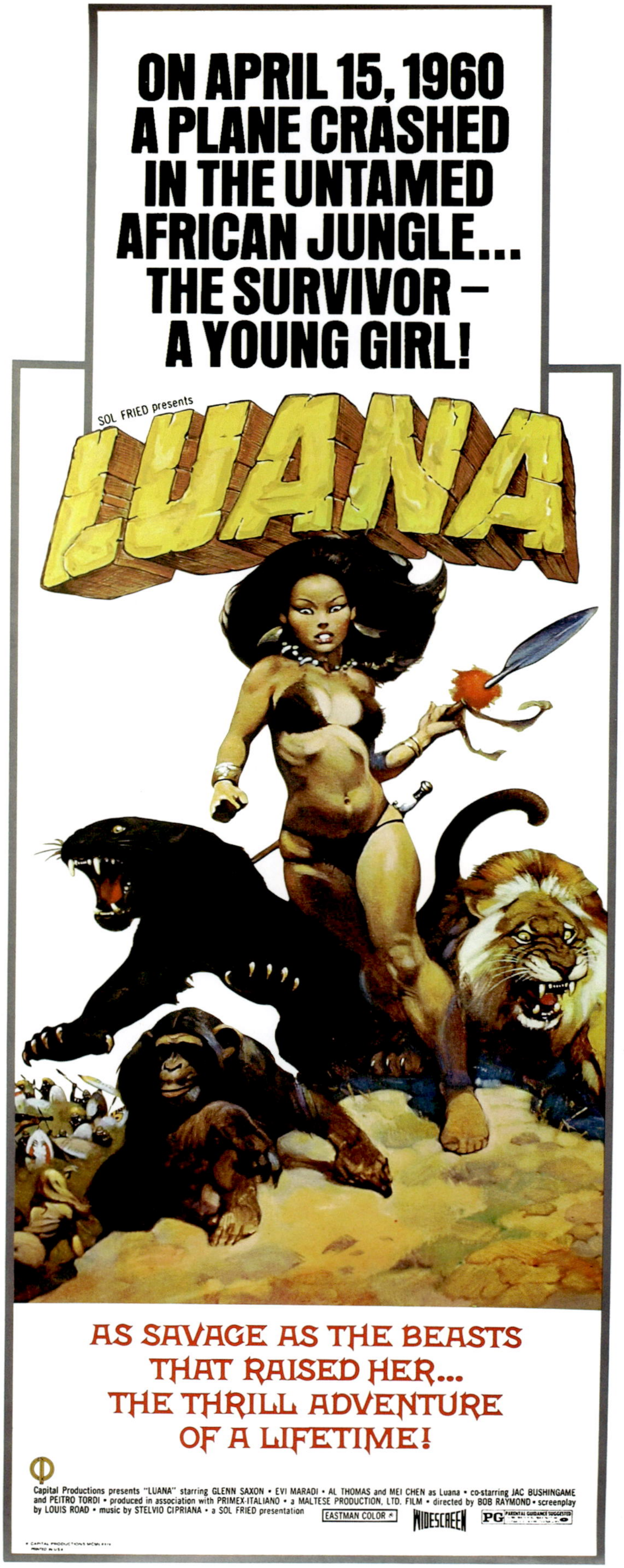

ON APRIL 15, 1960
A PLANE CRASHED
IN THE UNTAMED
AFRICAN JUNGLE...
THE SURVIVOR –
A YOUNG GIRL!

SOL FRIED presents
LUANA

AS SAVAGE AS THE BEASTS
THAT RAISED HER...
THE THRILL ADVENTURE
OF A LIFETIME!

Capital Productions presents "LUANA" starring GLENN SAXON • EVI MARADI • AL THOMAS and MEI CHEN as Luana • co-starring JAC BUSHINGAME and PEITRO TORDI • produced in association with PRIMEX-ITALIANO • a MALTESE PRODUCTION, LTD. FILM • directed by BOB RAYMOND • screenplay by LOUIS ROAD • music by STELVIO CIPRIANA • a SOL FRIED presentation

EASTMAN COLOR · WIDESCREEN · PG PARENTAL GUIDANCE SUGGESTED

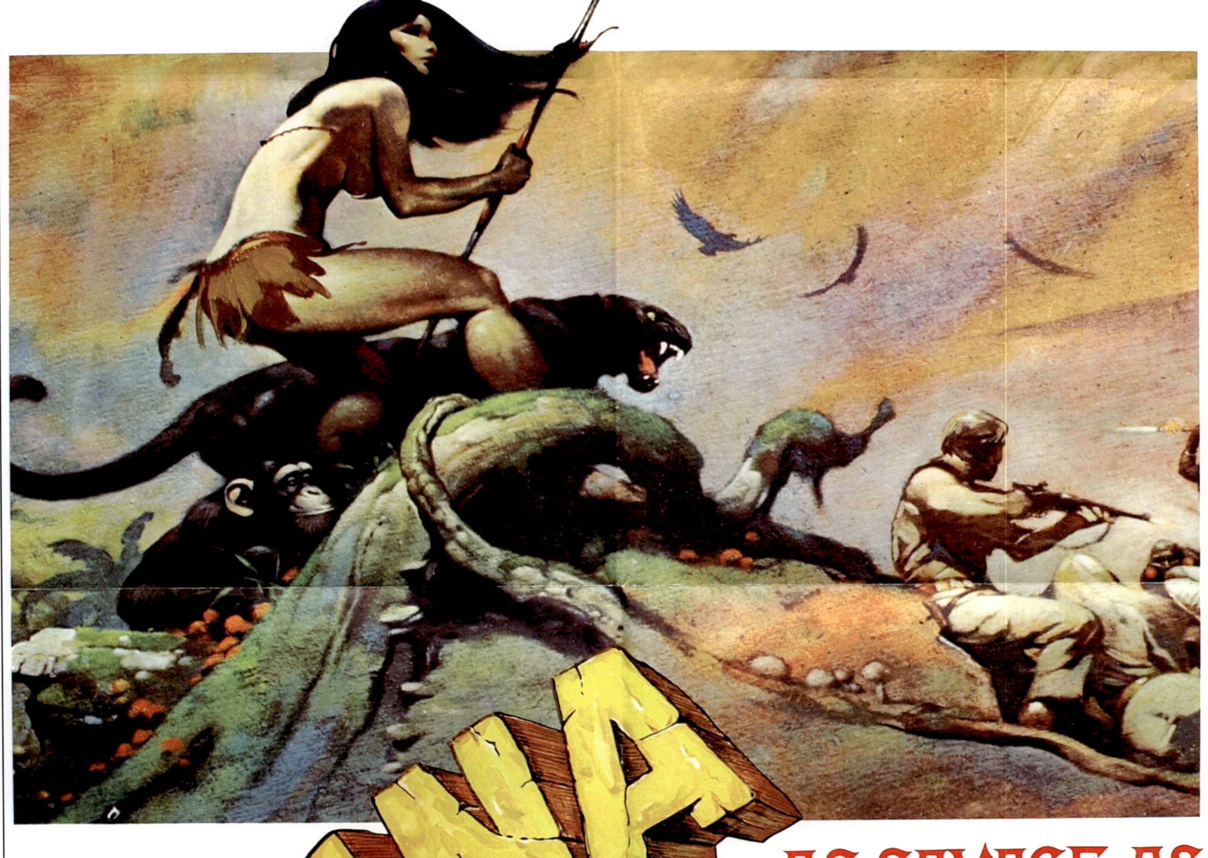
TOPS IN ACTION!
TOPS IN ADVENTURE!
TOPS IN EXCITEMENT!
SOL FRIED presents
LUANA
AS SAVAGE AS THE BEASTS THAT RAISED HER...
UNDERWATER ADVENTURE!
MAN-EATING PLANTS!
SPINE CHILLING ESCAPES!
FORBIDDEN JUNGLE TREACHERY!
ATTACK OF THE POISON DARTS!
DUEL AGAINST DEADLY SCORPIONS!
RIVER OF MADDENED CROCODILE HORDES!
Capital Productions presents "LUANA" starring GLENN SAXON • EVI MARADI • AL THOMAS and MEI CHEN as Luana • co-starring JAC BUSHINGAME and PEITRO TORDI • produced in association with PRIMEX-ITALIANO • a MALTESE PRODUCTION, LTD. FILM • directed by BOB RAYMOND • screenplay by LOUIS ROAD • music by STELVIO CIPRIANA • a SOL FRIED presentation
EASTMAN COLOR ®
WIDESCREEN
PG PARENTAL GUIDANCE SUGGESTED

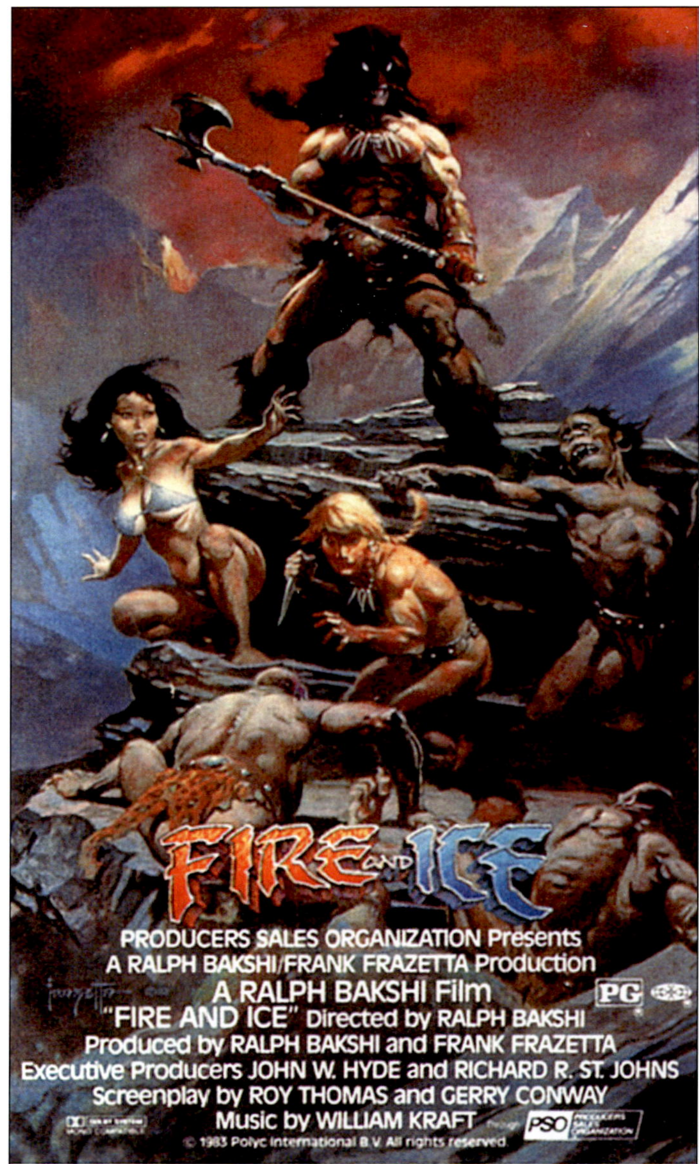

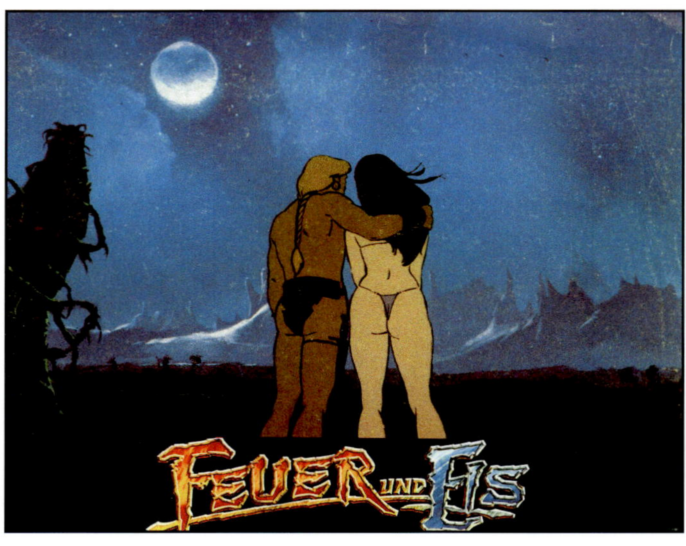

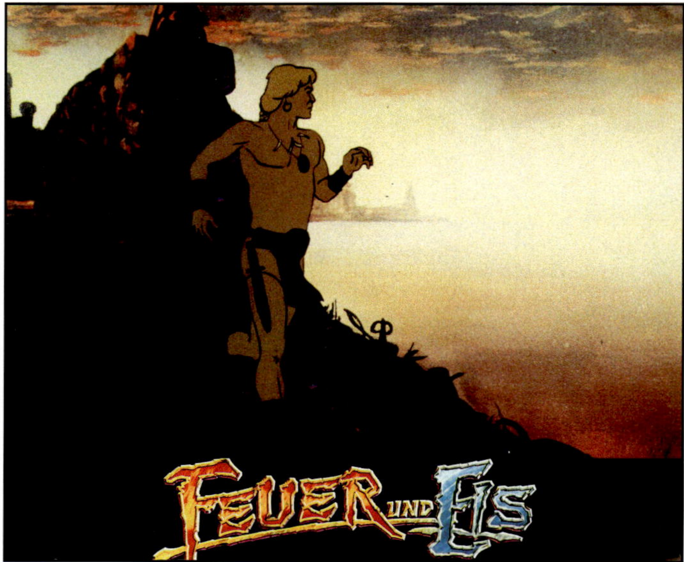

FIRE AND ICE. Ralph Bakshi's 1983 follow-up to his popular 1977 animated film Wizards. The art is based on Frazetta's paintings and co-directed by Frazetta himself. Screenplay by Roy Thomas and Gerry Conway. Some footage was also featured in the 2003 documentary film FRAZETTA: PAINTING WITH FIRE.

In the film Nekron, the evil Ice Lord uses his powers to conquer the Fire Keep, the great fortress ruled by the good King Jarol. When Jarol's beautiful daughter, Teegra, is abducted by Nekron's sub-human ape-like creatures, her only hope is a young warrior, Larn, who begins a daring search for her.

RIGHT: Lobby cards from the German release.
These were the only lobby cards ever issued for the film.

ABOVE: Theatrical one-sheet poster.

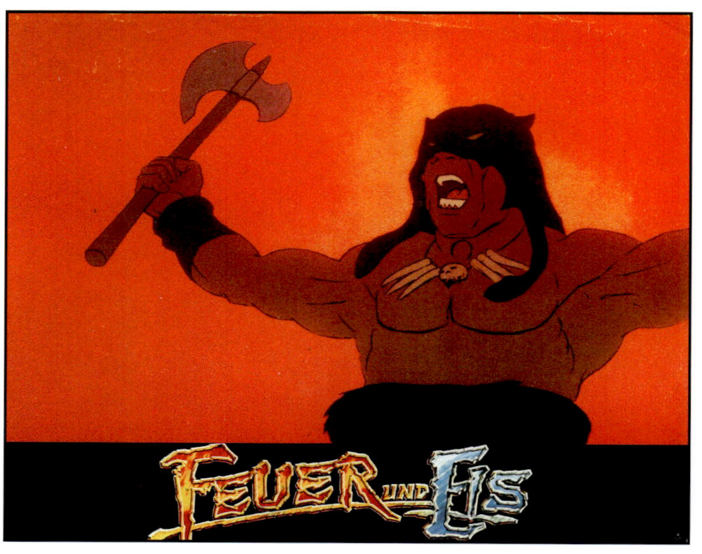

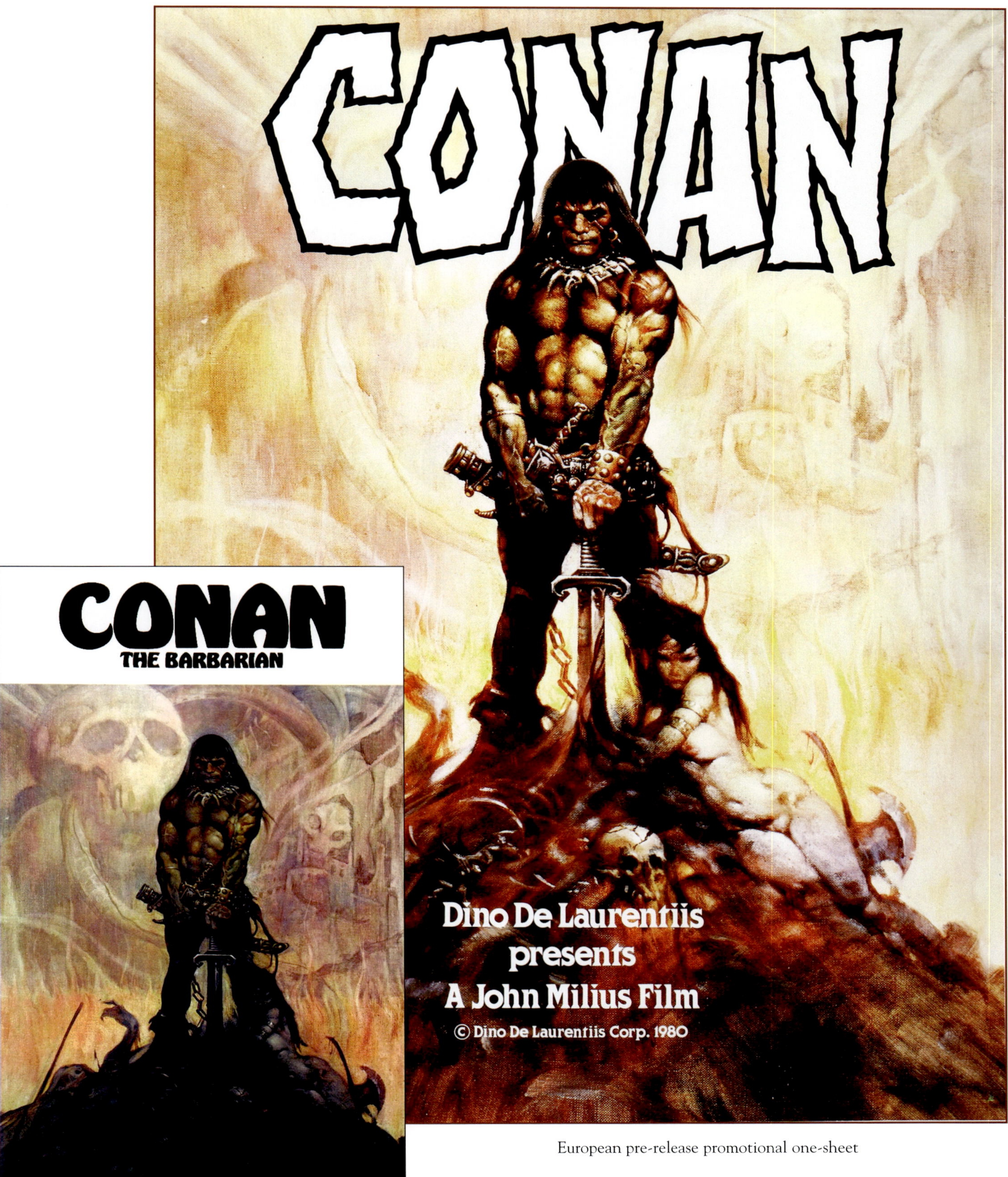

European pre-release promotional one-sheet

UK release promotional one-sheet

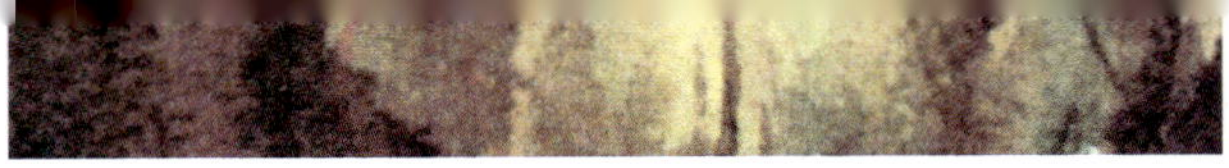

PAPERBACK DREAMS

Book Covers & Interior Illustration

BELOW: Frank at work on the cover painting for The Reign of Wizardry. *Photograph reproduced here from* The Frazetta Memory Book.

While it was his comic illustration that gave Frank Frazetta his career throughout the forties and fifties. It was his work in the sixties that helped push his career toward the realm of legend.

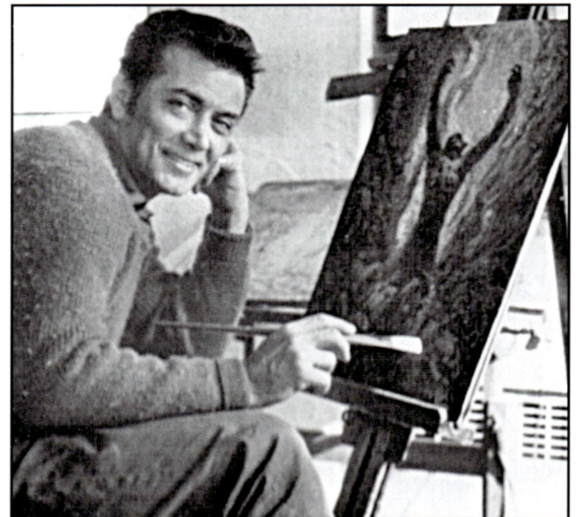

The early sixties was a time of experimentation for Frazetta. His techniques in oil and his work with brush and ink became even more exquisite. But, despite Frazetta's obvious talent, things didn't fall into place right away.

When Frazetta left Al Capp's studio in early 1961 he thought it would be no problem to land another illustration job, and so, with portfolio in hand, he went searching. But it seemed his work had become poison to any publisher he showed it to. His best stuff was rejected as being too "old style". He honestly believed he'd been blacklisted because of the way he left Capp's studio on a not-so-positive note.

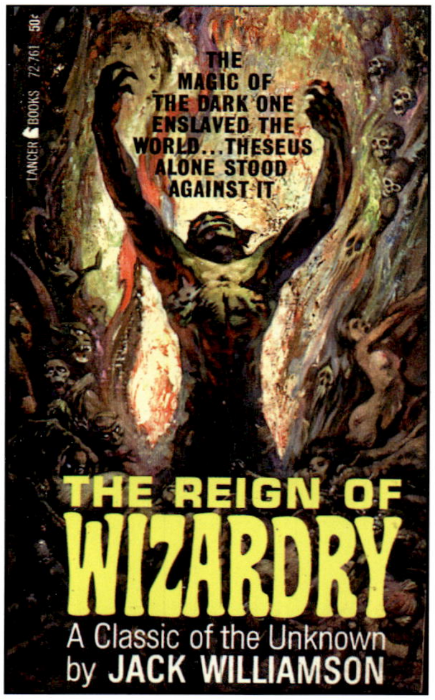

This down time in Frazetta's career can best be illustrated with the brushstrokes of his own Self Portrait (early 1962). The story goes that he painted it after yet another exhaustive day of searching for work. Look closely at the painting and you can see his frustration not only in his eyes but also in the explosive, staccato brushstrokes he used. It captures well the look of the troubled artist at the time. Ellie, Frank's wife, recalled the time. "He walked into the apartment, kissed me and went immediately into his small studio. A few hours later, the painting was finished." Ellie continued. "Look closely at that painting, look at the mouth. You can see a slight smirk of self confidence as if Frank is saying to the world I don't care what you think. I'm going to make it anyways."

Life for the Frazettas wasn't as bad as it could have been though. Frazetta wasn't completely out of work, he just wasn't able to land the jobs he really enjoyed doing. His work during 1961 consisted basically of men's magazine illustrations. Magazines such as GENT and CAVALCADE. He produced spot

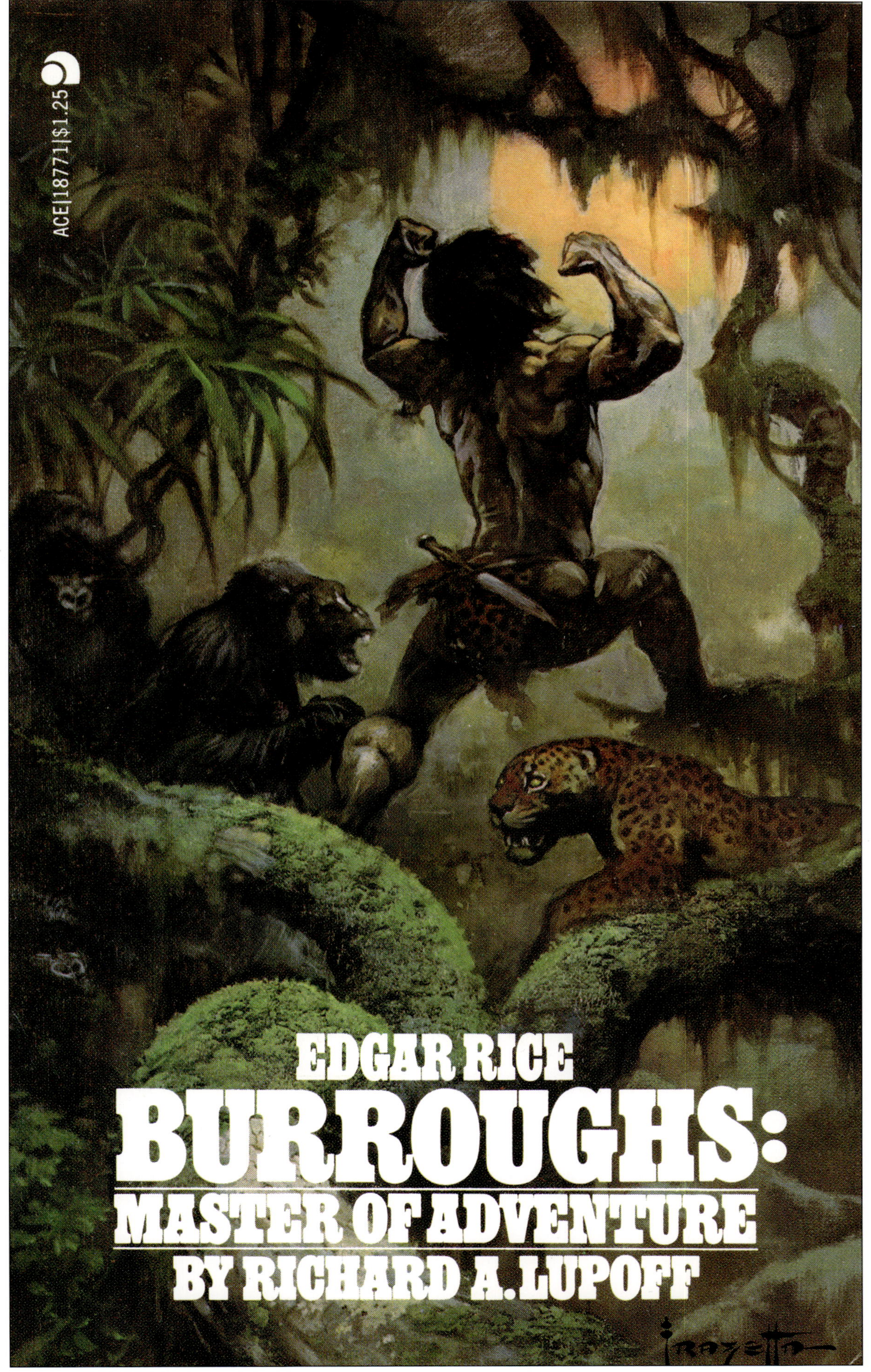
ACE|18771|$1.25
EDGAR RICE
BURROUGHS:
MASTER OF ADVENTURE
BY RICHARD A. LUPOFF
FRAZETTA

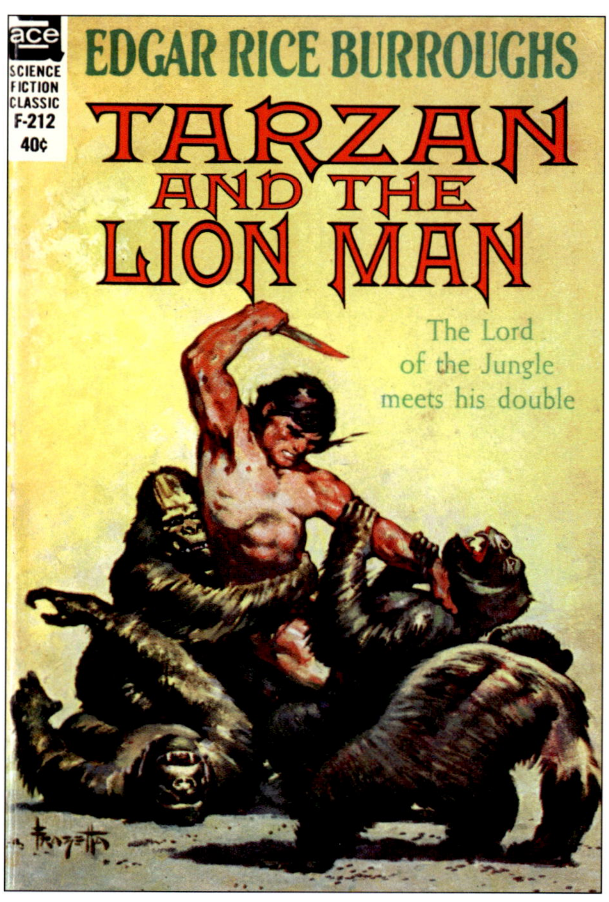

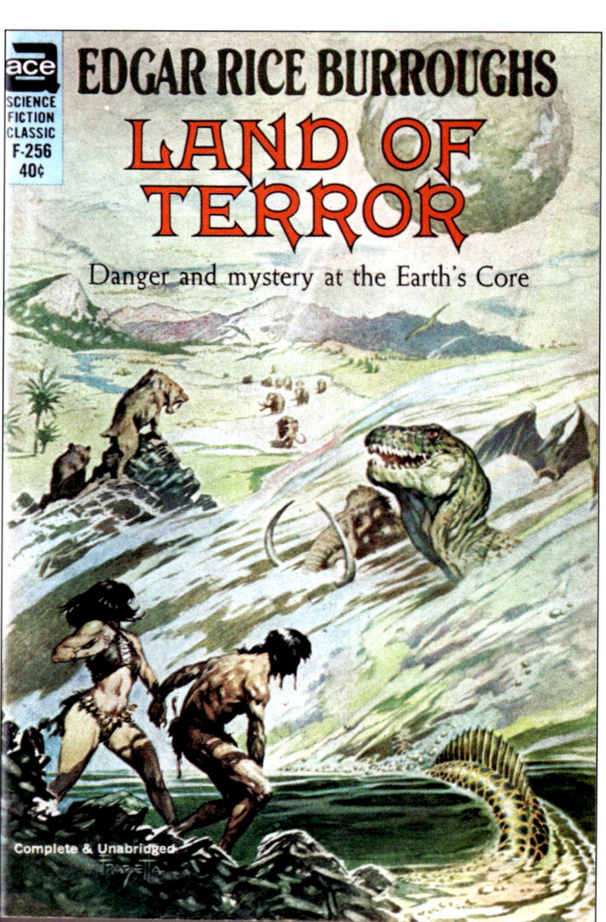

illustrations to punctuate the spicy stories and articles. These bawdy drawings led Frank to work for a company called Midwood. There he created beautiful illustrations to highlight the stories within. Books of that type were meant as throw away items back then. To find one today is very rare. On the market they can command premium prices due to their high demand and extremely low supply.

FINALLY–TARZAN!

The latter part of 1962 marked another watershed period in Frazetta's life when he was asked to provide interior illustrations for the Canaveral Press edition of TARZAN AT THE EARTH'S CORE. His illustrative style best reflected the original editions illustrated by J. Allen St. John (an icon of Frazetta's). It seemed the illustrators "old style", rejected by everyone else, was just the technique Canaveral Press was looking for. He was offered the book and Canaveral promised more work to come.

THE ACE YEARS

His good friend (and fellow Fleagle) Roy Krenkel came to Frank in late 1963 to ask for assistance. Ace books hired Krenkel to paint covers and provide interior illustrations for their entire line of Edgar Rice Burroughs books. Krenkel was quickly overwhelmed with the task and asked Frazetta to help him out. The two had been friends going way back to the fifties when they worked for E.C. Publications together. Krenkel was Frazetta's foot in the door and no sooner had Frank entered Ace Publications, he'd made himself at home.

Between the years of 1963-65 Frazetta produced twenty-five covers and twenty-two interior illustrations for Ace. Toward the end of 1965 his paperback contributions dwindled to a few pieces. However there was an explosion in other facets of his career. The most notable being his work on his first movie poster, "WHAT'S NEW PUSSYCAT?". He quickly learned that a single movie poster could pull an income equal to almost an entire year's worth of paperback work.

In 1964 Frank began his stint for Lancer Books when he produced the cover for THE SECRET PEOPLE and for Fawcett when he provided them the cover for THE REASSEMBLED MAN.

He returned to Canaveral Press in 1965 when they asked him to provide illustrations for three more Burroughs books (TARZAN AND THE CASTAWAYS, AT THE EARTH'S CORE and PELLUCIDAR.) Frank readily accepted the job. Only TARZAN AND THE CASTAWAYS saw print in its intended form. The other two book projects were shelved. Eventually, a few of the shelved illustrations appeared when Canaveral released EDGAR RICE BURROUGHS, MASTER OF ADVENTURE. What Frazetta created for those four books was a series of brush and ink drawings that, to this day, challenges anyone to outdo. His only other book contributions that year was for Ballantine when he sold them four covers. Three of those books reprinted stories from E.C. Comics.

His cover and illustrative work continued sporadically through 1966 with just a handful of contributions. He sold a couple of illustrations to House of Greystoke Publications for their books THE GIRL FROM FARRIS' and THE EFFICIENCY EXPERT. Frank also provided a single cover to Lancer for Ted White's book PHOENIX PRIME.

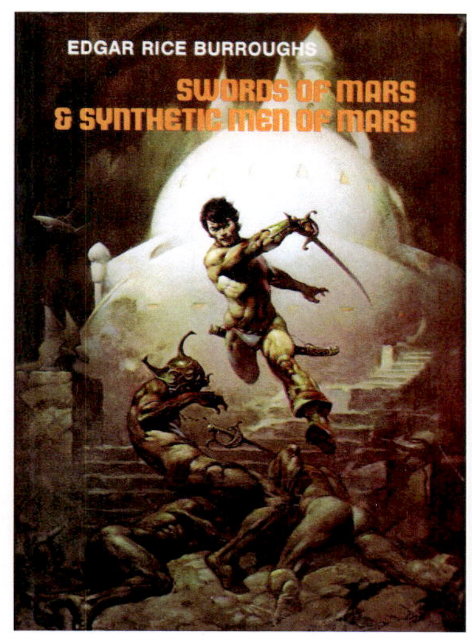

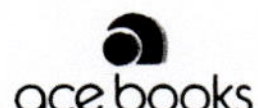

A division of Charter Communications Inc.
1120 AVENUE OF THE AMERICAS, NEW YORK 10036
· TELEPHONE (212) 867-5050 ·

OFFICE OF THE PRESIDENT

TAIL WAGS DOG

The Science Fiction readers are a world unto themselves. A Cult. An in-group. They have conventions. They have newsletters. Their own customs, their own heroes, their own styles.

And within this "world," there are "sub-worlds." The Perry Rhodan Cult is one. The Edgar Rice Burroughs Cult is another.

The Edgar Rice Burroughs Cult—huge in the United States and rapidly growing in 36 other countries—consists of hundreds of thousands of knowledgeable, involved people. They support numerous ERB newsletters, participate in ERB fan clubs, attend ERB conventions, debate ERB writings, see ERB movies, buy and sell items of all types in tremendous quantities—ERB books and posters and T-shirts and wigs and comics and coloring books and dolls and on and on.

And within this Cult, there reigns a High Priest of Art . . . FRANK FRAZETTA.

Although far and away the most famous and admired artist in the Science Fiction community at large, FRAZETTA totally dominates the Edgar Rice Burroughs Cult. His originals are treasured, priceless and essentially unavailable. His posters sell and sell and sell. And books with his covers are very different from "regular books."

Today, it has become hard—almost impossible—to commission an original FRAZETTA for a paperback cover. Money is not the only major issue—he must "feel" a sense of involvement with the publishing house.

Edgar Rice Burroughs: Master of Adventure therefore is truly an event. The entire Science Fiction world will immediately understand the significance of a **NEW FRAZETTA.** The Edgar Rice Burroughs Cult will be particularly turned-on.

Because Frazetta is FRAZETTA, Pocket Books-Ace did not receive covers in time to use for solicitation. FRAZETTA does not work by schedule. He could not complete this Work on time—and he probably did not even try. He believes it to be **his best work ever,** and took great pains to finish it with extraordinary care, and in his own good time.

In addition, but of somewhat less importance in this unique instance, **Edgar Rice Burroughs: Master Of Adventure** is acknowledged as the definitive biography of Edgar Rice Burroughs.

Also, the Ace Editorial Staff has updated the material by working unusually closely with the author and the Burroughs family.

The book has sold well and always will on its own merits. But the cover is where it's at on this edition from Ace.

The Tail Is Wagging The Dog.

A. Barry Merkin

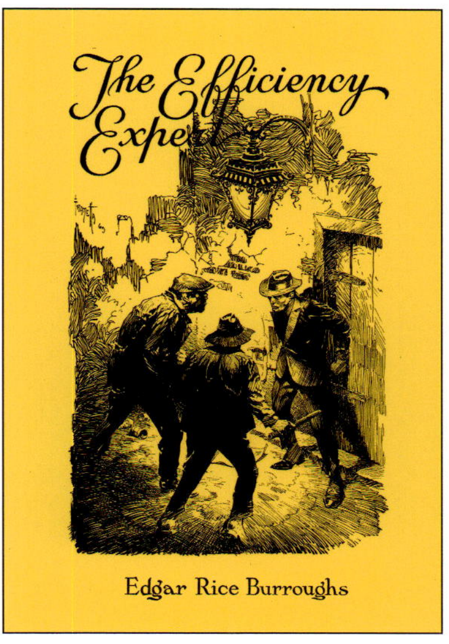

From the office of the President of Ace Books. This little gem simply titled "Tail Wags Dog" *was found on the reverse of an advertising slick for* Edgar Rice Burroughs: Master of Adventure.

For years it's been said that, in the sixties, it was Frank Frazetta's work which helped Ace Books become a number one bookseller. And here, for the first time, is PROOF of Ace's devotion and appreciation for Frazetta's numerous, outstanding contributions. Nothing more can really be said. This letter, WITHOUT A DOUBT, speaks for itself.

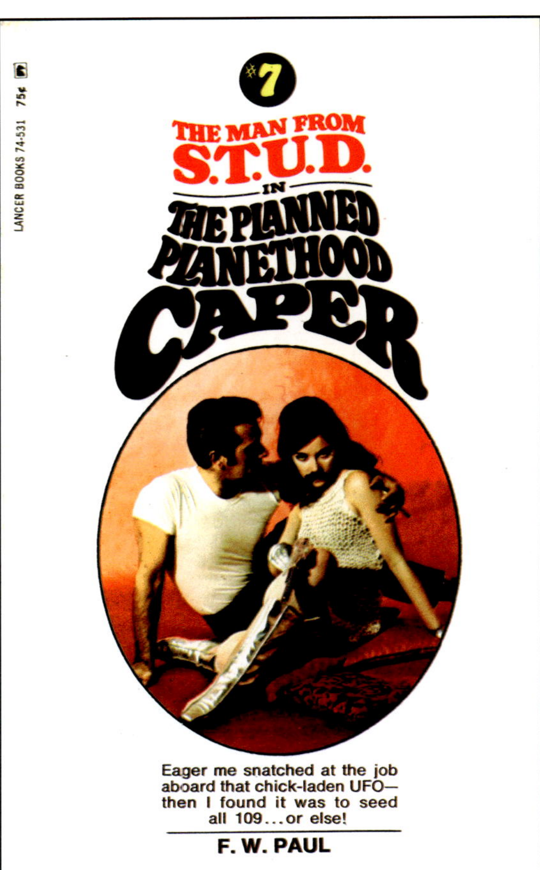

Frazetta modeled for these two rare photographic covers for The Man From S.T.U.D. *for Lancer Books in 1969.*

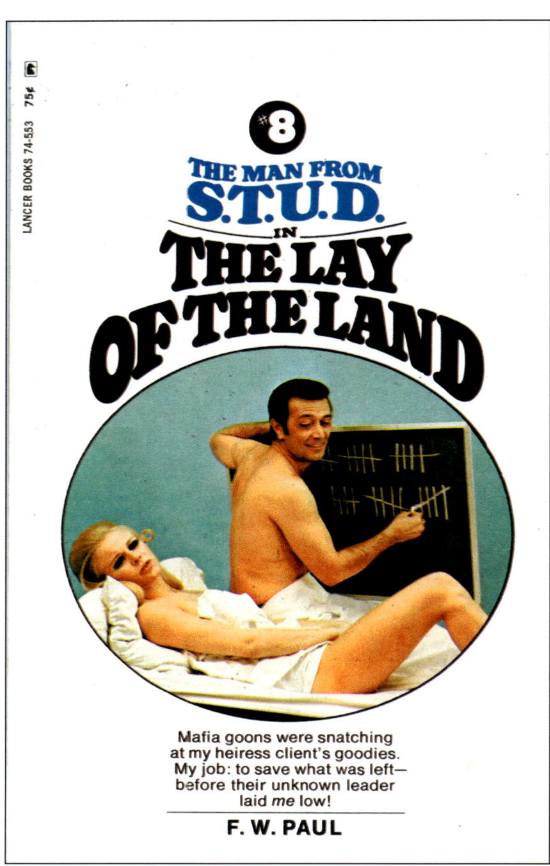

CONAN

Nineteen sixty-six through sixty-eight showed Frazetta again in full swing of paperback work when he went back to work for Lancer Books to paint covers for their CONAN series. Working with Ace this time, Frazetta produced far greater quality work than what he sold to them in the early sixties. This time around, Frazetta kept the originals as opposed. to handing them over for no extra money as he contractually was forced to do before.

Many claim it was the Frazetta covers that made those Conan books so popular. Sure, the covers caught the eye of the modern reader introducing them for the first time to the world of Howard, but the stories within those legendary volumes have been grabbing readers long before those Ace editions ever saw print. However, no one would ever argue the fact that when that series was published, giants walked the Earth. As well as his work for Ace, at the time Frazetta also worked for Lancer, Popular Library, Avon and Paperback Library.

In 1969 he finished his stint with Lancer when he sold them a painted cover for KAVIN'S WORLD and two very rare photo covers for THE MAN FROM S.T.U.D. He ended ties with Paperback Library with the cover for BRAK THE BARBARIAN VS. THE SORCERESS and began work for Dell Books with the cover for Robert E. Howard's BRAN MAK MORN.

In 1970 Doubleday looked up Frazetta about working on their line of Burroughs reprints for their book club. He sold Doubleday four covers and three illustrations that year. Frank sold Dell another cover (ETERNAL CHAMPION) and provided Popular Library four more covers. He also worked for Pinnacle Books when he painted the cover for THE GODMAKERS. The painting for that book is truly bizarre. Look closely and you see a mass orgy of intertwining arms and legs culminating toward a single female found at the tip of the human knot.

SLOWING DOWN

The years 1971-72 showed very little paperback work. He sold four covers and a handful of interiors to Doubleday Books and also began work on the Doubleday Book Club promo material. He did a cover for the Fawcett publication, CHILD OF THE SUN and another cover for Pinnacle's TO CATCH A CROOKED GIRL, another very difficult paperback to find.

His cover work continued well into the seventies when Ace again re-enlisted Frank to paint covers for yet another reissue series of the Burroughs novels. He also provided a few more paintings for Dell Books. A couple of these paintings (Death Dealer for FLASHING SWORDS #2 and Silver Warrior for SILVER WARRIORS) stand as two of the most popular paintings to come from the artist's brush. Frazetta then moved on to Warner Books to provide them seven covers. One of which (Dark Kingdom for DARK CRUSADE) was later turned into

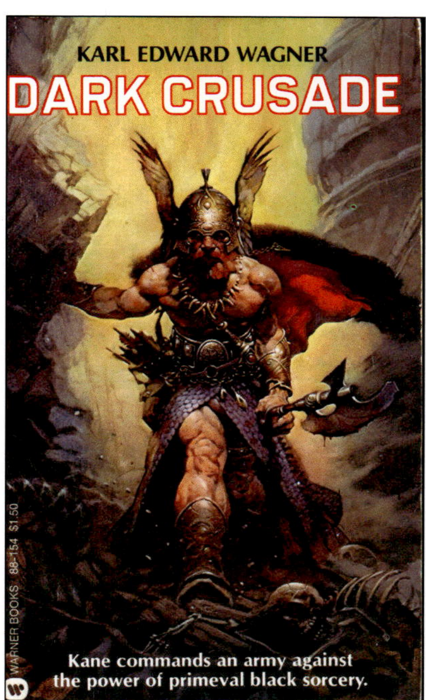

an album cover for the band Molly Hatchet.

It was around 1975 when he started slowing down the output of his paperback work. He was now established as one of the most talented artists in the history of heroic fantasy. After twelve years of working for publishing houses, During the sixties and early seventies, Frank Frazetta provided covers and illustrations for well over one hundred-fifty different books. Add to this the fact he was also doing movie posters and magazine covers and you might agree it was time to relax a bit and perhaps reap some well-deserved benefits.

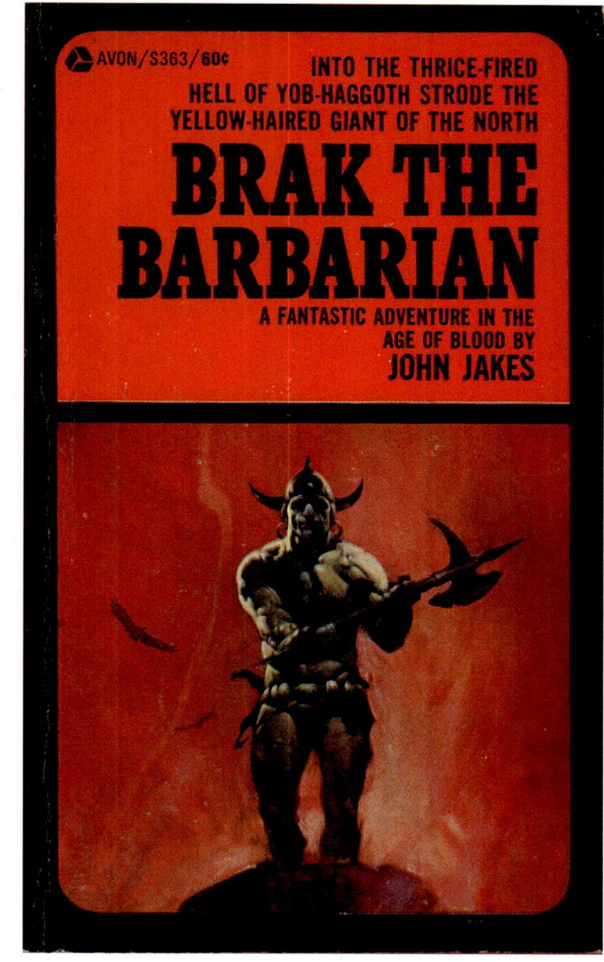

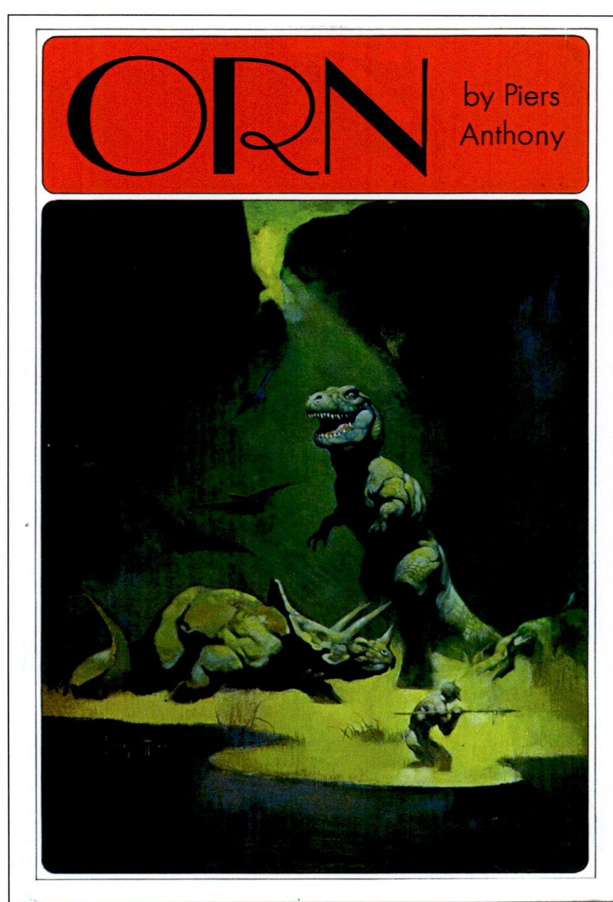

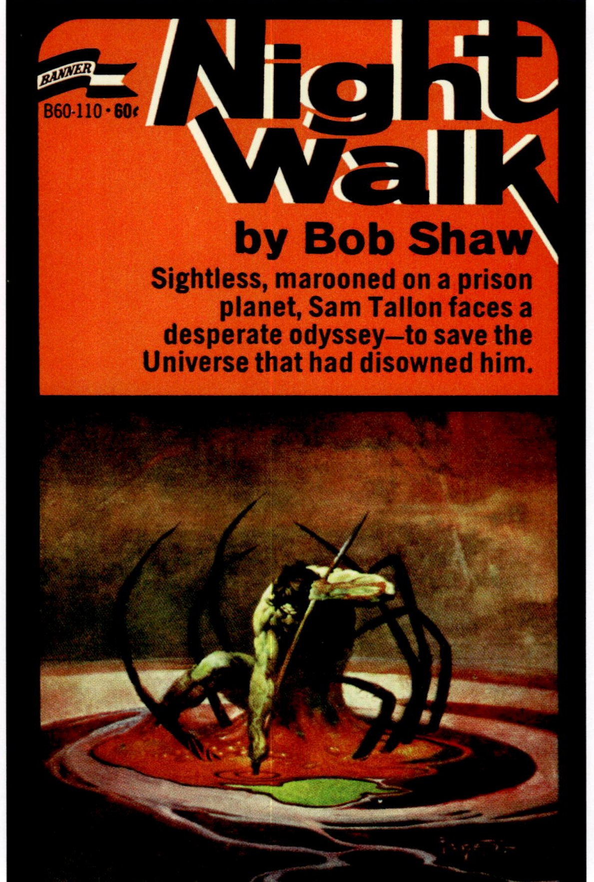

HARDCOVERS

ACE BOOKS
• EDGAR RICE BURROUGHS: MASTER OF ADVENTURE
by Richard A. Lupoff
1968
Expanded from the Canaveral Press Edition
interior illustrations include:
"David Innes, hyaenodons, and man-apes of Pellucidar"
"David Innes, Jubal the Ugly One, Dian the beautiful"
"A Mahar casts its sinister spell"
"Jacket design for a proposed edition of Pellucidar"
"David Innes faces a labrithodon in Pellucidar"
"David Innes, a hydrophidian, Ja the Mezop"

BRIDGE PUBLICATIONS
• FINAL BLACKOUT
by L. Ron Hubbard
1992
COVER - **The Lieutenant**

CANAVERAL PRESS
TARZAN AT THE EARTH'S CORE
by Edgar Rice Burroughs
1962
• First Printing - 236 pages, beige cloth, black lettering, early dust jacket without printed prices on front flap and rear panel

• Second Printing - 301pages, dark red cloth, gilt lettering, later dust jacket with printed prices on front flap and rear panel

Most interior illustrations have no page numbers. Therefore, they are shown here with an "a" to designate the corresponding page.

dust jacket	*"He caught them upon his tusks and tossed them high into the air."*
front end-paper	sabretooth tiger illustration (2 pp.)
title page	*"Tarzan swung the body over his head."*
pg. 53a	*"He caught them upon his tusks and tossed them high into the air."*
pg. 102a	Jana illustration reprinted in Frazetta #29 pg. 22
pg. 141	pterodactyl illustration (1/2 pg.)
pg. 150a	*"He struck suddenly upward with his blade."*
pg. 158a	*"The bear whirled about on the narrow ledge"*
pg. 216	lizard man riding on iguana creature (spot illo.)
pg. 272a	*"Tarzan swung the body over his head."*
back end-paper	monkey in a tree holding club (2 pp.)

EDGAR RICE BURROUGHS: MASTER OF ADVENTURE
by Richard A. Lupoff
1965
• standard edition

• signed and numbered limited edition (limited to 150 copies, signed by Lupoff)

Most interior illustrations have no page numbers. Therefore, they are shown here with an "a" to designate the corresponding page.

pg. 44a	*"David Innes, hyaenodons, and man-apes of Pellucidar"*
pg. 168a	*"David Innes, Jubal the Ugly One, Dian the beautiful"*
pg. 190a	*"A Mahar casts its sinister spell"*
pg. 212a	*"Jacket design for a proposed edition of Pellucidar"*
pg. 242a	*"David Innes faces a labrithodon in Pellucidar"*
pg. 256a	*"David Innes, a hydrophidian, Ja the Mezop"*

• TARZAN AND THE CASTAWAYS by Edgar Rice Burroughs
1965

Most interior illustrations have no page numbers. Therefore, they are shown here with an "a" to designate the corresponding page.

dust jacket	*"Itzl Cha saw in one terrifying glance that the god who bore her was flying through the air."*
frontis	reproduces dust jacket illustration
pg. 44a	*"He had me captured by an African Chief."*
pg. 82a	*"Tarzan took in the picture at a glance."*
pg. 86a	*"A great tiger emerged from the underbrush."*
pg. 158a	*"The ape-man dealt him a terrific blow on the side of the head with his open palm."*
pg. 196a	*"Tarzan in perfect calm, Raised his short, heavy spear above his right shoulder and waited."*

• TARZAN AND THE CASTAWAYS **promotional brochure**
"The silent creature drove a long knife again and again into his tawny side." (brochure illustration to advertise book)

DOUBLEDAY BOOK CLUB
• A PRINCESS OF MARS by Edgar Rice Burroughs
1970 dust jacket **A Princess of Mars**
frontis *"Nor could any apparel have enhanced the beauty of her figure!"*
pg. 55 *"Scarcely had his hideous laugh rung out when I was upon him..."*
pg. 156 *"Tal Hajus knows that you are here, and intends to see you tortured..."*

• DANCER FROM ATLANTIS by Poul Anderson
1971 dust jacket **Dancer From Atlantis**

• DOWNWARD TO THE EARTH by Robert Silverberg
1970 dust jacket **Downward To Earth**
frontispiece

• DRACULA - FRANKENSTEIN by Bram Stoker / Mary Shelly
1973 wrap-around dust jacket **Frankenstein - Dracula**

• FLASHING SWORDS #1 edited by Lin Carter
1973 dust jacket **The Norseman**

FLASHING SWORDS #2 edited by Lin Carter
1973 dust jacket
Three cover variations exist. They are:
- **Tree of Death**
- **Death Dealer**
- **Warrior With Ball and Chain**

• THE GODS OF MARS and THE WARLORD OF MARS
by Edgar Rice Burroughs
1971
wrap-around dust jacket **John Carter and the Savage Apes of Mars**
Also contains the following interior illustrations:

frontis	*"The great apes, towering in all their fifteen feet of height, had gone down before my sword."*
pg. 26	*"It launched its great bulk toward me, and met cold steel instead of the tender flesh its cruel jaws gaped so widely to engulf."*
pg. 96	*"I sprang into the arena, my long sword whirring through the air..."*
pg. 196	*"Her right hand went high with the gleaming blade and her sharp point pierced the vile heart of the great villain."*

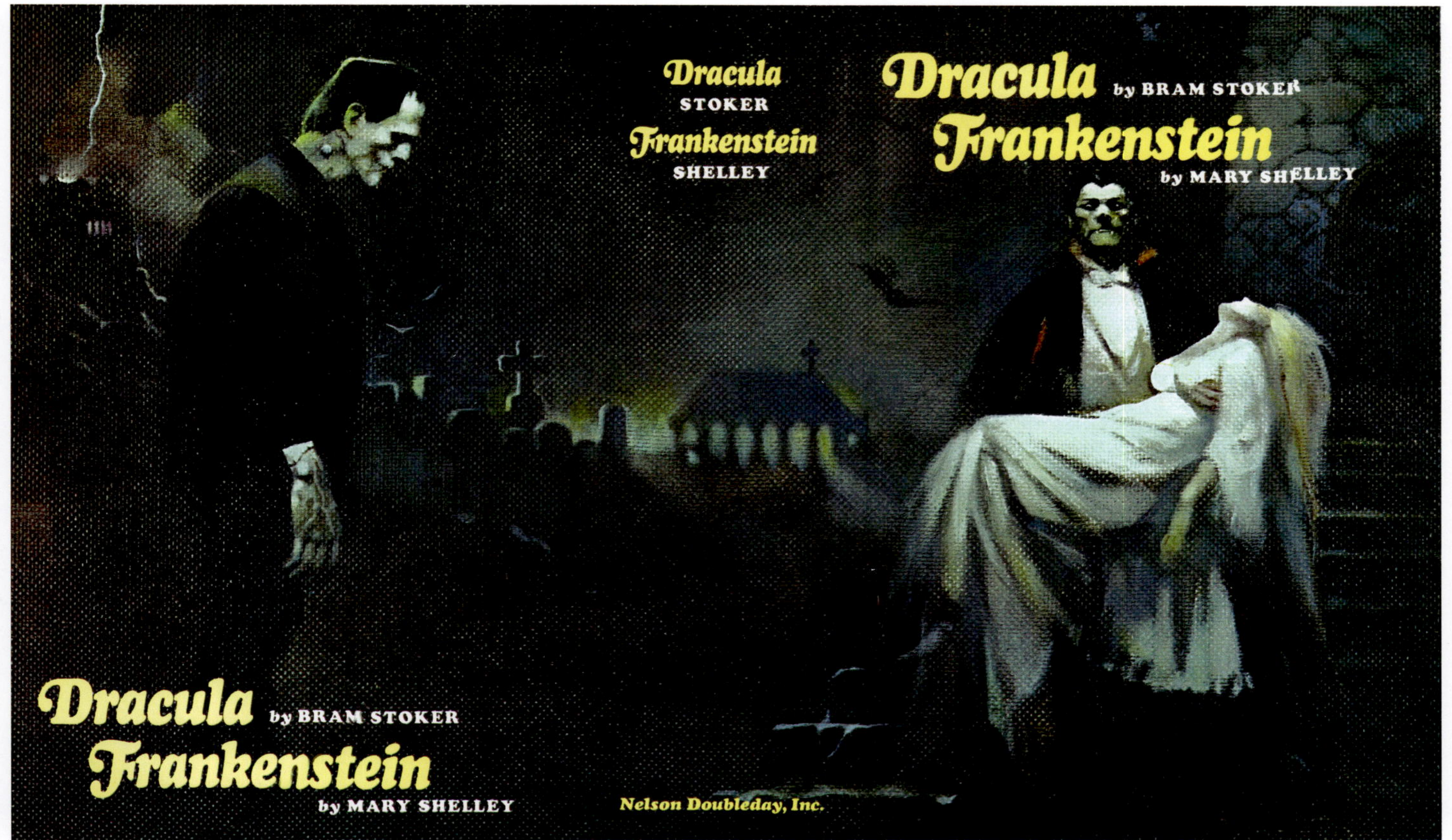

Dust jacket for Dracula-Frankenstein *Doubleday (1973)*

pg. 230 *"She called the fierce banths about her and led them as a shepherdess might lead her flock of meek and harmless sheep."*
pg. 292 *"A dozen of them felt the weight of my clenched fists, and then I went down, fighting, beneath a half-hundred warriors..."*

• THE MASTERMIND OF MARS and A FIGHTING MAN OF MARS by Edgar Rice Burroughs
1973 dust jacket **A Fighting Man of Mars**
Also contains the following interior illustrations:
frontis *"An attendant appeared bearing the body of the beautiful girl."*
pg. 12 *"So often did I stumble and fall sprawling."*
pg. 110 *"She raised her slim blade above the heart of Dar Tarus."*
pg. 138 *"With wide distended jaws, came the great white lizard."*
pg. 316 *"Behind us came the hunting men of U-Gor."*
pg. 340 *"Everywhere upon the stone flagging were heaps and mounds of human bones."*

• 1972 ANNUAL WORLD'S BEST SCIENCE FICTION
edited by Donald Wollheim
1972 dust jacket **New World**

• ORN by Piers Anthony
1970 dust jacket **Tyrannosaurus Rex**

• RED MOON AND BLACK MOUNTAIN by Joy Chant
1970 wrap-around dust jacket **Red Moon and Black Mountain**

• SWORDS OF MARS and SYNTHETIC MEN OF MARS
by Edgar Rice Burroughs
1970
dust jacket **Swords of Mars**
frontis *"...cleaving his skull as I raced past him!"*
pg. 42 *"I ran my sword through his heart from behind."*
pg. 139 *"Her veiled eyes seemed to read my very soul."*
pg. 192 *"...one of them carried a a woman in front of him on the neck of the great bird..."*
pg. 236 *"I threw him as high as I could."*
pg. 279 *"Janai saw the body of Var Daj lying on the cold ersite slab..."*

• THUVIA, MAID OF MARS and CHESSMEN OF MARS by Burroughs
1972 wrap-around dust jacket **Thuvia, Maid of Mars**
Also contains the following interior illustrations:
frontis *"With a savage cry of triumph, Thar Ban vaulted to the back of his throat, Thuvia of Ptarth still in his arms."*
pg. 72 *"Carthoris stepped between Thuvia and the banth, his sword ready to contest the beast's victory over them."*
pg. 90 *"Thewed like some giant god was Carthoris of Helium, yet in the clutches of these creatures he was helpless as a frail woman."*
pg. 126 *"As Gahan entered his square, Udor leaped toward him with drawn sword."*
pg. 187 *"To Tara's horror, the headless body moved, took the hideous head in its hands and set it on its shoulders."*
pg. 238 *"Twice Turan struck the Martian rat away, but both times it returned with increased ferocity to renew the attack.."*

DOUBLEDAY BOOK CLUB MEMBERSHIP PROMOTIONALS
see PROMOTIONAL COLLECTIBLES

DOUBLEDAY & COMPANY
• THE NEW VISIONS
with introduction by Fred Pohl
1982
pg. 2Frazetta biography (2pp.) contains the following:
rare self portrait (pen and ink)
Swords of Mars

MIRAGE
• CONAN SWORDBOOK, THE by L. Sprague DeCamp
1969
pg. 171sketch
pg. 172sketch

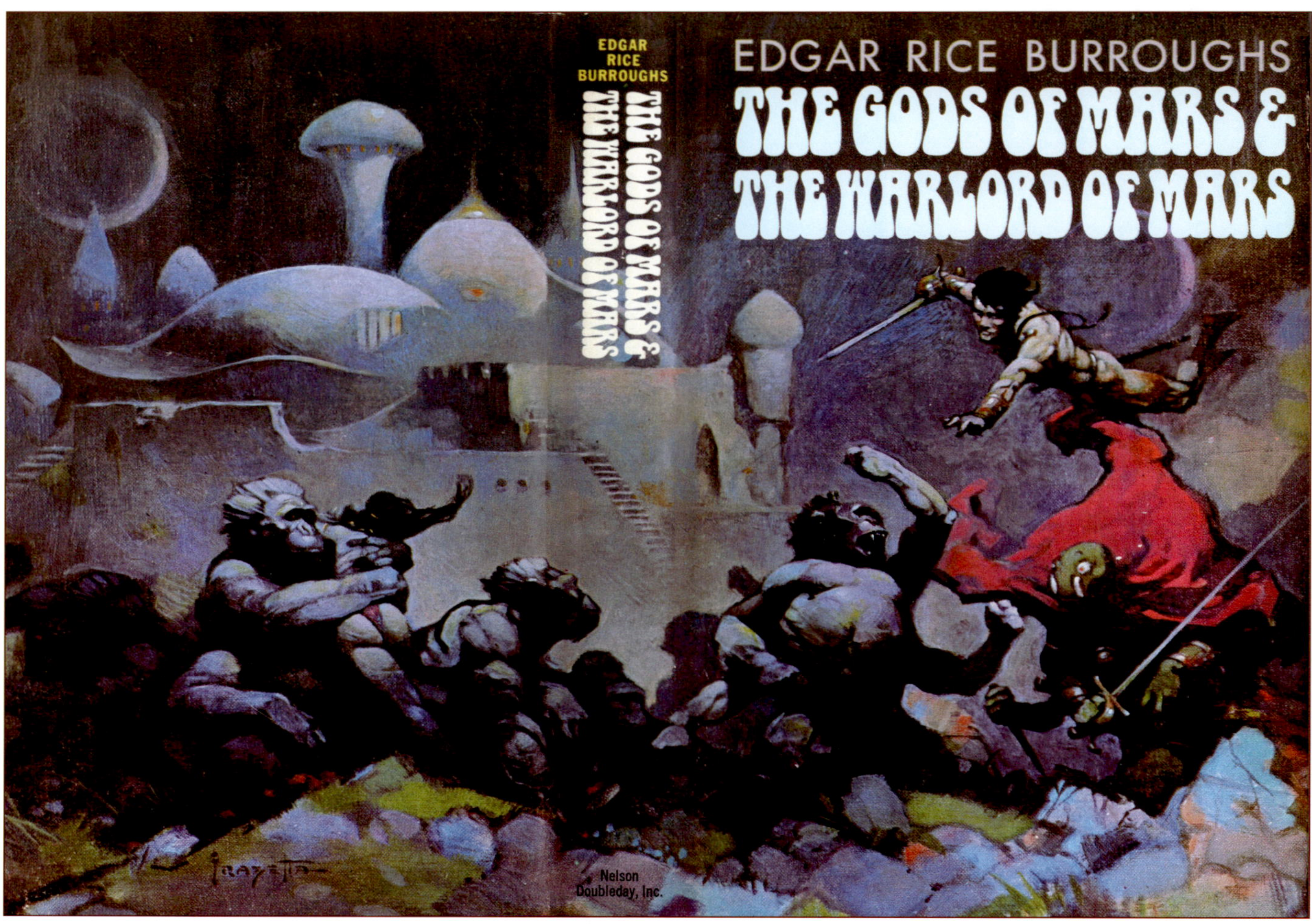

MORNINGSTAR PRESS

- NIGHT IMAGES

by Robert E. Howard (Limited Edition of 1000 copies)
1976
dust jacket **Thor's Flight**
COVER **Thor's Flight**

- Limited edition copy (first 250 copies)
  Both the slipcase and cover have silver embossed relief of **Thor's Flight**
  color, tipped in plate - watercolor Winged Nymph (never reproduced elsewhere)

RUSS COCHRAN PUBLICATIONS

- EDGAR RICE BURROUGHS - LIBRARY OF ILLUSTRATIONS Vol. 3

cover **Tarzan and the Jewels of Opar**
pg. 183 article - interview and photos 16 pp.
Reproduces the following Frazetta art:
pg. 201 **Self Portrait**
ACE BOOKS - covers and frontispiece illustrations
pg. 202 cover (**The Lost Empire**)
frontis for TARZAN AND THE LOST EMPIRE
pg. 204 cover (**Tarzan at the Earth's Core**)
frontis for TARZAN AT THE EARTH'S CORE
pg. 206 cover (**The Monster Men**)
frontis for THE MONSTER MEN
pg. 208 **Tarzan the Invincible** (color preliminary)
Tarzan the Invincible (finished version)
pg. 210 cover for TARZAN AND THE JEWELS OF OPAR
pg. 212 cover (**The Son of Tarzan**)
frontis for THE SON OF TARZAN
pg. 214 cover (**Jungle Tales of Tarzan**)
frontis for JUNGLE TALES OF TARZAN
pg. 216 cover (**Tarzan and the Lion Man**)
frontis for TARZAN AND THE LION MAN
pg. 218 cover (**Tarzan and the City of Gold**)
frontis for TARZAN AND THE CITY OF GOLD
pg. 220 cover (**Beasts of Venus**)
frontis for LOST ON VENUS
pg. 222 cover (**Lost Continent**)
frontis for THE LOST CONTINENT
pg. 224 cover (**Land of Terror**)
frontis for OUT OF TIME'S ABYSS
pg. 226 cover (**The Huntress**)
frontis for SAVAGE PELLUCIDAR
pg. 228 cover (**Beyond the Farthest Star**)
frontis for BEYOND THE FARTHEST STAR
pg. 230 alternate, unused frontis for Son of Tarzan
pg. 231 cover to TARZAN AT THE EARTH'S CORE
AKA - *"He caught them upon his tusks and tossed them high into the air."*
pg. 233 front, end paper illustration
pg. 234 interior illustration
pg. 235 interior Illustration
TARZAN AND THE CASTAWAYS
pg. 237 cover to TARZAN AND THE CASTAWAYS
AKA - *"Itzl Cha saw in one terrifying glance that the god who bore her was flying through the air."*
pg. 239 interior illustration
pg. 241 illustration from BURROUGHS PORTFOLIO plate 17.
(Never appeared in TARZAN AND THE CASTAWAYS.)
pg. 243 interior illustration
Miscellaneous
pg. 245 cover art to THE EFFICIENCY EXPERT
pg. 247 interior illustration
AKA - *"The silent creature drove a long knife again and again into his tawny hide."*

WANDERING STAR
THE ULTIMATE TRIUMPH by Robert E. Howard
2000
This book contains text by Howard and has over 120 previously unpublished illustrations by Frazetta

- Classic Edition - has 125 illustrations
- Collector's Edition - featuring all black and white illustrations found in the Classic edition, plus four previously unpublished color watercolor plates, gilt-edged paper, a golden foil stamped cover, durable stitch binding, an embossed slipcase cover, and a numbered bookmark. Each book is individually numbered and limited to 1,500 copies.
- Ultra Deluxe Edition - This ultra deluxe edition is complete with all the features of the Collector's Edition, plus one additional unpublished color plate, a beautiful fine leather binding tooled to look like snakeskin with matching slipcase. Each book is individually numbered and only 100 copies were printed.
- Limited Signed/Numbered Edition of 125
  Special Sleeve Cover

ACE BOOKS "F" series

- F-203 BEASTS OF TARZAN by Burroughs
  1963 COVER **Beasts of Tarzan**
  title page illustration
- F-282 BEYOND THE FARTHEST STAR by Burroughs
  1964 COVER **Beyond the Farthest Star** (1st version)
  title page illustration
- F-247 CARSON OF VENUS by Burroughs
  1963 COVER **Carson of Venus**
  title page illustration
- F-296 GULLIVER OF MARS by Edwin L. Arnold
  1964 COVER **Gulliver of Mars**
  title page illustration
- F-354 HUNTER OUT OF TIME, THE by Otis Adelbert Kline
  1964 title page illustration (sketch of Carson of Venus)
- F-206 JUNGLE TALES OF TARZAN by Burroughs
  1963 COVER **Jungle Tales of Tarzan**
  title page illustration
- F-256 LAND OF TERROR by Burroughs
  1964 COVER **Land of Terror** (2nd version)
  title page illustration
- F-235 LOST CONTINENT, THE (Beyond Thirty) by Burroughs
  1963 COVER **The Lost Continent**
  title page illustration
- F-221 LOST ON VENUS by Burroughs
  1963 COVER **Beasts of Venus**
  title page illustration
  back cover illustration
- F-270 MAD KING, THE by Burroughs
  1964 COVER **The Mad King** (1st version)
  title page illustration
- F-321 MAZA OF THE MOON by Otis Adelbert Kline
  1965 COVER **Maza of the Moon**
  title page illustration
- F-182 MONSTER MEN, THE by Burroughs
  1963 COVER **The Monster Men**
  title page illustration
- F-280 SAVAGE PELLUCIDAR by Burroughs
  1964 COVER **The Huntress**
  title page illustration
- F-193 SON OF TARZAN, THE by Burroughs
  1963 COVER **The Son of Tarzan**
  title page illustration
- F-311 SWORDSMEN IN THE SKY
  edited by Donald A. Wollheim
  1964 COVER **Swordsmen in the Sky**

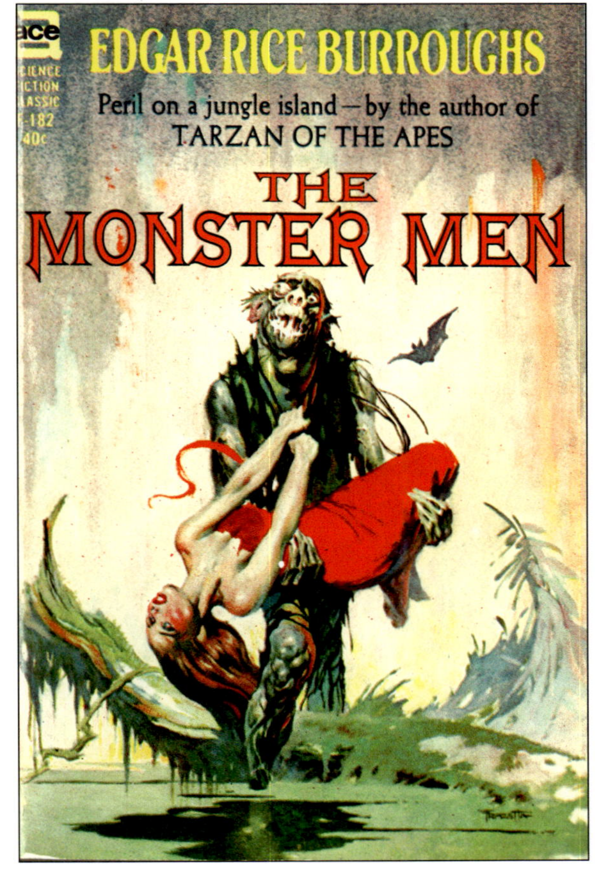

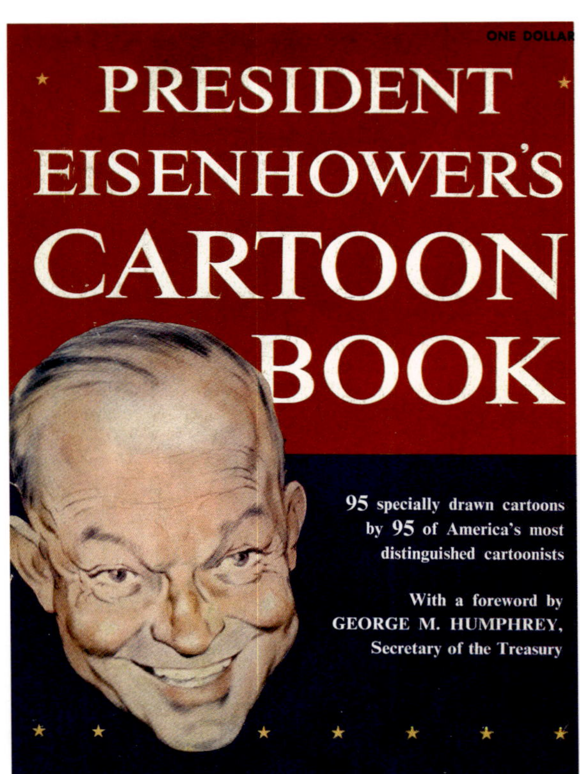

"In 1968 I discovered the paperback edition of Richard Lupoff's EDGAR RICE BURROUGHS: MASTER OF ADVENTURE, and within that volume the inked illustrations of Al Williamson, Reed Crandall - and Frank Frazetta. My life thereafter was turned to a new course, one that would open the world of classic illustration to me. As I had at the time no idea how bad reproduction deteriorates line work, it wasn't till years later that I learned what I initially took to be scratchy pen lines in Frazetta's Pellucidar plates were actually lush, gradated brush strokes! I doubt that any illustrator has mastered the vigorous use of the ink brush as completely as has Frazetta, his marks here muscular and slashing, there spidery and delicate, always singing with vitality. His confidence and spontaneity amaze and befuddle me, even as his rigorous technique inspires me. How does he manage to do it all? Studying the products of his enormous talents has helped lead me to many other classic illustrators, and has certainly informed my own limited skills."

Mark Schultz

Mark is the creator, artist and writer of Xenozoic Tales. *His fine art and dynamic writing style can be seen in two Dark Horse mini-series:* Aliens: Apocalypse Destroying Angels *and* Sub-Human. *Mr. Schultz has also written for D.C.'s* Superman, The Man of Steel.

- F-205 TARZAN AND THE CITY OF GOLD by Burroughs
  1963 COVER **Tarzan and the City of Gold**
  title page illustration
- F-204 TARZAN AND THE JEWELS OF OPAR by Burroughs
  1963 COVER **Tarzan and the Jewels of Opar**
  title page illustration
- F-212 TARZAN AND THE LION MAN by Burroughs
  1963 COVER **Tarzan and the Lion Man**
  title page illustration
- F-169 TARZAN AND THE LOST EMPIRE by Burroughs
  1962 COVER **Lost Empire**
  title page illustration
- F-180 TARZAN AT THE EARTH'S CORE by Burroughs
  1963 COVER **Tarzan at the Earth's Core**
  title page illustration
- F-189 TARZAN THE INVINCIBLE by Burroughs
  1963 COVER **Tarzan the Invincible**
  title page illustration
- F-194 TARZAN THE TRIUMPHANT by Burroughs
  1963 COVER by Roy Krenkel (Frazetta assists)
  title page illustration
- F-307 WARRIOR OF LLARN Gardner Fox
  1964COVER **Warrior of Llarn**
  title page illustration

ACE BOOKS - NUMBERED SERIES

- 03322 AT THE EARTH'S CORE by Burroughs
  1972 COVER **At The Earth's Core**
- 04635 BACK TO THE STONE AGE by Burroughs
  1973 COVER **The Mammoth**
- 0565-3 BEYOND THE FARTHEST STAR by Burroughs
  1973 COVER **Beyond the Farthest Star**
  (AKA: **God From the Sky**)
- 09203 CARSON OF VENUS by Edgar Rice Burroughs
  1973 COVER **Carson of Venus** (2nd version)
- 09282 CAVE GIRL, THE by Edgar Rice Burroughs
  1964COVER **The Huntress**

CONAN
by Robert E. Howard, De Camp and Carter
COVER **Man-Ape**
- 11671-X white border 1967
- 11577-2 black spine (#1) 1983

CONAN THE ADVENTURER
by Robert E. Howard and De Camp
COVER **The Barbarian**
- 11675-2 white border 1966
- 11598-5 black spine 1983

CONAN THE AVENGER
by Robert E. Howard, Bjorn Nyberg and De Camp
COVER **Sacrifice** (1st version)
- 11680-9 white border 1968
- 11608-6 black spine 1983

CONAN THE BUCCANEER
by De Camp and Carter
COVER **The Destroyer** (2nd version)
- 11676-0 white border 1971
- 11599-3 black spine 1983

CONAN THE CONQUEROR
by Robert E. Howard and De Camp
COVER **The Berserker**
- 11679- white border 1968
- 11466-0 black spine 1984

CONAN THE USURPER
by Robert E. Howard and De Camp
COVER **Chained**
- 11678- white border 1967
- 11459-8 black spine 1984

CONAN THE WARRIOR
by Robert E. Howard
COVER **Indomitable**

- 11677-9 white border 1967
- 11465-2 black spine 1984

CONAN OF CIMMERIA
by Robert E. Howard, De Camp and Carter
COVER **Snow Giants**

- 11672-8 white border 1967
- 11595-0 black spine 1983

EDGAR RICE BURROUGHS: MASTER OF ADVENTURE
by Richard A. Lupoff

- 1406/N-6 1968
  COVER **Beasts of Tarzan** (first printed in Ace F-203)
- 18771 1974
  COVER **Edgar Rice Burroughs - Master of Adventure**

Both editions contains 6 identical illustrations originally intended for CANAVERAL PRESS editions of AT THE EARTH'S CORE and PELLUCIDAR. See CANAVERAL PRESS hardcover edition for list of illustrations in this book.

- 21562 ESCAPE ON VENUS by Edgar Rice Burroughs
  1973 COVER **Escape on Venus**
- 44470 KING KONG by Edgar Wallace and Richard Lupoff
  1976 COVER **King Kong**
- 44472-5 KING KONG (movie script) by Lorenzo Semple jr.
  1976 COVER **King Kong and Snake**
- 47012 LAND OF HIDDEN MEN, THE (JUNGLE GIRL)
  by Edgar Rice Burroughs
  1973 COVER **Black Panther**
- 47000-9 LAND OF TERROR
  1973 COVER **Monster Out of Time**
  (AKA: **Land of Terror**)
- 47022 LAND THAT TIME FORGOT, THE
  By Edgar Rice Burroughs
  1973 COVER **Beyond the Farthest Star** (1st version)
- 49292 LOST CONTINENT, THE by Edgar Rice Burroughs
  1973 COVER **Lost Continent**
- 49502 LOST ON VENUS by Edgar Rice Burroughs
  1973 COVER **Beasts of Venus**
- 51402 MAD KING, THE by Edgar Rice Burroughs
  1970COVER **The Mad King**
  (rougher, duplicate painting of the original)
  title page illustration
- 53703 MOON MAID, THE by Edgar Rice Burroughs
  1973 COVER **The Moon Maid**
- 53752 MOON MEN, THE by Edgar Rice Burroughs
  1974 COVER **The Moon Men**
- 54460 MUCKER, THE by Edgar Rice Burroughs
  1974 COVER **The Mucker**
- 60563 OAKDALE AFFAIR, THE by Edgar Rice Burroughs
  circa mid 70's COVER **The Bear**
- 64512 OUTLAW OF TORN, THE by Edgar Rice Burroughs
  1973 COVER **The Outlaw of Torn**
- 64484 OUT OF TIME'S ABYSS by Edgar Rice Burroughs
  1973 COVER **Land of Terror**
- 65852 PELLUCIDAR by Edgar Rice Burroughs
  1973 COVER **Flying Reptiles**
- 65942 PEOPLE THAT TIME FORGOT, THE
  by Edgar Rice Burroughs
  1973 COVER **Captive Princess**
- 71815 RETURN OF THE MUCKER, THE
  by Edgar Rice Burroughs
  1974 COVER **Return of the Mucker**
- 72280 RIDER, THE by Edgar Rice Burroughs
  1974 COVER **The Rider**
- 75134 SAVAGE PELLUCIDAR by Edgar Rice Burroughs
  1973 COVER **Savage Pellucidar**
- 79796-2 TANAR OF PELLUCIDAR by Edgar Rice Burroughs
  1973 COVER **Tanar of Pellucidar**

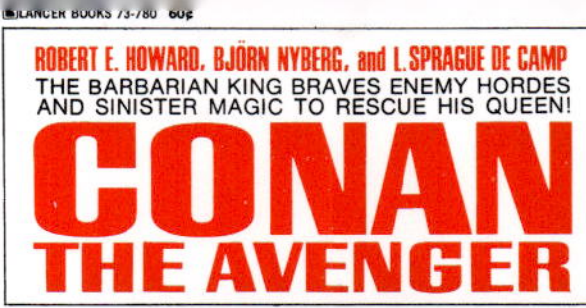

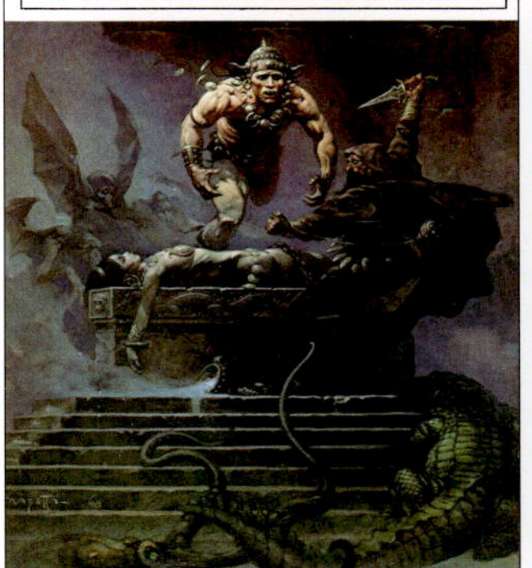
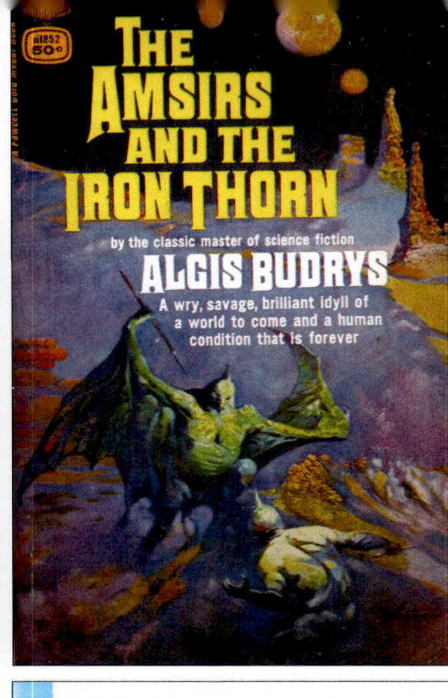

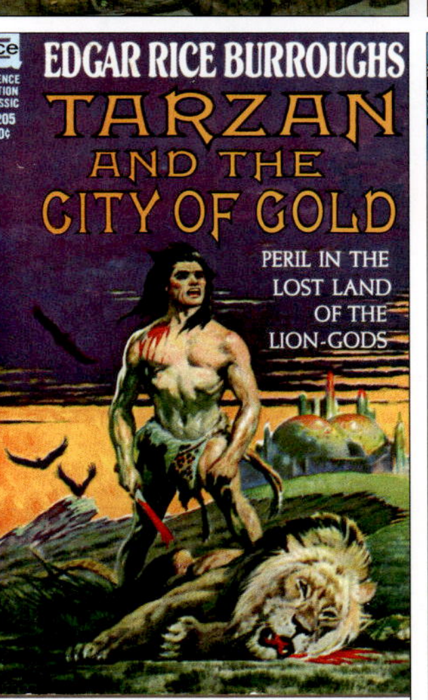

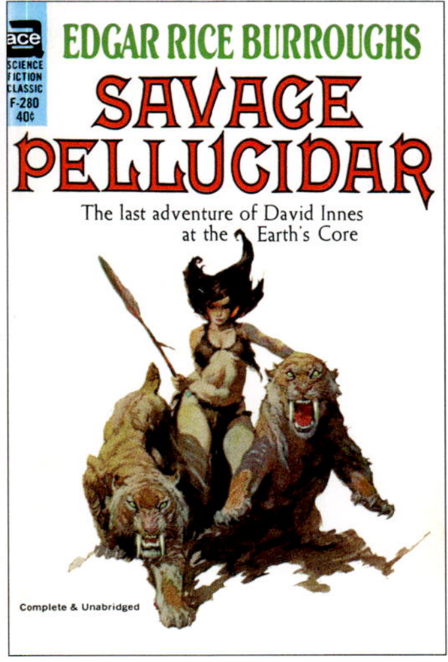

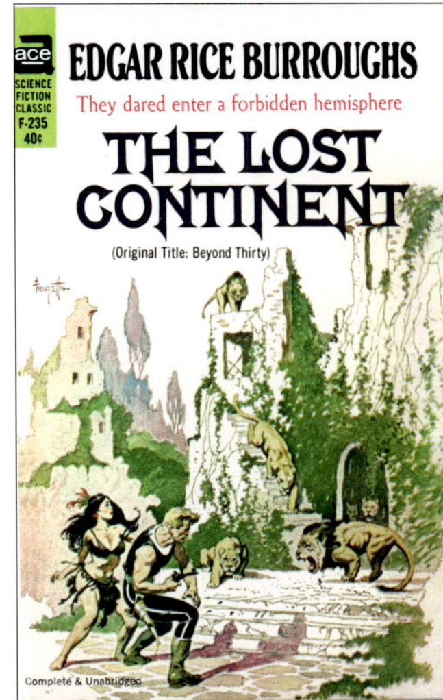

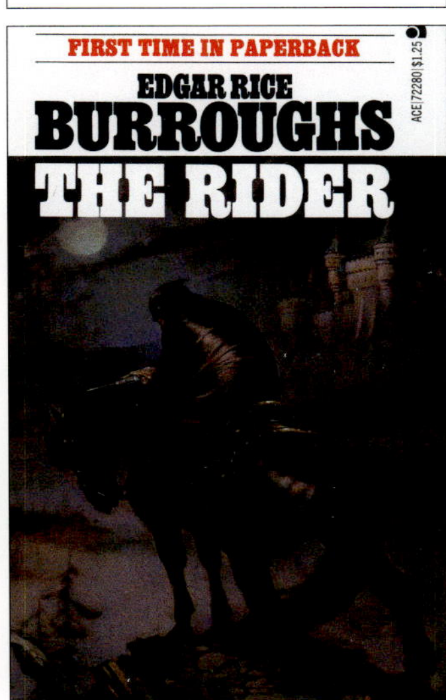

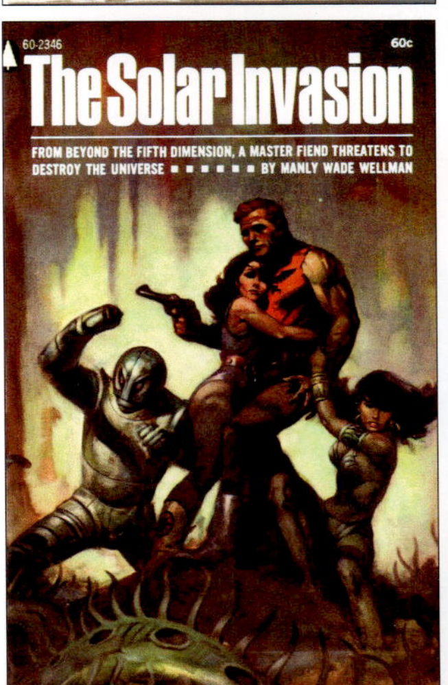

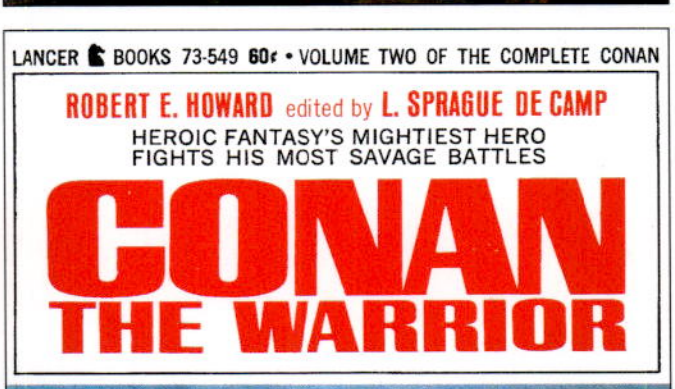

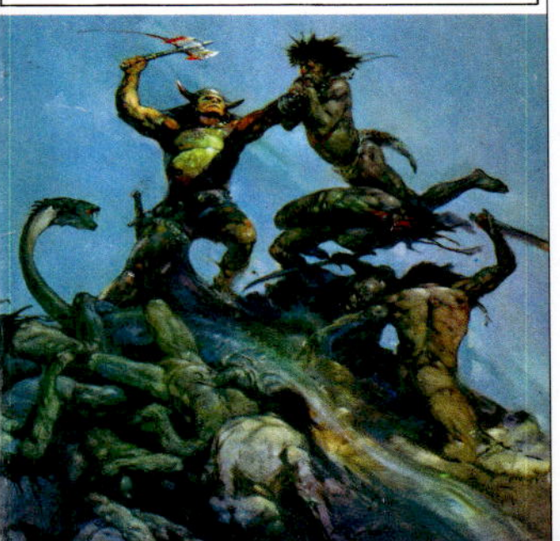

- 79852 TARZAN AT THE EARTH'S CORE
  by Edgar Rice Burroughs
  1973 COVER **Tarzan at the Earth's Core**

AIRMONT BOOKS
- CL-69 WONDERFUL WIZARD OF OZ by L. Frank Baum
  1965COVER with Roy Krenkel

AVON
- S363 BRAK THE BARBARIAN
  1968COVER **Brak The Barbarian**

BAEN
- 0-446-88154-6 DARK CRUSADE
  1991COVER **Dark Kingdom**

BALLANTINE BOOKS
- U2141 THE AUTUMN PEOPLE by Ray Bradbury
  1965COVER **The Autumn People**
- 23793 LUANA by Alan Dean Foster
  1974COVER **Luana** (A Sheet design)
- U2106 TALES FROM THE CRYPT
  1965COVER **Tales From the Crypt**
- U2140 TALES OF THE INCREDIBLE
  1965COVER
  "50 *Girls* 50" with Al Williamson and Roy Krenkel
  first printed in WEIRD SCIENCE #20
- U2142 TOMORROW MIDNIGHT by Ray Bradbury
  1966COVER **Tomorrow Midnight** (AKA - **Stranded)**
- U2107 THE VAULT OF HORROR
  1965COVER

BANNER BOOKS
- B60-110 NIGHT WALK by Bob Shaw
  1967COVER **Spiderman**

BANTAM
- 23311 RED MOON AND BLACK MOUNTAIN by Joy Chant
  1983COVER **Red Moon and Black Mountain**
  (wrap-around cover)

BERKLEY
BATTLESTAR GALACTICA 2 (THE CYLON DEATH MACHINE) by Glen Larson and Robert Thurston
1979COVER **Attack**
(wrap-around cover)
- 04080 uncensored cover
- censored cover shows clothing on girl covers her upper thigh.

BRIDGE PUBLICATIONS
- FINAL BLACKOUT by L. Ron Hubbard

L. RON HUBBARD PRESENTS - WRITERS OF THE FUTURE by various writers
- Vol. 3 1987 wrap-around COVER - **Dreamflight**
- Vol. 4 1988 wrap-around COVER - **Moon Rider**
- Vol. 5 1989 wrap-around COVER - **Encounter**
- Vol. 6 1990 wrap-around COVER - **Leaping Lizards**
- Vol. 7 1991 wrap-around COVER - **Dawn Attack**
  article by Frazetta on his art
- Vol. 10 1994 COVER - **Sound**
- Vol. 13 1997 wrap-around COVER - **A Fighting Man of Mars**

CHARTER PRESS
- 60565-6 THE OAKDALE AFFAIR by Edgar Rice Burroughs
  1979 COVER **The Bear**

DARK HORSE
- CONAN THE PHENOMENON by Paul Sammon
  2007 COVER **The Berserker**

DAW
- 04080 1972 ANNUAL WORLD'S BEST SCIENCE FICTION
  1972 COVER **New World**

DELL BOOKS
- 9461 WHAT'S NEW PUSSYCAT? by Marvin Albert
  (based on the movie)
  1965 COVER **What's New Pussycat?** (B sheet design)
- 0774 BRAN MAK MORN by Robert E. Howard
  1969 COVER **Bran Mak Morn**
- 2388 ETERNAL CHAMPION by Michael Moorecock
  1970 COVER **Eternal Champion**
- 0931 ARDOR ON AROS by Andrew J. Offutt
  1973 COVER **Serpent**
- 0932 THE BLACK STAR by Lin Carter
  1973 COVER **Black Star**
- 1182 ATLANTIS RISING by Brad Steiger
  1973 COVER **Atlantis**
- 2640 FLASHING SWORDS #1 edited by Lin Carter
  1973COVER **The Norseman**
- 3123 FLASHING SWORDS #2 edited by Lin Carter
  1974 COVER: three cover versions exist
  Tree of Death
  Death Dealer
  Warrior With Ball and Chain
- 3830 INTO THE AETHER by Richard A. Lupoff
  1974 COVER **Flying Galleon**
- 7994 SILVER WARRIORS Michael Moorcock
  1974 COVER **Silver Warrior**
- 08625 TIME WAR by Lin Carter
  1974 COVER **Invaders**
- 03343 BOOK OF PARADOX, THE by Louise Cooper
  1975 COVER **Paradox**

FAWCETT
- L1494 THE REASSEMBLED MAN by Herbert Kastle
  1964 COVER **Reassembled Man**
- D1852 THE AMSIRS AND THE IRON THORN by Algis Budrys
  1967 COVER **Iron Thorn**
- T1978 ROGUE ROMAN by Lance Horner
  1965 COVER **Rogue Roman**
- R2207 THE HIGH SIDE by Max Erlich
  1970 COVER **Devil Rider**
- 02219 STRANGE CREATURES FROM TIME AND SPACE
  by John A. Keel
  1970 COVER **Strange Creatures**
- P2623 CHILD OF THE SUN by Kyle Onsott and Lance Horner
  1972 COVER

HARPER & ROW
- SEA DEMONS by Lawrence (Michael)Yep
  1977 COVER **Sea Witch**

HOUSE OF GREYSTOKE
- THE EFFICIENCY EXPERT (6 3/4" x 9 3/4")
  by Edgar Rice Burroughs
  1966COVER
  title page illustration (same as cover)
- THE GIRL FROM FARRIS'S (6 3/4" x 9 3/4")
  by Edgar Rice Burroughs
  1965 COVER
  title page illustration (same as cover)

ILLUMINET PRESS
- MOTHMAN PROPHESIES by John A. Keel
  1991COVER **Mothman**

LANCER BOOKS
- 73-526 CONAN THE ADVENTURER
  by Robert E. Howard and De Camp
  1966 COVER **The Barbarian**

• 73-549 **CONAN THE WARRIOR** by Robert E. Howard
1967 COVER **Indomitable**
• 73-572 **CONAN THE CONQUEROR**
by Robert E. Howard and De Camp
1968 COVER **The Berserker**
• 73-599 **CONAN THE USURPER**
by Robert E. Howard and De Camp
1967 COVER **Chained**
• 73-685 **CONAN** by Robert E. Howard, De Camp and Carter
1967 COVER **Man-Ape**
• 73-780 **CONAN THE AVENGER**
by Robert E. Howard, Bjorn Nyberg and De Camp
1968 COVER **Sacrifice** (1st version)
• 73-972 **CONAN OF CIMMERIA**
by Robert E. Howard, De Camp and Carter
1967 COVER **Snow Giants**
• 75181-095 **CONAN THE BUCCANEER** by De Camp and Carter
1971 COVER **The Destroyer** (original version)
• 72-701 **SECRET PEOPLE, THE** by John Jakes
1964 COVER **The Secret People**
• 72-761 **REIGN OF WIZARDRY** by Jack Williams
1964 COVER
• 73-476 **PHOENIX PRIME** by Ted White
1966 COVER **Wolf Moon**
• 73-591 **BUSY BODY, THE** by Don Westlake
(based on the movie)
1967 COVER **The Busy Body**
• 73-721 **WOLFSHEAD** by Robert E. Howard
1968 COVER **Green Death**
• 75372 **KAVIN'S WORLD** by David Mason
1969 COVER **Kavin's World**
• 74-840 **TORTURE GARDEN** by Octave Mirbeau
1965 COVER **Torture Garden**
• 75165 **BLACK EMPEROR** by Stuart Jason
1973 COVER **Black Emperor**
• 15414 **WITCH OF THE DARK GATE** by John Jakes
1972 COVER **Swamp Demon**
• 75465 **THE DEVIL'S GENERATION** edited by Vic Ghidalia
1973 COVER **The Devil's Generation**
• 74-531 **THE MAN FROM S.T.U.D. #7**
The Planned Parenthood Caper by F.W. Paul
1969 PHOTO COVER - Frank Frazetta with model
• 74-533 **THE MAN FROM S.T.U.D. #8**
The Lay of the Land by F.W. Paul
1969 PHOTO COVER - Frank Frazetta
with semi-nude model

MAGNUM
• 15414 **WITCH OF THE DARK GATE** by John Jakes
1972 COVER **Swamp Demon**

MIDWOOD
• D-231 **THE WILD WEEK and IMITATION LOVERS**
by Jason Hytes and March Hastings
19638 sepia tone illustrations
• S-277 **PERFUMED and PAMPERED**
by Jason Hytes and Kimberly Kemp
196310 sepia tone illustrations
• 34-394 **THE DANGEROUS AGE and BAD BY CHOICE**
by Joan Ellis and Jason Hytes
19648 sepia tone illustrations
• 34-612 **PERFUMED and THE WILD WEEK** by Jason Hytes
19648 sepia tone illustrations

The illustrations in these books are reprinted in BABY, YOUR REALLY SOMETHING (comic book).Alternate combinations of these stories are rumored to exist yet only "Perfumed"/"The Wild Week" are known to exist for sure.

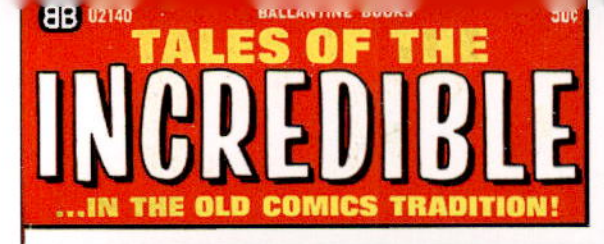

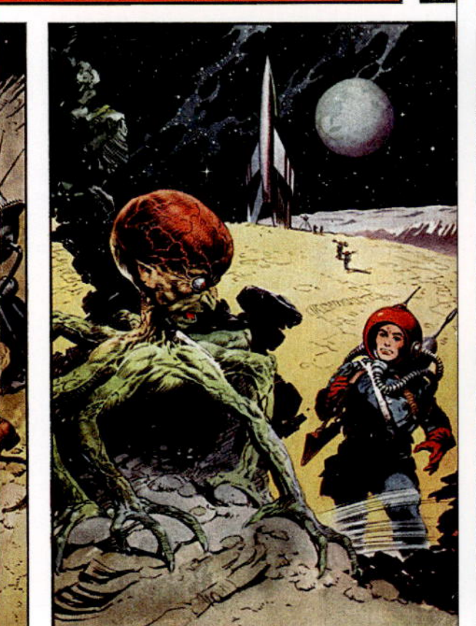
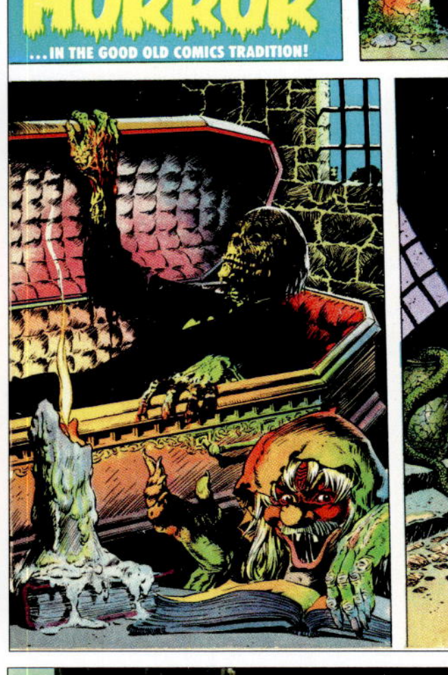

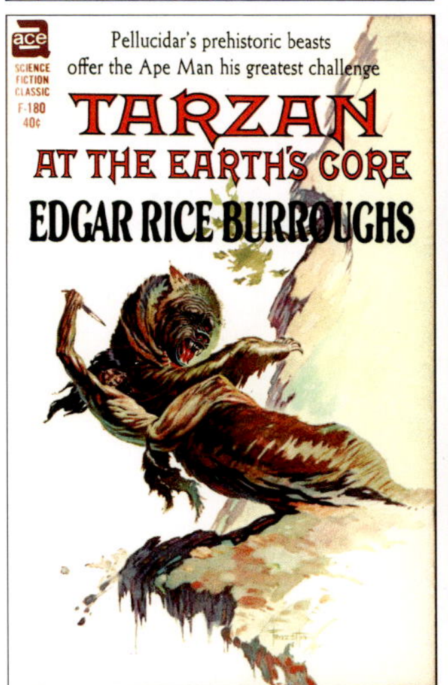

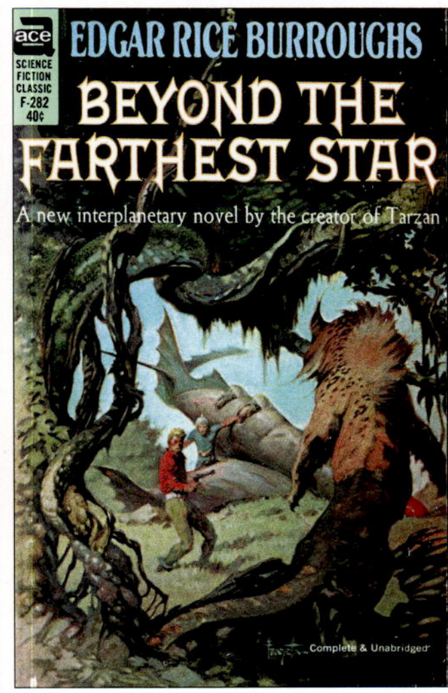

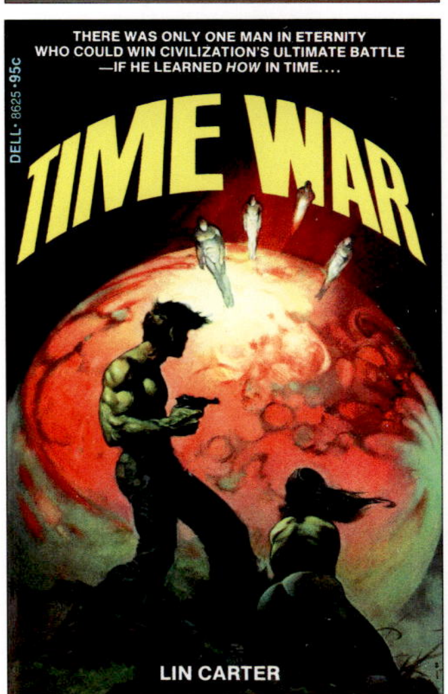

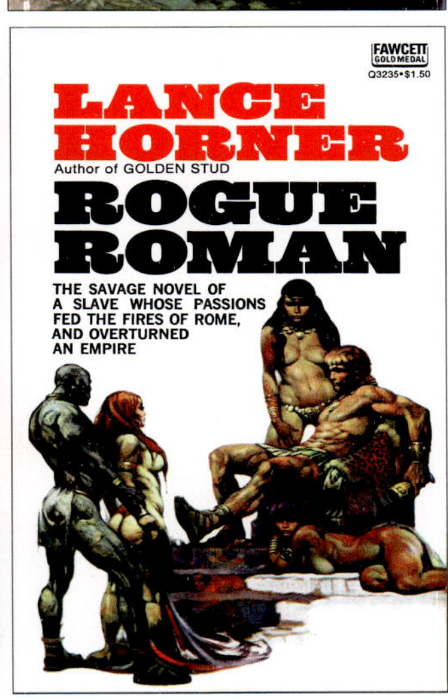

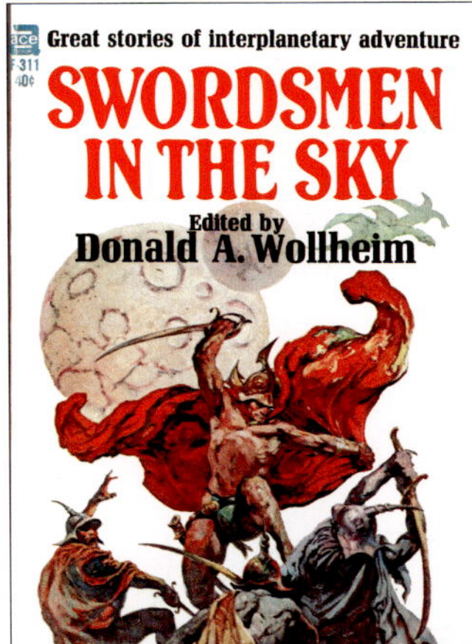

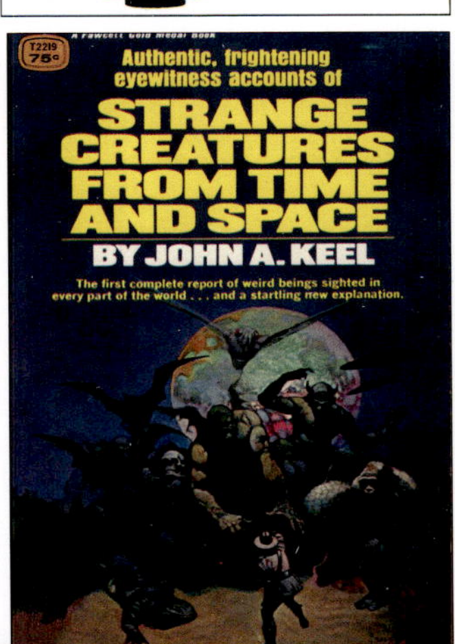

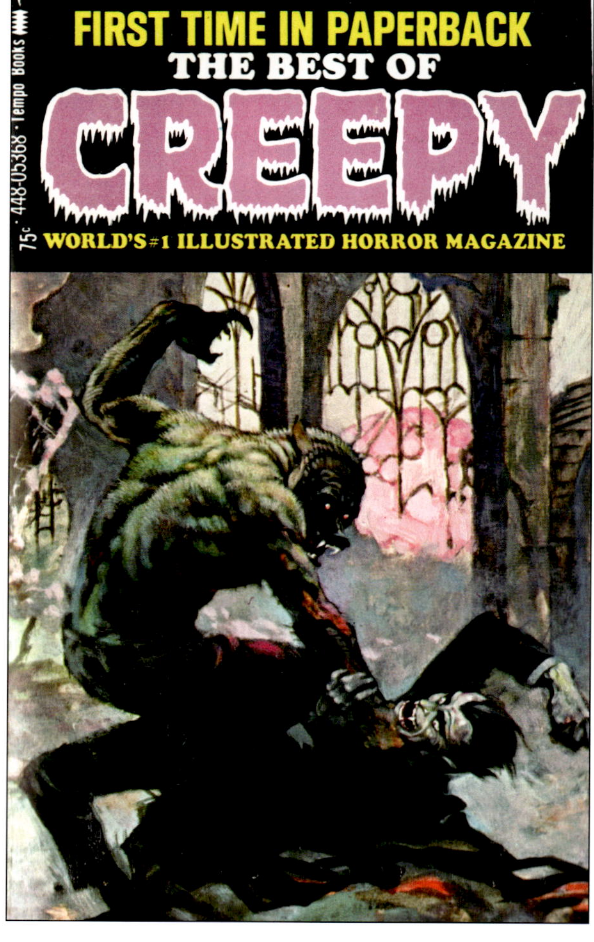

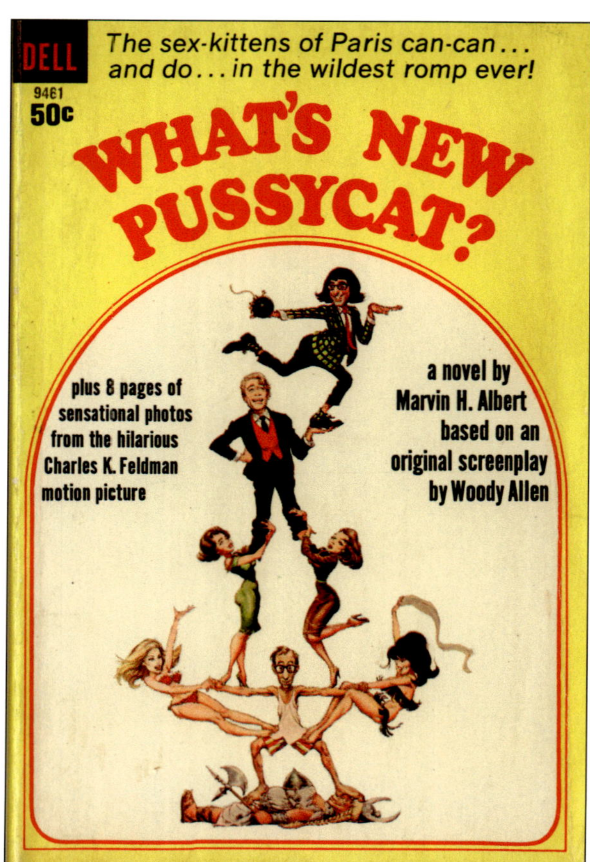

NOVA CLASSICS

- THE COMPLETION OF KUBLA KHAN by Julio Delatorre
  1997 illustrated by Frazetta
  reprinted from THE KUBLA KHAN PORTFOLIO (plates one through four)

PAPERBACK LIBRARY

- 55-738 ATLAN
  by Jane Gaskall
  1968 COVER **Wolfpack**
- 63-089 BRAK THE BARBARIAN VS. THE SORCERESS
  by John Jakes
  1969 COVER **The Apparition**
- 53-618 THE TRITONIAN RING
  by L. Sprague De Camp
  1968 COVER **Pony Tail**
- 52-586 THONGOR AGAINST THE GODS
  by Lin Carter
  1967 COVER **Against the Gods**
- 53-665 THONGOR IN THE CITY OF MAGICIANS
  by Lin Carter
  1968 COVER **Thor's Flight**
- 55-693 THE SERPENT
  by Jane Gaskall
  1968 COVER **Serpent**

PERRENIAL

- P477 SEA DEMONS
  by Lawrence (Michael) Yep
  1979 COVER **Sea Witch**

PINNACLE

- P010-N THE GODMAKERS
  by Dan Britain
  1970 COVER **The Godmakers**

- P020-N TO CATCH A CROOKED GIRL
  by Paul Fairman
  1971 COVER **To Catch a Crooked Girl**

POCKET BOOKS

PRESIDENT EISENHOWER'S CARTOON BOOK
1956

- hardcover edition — b/w caricature of Eisenhower (dust-jacket illo. on back and interior of book)
- softcover edition — color caricature of Eisenhower (front cover)

POPULAR LIBRARY

- 2335 DANGER PLANET
  by Brett Sterling
  1968 COVER **Alien Worlds**
- 2346 THE SOLAR INVASION
  by Manly Wade Wellman
  1968 COVER **Solar Invasion**
- 2355 THE CREATURE FROM BEYOND INFINITY
  by Henry Kuttner
  1968 COVER **Mastodon**
- 602376 OUTLAW WORLD
  by Edmond Hamilton
  1970 COVER **White Apes**
- 02474 MONSTER OUT OF TIME
  by Frank Belknap Long
  1970 COVER **Monster Out of Time**
- 02498 JONGOR OF LOST LAND
  by Robert Moore Williams
  1970 COVER
  later version of cover used for JAGUAR GOD #1

- 02511 **THE RETURN OF JONGOR**
  by Robert Moore Williams
  1970 COVER **The Return of Jongor**
- 02540 **JONGOR FIGHTS BACK**
  by Robert Moore Williams
  1970 COVER **Jongor Fights Back**

SPHERE (Lancer, CONAN overseas editions)

All Frazetta cover art is identical to those of the Lancer editions with the exception of CONAN OF AQUILONIA. This edition of CONAN OF AQUILONIA showcases the Frazetta painting that was stolen from the Lancer office. Sphere relied on a proof photo to reproduce the art. Since there was no original to match up to the proof, the cover was reproduced with a poor color match.

- 0 7221 4707 4 **CONAN THE ADVENTURER**
  by Robert E. Howard and De Camp
  1973 COVER **The Barbarian**
- 0 7221 4711 2 **CONAN THE WARRIOR**
  by Robert E. Howard
  1973 COVER **Indomitable**
- 0 7221 4708 2 **CONAN THE CONQUEROR**
  by Robert E. Howard and De Camp
  1974 COVER **The Berserker**
- 0 7221 4697 3 **CONAN THE USURPER**
  by Robert E. Howard and De Camp
  1974 COVER **Chained**
- 0 7221 4709 0 **CONAN**
  by Robert E. Howard, De Camp and Carter
  1974 COVER **Man-Ape**
- 0 7221 4693 0 **CONAN THE AVENGER**
  by Robert E. Howard, Bjorn Nyberg and De Camp
  1974 COVER **Sacrifice** (1st version)
- 0 7221 4695 7 **CONAN OF CIMMERIA**
  by Robert E. Howard, De Camp and Carter
  1974 COVER **Snow Giants**
- 0 7221 4705 8 **CONAN THE BUCCANEER**
  by De Camp and Carter
  1975 COVER **The Destroyer** (original version)
- 0 7221 4706 6 **CONAN OF AQUILONIA**
  by De Camp and Carter
  1978 COVER **Conan of Aquilonia**

SIGNET
- Y5491 **FLASH FOR FREEDOM**
  by George MacDonald Fraser
  1973 COVER
- Y6094 **FLASHMAN AT THE CHARGE**
  by George MacDonald Fraser
  1974 COVER **Flashman on the Charge**

TANDEM
- 5602 **MRS. POLLIFAX - SPY**
  by Dorothy Gillman (based on the movie)
  1971 COVER **Mrs. Pollifax - Spy**

TEMPO
- 12125 **THE BEST OF CREEPY**
  1971 COVER **Dracula Meets the Wolfman**
- **THE CAVE GIRL**
  1981 COVER **Savage Pellucidar**

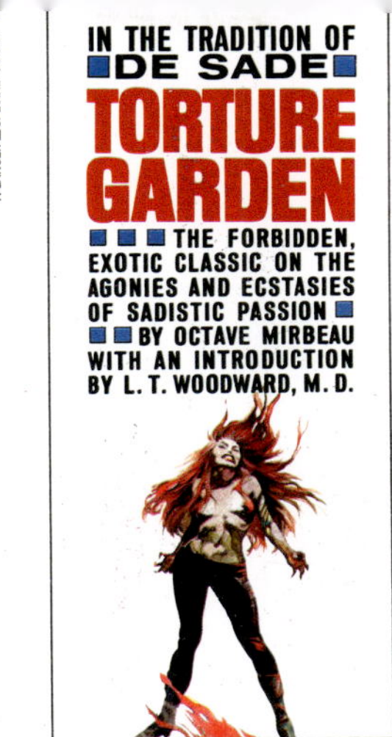

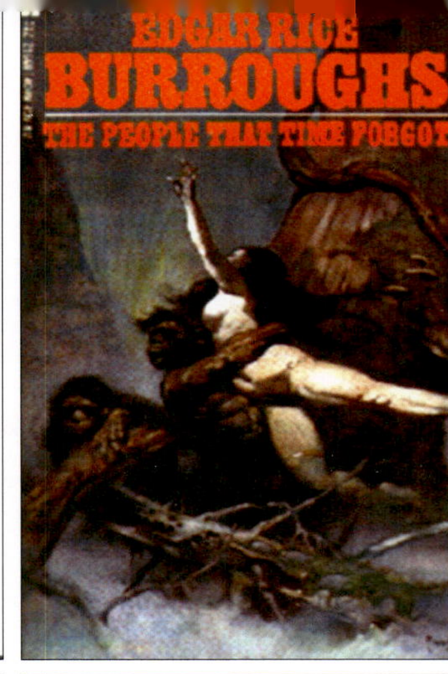

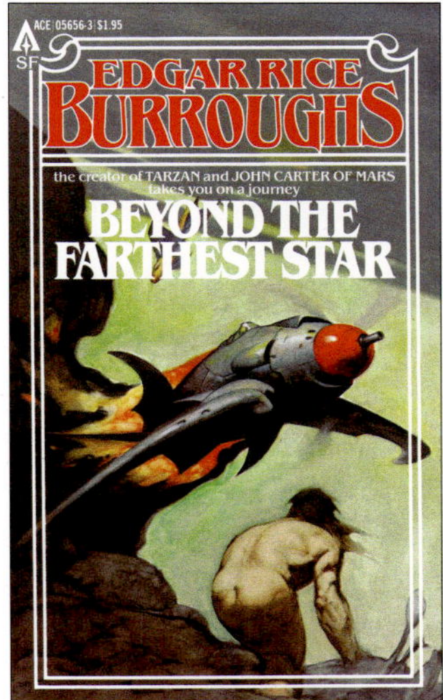

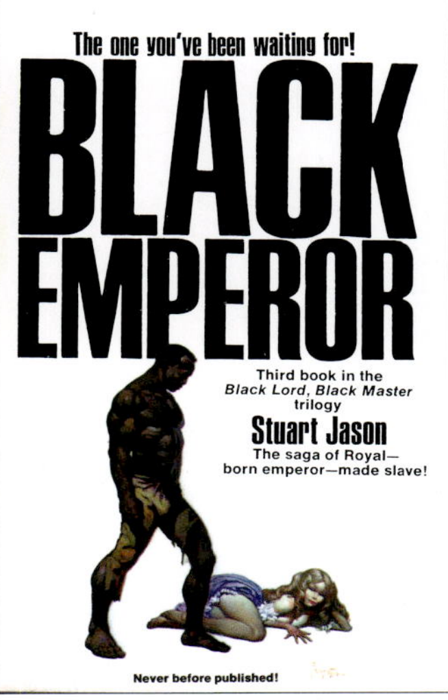

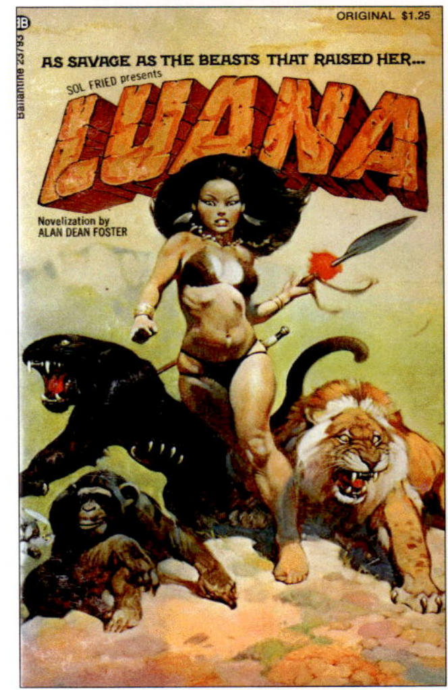

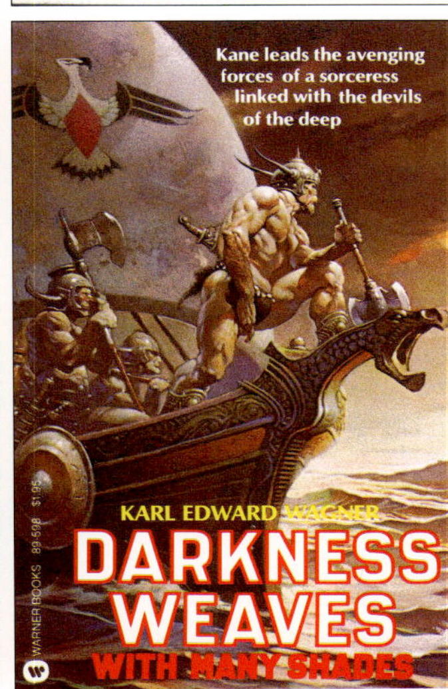

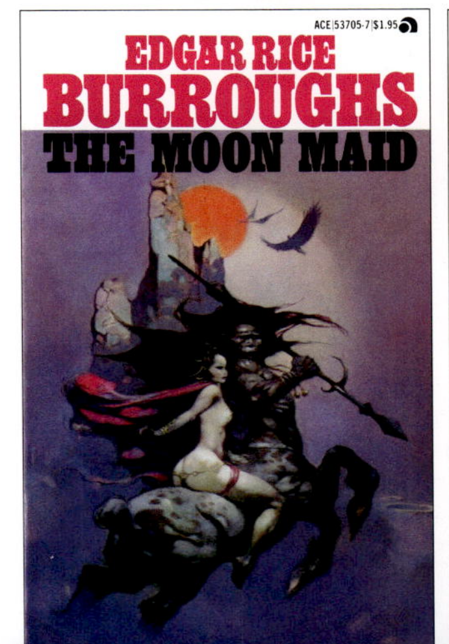

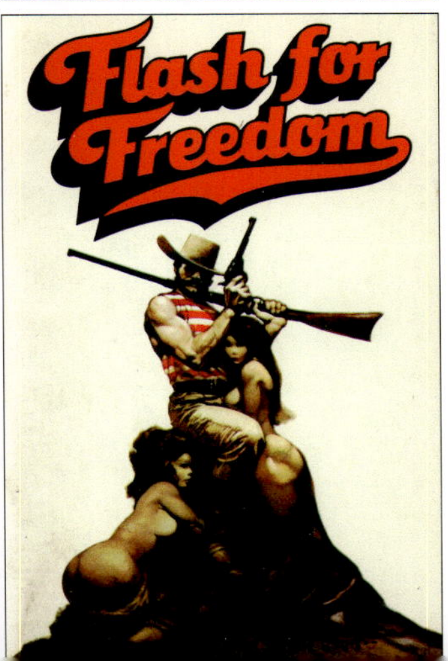

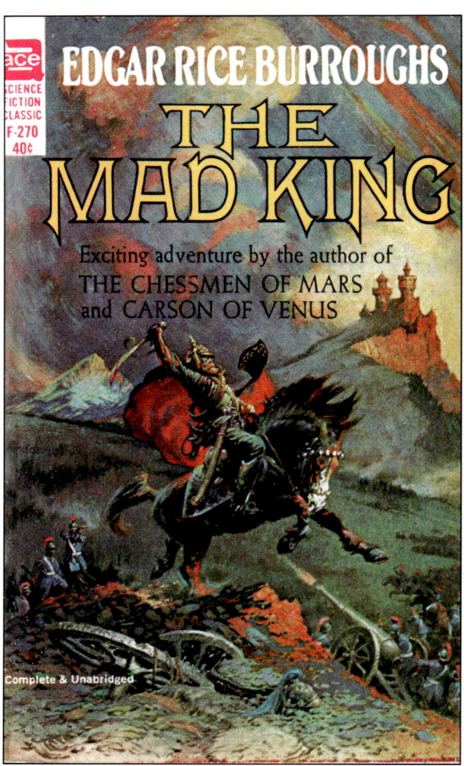

REPAINT / RECREATE

This isn't the only time Frazetta has repainted an already existing piece. The history of many of his works shows him either repainting a single figure, such as Conan on the Ace edition of CONAN THE BUCCANEER, or repainting an entire layout. Compare the cover of CREEPY #11 to it's repainted cousin; the paperback cover to KING KONG.

He does this for a couple of reasons. The first and foremost is probably the fact that he, like most artists, looks back on a piece of artwork and finds imperfections. Or perhaps the lack of modern technique shows certain characteristics, causing the artist to rethink his strategy.

In the case of the magazine cover for VAMPIRELLA #1 he simply disliked the costume that Jim Warren commissioned him to design for the character. So, as soon as Frazetta re-acquired the original from Warren, he took out his paints and re-painted her completely nude.

Another reason for an artist to re-paint an existing piece of work has to do with turning a quick dollar in order to devote time to other projects. Here Frazetta had this original art laying around collecting dust. He probably was paid a minimal fee for his efforts at Popular Library when he first painted it. Thirty five years later Glenn Danzig was searching for a cover to the first issue of JAGUAR GOD and didn't wish to pay a relatively exorbitant price. This way both parties were happy. Frank was able to sell a painting twice and Danzig acquired a Frazetta cover. Everyone walked away happy from the deal.

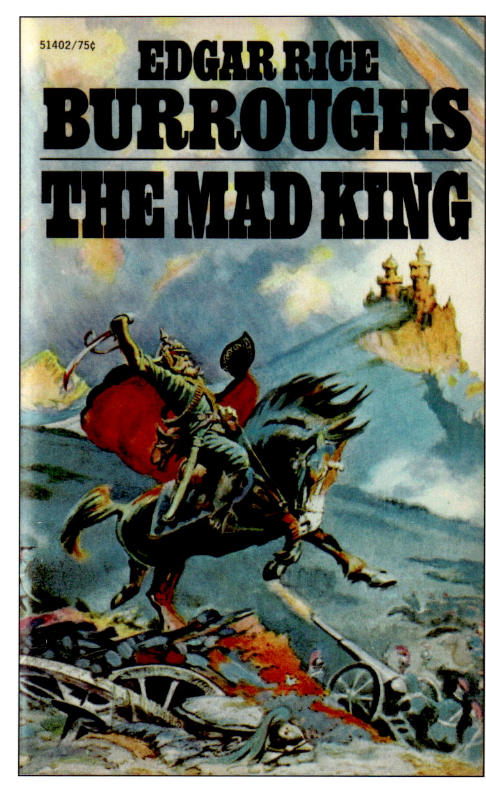

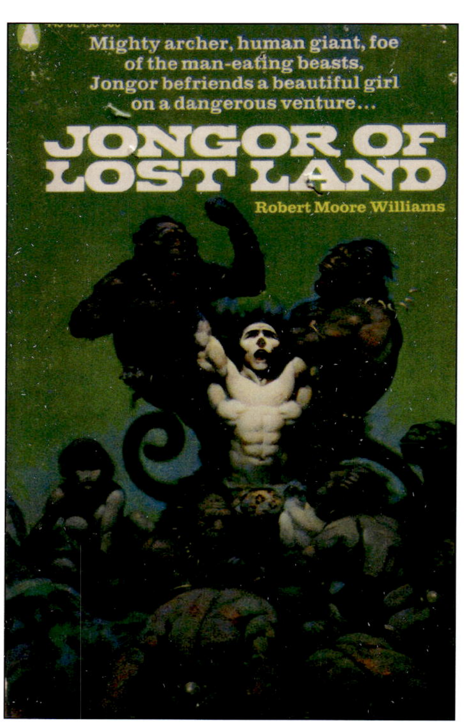

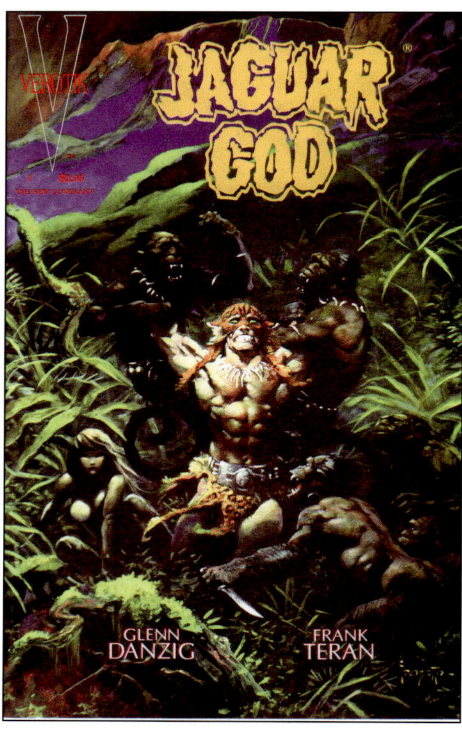

ABOVE: The Mad King *original edition and the repainted version.*

LOWER: Cover tc Jongor of Lost Land *and the repainted version (right) used 35 years later for the comic book* Jaguar God *#1.*

TOR BOOKS

All books feature Frank Frazetta's Death Dealer

- S3823-4 **PRISONER OF THE HORNED HELMET**
  by James Silke and Frank Frazetta
  1989 COVER **Death Dealer**
- S3821-8 **LORDS OF DESTRUCTION**
  by James Silke and Frank Frazetta
  1989 COVER **Death Dealer II**
- S0331-7 **TOOTH AND CLAW**
  by James Silke and Frank Frazetta
  1989 COVER **Death Dealer III**
- S0332-5 **PLAGUE OF KNIVES**
  by James Silke and Frank Frazetta
  1989 COVER **Death Dealer IV**

WARNER

- 0-446-78-711-6 **BLOODSTONE**
  by Karl Edward Wagner
  1975 COVER **Bloodstone**
- 88-154 **DARK CRUSADE**
  by Karl Edward Wagner
  1976 COVER **Dark Kingdom**
- 89-587 **NIGHT WINDS**
  by Karl Edward Wagner
  1978 COVER **Night Winds**
- 89-598 **DARKNESS WEAVES**
  by Karl Edward Wagner
  1978 COVER **Kane on the Golden Sea**
- 90-001 **DEATH ANGEL'S SHADOW**
  by Karl Edward Wagner
  1978 COVER **Cave Demon**
- 90-115 **WITHERWING**
  by David Jarrett
  1979 COVER **Witherwing**
- 82-633 **THE FLESH EATERS**
  by L.A. Mors
  1979 COVER **The Flesh Eaters**

ZEBRA

- 89083-239 **SWORDS AGAINST DARKNESS**
  by Robert E. Howard, others.
  1977 COVER **Fire Demon**

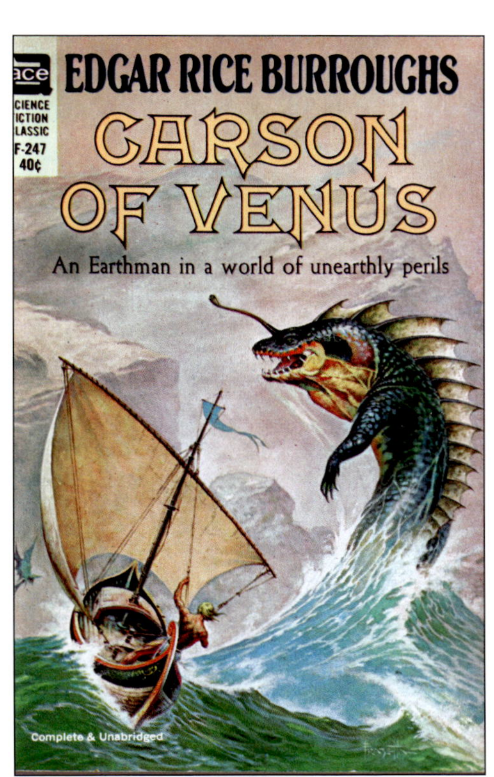

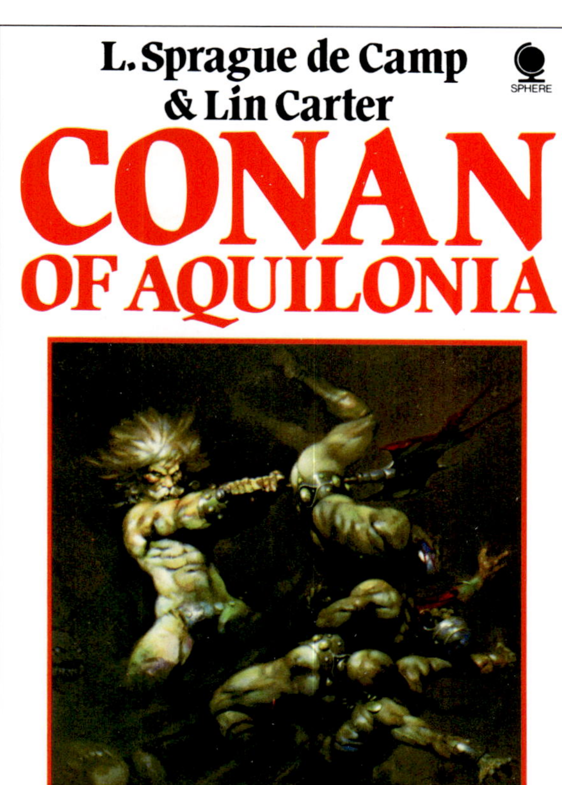

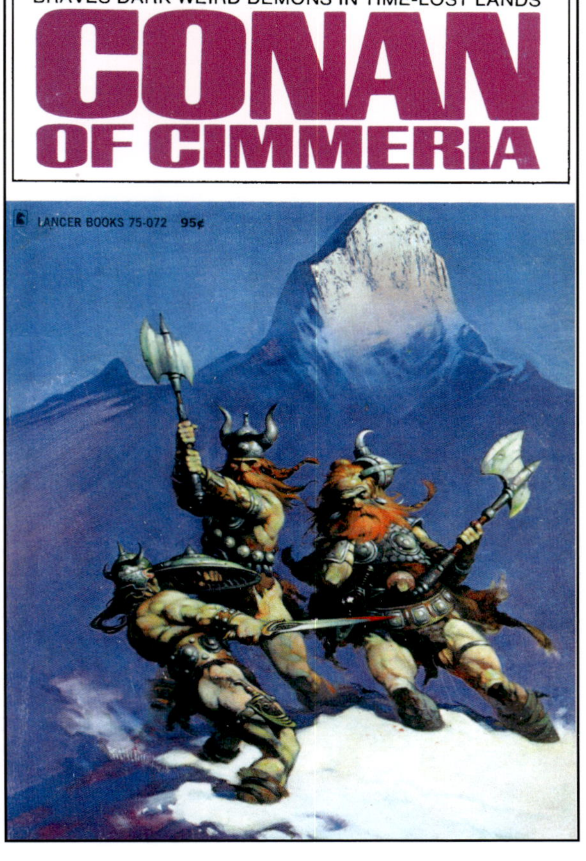

ART FOR ART'S SAKE

Prints & Portfolios

By Andrew Steven

ANDREW STEVEN is a clothing designer who owns a chain of boutiques that sell his creations. He lives and works in New York City. A collector of vintage model kits and Robert E.Howard esoterica, it's also rumored he has a weakness for Frank's work.

The last 40 years has offered an amazing array of posters, portfolios and prints of Frank Frazetta's art from which to choose. Images ranging from pencil to pen and ink to watercolor to oils are generously represented in a variety of formats. While some are just a click of a mouse pad away, others can take a life-time to track down; the remaining handful … let's just say it wouldn't hurt to be a cat with *nine* lives.

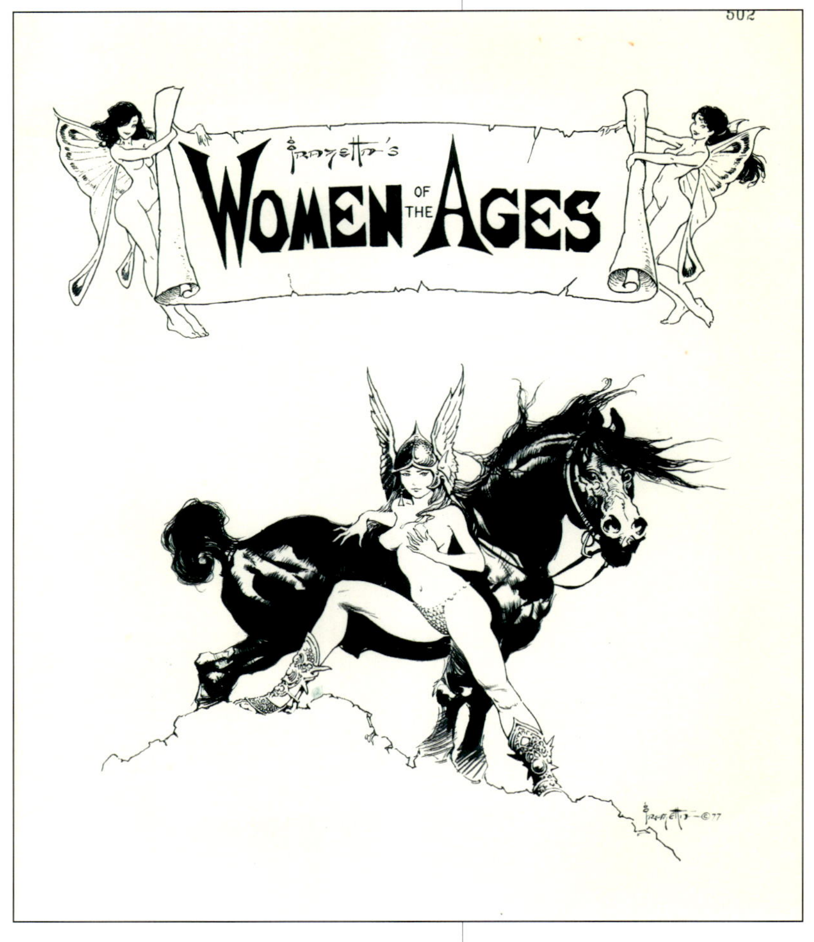

The Frazetta's themselves have issued the most readily available and most popular of all poster releases. Through their Frazetta Prints catalogue, well over one-hundred full color images are available, all with first rate reproduction from the original artwork. Many share the same dimensions as the oil paintings they facsimilate.

Exquisite pen and ink line work fill three of the more well-known signed and numbered portfolios: Lord of the Rings, Women of the Ages and Kubla Khan. While Women of the Ages and Kubla Khan were issued in editions of 1500, only 1000 sets of Lord of the Rings were released. Strong interest from J.R.Tolkien enthusiasts and a lower print run help this particular folio retain a stronger difficulty rating to acquire.

Prints released in quantities as low as 40, such as the hand-colored and remarqued Weird Science-Fantasy #29 cover, to editions numbering in the thousands, i.e. Golden Girl, have been published over the last five decades. While some of the images are available in other for-

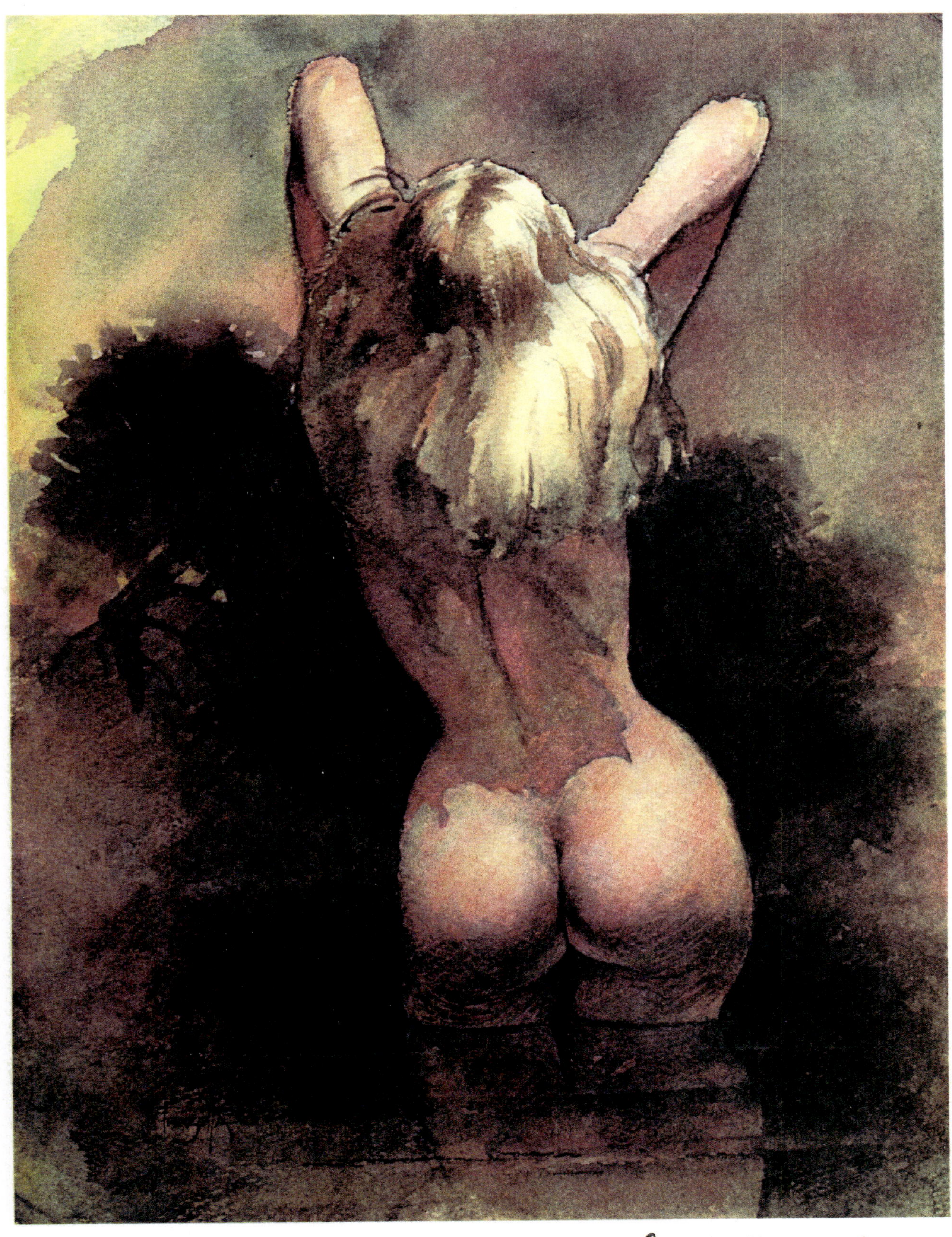

Land of Enchantment, Publisher
14164 W. Outer Drive, Detroit, MI 48239

Frazetta 51/100

mats many are unique to their specific issue. Nude Watercolor, published by Christopher Ent., limited to just 100 signed and numbered prints, is one example of an uncommon release.

The vast amount of material available in poster, portfolio and print form of Frank's artwork can keep a collector occupied for a life-time. It's a shame we can't trade places with that cat of nine lives… they would come in handy.

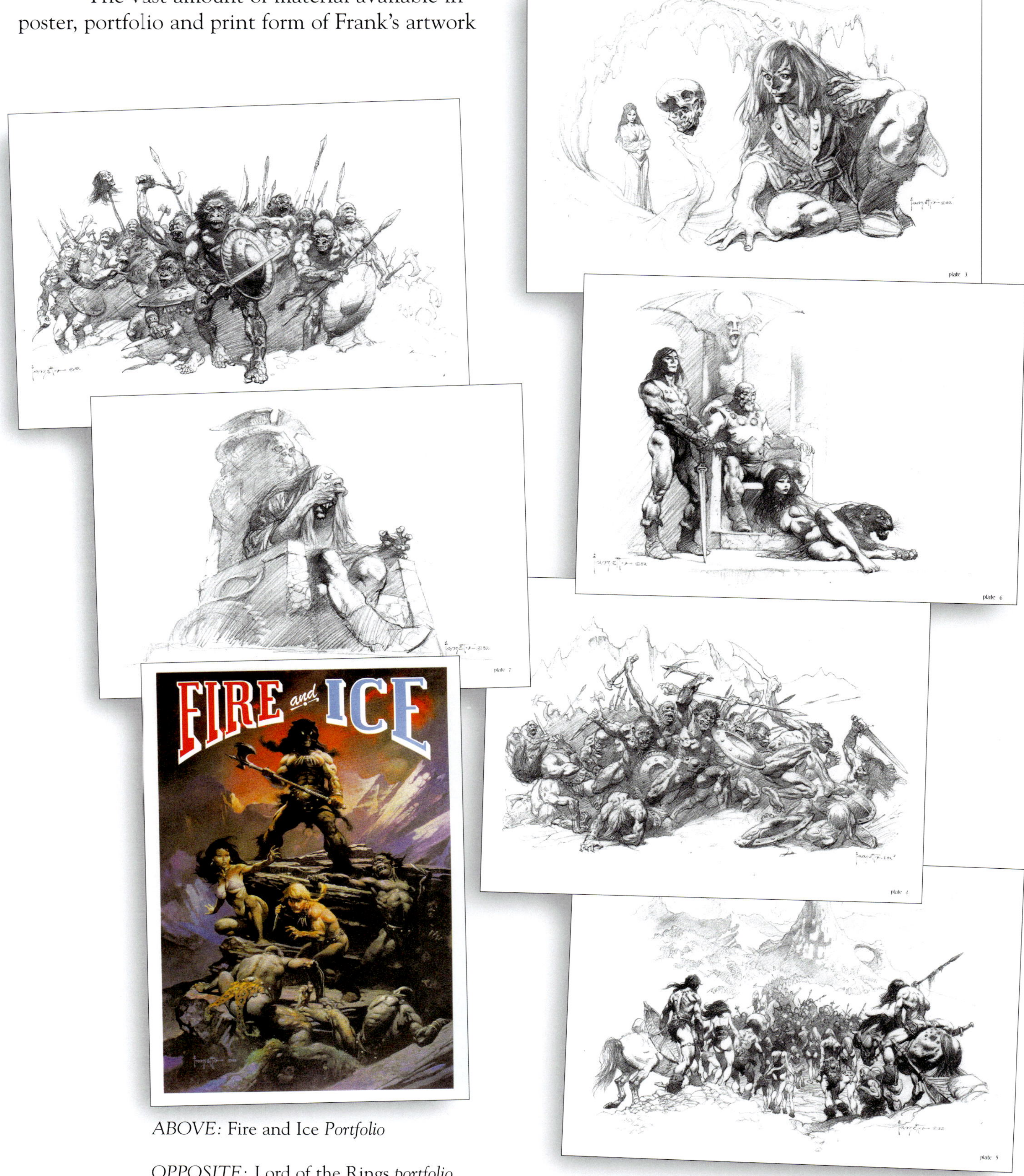

ABOVE: Fire and Ice *Portfolio*

OPPOSITE: Lord of the Rings *portfolio*

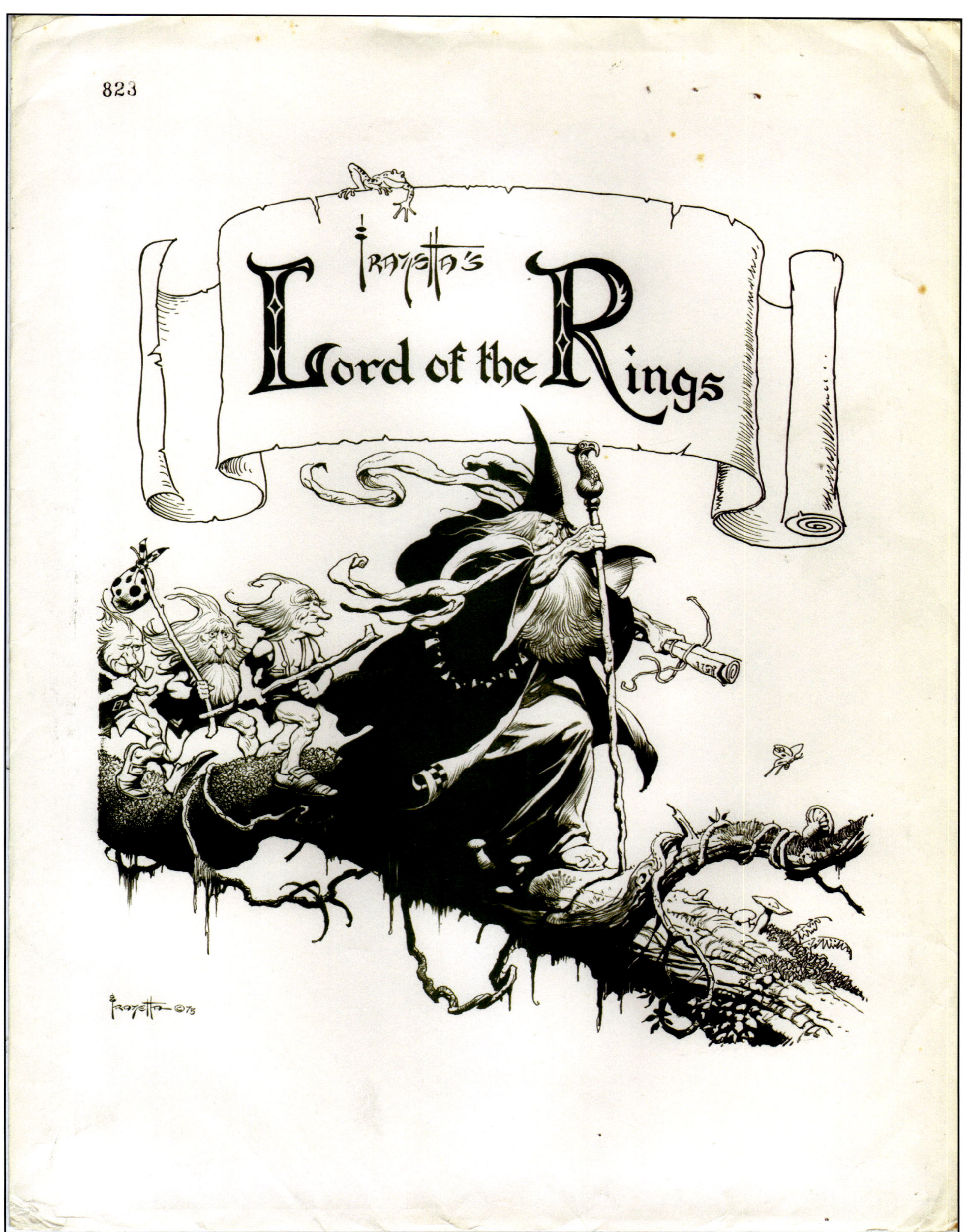
823
Frazetta's
Lord of the Rings
Frazetta ©75

FRAZETTA ART PRINTS - standard series

Available through the Frazetta catalog

TITLE	PRINT #
•Against the Gods	60
•Apparition, The	14
•A Princess of Mars	54
•Aros	74
•Arthur Rex	127
•Atlantis	23
•At the Earth's Core	35
•Autumn People	82
•Barbarian, The	40
•Battlefield Earth	124
•Battlestar Galactica: Attack	103
•Battlestar Galactica: Scramble	104
•Beauty and the Beast	148
•Berserker	15
•Beyond the Grave	96
•Birdman	64
•Black Star	93
•Bloodstone	73
•Brain, The	13
•Bran Mak Morn	84
•Bucking Bronco	65
•Captive Princess	143
•Carson of Venus	92
•Cat Girl	125
•Catwalk	146
•Cave Demon, The	107
•Chained	39
•Combat	62
•Count Dracula	94
•Countess, The	120
•Dark Kingdom	69
•Dawn Attack	138
•Day of Wrath	136
•Death Dealer	31
•Death Dealer II	129
•Death Dealer III	130
•Death Dealer IV	131
•Death Dealer V	145
•Death Dealer VI	137
•Destroyer, The	49
•Downward to Earth	66
•Dracula Meets The Wolfman	83
•Dream Flight	126
•Egyptian Queen	21
•Encounter, The	122
•Escape on Venus	53
•Eternal Champion	86
•Eve	108
•Fire & Ice	132
•Fire Demon	79
•Flashman on the Charge	101
•Flesh Eaters	117
•Flying Reptiles	43
•From Dusk Till Dawn	147
•Galleon, The	25
•Ghoul Queen	63
•Girl Bathing	78
•Golden Girl	59
•Gollum	90
•Green Death	12
•Gulliver of Mars	58
•Headless Horseman I	133
•Headless Horseman II	134
•Huns	123
•Huntress, The	68
•Indomitable	33
•Iron Thorn	87
•Jaguar God I	141
•Jaguar God II	142
•John Carter and the Savage Apes of Mars	55
•Jongor Fights Back	44
•Kane on the Golden Sea	99
•King Kong	119
•Land of Terror	47
•Las Vegas	112
•Leaping Lizards	139
•Lieutenant, The	140
•Madame Derringer	61
•Mad King, The	57
•Mammoth, The	32
•Man-Ape	34
•Mongol Tyrant	98
•Monster out of Time	51
•Moon Maid, The	48
•Moon Rider	121
•Mothman	118
•Neanderthal	8
•New World	106
•Nightstalker	76
•Night Winds	102
•Norseman, The	52
•Outlaw of Torn	95
•Paradox	50
•Pony Tail	45
•Princess and the Panther	149
•Reassembled Man	89
•Return of Jongor, The	109
•Return of the Mucker	67
•Rogue Roman	80
•Sacrifice	113
•Savage Pellucidar	38
•Sea Monster	9
•Sea Witch	42
•Secret People, The	114
•Serpent	75
•Seven Romans	116
•Silver Warrior	24
•Snow Giants	17
•Sorcerer, The	6
•Sound	115
•Spiderman	10
•Sun Goddess	22
•Swamp Demon	18
•Swords of Mars	85
•Tanar of Pellucidar	81
•Tempters, The	105
•Thor's Flight	110
•Thuvia, Maid of Mars	56
•Tomorrow Midnight	46
•Tree of Death	88
•Tyrannosaurus Rex	20
•Warrior With Ball and Chain	100
•Wild Ride	128
•Withering	111
•Wolfman	7
•Wolf Moon	5
•Wolf Pack	11
•Wolves Night	135
•Woman With a Scythe	19

A.C.B.A.A. SKETCHBOOK PORTFOLIO, THE 8 1/2" x 11", 36 plates Heritage
- 1 1973
  single b/w plate.
  see also page 1 illustration for FRANK FRAZETTA: BOOK FIVE (art book).
- 2 1974single b/w plate

AFRICAN HUNTER, THE Watercolor print set
2003 Frank Frazetta
These fabulous watercolors were done by Frank Frazetta between 1989 - 1995.
They were given to his wife Ellie on special occasions such as her birthday, Valentines etc.
- Standard Edition
  Six plates
  Limited print run of 950
  certificate of authenticity.
- Signed Edition
  Six plates
  Limited print run of 50
  certificate of authenticity.

ALAMO SUPER PRINTS SERIES (produced overseas)
1975 Alamo
The series includes the following:
- **The Return of the Mucker** 15 3/4" X 21 1/8"
- **Rogue Roman** 16 7/8" X 20 3/8"
- **At the Earth's Core** 18" X 24"
- **Jongor Fights Back** 15 3/8" X 22 7/8"
- **Tyrannosaurus Rex** 17" X 23"
- **The Rider** 18" x 24"

ARGENTINA PRINTS
Size is 16.5" x 11.7" (inches).
Printed on illustration paper
- GIANTESS PRINT
- VAMPIRELLA PRINT (Vampirella crouching with skull in hand)

ARTIST PROOF LITHOGRAPH
2003 Frank Frazetta
- **Countess**
- **Moon Rider**
- **Encounter**
- **Battlefield Earth**
- **The Lieutenant**

A SPARKLE OF QUICKSILVER 8 1/2" x 11", 7 plates
1975 Frodo's Press
Contains portfolio envelope with illustration, and 6 b/w, pen & ink illustrations.
- unsigned copy
- signed copy

- AT THE EARTH'S CORE and PELLUCIDAR PORTFOLIO

1968Opar Press
Contains portfolio envelope and 16 b/w illustrations from the Canaveral Press books.
Images are printed on both sides of each plate.
plate 1 side A proposed jacket design for PELLUCIDAR
side B *"We were assailed by enormous white bears."*
plate 2 side A *"I saw three mighty Thipdars."*
side B *"They buried their talons in his back."*
plate 3 side A *"The great man-brute seated himself upon a flat rock."*
side B *"I had my stone knife in my hand, and he had his."*
plate 4 side A *"The fierce beasts were upon the Thurian simultaneously."*
side B Jungle Woman
plate 5 side A dust jacket design for AT THE EARTH'S CORE
side B *"One of the creatures swung down headforemost, grasping me beneath my armpits."*
plate 6 side A *"I caught my first sight of the dominant race of the inner world."*
side B *"She moved as one in a trance straight toward the reptile."*
plate 7 side A *"His huge, fanged jaws grinned in pleasurable appreciation of my predicament."*
side B *"With all my strength I drove the spear straight into the gaping jaws of the hydrophidian."*
plate 8 side A *"My shaft pierced the sagoth's savage heart..."*
side B *"I let him have a left fair on the point of the jaw that sent him tumbling over on his back."*

- BARBARIAN WITH AXE b/w print 9" x 11"
  pencil illustration

- BATTLESTAR GALACTICA PROMO LITHOGRAPH SET

b/w
1978 T.V.Guide
This set was made available by T.V. Guide to promote the Battlestar Galactica series. Mail in coupons were found within the pages of the magazine. The set consists of the following black and white images:
Battlestar Galactica: Attack
Battlestar Galactica: Darkness at Time's Edge
Battlestar Galactica: Scramble

- BATTLESTAR GALACTICA PROMO POSTER

full color 17" x 22"
1978
ABC Television **Battlestar Galactica: Attack**

BEAUTY & THE BEAST b/w print
1972 Frank Frazetta
7" x 23"
- unsigned copy
- signed copy

- BURROUGHS ARTIST PORTFOLIO

1973 Opar Press
Contains 1 color plate, 21 b/w plates (from the Canaveral Press books) and 1 portfolio envelope w/3 illustrations
The images included are as follows:
* **The captions for plates 11 and 12 in the portfolio are switched.**

plate 1 (color) cover to the 1963 edition of CARSON OF VENUS titled: *"I saw monstrous creatures of the deep."*
plate 2 *"The bear whirled about on the narrow ledge"*
plate 3 *"For seconds he was a carved statue of bone and sinew and sun-bronzed flesh."*
plate 4 *"The silent creature drove a long knife again and again into his tawny side."*
plate 5 *"The ape-man dealt him a terrific blow on the side of the head with his open palm."*
plate 6 *"Tarzan in perfect calm, Raised his short, heavy spear above his right shoulder and waited."*

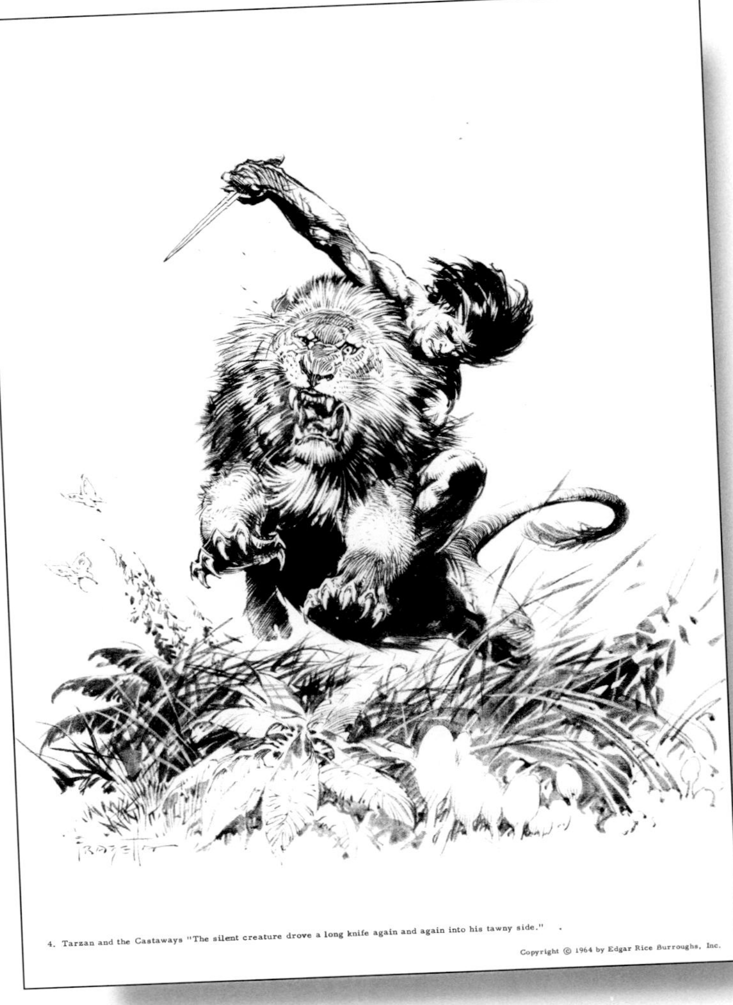

BURROUGHS ARTIST PORTFOLIO *cont'd*

plate 7 dust jacket design for AT THE EARTH'S CORE
plate 8 *"One of the creatures swung down headforemost, grasping me beneath my armpits."*
plate 9 *"I caught my first sight of the dominant race of the inner world."*
plate 10 *"She moved as one in a trance straight toward the reptile."*
*plate 11 *"His huge, fanged jaws grinned in pleasurable appreciation of my predicament."*
*plate 12 *"With all my strength I drove the spear straight into the gaping jaws of the hydrophidian."*
plate 13 *"My shaft pierced the sagoth's savage heart..."*
plate 14 *"I let him have a left fair on the point of the jaw that sent him tumbling over on his back."*
plate 15 proposed jacket design for PELLUCIDAR
plate 16 side A *"We were assailed by enormous white bears."*
side B a previously unpublished pencil rough
plate 17 *"I saw three mighty Thipdars."*
plate 18 *"They buried their talons in his back."*
plate 19 *"The great man-brute seated himself upon a flat rock."*
plate 20 *"I had my stone knife in my hand, and he had his."*
plate 21 *"The fierce beasts were upon the Thurian simultaneously."*
plate 22 Jungle Woman
envelope illustrations frontispiece from LAND OF TERROR
frontispiece from TARZAN AND THE LION MAN
White Indian illustration

CANVAS TEXTURED FANTASY ART PRINTS
Worldbeater / Frazetta Prints ltd.
THE FOLLOWING NUMBERING SYSTEM WAS USED BY RETAILER AS LOCATION NUMBERS

- 1-1 **Wolfman**
- 1-2 **The Apparition**
- 1-3 **Snow Giants**
- 1-4 **Berserker**
- 1-5 **Sea Monster**
- 2-1 **Spiderman**
- 2-2 **Neanderthal**
- 2-3 **Tyrannosaurus Rex**
- 2-4 **Egyptian Princess (Egyptian Queen)**
- 2-5 **Woman With a Scythe**
- 3-1 **The Sorcerer**
- 3-2 **Sun Goddess**
- 3-3 **Sea Witch**
- 3-4 **The Brain**
- 3-5 **Wolf Moon**
- nn display poster showing poster thumbnails with location #'s. The back of this display poster has a full image produced on the back. Not all display posters have the same image on the back. This may be done for window display or perhaps to save paper.

- CAT GIRL color print

Frank Frazetta
signed and numbered edition of 350, color, 15" x 16"
each print has original remarque at bottom

- CAVEMAN FIGHTING OFF WOLVES 11 x 17

Never published since this print.

CLOTH PRINTS
1968
Very limited quantity
These were printed on a Tyvek-like "cloth", with borders, and were designed to be stretched over a frame and framed like oil paintings.

- **Sea Witch**
- **Egyptian Queen**
- **The Apparition**

- cover to BUSTER CRABBE #5 print

Ed April, Jr.
b/w print reproduced from the original 17 1/2" x 22"

- CONAN color print

1974
Ken Baker
7" x 9", numbered edition of 350

DEATH DEALER color print signed and numbered edition of 345, color, 20" x 27 3/4"
Frank Frazetta

- gold edition (1 - 100)
- edition 101 - 345

- DRAGULA print (Bootleg)

early 1970's, 8.5" x 11" on heavy paper
first printed in NATIONAL LAMPOON November, 1971

EFFICIENCY EXPERT b/w print
House of Greystoke
1966
reproduces the frontispiece from THE EFFICIENCY EXPERT

- unsigned edition
- 4 signed copies are known to exist

EGYPTIAN QUEEN LITHOGRAPH
- Signed and numbered with remarque Limited to 500
- without remarque

- **EXECUTIONER, THE** b/w print
  8" x 8" later reproduced in FANTASTIC ART OF FRANK FRAZETTA Vol. 1 (art book)

- **FAMOUS FUNNIES COVERS** portfolio

Russ Cochran
1975
8 color plates
first printed in FAMOUS FUNNIES #209 - 216
These are re-colored by Frazetta for this edition
envelope with b/w image

- **FIRE & ICE** portfolio limited to 5000

Frank Frazetta
1991
7 b/w plates reproducing the introduction drawings beginning the FIRE & ICE movie
full color envelope reprinting the movie poster design

- **FRANK FRAZETTA: PORTFOLIO ONE**

Middle Earth
1971 7 plates limited to a print run of 500

- **FRANK FRAZETTA: PORTFOLIO II**

Falcon Press
1976
This portfolio is a rare item from England
envelope with 6 plates limited to a print run of 1000
plate titles are as follows:
1 - Tarzan Battles the Pterodactyl
2 - A Princess of Mars
3 - Cornered
4 - Pellucidar
5 - Portrait of a Native
6 - Tarzan at the Earth's Core

- **FRAZETTA MUSEUM** advertising poster

Frank Frazetta
uses **Cat Girl** - total size 16" x 24"

FRAZETTA MUSEUM LITHOGRAPH
- white background with remarque
- white background without remarque
- green background

- **FRAZETTA PORTFOLIO**

Kitchen Sink
1993
6 color plates 8 1/2" x 11"
released in conjunction with
THE FRAZETTA PILLOW BOOK
see also FRAZETTA PORTFOLIO PRINTS

FRAZETTA PORTFOLIO PRINTS 18" x 22"
1994
Kitchen Sink
two color prints released in conjunction with
THE FRAZETTA PILLOW BOOK
see also FRAZETTA PORTFOLIO
- print #1 **Familiars**
- print #2 **Morning Gallop**

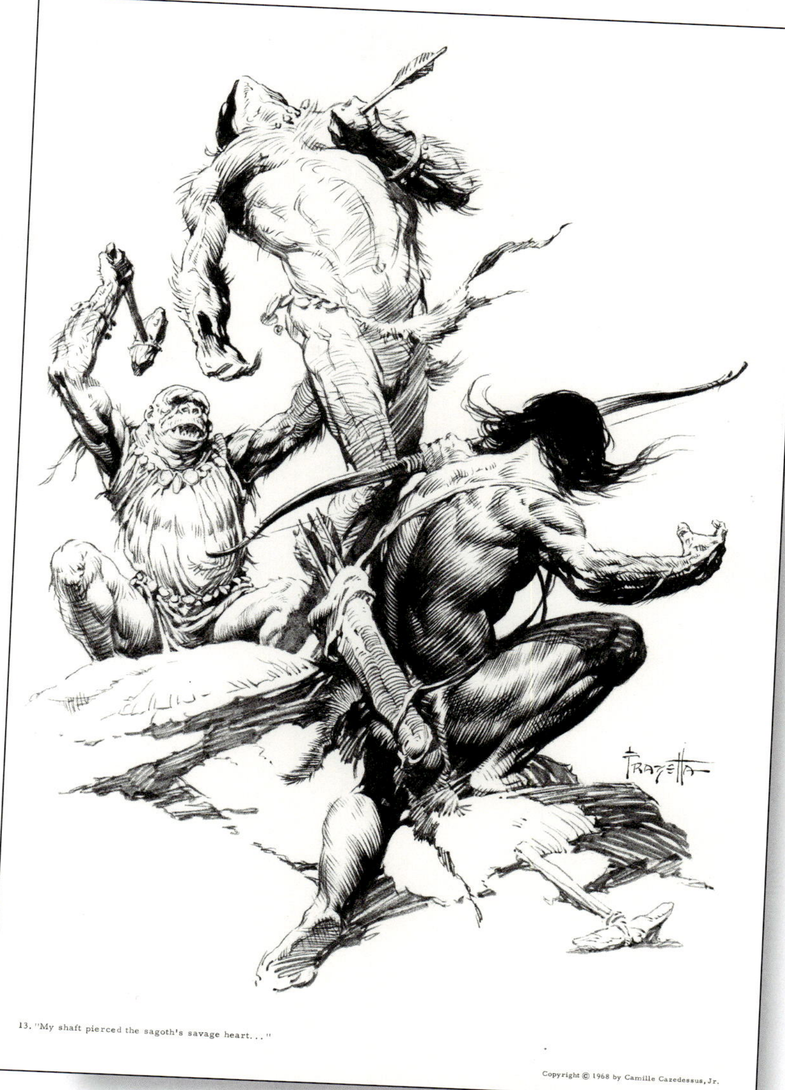

Plates from the Burroughs Artist Portfolio *Opar Press (1973)*

- **GIANTESS, THE** print

Frank Frazetta
Print size is 16.5" x 11.7"

GOLDEN GIRL LITHOGRAPH
Russ Cochran
- signed and numbered edition of 2,000, 17 3/8" x 18 1/2"

- **GOLFING NYMPHS** portfolio

Frank Frazetta
3 color plates 11" x 14"
plates are:
Better View
Great Form
Handicap

- **KUBLA KHAN PORTFOLIO** 12" x 15 1/2"

1977
Frazetta Prints
contents:
6 black and white plates (the first plate is signed and numbered by the artist) Limited to an edition of 1,500
1 folder with black and white image
1 envelope with black and white image same as folder (also numbered)

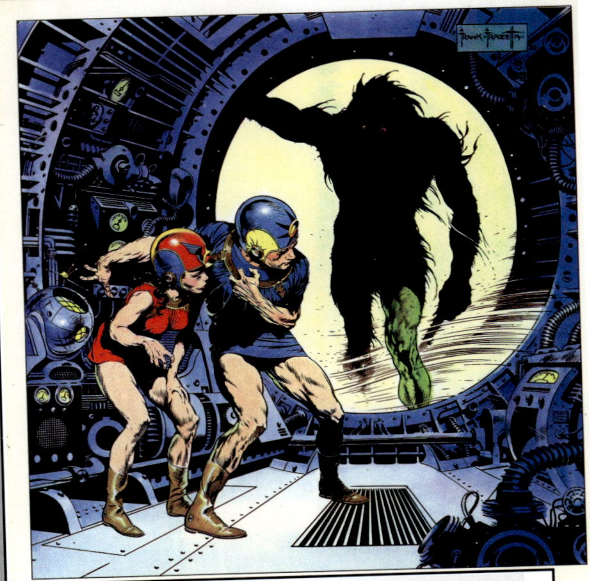

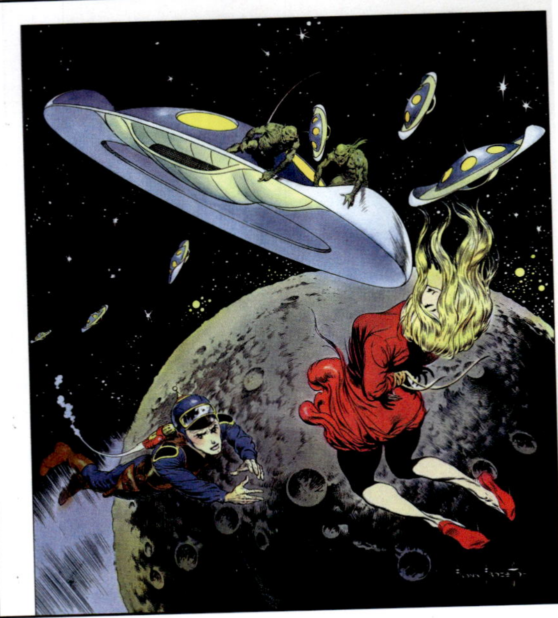

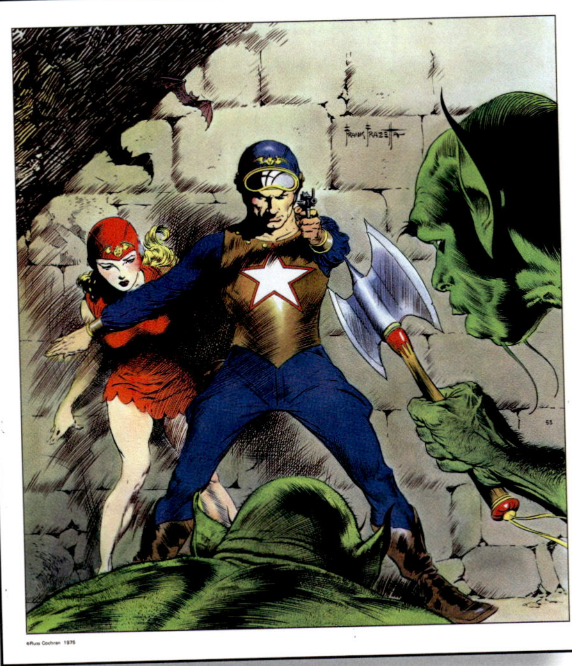

Love at First Sight

by Andrew Steven

In life the initial positive impact of an experience – "the grab" if you will, is of vital importance to the long term affinity with a person, place, or in this case, an artist's work. Every one of us has seen works of art that have stopped us dead in our tracks the instant that it came into view. Frank Frazetta, probably better than any other artist working in the fantasy field, has mastered that "grab." The initial impact of his work is so strong that to the uninitiated it truly is a case of "love at first sight."

What is fascinating is the fact that it really *is* all there on the canvas at first glance. The most captivating imagery is pushed right up front with the secondary elements, well, secondary! The bells and whistles are never distracting eye candy; they are only used to accent the genuine focus of the composition. Admittedly sometimes to the detriment of figural anatomy and the completeness of details depicted, it is as though Frank is telling us we were never meant to look that close anyway. Just as peripheral vision is distorted and never quite as clear as our primary focus, Frank's work is more faithful to true life *because* of the distortions. What we want and need to see is crystal clear while everything else is left for our brain to sort out at a later date, if ever.

The "grab" is the most arresting part of any experience. It is only later that we recognize the other pieces of the puzzle, whether good, bad or a combination of both. But by then, we've been hooked! Having done all the work, putting the best upfront, Frank makes it just that much easier on us. In a blink of an eye, love at first sight.

LEFT and OPPOSITE: From the
Famous Funnies Covers Portfolio
Russ Cochran (1975)

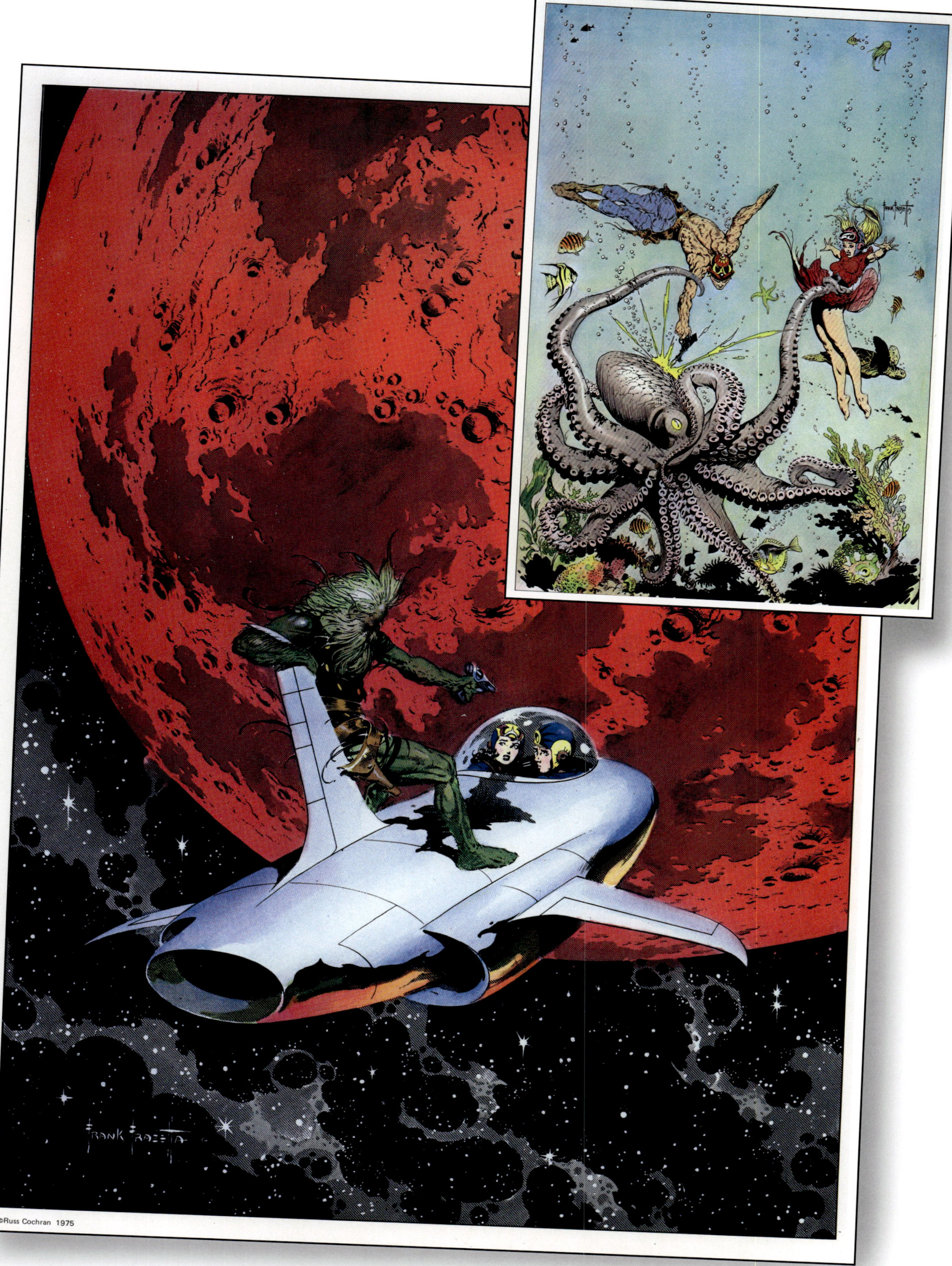
FRANK FRAZETTA
©Russ Cochran 1975

• LA OF OPAR color print
Attezarf Publications
color version of centerfold originally shown within FRAZETTA #1 (fanzine)

• LORD OF THE RINGS portfolio 12" x 15 1/2"
1975
Middle Earth
contents:
6 black and white plates (the first plate is signed and numbered by the artist)
1 folder with black and white image
1 envelope with black and white image same as folder (also numbered)
1 certificate of authenticity (also numbered)

• LOST CONTINENT color print
Worldbeaters
color print 7 1/8" x 10 1/8", 300 numbered prints

L. RON HUBBARD color prints
Author Services
a series of signed and numbered lithographs, each limited to an edition of 500
- **Battlefield Earth**
- **Dreamflight**
- **Moonrider**
- **The Countess**
- **The Encounter**
- **Lieutenant**
- **Leaping Lizards**
- **Man, the Endangered Species**

MASTERS COLLECTION ART PRINTS
2001
Frank Frazetta
Limited Edition of 300, each design
Printed on artist grade canvas, stamp signed and numbered by Frazetta.

The Barbarian
- Standard frame
- Museum duplicate frame

Snow Giants
- Standard frame
- Museum duplicate frame

Dark Kingdom
- Standard frame
- Museum duplicate frame

Sun Goddess
- Standard frame
- Museum duplicate frame

Destroyer
- Standard frame
- Museum duplicate frame

Swamp Demon
- Standard frame
- Museum duplicate frame

Death Dealer 5
- Standard frame
- Museum duplicate frame

Death Dealer
- Standard frame
- Museum duplicate frame

Princess & the Panther
- Standard frame
- Museum duplicate frame

Escape on Venus
- Standard frame
- Museum duplicate frame

Death Dealer 2
- Standard frame
- Museum duplicate frame

Moons Rapture
- Standard frame
- Museum duplicate frame

Las Vegas
- Standard frame
- Museum duplicate frame

Chained
- Standard frame
- Museum duplicate frame

Cat Girl
- Standard frame
- Museum duplicate frame

Princess of Mars
- Standard frame
- Museum duplicate frame

Huns
- Standard frame
- Museum duplicate frame

• NIGHT WINDS photo print
Frank Frazetta
photo copy of the cover to the book NIGHT WINDS
signed and numbered edition of 100, 11" x 14", color

• NUDE WATERCOLOR color print
1978
Christopher Ent.
signed and numbered edition of 100, 16" x 20", matted

• PORTFOLIO 8 1/2" x 11" poor quality bootleg
1972
Contains 10 plates. One of which (*Dragula*) is a comic cover parody.
first printed in NATIONAL LAMPOON November, 1971

• PORTFOLIO OF FINE COMIC ART
National Cartoonists Society
Contains a preliminary watercolor sketch of THE GAUNTLET movie poster artwork.
A signed and numbered portfolio limited to 1,500. Some plates are signed while others are not.
The Frazetta piece is not signed. Size is 11" x 16"

• REIGN OF WIZARDRY color print
8" x 8" revised version of paperback cover

• SCHLITZ BEER / RODEO promo poster 18" x 32"
1975 The poster image is **Bucking Bronco**
first printed in DOUBLEDAY BOOK CLUB WESTERN WRITERS *"The True Memoirs of Charley Blankenship"*

• SHI color poster
1996
Crusade
Reproduces the cover to SHI - SENRYAKU EDITION

• SILVER WARRIOR LIMITED EDITION FRAMED PRINT
2001
Frank Frazetta
Limited Edition of 500
Imported hardwood frame
Solid brass etched title plate
Individually numbered
Certificate of authenticity

• SOUTHWESTERN CON poster
1970 Conan sketch, limited print run of 250 8 1/2" x 11"

• TACO POSTERBOOK
COVER **Egyptian Queen**
Six plates by various artists.
Egyptian Queen plate by Frazetta, color, 12" x 17"

• TARZAN AND BOLGANI b/w print
Vern Coriell Publication
b/w print 8 1/2" x 11"

• **TARZAN AND THE ANT MEN** color print
first printed in BURROUGHS BULLETIN #29 (fanzine)

• **THUN'DA POSTER**
1973
Frank Frazetta
Size - 9"x13"
Reproduces cover (recolored) to A-1 COMICS #47
Lines on back of poster say
" © 1952 Sussex Publishing Co., Inc.
Entire Contents Copyright 1973 by Frank Frazetta"

• **VAMPIRELLA 1996** poster
1997
Harris Publications
reproduces the cover to
VAMPIRELLA 25th ANNIVERSARY

WARREN MAGAZINE COVER posters
Warren Publications
- Creepy #7 1972 **Dracula Meets the Wolfman**
- Creepy #10 1972 **Beyond the Grave**
- Creepy #11 1972 **King Kong**
- Eerie #23 1972 **Egyptian Queen**
- Eerie #81 1976 **Queen Kong**
- Vampirella #7 1972 **Sun Goddess**

• **WILLIAMSON & FRAZETTA - SPACE HEROES** portfolio
(limited to 1500 signed by Williamson and 1000 unsigned)
1976
September Publications
contains 10 previously un-published b/w plates by Williamson.
Plates 4-9 inked by Frazetta

WEIRD SCIENCE-FANTASY #29 b/w print
Russ Cochran
10" x 13" reproduced from the original
- unsigned copy
- signed copy

• **WEIRD SCIENCE-FANTASY #29** color print
Russ Cochran
signed and numbered edition of 50
(only 40 completed) 14" x 18"
each print hand colored by Frazetta
each print has additional hand drawn remarque at bottom
reprinted in cover to WEIRD SCIENCE-FANTASY #29 (b&w print)
reprinted in cover to WEIRD SCIENCE-FANTASY #29 (hand colored print)
reprinted in RUSS COCHRAN COMIC ART #23 (auction catalog)
reprinted in RUSS COCHRAN COMIC ART #33 (auction catalog)
reprinted in RUSS COCHRAN COMIC ART #58 (auction catalog)

• **WOMEN OF THE AGES** portfolio 12" x 15 1/2"
1977
Middle Earth
print run limited to 1,500 copies
contents:
6 black & white plates (the first plate is signed & numbered by the artist)
one folder with seventh black and white image
one envelope with black and white image same as folder
(also numbered)
one certificate of authenticity (also numbered)

• **YOUNG WORLD** color print 11" x 17"
first printed as wraparound cover to MONSTER MANIA #2

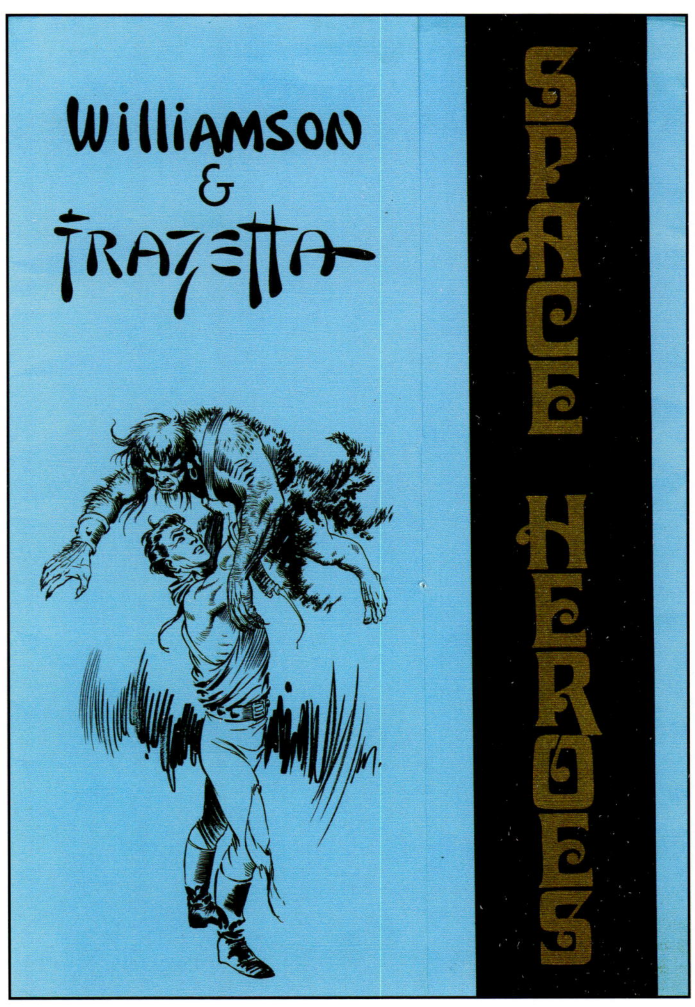

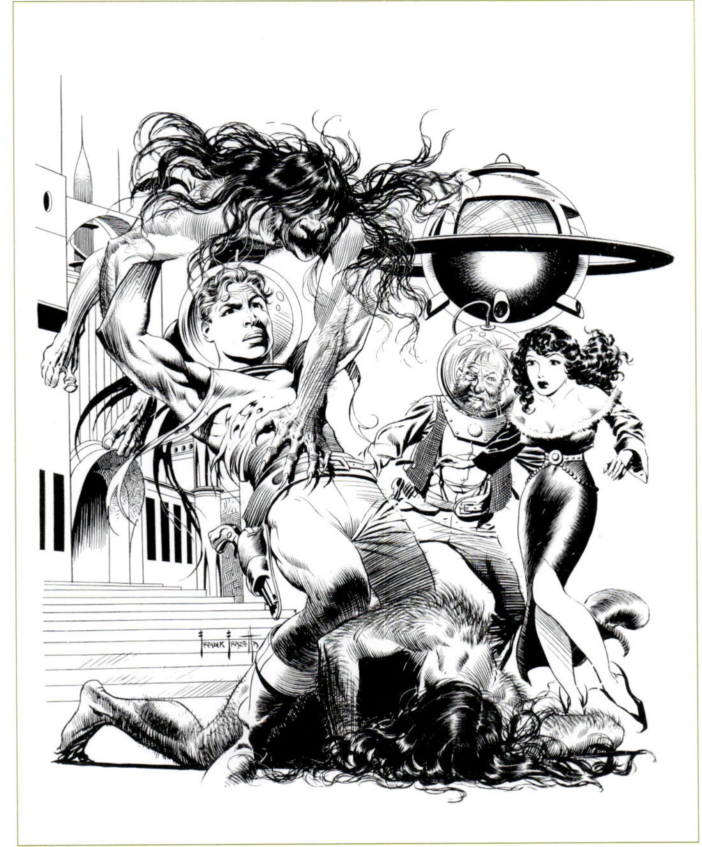

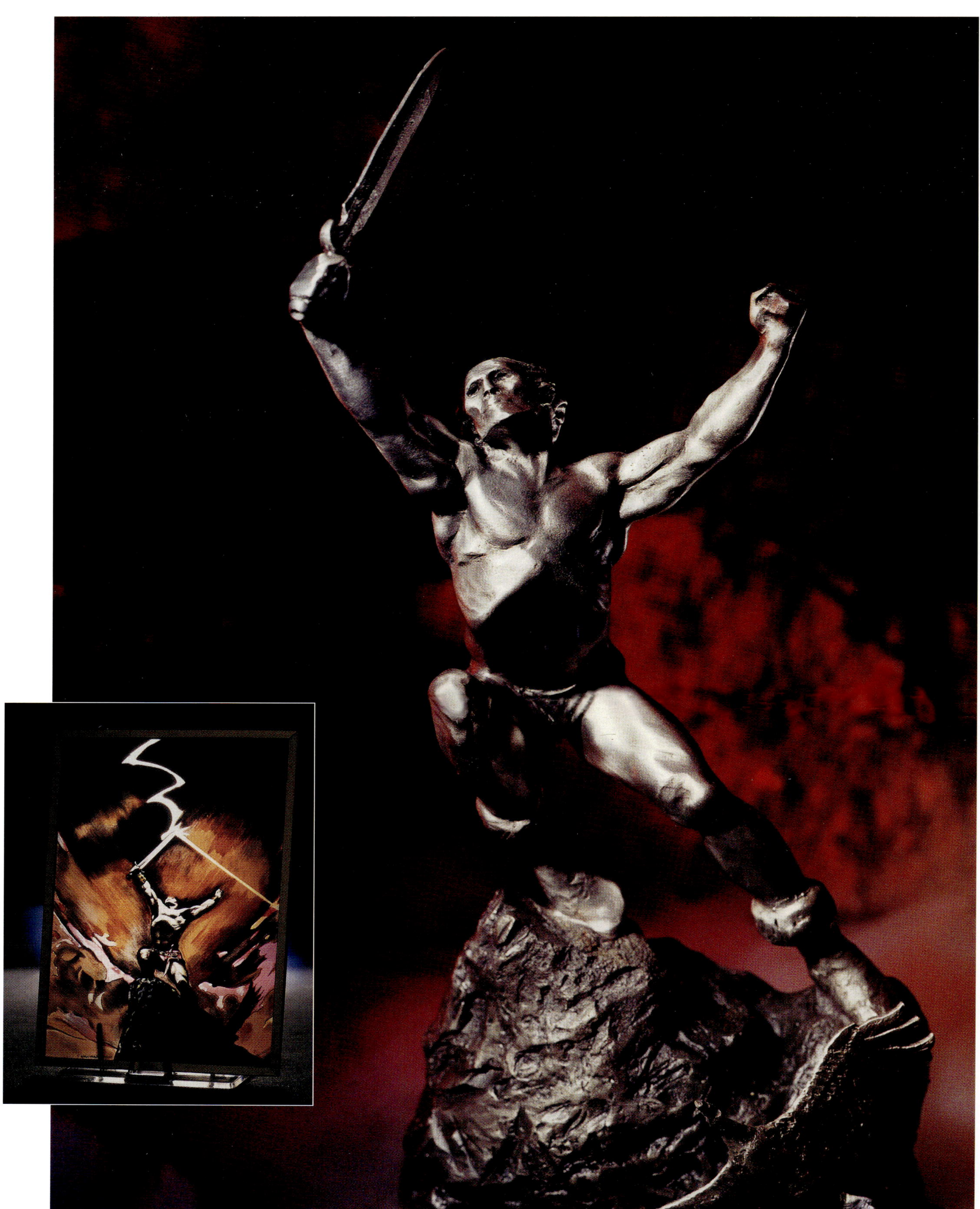

SCULPTURES & FIGURINES

By Randy Bowen

Over the past few years, RANDY BOWEN has carved an unbelievable number of sculptures for the comic book and fantasy industry. It seems as if there's a new Bowen sculpture coming out every week, every one of them testifies to his enormous talent.

Frank Frazetta was probably my single biggest influence. It was his dark fantasy images that ignited my imagination. When I was nine years old I stumbled upon a box of CREEPY magazines in the alley behind my father's store. Upon closer inspection I discovered that all the covers had been torn off (as was customary in those days for unsold stock mags in retail stores) In a nearby box were the covers. Even in their "dampened from being out of doors" state, Frazetta's images jumped off the page and became forever burned into my subconscious.

It was years later that I discovered who the artist was… Frazetta, of course. When I was older I bought all of his art books and collected a few of the paperbacks that bore his work. You can imagine how I felt as an adult to actually collaborate with the Man on a project.

OPPOSITE: War Against the Gods, *pewter statue sculpted by Frazetta. Stained glass image (inset.)*

BELOW LEFT: *Bronze Bust set sculpted by Frazetta.*

BELOW: Death Dealer *sculpted by Randy Bowen.*

Frazetta

Black Line Fever & Frank Frazetta present this limited edition set of 3 statue busts. Due to the extremely limited nature of this offer (75 sets) orders cannot be guaranteed unless verified by phone. Each set comes with a certificate of authenticity. These museum quality busts are sculpted by Frank Frazetta himself.
310.859-0658 fax: 310.859-1156
Make all checks payable to Black Line Fever
Only $2,000.00 postage paid.427 N. Canon Dr. Suite 204
Beverly Hills, CA 90210

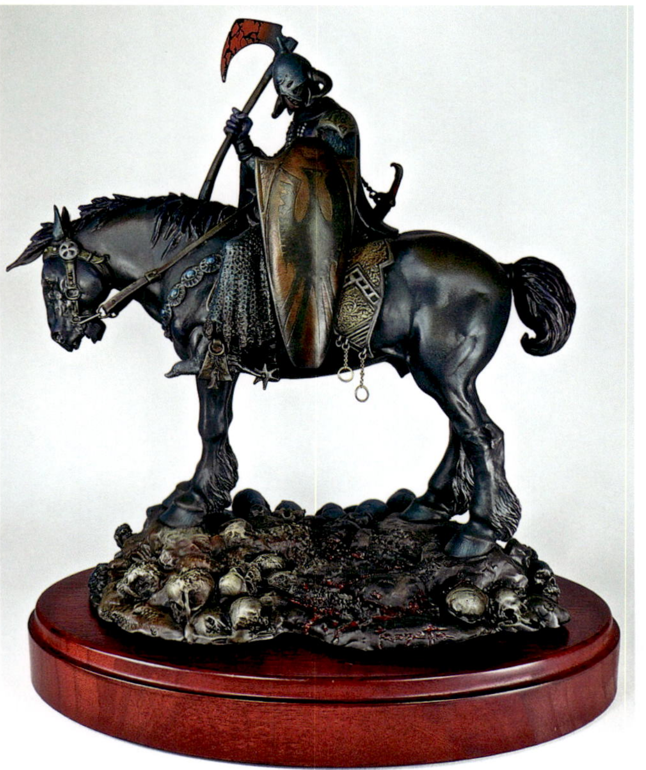

SCULPTURES & FIGURINES

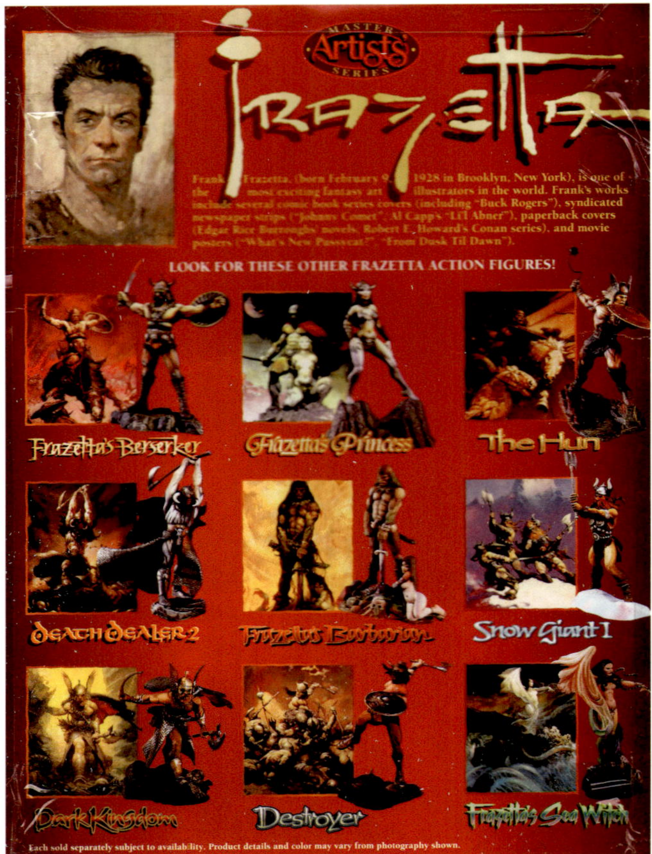

ABOVE: Master Artist Series *Frazetta action figures.*

BARBARIAN, THE porcelain figure (aka: Conan The Barbarian)
Moore Creations / CSM Studio
2000
Sculpted by Clayburn Moore, based on the painting **The Barbarian**.

- cold cast porcelain figure (6,500 castings)
- Artists proof - nude female (300 castings)
- Artists proof - clothed female (100 castings)

All artist proofs feature a ten karat gold dagger with 4 genuine rubies inlaid in the handle. The hilt and blade of the barbarian's sword are made of sterling silver.

- BRONZE BUST SET based on the characters from the movie

FIRE and ICE
(limited to 75 castings)
Black Line Fever \ Frank Frazetta
1996
3 busts, sculpted by Frazetta, sold as a set with a certificate of authenticity
set contains the following characters:
a sub-human (Nekron's minion)
Darkwolf
Teegra

- DEATH DEALER bronze figure (limited to 50 castings)

Dark Horse
1995 Sculpted by Randy Bowen
based on the painting **Death Dealer.**

- DEATH DEALER porcelain figure

Dark Horse
1997 Re-sculpted by Randy Bowen from the bronze figure

- DEATH DEALER mini porcelain figure (Limited to 5000 castings)

Dark Horse
2004 7 1/2" tall. Based on the original sculpture by Randy Bowen

- DEATH DEALER (Phantom Warrior) Life-sized fiberglass statue

2009
Deep in the Heart Foundry, based on the sculpture by Randy Bowen

- DEATH DEALER III mini porcelain figure

Work Shop Toys
2004
Sculpted by Kevin Johnson
12" tall. Based on **Death Dealer III**

- Standard Edition (Limited to 5000 castings)
- Signed/Numbered Edition (Limited to 125 castings, initialed by Frazetta)
- Extremely Limited Edition (10 castings)
  Painted by, signed & numbered by Frazetta. Comes with signed/numbered print

- DEATH DEALER STEIN Ceramic/metal

2003
12" tall
Limited edition stein Personally Signed & Numbered by Frank Frazetta - Limited edition of 125

- DRACULA MEETS THE WOLFMAN cold cast porcelain

2010
Dark Horse
Sculpted by Troy McDevitt
Paint Mastered by Joy & Tom Studios
10" tall

- EGYPTIAN QUEEN cold cast porcelain

2008
Dark Horse
Sculpted by Gabriel Marquez of Reel Art Studios
Prototype Painted by Alex Castro
Dimensions: 1/8 scale — 12" tall overall
Depth is 12"; Width is 12"
Queen figure is 9.25" tall
Guard figure is 8" tall; Cat figure is 6" long
Column is 6" tall; Base is 6" tall; Vase is 3" tall
limited edition of 2000 pieces

GHOUL QUEEN resin statue
2003
Frank Frazetta,The Art Farm & Spectrum Design
Sculpted by Tim Bruckner
8"H x 8"W on a 2" wooden base

- Standard Edition
- Personally Signed, Limited edition of 50

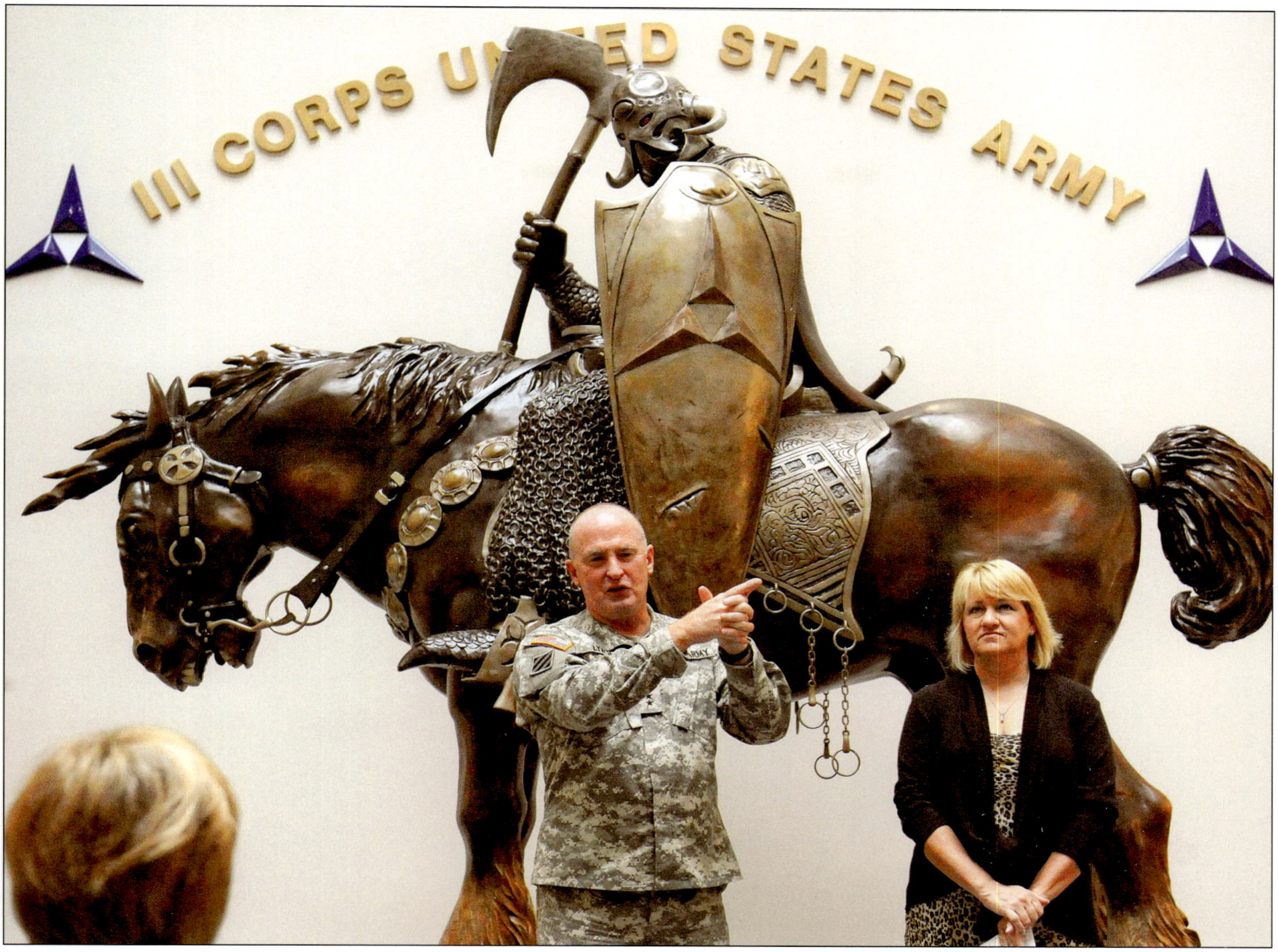

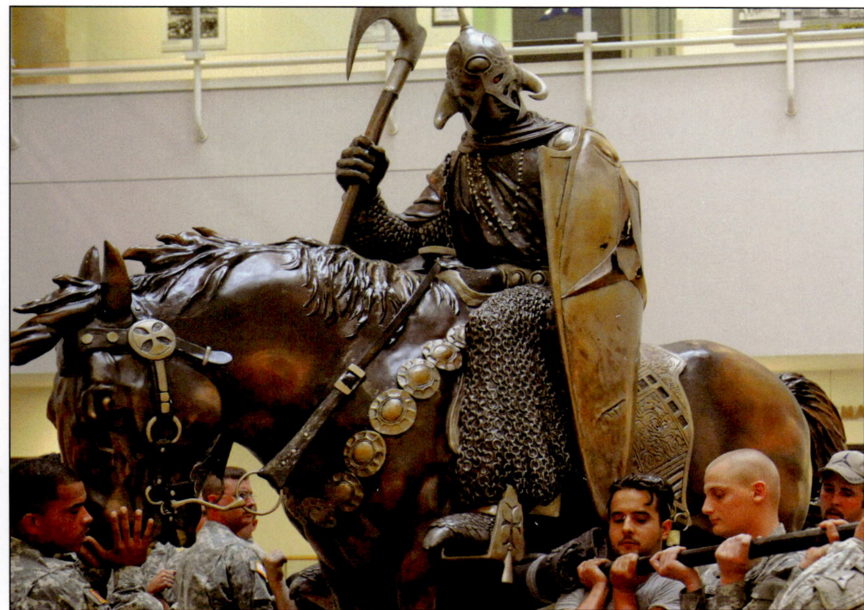

Photos by Michael Heckman for the U.S. Army's Fort Hood Sentinel.

The DEATH DEALER (Phantom Warrior) Life-sized fiberglass statue done in 2009 by the *Deep in the Heart Foundry*, based on the sculpture by Randy Bowen.

Created for the U.S. military's III Corps at Fort Hood Texas. The III Corps has used the image of The Death Dealer as a symbol since 1985.

It features an 18-hands tall horse with a 6-foot, 6-inch rider. The statue sits in the III Corps Headquarter's Atrium.

It was also reported by the Fort Hood *Sentinel* newspaper that: "A metal statue of the Phantom Warrior [Death Dealer] will be placed outside the headquarters in January 2010. A smaller version will deploy with troops." As of the time of this publication, these reports of additional statuary have yet been realized.

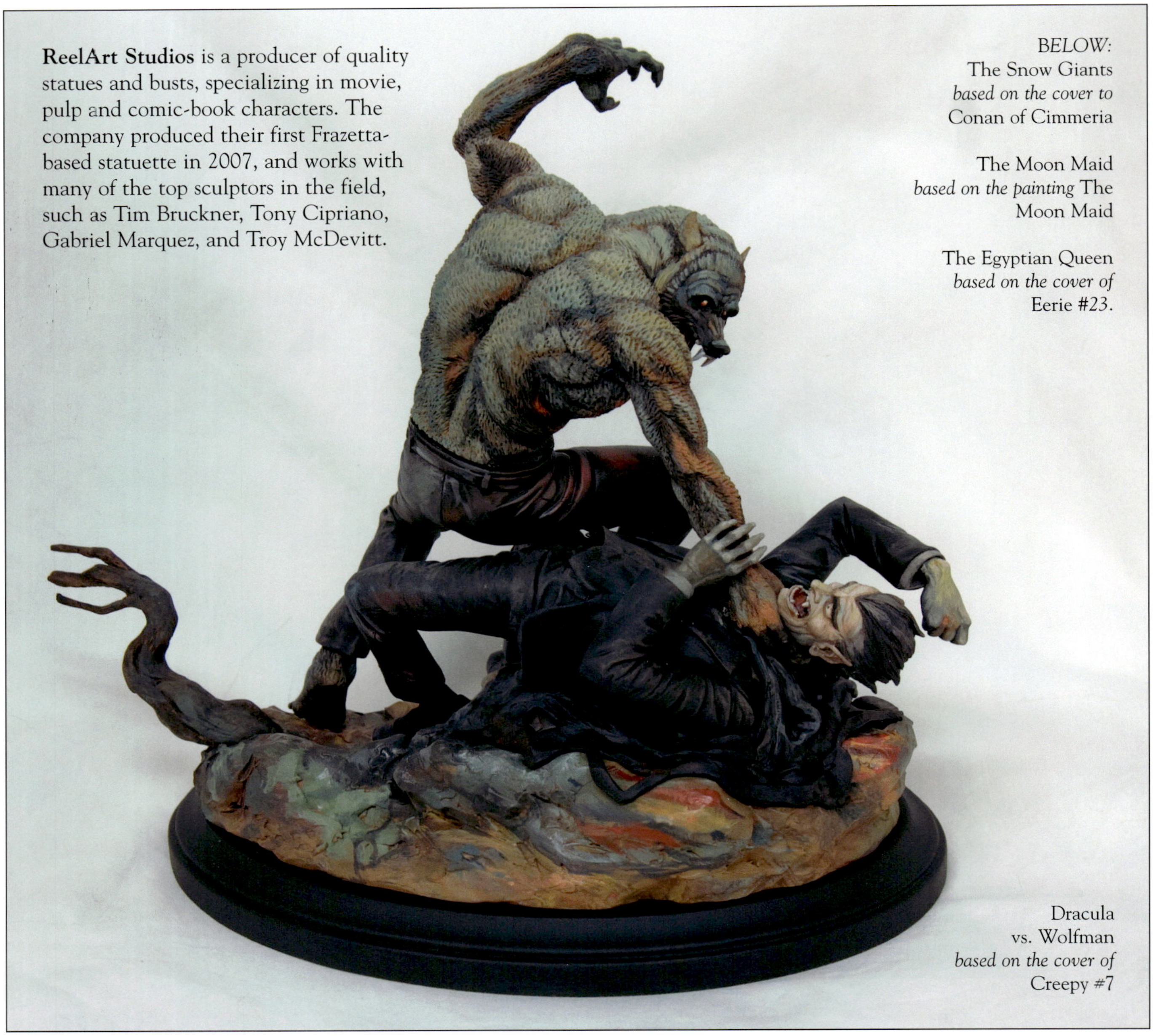

ReelArt Studios is a producer of quality statues and busts, specializing in movie, pulp and comic-book characters. The company produced their first Frazetta-based statuette in 2007, and works with many of the top sculptors in the field, such as Tim Bruckner, Tony Cipriano, Gabriel Marquez, and Troy McDevitt.

BELOW:
The Snow Giants
based on the cover to
Conan of Cimmeria

The Moon Maid
based on the painting The Moon Maid

The Egyptian Queen
based on the cover of
Eerie #23.

Dracula vs. Wolfman
based on the cover of
Creepy #7

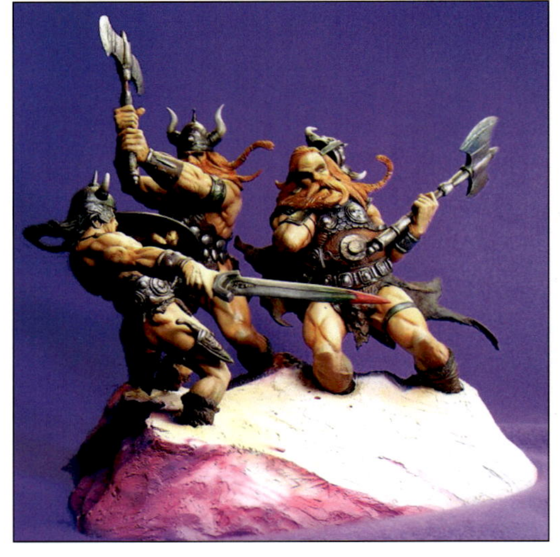

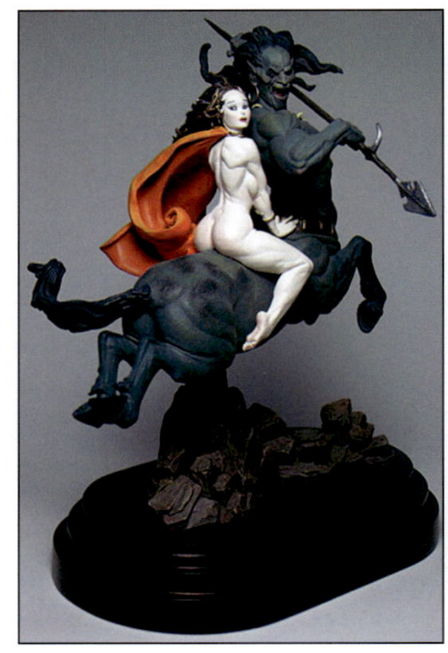

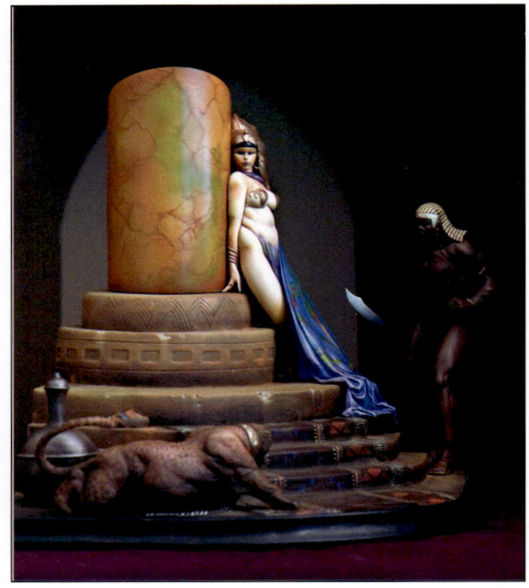

- MAN THE ENDANGERED SPECIES

Bronze Sculpture
Gentle Giant Studios
2003
Sculpted by Jeffrey Scott

Based on the painting **Man The Endangered Species**
Limited edition of 50
12.5"H - 18"L - 9"W

MASTER ARTIST FIGURE SERIES

8 Ball Studios
1999 - 2001

A series of collectable, plastic figures in display packaging.

- Death Dealer II
- Death Dealer II alternate
- Barbarian
- Berserker
- Princess
- Princess alternate
- Dark Kingdom
- Sea Witch
- The Destroyer
- The Snow Giant
- The Hun

- MOON MAID cold cast porcelain

2007
Dark Horse
Sculpted by Tim Bruckner of Reel Art Studios
Prototype Painted by Tim Bruckner
Dimensions: 1/12 scale — 10" tall
Depth is 6"
Width is 8"
limited edition of 2000 pieces

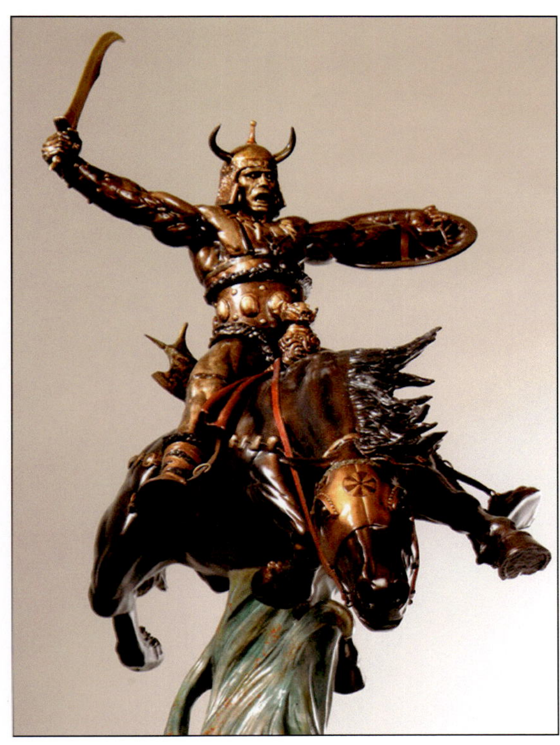

Conan the Conqueror
bronze, CSM Studio, 2009

- PRINCESS based on the painting - **A Fighting Man of Mars**

Moore Creations
1997
sculpted by Clayburn Moore

- bronze figure (75 castings)

10 1/4 inches tall, on a marble base

- cold cast porcelain figure (4000 castings)

10 1/4 inches tall, on a wood base

- cold cast porcelain figure with ruby in head dress

10 1/4 inches tall, on a wood base

- PRINCESS ORNAMENT

1997
Moore Creations

Cold cast porcelain, limited to 3000.

- SILVER WARRIOR musical snow globe

Moore Creations
Sculpted by the Shiflett Brothers
2000
limited to 3,000.
Plays Wagner's "Flight of the Valkeries"

- SNOW GIANTS cold cast porcelain

2007
Dark Horse
Sculpted by Tony Cipriano of Reel Art Studios
Prototype Painted by Dan Cope
Dimensions: 1/8 to 1/9 scale — 13.5" tall overall
Backside length is 13 1/2"
Giant figures are 11" tall
Barbarian figure is 9" tall

- SUN GODDESS cold cast porcelain

2008
Dark Horse
Sculpted by Tony Cipriano
Prototype Painted by Kat Sapene
Dimensions: 1/8 scale — 13" tall
Width is 9"
limited edition of 2000 pieces

- VAMPIRELLA cold cast porcelain figure

1997
Sculpted by Shawn Nagle

based on the painting - **Vampirella 1996**

- VAMPIRELLA RESIN MODEL KIT bootleg

2003
size - 4.5" H

Based on **Vampirella**

- WAR AGAINST THE GODS

pewter figure
Sculpted by Frank Frazetta
1991
Based on the painting **Against The Gods**

limited edition of 500
(less than 100 were actually sold)

Comes with stained glass plaque version of **Against the Gods** 9" x 5"

Related topic – JOVAN SEX APPEAL television commercial (movie and television)

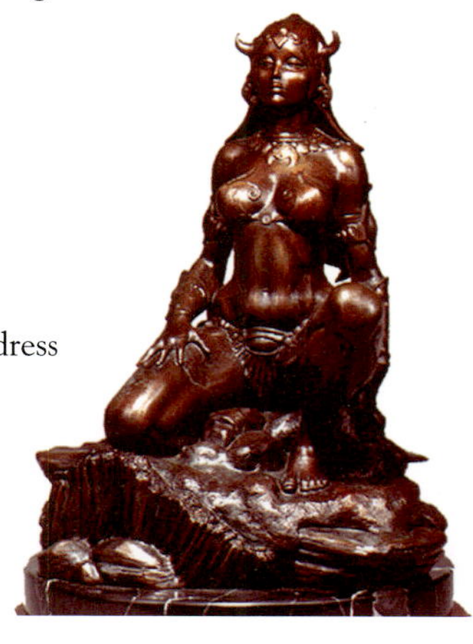

ABOVE: Princess *bronze based on the painting,* A Fighting Man of Mars

BELOW: The Barbarian *CSM Studio cold-cast porcelain sculpture based on the painting* The Barbarian

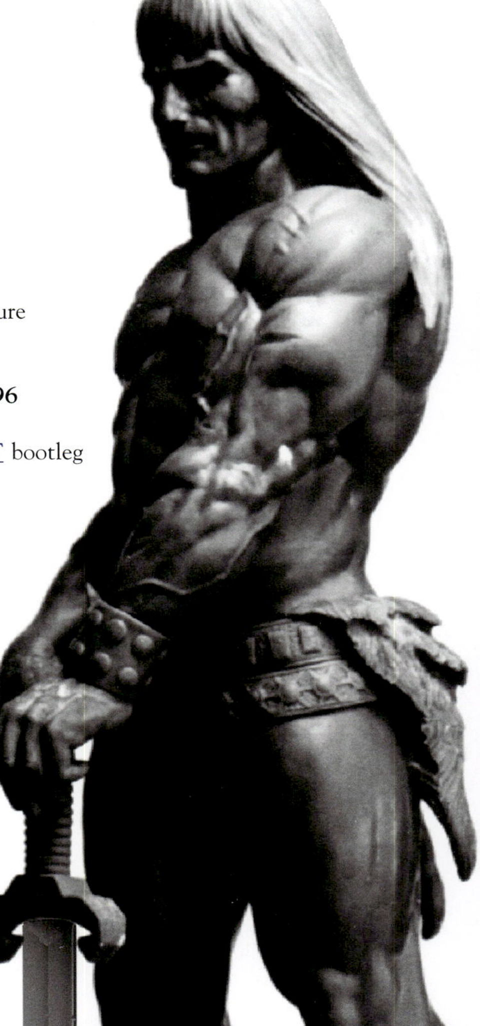

IN THE GROOVE

Frazetta's Record Covers

By Dean Motter

DEAN MOTTER *has designed hundreds of record jackets, first as executive art director for CBS Records Canada, and later as one of the country's top album cover designer* (Motorhead, Loverboy, Long John Baldry, The Nylons, Triumph, Anne Murray-- even Rich Little (and, yes... Anvil.) *During that time he was nominated for the industry's LP cover design awards nearly every year and won five of 'em. He is also known for his labors in the comic book mines via* Vertigo, Batman, Wolverine, Ray Bradbury and Mister X *and continues to toil therein.*

Most art directors in the music and movie promotion business during the 1960s were either uninterested or unaware of Frazetta's fantasy/horror illustration. They had him pegged strictly as a remarkable cartoonist who could paint like a sonovabitch. But it didn't take a Madison Avenue genius to see how such a colorful and robust style of illustration would appeal to film buffs, movie soundtrack afficionados and cartooning fans alike.

As movie posters were not considered particularly collectible at that time–they were usually trashed after the the theatrical run– the soundtrack LP covers were the only way many of us Frazetta fans were ever able to put our hands on copies of this art. As an avid consumer of record albums and Warren magazines in my youth, these items easily found their way into my archives (as was the case with many, many other collectors) pretty early on.

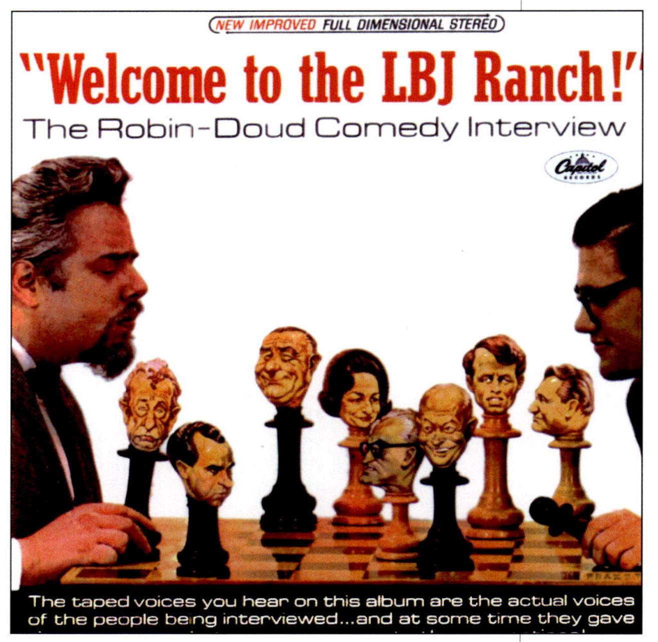

ABOVE:
Before Stewert or Colbert there was "Welcome to the LBJ Ranch!" *(1965)*

OPPOSITE:
Nazareth, Expect No Mercy *(1977)*

With the overnight success of Vaughn Meader's JFK spoof, *The First Family* (in 1962, over a decade before SNL) a new comedy genré was born. But in the aftermath of the Kennedy assassination the record's writer/producer Earl Doud stepped into the vacuum Meader's unfortunately forced retirement had left, with his own political comedy album, *Welcome to the LBJ Ranch*, featuring a roundtable of impressionists and comedians doing imitations of politicians of the day– and Frank supplying the likenesses for the cover. I was particularly fascinated by the deft composite work, seamlessly marrying illustration to photograph. Frazetta was quickly enlisted to do the covers for Doud's follow-up albums such as *Lyndon Johnson's Lonely Hearts Club Band* and others.

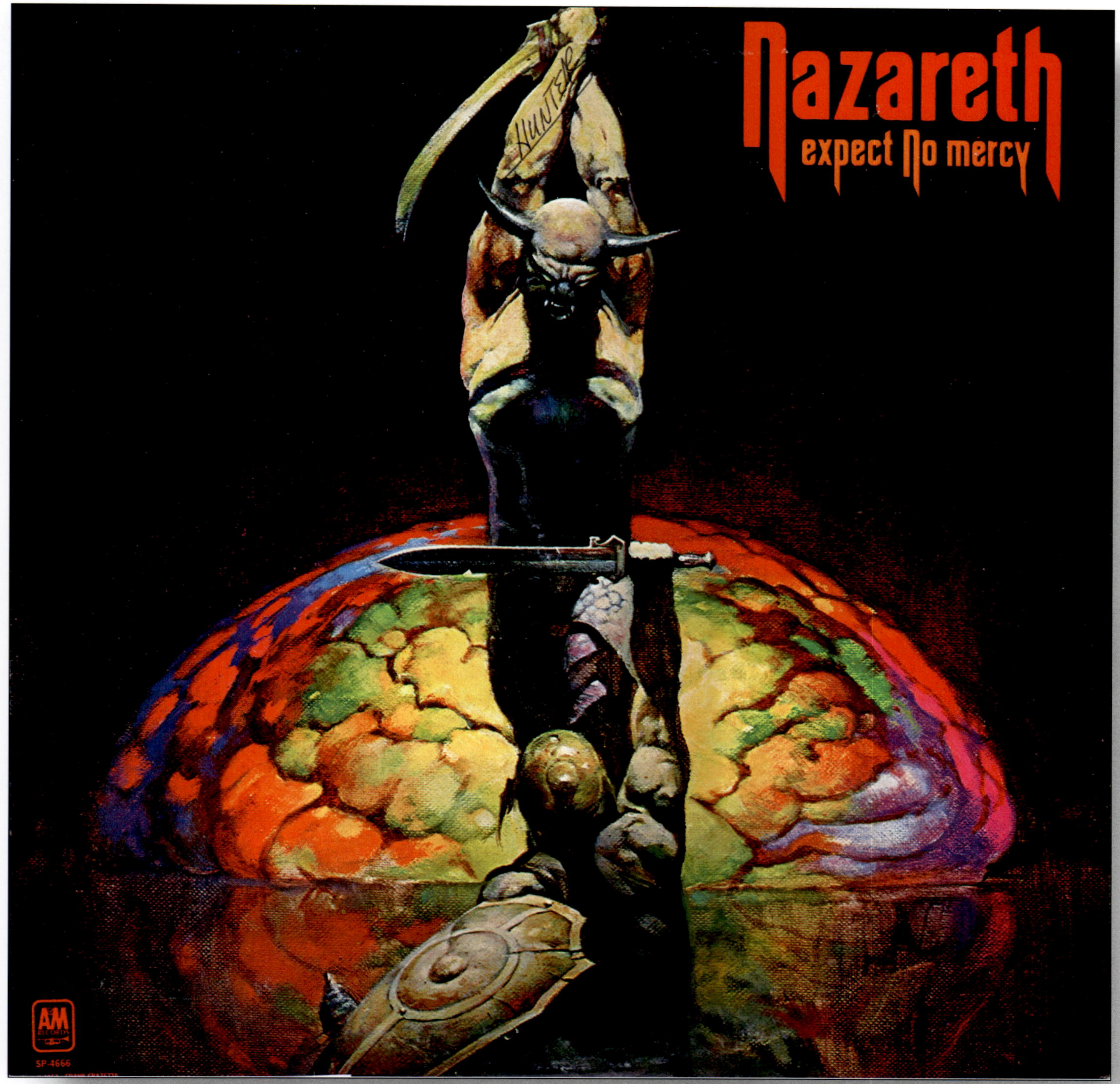

But as the *Mad Magazine* / Jack Davis style of movie poster, soundtrack and comedy album art gave way to more and more photography Frank's work gradually disappeared from the record shelves.

That is until 1972, when Kama Sutra records licensed *The Snow Giants* (the cover for CONAN OF CIMMERIA) for New York hard rock band Dust's second LP, *Hard Attack*. The cover not only featured a tastefully understated logo, but was embossed with a canvas texture, giving the entire sublime package an especially "artsy" nuance.

The label's art director was a long-time a fan of Frazetta's fantasy work and also happened to be in search of an American counterpart to the then king-of-the-LP-cover-hill, Roger Dean (of Yes and Uriah Heep fame, whose subject matter was often influenced by Frazetta.) Scotland's Nazareth followed suit a few years later, when A&M records licensed *The Brain* for the cover of their popular ninth album, *Expect No Mercy*.

But it was with the appearance of the art for *Death Dealer, Dark Kingdom* and *The Berserker* on the jackets of southern rock giants Molly Hatchet (1978's *Molly Hatchet*, 1979's *Flirtin' with Disaster* and 1980's *Beatin' the Odds* on Epic records) that Frazetta's work truly reached a new generation (and subculture) of record buyers. At the time of their release I was employed as executive art director with their Canadian record company, where, as the giant 42" point-of-purchase posters of these covers disappeared from the record stores, I was forced to constantly have them reprinted. My U.S. counterpart reported the same phenomena (matched at that time by Meat Loaf's *Bat Out of Hell* by Richard Corben and Bruce Springsteen's *Born in the U.S.A.* by photographer Annie Liebowitz. Of course I had my own framed "samples" on the office wall over my desk.) Gene Simmons and Kiss decided that they, too, wanted Frazetta covers, but when negotiations hit an impasse, the band turned to Frazetta protegee, Ken Kelly for *Destroyer* and *Love Gun*.

Frazetta's testosterone-fueled images of warriors, sorcerers and zaftig women continue to appeal to hard rock and heavy metal artists around the world–most recent being the Australian psychedelic rock band Wolfmother, who have displayed Frazetta imagery on their CD covers, posters and merchandise since 2006.

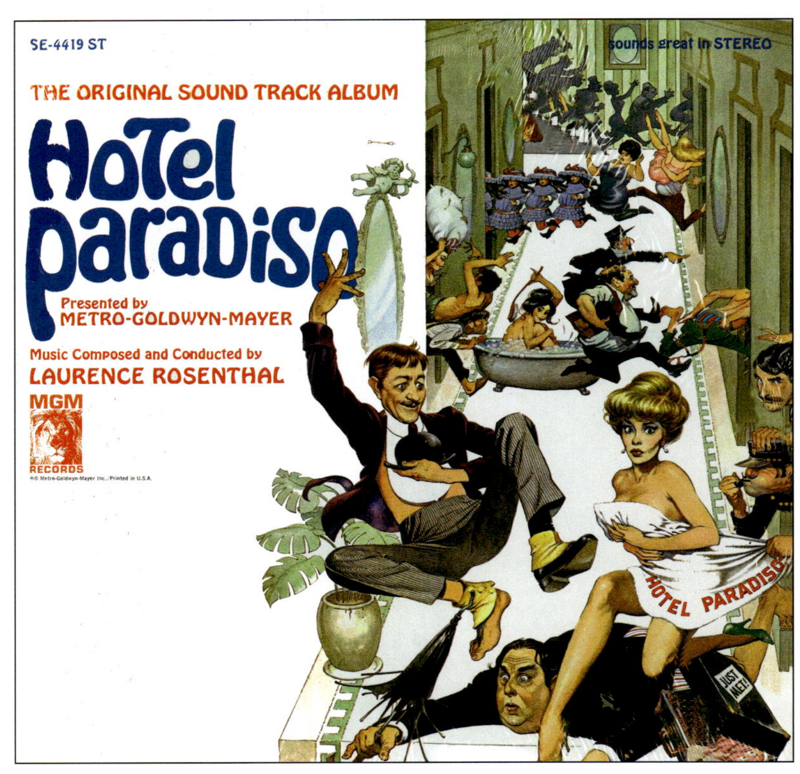

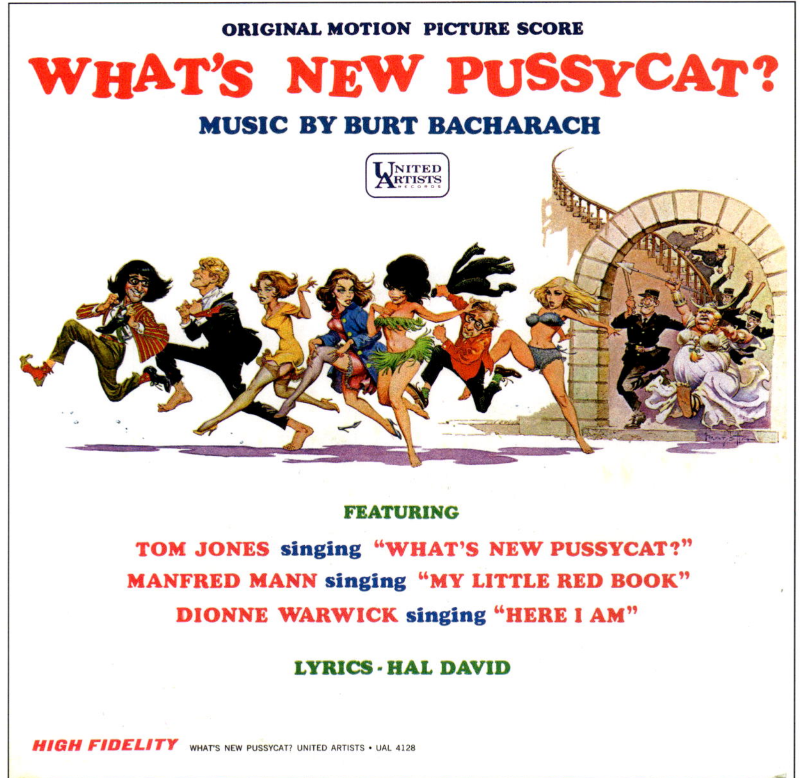

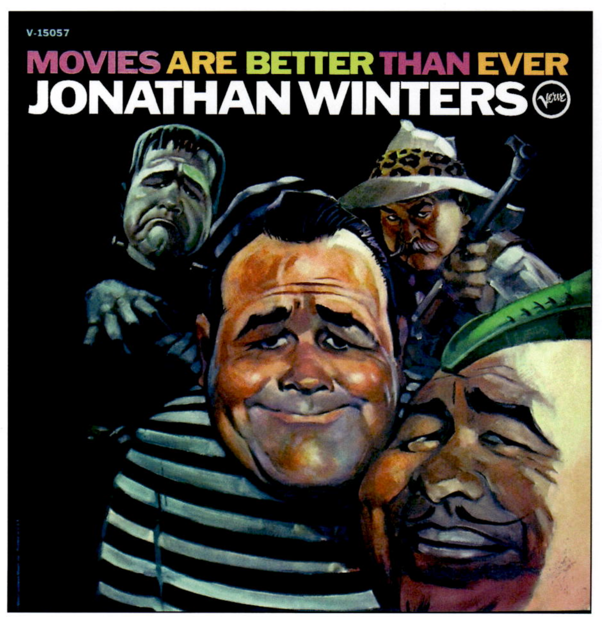

TOP: Soundtrack for Hotel Paradiso. *MGM Records (1966)*

ABOVE: What's New Pussycat? *United Artists (1965)*

RIGHT: Jonathan Winters - Movies are Better Than Ever. *Verve (1964)*

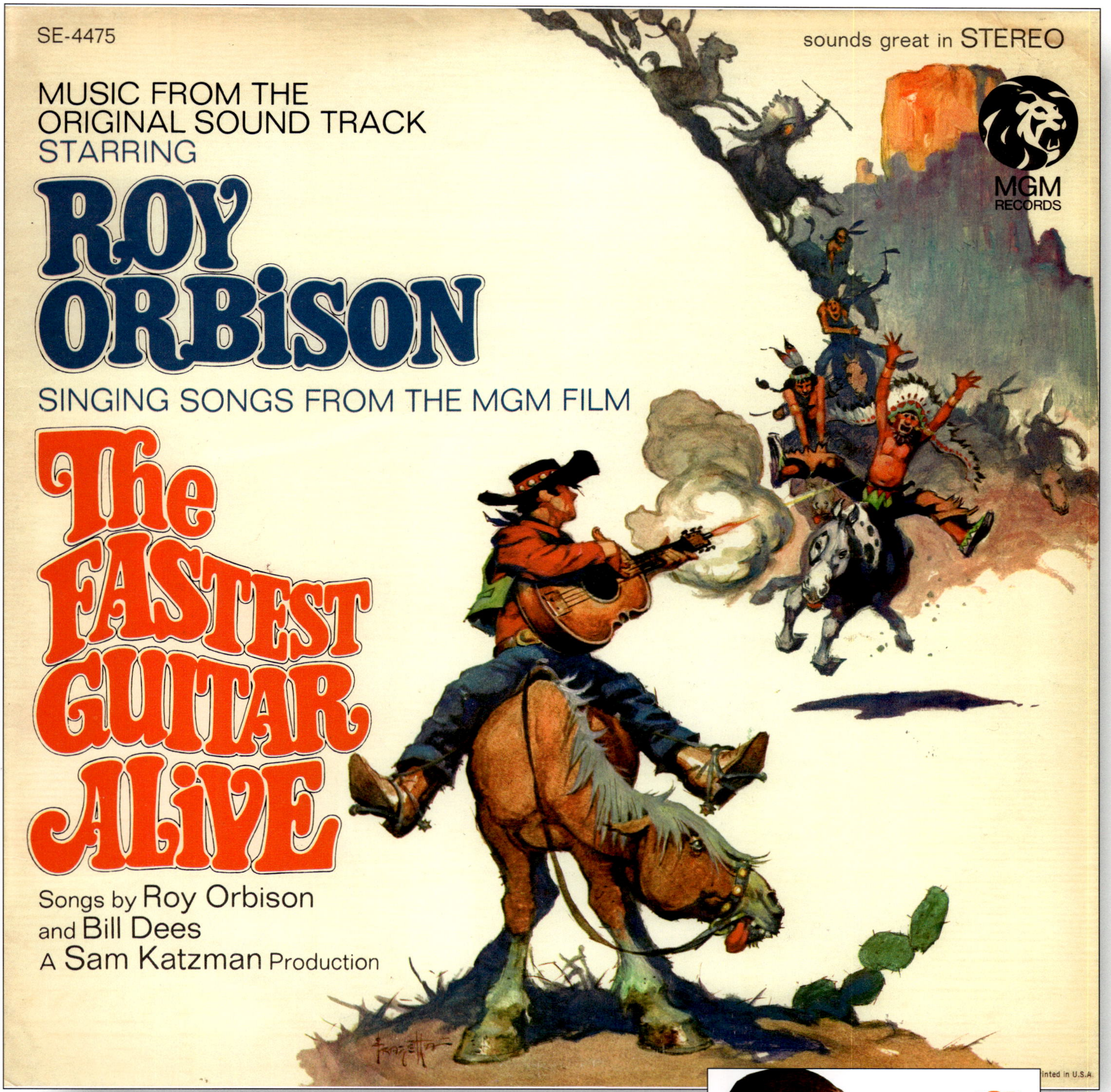

SE-4475

sounds great in STEREO

MUSIC FROM THE ORIGINAL SOUND TRACK STARRING

ROY ORBISON

SINGING SONGS FROM THE MGM FILM

The FASTEST GUITAR ALIVE

Songs by Roy Orbison and Bill Dees

A Sam Katzman Production

MGM RECORDS

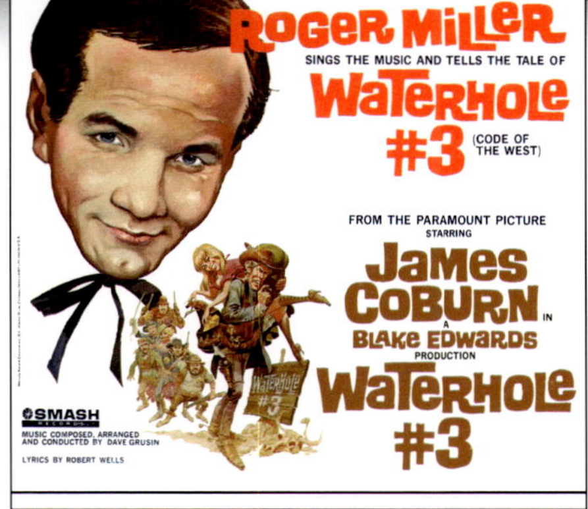

ABOVE:
Fastest Guitar Alive
soundtrack by Roy Orbison.
MGM Records (1968)

RIGHT:
With Jack Davis,
Waterhole #3
soundtrack by Roger Miller
Smash Records
(1967)

RECORD COVERS

- **AFTER THE FOX** (soundtrack)

United Artists UAS 5148
1966 front cover **After the Fox** (B sheet design)
back cover **After the Fox** (A sheet design)

- **DEAD ELVI, THE - Buddy Bought the Farm**

Chiller Theatre (2003)
CD Cover and Frazetta 'overlay' sleeve.

- **DUST - Hard Attack**

Kama Sutra Records KS BS 2059
1972
front cover **Snow Giants**
back cover detail of **"Snow Giants"**
Snow Giants Poster included with album

- Standard Edition
- Gatefold Edition

- **EARL DOUD & ALLEN ROBIN - Lyndon Johnson's Lonely Hearts Club Band**

Atco SD 33-230
1967
front cover Photo of military band with politicians faces (retouched by Frazetta) pasted over existing faces of band. Frazetta given credit for cover.

- **EARL DOUD & ALLEN ROBIN - Score 3 Points**

Capitol Records T 2629
1966
front cover Photo of Mt.Rushmore with Frazetta additions:
ALLEN Robin carving head of Lyndon B. Johnson
into
existing monument while Earl Doud looks down from above.

- **EARL DOUD & ALLEN ROBIN - Welcome to the L.B.J. Ranch!**

Capitol Records W 2423
1965
front cover Photo of Earl Doud and ALLEN Robin playing chess. The chess pieces have head caricatures of political figures painted by Frazetta. Cameos shown are (from L to R): Everett Dirkson, Richard Nixon, Lyndon Johnson, Lady Bird Johnson, Barry Goldwater, Dwight D. Eisenhower, Bobby Kennedy and Nelson Rockefeller.

- **FITZWILLY** (soundtrack)

United Artists UAS 5173 / UAL 4173
1967
front cover **Fitzwilly** (B sheet design)
back cover **Fitzwilly** (A sheet design) (b/w)

- **GAUNTLET, THE** (soundtrack)

(soundtrack)
Warner Brothers Records BSK 3144
1978 front cover **The Gauntlet**

- **HERMAN'S HERMITS -Both Sides of Herman's Hermits**

MGM Records SE-4386
1966
front cover **Herman's Hermits**
back cover

- **HOTEL PARADISO** (soundtrack)

MGM Records E/SE-4419 ST
1966 front cover **Hotel Paradiso**

- **JONATHAN WINTERS - Movies are Better Than Ever**

Verve V6-15057
1964 front cover **Jonathan Winters**

MOLLY HATCHET - Bounty Hunter

Epic PJE-35347
1979

- front cover **Death Dealer**
- picture disk.

  Used as a commemoration for high sales. Displayed inside chrome frame with engraved plaque which reads: "PRESENTED TO (SALES REPS NAME) IN COMMEMORATION OF SALES IN EXCESS OF (NUMBER OF) UNITS OF THE EPIC RECORD ALBUM "MOLLY HATCHET"
- picture disk retail version

MOLLY HATCHET - Flirtin' with Disaster

Epic AS-99-694
1979

- front cover **Dark Kingdom**
- picture disk

  Used as a commemoration for high sales. Displayed inside chrome frame with engraved plaque which reads: "PRESENTED TO (SALES REPS NAME) IN COMMEMORATION OF SALES IN EXCESS OF (NUMBER OF) UNITS OF THE EPIC RECORD ALBUM "MOLLY HATCHET – FLIRTIN' WITH DISASTER"

MOLLY HATCHET – Beatin' The Odds

Epic

- front cover **The Berserker**
- picture disk

- **NAZARETH - Expect No Mercy**

A&M SP-4666
1977 front cover **The Brain**

- **NIGHT THEY RAIDED MINSKY'S, THE** (soundtrack)

United Artists UAS 5191
1968 front cover **The Night They Raided Minsky's**
Back cover b/w version of same art.

- **ROGER MILLER - Sings the Music and Tells the Tale of Waterhole #3** (soundtrack)

Smash Records MGS 27096 / SRS 67096
1967 front cover Includes **Roger Miller** caricature by Frazetta.

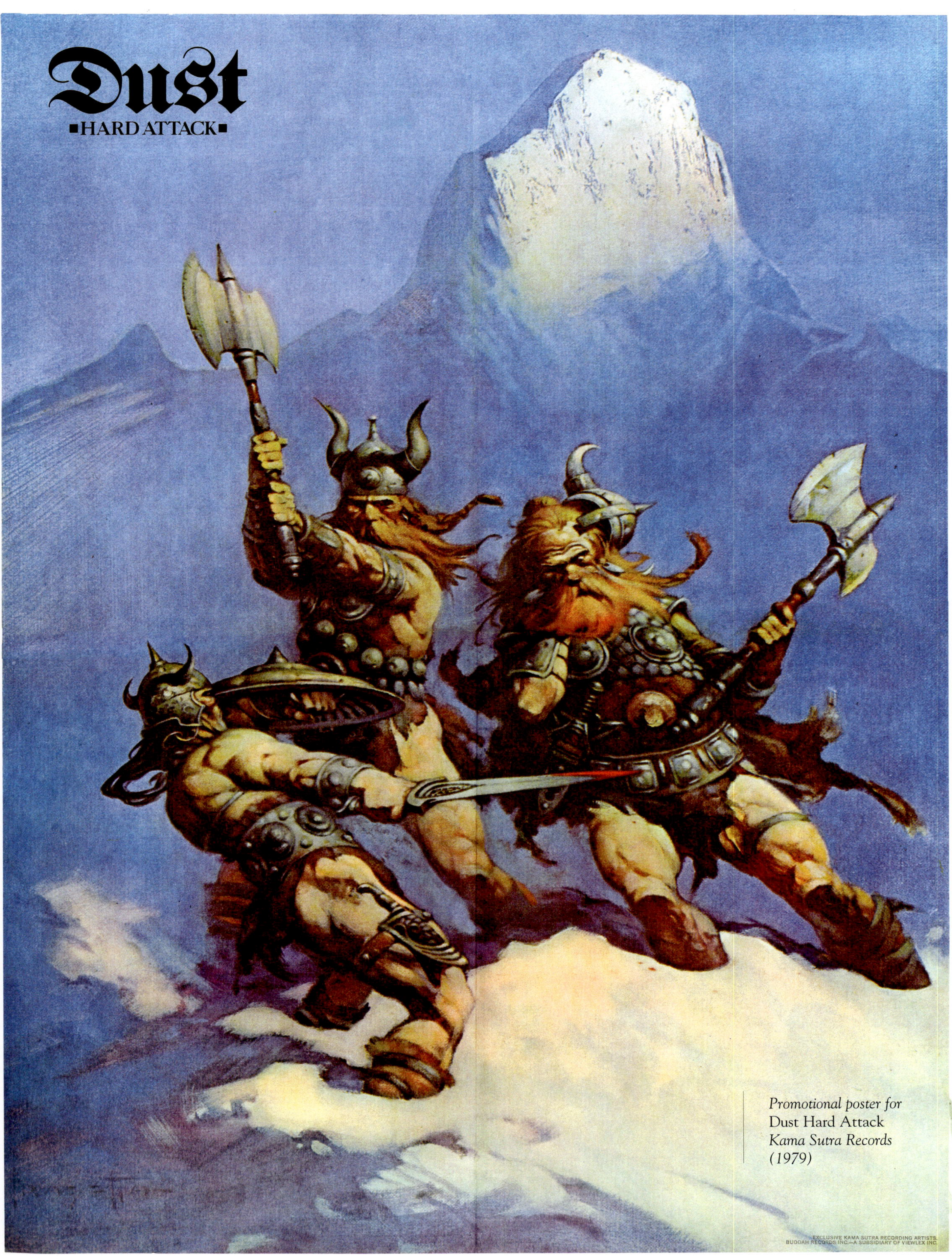

Promotional poster for
Dust Hard Attack
Kama Sutra Records
(1979)

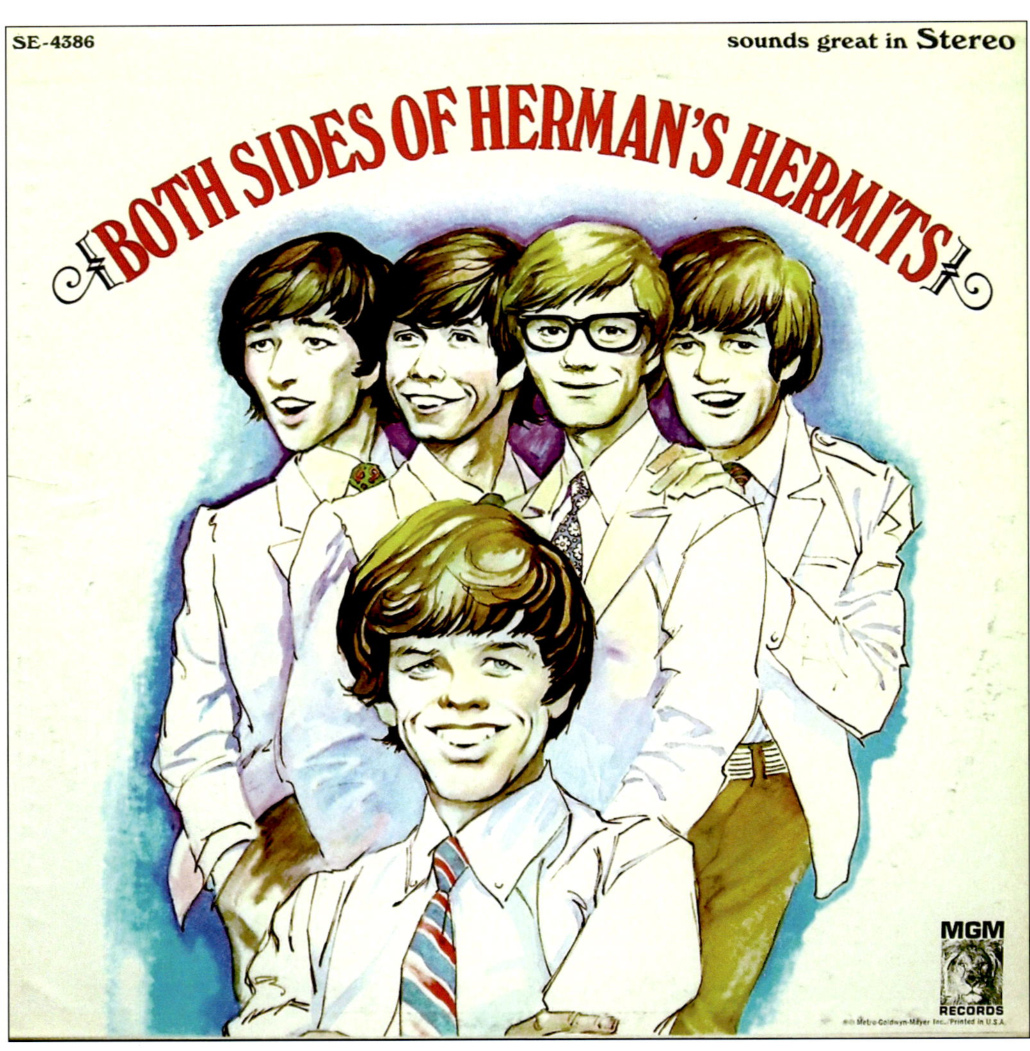

ABOVE: *Front cover to* Both Sides of Herman's Hermits. MGM *Records (1966)*

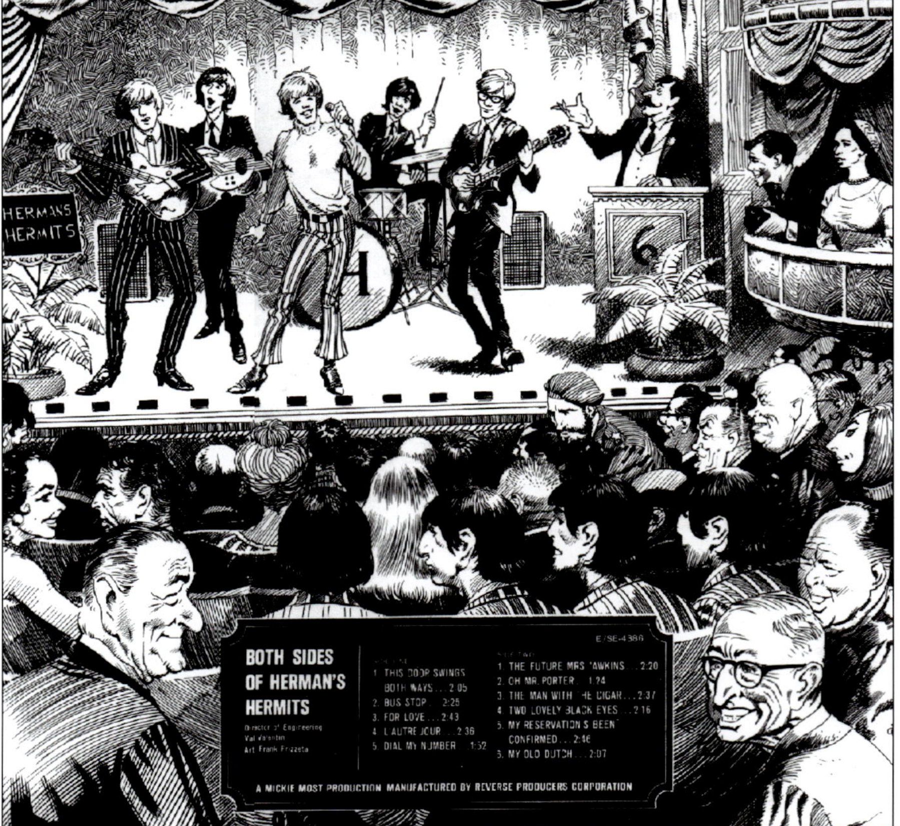

RIGHT: *Back cover of* Both Sides of Herman's Hermits *in which Frazetta included, notables of the era in the audeance: The Beatles, President Johnson, Liz Taylor, Richard Burton, Barbra Streisand, Fidel Castro and more.*

STEREO YOURS, MINE AND OURS • ORIGINAL MOTION PICTURE SOUNDTRACK • UNITED ARTISTS • UAS 5181

ORIGINAL MOTION PICTURE SOUNDTRACK

Yours, Mine and OURS

Composed and Conducted by
FRED KARLIN

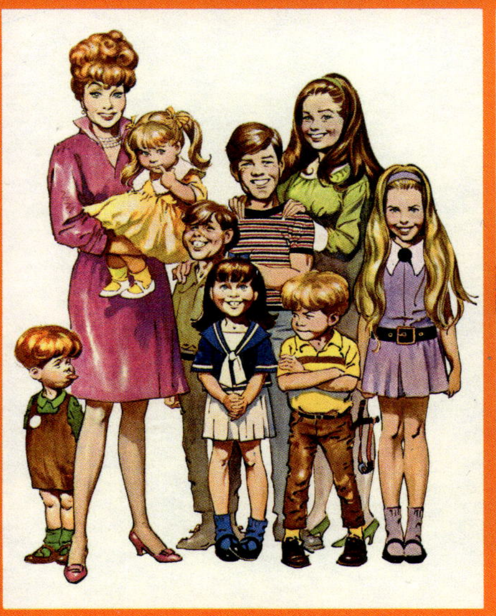

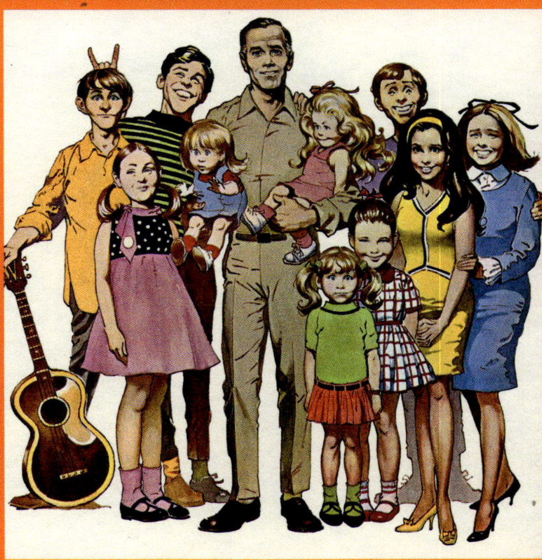

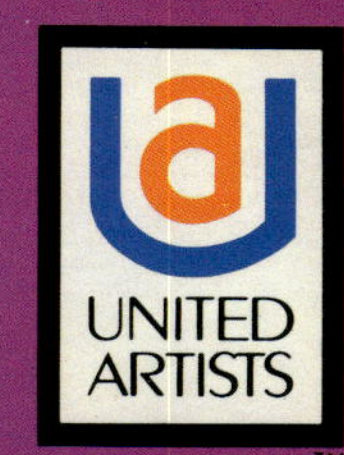

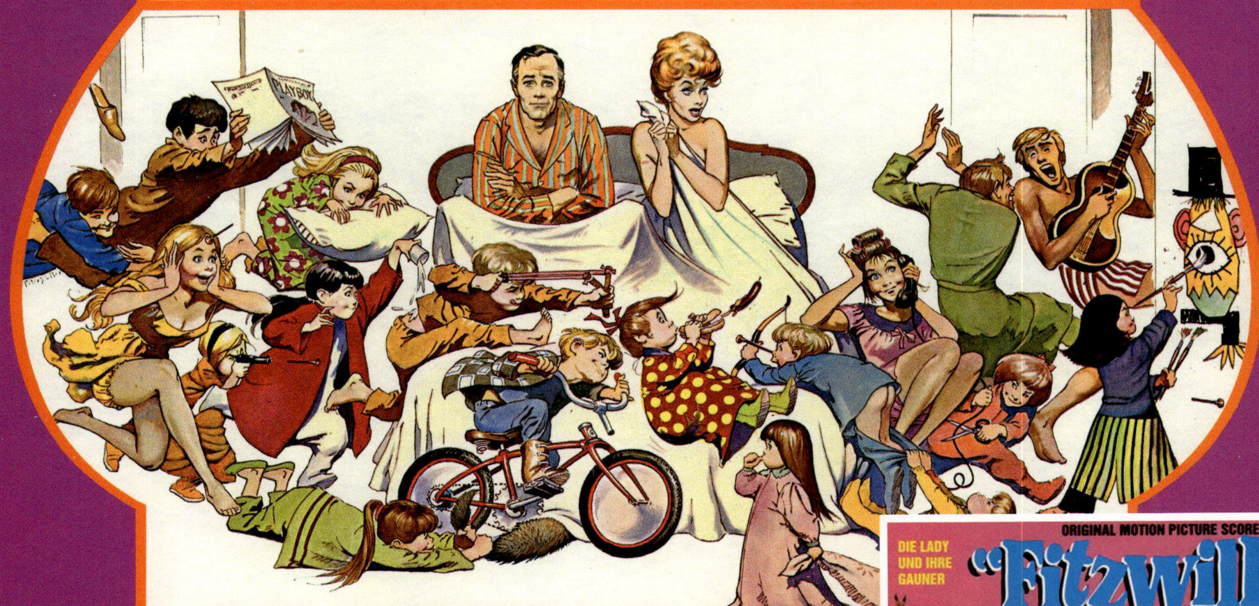

ORIGINAL MOTION PICTURE SCORE

DIE LADY UND IHRE GAUNER

"Fitzwilly"

MUSIC COMPOSED AND CONDUCTED BY
JOHNNY WILLIAMS

TSUNAMI

ABOVE: *Soundtrack for* Yours, Mine and Ours. *United Artists (1968)*

RIGHT: Fitzwilly *soundtrack. United Artists (1967)*

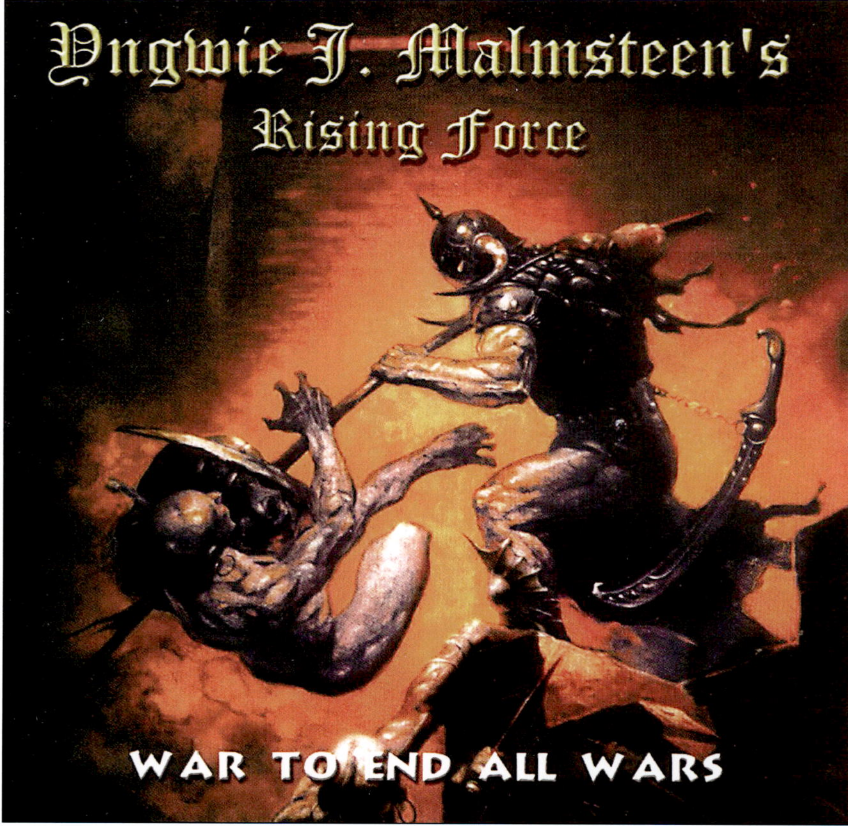

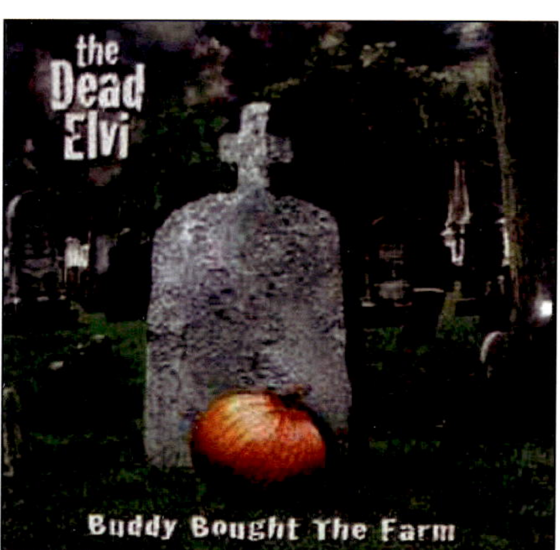

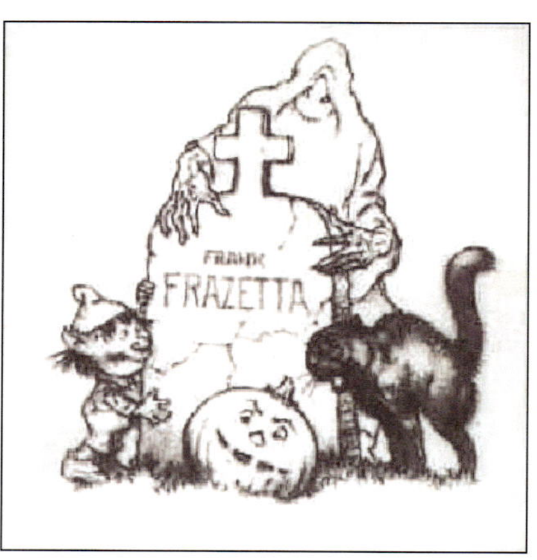

Perhaps Frank's most *curious* record sleeve is actually quite recent. A very tongue-in-cheek graveyard tableau, harkening back to his CREEPY/ EERIE epoch, for *The Dead Elvi,* a cult rockabilly/surf/horror band. This was Frank's first "original" musical cover since the old Herman's Hermits' days. *Buddy Bought The Farm* completes the cycle— for the moment, that is.

• ROY ORBISON - The Fastest Guitar Alive
(soundtrack)
MGM Records SE-4475
1968 front cover **The Fastest Guitar Alive**

Shows complete artwork intended for the movie poster (the movie poster design only shows a portion of artwork)

WHAT'S NEW PUSSYCAT? (soundtrack)
United Artists UAL 4128 (1965)

- front cover ***What's New Pussycat?*** (A sheet design)
  back cover ***What's New Pussycat?*** (A sheet design)
  Includes the pressbook b/w caricatures of Peter Sellers, Peter O'Toole, Romy Schneider, Capucine, Paula Prentiss, Woody Allen and Ursula Andress from the pressbook art.
- 45 single picture sleeve ***What's New Pussycat?*** (B sheet design)

WOLFMOTHER
Modular Records (Australia 2006)
Self-titled debut CD
CD Picture-sleeve singles

- White Unicorn
- Love Train
- Woman
- Joker & the Thief

• YNGWIE MALMSTEEN - War to end All Wars
Spitfire Records (Sweden 2000)
front cover **Death Dealer V**

• YOURS, MINE, AND OURS (soundtrack)
United Artists UAS 5181 (1968)
front cover ***Yours, Mine and Ours***
(color A sheet design)
back cover **Yours, Mine and Ours**
(b/w A sheet design)

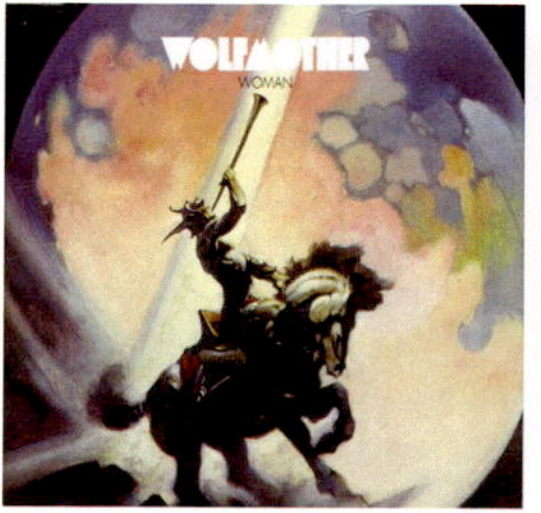

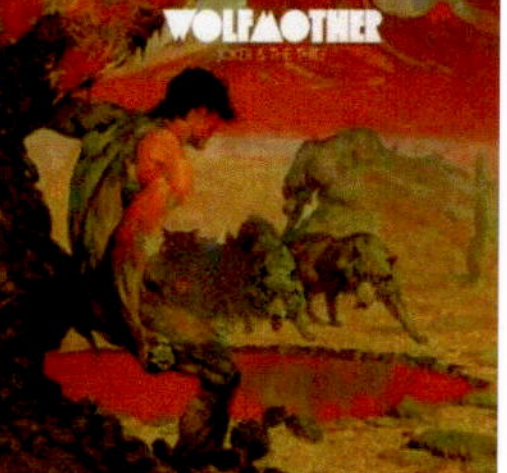

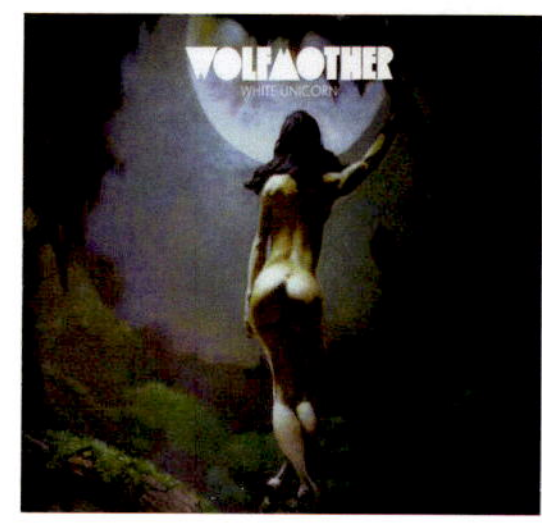

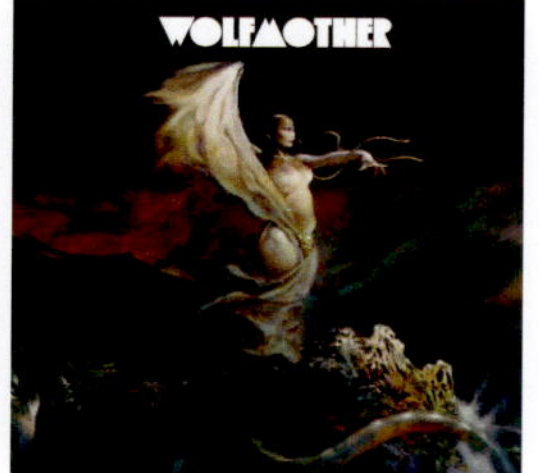

TOP LEFT:
Yngwie J. Malmsteen's Rising Force,
War to End All Wars, *Spitfire Records (2000)*

LEFT: The Dead Elvi, Buddy Bought the Farm.
CD Cover and Frazetta 'overlay' sleeve.
Chiller Theatre (2003)

ABOVE: Wolfmother *CD covers Modular Records (2006 Australia)*

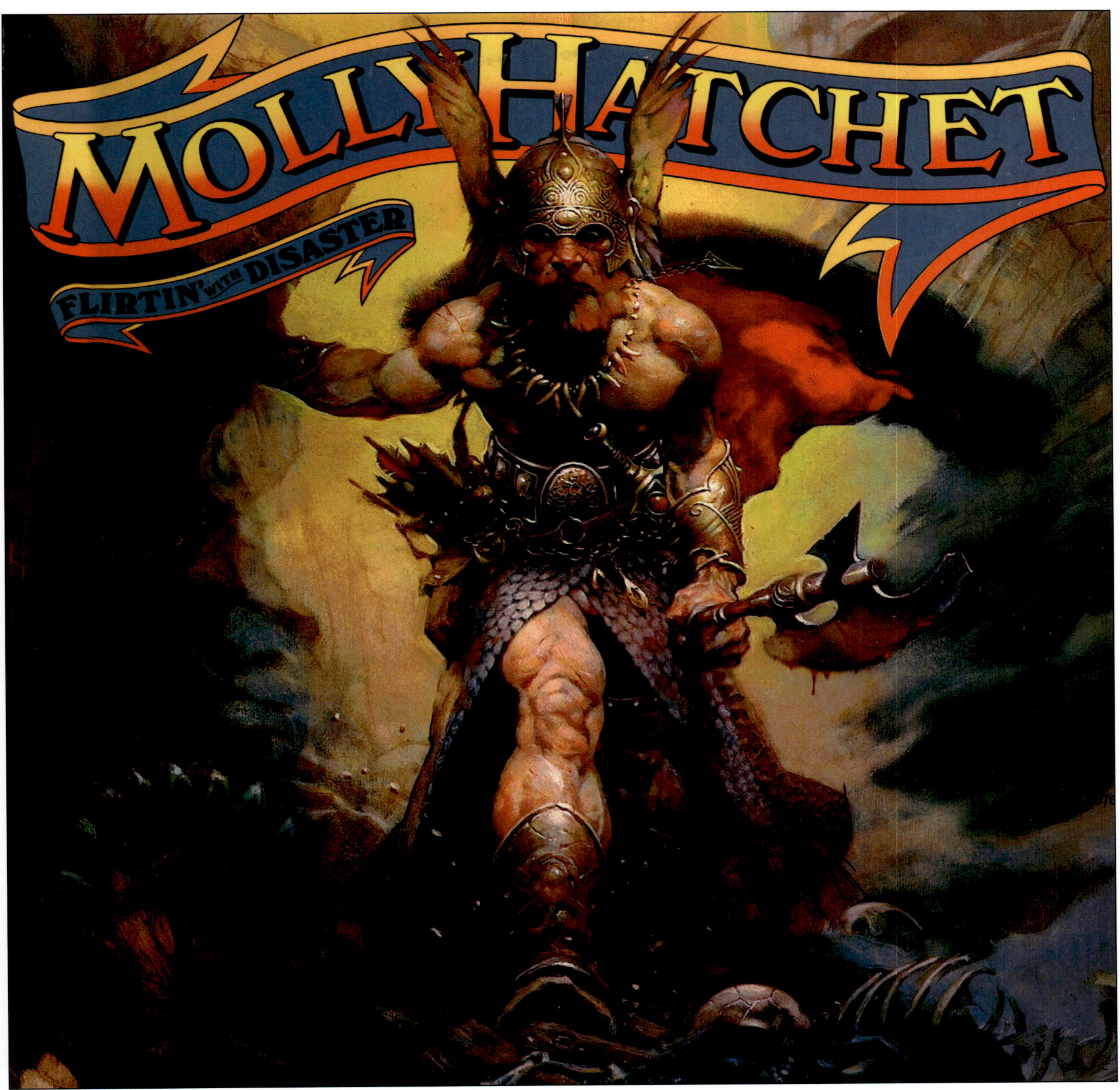

"To tell you the truth, I liked Frazetta. People were painting their houses like our album covers, and their cars, dragsters, and everything. To this day, we have people come up with their funny cars and I'll go to drag strips and see '*Flirting With Disaster*' funny cars. Frazetta's really cool."

Dave Hlubek

guitarist / founder, Molly Hatchet

From an interview with Philip Anderson in KAOS 2000 magazine, 1999.

ABOVE:
Molly Hatchet, Flirtin' with Disaster *(1979)*

THE FRAZETTA CANON

BY DR. DAVID WINIEWICZ

DAVID WINIEWICZ is a creative consultant, doctor of Mediaeval Philosophy and a close personal friend to Frank Frazetta. His essays and information grace numerous volumes of work pertaining to the artist. David also boasts a large collection of original Frazetta art including a number of legendary pieces for Canaveral Press.

That single, magical word "Frazetta" conjures up many things to many people. For me, I think of a man who is a genuine phenomenon, a legend, creative genius, former child prodigy, and my very good friend for many years. There will never again be anyone even remotely like Frazetta. Of course, I am biased, but this does not affect the objectivity of my opinion toward his art. Frank's 50-plus year career established a new standard for imaginative art.

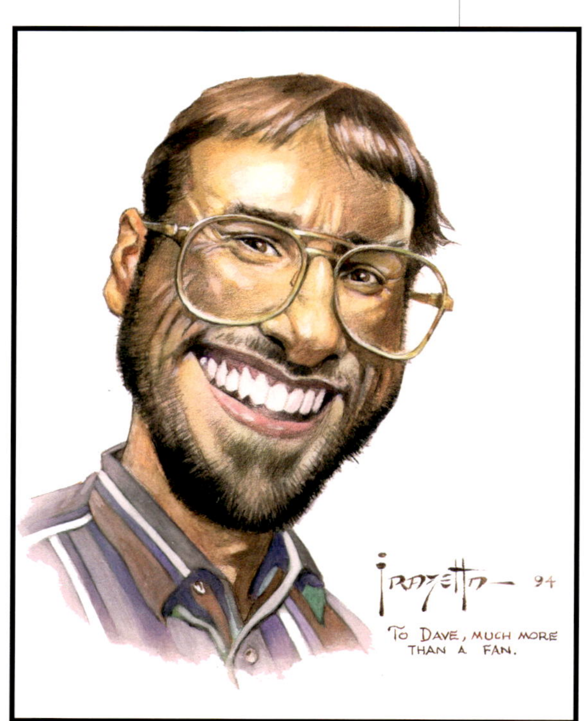

Portrait of David Winiewicz by his friend Frank.

He attained a level of creative excellence that few artists in history could match or even approach. His name will endure and continue to grow far into the future. His total mastery of pencil, watercolor, ink, and oil has influenced generations of artists. Many artists began their careers as Frazetta-imitators. Frazetta's style is so affecting, so beguiling; everyone wants to draw and paint like Frazetta. Look at the work of Berni Wrightson, Jeff Jones, Mike Kaluta, Boris Vallejo, Mark Schultz, Art Suydam, Alex Horley, Simon Bisley, just to name a few, and you will see the strong, heavy influence of Frazetta. Some artists are content just to mimic his style, copy some superficial characteristics, and pick-up a paycheck.

The more serious artist uses Frank as an initial inspiration and then moves on to capture their own singular voice and approach. Frazetta is the model for any true creative artist. Reach into yourself and create- that is Frazetta's message to other artists. Do it your own way and follow your own path. After all, no one can be Frazetta except Frazetta. His mark is made; he is a giant; he is part of history, and rightly so.

LEGACY

Selected Paintings & Drawings by the Grand Master of Fantastic Art

FRANK FRAZETTA

EDITED BY

Arnie Fenner & Cathy Fenner

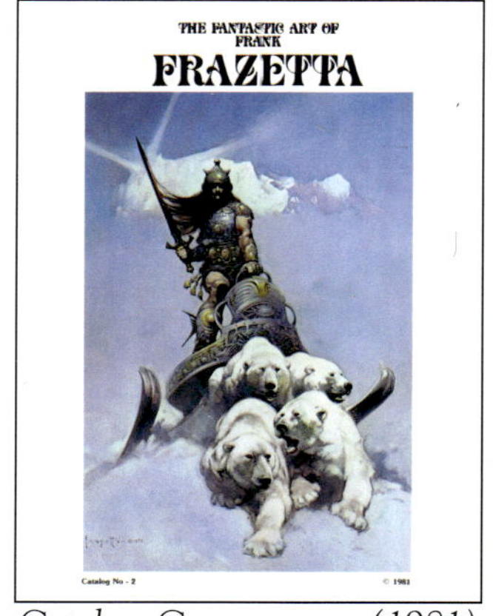

Catalog C *(1981)*

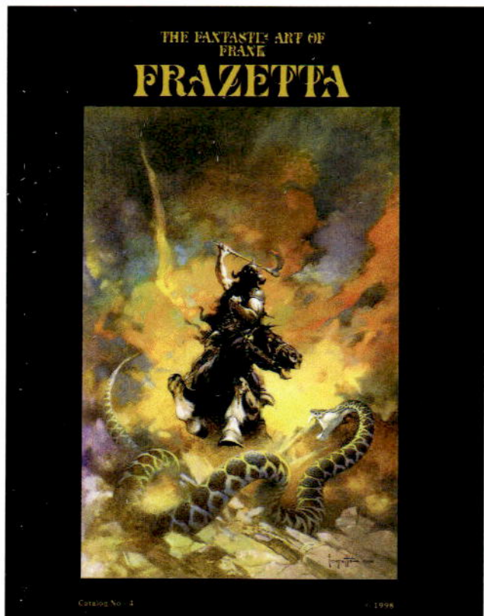

Catalog U *(1998)*

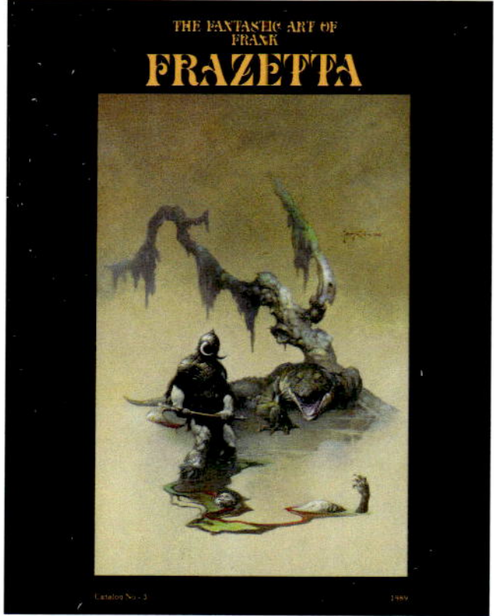

Catalog S *(1989)*

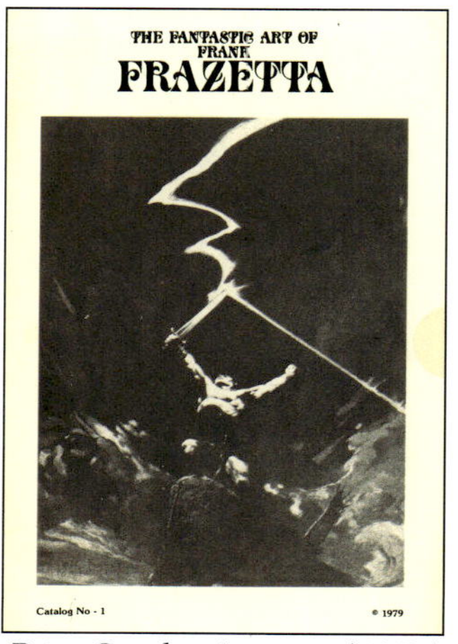

Print Catalog 1 *(1979)*

The vast output of Frazetta reflected in this index demonstrates how deep and prodigious his creativity is. No other artist has brought forth so many truly memorable images. Many people consider Picasso's GUERNICA to be the finest painting of the twentieth century concerning the theme of war. I disagree. Look into the face of Frazetta's THE BARBARIAN and you will see the haunting visage of the twentieth century; indeed, one will see straight into the dark side of human nature. It is, at once, both wonderful and terrible. The image is powerful, disturbing, and unforgettable. Of course, much has been written about those great Frazetta oils, and they guarantee him a permanent place in art history. However, another facet of Frazetta is even more outstanding, namely, his sublime pen and brush drawings. His Canaveral Press drawings executed between 1962-1965 represent a creative peak that will never be approached. These drawings are unprecedented; a virtuoso combination of power and subtlety. Look at them. What an interesting period in Frazetta's career. He was attempting to show the world what he could do. The result was a series of perfect little miracles. Yes, Frazetta achieved perfection in those drawings. I have often thought that there were two angels on either side of Frank's drawing board during their creation, and they were constantly at war in the tip of Frazetta's brush. The result were works that combined incredible beauty, violence, and pure magic. A major artist working on a sophisticated theme at the apex of his mature powers. Frazetta never bores the viewer; his artistic ideas are always sound, interesting, and lively.

Frazetta, the man, is just as interesting and impressive as Frazetta the artist. I have spent countless hours talking with Frazetta about everything under the sun. Frazetta has a razor-sharp intellect and he doesn't suffer fools, or foolishness, gladly. Frank is a born raconteur, filled with stories, observations, opinions, and a wonderful ability to impersonate. Frank's rubbery, expressive face can imitate anything or anybody. Always present is a devilish twinkle in his eye. Frazetta has always had the bubbling imagination of a 5-year old with his first set of watercolors. This is allied with the body of a world class athlete–a golden boy who strode through life like a giant. Bill Gaines' wife once confided to Frank that he was the most handsome man she had ever seen. A look at some of his early photos will easily confirm Frazetta's movie-star good looks. Some people have it all. Frank was one of those people. It was incredible to walk-around with Frank during the big San Diego Comic Convention of 1995. He was treated like a God. People would shake, tremble, and cry when they realized who they were meeting. Even Boris Vallejo was there and upon meeting Frank for the very first time said: "You are the ultimate master. There will never be another as great as you." A very gracious and heartfelt comment that really sums it all up.

Frazetta's opinions of other artists are typically no-nonsense and direct. He dislikes the "barn painter" mentality because it is so repetitious and unaffecting. What are these artists saying? Frank's highest praise is reserved

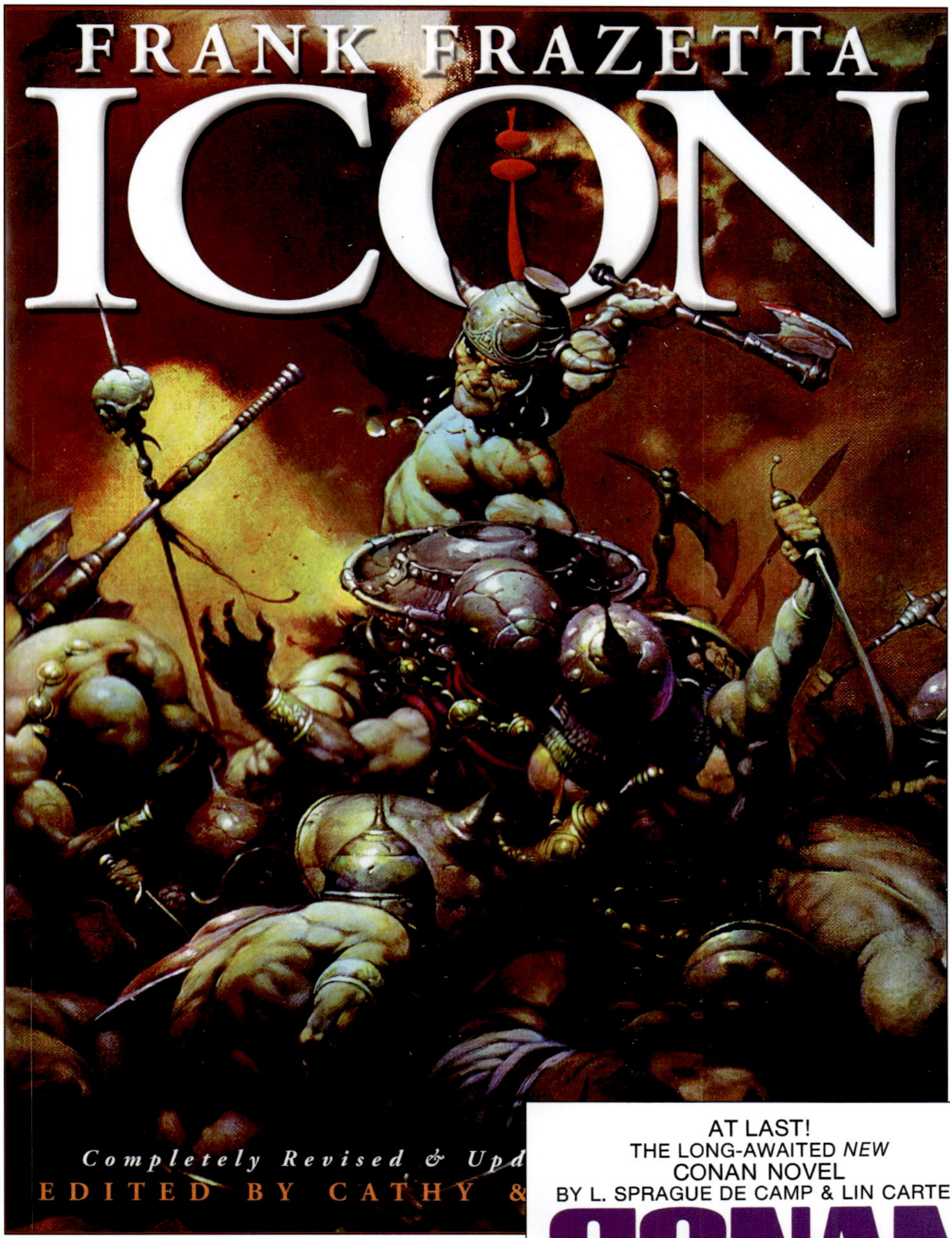

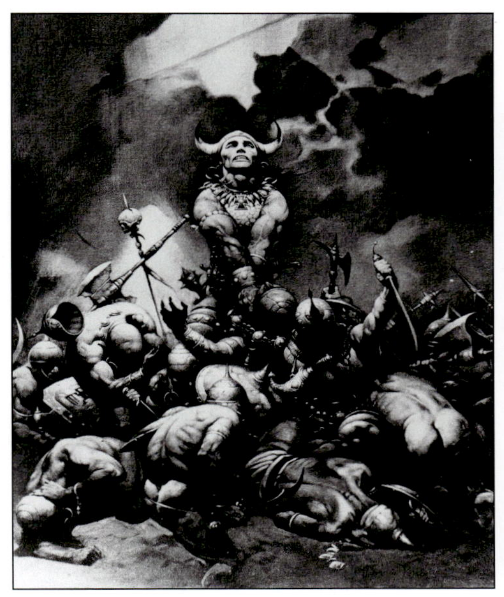

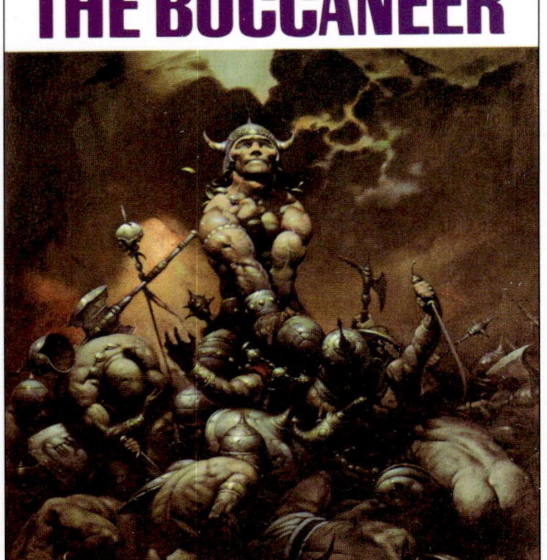

THIS PAGE: One can follow the evolution of Frazetta's painting, The Destroyer, *through its various incarnations; from the original appearance on the Lancer book,* Conan the Buccaneer *to the rare, Fairfax black & white canvas print, to the current version on the cocer of the Underwood book,* Icon.

"I took a college credit art course in my last year in high school and the last half of the year was spent in a personal focus area. I chose fantasy art, at the suggestion of my art teacher. I had seen Frazetta's first art book in the store and wanted it but couldn't afford to buy it. The art teacher, Bruce Ray, and I bought it together. He paid half and I paid half. We did this with the intention of having a contest: we would each do a fantasy painting, whoever did the best one got to keep the book. He actually did a painting on his own time, which now I realize was for the sole purpose of motivating me, but at the time I thought he was competing for the book (naive youth!) Anyway, as I'm sure he planned, I won the contest and got to keep the book. So, my art teacher was the one that pointed me on my career path in fantasy art, and the Frazetta book."

Keith Parkinson

Keith first carved a niche for himself at TSR as a staff artist. He contributed to a wide variety of projects. These range from book and magazine covers to calendars. After five years at TSR, Keith decided it was time to move on to a freelance career. The next seven years were spent primarily doing book covers for the New York publishing market. This work eventually earned Keith Chelsey awards for the years '88, '89 for best hard cover jacket. FPG has also published an art book of all of Keith's best cover work.

for the early TARZAN Sunday pages of Hal Foster. He credits Foster's realistic approach with influencing his approach to art. Make it real; make it believable; make it move, jump, and live. Of course, Frazetta transcended and surpassed Foster by not limiting himself to one character, or genre, or medium. For over 40 years, Frazetta has had a great TARZAN original by Foster hanging in his family room. It is the page dated January 21, 1934, "The Captive King." The page is one of Frank's all-time favorites and features jungle, apes, beautiful design, and lots and lots of energy. Over the years, Frank has drawn much inspiration from that page. Some have even maintained that, in the end, Frazetta is just an imitator of Foster. This is patently absurd. Frazetta's answer to this nonsense is simply to point to the walls of his studio and ask: "Where do you see Foster in any of this? The colors? The figure-work? It is not there." Frazetta does praise the TARZANs and the early PRINCE VALIANTs with the fantasy-magical themes, but Foster simply pointed him in a direction. Anchor your art in realism and believability; give people something that they can feel and relate to.

Other originals hanging in the Frazetta home include a lovely wash-drawing of idiosyncratic robots by Wally Wood, a double-page splash spread from AMAZING STORIES by St. John, and a large 16x20 conte pencil drawing of old Cimmeria by Roy Krenkel. Frazetta also admires the early comic strips such as HENRY ("wonderful simplicity in that strip"), and those wild POPEYE strips by Segar. The young Frazetta absorbed so many influences from the pulps, books, comics, strips, and from the hard streets of Brooklyn. His imagination was well-stocked with vibrant images of heroism and terror. There was a purity of influence in Frazetta's childhood that is lost today. Television and computer games have replaced the traditional Childhood influences and

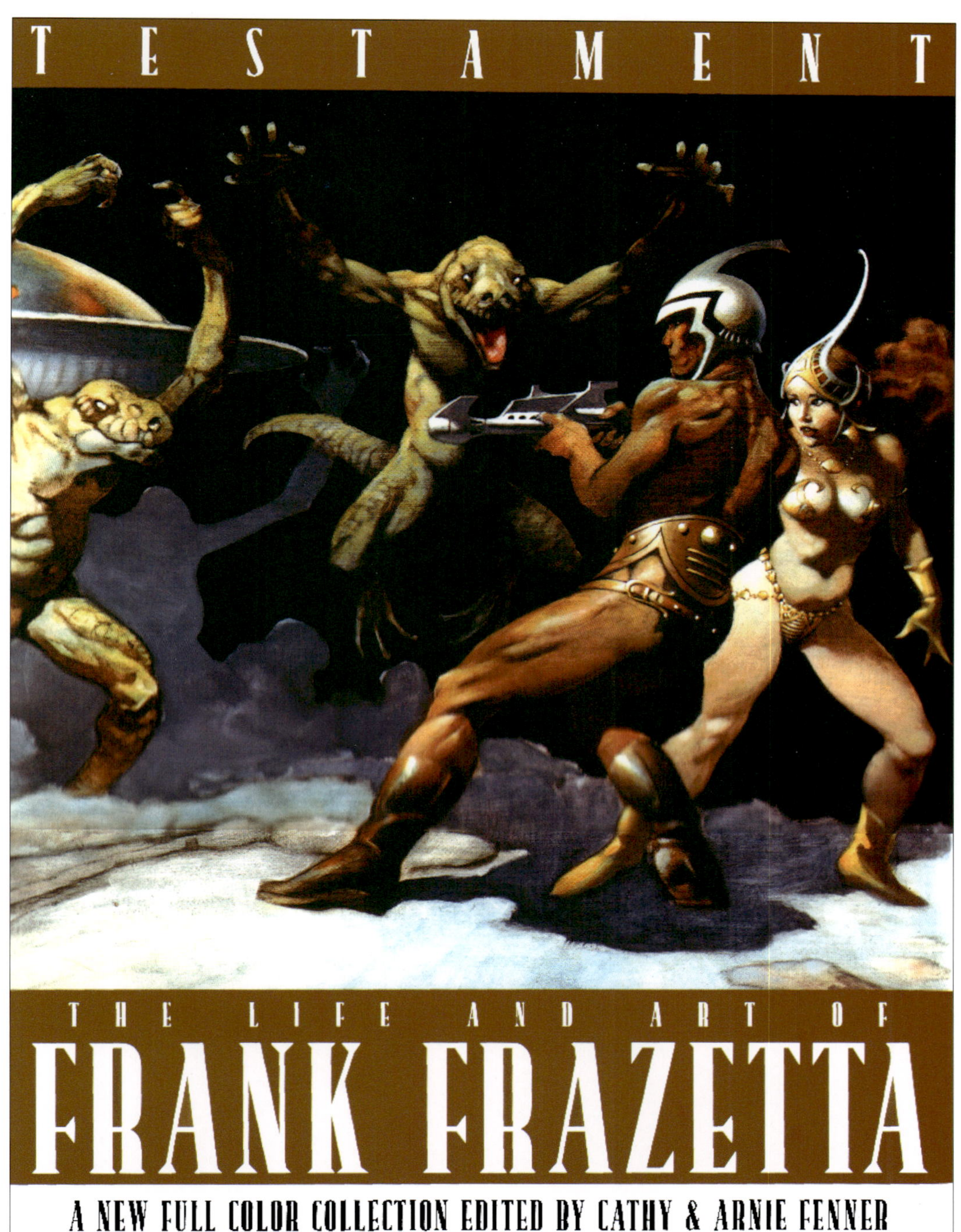

destroyed an important part of our imaginative life. Frazetta comments: "I've always looked backward. From the great artists of the pulps and Walt Disney to the wonderfully painted toys of the 20s to the 40s—these are the things that appealed to me and affected me." Yes, it is the great, good things of childhood that form us, define us, and place us, finally, on a pathway to ourselves.

It was years later that I discovered who the artist was... Frazetta, of course. When I was older I bought all of his art books and collected a few of the paperbacks that bore his work. You can imagine how I felt as an adult to actually collaborate with the Man on a project.

THE ART BOOKS

FANTASTIC ART OF FRANK FRAZETTA, THE - VOL.1

(softcover edition)
August 1975 (first printing date)
Rufus Publishing / Peacock Press / Bantam Books

- softcover edition
- hardcover edition limited to 1,000 copies (published by Charles Scribner & Sons, September 1975)

COVER **Egyptian Queen**
pg. 1 sketchbook drawing
pg. 5 sketchbook drawing
pg. 7 "*Cindy is Saved*" 2 pp. b/w
first printed in HEROIC COMICS #94
pg. 11 sketchbook drawing
pg. 13 The Executioner – sketchbook drawing (not to be confused with the painting of the same name)
pg. 15 Stone Age
AKA - *"He caught them upon his tusks and tossed them high into the air."*
first printed in TARZAN AT THE EARTH'S CORE interior illo.
pg. 17 Caveman
first printed in WEIRD SCIENCE-FANTASY #29 comic book cover
pg. 19 Apeman
AKA - *"Itzl Cha saw in one terrifying glance that the god who bore her was flying through the air."*
first printed in TARZAN AND THECASTAWAYS dust jacket
pg. 21 **Wolf Moon**
pg. 23 **The Sorcerer**
pg. 25 **Wolfman**
pg. 27 **Neanderthal**
pg. 29 **Sea Monster** (repainted version)
pg. 31 **Spiderman**
pg. 33 **Wolfpack**
pg. 35 **Green Death**
pg. 37 **The Brain**
pg. 39 **The Apparition**
pg. 41 **Berserker**
pg. 43 detail from "**Snow Giants**"
pg. 45 **Snow Giants**
pg. 47 **Swamp Demon** (2nd version)
pg. 49 **Woman with a Scythe**
pg. 51 **Tyrannosaurus Rex**
pg. 53 **Egyptian Queen**
pg. 55 **Sun Goddess**
pg. 57 **Atlantis**
pg. 59 **Silver Warrior**
pg. 61 **The Galleon**
pg. 63 Banth
first printed in THUVIA, MAID OF MARS and CHESSMEN OF MARS
pg. 65 *"Behind us came the fighting [hunting] men of Ugor."*
first printed in A FIGHTING MAN OF MARS interior book illo.
pg. 67 *"With wide, distended jaws came the great white lizard."*
first printed in A FIGHTING MAN OF MARS interior book illo.
pg. 69 *"Her veiled eyes seemed to read my very soul."*
first printed in SWORDS OF MARS interior book illustration
pg. 71 Detail from "**Death Dealer**"
pg. 73 **Death Dealer**
pg. 75 **The Mammoth**
pg. 77 **Indomitable**
pg. 79 **Man-Ape**
pg. 81 **At the Earth's Core**
pg. 83 Middle Earth
first printed in the LORD OF THE RINGS portfolio
pg. 85 **The Bear**
pg. 87 **Savage Pellucidar**
pg. 89 **Chained**
pg. 91 **The Barbarian**
pg. 93 Detail from "**The Barbarian**"
pg. 95 **Sea Witch**
back cover **Chained**

FRANK FRAZETTA: BOOK TWO

June 1977 (first printing date)
Peacock Press / Bantam Books

- softcover edition
- hardcover edition limited to 1,000 copies (September 1977)

COVER **Dark Kingdom**
pg. 1Duel
first printed in DOUBLEDAY, BURROUGHS interior book illo.
Title page Kubla Khan
first printed in KUBLA KHAN portfolio
pg. 6 sketchbook drawing
pg. 8 sketchbook drawing
pg. 9 sketchbook drawing
pg. 11 **Flying Reptiles**
pg. 13 **Jongor Fights Back**
pg. 15 **Pony Tail**
pg. 17 **Stranded**
pg. 19 **Land of Terror**
pg. 21 **The Moon Maid**
pg. 23 detail from "**The Moon Maid**"
pg. 25 **The Destroyer** (repainted version)
pg. 27 detail from "**The Destroyer**"
pg. 29 **Paradox**
pg. 31 **Monster out of Time**
pg. 33 **The Norseman**
pg. 35 **Escape on Venus**
pg. 37 **A Princess of Mars**
pg. 39 **John Carter and the Savage Apes of Mars**
pg. 41 **Thuvia, Maid of Mars**
pg. 43 *"To Tara's horror, the headless body moved, took the hideous head in it's hands and set it on its shoulders."*
first printed in THUVIA, MAID OF MARS and CHESSMEN OF MARS
pg. 45 *"As Gahan entered his square, U-dor leaped towards him with drawn sword."*
first printed in THUVIA, MAID OF MARS and CHESSMEN OF MARS
pg. 47 Sheba
pg. 49 Scene from "Lord of the Rings"
first printed in LORD OF THE RINGS portfolio.
pg. 51 Kubla's Anguish
first printed in KUBLA KHAN portfolio
pg. 53 **The Mad King** (original version)
pg. 55 **Gulliver of Mars**
pg. 57 **Jungle Tales of Tarzan**
pg. 59 **Golden Girl**
pg. 61 detail from "**Golden Girl**"
pg. 63 **Against the Gods**
pg. 65 **Madame Derringer**
first printed in DOUBLEDAY BOOK CLUB'S *"The Legend of Baby Doe"*

pg. 67 **Combat**
pg. 69 **Beasts of Venus**
pg. 71 **Ghoul Queen**
pg. 73 **Birdman**
pg. 75 **Bucking Bronco**
first printed in DOUBLEDAY BOOK CLUB'S "*The Trials of Judas Wiley*"
pg. 77 **Beyond the Forest (Farthest) Star**
pg. 79 **Downward to Earth**
pg. 81 **The Return of the Mucker**
pg. 83 **The Lost Empire**
pg. 85 Spaceman
first printed in DOUBLEDAY BOOK CLUB insert advertisement
pg. 87 Duel
first printed in DOUBLEDAY, BURROUGHS interior illo.
pg. 89 Kubla Khan
first printed in KUBLA KHAN portfolio
pg. 91 **The Huntress**
pg. 93 **Dark Kingdom**
pg. 95 detail from "**Dark Kingdom**"
back cover **The Moon Maid**

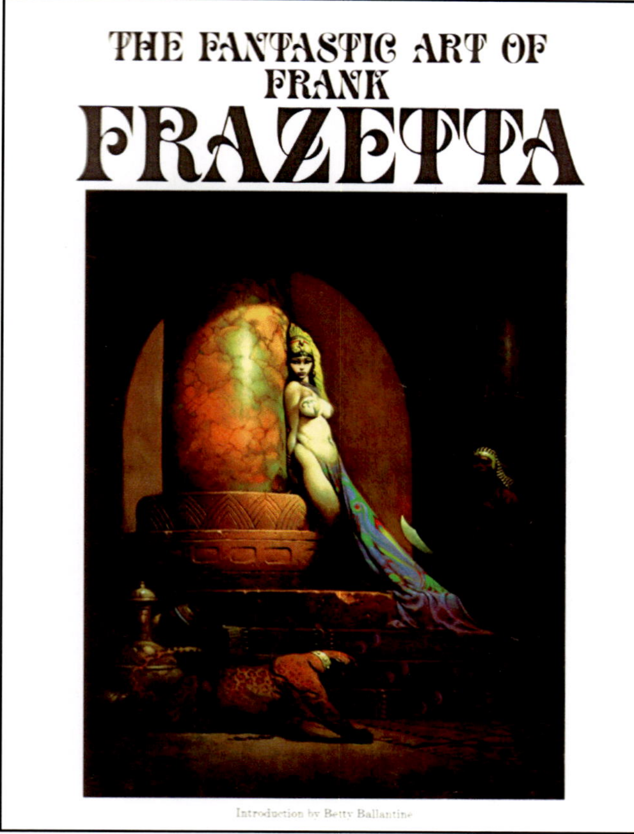

- FRANK FRAZETTA: BOOK THREE softcover edition only

August 1978 (first printing date)
Peacock Press / Bantam Books
COVER **Night Winds**
pg. 1 sketchbook drawing
Title sketchbook drawing
pg. 4 sketchbook drawing
pg. 5 sketchbook drawing
pg. 6 sketchbook art 10 pp.
pg. 17 **Dracula Meets the Wolfman**
pg. 19 **Swords of Mars**
pg. 21 **Girl Bathing** (notice the happy shrubbery)
pg. 23 **Bloodstone**
pg. 25 **Aros**
pg. 27 **Bran Mak Morn**
pg. 29 **Nightstalker**
pg. 31 **Serpent**
pg. 32 sketchbook art 4 pp.
pg. 37 **Black Panther**
pg. 39 **Autumn People**
pg. 41 **Tanar of Pellucidar**
pg. 43 **Fire Demon**
pg. 45 **Rogue Roman**
pg. 47 Image of KUBLA KHAN
first printed in KUBLA KHAN portfolio
pg. 49 Lioness Watching Cabin
pg. 51 Girl and Black Horse
first printed in WOMEN OF THE AGES portfolio
pg. 53 illustration from THE CHESSMEN OF MARS
first printed in THE THUVIA, MAID OF MARS and CHESSMEN OF MARS
pg. 55 **The Night They Raided Minsky's**
(previously unpublished, uncensored version)
pg. 57 **Tarzan and the Ant Men**
pg. 59 **Girl with Sword**
Indian with Long Rifle
pg. 61 **Nude with Dagger Raised**
Nude with Sword
pg. 63 **Bear Watching Caveman Threaten Cub**
Girl Observed by Undressed Man with Hat
pg. 65 **Indian with Bow**
AKA - **The Archer**
reprinted in RETROSPECTIVE
Nude in Pond
AKA - **Silent Breeze**
reprinted in RETROSPECTIVE
pg. 66 sketchbook art 4 pp.

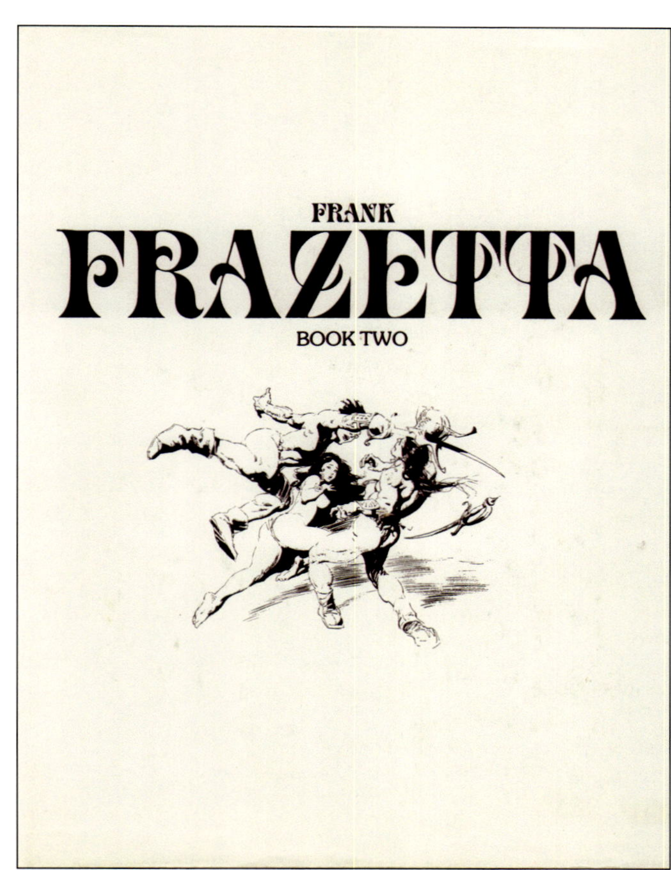

pg. 70 Monster Entering Space Vehicle
first printed as cover to FAMOUS FUNNIES #213 (comic book)
pg. 71 Attack
first printed as cover to FAMOUS FUNNIES #214 (comic book)
pg. 73 **The Fastest Guitar in the West**
pg. 75 **Roman Chariot**
pg. 77 **Tarzan and the Jewels of Opar**
pg. 79 **Land of Terror**
pg. 81 **Lost Continent**
pg. 82 sketchbook art 6 pp.
pg. 89 **Torture Garden**
pg. 91 **Kane on the Golden Sea**
pg. 93 **Warrior with Ball and Chain**
pg. 95 **Flashman on the Charge**
pg. 96 image from LORD OF THE RINGS
first printed in LORD OF THE RINGS portfolio
pg. 97 Orcs
first printed in LORD OF THE RINGS portfolio
pg. 99 detail from **"Night Winds"**
back cover **Serpent**

• **FRANK FRAZETTA: BOOK FOUR** (softcover edition only)
August 1980 (first printing date)
Peacock Press/Bantam Book
COVER **Sacrifice**
pg. 1 sketchbook drawing
pg. 3 sketchbook drawing
pg. 4 three sketchbook drawings
pg. 5 sketchbook drawing
pg. 6 sketchbook pages 2 pp.
pg. 8 sketchbook drawing
pg. 9 **Eternal Champion**
pg. 11 **Iron Thorn**
pg. 12 sketchbook drawing
pg. 13 **Tree of Death**
pg. 14 sketchbook page
pg. 15 **Reassembled Man**
pg. 17 **Gollum**
pg. 18 sketchbook page
pg. 19 **Fantasy World**
pg. 21 **Carson of Venus** (2nd version)
pg. 22 sketchbook page
pg. 23 **Black Star**
pg. 24 sketchbook page
pg. 25 **Count Dracula**
pg. 27 **Outlaw of Torn**
pg. 28 sketchbook drawing
pg. 29 **Beyond the Grave**
pg. 30 sketchbook page
pg. 31 **Winged Terror**
pg. 32 sketchbook drawing
pg. 33 **Mongol Tyrant**
pg. 34 sketchbook pages 9 pp.
pg. 43 preliminary for **Green Death**
preliminary for **A Princess of Mars**
pg. 44 2 illustrations from WOMEN OF THE AGES
first printed in WOMEN OF THE AGES portfolio
pg. 47 **God From the Sky**
pg. 48 preliminary sketches for *"He struck suddenly upward with his blade!"*
pg. 49 *"He struck suddenly upward with his blade!"*
first printed in TARZAN AT THE EARTH'S CORE interior book illo.
pg. 50 sketchbook pages 4 pp.
pg. 55 **Space 103 - Attack**
pg. 57 **Space 104 - Scramble**
pg. 58 sketchbook drawing
pg. 59 **The Tempters**
pg. 61 **Circle of Terror**
pg. 62 sketchbook page
pg. 63 **New World**
pg. 64 sketchbook drawing
pg. 65 **The Cave Demon**
pg. 66 sketchbook drawing
pg. 67 **Eve**
pg. 68 sketchbook page
pg. 69 **The Return of Jongor**
pg. 70 sketchbook drawing
pg. 71 **Thor's Flight**
pg. 72 sketchbook page
pg. 73 **Witherwing**
pg. 74 sketchbook page
pg. 75 **Frankenstein and Dracula**
pg. 77 **Las Vegas**
pg. 78 sketchbook page
pg. 79 **Devil Rider**
pg. 81 **Sacrifice**
pg. 82 sketchbook drawing
pg. 83 **The Secret People**
pg. 85 **Sound**
pg. 86 sketchbook page
pg. 87 **Seven Romans**
pg. 88 sketchbook drawing
pg. 89 **Flesh Eaters**
pg. 91 **Mothman**
pg. 93 **King Kong** (2nd version)
pg. 95 **Self Portrait**
back cover **King Kong** (2nd version)

• **FRANK FRAZETTA: BOOK FIVE** softcover edition only
June 1985
Peacock Press / Bantam Books
COVER **Charging Huns**
Pg. 1 sketchbook drawing
first printed in THE A.C.B.A. PORTFOLIO.
pg. 5 *"Dialog with Frank Frazetta"* 3 pp.
pg. 8 **Young World** 2 pp.
pg. 10 **Red Moon, Black Mountain** 2 pp.
pg. 12 sketchbook drawing
pg. 13 **King Kong and Snake**
pg. 14 b/w sketch
pg. 15 **The Amali Legend**
pg. 16 sketchbook drawing
pg. 17 **The Indian Brave**
pg. 18 sketchbook drawing
pg. 19 **The Defender** (unfinished)
pg. 20 sketchbook drawing
pg. 21 **Kavin's World** (unfinished)
pg. 22 sketchbook drawing
pg. 23 **Mastodon**
pg. 24 sketchbook drawing
pg. 25 **Captive Princess**
pg. 26 sketchbook drawing
pg. 27 **Pharoah's Tomb**: Battlestar Galactica
pg. 28 **Castle of Sin** 2 pp.
pg. 30 sketchbook drawing
pg. 31 **The African Elephant**
pg. 32 **Girl on the River** 2 pp.
pp. 34 Collected Book Covers include:
WARRIOR OF LLARN
TALES OF THE INCREDIBLE
MAZA OF THE MOON
OUTLAW WORLD
TARZAN AND THE LION MAN

THE SON OF TARZAN
TARZAN THE INVINCIBLE
TARZAN AND THE CITY OF GOLD
THE BEASTS OF TARZAN
JUNGLE TALES OF TARZAN
SWORDSMAN IN THE SKY
THE DEVIL'S GENERATION
LOST ON VENUS
CARSON OF VENUS
THE MUCKER
cover to BEYOND THE FARTHEST STAR (1st version)
cover to BEYOND THE FARTHEST STAR (2nd version)

pg. 37 **Battlefield Earth**
pg. 38 **Cat Girl** 2 pp.
pg. 40 sketchbook drawing
pg. 41 Attack on the Spaceship
AKA - *"Her right hand went high with the gleaming blade...and her sharp point pierced the vile heart of the great villain."*
first printed in THE GODS OF MARS / THE WARLORD OF MARS
pg. 42 sketchbook drawing
pg. 43 **Darkness at Time's Edge**
pg. 44 sketchbook drawing
pg. 45 **Swamp Demon** (1st version)
pg. 46 **Orka, Killer Whale** 2 pp.
pg. 48 sketchbook drawing
pg. 49 sketchbook drawing
pg. 50 sketchbook drawing
pg. 51 **Alien Worlds**
pg. 52 sketchbook drawing
pg. 53 **Alien Crucifixion**
pg. 54 sketchbook drawing
pg. 55 **Conan**
pg. 56 3 b/w sketches
pg. 57 2 b/w sketches
pg. 58 sketchbook drawing
pg. 59 Windblown
pg. 61 **Deina**
pg. 62 **Family Portrait**
pg. 63 **The Gang's All Here**
pg. 64 preliminaries for DEATH DEALER book cover
pg. 65 preliminary for **Death Dealer II**
pg. 66 sketchbook drawing
pg. 67 **A Fighting Man of Mars**
pg. 68 The Giantess
first printed in CAVALCADE vol. 4 #18 (magazine)
pg. 69 6 b/w illustrations
pg. 70 sketchbook drawing
pg. 71 On the Stairs
first printed as cover to FAMOUS FUNNIES #209 (comic book)
pg. 72 Space Octopus
first printed as cover to FAMOUS FUNNIES #215 (comic book)
pg. 73 To the Rescue
first printed as cover to FAMOUS FUNNIES #210 (comic book)
pg. 74 Free Fall
first printed as cover to FAMOUS FUNNIES #212 (comic book)
pg. 75 Asteroid Explosion
first printed as cover to FAMOUS FUNNIES #216 (comic book)
pg. 76 "*-Primitive ape men...*" sketchbook drawing
pg. 77 "*...and prehistoric birds-*"
AKA - "proposed dust jacket design for AT THE EARTH'S CORE"
first printed in BURROUGHS ARTIST PORTFOLIO
pg. 78 Captured
AKA - *"I caught my first sight of the dominant race of the inner world."*
first printed in BURROUGHS ARTIST PORTFOLIO
pg. 79 Princess and the Swamp Thing
AKA - *"A Mahar casts her sinister spell"*
first printed in E. R. BURROUGHS: MASTER OF ADVENTURE
pg. 80 Tarzan Against the Giant Alligator
AKA - *"David Innes faces a labrynthodon in Pellucidar"*
first printed in E. R. BURROUGHS: MASTER OF ADVENTURE

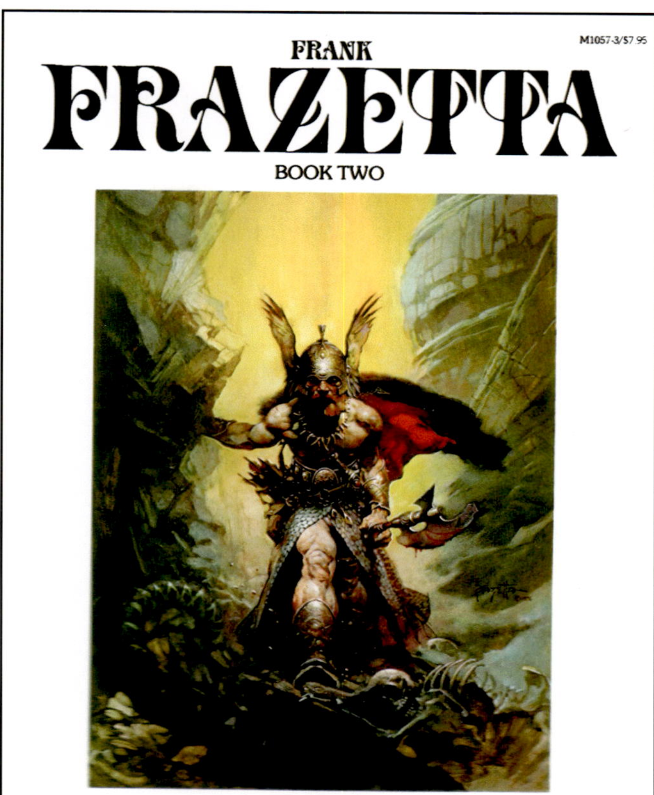

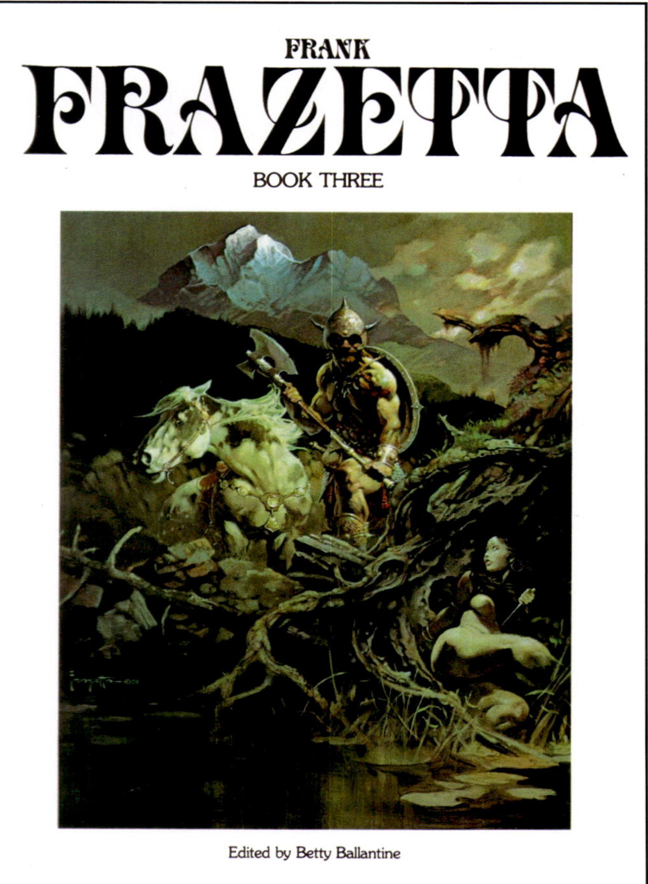

pg. 81 Killing the Giant Eel
AKA - *"David Innes, a Hydrophidian, Ja the Mezop"*
first printed in E. R. BURROUGHS: MASTER OF ADVENTURE
pg. 82 Woman with Spear
AKA - proposed jacket design for the book "PELUCIDAR"
first printed in E. R. BURROUGHS: MASTER OF ADVENTURE
pg. 83 Pterodactyls to the rescue
AKA - *"I saw three mighty Thipdars."*
originally intended for PELLUCIDAR interior illo.
first printed in BURROUGHS ARTIST PORTFOLIO
pg. 84 Sabretooth Being Bitten
AKA - *"They buried their talons in his back."*
originally intended for PELLUCIDAR interior illo.
first printed in BURROUGHS ARTIST PORTFOLIO
pg. 85 Tarzan and the Golden Lion
AKA - *"Tarzan in perfect calm, Raised his short, heavy spear above his right shoulder and waited."*
first printed in TARZAN AND THE CASTAWAYS interior book illo.
pg. 86 Tarzan Confronts an Enemy
AKA - *"I had my stone knife in my hand, and he had his."*
originally intended for PELLUCIDAR interior illo.
first printed in BURROUGHS ARTIST PORTFOLIO
pg. 87 Ape Men Grab the Explorer
AKA - *"David Innes, hyaenodons, and man-apes of Pellucidar"*
first printed in E. R. BURROUGHS: MASTER OF ADVENTURE
pg. 88 Native Overwhelmed by Giant Wild Dogs
AKA - *"The fierce beasts were upon the Thurian simultaneously."*
originally intended for PELLUCIDAR interior illo.
first printed in BURROUGHS ARTIST PORTFOLIO
pg. 89 Tarzan Kills Lion
AKA - *"The silent creature drove a long knife again and again into his tawny side."*
first printed in CANAVERAL PRESS brochure advertisement
pg. 90 sketchbook drawing
pg. 91 **Nude**
pg. 92 sketchbook drawing
pg. 93 **Charging Huns**
pg. 95 **Flying Alligator**
back cover **Flying Alligator**

- **FRANK FRAZETTA: A RETROSPECTIVE**

1994
Alexander Gallery
This volume was released in cooperation with a gallery showing of this work from November 1 to December 10, 1994.

COVER **Catwalk**
pg. 4 **Catwalk**
pg. 11 *"The Red Devil and Goldy vs. The Monster"*
"Snowman" 1 pg. (color sketch by 8 year old Frazetta)
pg. 12 four panels from *"Snowman"* story
(not the same story from TALLY HO)
pg. 15 model sheet 1 pg.
pg. 16 DURANGO KID model sheet 1 pg.
pg. 17 STRAIGHT ARROW and PACCI model sheet 1 pg.
pg. 18 NINA tryout panels 4 pp.
pg. 23 cover to TIM HOLT #17 (comic book), b/w
pg. 24 cover to TIM HOLT #21 (comic book), b/w
pg. 25 cover to TIM HOLT #23 (comic book), b/w
pg. 26 cover to A-1 COMICS #29
pg. 27 cover to A-1 COMICS #31
pg. 28 cover to A-1 COMICS #37
pg. 29 cover to BUSTER CRABBE COMICS #5
pg. 30 cover to FAMOUS FUNNIES #212 (comic book)
pg. 31 cover to FAMOUS FUNNIES #215 (comic book)
pg. 33 art intended for FAMOUS FUNNIES #217
pg. 35 Doodle Books #1 & #2 (1953-1959) 55 pp.
pg. 91 ink illustration
AKA - *"David Innes, hyenodons and man-apes of Pellucidar"*
first printed in E. R. BURROUGHS MASTER OF ADVENTURE
pg. 93 ink illustration
AKA - *"The silent creature drove a long knife again and again into his tawny side."*
first printed in CANAVERAL PRESS brochure advertisement.
pg. 94 ink illustration
AKA - *"A dozen of them felt the weight of my clenched fists, and then I went down, fighting, beneath a half-hundred warriors..."*
first printed in THE GODS OF MARS & THE WARLORD OF MARS
pg. 95 ink illustration
AKA - *"I sprang into the arena, my long sword whirring through the air..."*
first printed in THE GODS OF MARS & THE WARLORD OF MARS
pg. 96 Kubla Khan
first printed in THE KUBLA KHAN PORTFOLIO
pg. 98 ink illustration
AKA - *"She called the fierce banths about her and led them as a shepherdess might lead her flock of meek and harmless sheep."*
first printed in THE GODS OF MARS & THE WARLORD OF MARS
pg. 99 ink illustration
AKA - *"She raised her slim blade above the heart of Dar Tarus."*
first printed in THE MASTERMIND OF MARS AND A FIGHTING MAN OF MARS interior illo.
pg. 100 sketchbook drawing
pg. 101 ink illustration
pg. 103 LI'L ABNER greeting card illustrations

COLORED PENCIL RENDERINGS

pg. 109 **Golden Girl**
pg. 110 **Tyrannosaurus Rex**
pg. 111 **Survivor**
pg. 112 **Massai Warrior**
pg. 113 **The Challenge**
pg. 114 **Silent Breeze**
pg. 115 **The Archer**

THE PRELIMINARIES

pg. 116 **Tarzan the Invincible**
pg. 118 **Thuvia, Maid of Mars**
pg. 119 sketches for **At the Earth's Core** and **Tanar of Pellucidar**
pg. 120**Alien Crucifixion**
pg. 121 **Darkness at Time's Edge**
pg. 122 **Tanar of Pellucidar**
pg. 123 **Swords of Mars**
pg. 124 **Battlefield Earth**
pg. 125 **Sound**
pg. 126 sketches for **Death Dealer**
pg. 127 **Death Dealer with Alligator (Death Dealer**
pg. 128 **Death Dealer with Serpent**
pg. 129 **Death Dealer**

THE OIL PAINTINGS

pg. 131 **Tales From the Crypt**
pg. 133 **Dracula**
pg. 135 **Flashman on the Charge**
pg. 137 **Wolf Moon**
pg. 139 **Tarzan and the Jewels of Opar**
pg. 141 **Black Panther**
pg. 143 **Sun Goddess**
pg. 145 **Jongor Fights Back**
pg 147 **Tanar of Pellucidar**
pg. 149 **Bran Mak Morn**
pg. 151 **Neanderthal**
pg. 153 **Captive Princess**
pg. 155 **The Mammoth**
pg. 157 **Young World**
pg. 159 **Carson of Venus**
pg. 161 **Tree of Death**
pg. 163 **Serpent**
pg. 165 **Spiderman**
pg. 167 **Fantasy World**
pg. 169 **John Carter and the Savage Apes of Mars**
pg. 171 **The Moon Maid**

pg. 173 **Man-Ape**
pg. 175 **Charging Huns**
pg. 177 **Berserker**
pg. 179 **The Destroyer**
pg. 181 **Egyptian Queen**
pg. 183 **Sea Witch**
pg. 185 **Death Dealer** IV
pg. 187 **Death Dealer**
pg. 189 **Mongol Tyrant**
pg. 191 **Sacrifice**
pg. 193 **The Barbarian**
pg. 195 **Catgirl** repainted version
pg. 196 The auction price index for the items for sale in the book.

- FRANK FRAZETTA: BOOK ONE

November 1996 (first printing date)
Frazetta Publications / Sun Litho-Print / Frazetta Books
COVER **Wolves Night**
pg. 1 b/w drawing
pg. 5 portrait **David Winiewicz**
pg. 7 **Princess and the Panther**
pg. 9 **Headless Horseman II**
pg. 11 **Wolves Night**
pg. 13 **Day of Wrath**
pg. 15 Tarzan Triumphant (b/w)
pg. 17 **Death Dealer VI**
pg. 19 **Huns**
pg. 21 **Moon Rider**
pg. 23 **Encounter**
pg. 25 **The Countess**
pg. 27 **Dream Flight**
pg. 29 **Battlefield Earth**
pg. 31 **Dawn Attack**
pg. 33 **Leaping Lizards**
pg. 35 **The Lieutenant**
pg. 37 **Jaguar God I**
pg. 39 **Jaguar God II**
pg. 41 Tarzan and Bolgani (b/w)
pg. 43 **Captive Princess**
pg. 45 Tooth and Claw (b/w)
pg. 47 **Death Dealer II**
pg. 49 **Death Dealer III**
pg. 51 **Death Dealer IV**
pg. 53 **Death Dealer V**
pg. 55 **Death Dealer**
pg. 57 **Death Dealer II** (revised)
pg. 59 **Fire & Ice**
pg. 61 **The Moon's Rapture**
pg. 63 **From Dusk till Dawn** (movie poster design)
pg. 65 **Beauty and the Beast**
pg. 67 **Wild Ride**
pg. 69 **Headless Horseman I**
back cover **Self Portrait**

- FRANK FRAZETTA - THE LIVING LEGEND (b/w)

1981
Frazetta Prints / Sun Litho
COVER b/w illustration
Title page b/w illustration
Vampirella promo illustration
pg. 5 article "*About the Artist*" 12pp.
Article includes the following:
pg. 5 sketchbook drawing
pg. 6 sketchbook drawing
pg. 7 sketchbook drawing
two tryout strips from AMBI DEXTER

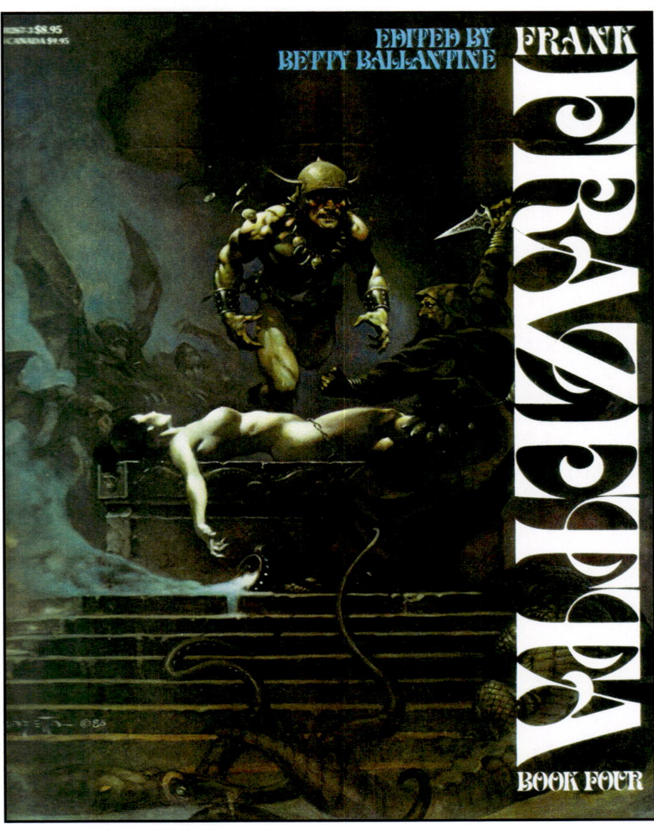

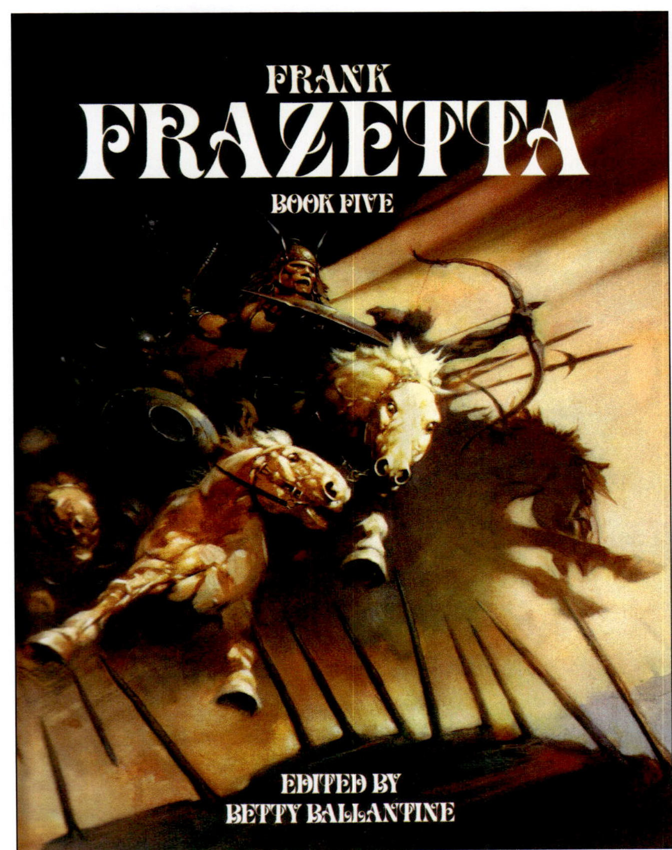

pg. 9 NINA unpublished tryout page in its entirety
pg. 12 ink illustration
AKA - Sword Woman
first printed in AT THE EARTH'S CORE AND PELLUCIDAR PORTFOLIO
pg. 13 cover to A-1 COMICS #47
pg. 14 *"King of the Lost Lands"* 10 pp.
first printed in A-1 COMICS #47
pg. 25 cover to FAMOUS FUNNIES #209 (comic book)
pg. 26 cover to FAMOUS FUNNIES #215 (comic book)
pg. 27 cover to FAMOUS FUNNIES #210 (comic book)
pg. 28 cover to FAMOUS FUNNIES #212 (comic book)
pg. 29 cover to FAMOUS FUNNIES #216 (comic book)
pg. 30 comic strips JOHNNY COMET 2 pp.
pg. 32 painting from 1950
pg. 34 sketchbook drawing
pg. 35 proposed dust jacket design for AT THE EARTH'S CORE
first printed in AT THE EARTH'S CORE AND PELLUCIDAR PORTFOLIO
pg. 36 untitled ink illustration
AKA - *"I caught my first sight of the dominant race of the inner world."*
first printed in AT THE EARTH'S CORE AND PELLUCIDAR PORTFOLIO
pg. 37 untitled ink illustration
AKA - *"A Mahar casts her sinister spell"*
first printed in E.R. BURROUGHS MASTER OF ADVENTURE
pg. 38 untitled ink illustration
AKA - *"David Innes faces a labrithodon in Pellucidar"*
first printed in E.R. BURROUGHS MASTER OF ADVENTURE
pg. 39 untitled ink illustration
AKA - *"David Innes, a hydrophidian, Ja the Mezop"*
first printed in E.R. BURROUGHS MASTER OF ADVENTURE
pg. 40 **Carson of Venus** (1st version)
pg. 42 illustration for 1940's funny animal book
pg. 43 cover to RETURN OF THE MUCKER
Ringo Starr
Thuvia, Maid of Mars
pg. 44 sketchbook drawing
pg. 45 illustrations for E.C. Comics "Picto-Fiction" incomplete, unpublished story (2 pp.)
pg. 47 untitled ink illustration
AKA - proposed jacket design for PELLUCIDAR
first printed in E.R. BURROUGHS MASTER OF ADVENTURE
pg. 48 untitled ink illustration
AKA - *"I saw three mighty Thipdars."*
first printed in AT THE EARTH'S CORE AND PELLUCIDAR PORTFOLIO
pg. 49 untitled ink illustration
AKA - *"They buried their talons in his back."*
first printed in AT THE EARTH'S CORE AND PELLUCIDAR PORTFOLIO
pg. 50 untitled ink illustration
AKA - *"Tarzan in perfect calm, Raised his short, heavy spear above his right shoulder and waited."*
first printed in TARZAN AND THE CASTAWAYS interior illo.
pg. 51 untitled ink illustration
AKA - *"I had my stone knife in my hand, and he had his."*
first printed in AT THE EARTH'S CORE AND PELLUCIDAR PORTFOLIO
pg. 52 untitled ink illustration
AKA - *"David Innes, hyaenodons, and man-apes of Pellucidar"*
first printed in E.R. BURROUGHS MASTER OF ADVENTURE
pg. 53 untitled ink illustration
AKA - *"The fierce beasts were upon the Thurian simultaneously."*
first printed in AT THE EARTH'S CORE AND PELLUCIDAR PORTFOLIO
pg. 54 untitled ink illustration
AKA - *"We were assailed by enormous white bears."*
first printed in AT THE EARTH'S CORE AND PELLUCIDAR PORTFOLIO
pg. 55 untitled ink illustration
AKA - *"The silent creature drove a long knife again and again into his tawny side."*
first printed in CANAVERAL PRESS brochure advertisement.
pg. 56 untitled ink illustration
AKA - *"My shaft pierced the Sagoth's savage heart…"*
first printed in AT THE EARTH'S CORE AND PELLUCIDAR PORTFOLIO
pg. 57 untitled ink illustration
AKA - *"David Innes, Jubal the Ugly One, Dian the beautiful"*
first printed in E.R. BURROUGHS MASTER OF ADVENTURE
pg. 58 untitled ink illustration
AKA - *"The great man-brute seated himself upon a flat rock."*
first printed in AT THE EARTH'S CORE AND PELLUCIDAR PORTFOLIO
pg. 59 sketchbook drawing
pg. 62 untitled painting b/w
pg. 63 LORD OF THE RINGS entire portfolio 7 pp.
pg. 70 sketchbook drawing
pg. 71 KUBLA KHAN entire portfolio 5 pp.
pg. 76 preliminary sketches for Doubleday Books' John Carter series
pg. 77 interior illustration for Doubleday Books' John Carter series
pg. 78 sketchbook drawing
pg. 79 sketchbook drawing
pg. 80 sketchbook drawing
pg. 81 WOMEN OF THE AGES *entire* portfolio 7 pp.
pg. 94 **Svengali**

- **FRAZETTA: ILLUSTRATIONS ARCANUM** (b/w)

1994
Verotik THIS VOLUME CONTAINS 30 UNTITLED, PENCIL ILLUSTRATIONS

- **FRAZETTA PILLOW BOOK, THE**

March 1994 (first printing date)
Kitchen Sink
THIS VOLUME CONTAINS 32 UNTITLED, FULL COLOR ILLUSTRATIONS
see also THE FRAZETTA PORTFOLIO
see also FRAZETTA PORTFOLIO PRINTS

ICON

1998
Frank Frazetta/Underwood
Four versions of this book exist.

- Deluxe edition hardcover - Includes tooled leather slipcase, tray-case, and one additional illustration. Signed by practically everyone except Frazetta. Limited to 100 copies.
- Limited edition hardcover - Includes slipcase hardcover edition with additional, stamped page and extra pages of art. limited to 1,200 copies.

COVER **Sea Witch** detail

- Regular edition hardcover
COVER **Encounter**
- Regular edition softcover
COVER **Encounter**

inside f.c. Tarzan and Bolgani
authentication page with pencil drawing and facsimile of Frazetta's signature
pg. I promotional Vampirella drawing
pg. II **The Barbarian** detail
pg. IV untitled pencil drawing 2 pp.
pg. VI **Maza of the Moon**
pg. VIII Tarzan illustration
AKA - *"Tarzan took in the picture at a glance."*
first printed in TARZAN AND THE CASTAWAYS interior book illo.
pg. 1 article ***"Frank Frazetta – Master of Imagination"***
by Arnie Fenner
Article includes the following:
pg. 2 color illustration from "*Snowman*" (not from Tally Ho)
untitled still life done by an eight year old "Frazetta"

pg. 3 first page from "*Barney Rooster*"
first printed in BARNYARD COMICS' #20
pg. 4 cover to A-1 COMICS #31.
pg. 5 first page from "*King of the Lost Lands*"
first printed in A-1 COMICS #47
pg. 6 cover to FAMOUS FUNNIES #214 (comic book)
pg. 7 panel from TIGA tryout strip
pg. 8 SWEET ADELINE tryout strip
AMBI DEXTER tryout strip
JOHNNY COMET newspaper strip
pg. 9 single panel from NINA tryout strip
first printed in WITZEND #8
pg. 10 Moonbeam McSwine greeting card cover
"*The Giantess*" illustration
first printed in CAVALCADE vol. 4 #18 (magazine)
pg. 11 "*Little Annie Fannie*"
first printed in PLAYBOY (magazine) May, 1965
pg. 12 cover to TARZAN AND THE LOST EMPIRE.
pg. 13 cover to BLAZING COMBAT #3 (comic book)
cover to BLAZING COMBAT #4 (comic book)
pg. 14 first page from "*Werewolf*"
first printed in CREEPY #1 (comic book)
pg. 15 **Ringo Starr**
letter column header
first printed in FAMOUS MONSTERS OF FILMLAND (magazine)
pg. 17 detail of intro drawing used in the movie FIRE & ICE
pg. 19 **The Countess and the Green Man**
pg. 22 **After the Fox**
pg. 23 article - **"*Frank Frazetta – Motion Picture & Television Advertising Artist*"** by William Stout
Article includes the following:
pg. 24 **What's New Pussycat?** A sheet version
pg. 25 **Hotel Paradiso**
pg. 26 **The Fearless Vampire Killers**
pg. 27 **The Busy Body**
pg. 29 **The Gauntlet**
pg. 30 **Pharoah's Tomb**
pg. 31 poster for LUANA (A sheet version)
From Dusk Till Dawn
pg. 32 chapter - "*Gallery of Works*"
detail from **Egyptian Queen**. 2 pp
pg. 34 "*Creepy's Loathsome Lore*"
first printed in CREEPY #7 (comic book)
pg. 35 **Winged Terror**
pg. 36 cover to EERIE #5 **Swamp God**
Swamp God
pg. 38 **Sea Witch** 2 pp.
pg. 40 pencil roughs for cover to CREEPY #7 by Roy Krenkel
pg. 41 cover to CREEPY #7 **Dracula Meets the Wolfman**
pg. 42 Creepy Fan Club premium **Uncle Creepy** portrait
pg. 43 **Neanderthal**
pg. 44 plate six from the WOMEN OF THE AGES portfolio
pg. 45 **Egyptian Queen**
pg. 46 **Vampirella** (1st version)
Vampirella (2nd version)
pg. 47 **Cornered**
pg. 48 sketchbook drawing
pg. 49 **Sun Goddess**
pg. 50 art from ILLUSTRATIONS ARCANUM (art book)
pg. 51 **The Executioner**
pg. 53 **Queen Kong**
pg. 54 promotional Vampirella drawing
pg. 55 **Vampirella 1996**
pg. 56 CONAN THE ADVENTURER Preliminary color rough
not the final concept
pg. 57 **The Barbarian**
pg. 59 **Man-Ape**
pg. 60 Conan sketchbook drawing

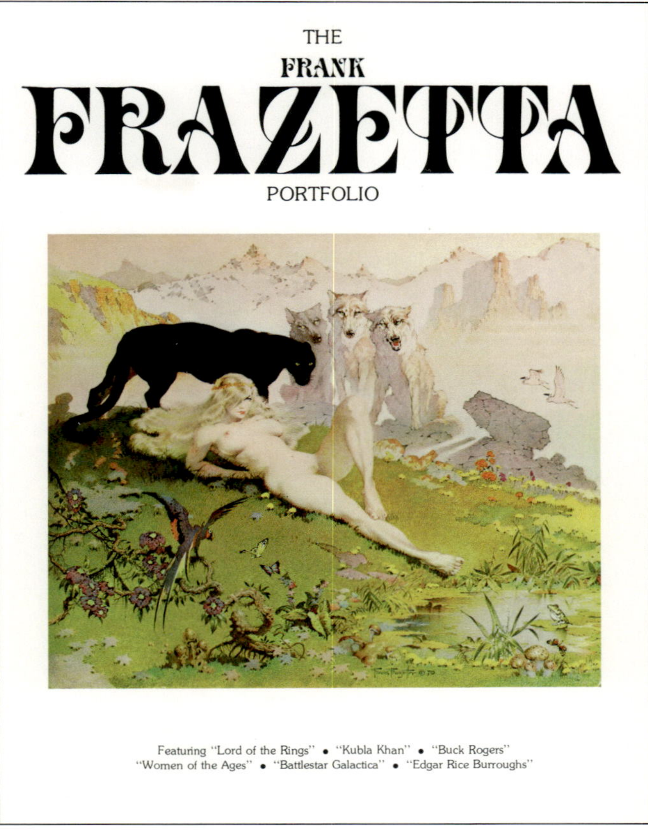

ABOVE: The Frank Frazetta Portfolio *unauthorized (1979)*

BELOW: Frank Frazetta: Book One *Frazetta Publications (November 1996)*

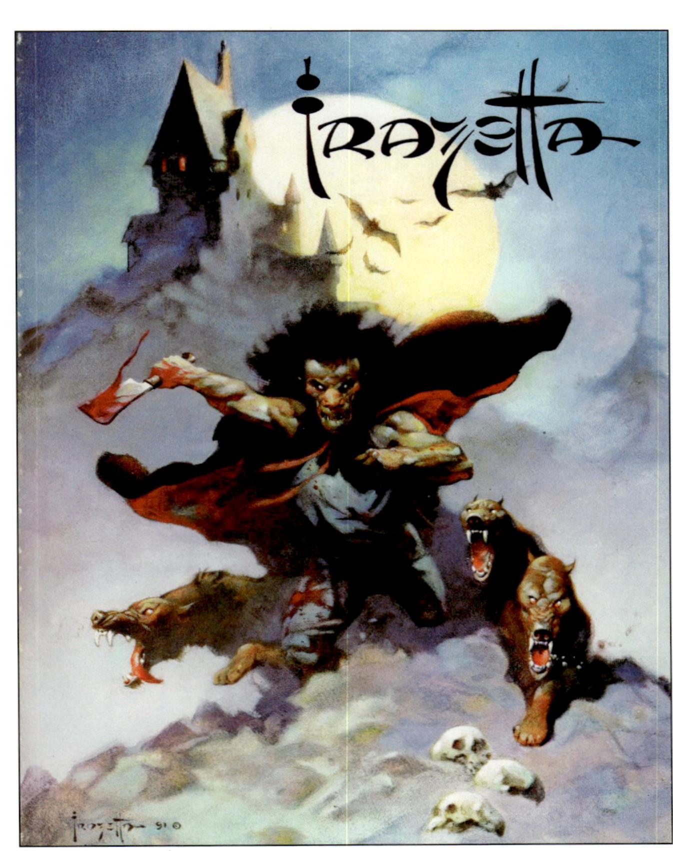

ILLUSTRATIONS ARCANUM
see FRAZETTA: ILLUSTRATIONS ARCANUM

LEGACY
1999
Frank Frazetta/Underwood
Four versions of this book exist.
• Deluxe leatherbound edition - Includes signatures by Danton Burroughs, Arnie Fenner, Cathy Fenner, Nick Meglin, and Michael Friedlander. Cover is leather, textured as snakeskin. Traycase bound in black iris linen.
limited to 100 copies
• Limited edition hardcover - Includes slipcase hardcover edition with additional, stamped page and extra pages of art.
limited to 2,500 copies.
COVER **At the Earth's Core**
• Regular edition hardcover
COVER **Savage Pellucidar**
• Regular edition softcover
COVER **Savage Pellucidar**
Endpapers intro illustration from the movie FIRE & ICE
Authentication page - untitled ink illustration
AKA - *"The great man-brute seated himself upon a flat rock."*
first printed in BURROUGHS ARTIST PORTFOLIO
Frontis **The Apparition**
Contents detail of sculpture "Death Dealer"
pg. 7 **The Mad King** (1st version)
pg. 8 **Tarzan and the City of Gold**
pg. 9 **The Monster Men**
pg. 11 **The Secret People**
pg. 13 LI'L ABNER newspaper strip featuring Marilyn Monroe
pg. 16 illustration from BARNYARD COMICS
pg. 17 cover to FAMOUS FUNNIES #215 (comic book)
pg. 19 cover to A-1 COMICS #47
pg. 20 LI'L ABNER greeting card artwork
pg. 21 **Deina**
pg. 22 untitled ink illustration
AKA - *"Tarzan swung the body over his head."*
first printed in TARZAN AT THE EARTH'S CORE interior book illo.
pg. 23 **Herman's Hermits**
"*The Perfect Gentleman*" interior illustration
first printed in CAVALCADE (magazine) Feb. 1964
pg. 24 photo - Death Dealer toy
pg. 25 cover to FAMOUS FUNNIES #213 (comic book)
pg. 26 **Lost on Venus**
pg. 29 cover to FAMOUS FUNNIES #209
pg. 30 **Ellie Frazetta** circa 1960
previously unpublished
pg. 31 untitled ink illustration
AKA- *"The ape-man delt him a terrific blow on the side of the head with his open palm."*
first printed in TARZAN AND THE CASTAWAYS interior book illo.
pg. 32 illustration from comic story "*Untamed Love*"
first printed in PERSONAL LOVE #32 (comic book)
pg. 34 cover to BUSTER CRABBE COMICS #4
cover to A-1 COMICS #34
cover to BOBBY BENSONS B-BAR-B RIDERS #9
cover to STRAIGHT ARROW #22 (comic book)
pg. 35 page of character studies for unsold newspaper series, AMBI DEXTER
pg. 36 BUSTER CRABBE COMICS
previously unpublished try-out page
SWEET ADELINE
sample newspaper strip for unsold series
pg. 37 "*Brothers of the Wilderness*" splash page
first printed in DURANGO KID #4 (comic book)
pg. 38 "*A Love of My Own*" 8 pp.
first printed in PERSONAL LOVE #24 (comic book)
pg. 46 detail from "**Night Winds**"
pg. 48 **Tarzan the Invincible** (1963)
preliminary painting
pg. 49 **Tarzan the Invincible** (1963)
pg. 51 **Tarzan and the Jewels of Opar**
pg. 52 untitled ink illustration
AKA - *"He struck suddenly upward with his blade"*
first printed in TARZAN AT THE EARTH'S CORE interior book illo.
pg. 53 **Tarzan at the Earth's Core**
pg. 54 **Tarzan and the Lion Man**
pg. 55 **Jungle Tales of Tarzan**
pg. 56 Tarzan sketchbook drawing
pg. 57 **The Lost Continent**
pg. 58 Tarzan and Dum-dum - Previously unpublished art
pg. 60 **Swordsmen in the Sky**
pg. 61 **Land of Terror**
pg. 63 **Savage Pellucidar**
pg. 64 **Beyond the Farthest Star** (2nd version)
preliminary painting
Beyond the Farthest Star (2nd version)
pg. 65 **Beyond the Farthest Star** (1st version)
pg. 66 **The Mucker**
pg. 67 **Return of The Mucker**
pg. 68 **Swords of Mars**
preliminary painting
pg. 69 **Swords of Mars**
pg. 70 **John Carter and the Savage Apes of Mars**
pg. 72 **The Moon Men**
pg. 73 **Escape on Venus**
pg. 75 **Outlaw of Torn**
pg. 76 cover to **E.R..BURROUGHS: MASTER OF ADVENTURE**
pg. 77 **Black Panther**
pg. 78 **Tanar of Pellucidar**
preliminary painting
sketchbook drawing
pg. 79 **Tanar of Pellucidar**
pg. 80 Tarzan sketchbook drawing
pg. 81 **At the Earth's Core**
pg. 82 **Tarzan Meets La of Opar** - Previously unpublished art
pg. 84 **Pellucidar**
preliminary painting
pg. 85 **Flying Reptiles**
pg. 87 **Savage Pellucidar**
pg. 88 **Tales From the Crypt**
pg. 89 **Sorcerer**
pg. 90 **Sea Monster** (1st version)
pg. 91 **Sea Monster** (2nd version)
pg. 92 Vampirella promotional drawing
pg. 93 **Woman With a Scythe**
pg. 95 **Gargoyle**
pg. 96 plate from the Kubla Khan portfolio
rough drawing
pg. 97 **Mongol Tyrant**
pg. 99 **Nightstalker**
pg. 100 Vampirella drawing
pg. 101 **The Brain**
pg. 102 cover to BLAZING COMBAT #4 (comic book)
pg. 103 **Combat**
pg. 105 **Count Dracula**
pg. 107 **Beyond the Grave**
pg. 108 **Creatures of the Night**
pg. 110 **The Eighth Wonder**
preliminary painting
pg. 111 **The Eighth Wonder**
pg. 112 character study for Dracula
pg. 113 **Dracula**
pg. 114 MAD MONSTER PARTY (A sheet design)
pg. 115 unused poster art for MAD MONSTER PARTY

pg. 116 **After the Fox** (B sheet design)
pg. 117 **3000 AD** - Movie poster for unreleased movie
pg. 118 **Mrs. Pollifax - Spy**
pg. 119 **Jonathan Winters**
pg. 120 WELCOME TO THE L.B.J. RANCH - Record album
pg. 121 **The Secret of My Success**
pg. 122 photo - trio of sculptures used as character studies for the movie FIRE & ICE
pg. 125 **Flash For Freedom**
pg. 126 **Flashman at the Charge** (1st version)
pg. 127 **Flashman at the Charge** (2nd version)
pg. 128 sketchbook drawings
pg. 129 **Pony Tail**
pg. 131 **Masai Warrior**
pg. 132 **Predators**
previously unpublished
pg. 134 previously unpublished sketchbook rough
pg. 135 **Wolf Pack**
pg. 136 sketchbook drawing
pg. 137 **Tree of Death**
pg. 138 character study of Darkwolf for FIRE & ICE
pg. 139 **Victorious**
pg. 140 sketchbook drawing
pg. 141 **Black Star**
pg. 142 sketchbook drawing
pg. 143 **Wolf Moon**
pg. 144 sketchbook drawing
pg. 145 **Reassembled Man**
pg. 146i illustration for "*The Gent Zodiac*"
first printed in GENT vol.6 #16 (magazine)
pg. 147 **Pinup**
previously unpublished
pg. 148 Painting
first printed in THE RARE FRAZETTA (fan publication)
pg. 149 **Las Vegas**
pg. 150 pencil drawing of Ellie Frazetta
pg. 151 **Nude**
pg. 152 **Green Death**
preliminary painting
pg. 153 **Green Death**
pg. 154 **The Eternal Champion** (1st version)
pg. 155 **The Eternal Champion** (2nd version)
pg. 156 **Arthur Rex**
preliminary painting
pg. 157 **Paradox**
pg. 158 **Arthur Rex**
pg. 160 sketchbook drawing
pg. 161 **Fire Demon**
pg. 162 **Alien crucifixion**
Alien Crucifixion
preliminary painting
pg. 163 **Ghoul Queen**
pg. 164 sketchbook drawings
pg. 165 **Seven Romans**
pg. 166 **Solar Invasion**
Alien Worlds
pg. 167 **Invaders**
pg. 168 **Mastodon**
pg. 170 sketchbook drawing
pg. 171 **Bloodstone**
pg. 172 sketchbook drawing
pg. 173 **Night Winds**
pg. 174 sketchbook drawing
pg. 175 **Cave Demon**
pg. 176 **Kane on the Golden Sea**
preliminary painting
pg. 177 **Kane on the Golden Sea**
pg. 178 **Frogs on the Moon**
pg. 179 **A Requiem for Sharks**
pg. 180 **Lost City** - Previously unpublished in color.
pg. 181 detail from **"Lost City"**
pg. 182 **The Norseman**
preliminary painting
pg. 183 **The Norseman**
pg. 184 sketchbook drawing
pg. 185 **Warrior With Ball and Chain**
pg. 186 **Jongor of Lost Land**
pg. 187 **The Return of Jongor**
pg. 188 cover to BLACK EMPEROR
pg. 189 **Black Emperor** - (2nd version)
pg. 193 *COLLECTORS EDITION PORTFOLIO*
Includes 16 pages of previously unpublished works

SMALL WONDERS: The Funny Animal Art of Frank Frazetta
Kitchen Sink Press
1991
"*Snowman*" 8pp. with John Giunta
first printed in TALLY HO
* "*Flippy the Monk*"
first printed in HAPPY COMICS #29
* "*The Silent Monkey*"
first printed in HAPPY COMICS #26
* "*Bobby the Cheetah*"
* "*The Quiet Pup*"
first printed in SUPERMOUSE #2
* "*Small Fry*"
first printed in COO COO COMICS #43
* "*Golden Horse*"
first printed in HAPPY COMICS #24
* "*Chocolate and Vanilla*"
first printed in HAPPY COMICS #27
* "*The Mouse and the Moose*"
* "*The Talkative Mouse*"
first printed in HAPPY COMICS #29
* "*President Mouse*"
first printed in HAPPY COMICS #30
Hucky Duck in "*Barney's Little Helper*" 7 pp.
first printed in BARNYARD COMICS #22
* "*The Reckless Horse*" 2 illos.
first printed in GOOFY COMICS #27
* "*The Ghost*"
first printed in GOOFY COMICS #30
* "*Scaredy Cat*"
first printed in BARNYARD COMICS #23
* "*Miggles and Bojo*"
first printed in BARNYARD COMICS #23
* "*Freddy Bear to the Rescue*"
first printed in BARNYARD COMICS #22
* "*The Strange Little Creature*"
first printed in COO COO COMICS #42
* "*High Flying Squirrel*"
first printed in HAPPY COMICS #21
* "*The Bully and the Blowfish*"
first printed in GOOFY COMICS #30
* "*Ferdinand the Bullfrog*"
first printed in SNIFFY THE PUP #5
* "*Percy the Puffer-fish*"
"*Barney Rooster*" 7 pp.
first printed in BARNYARD COMICS #19
* "*Crooner Cat*"
first printed in HAPPY COMICS #20
* "*The Forest Concert*"
first printed in BARNYARD COMICS #20
* "*The Poor Little Woodpecker*"
first printed in GOOFY COMICS #21
* "*The Just-the-Same Mouse*" 2 illos.
first printed in HAPPY COMICS #27
* "*Mike and Jerry*"
first printed in BARNYARD COMICS #22

* "*Roaring Cat*"
first printed in GOOFY COMICS #28

* "*The Timid Caterpillar*"
first printed in HAPPY COMICS #33

Munchy the Squirrel in "*Spare That Tree*" 5 pp.
first printed in COO COO COMICS #47

* "*Unhappy Animal*" 2 illos.
first printed in SUPERMOUSE #3

* "*A Word to the Wise*"
first printed in COO COO COMICS #35

* "*Eager Beaver*"
first printed in HAPPY COMICS #29

* "*The Lost Chipmunk*"
first printed in SUPERMOUSE #2

* "*The Homeless Cat*"
first printed in BARNYARD COMICS #15

* "*Butch the Bully*"
first printed in GOOFY COMICS #33

* "*The Big Race*"
first printed in BARNYARD COMICS #24

* "*The Bold Little Antelope*"
first printed in GOOFY COMICS #24

* "*Monkey Business*"
first printed in SNIFFY THE PUP #5

"*Dodger de Squoil*" 5 pp.

* "*Big Ears and Little Ears*" 2 illos.
first printed in BARNYARD COMICS #20

* "*Coalie the Lamb*"
first printed in HAPPY COMICS #30

* "*Ferocious Lamb*"
first printed in COO COO COMICS #39

* "*The Cowardly Lamb*"

* "*The Big Badger Hunt*"
first printed in HAPPY COMICS #20

* "*Barnyard Hero*"
first printed in COO COO COMICS #39

* "*The Colt Who Was Too Good*"
first printed in BARNYARD COMICS #24

* "*Nothing at All*"
first printed in COO COO COMICS #49

* "*The Nightingale Who Couldn't Sing*"
first printed in HAPPY COMICS #36

* "*The Walking Stick*"
first printed in BARNYARD COMICS #15

* "*Lucky Bird*"
first printed in GOOFY COMICS #20

Hucky Duck in "*Circus Ticket*" 6 pp.
first printed in BARNYARD COMICS #25

* "*Wally the Whale*"
first printed in GOOFY COMICS #33

* "*Abbott the Rabbit*"
first printed in HAPPY COMICS #28

* "*Herbie*"
first printed in HAPPY COMICS #32

* "*The Elephant Who Wouldn't Help*"
first printed in HAPPY COMICS #28

* "*Cleverest One*"
first printed in BARNYARD COMICS #19

* "*Unsociable Turtle*"
first printed in COO COO COMICS #47

* "*The Turtle and the Pelican*"
first printed in COO COO COMICS #34

* "*Slippy the Seal*"

"*Hucky Duck*" 7 pp.

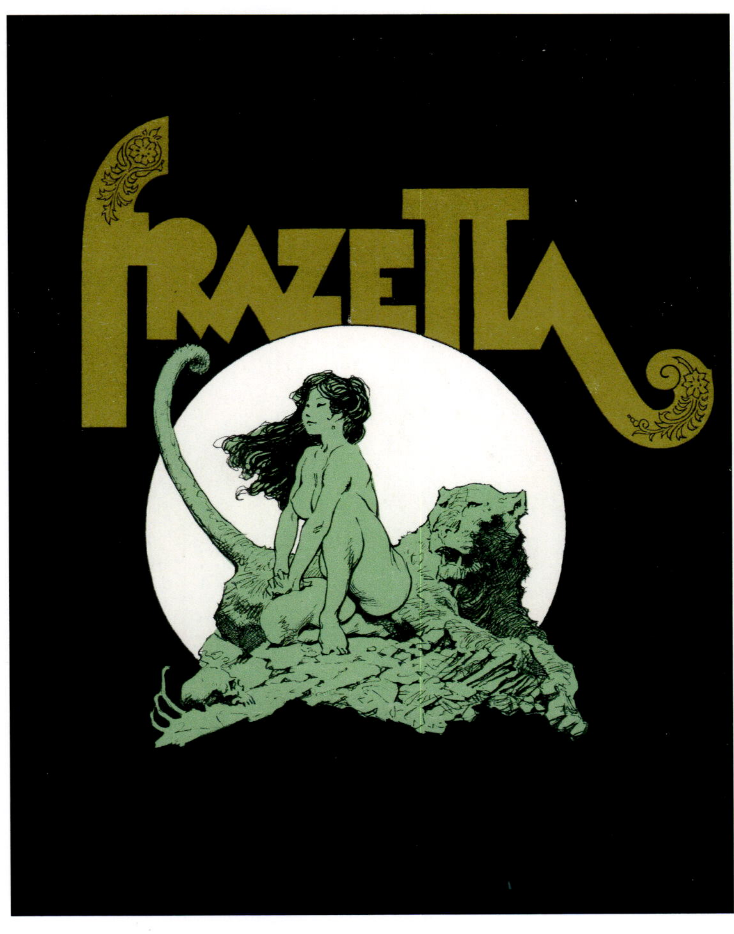

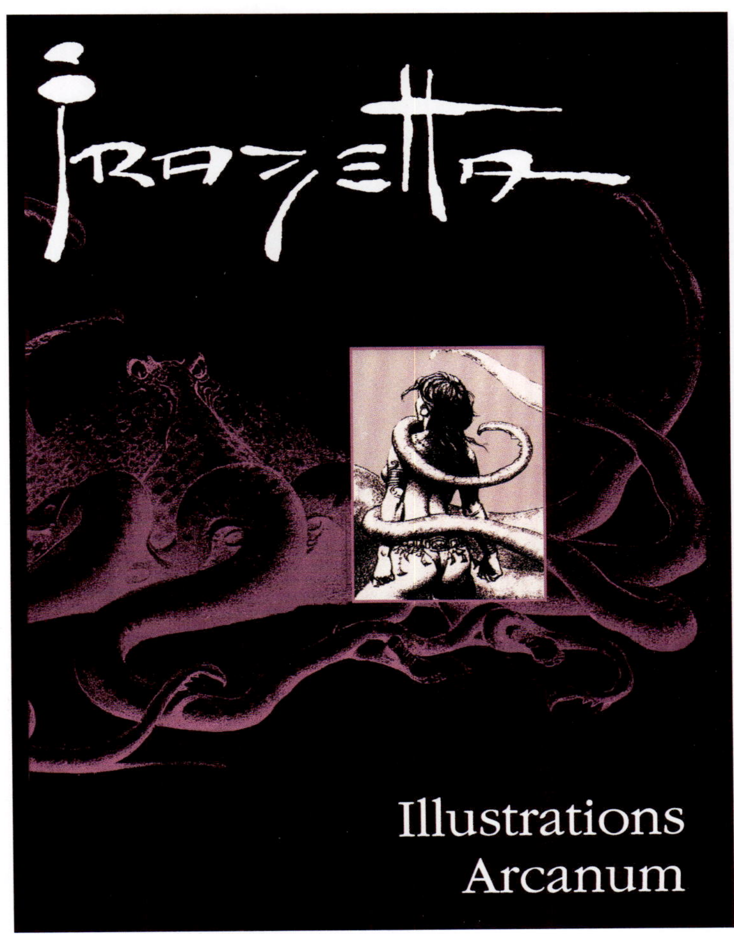

TOP:
Frazetta: The Living Legend
Frazetta Prints / Sun Litho (1981)

BOTTOM:
Frazetta: Illustrations Arcanum
Verotik (994)

TESTAMENT: The Life and Art of Frank Frazetta
2001
Underwood Press
• Deluxe leatherbound edition - Each with slipcase, Authentication page, and additional pages of artwork not found in trade edition.. Cover is leather, textured as snakeskin. Traycase bound in black iris linen.
  Limited to 100 copies
• Limited Edition - Each with slipcase, Authentication page, and additional pages of artwork not found in trade edition.
  Limited to 1,200 copies.
• Trade Hardcover Edition
  f-cover **Leaping Lizards**
  d.j. end sleeve photo - Frank with second version of **The Destroyer**
  endpapers Plate from the Kubla Khan Portfolio
  pg. 1 logo intended for Ellie Frazetta's letterhead
  pg. 2 upper left - cover to FRANK FRAZETTA FANTASY ILLUSTRATED #1
  large photo - Frank with knife in hand and loin cloth
  upper right photo - Frank with Ellie (early 60's)
  lower right - rough of **Jongor Fights Back**
  pg. 3 cover to FRAZETTA fanzine #1
  "With Only a Shovel" detail
  first printed in HEROIC COMICS #72
  pg. 4 **Angel Hair**
  pg. 5 **Encounter**
  pg. 6 **Death Dealer III** detail
  contents Beauty & the Beast ink illustration
  pg. 10 cover to CREEPY #9
  pg. 11 **New World**
  pg. 12 **King Kong** version for Ace Books
  pg. 13 painting that eventually became **Mongol Tyrant**
  pg. 14 untitled early drawing of savage girl with panther
  (Caption dates the piece at 1945. Date is closer to 1950.)
  pg. 15 Thun'da character sheet.
  pg. 20 *"The Scared Life Saver"* page 1
  first printed in HEROIC COMICS #67
  pg. 21 artwork for FAMOUS FUNNIES #210
  recolored by Frazetta
  pg. 22 artwork for LI'L ABNER Greeting Card
  pg. 23 artwork for *"Early one Morning in the Jungle"* 1 pg.
  first printed in MAD MAGAZINE #106
  pg. 24 covers to the five "Fantastic Art" books
  see individual books for cover listings
  pg. 25 cover to ICON - **Dreamflight**
  cover to AMERICAN ARTIST, May 1976 - **Death Dealer**
  interior of 1978 CALENDAR - **Bloodstone**
  cover to ILLUSTRATIONS ARCANUM
  packaging and obverse of card from FRAZETTA II series
  HOLOGRAM SET images are:
  Dreamflight
  The Countess
  Dawn Attack
  pg. 27 **Portrait of Ellie 1960**
  pg. 30 sketch of a pregnant Ellie
  pg. 31 **King of Kings**
  pg. 32 THE FRANK FRAZETTA PORTFOLIO
  fanzine cover featuring **Golden Girl**
  pg. 33 FRAZETTA'S WOMEN fanzine
  fanzine cover featuring **Savage Pellucidar**
  FRANK FRAZETTA: MASTER OF PEN AND INK
  fanzine cover
  THE RARE FRAZETTA
  fanzine cover featuring **Temptation**
  THE MAGIC OF FRANK FRAZETTA
  fanzine cover
  THE SENSUOUS FRAZETTA
  fanzine cover
  THE COMIC STRIP FRAZETTA
  fanzine cover
  pg. 34 cover to THE FRAZETTA TREASURY
  fanzine cover featuring **Conan of Aquilonia**
  HEROIC FANTASY: FRANK FRAZETTA
  unpublished fanzine cover featuring **Moon Maid**
  pg. 35 drawing
  first printed in A.C.B.A.A. SKETCHBOOK PORTFOLIO
  pp. 36,37 **Red Moon, Black Mountain**
  pg. 38 article *"Frazetta"* by Michael Kaluta 4pp.
  article includes the following:
  frontispiece to CARSON OF VENUS paperback
  pg. 39 **Jongor Fights Back**
  pg. 40 **The Beasts of Tarzan**
  The Warrior of Llarn
  pg. 41 frontispiece to TARZAN AND THE LION MAN
  pg. 42 **Carson of Venus**
  rough and sketches
  pg. 43 **Carson of Venus**
  pg. 44 **Iron Thorn**
  pg. 45 **Gulliver of Mars**
  pg. 46 **Roman Chariot**
  pg. 47 detail of **Roman Chariot**
  pg. 48 Tarzan and the Golden Lion
  AKA - *"Tarzan in perfect calm, raised his short, heavy spear above his right shoulder and waited."*
  first printed in TARZAN AND THE CASTAWAYS interior book illo.
  pg. 49 **Land of Terror**
  pg. 50 **Witherwing** - original version
  pg. 51 **Witherwing** - repainted version
  pg. 52 **Leaping Lizards**
  pg. 53 detail of **Leaping Lizards**
  pp. 54-5 **Dream Flight**
  pg. 56 rough to **Battlefield Earth**
  pg. 57 **Battlefield Earth**
  pg. 58 three plates from the LORD OF THE RINGS portfolio
  pg. 59 **The Gollum**
  pg. 60 Stand Off
  cover art **first printed in** FAMOUS FUNNIES #211
  pg. 61 Free Fall
  cover art **first printed in** FAMOUS FUNNIES #212
  pg. 62 On the Stairs
  cover art **first printed in** FAMOUS FUNNIES #209
  pg. 63 **In Pharaoh's Tomb**
  AKA - **Battlestar Galactica: Pharaoh's Tomb**
  pp. 64 **Attack**
  AKA - **Battlestar Galactica: Attack**
  pg. 66 **Scramble**
  AKA - **Battlestar Galactica: Scramble**
  pg. 67 detail of **Scramble**
  pg. 68 article *"Ground Zero"* 1 pg. by Dave Stevens
  article includes the following:
  cover to CONAN paperback - **Man Ape**
  pg. 69 drawing for the proposed "NINA" newspaper strip
  previously unpublished
  pg. 70 **Devil Rider** (1st version)
  pg. 71 **Devil Rider** (2nd version)
  pg. 72 **The Destroyer** (1st version)
  cover art **first printed in** CONAN THE BUCCANEER
  pg. 73 **The Destroyer** (2nd version)
  pg. 74 **Eve**
  pg. 75 **Girl Bathing**
  pg. 76 **Spirit of the Forest**
  pg. 77 **The Tempters**
  pg. 78 **Svengali Letterhead**
  detail of **Svengali Letterhead**
  pg. 80 drawing - Queen of the Nile

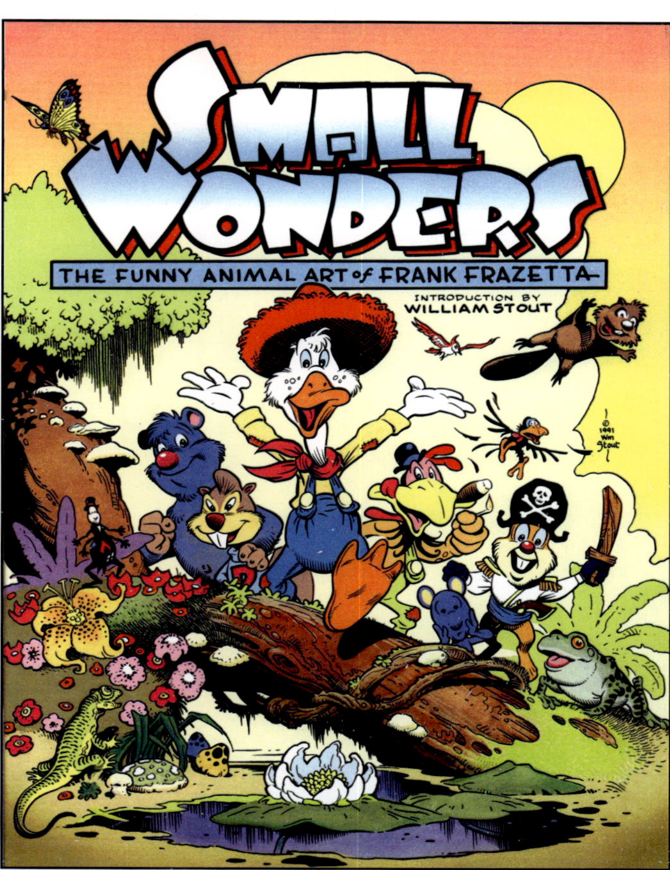

Small Wonders: The Funny Animal Art of Frank Frazetta
Kitchen Sink Press (1991)

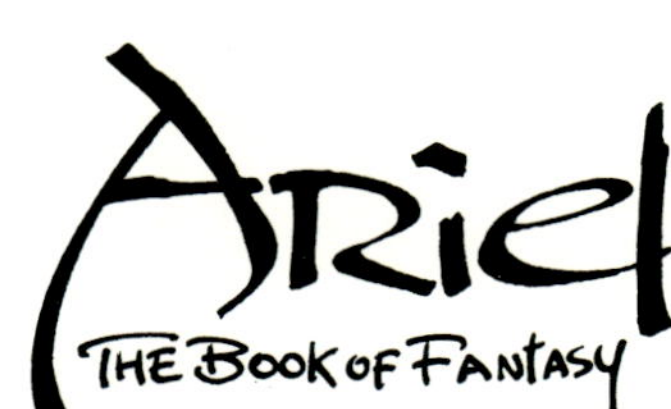

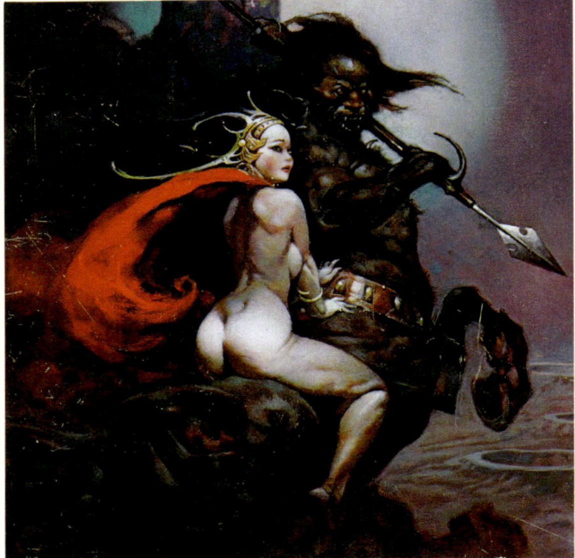

RAY BRADBURY RICHARD CORBEN HARLAN ELLISON
FRANK FRAZETTA URSULA LE GUIN
MICHAEL MOORCOCK J.R.R. TOLKIEN

Ariel *Volume 2 Morning Star Press (1977)*

OTHER ART BOOK APPEARANCES

- ARIEL: THE BOOK OF FANTASY VOL. 1

1976 (first printing date)
The Morning Star Press Ltd.
pg. 1 sketchbook drawing
pg. 6 article *"A hero lives in Brooklyn"* 5 pp.
Article includes the following:
detail of "**The Barbarian**" b/w
pg. 11 article *"Interview with Frank Frazetta"* 11 pp.
Article includes the following:
panel from *"Monsters from the Mists"* b/w
first printed in A-1 COMICS #47
sketchbook drawing
first printed in FANTASTIC ART OF FRANK FRAZETTA VOL. 1
panel from *"Gods of the Jungle"* b/w
first printed in A-1 COMICS #47
detail of "**Berserker**" b/w
panel from *"Empty Heart"* b/w
first printed in PERSONAL LOVE #28
six consecutive panels from *"Monsters from the Mists"* b/w
first printed in A-1 COMICS #47
last page from the story *"Untamed Love"* b/w
first printed in PERSONAL LOVE #32
pg. 22 article *"On Frazetta's art"* by Margaret Cline 5 pp.
Article includes the following:
Egyptian Queen b/w
six consecutive panels from *"King of the Lost Lands"* b/w
first printed in A-1 COMICS #47

Savage Pellucidar b/w
(mis-titled "Sun Goddess")
The Brain b/w
Atlantis b/w
Panel from NINA tryout page
first printed in WITZEND #8 *"The City in the Sea"*

- ARIEL: THE BOOK OF FANTASY VOL.2

1977 (first printing date)
The Morning Star Press Ltd.
cover **The Moon Maid**
Title page Dejah Thoris detail
contents pg. detail of "**La of Opar**"
first printed in FRAZETTA #1 (fanzine)
pg. 14 **Spiderman**
pg. 15 article *"Frazetta"* part two - 12 pp.
Article includes the following:
close detail of "**Self Portrait**" b/w
Self Portrait
Outlaw of Torn
Sketchbook drawing
illustration from *"The Giantess"*
first printed in CAVALCADE VOL. 4 #18
color Illustration
Detail of "Tarzan and Bolgani"
first printed in FRAZETTA #2 (fan publication)
Flash Gordon b/w
The Death Dealer
The Giantess
first printed in CAVALCADE VOL. 4 #18
detail of "**Luana**"
"He struck suddenly upward with his blade."
Tarzan illustration early version.
first printed in WITZEND #4 back cover.
John Carter and the Savage Apes of Mars

- ART OF PLAYBOY, THE

1985
Alfred Van Der March Editions
reproduces art - **Castle of Sin**

- ART OF AL WILLIAMSON, THE

1983
James Van Hise
Interview with Frazetta
"The Vicious Space Pirates" 6 pp. by Williamson and Frazetta
first printed in DANGER IS OUR BUSINESS comic book

CLASSIC COMICS ILLUSTRATORS
Fantagraphics Books
2005

- Vol. 5 Featuring artists: Burne Hogarth, Russ Heath, Russ Manning, Mark Schultz and Frank Frazetta.

pg. 103 Article "Separating the Men from the Boys"
pg. 143 Article "Fantasy's Michelangelo"

- COLLECTIBLY MAD

Kitchen Sink Press
April 1995 Reprints all Frazetta material to date.

- COLLECTOR'S GUIDE TO THE ARTISTS, A

1977
Jeffrey Merrihue
Lists major works of comic book artists, including Frazetta.
COVER Flash Gordon illustration

- COLLECTING EDGAR RICE BURROUGHS

2000
Schiffer Publishing
pg. 9 Beasts of Venus
pg. 12 **Carson of Venus** (1st version)
Carson of Venus (2nd version)
pg. 16 **Escape on Venus** (2nd version)
pg. 21 **At the Earth's Core**
pg. 23 **Flying Reptiles**
pg. 30 **Tanar of Pellucidar**
pg. 33 **Back to the Stone Age** old series
pg. 36 **Land of Terror** (1st version)
pg. 38 **The Huntress**
pg. 42 **Outlaw of Torn**
pg. 45 **The Mad King**
pg. 47 **The Bear**
pg. 48 **The Rider**
pg. 53 **The Moon Maid** (2nd version)
pg. 55 **Beyond the Farthest Star**
pg. 55 **God from the Sky**
pg. 88 **Thuvia, Maid of Mars**
pg. 97 **A Fighting Man of Mars**
pg. 128 **The Return of the Mucker**
pg. 130 **Lost Continent**
pg. 133 cover art for THE GIRL FROM FARRIS'
pg. 137 cover art for THE EFFICIENCY EXPERT
pg. 141 **Black Panther**

COMPLETE E.C. LIBRARY, THE

Russ Cochran

- Crime Suspenstories Vol. 4
  "*Fired*" 6 pp.with Al Williamson
  first printed in CRIME SUSPENSTORIES #17
- Shock Suspenstories Vol. 3
  "*Squeeze Play*" 7 pp.
  first printed in SHOCK SUSPENSTORIES #13
- Weird Fantasy Vol. 3
  "*Mad Journey*" 7 pp. with Al Williamson and Roy Krenkel
  first printed in WEIRD FANTASY #14
- Weird Fantasy Vol. 4
  "*I Rocket*" 7 pp. with Al Williamson and Roy Krenkel
  first printed in WEIRD FANTASY #20
  COVER with Al Williamson
  first printed in WEIRD FANTASY #21
- Weird Science Vol. 4
  "*The One Who Waits*" 7 pp. with Al Williamson
  first printed in WEIRD SCIENCE #19
  "*50 girls 50*" 7 pp. with Al Williamson and Roy Krenkel
  first printed in WEIRD SCIENCE #20
  "*Two's Company*" 7 pp. with Al Williamson
  first printed in WEIRD SCIENCE #21
  "*A New Beginning*" 8 pp. with Al Williamson
  first printed in WEIRD SCIENCE #22
- Weird Science-Fantasy Vol. 1
  COVER
  first printed in WEIRD SCIENCE-FANTASY #29

- COMPLETE JOHNNY COMET, THE

Vanguard Productions
2010
- softcover
- hardcover

COMPLETELY MAD

1991
Little Brown and Co.
pg. 53 **Ringo Starr** Blecch Ad
- hardcover
- softcover

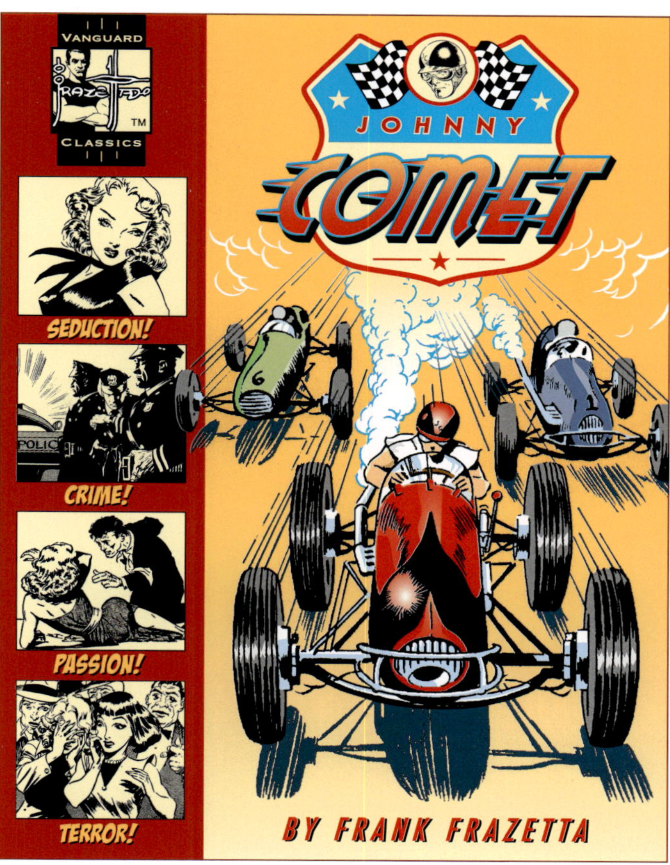

ABOVE: The Complete Johnny Comet
Softcover. Vanguard Productions (2010)

BELOW: The Complete Johnny Comet
Hardcover. Vanguard Productions (2010)

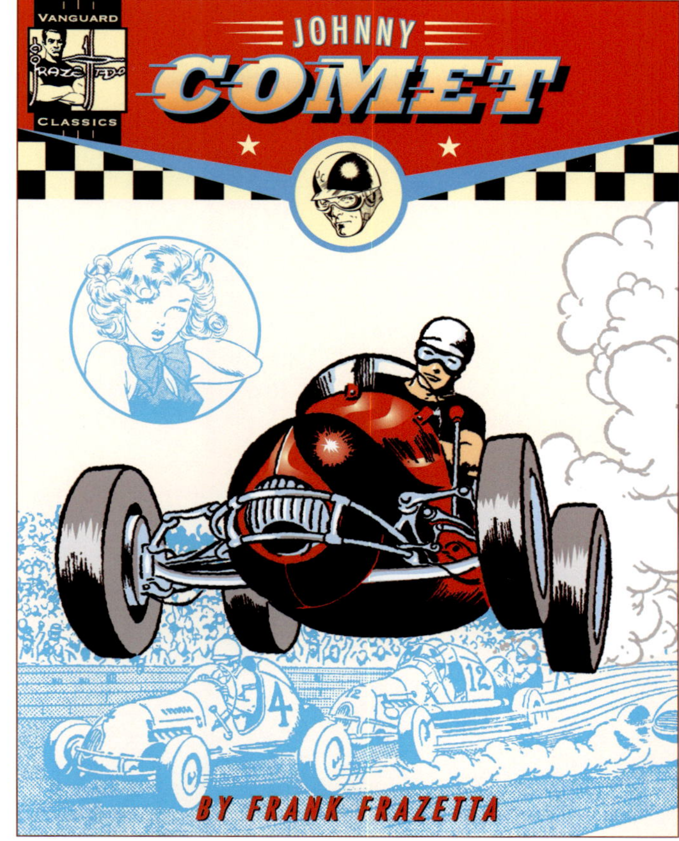

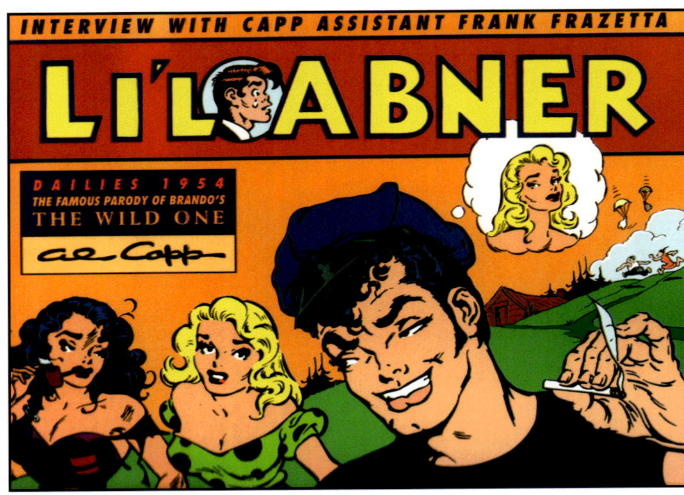

Li'l Abner Dailies: Volume 20
Kitchen Sink Press/ Capp Enterprises

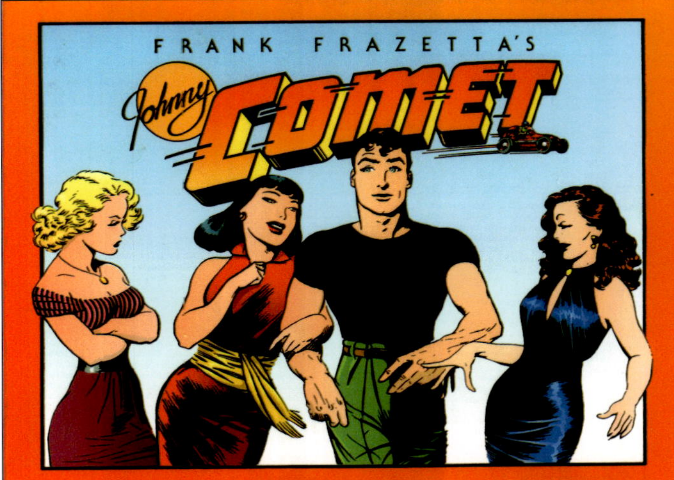

Frank Frazetta's Johnny Comet
Eclipse Books (1991)

- DINOSAUR SCRAPBOOK, THE

1980
Citadel Press
pg. 192 *"King of the Lost Lands"* pg. 2
first printed in A-1 COMICS #47

- E.C. HORROR LIBRARY OF THE 1950's

Nostalgia Press
1971 *"Squeeze Play"* 7 pp.
first printed in SHOCK SUSPENSTORIES #13

E.C. PORTFOLIO
Russ Cochran

- 2 1972
  F. COVER/B. COVER - cover to Weird Science-Fantasy #29
  (unretouched version)
  Front and back covers are colored differently.
  "Squeeze Play" 7 pp.
  first printed in SHOCK SUSPENSTORIES #13
- 3 1972
  cover to Weird Fantasy #21 with Al Williamson
  "50 Girls 50" 7 pp. with Al Williamson and Roy Krenkel
  first printed in WEIRD FANTASY #20

- FLASH GORDON the complete daily strips November 1951 - April 1953

1988
Kitchen Sink Press
pg. 103 daily strip reprints from 2\18\53 - 2\28\53 (2 pp.)
pg. 123 reprints the original pencil layouts for the above mentioned strips
reprinted in SQUA TRONT #3

- FRANK COLLECTION, THE by Howard and Jane Frank

1999
Paper Tiger
pg. 82 **Warrior with Ball and Chain**
pg. 85 **Fire & Ice**

- FRANK FRAZETTA'S JOHNNY COMET

1991
Eclipse Books
Reprints the entire run (1/28/52 – 2/1/53) in b/w including Sunday pages with the exception of the following:
dailies - 12/12/53, 1/20/53
Sundays - 2/10/52, 2/17/52, 1/11/53

- FRANK FRAZETTA SKETCHBOOK

April 2001
Spanish publication comic book size
56 pages in black/white full with sketches, preliminary art, cover and pages reproductions, rare drawings, unseen art.
Also contains an interview with Frazetta (texts in spanish).

FROM AARGH! TO ZAP!
1991
- Kitchen Sink hardcover
- Prentice Hall Press softcover

pg. 35 pg. 5 from *"50 Girls 50"*
first printed in WEIRD SCIENCE #20 comic book
"Two's Company" partial page
first printed in WEIRD SCIENCE #21 comic book
pg. 36 cover to WEIRD SCIENCE-FANTASY #29 comic book
"Untamed Love" splash page
first printed in PERSONAL LOVE #32 comic book
"Squeeze Play" splash page
first printed in SHOCK SUSPENSTORIES #13
pg. 37 cover to FAMOUS FUNNIES #210 comic book
cover to FAMOUS FUNNIES #213 comic book
cover to FAMOUS FUNNIES #214 comic book
cover to FAMOUS FUNNIES #215 comic book

GLAMOUR INTERNATIONAL
1985
- 2 April 1985
  pg. 22 Midwood paperback interior illustration
  pg. 23 Midwood paperback interior illustration
  pg. 24 Midwood paperback interior illustration
  pg. 25 Midwood paperback interior illustration
  pg. 26 Midwood paperback interior illustration
- 3 September 1985
  pg. 17 **Flashman on the Charge** (2nd version)
  The Moon Maid (2nd version)
  2 untitled ink illustrations
  untitled ink illustration
  AKA - *"I let him have a left fair on the point of the jaw that sent him tumbling over on his back."*
  first printed in E. R. B.: MASTER OF ADVENTURE interior book illo.
- 10 October 1987
  pg. 60 **Golden Girl**
  pg. 61 detail of **Cat Girl**

- 13 March 1989
  - pg. 4 **Nude**
  - pg. 10 comic book panel
    first printed in PERSONAL LOVE #27 comic book
  - pg. 20 untitled sketchbook drawing
  - pg. 32 untitled sketchbook drawing
- 17 October 1991
  - pg. 45 Midwood paperback interior illustration
  - pg. 46 **Girl Bathing**
    cover art to FAMOUS FUNNIES #209 comic book
    (AKA - On the Stairs)
  - pg. 47 Jungle Woman (Canaveral Press ink illustration)
- 18 May 1992
  - pg. 7 **Sea Witch**
  - pg. 11 **Paradox**
- 23 October 1996
  - pg. 8 LI'L ABNER daily 8-26-54
  - pg. 11 untitled watercolor
    first printed in THE FRAZETTA PORTFOLIO

- GREAT COMIC BOOK ARTISTS, THE by Ron Goulart

1986
St. Martin's Press
vol. 1
pg. 45 Contains one page biography on Frazetta. Article includes single comic panel from "*Squeeze Play*"
first printed in SHOCK SUSPENSTORIES #13

GREATEST 1950'S STORIES EVER TOLD

National Periodical Pub
reprints two Frazetta stories

- hardcover
- softcover

- HILLS OF FARAWAY, THE : **A Guide to Fantasy** by Diana Waggoner

Atheneum
1978 re produces painting - **Swords of Mars**

- INFINITE WORLDS The Fantastic Visions of Science Fiction Art by Vincent Di Fate

1997
Penguin

- pg. 70 **The Moon Maid**
  Gulliver of Mars
- pg. 172 **Sea Monster**
  Beyond the Farthest Star
- pg. 173 **Thuvia, Maid of Mars**
  A PRINCESS OF MARS interior illustration
  THE MASTERMIND OF MARS / A FIGHTING MAN OF MARS interior illustration
- pg. 174 **Carson of Venus** (original version)
  King Kong and Snake
  Downward to the Earth
- pg. 175 **Battlefield Earth**

LI'L ABNER DAILIES

Kitchen Sink Press / Capp Enterprises

- volume 20 reprints Frazetta's first work on the strip from 12\16\53 - 11\20\54
- volume 21 reprints 11\21\54 - 10\17\55
- volume 22 reprints 10\18\55 - 9\12\56
- volume 23 reprints 9\13\56 - 8\7\57
- volume 24 reprints 8\8\57 - 7\2\58
- volume 25 reprints 7\3\58 - 5\30\59
- volume 26 reprints 5\31\59 - 4\27\60
- volume 27 reprints 4\28\60 - 3\24\61
- volume 28 reprints 3\25\61 - 2\21\62

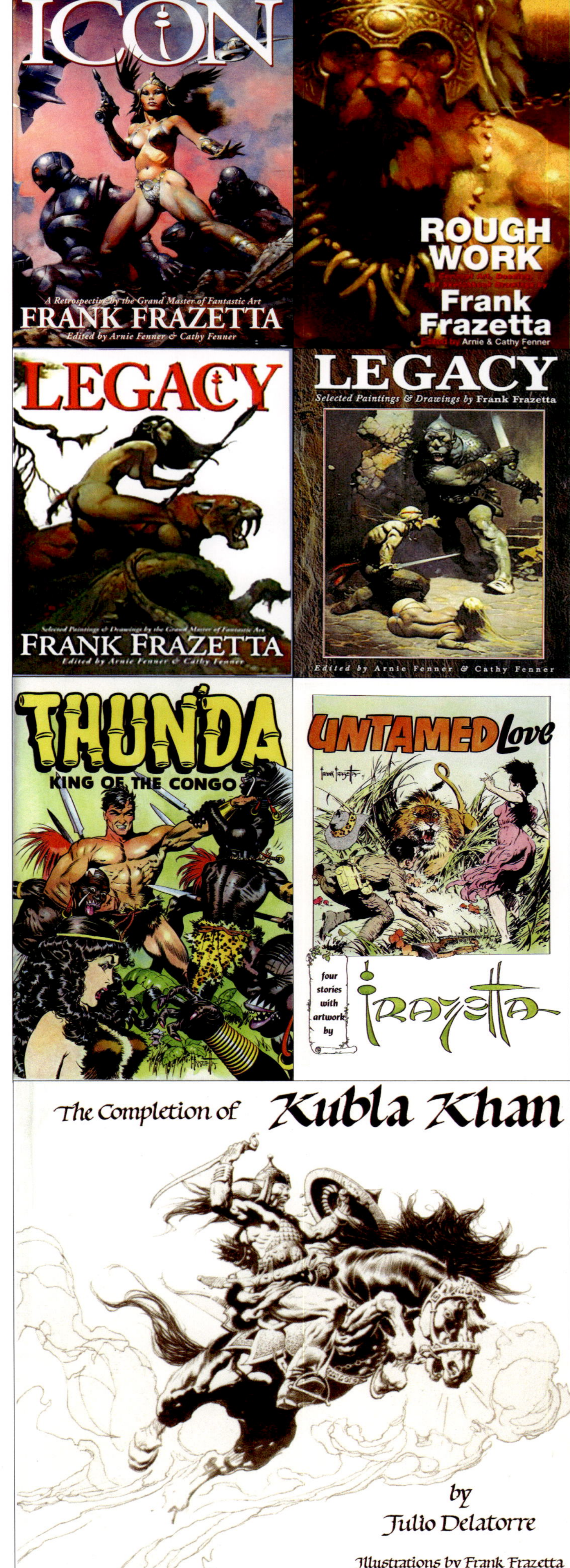

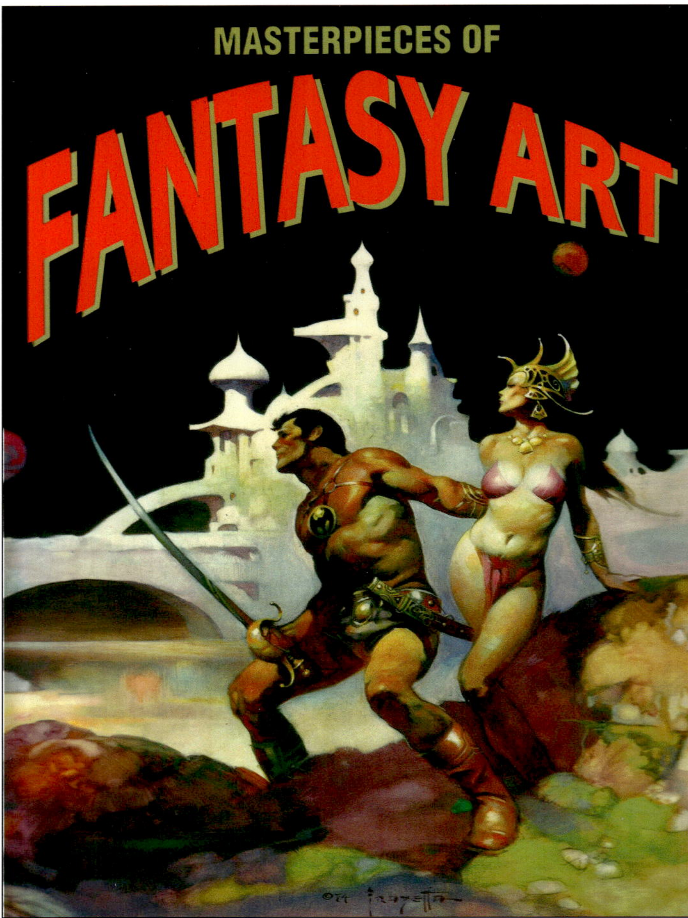

MasterPieces of Fantasy Art
Taschen (1991)

LI'L ABNER - THE FRAZETTA YEARS
2003
Dark Horse
- volume 1, 1954 - 1955
- volume 2, 1956 - 1957
- volume 3, 1958 - 1959
- volume 4, 1960 - 1961

- MASTERPIECES OF FANTASY ART

1991
Benedikt Taschen
COVER **Thuvia, Maid of Mars**
pg. 11 **The Galleon**
pg. 12 **Flying Reptiles**
pg. 13 **Thuvia, Maid of Mars** (2 page spread)
pg. 17 **A Princess of Mars**

- PHOTO JOURNAL GUIDE TO COMIC BOOKS, THE

volumes one and two
1989
Gerber Publishing Company
Reprints all Frazetta and collaborative comic book covers up to the year 1955.

- PLAYBOY'S LITTLE ANNIE FANNIE

Playboy Press
1966
pg. 49 *"Surf Party"* 5 pp. with Jack Davis
first printed in PLAYBOY July 1965
pg. 86 *"James Bomb in Russia"* part two 3 pp. with Russ Heath
first printed in PLAYBOY February 1965
pg. 105 *"Topless Bathing Suit Trial"* 5 pp. with Jack Davis
first printed in PLAYBOY May 1965

- SCIENCE FICTION COLLECTORS CATALOG, THE

by Jeff Rovin
1982
A.S. Barnes & Co.
pg. 139 cover to LOST ON VENUS
pg. 142 cover to E.R.B.DOM #88 sketch from PELLUCIDAR
pg. 164 photo Vampirella model kit

- SEX IN THE COMICS by Maurice Horn

Chelsea House
comic panel
first printed in PERSONAL LOVE #28 comic book

- SPECTRUM VOL. 2

1996
Underwood Press
Berserker

- SPECTRUM VOL. 3

1997
Underwood Press
Beauty and The Beast

- SPECTRUM PRESENTS: Frank Frazetta: Rough Works

2007
Spectrum Fantastic Art

- SPECTRUM PRESENTS: The Comic Art of Frank Frazetta

2007
Spectrum Fantastic Art

- TALES FROM THE CRYPT

St. Martin's Press
1996
pg. 231 WEIRD SCIENCE-FANTASY #29
lithograph reproduction. Originally hand colored by Frazetta with remarque of nude female.
first printed in WEIRD SCIENCE-FANTASY #29
pg.157 same as above without remarque

- TELLING STORIES: The Classic Comic Art of Frank Frazetta

Underwood Books
2008

- THUN'DA

1973
Russ Cochran entire contents **first printed in** A-1 COMICS #47
"King of the Lost Lands" 10 pp.
"The Monsters From the Mists" 7 pp.
"When the Earth Shook" 6 pp.
"Gods of the Jungle" 8 pp.

- UNTAMED LOVE

1973
Russ Cochran
"Too Late for Love" 7 pp.
first printed in PERSONAL LOVE #25
"The Wrong Road" 8 pp.
first printed in PERSONAL LOVE #27
"Empty Heart" 6 pp.
first printed in PERSONAL LOVE #28
"Untamed Love" 8 pp.
first printed in PERSONAL LOVE #32

ALL STAR AUCTIONS
All Star, Joe Mannarino, Nadia Mannarino
- 7 2003
  Cover **The Tempest** (a re-rendered version of Against the Gods)
  Back Cover Cover to A-1 COMICS #47 (original art version)
Limited edition of 500

CHRISTIE'S AUCTION catalog
- October 31, 1992
  cover **A Fighting Man of Mars**
  essay by Winiewicz
  Monster Men
  Defender
  Fantasy World
  sketches
- October 30, 1993
  cover **Princess of Mars**
  essay by Winiewicz
  watercolor of nude
  watercolor of jaguar
  back cover - **Mothman**
- October 29, 1994
  The Rider
  essay by Winiewicz
  watercolor study of early **Conan The Adventurer**
- November 17,1995
  cover **Tarzan and the Jewels of Opar**
  Vampirella rough
  Judge Dredd with Alfred E. Neuman
- November 1, 1996 Frazetta pencils and sketches
- December 18, 1997 Frazetta pencils JOHNNY COMET Sunday

CHRISTIE'S EAST catalog
- December 18, 1992
  "*The Art of Mad*" contains:
  "*Early one Morning in the Jungle*" (1 pg.)
  first printed in MAD MAGAZINE #10

COCHRAN, RUSS - COMIC ART AUCTION
- 1 October 1980
  JOHNNY COMET Daily 2/25/52
  SWEET ADELINE Daily; never used
- 2 December 1980
  JOHNNY COMET Sunday 4/27/52
  Cave Man Illo
  "*Efficiency Expert*" illustration
- 3 February 1981
  JOHNNY COMET Daily 2/8/52
  Two Frazetta ink drawings
- 4 April 1987
  JOHNNY COMET Sunday 3/16/52
  page 4 from "*Captain Comet*"
  first printed in DANGER IS OUR BUSINESS #1
  frontis to DOWNWARD TO THE EARTH
- 5 June 1981
  ACE McCOY Sunday 12/21/52
  ACE McCOY Daily 12/26/52,
  sci-fi tryout page (with Williamson)
  page from WHITE INDIAN comic book

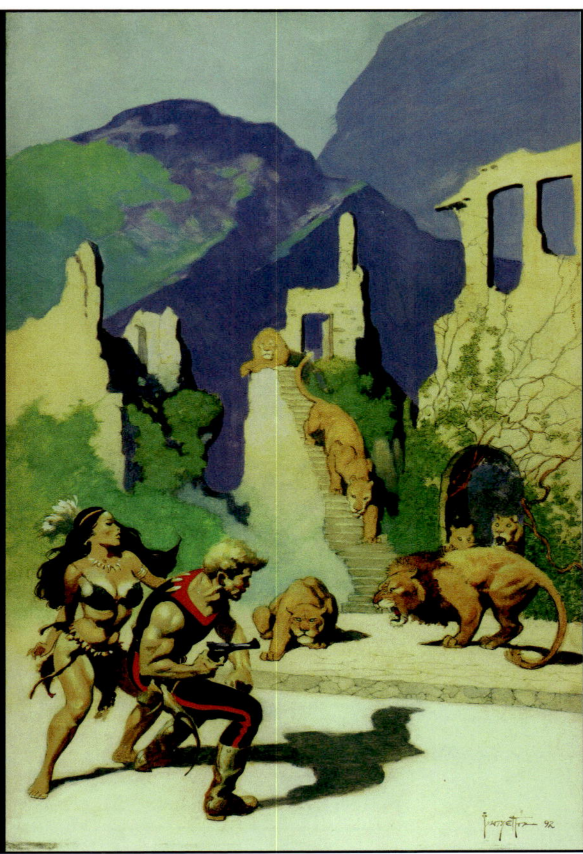

- 8 December 1981
  JOHNNY COMET Daily 2/11/52
  Brak The Barbarian
- 9 March 1982
  JOHNNY COMET Daily 9/15/52
- 10 May 1982
  Gauntlet color rough
  Yours, Mine & Ours watercolor prelim.
  Cavemen sketch
  Circle of Terror
- 11 September 1982
  color versions of Indian & Cowboy from
  Book Club Flyer
  LI'L ABNER 11/27/55 Sunday
  Frazetta inks
- 12 December 1982
  JOHNNY COMET Dailies 5/5/52 & 5/6/52
  ACE McCOY Sunday 12/21/52
  2 sketches
- 13 November 1983
  4 sketches
  pen & ink illustration
- 15 October 1983
  ACE McCOY Sunday 2/1/53 Untitled daily never used.
  Notice of Frazetta forgeries existing.
  splash page from "*A Dog's Best Friend*"
  first printed in HEROIC COMICS

- 16 December 1983
  JOHNNY COMET Sunday 3/30/52
  Proposed cover to PELLUCIDAR
  first printed in E.R..BURROUGHS: MASTER OF ADVENTURE
  men's magazine illustration
- 17 April 1984
  illustration from CANAVERAL PRESS
  Western painting
- 18 August 1984
  JOHNNY COMET Dailies 2/29/52, 3/5/52, 11/11/52
- 19 November 1984
  "*Squeeze Play*" (7 pp.)
  first printed in SHOCK SUSPENSTORIES #13
  page from WHITE INDIAN comic book
- 21 July 1985
  Frazetta sketches
  Uncle Creepy
  Gollum
- 22 October 1985
  one sketch
  one JOHNNY COMET Daily (reprint from #18)
- 23 December 1985
  5 original concept illustrations for
  The Night They Raided Minsky's
  tryout page for romance comic
  JOHNNY COMET Sunday 4/13/52
  JOHNNY COMET Daily 3/6/52
  Hand Colored print - WEIRD SCIENCE-FANTASY #29
  page from HEROIC COMICS
- 25 June 1986
  illustration from CANAVERAL PRESS
- 26 September 1986
  JOHNNY COMET Dailies 3/11/52 & 3/20/52
  ACE McCOY Dailies 12/4/52, 12/9/52, 12/15/52, 1/6/53, 1/12/53, 1/14/53, 1/15/53, 1/16/53, 1/17/53
- 27 November 1986 **FRANK FRAZETTA AUCTION ONE**
  Many oils, drawings, and sketches
  Three comic books tryout pages
  JOHNNY COMET Daily 10/14/52
  ACE McCOY Dailies 11/19/52, 12/17/52 & 12/18/52
- 28 December 1986
  Frogs on the Moon
- 30 June 1987
  WHITE INDIAN story
- 32 December 1987
  JOHNNY COMET dailies 7/14/52, 8/9/52
- 33 March 1988
  hand colored, reworked WEIRD SCIENCE-FANTASY #29 print
  Doubleday illustration
- 34 June 1988
  JOHNNY COMET dailies 10/6/52, 10/18/52
- 37 March 1989
  JOHNNY COMET Sunday 11/9/52
- 40 December 1989
  JOHNNY COMET Daily 12/26/52
- 41 March 1990
  Dead of Night
- 42 June 1990
  LI'L ABNER Sunday 7/7/54 Frazetta inks
  JOHNNY COMET Sunday 5/4/54
- 43 October 1990
  JOHNNY COMET Sunday 3/23/52, dailies12/3/52, 1/8/53
  WHITE INDIAN page
- 44 February
  1991 JOHNNY COMET daily 7/8/52
- 45 June 1991
  5 pencil illustrations
  JOHNNY COMET daily 7/17/52
- 46 October 1991
  5 pencil illustrations
- 48 May 1996
  pen & ink illustration
  2 ACE frontispieces
  2 ink sketches
  JOHNNY COMET dailies 3/29/53, 7/18/53
  page from WHITE INDIAN
- 49 October 1996
  2 WHITE INDIAN pp.
  JOHNNY COMET daily 7/25/52
- 50 December 1996
  JOHNNY COMET dailies 3/17/52, 5/29/52
  Tanar of Pellucidar color rough
- 51 April 1997
  LI'L ABNER Sunday 5/15/55 Frazetta inks
  Doubleday illustration
  hand colored FAMOUS FUNNIES cover
  LI'L ABNER AND THE CREATURES FROM DROP OUTER SPACE entire book (28 pp.)
- 52 June 1997
  JOHNNY COMET dailies 6/7/52, 7/23/52
  2 sketches
  Flesh Eaters color rough
- 53 October 1997
  JOHNNY COMET dailies 4/9/52, 6/11/52, 6/18/52, 1/23/53
  Vampirella #1 color rough
- 54 March 1998
  Cat Girl w/remarque
- 55 August 1998
  JOHNNY COMET dailies 10/23/52, 12/30/52
  Williamson, Frazetta try out page for TRAIL COLT
- 56 December 1998
  alternate version of **Tarzan at the Earth's Core**
  JOHNNY COMET dailies 5/10/52, 7/31/52
  3 ACE frontispieces
- 57 April 1999
  ink illustration
- 58 September 1999
  hand colored FAMOUS FUNNIES cover
  hand colored WEIRD SCIENCE FANTASY#29 cover
  JOHNNY COMET daily 9/15/52
  Pappy Yokum watercolor
- 59 December 1999
  "*The Trail of the Traitor*" 7 pp.
  first printed in DURANGO KID #13
- 60 May 2000
  "*The White Wolf*" 6 pp.
  first printed in DURANGO KID #15
  Mammy and Pappy watercolor
- 62 July 2001
  LI'L ABNER Sunday 8/15/54
  Lost Continent second version

COLLECTOR'S SHOWCASE

- 2 1975 JOHNNY COMET daily 4/9/52

COMIC ART SHOWCASE

- 4 1975 JOHNNY COMET dailies 6/24/52, 7/1/52
  "*Claws of Death*" 4 pp. with Williamson
  first printed in JOHN WAYNE ADV. COMICS #3

- 5 1976 JOHNNY COMET dailies 6/25/52, 9/6/52

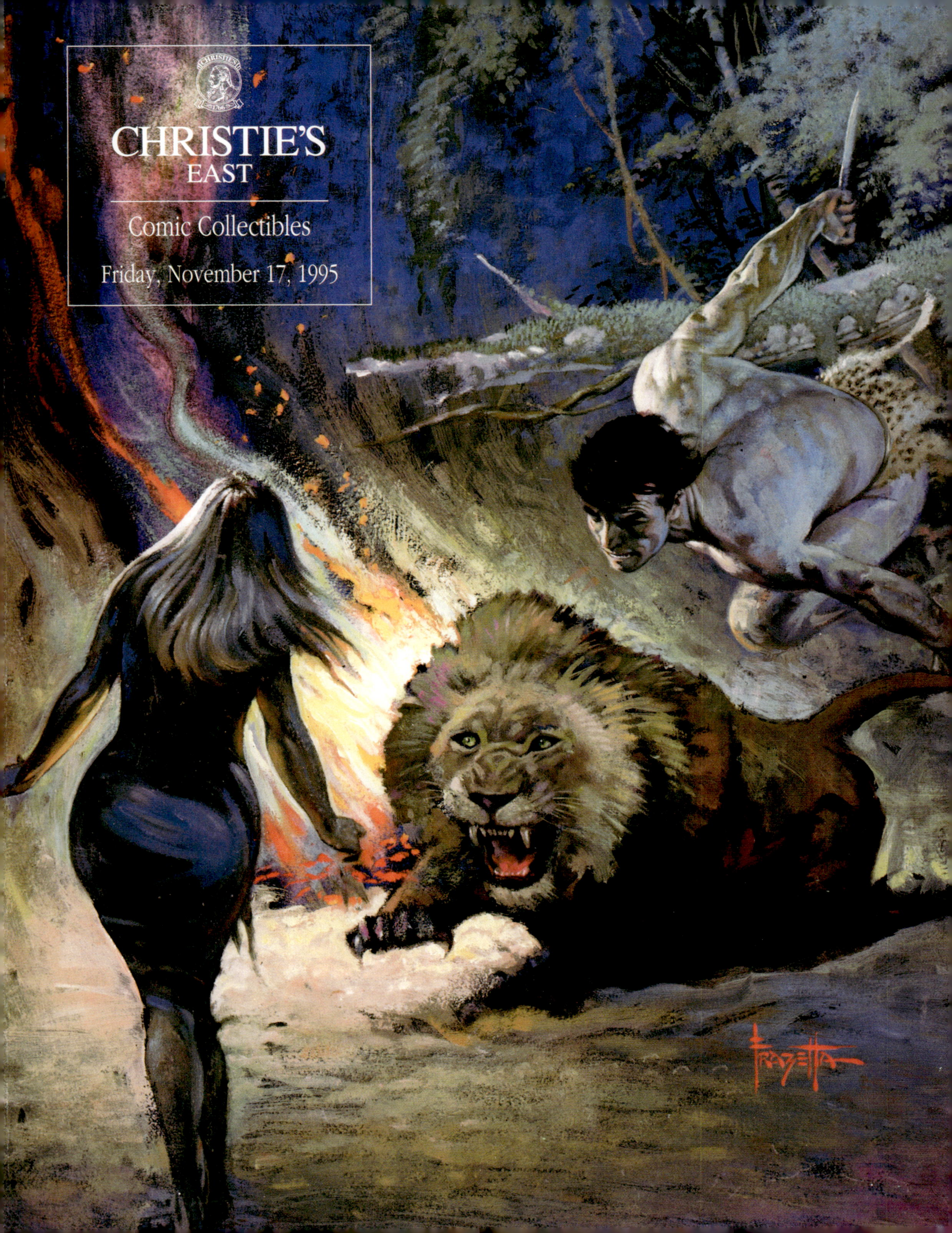
CHRISTIE'S
EAST
Comic Collectibles
Friday, November 17, 1995
Frazetta

GRAPHIC COLLECTIBLES
- 3 1984 JOHNNY COMET daily 9/25/52
- 4 1985 watercolor prelim for "**Solar Invasion**"

GRAPHIC GALLERY
Russ Cochran Publishing
No. 1, 1973 - No. 13, 1979
- 1 1973
  24 pen & ink illustrations
  5 watercolors
  Cornered
  Brak the Barbarian
  The Executioner
  Alien Worlds
- 2 1973
  3 sketches
  watercolor
- 3 1974
  JOHNNY COMET Sunday strips 5-4-52 & 7-20-52
  4 watercolors
  6 sketches
  Beyond the Farthest Star (2nd version)
- 4 1974
  JOHNNY COMET Sunday strips 3-9-52 & 11-23-52
  2 color photos of Frank
  Outlaw of Torn
  High Side (revised)
  Cowboys
  Thor's Flight
  Blazing Combat #3
  7 sketches
- 5 1975
  JOHNNY COMET Sunday strip (9-21-52)
  JOHNNY COMET daily strips
  8-9-52, 9-29-52, 9-30-52, 10-8-52 & 10-30-52
  2 Doubleday interior illustrations
  New World
- 6 1976
  JOHNNY COMET Sunday strips 3-16-52 & 6-1-52
  JOHNNY COMET daily strips
  4-14-52, 4-15-52, 4-16-52, 3-25-52 & 6-3-52
  cover to TALES OF THE INCREDIBLE paperback
  Cowboys
- 7 1976
  JOHNNY COMET daily strips
  2-21-52, 11-14-52, & 11-25-52
  ACE McCOY daily strip (12-25-52)
  2 sketches
- 9 1976 JOHNNY COMET Sunday strip (11-16-52)
  4 sketches
  pen & ink illustration
  "*Claws of Death*" 2 pp.
  first printed in JOHN WAYNE ADVENTURE COMICS #3
- 10 1977
  3 Sample sci-fi art pages (with Williamson)
  1 sample romance page
  1 WHITE INDIAN page
  JOHNNY COMET daily strips (5-19-52, & 5-20-52)
  ACE McCOY daily strips (1-22-53 & 1-23-53)
  CANAVERAL PRESS illustration
  2 sketches
- 11 1977
  LI'L ABNER Sunday strip (5-29-55)
  2 western pages
  2 CANAVERAL PRESS illustrations

GUERNSEY'S: The Art of Popular Culture
- January 28 - 31, 1998
  Judge Dredd with Alfred E. Neuman
  Eternal Champion (repainted version)
  3000 A.D.

HERITAGE COMICS
- March 16, 2002
  6543 Original Art for L'il Abner Daily dated 6-17-57
  6700 Original Illustration (Canaveral Press, 1962)
  AKA - lizard man riding on iguana creature
  First printed in TARZAN AT THE EARTH'S CORE
  6701 Original Illustration of Tarzan and the Golden Lion
  (Canaveral Press, 1962)
  AKA - *"Tarzan in perfect calm, Raised his short, heavy spear above his right shoulder and waited."*
  First printed in TARZAN AND THE CASTAWAYS
  6702 Original Illustration Tarzan of the Apes (1991)
  6704 Unpublished Original Art from Shock Illustrated #4
  6707 Original **Cat Girl** rough (undated)
  6708 Original Illustration (undated)
  6709 Original Oil Painting **Thor's Flight**
  6710 Original Cover Art for Famous Funnies #213
- July 7, 2002
  5800 Original Comic Strip Art for Johnny Comet
  5801 Original Comic Strip Art for Johnny Comet
  5802 Original Art Comic Strip Art For Johnny Comet
  5804 Original Comic Strip Art for L'il Abner
  5805 Original Comic Strip Art for L'il Abner
  6126 Original Art for The Durango Kid #15
  6191 Original Art for the Back Cover of Mad
  6230 Original Illustration "Trail Colt"
  6232 Original Illustration of Conan
  6233 Original Watercolor Rough for **A Requiem for Sharks**
  6234 Original Oil Painting **Carson of Venus**
  6235 Original Oil Painting **Winter of the Coup**
- October 12, 2002
  7511 Original Pencil Rough for **The African Elephant**
  7512 Original Art for John Wayne #36, page 1 (with Williamson)
  7515 Original Illustration From *The Night They Raided Minsky's* Pressbook
  7516 Original Illustration (Canaveral Press, 1965)
  7517 Original Illustration (Sun Litho, 1981)
  7571 Original Oil Painting, **The Countess and the Green Man**
  7572 Original Watercolor Painting, **The Secret People**
- December 7, 2002
  6448 Original Oil Painting, **Brooklyn Dreams**
  6449 Original Illustration for E.R. Burroughs' Chessmen of Mars
  AKA - *"Twice Turan struck the Martian rat away, but both times it returned with increased ferocity to renew the attack.."*
  6450 Illustration for Shock Illustrated #4, "Came the Dawn"
  6451 Illustration for Shock Illustrated #4, "Came the Dawn"
  6452 Original Illustration for Tarzan and the Lost Empire (title page illustration)
- March 6, 2003
  6663 Original Comic Strip Art for Johnny Comet Daily, dated 2/6/52
  6664 Original Comic Strip Art for Johnny Comet daily, Dated 2/7/52
  6812 Original Illustration
  AKA - Jungle Woman
  First printed in BURROUGHS ARTIST PORTFOLIO
  6813 Original Cover Art for Ghost Rider #3
  6814 Original art for Mastermind of Mars
  AKA - *"An attendant appeared bearing the body of the beautiful girl."*
  6815 Original Art for Thuvia, Maid of Mars
  AKA - *"With a savage cry of triumph, Thar Ban vaulted to the back of his throat, Thuvia of Ptarth still in his arms."*

6821 Original Art for "Came the Dawn"
6822 Original Art for "Came the Dawn"
6823 Original Art Prints **Nude**
6824 Original Painting, **Savage World**

- April 20, 2003
  16761 Original Preliminary Sketch for Midwood Paperback Series #1 of 2
- May 4, 2003
  17658 Original Preliminary Sketch for Midwood Paperback Series #2 of 2
- June 15, 2003
  16017 Original Sketch of Indian
  16018 Original Lion Sketch
  16019 Original Lion Sketches
  Pencil preliminaries for Canaveral Press illustrations
  16020 Original Preliminary Sketch for **Winter of the Coup**
- July 6, 2003
  17801 Original Gesture Drawings
  17802 Original Sketches of Male Figures
- July 17, 2003
  9325 Original Illustration, "Girl and Lion"
  9326 Original Illustration for "The Hunter Out of Time"
  9328 Original Sketch of a Nude Woman
  9329 Original Preliminary Painting, **Battlestar Galactica**
  9330 Original Illustration
  9331 Original Preliminary Painting, **Thor's Flight**
  9333 Original Illustration
  9721 Original Art for Weird Science Fantasy #20, Complete 7-page Story, *I, Rocket*
- July 20, 2003
  16711 Original Sketch
  16713 Original Preliminary Art for **The Indomitable**
  16715 Original Preliminary Sketch for **Bloodstone**
  16716 Original Preliminary Sketches for Canaveral Press illos.
  16717 Original Sketches
  16719 Original Sketch Art
  16720 Original Sketch Art (preliminaries for Midwood illos)
- August 3, 2003
  17588 Original Illustration, Bear-Back Rider
  17589 Original Sketches, Horses and Riders
  17591 Original Sketches, Sorcerer
  17592 Original Sketch, Nude Woman
  17593 Original Sketches, Nudes and Caveman
  17594 Original Sketches, Three Nude Women
  17595 Original Sketches, Figures in Motion
- August 13, 2003
  1424 Original Sketches, Nude Woman
  1425 Original Sketches, Beauties and Beasts
  1426 Original Sketches, Nudes in Motion
  1427 Original Sketches, Doodle Book Title Page
  1428 Original Sketches, Tarzan and Dinosaurs
  1430 Original Sketch, Caveman
  1433 Original Illustration, Rescue
  1434 Original Preliminary Sketch, Frontier Conflict
- August 17, 2003
  15886 Original Illustration, African with Parasol
  15887 Original Sketches, Nudes
  15888 Original Sketches, Multiple Nudes
  15889 Original Sketches, Horses and Riders
  15891 Original Sketches, Bathroom Studies
  15892 Original Sketch, Study for Masai Warrior
- September 7, 2003
  18210 Original Preliminary Sketch, "Pellucidar"
  18212 Original Preliminary Sketch, "Mastodon"
  18214 Original Sketch, Caveman$207.00
  18216 Original Sketch, "Chasing the Girl"
  18218 Original Art, Pencil Studies

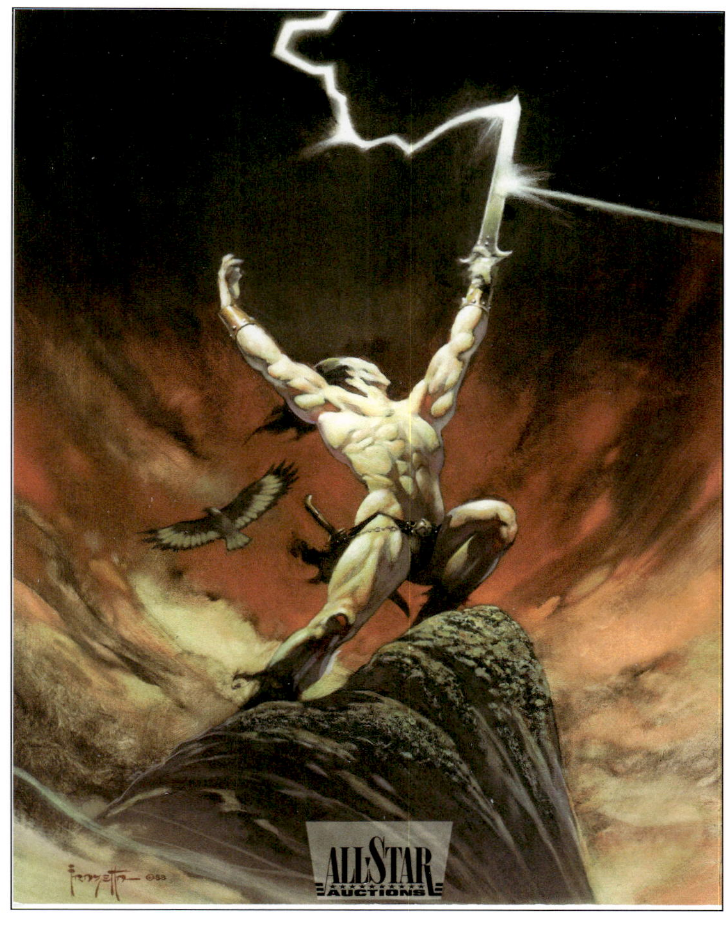

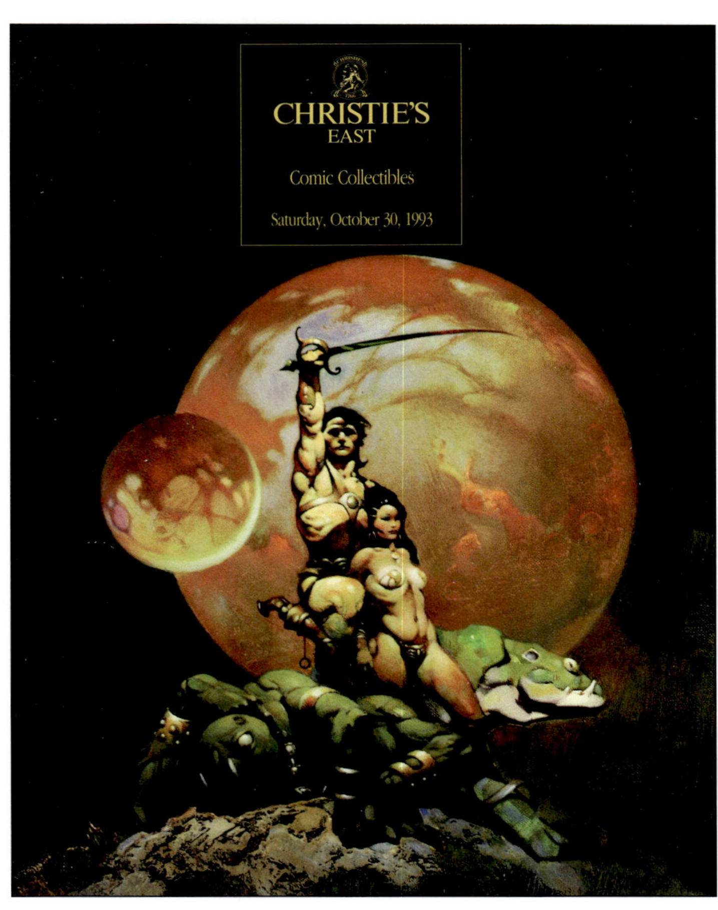

- September 21, 2003
  - 17195 Original Sketch, Zaftig Nude
  - 17196 Original Sketches, Three Nude Ladies
  - 17201 Original Illustration, Archer
  - 17202 Original Sketches, Two Lions
- October 5, 2003
  - 17894 Original Illustration, Fallen Gladiator
  - 17897 Original Illustration, Warrior
  - 17898 Original Illustration, Caveman Summit
  - 17899 Original Illustration, Two Women
  - 17900 Original Illustration, Cowboy/Nude/Dracula
  - 17901 Original Illustration, Lioness
  - 17902 Original Sketches, Caveman Chasing Nude
  - 17903 Original Sketches, Funny Faces
  - 17904 Original Sketch Art, Family Gathering
- October 19, 2003
  - 17284 Original Preliminary Art for Paradox
  - 17285 Original Sketch, "Cloak and Dagger"
  - 17286 Original Sketch, "Longing"
  - 17287 Original Sketch, "Caveboy and Cavegirl"
  - 17288 Original Sketch, "Masai Sketch"
  - 17289 Original Sketch, "Wrestlers"
  - 17290 Original Sketch, "Hair Pulling"
  - 17291 Original Sketch, "Kidnapped"
  - 17292 Original Sketch, "Conflict"
- November 2, 2003
  - 17663 Original Sketches of Thighs and Lions
  - 17664 Original Sketch of Woman
  - 17666 Original Sketch of Males Fighting
- November 16, 2003
  - 17238 Original Pencil Prelim, "Masai Warrior"
  - 17240 Original Sketch, Two Cavewomen
  - 17241 Original Sketch, Two Torsos
  - 17242 Original Sketch, Head and Body
  - 17243 Original Sketch, Reclining Figure
  - 17244 Original Sketch, Pursuit
- November 20, 2003
  - 4944 Original Art for L'il Abner Daily dated 6-17-57
  - 5209 Original Sketch, Woman Escaping
  - 5210 Original Art Color Prelim for Verotika #3
  - 5211 Original Sketch of Female Figures
  - 5212 Original Art Sketch, Cavemen
  - 5214 Original Art Illustration, Zoot Suit & Dame
  - 5215 Original Art Sketch of a Gorilla
  - 5216 Original Art for Durango Kid #13
  - 5217 Original Art for Durango Kid #14
  - 5218 Original Art of Nude Woman with Sword
  - 5219 Original Illustration, Sabretooth Tiger
  - 5220 Original Art Sketch "Shootist"
  - 5222 Original Art Sketch "Two Men"
  - 5223 Original Sketch "Death Dealer"
  - 5224 Original Art Sketch "Femme Fatale"
  - 5225 Original Art Sketch "Men & Lizards"
  - 5226 Original Illustration, Awakening
  - 5227 Original Illustration, "Attack"
  - 5228 Original Preliminary Painting for "The Flesh Eaters"
  - 5229 Unfinished Original Painting for Little Annie Fanny
- December 7, 2003
  - 17869 Original Sketch, "Man Carrying Sack"
  - 17870 Original Sketches, "Whimsical Fantasy Figures and Dinosaurs"
  - 17872 Original Sketches, "African Sketches"
  - 17873 Original Sketches, "Humorous Caveman"
- December 21, 2003
  - 16769 Original Sketches, Western Gunfighters
  - 16770 Original Sketches, Fighting Savages and Cloaked Figure
  - 16771 Original Sketches, Well-Dressed Gunman
  - 16772 Original Sketches, Cheerful Nude Girl
  - 16799 Original Art Sketch, Cave Men and Women
- January 18, 2004
  - 17891 Original Art Sketch, "Little Dinosaur"
  - 17892 Original Art Sketches, "Horses"
  - 17893 Original Art Sketch "Boots"
  - 17894 Original Art Sketches "Nude and Profile"
- February 1, 2004
  - 16556 Original Cute Nude Sketch
  - 16557 Original Man with Guitar Sketches
  - 16559 Original Sketch of Comical Caveman
  - 16560 Original Squatting Figure Sketches
  - 16561 Original Sketches of Males in Motion
  - 16562 Original Viking Sketch
- February 8, 2004
  - 4265 Original Sketch, "Death Dealer"
  - 4266 Original Preliminary Sketch for Death Dealer #3
  - 4269 Original Illustration, Riders on Horseback
  - 4271 Original Sketch of Two Cavemen and a Dinosaur
  - 4272 Original Sketch, "Lion Hunt"
  - 4273 Original Sketch, "Dark Woman"
  - 4274 Original Sketches of Nude Studies
  - 4275 Original Sketches of Fighting Figures
  - 4276 Original Sketches of Female Nudes
  - 4278 Original Sketch of The Defiant One
  - 4279 Original Sketches of Four Men and a Horse
  - 4282 Original Color Preliminary Sketch "Masai Warrior"
- February 15, 2004
  - 17513 Original Art Sketch Portrait of a Centurion
  - 17514 Original Art Sketches "Seated Nude"
  - 17515 Original Art Sketch of 4 Zaftig Women
  - 17516 Original Art Sketch of Female Torso
  - 17518 Original Art Sketch Page, 7 Figures and Head Study
  - 17520 Original Art Sketch of Two Cavemen
  - 17521 Original Nude Man with Big Pig Art Sketch
- March 7, 2004
  - 16836 Original Art Sketch, Standing Girl Nude in Profile
  - 16837 Original Art Sketch, Female Nude Study
  - 16838 Original Art Sketch, Tarzan Pencil Study
  - 16839 Original Art Sketch, Victory Dance, 2 Cavemen
  - 16840 Original Art Sketch, Whimsical Standing Caveman
  - 16841 Original Art Sketch, 3 Humorous Cavemen Figures
  - 16842 Original Art Sketch Page, Cavemen, Horse and Warriors
- March 21, 2004
  - 17783 Original Sketch, "Cavemen and Cavewomen"
  - 17784 Original Sketch, "Warrior Woman"
  - 17785 Original Sketch, "Saber-Tooth Tiger"
  - 17786 Original Sketch, "Pouting Girl Studies"
  - 17787 Original Sketch, "Nomad"
  - 17788 Original Art Sketch, "Brawl"
  - 17789 Original Sketch, "Punching Man"
- April 4, 2004
  - 1040 Original Comic Strip Art for Johnny Comet Daily dated 2-7-52
  - 1041 Original Comic Strip Art for Johnny Comet Sunday dated 12-7-52
  - 1276 Original Sketches of Cavemen, Female Nudes, and a Horse
  - 1277 Original Color Prelim for Conan the Usurper
  - 1278 20 Page Sketchbook of Original Art
  - 1280 Original Color Prelim for "Pony Tail"
  - 1281 Original Illustration, The Mad King
  - 16709 Original Sketch of Standing Small Nude
  - 16710 Original Sketch of a Mounted Hunter
  - 16712 Original Sketch of a Gunfight
  - 16713 Original Sketch of Standing Comical Caveman
  - 16714 Original Sketch Studies of a Figure's Head and Arm
  - 16715 Original Sketch of a Tree

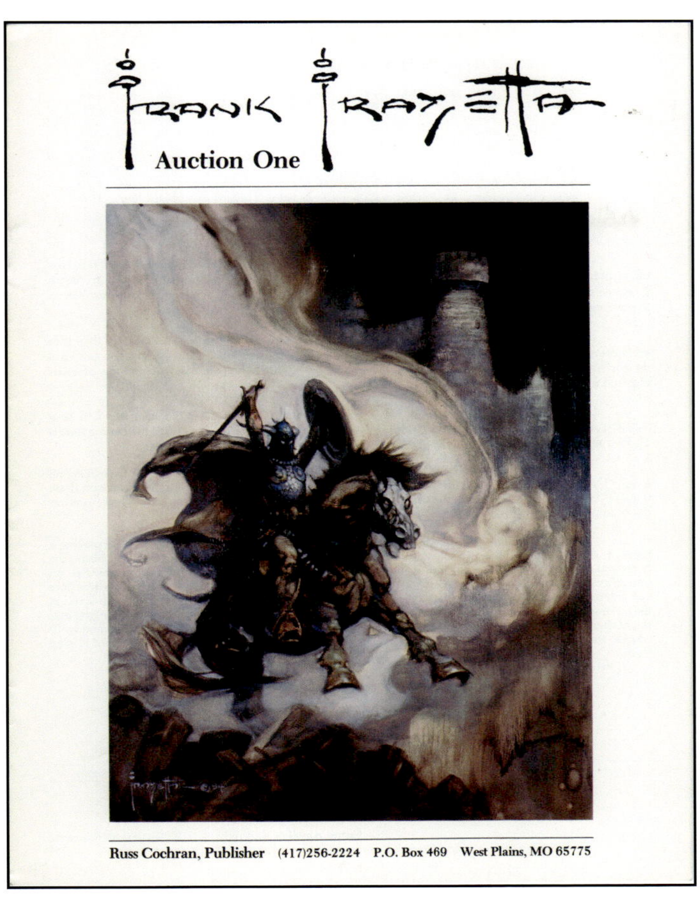
Frank Frazetta
Auction One
Russ Cochran, Publisher (417)256-2224 P.O. Box 469 West Plains, MO 65775

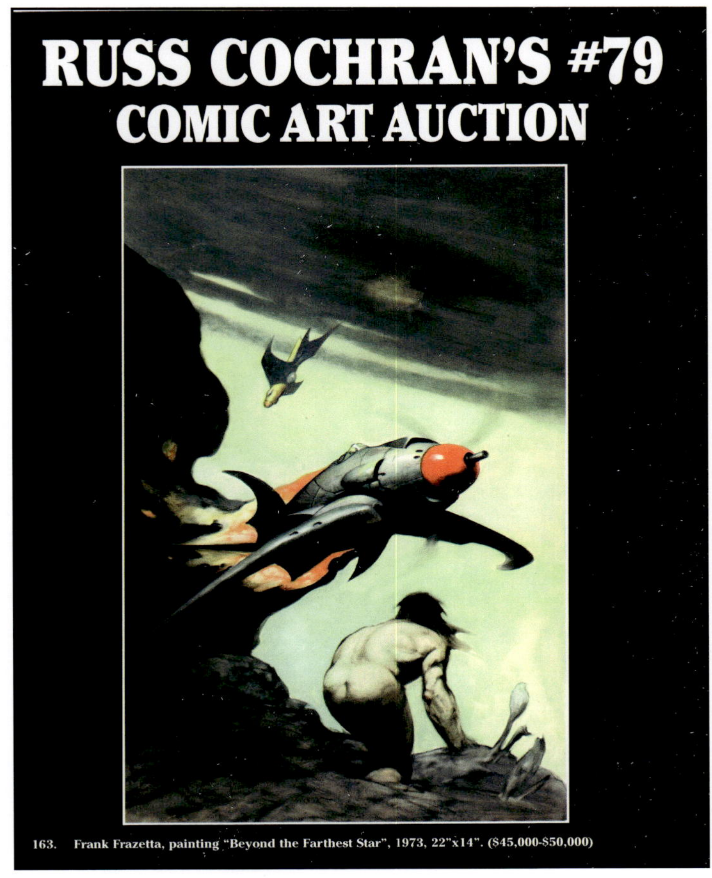
RUSS COCHRAN'S #79
COMIC ART AUCTION
163. Frank Frazetta, painting "Beyond the Farthest Star", 1973, 22"x14". ($45,000-$50,000)

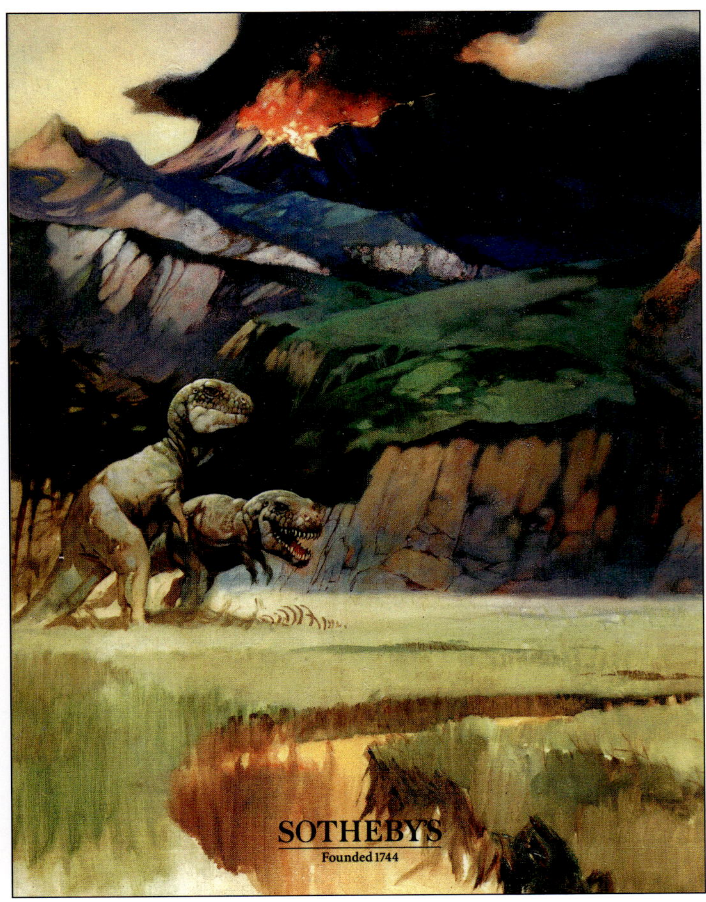
SOTHEBYS
Founded 1744

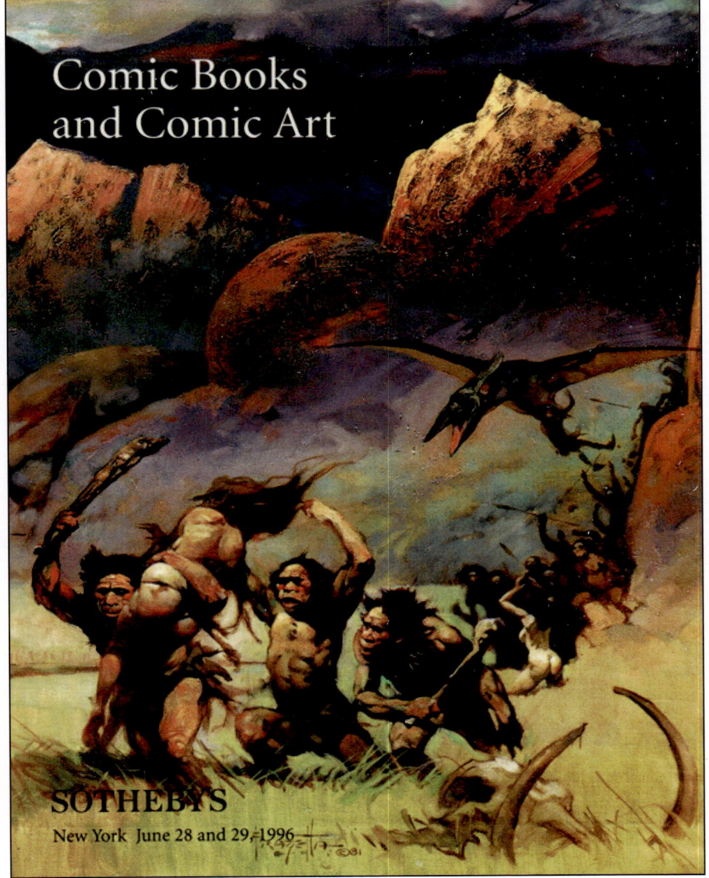
Comic Books
and Comic Art
SOTHEBYS
New York June 28 and 29, 1996

- April 18, 2004
  - 17816 Four Female Figures Sketch Original Art
  - 17817 Cute Cave Couple Sketch Original Art
  - 17818 Ape Dance Sketch Original Art
  - 17819 Nude Male Figures Sketches Original Art
  - 17820 Sketchbook Covers with Couches Original Art Drawings
- May 2, 2004
  - 16648 "Mongol Head" Sketch Original Art
  - 16649 "Flash" Sketch Original Art
  - 16650 "Cliffhanger" Sketch Original Art
  - 16651 Two Quick Female Nude Studies Original Sketch
  - 16652 "Devil and Dinosaur" Original Sketches
  - 16653 Three Cave Goofs Original Sketch
- May 16, 2004
  - 18009 Nude Male and Female Figures Sketch Original Art
  - 18010 "Flash Gordon Studies" Original Art
  - 18012 Nude Female Torso Sketch Original Art
  - 18013 Four Whimsical Cavemen Sketches Original Art
  - 18015 T-Rex and Caveman Sketch Original Art
- June 6, 2004
  - 16771 Caveman Profile Sketch Original Art
  - 16772 Cute Caveman Sketch Original Art
  - 16773 Female Figure Back Study Sketch Original Art
  - 16774 Three Detailed Nude Figure Studies Sketch Original Art
  - 16775 Car, Gangster, Nudes, and American Indian Studies Sketch Original Art
  - 16776 Man with Knife Sketch Original Art
- June 13, 2004
  - 5018 Li'l Abner's Women Magazine Illustration Original Art
  - 8203 Woman With a Scythe Study Sketch Original Art
  - 8204 "Awakening" Illustration Original Art
  - 8207 Little Annie Fanny Unfinished Painting Original Art
- June 20, 2004
  - 18287 Galloping Horse Sketch Original Art
  - 18288 Flash Gordon Study Sketch Original Art
  - 18289 Fallen Gladiator Sketch Original Art
  - 18290 Demon Preliminary Sketch Original Art
  - 18291 "Gaucho" Sketch Original Art
  - 18292 Trio of Figures Sketch Original Art
  - 18293 African Figure Studies Sketch Original Art
  - 18294 Gesture Drawings Sketch Original Art
  - 18295 Minsky's Study Sketch Original Art
- July 4, 2004
  - 17273 Tarzan Head Sketch Original Art
  - 17274 Champion Sketch Original Art
  - 17275 Cute Caveman Clan Sketch Original Art
  - 17276 Two Horse Studies Sketch Original Art
  - 17277 Demon Sketch Original Art
  - 17278 Standing Female Nude Sketch Original Art
  - 17279 Seated Female Nude Sketch Original Art
  - 17280 Standing Nude Couple Sketch Original Art
  - 17281 Standing Male Nude Sketch Original Art
  - 17282 Two Male Nudes Sketch Original Art
- July 18, 2004
  - 18231 3 Female Nudes Sketch Original Art
  - 18232 Female Nude Pencil Sketch Original Art
  - 18233 Witch Study Sketch Original Art
  - 18234 Three Figure Studies Sketch Original Art
  - 18235 Fantastic 8 Figures Sketch Original Art
  - 18236 Heads and Figure Sketch Original Art
  - 18237 Arabian Fight Sketch Original Art
  - 18238 Cute Cave Couple Sketch Original Art
  - 18239 Crawling Caveman Sketch Original Art
  - 18240 Man's Torso Sketch Original Art
- July 29, 2004
  - 3753 Kubla Khan Preliminary Sketch
  - 3754 Back endpaper illustration for Tarzan at the Earth's Core
    AKA - Monkey in a tree holding club (2 pp)
    First printed in TARZAN AT THE EARTH'S CORE
  - 3755 Tarzan Illustration Original Art
    AKA - *"The silent creature drove a long knife again and again into his tawny side."*
    First printed in TARZAN AND THE CASTAWAYS (promotional brochure)
  - 3756 Tarzan and Bolgani Illustration Original Art
  - 3757 Color Preliminaries for **Reign of Wizardry)**
  - 3758 Popcorn Man Sketch Original Art

ILLUSTRATION HOUSE

- September 19, 1992 **Frogs on the Moon**
- May 9, 1998 watercolor
  first printed in FRAZETTA fanzine
- November 7, 1998 Ace frontispiece
  "Came the Dawn" 1 panel

LOWERY, HOWARD

- February 26-27 1994 COVER pencil sketch of female

PHILIP WEISS AUCTIONS

- December 12, 1998 **The Defender**

SOTHEBY'S AUCTION

- 6261 December 18, 1991
  Vampirella (repainted nude)
  two WHITE INDIAN Stories
  ink sketch
- 6338 September 30, 1992
  Eternal Champion
  Green Jade and Soft Ivory
  Beyond the Farthest Star
  The Night They Raided Minsky's
  two WHITE INDIAN stories
- 6446 June 26,1993
  Cowboy Sunset
  Battlestar Galactica
  The Busy Body
  complete sketchbook
  two WHITE INDIAN stories
- 6588 June 18, 1994
  The Godmakers
  six rough sketches
- 6727 June 17, 1995
  various pen and ink illustrations
- 6872 June 28-29, 1996
  Young World
  three LI'L ABNER watercolors
  Ghoul Queen
  Tarzan illustration
  various sketches
- 7018 June 13, 1997
  JOHNNY COMET Sunday strip
- 7145 June 5, 1998
  watercolor study for **Against the Gods**
- 7330 June 28, 1999
  watercolor study for **Jungle Tales of Tarzan**
  Silver Warrior rough

• TRH GALLERY AUCTION

1980's Includes several Frazetta items plus others

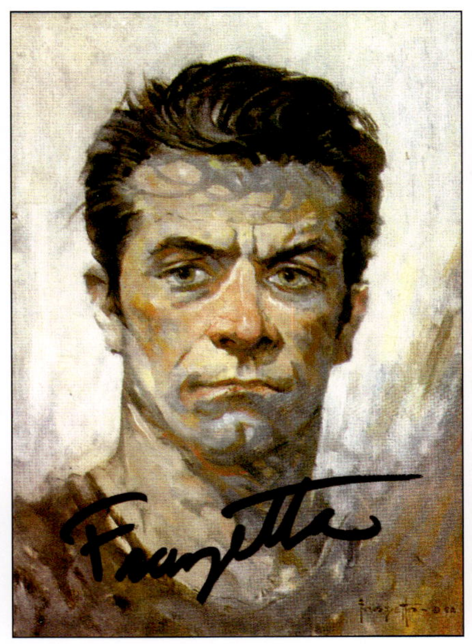

CONGRATULATIONS!
You've found
a rare
Best of Frazetta
Autographed
card!
This certifies that
this card bears
the authentic
signature of
Frank Frazetta,
and that no
reproductive
means were used

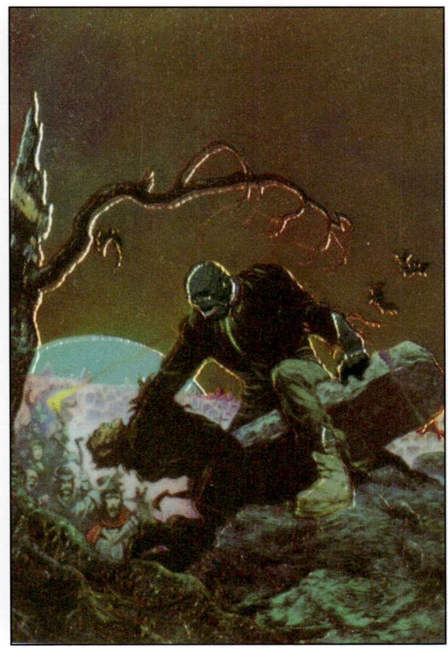

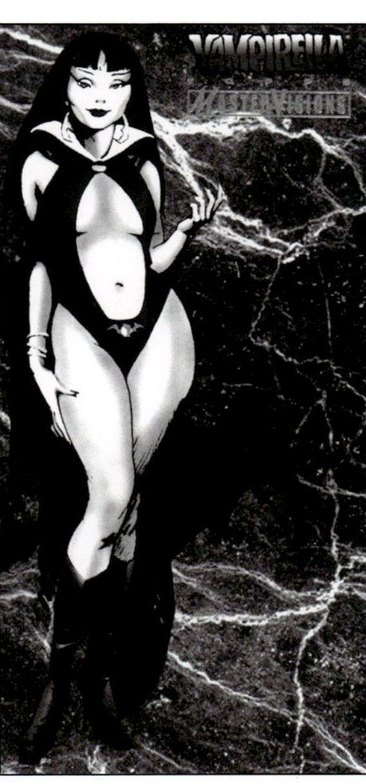

BATTLESTAR GALACTICA
1996
Dart Flipcards Inc.
- 6 **Warriors of the Galactica**
  AKA - **Space 103 - Attack**

COMIC IMAGES ARTIST CHOICE COLLECTOR CARDS
1997
Comic Images
- 1 **Las Vegas**
- 2 **Iron Thorn**
- 3 **Tree of Death**
- 4 **Death Dealer**

COMIC IMAGES SUPREME COLLECTOR CARDS (chromium)
1996
Comic Images
- F-1 King of the Jungle
- F-2 Bareback
- F-3 Ship Ahoy
- F-4 Two Nudes
- F-5 Dracula
- F-6 Queen of the Jungle
- F-7 Boy With Frog
- F-8 Delicate Negotiation
- F-9 Classic
- F-10 Self Portrait (checklist)

GOLDEN AGE OF COMICS, THE (chromium)
1995
Topps
- 86 cover to BUSTER CRABBE COMICS #5
- 89 cover to FAMOUS FUNNIES #214 (comic book)

JOE JUSKO'S EDGAR RICE BURROUGHS COLLECTION
1994
FPG
All Frazetta art is on back of cards.
- 3 **Tarzan and the Lion Men**
- 4 **Savage Pellucidar**
- 8 **Tarzan and the Lost Empire**
- 10 **The Lost Continent**
- 21 **Tarzan at the Earth's Core**
- 25 **Land of Terror**
- 31 **Tarzan and the Jewels of Opar**
- 35 **The Son of Tarzan**
- 36 **Tarzan and the City of Gold**
- 39 **Tarzan the Invincible**
- 48 **Jungle Tales of Tarzan**
- 54 **Beyond the Farthest Star**
- 95 **The Lost Continent**
- 97 **The Monster Men**
- 109 **Lost on Venus**

- KEEPSAKES (oversized, 6"x9")

1996
Comic Images
six card set limited to 2500
The images used are like those shown in THE PILLOW BOOK

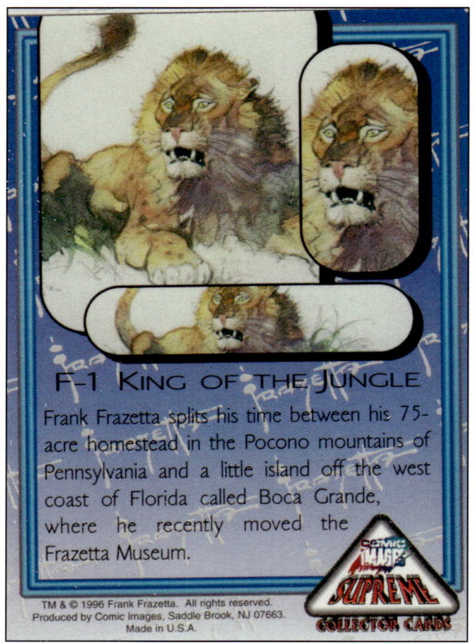

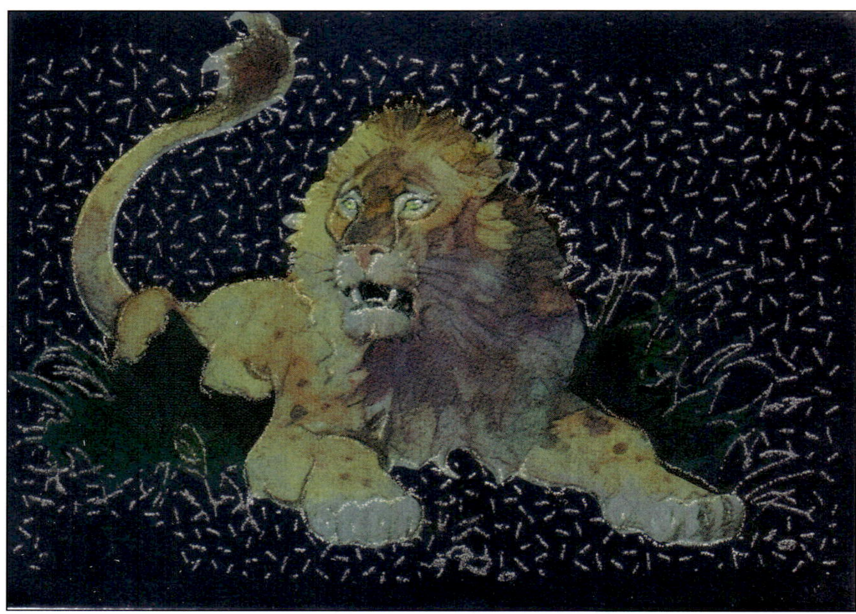

LIMITED EDITION FRAZETTA HOLOGRAMS
1993
21st Century Archives Inc.
comes with numbered certificate of authenticity
each set contains:
Dreamflight
The Countess
Dawn Attack
- silver edition limited to 50,000 sets
- gold edition limited to 3,000 sets

MADMAN x 50 BUBBLEGUM CARDS SET 2 available only as a set
1996
Dark Horse Comics
- card #50
  first printed in MADMAN COMICS #11 (comic book)

MORE THAN BATTLEFIELD EARTH
1995
Comic Images
Contains Frazetta artwork in the basic card set plus 6 sub-set cards.
six chromium card sub-set
- C1 **Man, The Endangered Species**
- C2 **The Countess**
- C3 **Leaping lizards**
- C4 **Encounter**
- C5 **The Lieutenant**
- C6 **Dawn Attack**

NATIONAL LAMPOON
1993
NL Communications / 21st Century Archives
- SC4 prototype card - **Alien Crucifixion**
- #6 **Desperation**

PHANTOM, THE
1996
Intrepid
- chase card created exclusively for this card set.

- REDEMPTION Collectible Card Game
1995
This bible based card game contains artwork from some of the best names in the business.

STARQUEST Collectible Card Game
1995
Comic Images
- 2 **Atlantis**
- 11 **Wolf Moon**
- 27 **Fantasy World**
- 157 Spaceman
  first printed in Doubleday Science Fiction Book Club promo pamphlet

VAMPIRELLA
1995
Topps
- 3 **Vampirella**
  first printed in VAMPIRELLA #1 (comic book)
  card back shows preliminary sketch

- VAMPIRELLA: MASTER VISIONS
1996
Topps
No number single card image.
Oversized cards available only as a set

FRAZETTA 1
1991
Comic Images

•complete set
•1 A Princess of Mars
•2 Self Portrait
•3 Stranded
•4 Count Dracula
•5 Autumn People
•6 Land of Terror
•7 Reassembled Man
•8 Jongar Fights Back
•9 Pony Tail
•10 King Kong and Snake
•11 Golden Girl
•12 Dracula Meets Wolfman
•13 Iron Thorn
•14 Man-Ape
•15 Swamp Demon
•16 Snow Giants
•17 Berserker
•18 The Apparition
•19 The Brain
•20 Green Death
•21 Neanderthal
•22 Sea Monster
•23 Wolf Pack
•24 Spiderman
•25 Caveman
•26 Sun Goddess
•27 Egyptian Queen
•28 Outlaw of Torn
•29 Tyrannosaurus Rex
•30 Woman with a Scythe
•31 Girl Bathing
•32 The Mad King
•33 Gulliver of Mars
•34 Combat
•35 Black Panther
•36 The Sorcerer
•37 Bran Mak Morn
•38 Atlantis
•39 Tree of Death
•40 Eternal Champion
•41 John Carter and the Savage Apes of Mars
•42 Downward to Earth
•43 Flying Reptiles
•44 The Destroyer
•45 Thuvia, Maid of Mars
•46 Tanar of Pellucidar
•47 Ghoul Queen
•48 The Mammoth
•49 Birdman
•50 Silver Warrior
•51 Swords of Mars
•52 Bucking Bronco
•53 Death Dealer
•54 Chained
•55 The Bear
•56 Dark Kingdom
•57 At The Earth's Core
•58 Sea Witch
•59 Against the Gods
•60 The Return of the Mucker
•61 Paradox
•62 Madame Derringer
•63 Fire Demon
•64 Bloodstone
•65 The Huntress
•66 Flesh Eaters
•67 Young World
•68 Flying Alligator
•69 Indomitable
•70 The Galleon
•71 Gollum
•72 Serpent
•73 Wolf Moon
•74 Carson of Venus
•75 Black Star
•76 Escape on Venus
•77 The Norseman
•78 Monster out of Time
•79 The Moon Maid
•80 The Barbarian
•81 Savage Pellucidar
•82 Mothman
•83 The Cave Demon
•84 Withering
•85 Sound
•86 Seven Romans
•87 Captive Princess
•88 A Fighting Man of Mars
•89 Aros
•90 CHECKLIST

FRAZETTA 2
1993
Comic Images

• complete set without chase cards
•1 Tarzan and the Golden Lion
•2 Tarzan Kills Lion
•3 Tarzan confronts an Enemy
•4 Tarzan Against the Giant Alligator
•5 Tarzan and the Ant-Men
•6 Tarzan and the Jewels of Opar
•7 Tarzan and the Cave Bear
•8 The Lost Empire
•9 Jungle Tales of Tarzan
•10 Land of Terror
•11 Tarzan and the City of Gold
•12 Tarzan the Invincible
•13 Tarzan and the Lion Men
•14 The Son of Tarzan
•15 Woman with Spear
•16 Wolfman
•17 Luana
•18 Beyond the Farthest Star
•19 Beasts of Venus
•20 Nightstalker
•21 Rogue Roman
•22 Kane on the Golden Sea
•23 Night Winds
•24 King Kong
•25 Captured
•26 The Night They Raided Minsky's
•27 The Fastest Guitar in the West
•28 Girl with Sword
•29 Indian with Long-Rifle
•30 Nude with Dagger Raised
•31 Bear Watching Caveman Threaten Cub
•32 Girl Observed by Undressed Man with Hat
•33 Indian with Bow (The Archer)
•34 Mongol Tyrant
•35 Roman Chariot
•36 Torture Garden
•37 Winged Terror
•38 Nude in Pond (Silent Breeze)
•39 Scramble
•40 The Tempters
•41 New World
•42 Eve
•43 Orca, Killer Whale
•44 The Return of Jongar
•45 Thor's Flight
•46 Sacrifice
•47 African Warrior
•48 The Secret People
•49 Circle of Terror
•50 God From the Sky
•51 Huns
•52 Fantasy World
•53 Frankenstein and Dracula
•54 Two of a Kind
•55 Green Death
•56 Caveman Fight
•57 T-Rex
•58 Castle of Sin
•59 The Gangs all Here
•60 Nude
•61 Windblown
•62 Conan
•63 Alien Worlds
•64 Deina
•65 Swamp Demon
•66 Darkness at Time's Edge
•67 Girl on the River
•68 The African Elephant
•69 Pharaoh's Tomb
•70 Family Portrait
•71 Luana
•72 Mastodon
•73 Kavin's World
•74 Attack
•75 Death Dealer II
•76 Death Dealer III
•77 Death Dealer IV
•78 The Defender
•79 The Indian Brave
•80 The Amali Legend
•81 Red Moon, Black Mountain
•82 Lost Continent
•83 Fire & Ice
•84 Wildride
•85 Handicap
•86 Better View
•87 Great Form
•88 Princess and the Swamp Thing
•89 The Giantess
•90 CHECKLIST
• promo card

Prism 3 card sub-set
•S1 Warrior with Ball and Chain
•S2 Flashman on the Charge
•S3 The Return of the Mucker

Chromium 3 card sub-set
•C1 Las Vegas
•C2 Devil Rider
•C3 Beyond the Grave

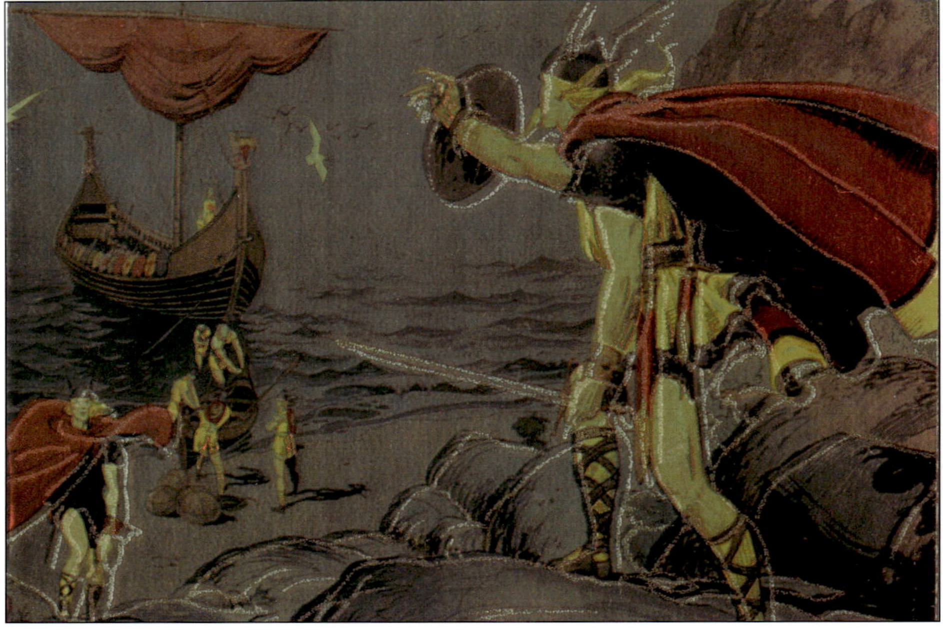

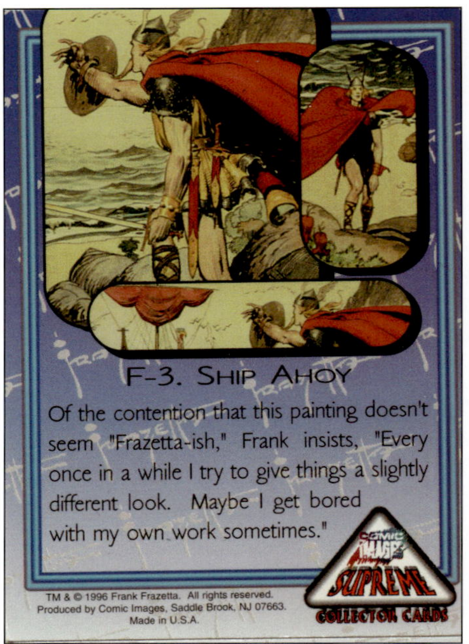

BEST OF FRAZETTA, ALL CHROMIUM COLLECTOR CARDS

1996

Comic Images

- •complete set without chase cards
- •0 Destroyer (bonus card)
- •1 Catwalk (The Moon's Rapture)
- •2 The Moon Maid
- •3 Monster Out of Time
- •4 Escape on Venus
- •5 Atlantis
- •6 Gollum
- •7 The Apparition
- •8 Fire Demo
- •9 Bloodstone
- •10 Pillow Book
- •11 Eternal Champion
- •12 The Galleon
- •13 Snow Giants
- •14 Man-Ape
- •15 Dracula Meets Wolfman
- •16 Dark Kingdom
- •17 Spiderman
- •18 Berserker
- •19 Tree of Death
- •20 Alien Crucifixion
- •21 Carson of Venus
- •22 Young World
- •23 Black Panther
- •24 Golden Girl
- •25 The Huntress
- •26 The Brain
- •27 Silver Warrior
- •28 At the Earth's Core
- •29 Outlaw of Torn - 95
- •30 Cat Girl
- •31 The Barbarian
- •32 Flying Reptiles
- •33 Princess of Mars
- •34 The Sorcerer
- •35 Black Star
- •36 Sea Witch
- •37 Jongar Fights Back
- •38 Bran Mak Morn
- •39 Sun Goddess
- •40 Massai Warriors
- •41 John Carter and the Savage Apes of Mars
- •42 Madame Derringer
- •43 Tanar of Pellucidar
- •44 Wolf Moon - 5
- •45 Swords of Mars
- •46 Egyptian Queen - 21
- •47 Tyrannosaurus Rex
- •48 Against the Gods
- •49 Reassembled Man
- •50 Tales from the Crypt
- •51 Swamp Demon
- •52 Wolf Pack
- •53 Thuvia, Maid of Mars
- •54 Chained
- •55 Autumn People
- •56 The Norseman
- •57 Land of Terror
- •58 Serpent
- •59 The Mammoth
- •60 Straight Arrow
- •61 Neanderthal
- •62 Count Dracula
- •63 King Kong and Snake
- •64 Huns
- •65 The Secret People
- •66 Kane on the Golden Sea
- •67 Green Death
- •68 Mongol Tyrant
- •69 A Fighting Man of Mars
- •70 Wonder Years
- •71 Wolfman
- •72 Sacrifice
- •73 The Challenge
- •74 King Kong
- •75 Death Dealer
- •76 Death Dealer II
- •77 Death Dealer III
- •78 Death Dealer IV
- •79 Beasts of Venus
- •80 Survivor
- •81 Pharaoh's Tomb
- •82 Scramble
- •83 Withering
- •84 Seven Romans
- •85 Sound
- •86 Mothman
- •87 Savage Pellucidar
- •88 God From the Sky
- •89 Fire & Ice
- •90 CHECKLIST

•promo Tales From the Crypt

"Uncivilized" 6 card sub-set
- •M1 Tarzan Against the Giant Alligator
- •M2 Woman with Spear
- •M3 Captured
- •M4 Tarzan Kills the Lion
- •M5 Orcs
- •M6 Tarzan Confronts an Enemy

"Comic Covers" 3 card sub-set
- •S1 Free Fall
- •S2 Space Octopus
- •S3 Weird Science-Fantasy #29

•uncut 6 card press sheet NOT CHROMIUM contains:
Aros
Birdman
Flesh Eaters
The Bear
Indomitable
Paradox

•Autographed card
Self Portrait

•Binder cover Death Dealer
back cover The Moon's Rapture

THE FRANK
FRAZETTA
CALENDAR
1977

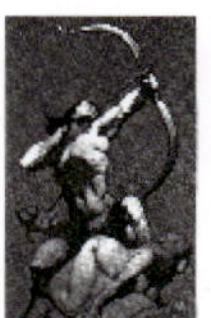

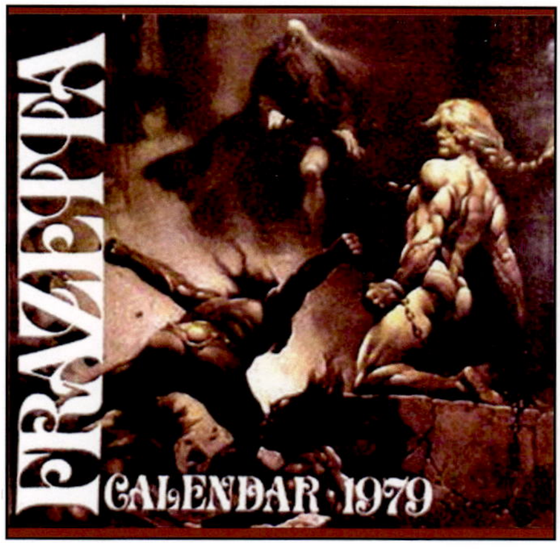

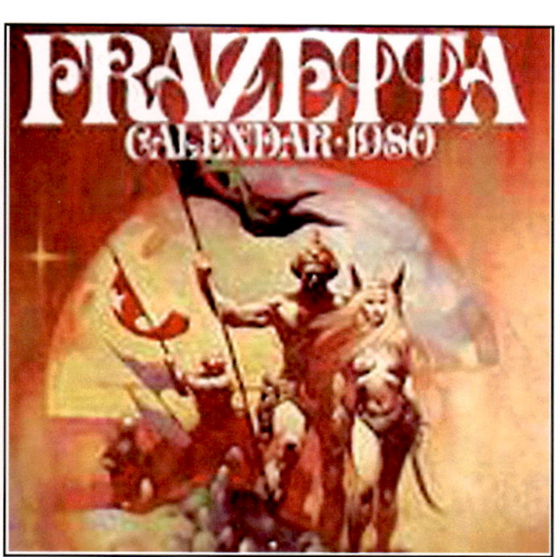

ARCOT A.G. Germany 18" x 23"
1991
Arcot A.G.
- Egyptian Princess on cover
- Death Dealer III on cover

- 1980 CBS ONE SHEET CALENDAR

CBS
One sheet image is **Dark Kingdom**

PEACOCK PRESS SERIES

- 1977 FRAZETTA CALENDAR

1977
Peacock Press
Packaged in box with Frazetta image

Jan. **Flying Reptiles**	Jul. **Paradox**
Feb. **Jongar Fights Back**	Aug. **Monster out of Time**
Mar. **Pony Tail**	Sep. **The Norseman**
Apr. **Tomorrow Midnight**	Oct. **Escape on Venus** (2nd version)
May **Land of Terror**	Nov. **A Princess of Mars**
Jun. **The Moon Maid** (2nd version)	Dec. **John Carter and the Savage Apes of Mars**
c-fold - **The Destroyer** (3rd version)	

- 1978 FRAZETTA CALENDAR

1978
Peacock Press
Packaged in box with Frazetta image

Jan. **Bloodstone**	Jul. **Rogue Roman**
Feb. **Aros**	Aug. **Tanar of Pellucidar**
Mar. **Serpent**	Sep. **Autumn People**
Apr. **Nightstalker**	Oct. **Dracula Meets the Wolfman**
May **Black Panther**	Nov. **Bran Mak Morn**
Jun. **Girl Bathing**	Dec. **Swords of Mars**
c-fold - **Fire Demon**	

- 1979 FRAZETTA CALENDAR

1979
Peacock Press
Packaged in box with Frazetta image

Jan. **Eternal Champion** (1st version)	Jul. **Black Star**
Feb. **Iron Thorn**	Aug. **Count Dracula**
Mar. **Tree of Death**	Sep. **Outlaw of Torn**
Apr. **Reassembled Man**	Oct. **Beyond the Grave**
May **Gollum**	Nov. **Winged Terror**
Jun. **Fantasy World**	Dec. **Mongol Tyrant**
c-fold - **Carson of Venus** (2nd version)	

- 1980 FRAZETTA CALENDAR

1980
Peacock Press
Packaged in box with Frazetta image

Jan. **The Gargoyle**	Jul. **Eve**
Feb. **The Tempters**	Aug. **The Return of Jongor**
Mar. **Circle of Terror**	Sep. **Alien Worlds**
Apr. **New World**	Oct. **Thor's Flight**
May **Battlestar Galactica - Attack**	Nov. **Tarzan and the Cave Bear**
Jun. **Battlestar Galactica - Scramble**	Dec. **Witherwing**
c-fold - **The Cave Demon**	

- 1982 FRAZETTA CALENDAR

1982
Peacock Press
Packaged in box with Frazetta image

Jan. **Young World**	Jul. **Red Moon / Black Mountain**
Feb. **Kavin's World**	Aug. **The Amali Legend**
Mar. **Arthur Rex**	Sep. **The African Elephant**
Apr. **The Defender**	Oct. **Girl on the River**
May **The Indian Brave**	Nov. **Captive Princess**
Jun. **Pharaoh's Tomb**	Dec . **Mastodon**
c-fold - **King Kong and Snake**	

LANDMARK CALENDAR SERIES

- 1995 FRAZETTA CALENDAR

1995
Landmark

Jan. **The Huntress**	Jul. **Moon Maid**
Feb. **Indomitable**	Aug. **Battlefield Earth**
Mar. **Witherwing**	Sep. **A Princess of Mars**
Apr. **Barbarian**	Oct. **Berserker**
May **Death Dealer IV**	Nov. **Warrior with Ball and Chain**
Jun. **Dark Kingdom**	Dec. **Chained**

- 1996 FRAZETTA CALENDAR

1996
Landmark

Jan. **Outlaw of Torn**	Jul. **Mothman**
Feb. **Las Vegas**	Aug. **The Apparition**
Mar. **Green Death**	Sep. **The Destroyer**
Apr. **Against the Gods**	Oct. **Jongar Fights Back**
May **Snow Giants**	Nov. **Black Star**
Jun. **Death Dealer**	Dec. **Tree of Death**

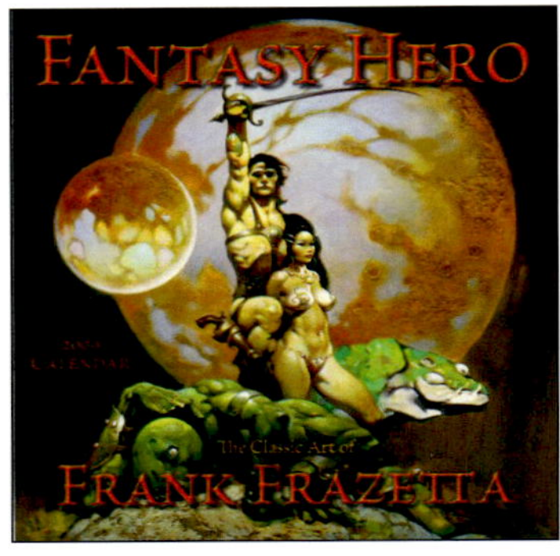

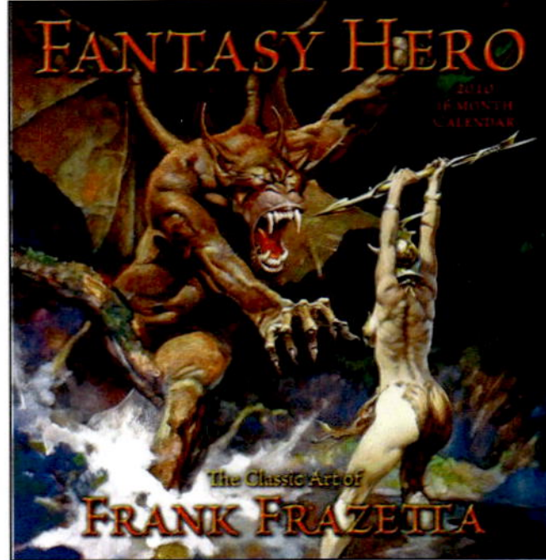

ABOVE: 2009 and 2010 Fantasy Hero calendars

- **1997 FRAZETTA CALENDAR**

1997
Landmark
Jan. **Silver Warrior**
Feb. **Seven romans**
Mar. **Swamp Demon**
Apr. **The Mad King**
May **Norseman**
Jun. **The Brain**
Jul. **Swords of Mars**
Aug. **The Cave Demon**
Sep. **Winged Terror**
Oct. **Night Winds**
Nov. **Eternal Champion** (1st version)
Dec. **Man-Ape**

- **1998 FRAZETTA CALENDAR**

1998
Landmark
Jan. **Huns**
Feb. **The Mammoth**
Mar. **Death Dealer II**
Apr. **John Carter and the Savage Apes of Mars**
May **Spiderman**
Jun. **Kane on the Golden Sea**
Jul. **Monster out of Time**
Aug. **Woman with a Scythe**
Sep. **Flesh Eaters**
Oct. **Bran Mak Morn**
Nov. **Death Dealer III**
Dec. **Tanar of Pellucidar**

- **1999 FRAZETTA CALENDAR**

1999
Landmark
Jan. **Carson of Venus** (2nd version)
Feb. **Pony Tail**
Mar. **New World**
Apr. **Mongol Tyrant**
May **The Return of Jongor**
Jun. **Warrior with Ball and Chain**
Jul. **Serpent**
Aug. **Sorcerer**
Sep. **Sound**
Oct. **Bloodstone**
Nov. **Birdman**
Dec. **Iron Thorn**

- **2004 FRAZETTA CALENDAR**

2004
Tide-Mark
Cover **Death Dealer**
Jan. **The Moon Maid**
Feb. **Warrior with Ball and Chain**
Mar. **Death Dealer**
Apr. **Escape on Venus**
May **Flesh Eaters**
Jun. **Black Panther**
Jul. **Swamp Demon**
Aug. **Jaguar God I**
Sep. **Dark Kingdom**
Oct. **Mongol Tyrant**
Nov. **Woman With Scythe**
Dec. **Night Winds**
Back Cover reproduces all 12 paintings within

- **2005 FRAZETTA CALENDAR**

2005
Tide-Mark
Cover **Death Dealer IV**
Jan. **Snow Giants**
Feb. **Indomitable**
Mar. **Death Dealer IV**
Apr. **Beauty and the Beast**
May **A Princess of Mars**
Jun. **Fire & Ice**
Jul. **Land of Terror**
Aug. **Sacrifice** (revised version)
Sep. **Huns**
Oct. **Death Dealer III**
Nov. **The Destroyer** (revised)
Dec. **Silver Warrior**
Back Cover reproduces all 12 paintings within

- **2006 FRAZETTA CALENDAR**

2006
Welcome Books
Cover **Egyptian Queen**
Jan. **Against the Gods**
Feb. **A Fighting Man of Mars**
Mar. **Chained**
Apr. **Atlantis**
May **Jaguar God II**
Jun. **Sound**
Jul. **Sun Goddess**
Aug. **Mammoth**
Sep. **Egyptian Queen**
Oct. **The Barbarian**
Nov. **Death Dealer V**
Dec. **Spider Man**
Centerfold **Moon's Rapture**
Back Cover reproduces all 12 paintings within

- **2009 FANTASY HERO classic art of Frank Frazetta**

2009
Sellers Publishing
Cover **Princess of Mars**
Jan. **Silver Warrior**
Feb. **Iron Thorn**
Mar. **Eternal Champion** (2nd)
Apr. **Tree of Death**
May **Gollum**
Jun. **Black Star**
Jul. **Winged Terror**
Aug. **The Mammoth**
Sep. **Seven Romans**
Oct. **Beyond the Grave**
Nov. **Atlantis**
Dec. **A Princess of Mars**
Back Cover reproduces all 12 paintings within

- **2010 FANTASY HERO classic art of Frank Frazetta**

2010
Sellers Publishing
Cover **Beauty and the Beast**
Jan. **Mothman**
Feb. **Cat Girl**
Mar. **Blazing Combat**
Apr. **Beauty and the Beast**
May **At the Earth's Core**
Jun. **Kane on the Golden Sea**
Jul. **Fire Demon**
Aug. **King Kong and Snake**
Sep. **Princess and the Panther**
Oct. **Night Stalker**
Nov. **Return of the Mucker**
Dec. **From Dusk Till Dawn**
Back Cover reproduces all 12 paintings within

OTHER CALENDAR APPEARANCES

- **EVERWAY CALENDAR**

1996
Wizards of the Coast
Beauty and the Beast

- **SCIENCE FICTION CALENDAR**

1984
Bridge Publications
Tear away calendar pages mounted on single backer. The image on the backer is **Battlefield Earth**

- **SCIENCE FICTION CALENDAR**

(paintings from the L. Ron Hubbard Gallery)
1994
Avalanche Publishing
Leaping Lizards
Dreamflight
Dawn Attack

- **SCIENCE FICTION CALENDAR**

(paintings from the L. Ron Hubbard Gallery)
1995
Avalanche Publishing
Encounter
Moon Rider
Countess

- **VAMPIRELLA CALENDAR**

1995
Harris Publications
Vampirella

- **WORLDS OF FANTASY CALENDAR**

1976
Sea Witch (1st version)

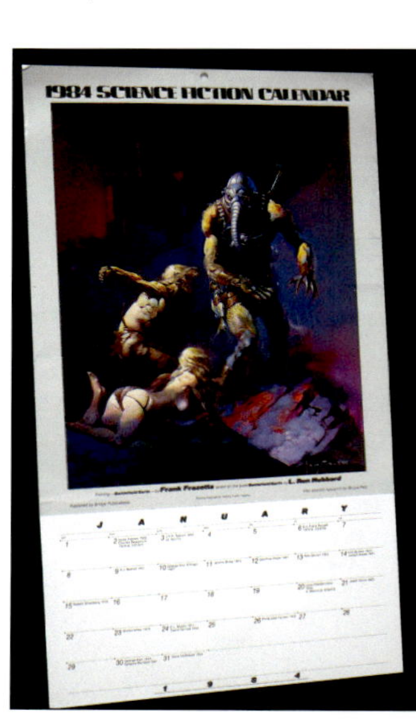

RIGHT: 1984 Science Fiction Calendar from Bridge Publications

INTERNATIONAL PUBLICATIONS

• DIE COMICWELT DES FRANK FRAZETTA
Abi Helzer's Productions, Germany
106 pp. reprints numerous comic stories and illustrations

• FRANK FRAZETTA: HEROIC FANTASY (softcover)
Nov. 1987
Editions Corentin, 80 pp.

• FRAZETTA: AMOUR INDOMITABLE, THUN'DA (hardcover)
1983
Xanadu: Les Humanoides Associes, Paris, 120 pp.

FRAZETTA FASCINATION
1984
Zoom
• 6 1984

cover **The Huntress**
title pg. untitled illustration
indicia untitled ink illustration
pg. 1 untitled ink illustration
pg. 3 Kubla Khan illustration
first printed in KUBLA KHAN PORTFOLIO (plate 4)
pg. 5 Women of the Ages illustration
first printed in WOMEN OF THE AGES PORTFOLIO (plate 3)
pg. 7 untitled ink illustration
AKA - *"Carthoris stepped between Thuvia and the banth, his sword ready to contest the beast's victory over them."*
first printed in THUVIA, MAID OF MARS/CHESSMEN OF MARS
pg. 9 **Las Vegas**
pg. 11 **Son of Tarzan**
pg. 13 **Reassembled Man**
pg. 14 **Golden Girl** (2 pp.)
pg. 17 **Tarzan the Invincible**
pg. 19 **Ghoul Queen**
pg. 21 **Beyond the Farthest Star**
pg. 22 untitled watercolor
pg. 23 **Land of Terror** (1st version)
pg. 24 **Monster out of Time**
pg. 26 **Carson of Venus** (2nd version)
pg. 27 **Thuvia, Maid of Mars** (2pp.)
pg. 31 **Land of Terror** (2nd version)
pg. 33 **Jongor Fights Back**
pg. 35 **The Silver Warrior**
pg. 36 **John Carter and the Savage Apes of Mars** (2pp.)
pg. 39 **Black Star**
pg. 41 **Tree of Death**
pg. 43 **Flesh Eaters**
pg. 45 **Iron Thorn**
pg. 47 **Gollum**
pg. 49 **Count Dracula**
pg. 51 **Beyond the Grave**
pg. 53 **Winged Terror**
pg. 54 **Combat**
pg. 56 **Flashman on the Charge** (2nd version)
pg. 58 **The Return of the Mucker**

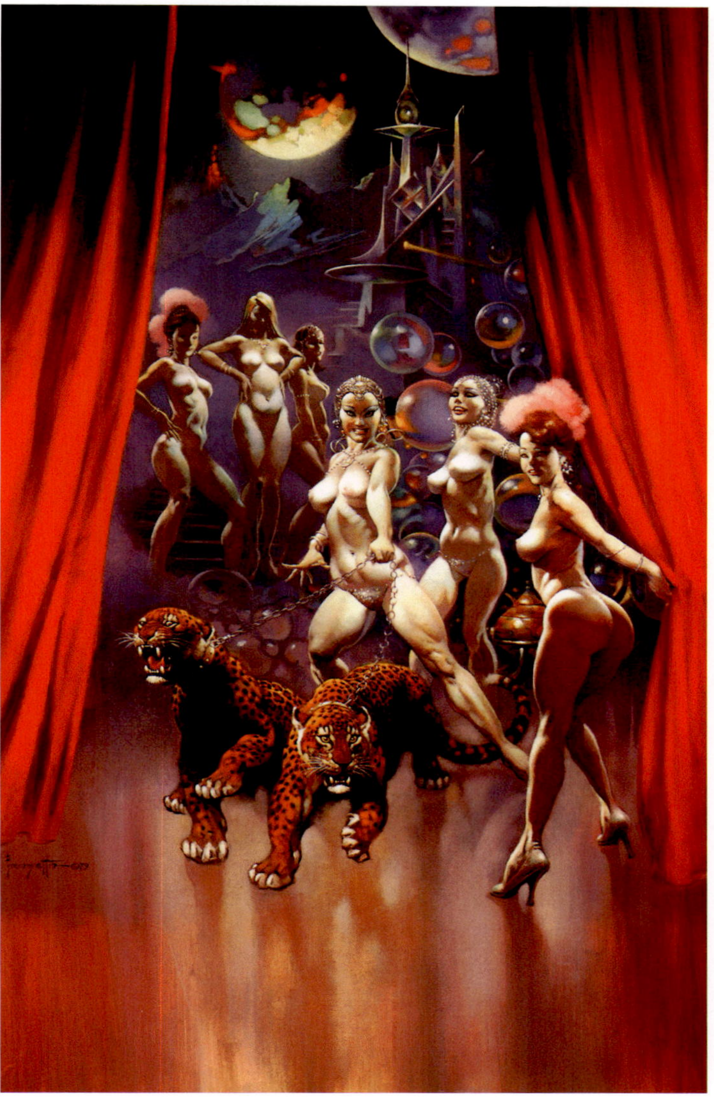

ABOVE: Las Vegas. *Originally commissioned by the Las Vegas Chamber of Commerce for a billboard, it was never used due to reservations about the sexuality. It was, however, eventually printed in* Frazetta Fascination, Legacy *and as a fine art print and trading card.*

pg. 60 **Eternal Champion**
pg. 62 **Kane on the Golden Sea**
pg. 64 **Seven Romans**
pg. 66 **Bran Mak Morn**
pg. 68 **Mongol Tyrant**
pg. 70 **Pony Tail**
pg. 72 **Nightwinds**
pg. 74 **Paradox**
pg. 76 FIRE & ICE movie poster (French edition titled "Tygra")
pg. 77 untitled ink illustration

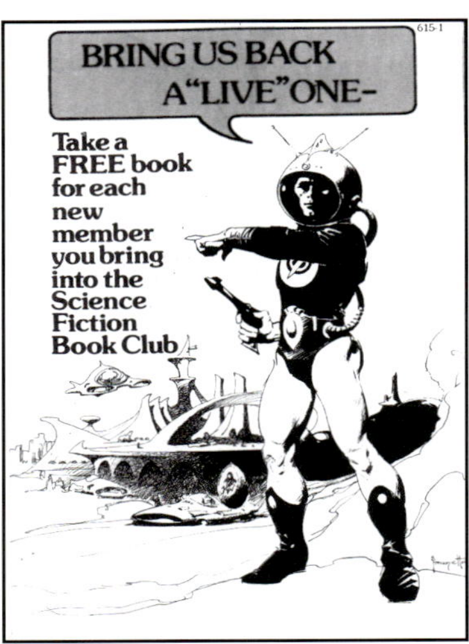

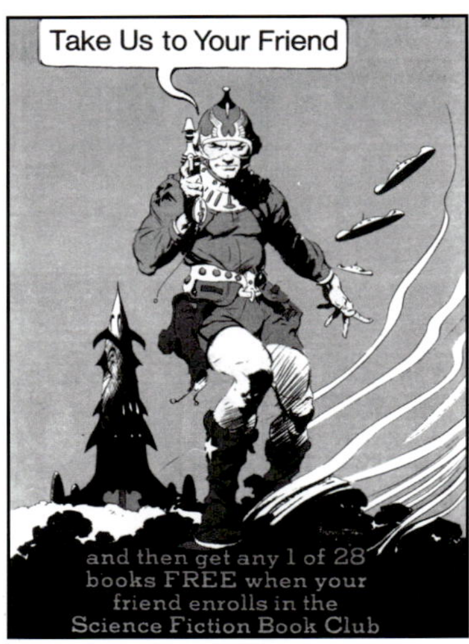

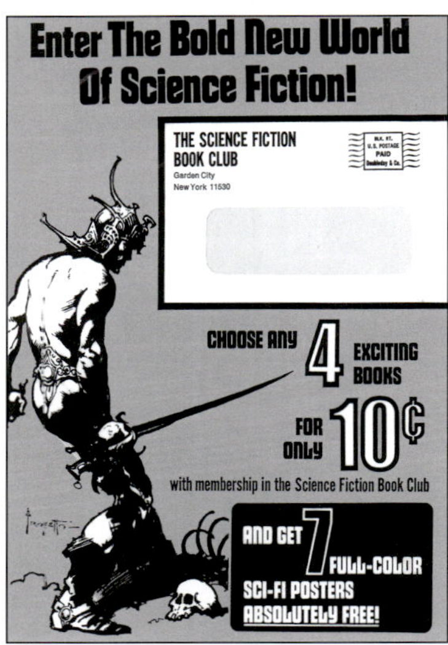

ABOVE: Promotional inserts and an envelope used by Doubleday Books for the Science Fiction Book Club. These small brochures were the predecessors to the modern magazine lap cards; those small advertisements that drop into your lap when you first open a magazine.

• L'INDIAN BLANC (The White Indian) (softcover)
Paris: Les Edition Du Fromage
1978 reprints the following stories:
untitled first "White Indian" story 7 pp.
first printed in DURANGO KID #1
"Blood on the Frontier" 7 pp.
first printed in DURANGO KID #2
"The War on the River" 7 pp.
first printed in DURANGO KID #3
"Brothers of the Wilderness" 7 pp.
first printed in DURANGO KID #4
"Trees of Doom" 7 pp.
first printed in DURANGO KID #5
"Tory Treachery" 7 pp.
first printed in DURANGO KID #9
"Sleep of Death" 8 pp.
first printed in DURANGO KID #10
"The Blood of Valley Forge" 7 pp.
first printed in DURANGO KID #11
"River Gauntlet" 7 pp.
first printed in DURANGO KID #12
"The Trail of the Traitor" 7 pp.
first printed in DURANGO KID #13
"The Voyage into Danger" 8 pp.
first printed in DURANGO KID #14
"Underworld of the Wilderness" 7 pp.
first printed in DURANGO KID #16

LONDON TELEGRAPH SUNDAY MAGAZINE
• 58 Nov. 23, 1977
pg. 46 article *"Frank Frazetta: Master of Fantasy"* 7 pp.

• METAL HURLANT (Heavy Metal) special TYGRA (FIRE & ICE) (softcover)
March 1983
80 pp.
contains photos, art and interviews for the movie FIRE & ICE

STARLOG (Japan)
Starlog Press Incorporated
• May 1979
• February 1980
• September 1981
• October 1981 COVER **Death Dealer**

UK ACTION COMICS
• 7 2 White Indian stories
Thun'da story
• 8 2 White Indian stories

NEWSPAPER ARTICLES and STRIPS

• ACE McCOY known as JOHNNY COMET thru Nov. 29, 1952.
Ran as Ace McCoy from Dec. 1, 1952 to Feb. 1, 1953
Frazetta drew all strips with the exception of the following three:
Jan. 4, 1953 drawn by Wally Wood
Jan. 11, 1953 drawn by Wally Wood
Jan. 18, 1953 drawn by Wally Wood with Frazetta touches

CHICAGO TRIBUNE MAGAZINE newspaper supplement
The Chicago Tribune
• Nov. 26, 1978
COVER **Berserker**
pg. 20 **Stranded**
pg. 21 article *"Demons, Warriors, Babes, and Frank"* 4 pp.
contains the following images:
The Destroyer
Madame Derringer
Swamp Demon

EXPRESS, THE Pocono area newspaper
- March 29, 1985
  cover, pp. D10, D11, D15 all have photos of Frazetta in museum
  interview with Frazetta

FLASH GORDON
- penciled 2 weeks of daily strips (2\18\53 - 2\28\53) written by Harvey Kurtzman and inked by Dan Barry
  reprinted in SQUA TRONT #3
  reprinted in FLASH GORDON the complete daily strips

JOHNNY COMET becomes ACE McCOY November 29, 1952
this strip ran from Jan. 28, 1952 to Nov. 29, 1952
  reprinted in FRANK FRAZETTA'S JOHNNY COMET
ran in the following newspapers:
  Chicago Sun Times
  L.A.Times - The Sunday strip was sometimes replaced with an ad.
  Oakland Tribune
  Detroit Free Press
  Baltimore Evening Sun - Dropped one week after strip became ACE McCOY
Some newspapers carried the strip in three row strips. Others printed only two thirds of a strip and deleted the top row.

LI'L ABNER
Frazetta worked on this strip between early 1954 through 1961. Most of the work was collaboration with other artists (Al Capp of course, Andy Amato, Walter Johnson and Harvey Curtis. Frazetta's first work appeared during the Marlon Brando parody (above). His only solo work was the Marilyn Monroe storyline which appeared about a year later.

NEW YORK TIMES
- May 1, 1977 article Paperback Talk (book review)

POCONO TODAY Stroudsberg Pa. newspaper
- March 24, 1985 COVER **Cat Girl**
  inside photo of Frazetta with comments by Ellie Frazetta

WASHINGTON POST
- Oct. 10, 1976
  article *"The Fantastic Frazetta, Art as Dread, Dread as Art"* by Henry Allen

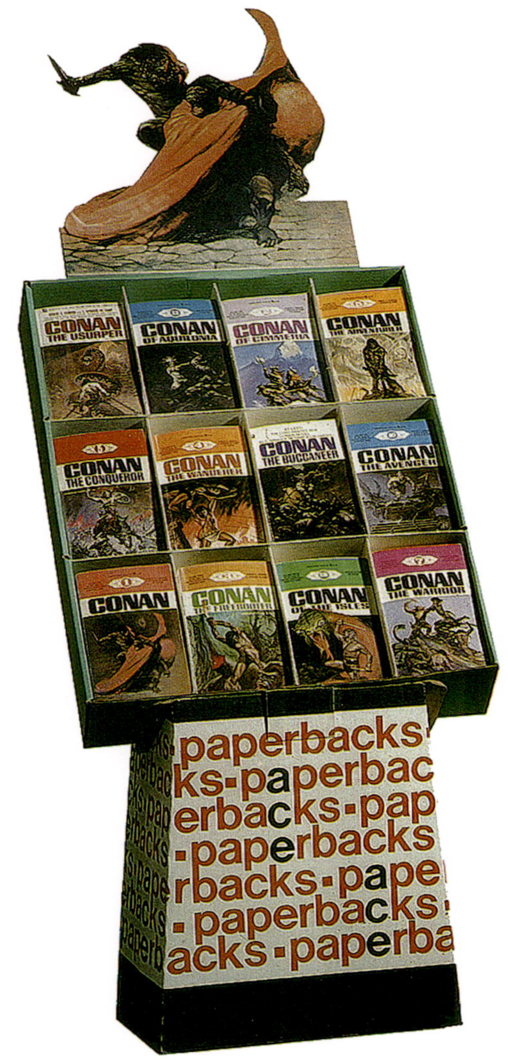

Ace Conan paperback display.

PROMOTIONAL COLLECTIBLES

ACE BOOKS
- **CONAN BOOK SERIES PROMO POSTER** 18" x 23"
  reproduces **Man Ape** in color
- **CARSON OF VENUS PROMO POSTER** 8 3/4" x 11 1/2"
- **KING KONG PROMO POSTER** 9 1/2" x 16"
- **BURROUGHS ADVENTURE booklet** 8 1/2" x 11 1/2"
  Shows Frazetta covers among others.

BERKLEY
- Battlestar Galactica folder (9" x 12")
  reproduces **Battlestar Galactica: Attack**
- 1978 color promo poster (17" X 22")
  reproduces **Battlestar Galactica: Attack** (Censored version with girls upper thigh covered)

- CANAVERAL PRESS BROCHURE
  TARZAN AND THE CASTAWAYS **promotional booklet**
  includes ink illustration
  AKA *"The silent creature drove a long knife again and again into his tawny side."*

- CARLSBERG BEER advertising poster
  The Disagreement 20" x 30"

- CHRISTIE'S AUCTION HOUSE – LTD. EDITION PIN
1993
  This limited edition pin was released to commemorate the CHRISTIE'S "Comic Collectibles Sale" Oct. 30, 1993
  Reproduces artwork from **A Princess of Mars**.

- CONAN PAPERBACK DISPLAY
1970s
Ace Books
  Display topper measuring 17 1/2" x 19 1/2". Image is **Man-Ape**

- DEATH DEALER POSTER 11"x16"
1995
Verotik
  used to promote DEATH DEALER (comic book)
  image shows cover of #1 - **Death Dealer II**

- DEATH DEALER STICKER 3"x5"

1995
Verotik
used to promote DEATH DEALER (comic book)
image shows cover of #1 - **Death Dealer II**
available in HERO ILLUSTRATED (Magazine)

DOUBLEDAY BOOK CLUB MATERIAL
promotional material for members only
CLUES - Mystery Guild
- Nov 1973
  A Requiem for Sharks
  to promote "*A Requiem for Sharks*" by Patrick Buchanan
- 1975
  Torment

SPURS - Western Writers of America
- August 1972
  Bucking Bronco
  to promote "*The True Memoirs of Charlie Blankenship*" by Benjamin Capp
  Trials of Judas Wiley
  to promote "*Trials of Judas Wiley*" by Lewis Patton
- April 1973
  Winter of the Coup
  to promote "*Winter of the Coup*" by Carter Travis Young
- Winter 1973
  Indian Brave
  to promote "*Summer of the Drums*" by Theodore V. Olson
- May 1974
  Madame Derringer
  to promote "*Legend of Baby Doe*" by John Burke

SCIENCE FICTION BOOK CLUB
- June 1972
  Birdman
  to promote "*Midsummer Century*" by James Blish
- 1971-1975
  "*Things to Come*"
  reproduces all dust jackets for the Doubleday Book Club
  each Doubleday book has its own flyer. 13 in all
  (i.e. "Things to Come - Downward to Earth")
- no date
  "*Are There Frogs on the Moon?*" color book club envelope 6" x 9"
- no date
  "*Frogs on the Moon?*" promotional flyer 10" x 21" unfolded
  COVER - **Frogs on the Moon?**
  reprinted in b/w in THE FRAZETTA TREASURY (fanzine)
  "*Limitless Horizons of Science Fiction*"
  COVER **Fantasy World** (b/w)
  reprinted in color in FRANK FRAZETTA: BOOK FOUR
- no date
  membership lap card placed within Doubleday books
  design 1
  AKA - "Spaceman"
  reprinted in FRANK FRAZETTA: BOOK TWO (art book)
  many different color versions exist
- no date
  membership lap card placed within Doubleday books
  design 2
- no date
  club membership print (8" x 10")
  John Carter and the Savage Apes of Mars

- DUST - Hard Attack promotional poster

Kama Sutra Records
1972 **Snow Giants**

- FRAZETTA'S FANTASY CORNER BUSINESS CARD
  Card image shows creature caricatures in graveyard

- FRAZETTA'S FANTASY CORNER SHOPPING BAG
  Bag image shows creature caricatures in graveyard

- GREAT PLAINS RENAISSANCE FESTIVAL POSTER

2000 Uses the image **Outlaw of Torn.** Authorized by the Frazettas.

HONDA RUNE - MOTORCYCLE ADVERTISING
2004
Honda Motor Sports
- 200 ft. billboard over Times Square featuring **Death Dealer III**
- Signed/Numbered poster featuring **Death Dealer III** Limited to 50 copies.
- Regular edition poster featuring **Death Dealer III**

- ILLUSTRATIONS ARCANUM ASHCAN

1994
Verotik
COVER
6 pp. reproduces illustrations found inside the book

- JOHNNY COMET PRESSBOOK

Sent to the feature editor of many newspapers. Contained teaser ads for promotion, some ads were possibly never reproduced.

- L. RON HUBBARD PROMOTIONAL BROCHURE

1990's
L. Ron Hubbard
6 pp. w/foldout. Advertises the L. Ron Hubbard prints

MOLLY HATCHET PROMOTIONALS
CBS / Epic Records

FLIRTIN' WITH DISASTER
1979
- 33" x 40" Cardboard Standee
  Features a die-cut image of **Dark Kingdom.**
- 48" x 48" Cardboard Standee
  Features a die-cut image of **Dark Kingdom.**
- 48" x 48" poster advertisement **Dark Kingdom**
- 24" x 24" poster advertisement **Dark Kingdom**

BEATIN' THE ODDS
1979
- 33" x 36" Cardboard Standee
  Features a die-cut image of **Berserker**.
- 48" x 48" poster advertisement **Berserker**
- 24" x 24" poster advertisement **Berserker**

BOUNTY HUNTER
1979
- 48" x 48" Cardboard Standee
  Features a die-cut image of **Death Dealer**
- 48" x 60" poster advertisement **Death Dealer**
- 48" x 48" poster advertisement **Death Dealer**
- 24" x 36" poster advertisement **Death Dealer**
- 12" x 19" B&W Tour Poster **Death Dealer**

- MOLLY HATCHET CONCERT ADVERTISEMENT 2-sided

postcard
CBS / Epic Records
One side shows Molly Hatchet concert for Dec. 17 (year unknown) at BB Kings Nightclub in N.Y. City. The other side shows concert for Hank Williams III.
Images shown are:
Dark Kingdom
Death Dealer

NAZARETH PROMOTIONALS
A&M
EXPECT NO MERCY
- 24" x 24" poster advertisement **The Brain**
- 24" x 36" poster advertisement **Death Dealer**

PILLOW CASE - From the Frazetta Pillow Book
Kitchen Sink
1993
Features art work **Familiars**
first printed in FRANK FRAZETTA'S PILLOW BOOK

- Russ Cochran Presents FRANK FRAZETTA'S GOLDEN GIRL (full color 5x7 card)

1983
Russ Cochran

- TARZAN PIN 3" diameter

1973
Edgar Rice Burroughs
Reproduces *"The silent creature drove a long knife again and again into his tawny side."*
first printed in CANAVERAL PRESS - TARZAN AND THE CASTAWAYS promotional booklet illustration

- VEROTIK PIN b/w

1994
Verotik
shows an image from the book ILLUSTRATIONS ARCANUM

- YNGWIE MALMSTEEN: Rising Force Promotional Poster (36"x24")

Epic records
1998
This item was made available only to record stores.
Uses the image **Death Dealer V**.

CLOTHING

CINEMACHINE / FRAZETTA SHIRTS
2003
CineMachine
- T-Shirt

Each shirt has red Death Dealer helmet on front upper chest, red movie poster image on back and red cinemachine logo on left sleeve

- DEATH DEALER T-SHIRT

1986
Wild Oats
Reproduces **Death Dealer II**

L. RON HUBBARD PRINT T SHIRTS
- **Dream Flight**
- **Countess**
- **Leaping Lizards**
- **Dawn Attack**
- **Encounter**

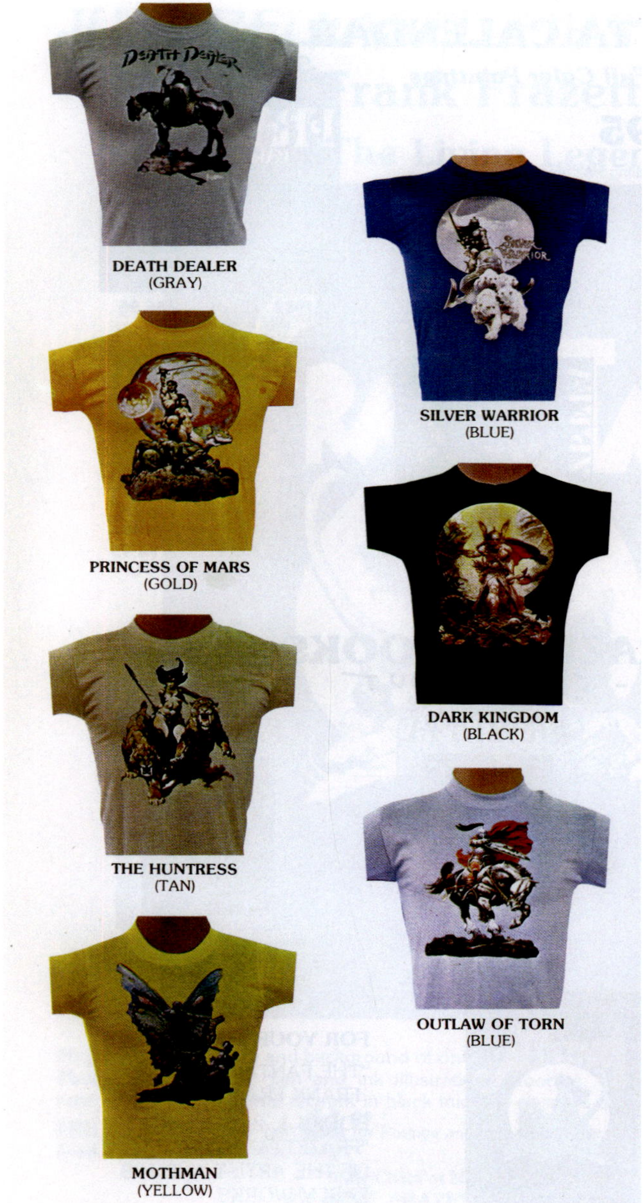

JIGSAW PUZZLES

FANTASTIC ART PUZZLES
American Publishing Corporation
- 6146 **Silver Warrior**
- 6138 **The Huntress**
- 6148 **Death Dealer**
- 6139 **Dark Kingdom**
- **Sound**
- **Flying Reptiles**
- **The Destroyer**
- **Berserker**
- **A Princess of Mars**
- **Against the Gods**

GIANT POSTER PUZZLE
International Polygonics
1972
- #E101 cover to Eerie #23 **Egyptian Queen**

WARREN MAGAZINE COVERS
Warren Publishing Co.
1977
- cover to Eerie #23 **Egyptian Queen**

LETTERHEADS

- BURROUGHS BIBLIOPHILE
  comic ape at typewriter

- CARNIVORE PRESS
  illustration of sabre-tooth tiger

- GARY FAIRFAX
  frontispiece illustration from BEASTS OF TARZAN

RUSS COCHRAN
- letterhead illustration of a fox (three versions exist)
- business card watercolor of barbarian and castle
- postcard reprints frontispiece from TARZAN AND THE JEWELS OF OPAR

- ROBERT BARRETT
  three illustrations: Tarzan, Lord Grandrith and John Gribardsum

- SVENGALI stationary header
John and Bo Derek film company
reprinted in FRAZETTA - THE LIVING LEGEND (art book)

PHONE CARDS

L. RON HUBBARD HOLOGRAM PHONE CARDS
1994
Global Link
Silver Edition - Limited to 4,000
Gold Edition - Limited to 800

• **Dream Flight**	• **Dream Flight**
• **The Countess**	• **The Countess**
• **Dawn Attack**	• **Dawn Attack**

FRANK FRAZETTA PHONE CARDS
1995
Celestial Communications
Each card limited to 5,000/numbered. 6 cards in set
Spiderman
The Norseman
Tanar of Pellucidar
Mastermind of Mars
Captive Princess

MISCELLANEOUS

- AD&D - LICH LORDS Role Playing Manual
1985
Mayfair Games
Cover **The Norseman**

- AGAINST THE GODS Stained Glass Reproduction 9"x5"
1991
Frank Frazetta
This item was initially distributed with a pewter sculpture of Frazetta's **Against the Gods.** The sculpture sold poorly and the manufacturer of the stained glass sold the remaining lot on EBAY.

ARMS & ARMOR
Albion Armorers
2003
- DEATH DEALER HELMET Full scale reproduction
  Based on the painting **The Death Dealer**
  Limited edition of 1,000

From the Albion website:
Hand-hammered by Lars Hansen from 16 gauge steel, this helm is totally handmade and hand-finished. The top spike is solid, the horns cast in an ivory resin.

Though certainly a striking display item, each helm is fully functional and wearable. They are fully lined with leather suspension and chinstrap and are available in small, medium and large sizes.
Each helm is numbered and comes with a Certificate of Authenticity.

- DEATH DEALER AXE Full scale reproduction
  Based on the painting **The Death Dealer**
  Limited edition of 1,000

From the Albion website:
Each axe is handmade by the talented artisans at Albion with a carbon steel (hand-ground blade) and mild steel (investment cast socket and spike), with an antiqued, hand-finished and hand-rubbed haft.

Though certainly a striking display item, the Death Dealer is fully functional.

Each is numbered and comes with a Certificate of Authenticity.
Specifications
Overall length: 47"
Edge: 14"
Weight: 12 lbs.

- SNOW GIANT SWORD Full scale reproduction
Based on the painting **The Snow Giants**
- THE BRAIN SWORD Full scale reproduction
  Based on the painting **The Brain**
- THE BARBARIAN SWORD Full scale reproduction
  Based on the painting **The Barbarian**
- BERSERKER SWORD Full scale reproduction
  Based on the painting **Berserker**
- BLOODSTONE SWORD Full scale reproduction
  Based on the painting **Bloodstone**
- BLOODSTONE SWORD (MARK ii) Full scale reproduction
  Based on the painting **Bloodstone**
  Redesigned by Lars Hansen. Limited Edition of 1000.

From the Albion website:
Each sword is handmade by the talented artisans at Albion of high carbon steel (hand-ground blade) and mild steel (investment cast) guard and pommel, with a cord and red leather wrapped grip of stabilized birch. The pommel features a real bloodstone gem set into recesses on each side.

Though certainly a striking display item, Bloodstone is fully functional and is sold sharp, unless otherwise requested by the customer.

MARTIAN LONGSWORD Full scale reproduction
Created by Jody Samson
- Standard Edition (limited to 1000 hand ground by Albion staff)
- Limited Edition (limited to 10, hand ground by Jody)

- ART OF KEN KELLY, THE
  Frazetta wrote a two page introduction for this collection of Ken Kelly paintings.

- BOOKMARKS - UNCUT, FRAMED
2001
Frank Frazetta
1st Edition
Limited Stamp Signed/Numbered Edition of 250

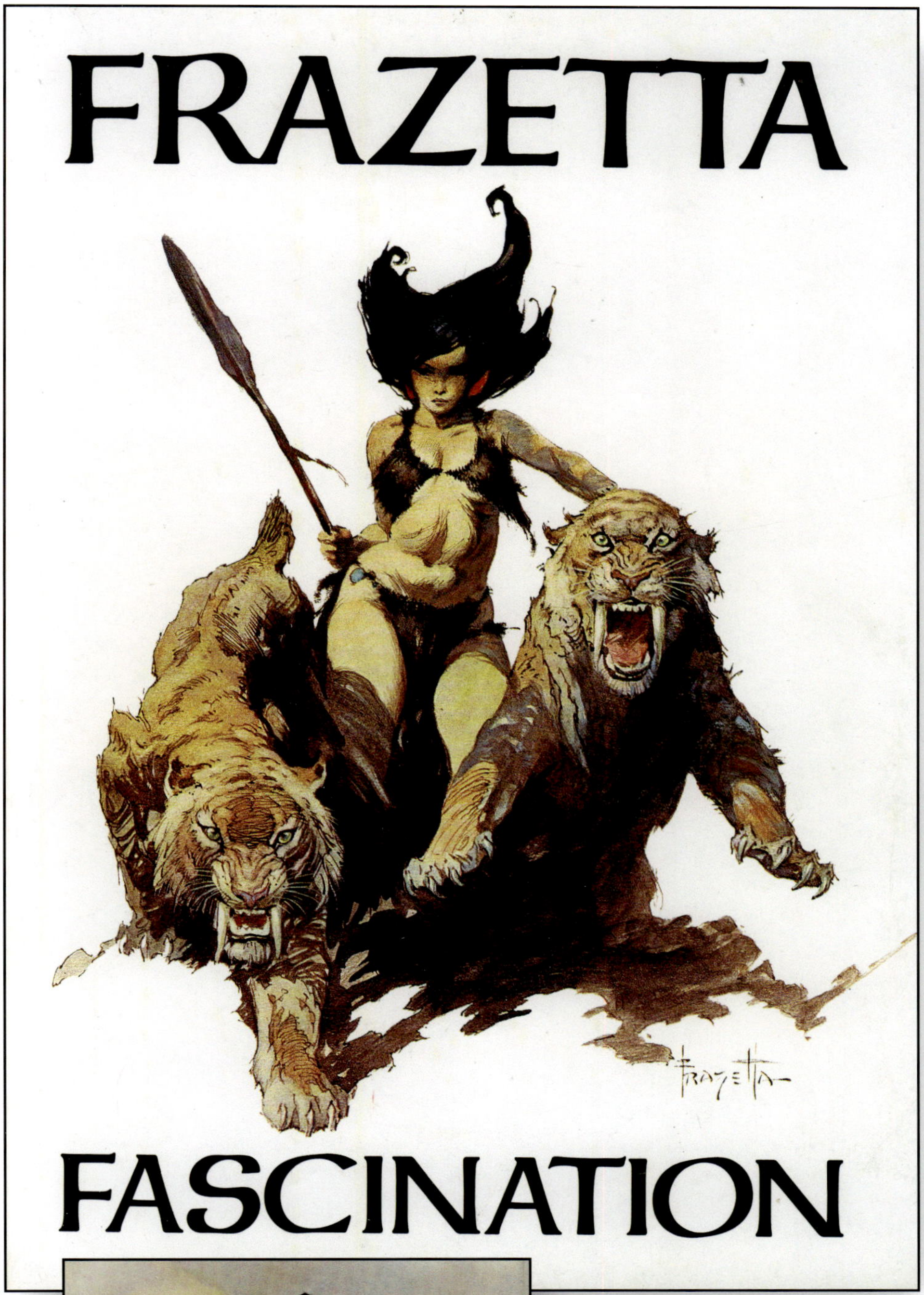

FRAZETTA

FASCINATION

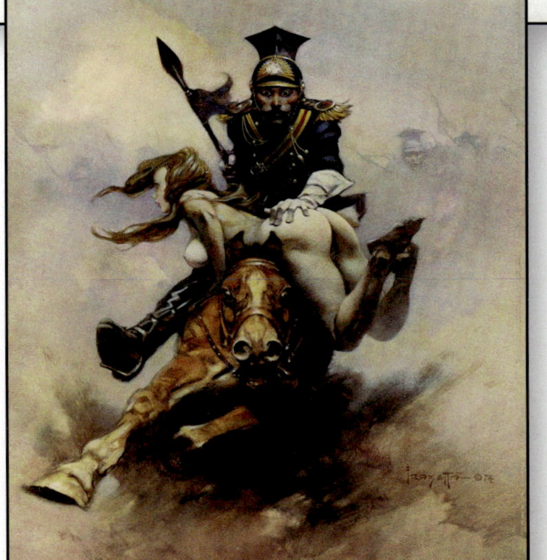

ABOVE:
Frazetta
Fascination
front cover.
Art from cover of
Pellucidar
(Zoom 1984)

RIGHT:
Frazetta
Fascination
back cover
Art from cover of
Flashman on
the Charge

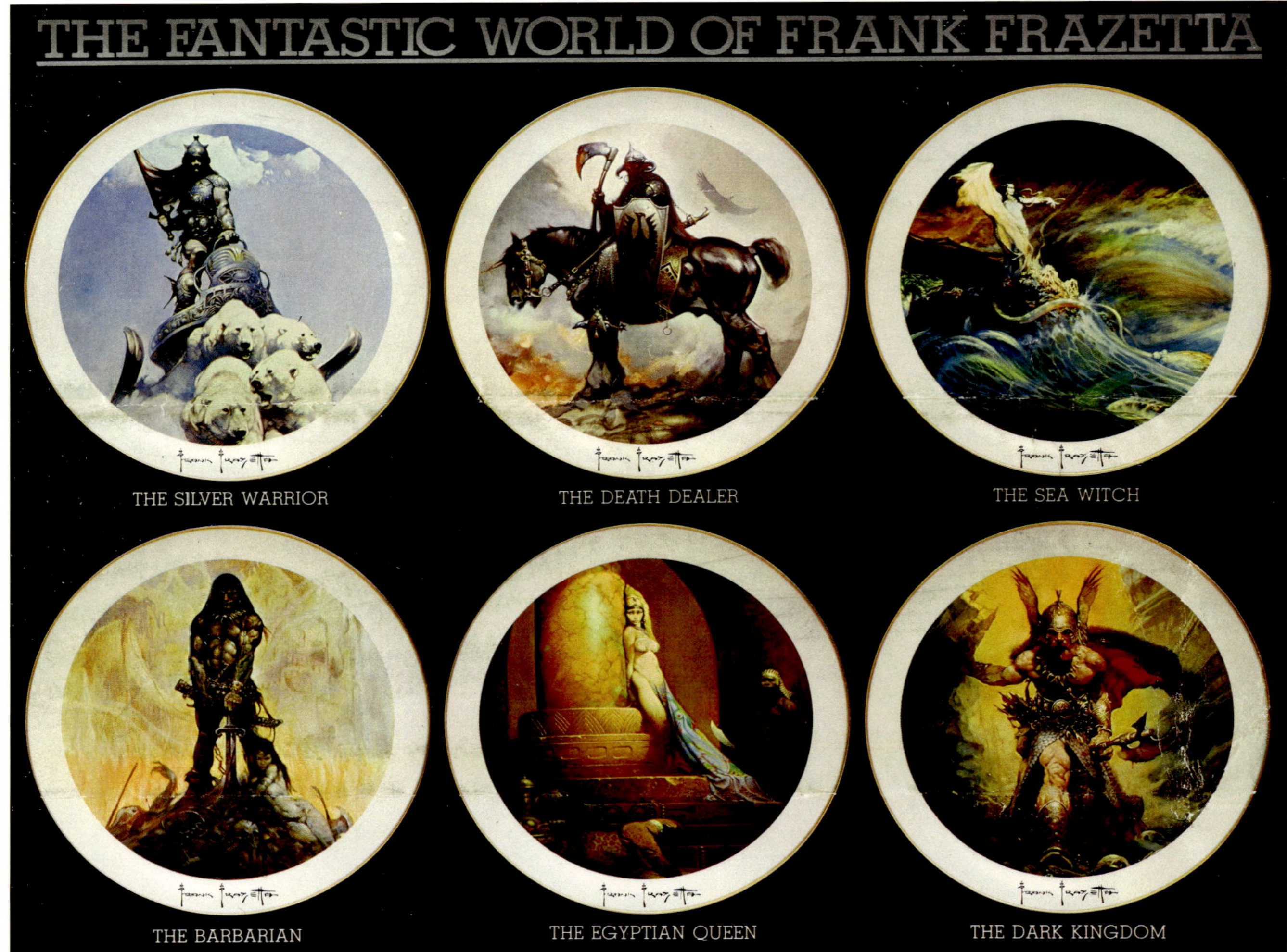

A promotional flyer for a selection of unproduced Frazetta collector plates.

• BOOTLEG DUST JACKET
Tarzan Alive: A Definitive Biography of Lord Greystoke by Philip Jose Farmer
1972
Not happy with the commercial design, a Burroughs fan created a bootleg dustjacket for the book. Only a few copies were produced. Contains a spine illustration by frazetta. The image is of the same design as an ACE paperback frontispiece.

• CD ROM COMICS
2003
Comics On CD Rom
Frazetta Special disc series #1 includes: Thun'da #1, White Indian #12, 13, Durango Kid #3 & Personal Love #32

• CERAMIC TILE bootleg
2003
size - 6"x6"
pencil illustration of Girl with Gorilla
first printed in ILLUSTRATIONS ARCANUM

CHINA PLATES PROTOTYPES
1980
10" plate with 8" image and 24k gold trim
These are one-of-a-kind prototype china plates with Frazetta images on them. EXTREMELY RARE!
The images on the only known plates are as follows:
• DARK KINGDOM
• SILVER WARRIOR
• EGYPTIAN PRINCESS

• CREEPY FAN CLUB
1960s
Warren Publishing
Uncle Creepy portrait (full color 8.5" x 11")

• FAMOUS CARTOONIST'S COURSE
1960s
Panel from HEROIC COMICS story *"Stranded in a Mine Field"*. The Famous Cartoonists Course was produced by the same company that did The Famous Artists Course. Do you remember the *"We're looking for people who like to draw"* advertisement on the back cover of certain comic books? This course followed the same premise.

• FRAZETTA MEMORY BOOK
1977
Frank Frazetta, (40 pp.)
collection of photos and artwork bound into a 5 1/2 x 8 1/2 book comes with envelope

FRAZETTA PRINTS CATALOG
• Volume 1
• Volume 2
• Volume 3

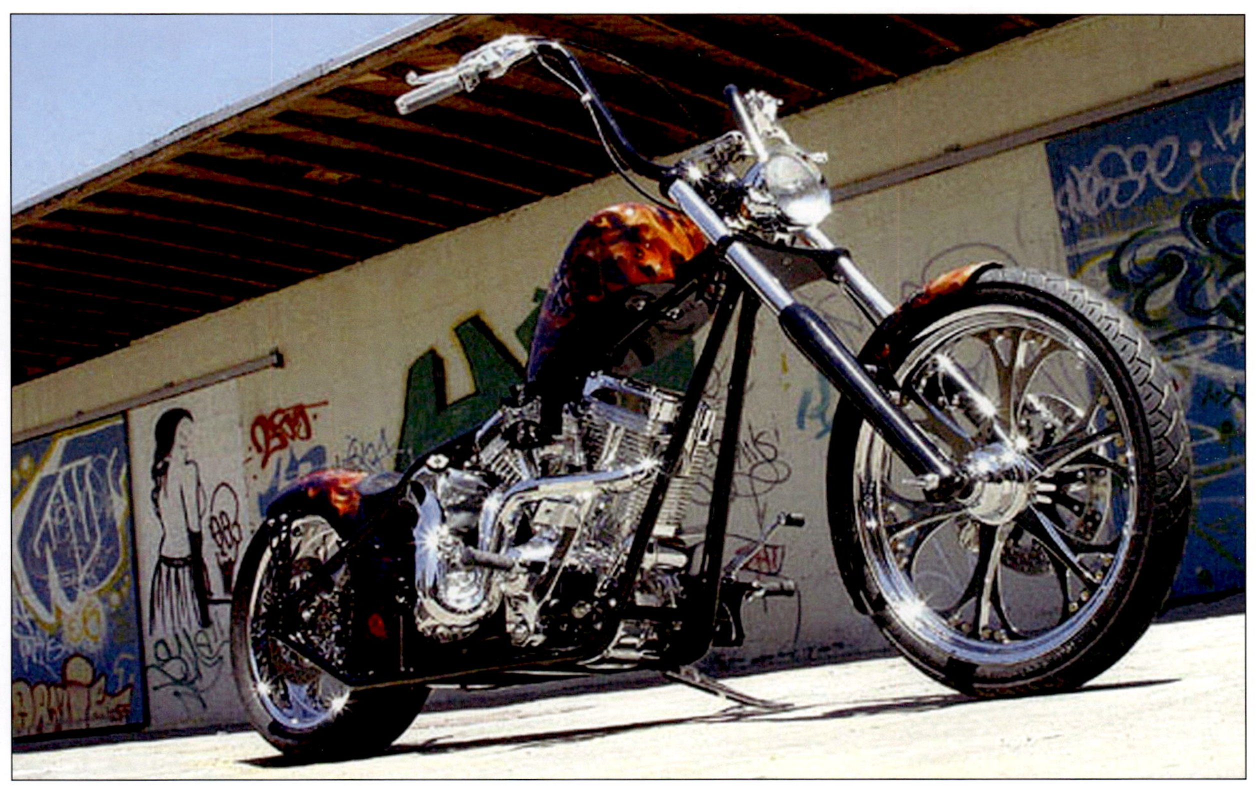

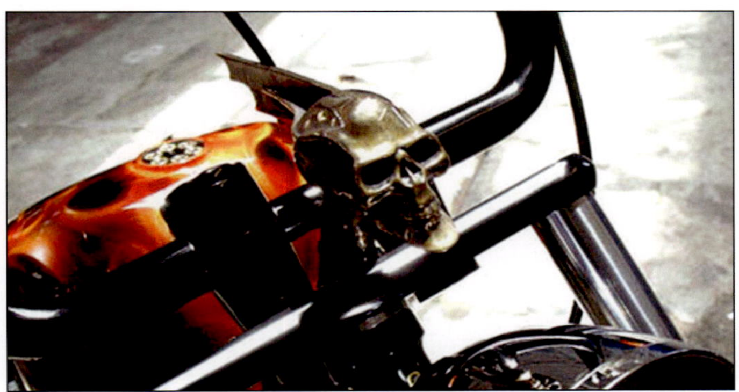

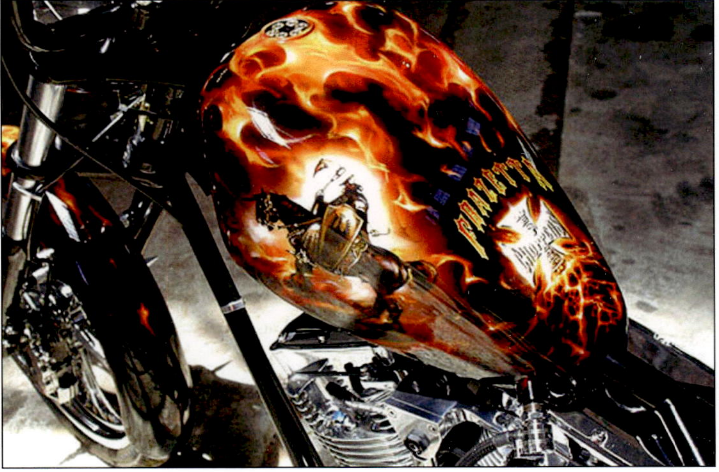

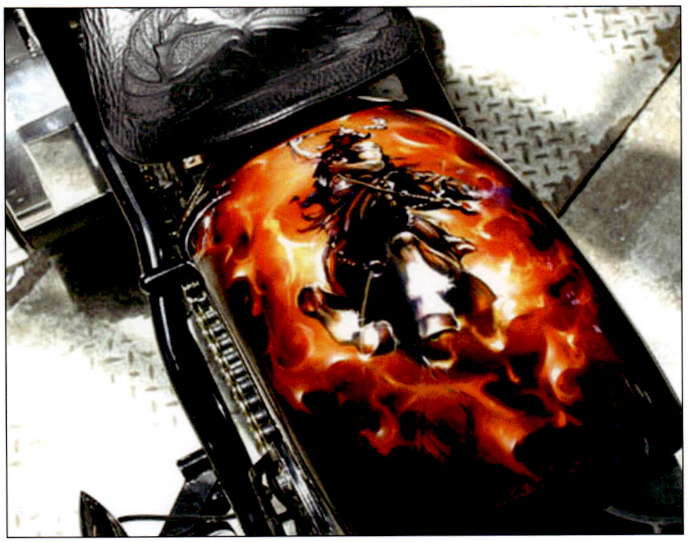

DEATH DEALER CHOPPER
built in 2005 by Jesse James and West Coast Choppers. Airbrushed by Mike Lavallee.

A *Death Dealer* themed, custom built chopper featuring airbrushed reproductions of Frank Frazetta's ***DEATH DEALER*** paintings.

The bike features the Frazetta name and ***DEATH DEALER*** on the gas tank, and ***DEATH DEALER 4*** on the rear fender.

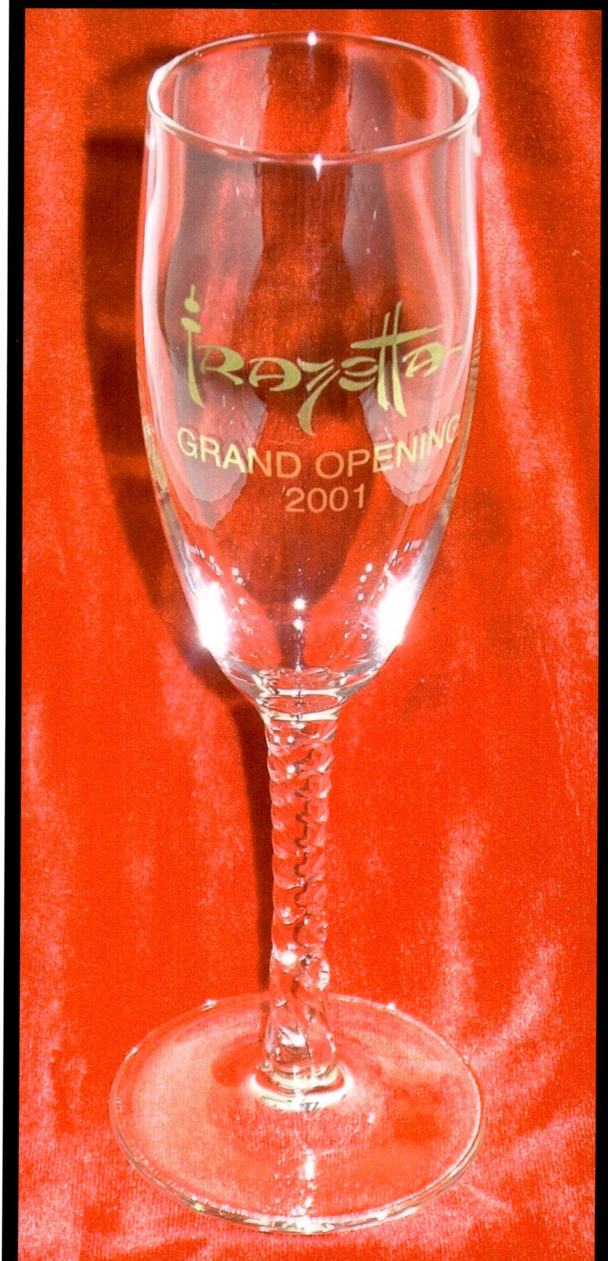

Commemorative champagne flute from 2001 grand opening of Frazetta Museum.

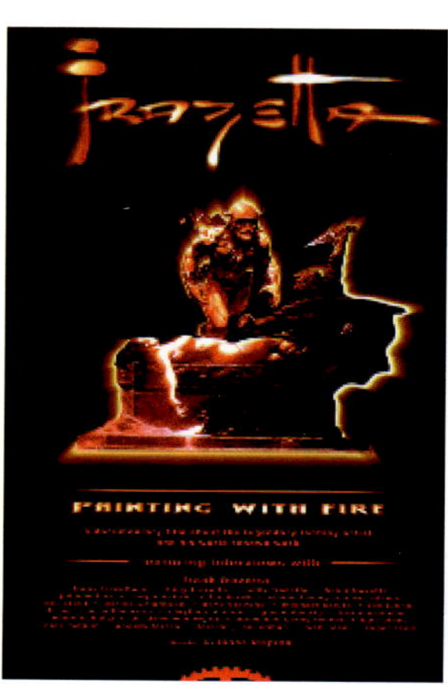

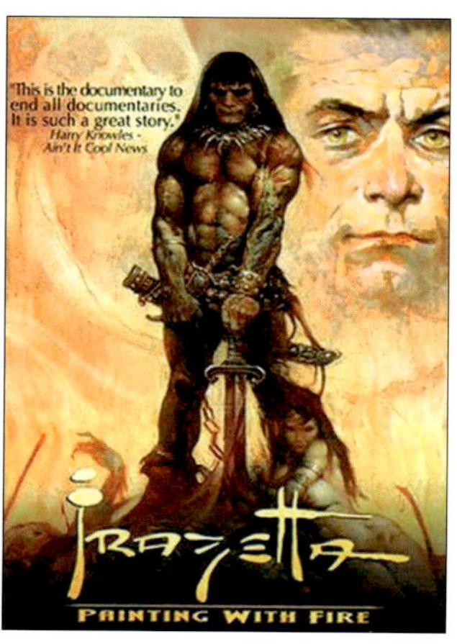

• HALLOWEEN MASK (DARKWOLF)
1982
Bakshi Prod.

This is a child's plastic Halloween mask with rubber band. Originally sold unpackaged and loose. It is the Darkwolf character from the animated feature FIRE & ICE. The mask is marked 1982. The movie was released in 1983.

IRON ON T- SHIRT TRANSFERS
- 1975 **Luana** (A sheet movie poster design)
- 1980 **Dark Kingdom**

• JERK, THE Movie starring Steve Martin
1979
Universal Pictures

The painting of **Sea Monster** is shown above Navin R. Johnson's (Steve Martin's) bed. Painting is altered. Sea creature is replaced with topless mermaid. The mermaid is not painted by Frazetta.

• LATER, WITH BOB COSTAS (TV interview program)
Bill Gaines interview mentions FAMOUS FUNNIES
and shows issue #211

LI'L ABNER GREETING CARDS
1950's

A series of cards featuring the cast of the LI'L ABNER newspaper strip. Each sold separately.

MIRRORS
- Madame Butterfly
- Elf with Sword

MOTORCYCLE, DEATH DEALER
2005
West Coast Choppers, Jesse James

• SHEET MUSIC - THE NIGHT THEY RAIDED MINSKY'S - love theme
1968
United Artists

Cover **The Night They Raided Minsky's**
first printed as one-sheet movie poster

Caricatures include - Jason Robards, Britt Ekland, Norman Wisdom, Bert Lahr. Elliott Gould and Denholm Elliot.

• SHEET MUSIC - WOLFMOTHER
(guitar book)
2006

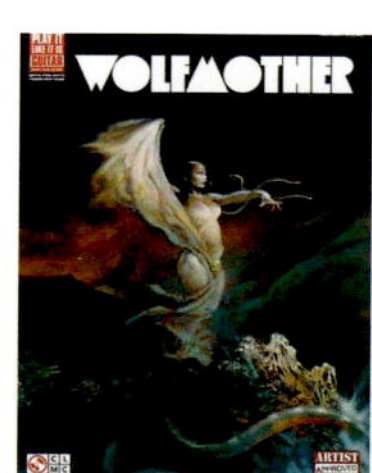

TAPESTRIES
Early 80's
36" x 54"
Black Velvet
- **Battlestar Galactica** black velvet
- **Battlestar Galactica** black cotton
- **Silver Warrior** black velvet
- **Silver Warrior** black cotton

FAR LEFT: Poster for Frazetta: Painting with Fire *(2003)*

LEFT: DVD cover for Frazetta: Painting with Fire *(2004)*

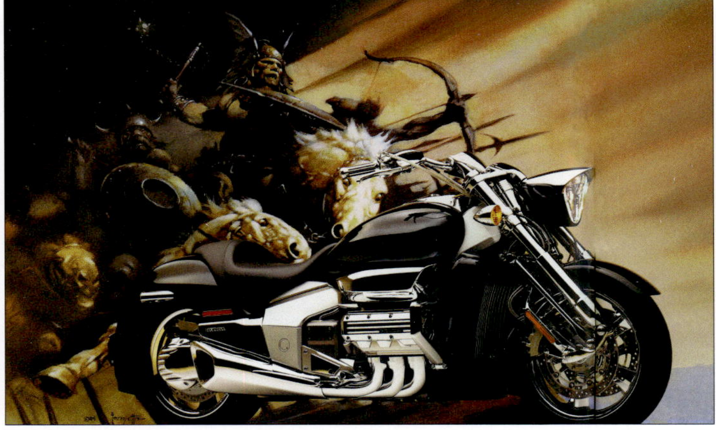

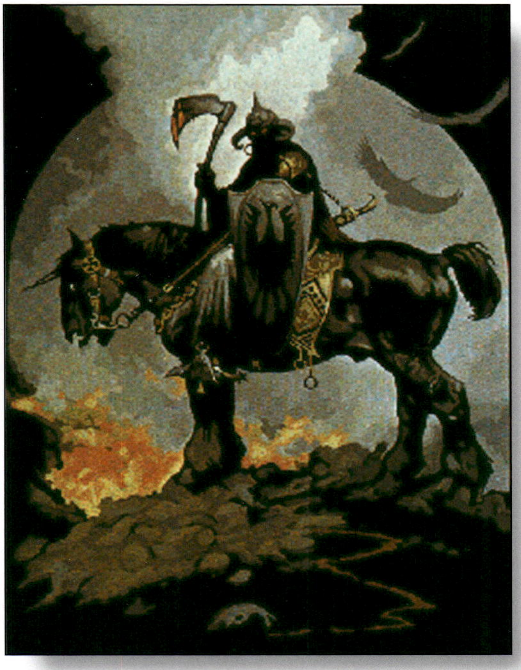

- OIL PAINT BY NUMBER SET

1978
Irwin Toys (Canadian)

These are black velvet versions of Frazetta paintings. Each set comes with 20 oil paints and a brush.

The black velvet panel is 30 x 41 cm.

- 18210 **Death Dealer**
- 18220 **Silver Warrior**

- WAR PINBALL MACHINE table size is 4' X 3', 2' tall

1978
Viza

This is a cocktail table pinball machine called "War". Players sit at opposite ends of the table and try to force the ball into their opponents goal.

Table graphic **Berserker**

- ZIPPO LIGHTERS

2003
Dark Horse

Each lighter comes in tin case and has slipcase with same image as lighter.

- Woman with Spear
- **Death Dealer**
- **Silver Warrior**
- **The Brain**

TOP LEFT: Honda Motor Sports 2004 Rune motorcycle promotional brochure image.

BELOW LEFT: Now you too can paint like Frazetta! Well, probably not. Here is one of the more esoteric collectibles; oil paint-b- number kits from Canada. Individually sold, they came complete with instructions, paint, and a small plastic brush. Here is the original package for the Silver Warrior *paint-by-numbers kit.*

ABOVE: The finished Death Dealer *paint-by-number painting.*

BELOW: Ad for Frazetta clocks and mirrors that appeared in The Fantastic Art of Frank Frazetta: Book One *(first edition.)*

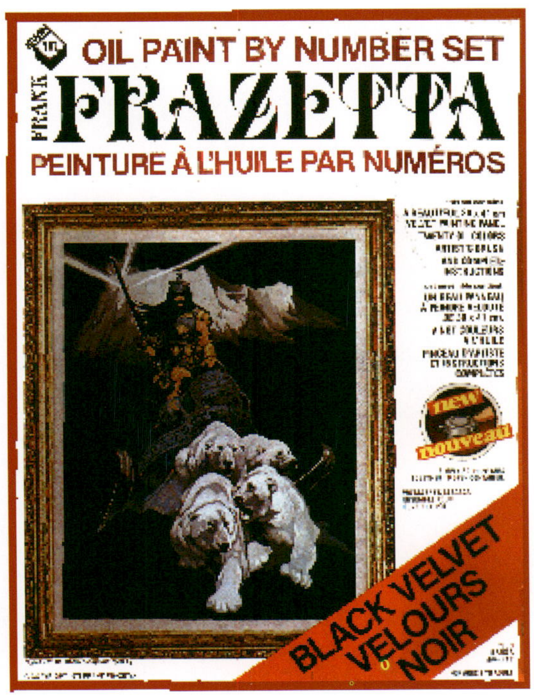

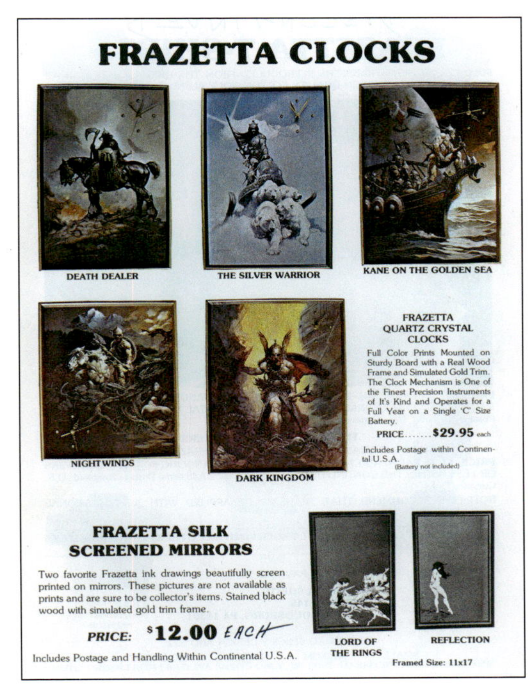

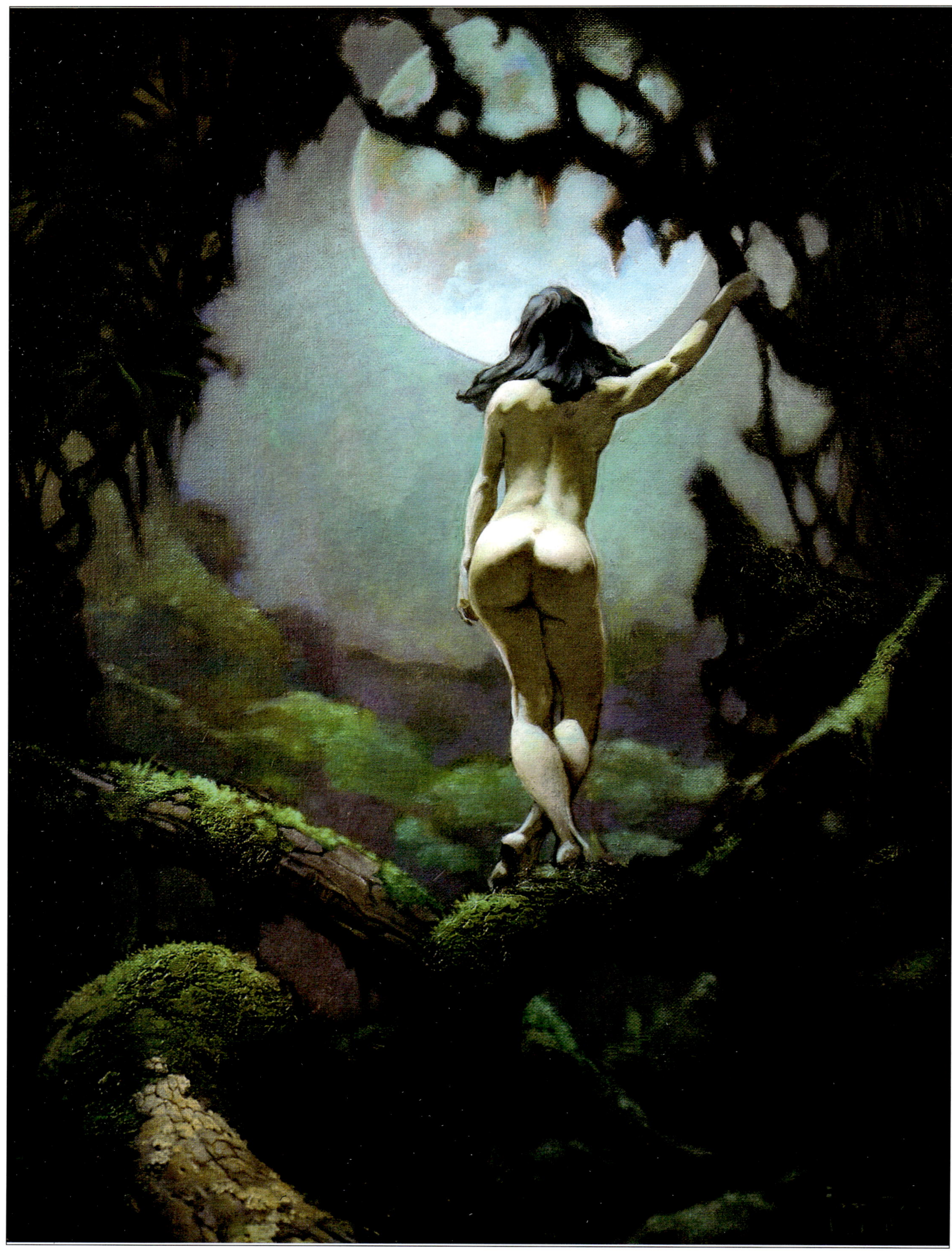

AFTERWORD

By James A. Bond

Origins: From list to book in a mere 28 years.

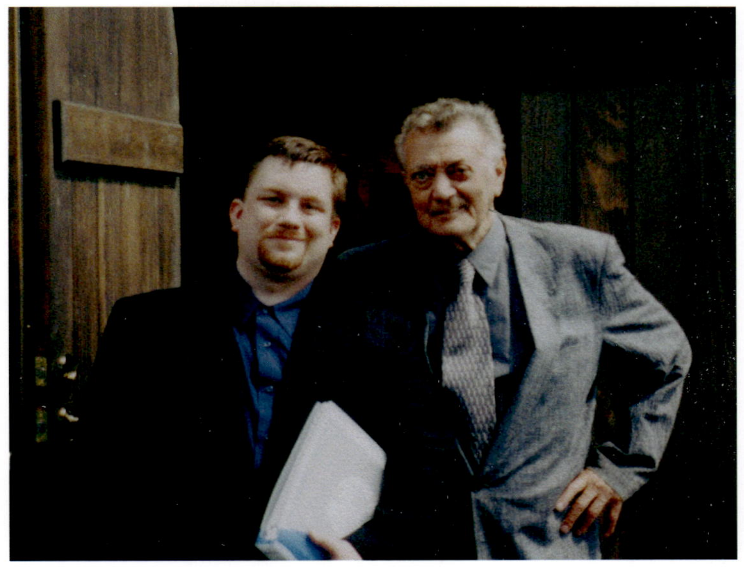

Strange things can happen when the humble hobby of collecting becomes larger than the sum of it's own collection. What originally started out as a simple list has turned into something with a life of its own. To me personally, this book has been many things; A time devouring monster, a passageway to friendship, a reason for anguish, a saviour from strife. For a long time it was the only driving force in my life. This book was my drug of choice.

In 1980 It started out as nothing more than a single page, torn from a spiral notebook. a mere list of Frazetta's art from the first three *Fantastic Art of Frazetta* books. As you might know, those particular books had no indexes of their own, so I filled a need and indexed them for my own use. It had no aspirations, no illusions of grandeur. It was merely a scribbled list.

But one day, I looked at the list, and it had grown a bit larger. By 1984 book titles had appeared on the list. At the same time, nearby used bookstores reported sales of dozens of paperbacks with Frazetta covers. One morning I awoke to find teetering stacks of paperbacks, threatening to engulf my bed like a tidal wave. Upon closer inspection of this motley hoard, I glimpsed not just books but record albums as well, and there, at the base of the tallest wobbly

ABOUT THE AUTHOR

James A. Bond is an afficionado and historian of fantasy art, specializing in the work of Frank Frazetta, his peers and his contemporaries..

Currently living in the waterfall quenched Adirondack Mountains of upstate New York, James continues to hold a constant passion for virtually all classic and modern fantasy art.

ABOVE: James Bond, holding a manuscript of this with Frank Frazetta, standing in front of the Frazetta Museum during its Grand Opening Celebration, June 23, 2001.

OPPOSITE:FRANK Frazetta: A retrospective. Alexander Art Gallery exhibit catalog (1994)

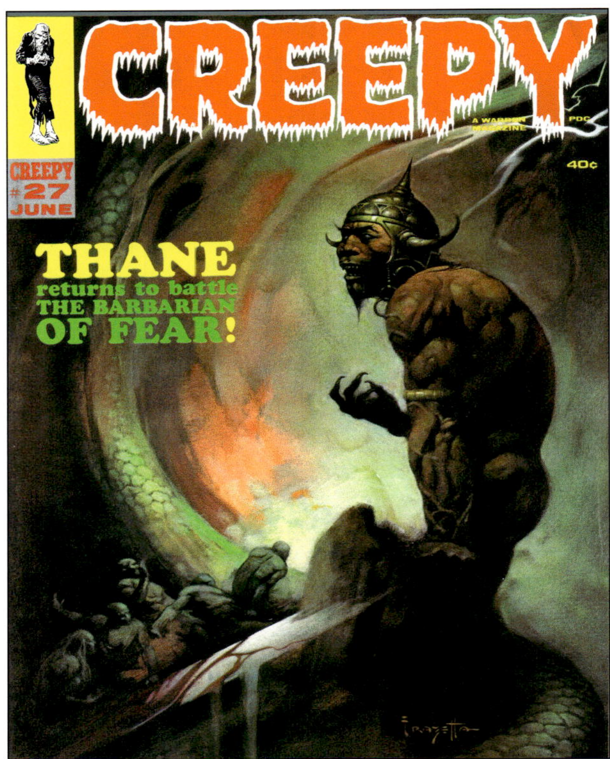

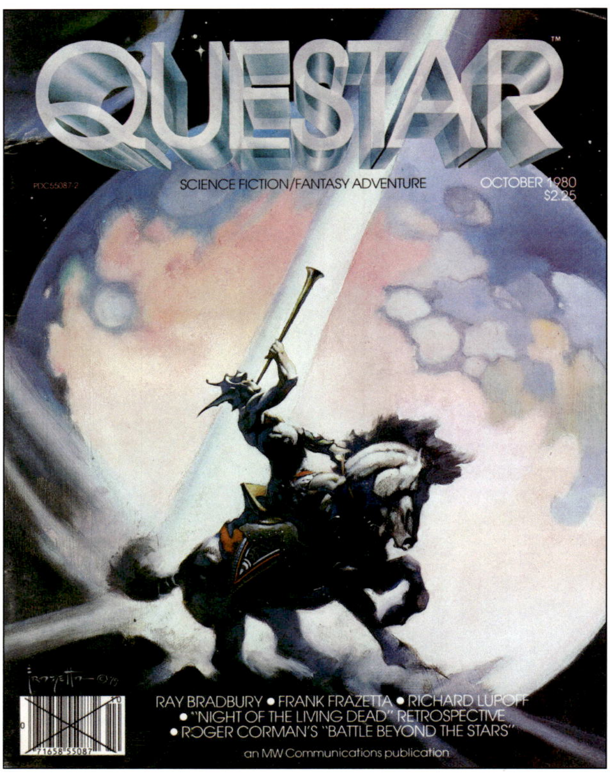

TOP: Creepy #27
Warren Publications (1969)

ABOVE: Questar Magazine
(October 1980)

OPPOSITE: Back Cover to Burroughs Bulletin #29
Tarzan & the Ant Men, also a print.

stack, was a jigsaw puzzle that I swear wasn't there the day before! And damned if I didn't see a Playboy in the mix (How did that get there?). Of course, with every new acquisition there appeared new items on the list.

And the list grew larger.

By 1995, the list was now in control. It forced me to travel the country, attending hundreds of comic book conventions, gathering more information. I'd spend days walking the convention floors, cross checking data. Oftentimes, I'd find information no one knew about, or bring to light myths that had no bearing on reality.

Eventually, around 1998 I could no longer afford every item on the list and pictures of items had to suffice. The illustrated version was born. After about fourteen years of research, and through the encouragement of friends and dealers, I mailed my small, 120 page list to the only address that had ties with Frank Frazetta, the P.O. box from which to order his prints.

Nothing happened.

Eight months passed and absolutely nothing happened. No word from Frank. The time was during Frank's health issues. To most of the fans he'd become semi-reclusive, accessible only to those who knew him very well. It was a shot in the dark, who was I kidding?

Then, one Saturday morning, the phone rang.

"James?" It was a woman's voice, distinct with a New York style accent.

"Yes?"

"James, this is Ellie Frazetta, Frank Frazetta's wife. We got your package in the mail."

"Oh, um, well, good!" I quickly turned off Peewee's Playhouse to focus on the conversation.

"What do you think of it?" I continued, sitting up straight on the edge of my recliner.

"It's wonderful! You did this all yourself?"

"Yeah! It's taken years, but yeah!"

"Well, Frank and I think what you did is great…"

(Omigod, Frank Frazetta read the list and thinks it's great!)

"…and we want to meet you. Can you come out to the house sometime so we can talk about your book?"

"… (book?)"

"James?"

"Yeah, sorry, I, uh, dropped the phone. Um, you were saying?"

"You should come out and see the new museum. It's not quite finished yet, but some of Frank's art is already inside. We can sit and talk about your book."

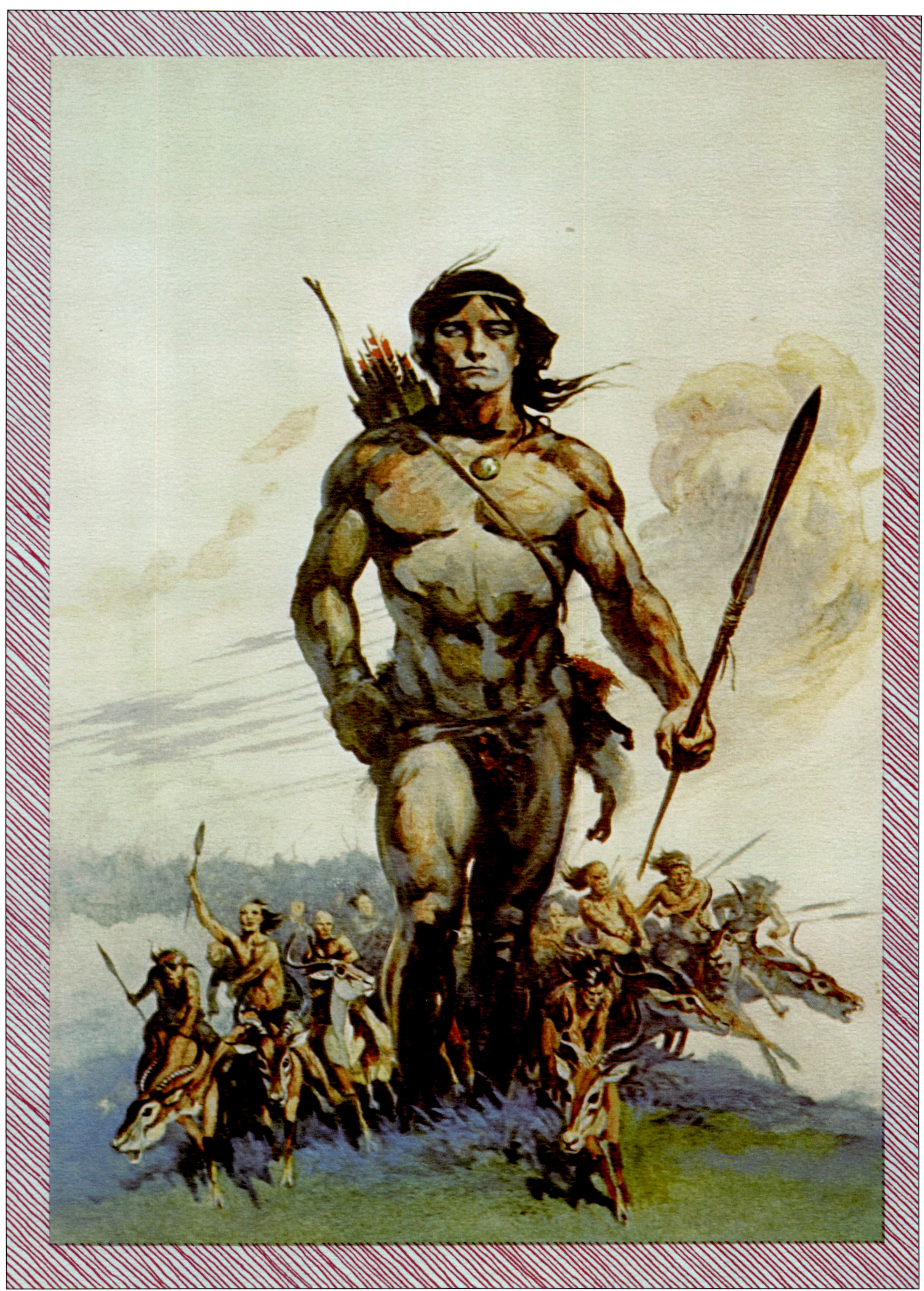

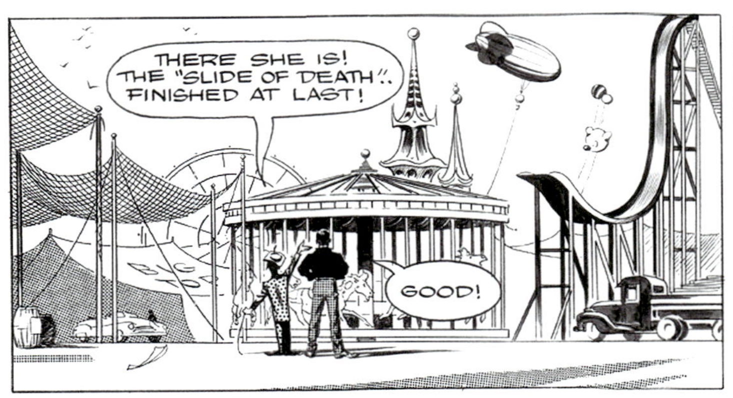

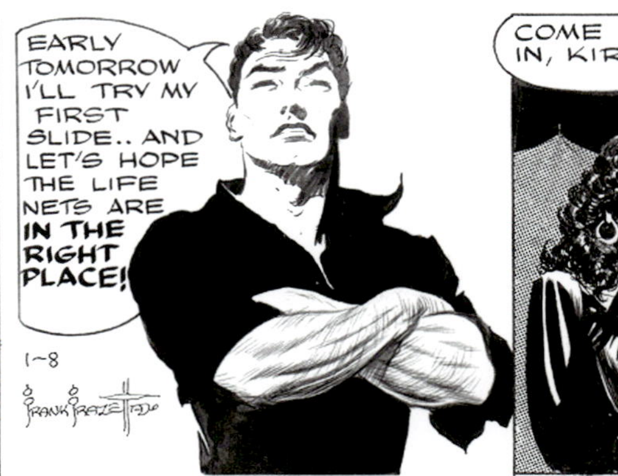

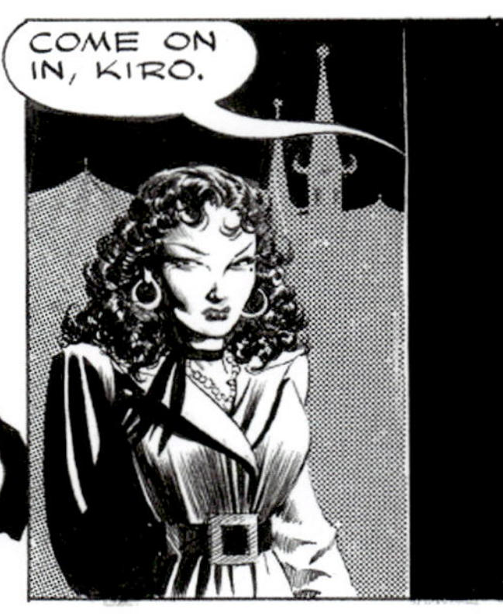

The rest of the conversation was a blur of addresses and phone numbers, discussions of details and dates.

Eventually, thanks to Ellie Frazetta, I met David Winiewicz and J. David Spurlock. She was actually the person who first suggested that Vanguard publish this very book. Through Winiewicz I met Andrew Steven. It was only a matter of time before my list met theirs and it became a match made in heaven. A ménage à trois of collectibles, a three-way dance of data. Since I had an existing format already designed, it was up to me to culminate all of that data together into one enormous, all encompassing book.

It wasn't long before we all began nurturing the project, guiding it, if you will, toward it's destination, as a father might guide his offspring to take those first steps on its own. And now, twenty eight years later, that day has finally come.

They grow up so fast...

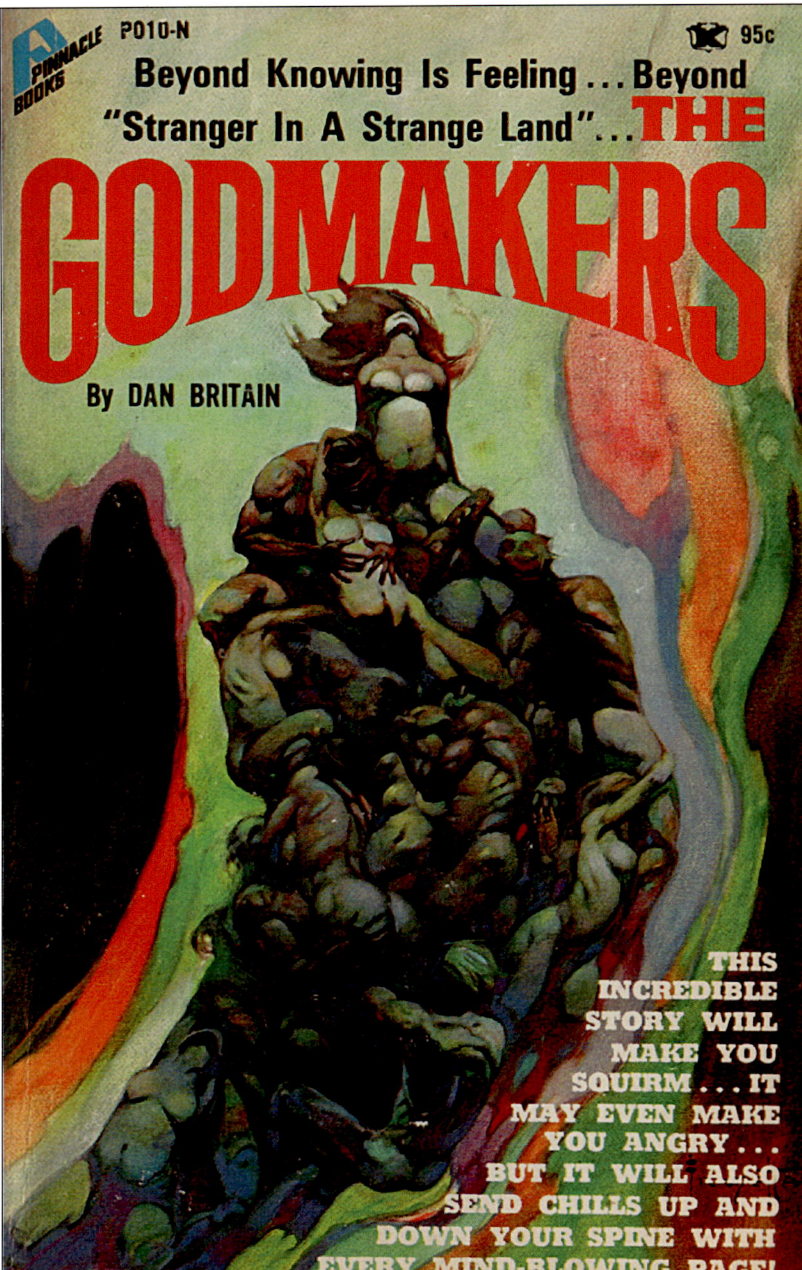

TOP: Johnny Comet *daily strip*

RIGHT: The Godmakers
Pinnacle Books (1970)

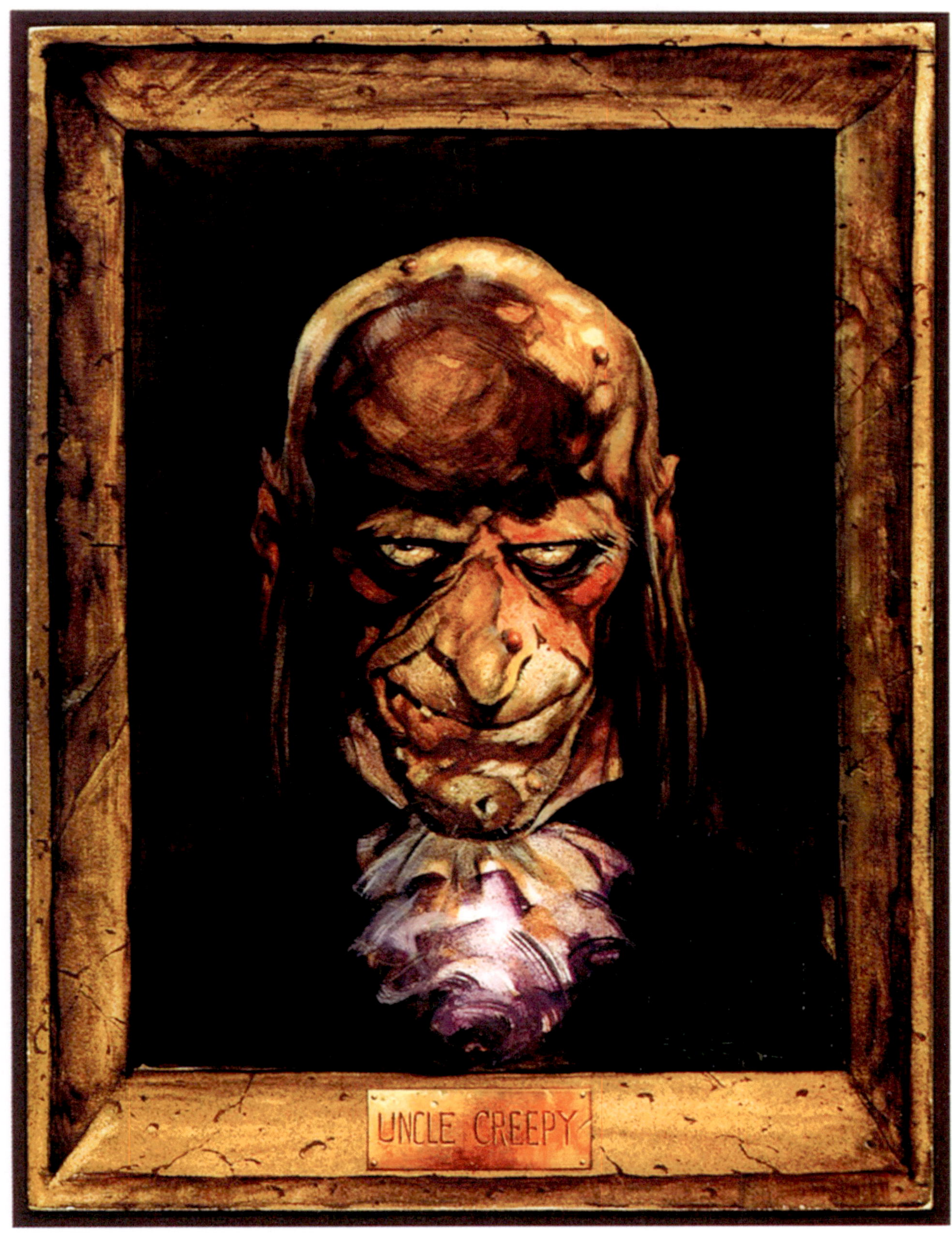

ABOVE: Uncle Creepy portrait
Warren Publishing Co. (1966)

Appendix A

An alphabetical listing of Frazetta's painted work.

Painting title	Year painted	Intended for	First published appearance
...			
3000 AD (unused)	1985	movie poster	Legacy
A			
A Fighting Man of Mars	1973	dust jacket	Mastermind of Mars / A Fighting Man of Mars
African Elephant, The (unused)	1971	movie poster	Frank Frazetta: Book Five
African Warrior			
see Masai Warrior			
After the Fox (A sheet design)	1966	movie poster	After the Fox
After the Fox (B sheet design)	1966	movie poster	After the Fox
Against the Gods	1967	paperback	Thongor Against the Gods
Alien Crucifixion	1972	magazine	National Lampoon June 1972
Alien Worlds	1968	paperback	Danger Planet
Amali Legend, The	1980	magazine	Animal Kingdom
Angel Hair		personal work	Testament
Apparition, The	1969	paperback	Brak vs. The Sorceress
A Princess of Mars	1970	dust jacket	A Princess of Mars
Archer, The			
see Indian With Bow			
A Requiem for Sharks	1973	promo item	Doubleday book club
A Requiem for Sharks (revised)	2001	art book	Legacy
Are There Fogs on the Moon?	1973	promo item	Doubleday book club pamphlet
Aros	1967	paperback	The Serpent
Arthur Rex	1978	magazine	Playboy
AKA - Playboy			
AKA - Castle of Sin			
Atlantis	1973	paperback	Atlantis Rising
At the Earth's Core	1972	paperback	At the Earth's Core
Autumn People	1965	paperback	The Autumn People
B			
Barbarian, The	1966	paperback	Conan the Adventurer
Battlefield Earth	1982	paperback	Battlefield Earth
AKA - Man, the Endangered Species			
Battlestar Galactica: Attack	1978	advertisement	TV Guide
AKA - Space 103 - Attack		art book	Frank Frazetta: Book Four
Battlestar Galactica: Darkness at Time's Edge	1978	advertisement	TV Guide
AKA - Darkness at Time's Edge			
Battlestar Galactica: Scramble	1978	advertisement	TV Guide
AKA - Space 104 - Scramble		art book	Frank Frazetta: Book Four
Battlestar Galactica: Pharoah's Tomb	1978	advertisement	TV Guide
AKA - Pharoah's Tomb			
Bear, The	1974	paperback	The Oakdale Affair
Beauty and the Beast	1995	calendar	Wizards of the Coast
Beasts of Tarzan	1964	paperback	The Beasts of Tarzan
Beasts of Venus	1963	paperback	Lost on Venus
AKA - Lost on Venus		art book	Legacy
Beauty and the Beast	1996	art book	Frank Frazetta: Book One
Berserker	1968	paperback	Conan the Conqueror
Better View	1996	portfolio	Golfing Nymphs

Painting title	Year painted	Intended for	First published appearance
Beyond the Farthest Star (1st version)	1964	paperback	Beyond the Farthest Star
AKA - **Beyond the Forest Star**			
Beyond the Farthest Star (2nd version)			
see **God from the Sky**			
Beyond the Grave	1966	comic book	Creepy #10
Birdman	1972	promo item	Doubleday Science Fiction Book Club
Black Emperor (1st version)	1973	paperback	Black Emperor
Black Emperor	1998	revision	Legacy
Black Panther	1973	paperback	Land of Hidden Men
Black Star	1973	paperback	The Black Star
Blecch ad			
see **Ringo Starr**			
Bloodstone	1975	paperback	Bloodstone
Brain, The	1967	comic book	Eerie #8
Bran Mak Morn	1969	paperback	Bran Mak Morn
Brak the Barbarian	1968	paperback	Brak the Barbarian
Brave, The	1973	promo item	Doubleday book club - Western Writers
Brooklyn Dreams (unused for Tower Books)	1962	paperback	Legacy
AKA - **Pinup**			
Bucking Bronco	1972	promo item	Doubleday book club - Western Writers
Busy Body, The	1967	movie poster	The Busy Body
By Dawn's Early Light	1963	personal work	Testament
C			
Captive Princess	1973	paperback	The People that Time Forgot
Carson of Venus (1st version)	1963	paperback	Carson of Venus
Carson of Venus (2nd version)	1973	paperback	Carson of Venus
Castle of Sin			
see **Arthur Rex**			
Cat Girl (1st version)	1967	comic book	Creepy #16
Cat Girl		revision	Frank Frazetta: Book Five
Catwalk	1994	art book	Retrospective
AKA - **The Moon's Rapture**			
Cave Demon, The	1978	paperback	Death Angel's Shadow
Chained	1967	paperback	Conan the Usurper
Charging Huns			
see **Huns**			
Circle of Terror	1965	comic book	Creepy #5
Combat	1965	comic book	Blazing Combat #1
Conan	1966	concept art	
Conan of Aquilonia	1973	paperback	Conan of Aquilonia (SPHERE BOOKS edition)
Cornered	1970	comic book	Vampirella #5
Count Dracula	1965	comic book	Creepy #5
Countess, The	1991	paperback	Mission Earth
Countess and the Green Man, The			Icon
Cowboy Sunset (unused)	1972	promo item	Doubleday book club - Western Writers
Creatures of the Night			
see **Frankenstein and Dracula**			
D			
Dancer from Atlantis, The (1st version)	1971	dust jacket	The Dancer from Atlantis
Dancer from Atlantis, The		revision	Testament
Dark Kingdom	1976	paperback	Dark Crusade
Darkness at Time's Edge			
see **Battlestar G.: Darkness at Time's Edge**			
Dave Winiewicz	1994	art book	Frank Frazetta: Book One
Dawn Attack	1991	paperback	L. Ron Hubbard - Writers of the Future Vol. 7
Day of Wrath	1996	comic book	Jaguar God #0
Dead of Night	1964	comic book	Creepy #3

Painting title	Year painted	Intended for	First published appearance
Death Dealer	1973	dust jacket	Flashing Swords 2
Death Dealer II	1987	paperback	Death Dealer: Prisoner of the Horned Helmet
Death Dealer III (1st version)	1987	paperback	Death Dealer: Lords of Destruction
Death Dealer III	1987	revision	Frank Frazetta: Book One
mis-titled "Death Dealer II (revised)"			
Death Dealer III	1987	rough	Testament
Death Dealer IV	1987	paperback	Death Dealer: Tooth and Claw
Death Dealer V	1989	paperback	Death Dealer: Plague of Knives
Death Dealer VI	1996	comic book	Death Dealer #2
Defender, The (unfinished Death Dealer)		art book	Frank Frazetta: Book five
Deina	1973	magazine	Elements vol. 1 #3 (Dow Chemicals)
Desperation (1st version)	1971	magazine	National Lampoon April 1971
Desperation (nude variant)		revision	Icon
Destroyer, The (1st version)	1971	paperback	Conan the Buccaneer
Destroyer, The (2nd version)	1974	revision	Testament
Destroyer, The (3rd version)	1977	revision	Frank Frazetta: Book Two
Devil Rider	1970	paperback	Ride the High Side
Devil Rider		revision	
Devil's Generation	1973	paperback	The Devil's Generation
Disagreement, The	1986	advertisement	Carlsberg Beer ad in Rolling Stone Magazine
Downward to Earth	1970	paperback	Downward to the Earth
Dracula Meets The Wolfman	1965	comic book	Creepy #7
Dream Flight	1987	paperback	L. Ron Hubbard's -Writers of the Future vol. 3
E			
Edgar R. Burroughs - Master of Adventure	1974	paperback	Edgar Rice Burroughs - Master of Adventure
Egyptian Queen	1969	comic book	Eerie #23
AKA - **Egyptian Princess**			
Eighth Wonder, The			
see King Kong and Snake			
Ellie Frazetta Portrait	1960	art book	Testament
Encounter, The	1989	paperback	L. Ron Hubbard's - Writers of the Future vol. 5
Escape on Venus	1973	paperback	Escape on Venus
Eternal Champion (1st version)	1970	paperback	Eternal Champion
Eternal Champion		revision	Legacy
Eve	1973	personal work	Frazetta #2
Executioner, The	1967	comic book	Creepy #17
F			
Familiars	1994	art book	Frazetta Pillow Book
Family Portrait			
see Yours, Mine, and Ours			
Fantasy World	1972	promo item	Doubleday book club -"*Limitless horizons of SF.*"
Fastest Guitar Alive, The (detail)	1968	movie poster	The Fastest Guitar Alive
Fastest Guitar Alive, The (full image)	1968	art book	Frank Frazetta: Book Three
Fearless Vampire Killers, The	1967	movie poster	The Fearless Vampire Killers
Fire & Ice	1982	movie poster	Fire & Ice
Fire Demon	1977	paperback	Swords against Darkness
Fitzwilly	1969	movie poster	Fitzwilly
Flash for Freedom	1973	paperback	Flash for Freedom
Flashman on the Charge (1st version)	1974	paperback	Flashman at the Charge
Flashman on the Charge		revision	Frank Frazetta: Book Three
Flesh Eaters	1979	paperback	The Flesh Eaters
Flying Alligator	1983	promo item	brochure for South Carolina amusement park ride
Flying Galleon	1974	paperback	Into the Aether
Flying Reptiles	1973	paperback	Pellucidar
Frankenstein and Dracula	1973	dust jacket	Dracula - Frankenstein
AKA - **Creatures of the Night**		art book	Icon
Frogs on the Moon?	1973	promo item	Doubleday book club envelope
From Dusk Till Dawn (unused)	1996	movie poster	Frank Frazetta: Book One

Painting title	Year painted	Intended for	First published appearance
G			
Galleon, The	1974	paperback	Into the Aether
Galleon, The	1974	rough	Testament
Gargoyle	1965	comic book	Creepy #6
Gauntlet, The	1977	movie poster	The Gauntlet
Geisha	1983	art book	Frank Frazetta: Book One
Ghoul Queen	1973	magazine	National Lampoon - August 1973
Girl Bathing	1962	personal work	Frank Frazetta: Book Three
Girl on the River	1981	movie concept	Frank Frazetta: Book Five
God from the Sky	1973	paperback	Beyond the Farthest Star
AKA - **Beyond the Farthest Star** (1st version)			
Godmakers, The	1970	paperback	The Godmakers
Golden Girl	1977	personal work	Frank Frazetta: Book Two
Gollum	1975	personal work	Testament
Great Form	1996	portfolio	Golfing Nymphs
Green Death	1968	paperback	Wolfshead
Gulliver of Mars	1964	paperback	Gulliver of Mars
H			
Handicap	1996	portfolio	Golfing Nymphs
Headless Horseman I	1996	personal work	Frank Frazetta: Book One
Headless Horseman II	1996	personal work	Frank Frazetta: Book One
Herman's Hermits	1966	record album	Both Sides of Herman's Hermits
Hotel Paradiso	1966	movie poster	Hotel Paradiso
Huns (unused) (intended for Son of Conan)	1985	paperback	Frank Frazetta: Book Five
AKA - **Charging Huns**			
Huntress, The	1964	paperback	Savage Pellucidar
I			
Indian Brave	1973	promo item	Doubleday book club - *"Summer of the Drums"*
Indian with Bow	1978	personal work	Frank Frazetta: Book Three
AKA - **The Archer**		personal work	Retrospective
Indomitable	1967	paperback	Conan the Warrior
Invaders	1977	paperback	Time War
Iron Thorn	1967	paperback	The Amsirs and the Iron Thorn
J			
Jaguar God I	1995	comic book	Jaguar God #1
Jaguar God II	1995	comic book	Jaguar God #2
Jonathan Winters	1964	record album	Movies are Better Than Ever
John Carter and the Savage Apes of Mars	1971	dust jacket	The Gods of Mars / Warlord of Mars
Jongor Fights Back	1966	paperback	Jongor Fights Back
Judge Dredd with Alfred E. Neuman	1995	comic book	Mad Magazine #338
Jungle Tales of Tarzan	1963	paperback	Jungle Tales of Tarzan
K			
Kane on the Golden Sea	1978	paperback	Darkness Weaves
Kavin's World	1969	paperback	Kavin's World
King Kong (1st version)	1966	comic book	Creepy #11
King Kong (2nd version)	1976	paperback	King Kong
King Kong and Snake	1976	paperback	King Kong movie transcript
AKA - **The Eighth Wonder**			
King of Kings	1986	personal work	Testament
L			
La of Opar	1969	personal work	Frazetta #1
AKA - **Primitive Beauty**		personal work	Icon
Land of Terror (1st version)	1964	paperback	Out of Time's Abyss
Land of Terror (2nd version)			

Painting title	Year painted	Intended for	First published appearance
Land of Terror (3rd version)			
see **Monster out of Time**			
Las Vegas	1980	personal work	Frank Frazetta: Book Four
Leaping Lizards	1989	paperback	L. Ron Hubbard - Writers of the Future vol. 6
Lieutenant, The	1989	paperback	Final Blackout
Lost City	1964	personal work	Legacy
Lost Continent, The	1963	paperback	The Lost Continent
Lost Empire, The	1962	paperback	Tarzan and the Lost Empire
Lost on Venus			
see **Beasts of Venus**			
Luana (A Sheet design)	1973	movie poster	Luana
Luana (B Sheet design)	1973	movie poster	Luana
Luana (Teaser card design)	1973	teaser card	Luana
M			
Madame Derringer	1974	promo item	Doubleday book club - The Legend of Baby Doe
Mad King, The (1st version)	1964	paperback	The Mad King
Mad King, The (2nd version)	1973	paperback	The Mad King
Mammoth, The	1973	paperback	Back to the Stone Age
Man-Ape	1967	paperback	Conan
Man, The Endangered Species			
see **Battlefield Earth**			
Man Impaled by Sculpture			
see **Torment**			
Masai Warrior		personal work	Legacy
AKA - **African Warrior**			
Master of Adventure			
see **Beasts of Tarzan**			
Mastodon	1968	paperback	The Creature from Beyond Infinity
Maza of the Moon	1965		paperback Maza of the Moon
Mixed Company	1974	movie poster	Mixed Company
Mongol Tyrant	1969	comic book	Creepy #27
Mongol Tyrant		revision	Testament
Monster out of Time	1973	paperback	Land of Terror
AKA - **Land of Terror**			
Moon Maid, The (1st version)	1973	paperback	The Moon Maid
Moon Maid, The		revision	Fantastic Art of Frank Frazetta, Vol. 1
Moon Men, The	1974	paperback	The Moon Men
Moon Rider	1988	paperback	L. Ron Hubbard's -Writers of the Future vol. 4
Moon's Rapture, The			
see **Catwalk**			
Mothman	1980	magazine	High Times #57
Mrs. Pollifax, Spy	1971	movie poster	Mrs. Pollifax, Spy
Mucker, The	1974	paperback	The Mucker
Muse, The	1978	personal work	Testament
N			
Neanderthal	1967	comic book	Creepy #15
New World	1972	dust jacket	The 1972 Annual World's Best SF
Nightstalker	1970	comic book	Creepy #32
Night They Raided Minsky's, The (censored)	1968	movie poster	The Night They Raided Minsky's
Night They Raided Minsky's, The (uncensored)	1968		Frank Frazetta: Book Three
Night Winds	1967	paperback	Night Winds
Norseman, The	1973	dust jacket	Flashing Swords #1
Nude	1964	personal work	
Nude in Pond		personal work	Frank Frazetta: Book Three
AKA - **Silent Breeze**			Retrospective
O			
Outlaw of Torn	1973	paperback	The Outlaw of Torn

Painting title	Year painted	Intended for	First published appearance
Orca, Killer Whale (unused)	1977	movie poster	Frazetta: Book Five
P			
Paradox	1975	paperback	Book of Paradox
Patty Duke (unused)	1965	movie poster	currently unpublished
Phantom, The	1996	chase card	The Phantom - card set
Pharoah's Tomb			
see **Battlestar Galactica: Pharoah's Tomb**			
Pinup			
see **Brooklyn Dreams**			
Playboy			
see **Arthur Rex**			
Pony Tail	1970	paperback	The Tritonian Ring
Predators		personal work	Frazetta #2 (fanzine)
Primitive Beauty			
see **La of Opar**			
Prince of Darkness (unused)	1975	movie poster	Testament
Princess and the Panther (1st version)	1990	comic book	Heavy Metal
Princess and the Panther		revision	Icon
Q			
Queen Kong	1976	comic book	Eerie #81
R			
Reassembled Man	1964	paperback	Reassembled Man
Red Moon, Black Mountain	1983	dust jacket	Red Moon, Black Mountain
Return of Jongor, The	1970	paperback	The Return of Jongor
Return of the Mucker	1974	paperback	The Return of the Mucker
Rider, The	1974	paperback	The Rider
Ringo Starr	1964	comic book	Mad Magazine
Roger Miller	1967	record album	Waterhole #3
Roman Chariot	1972	paperback	Child of the Sun
Rogue Roman	1965	paperback	Rogue Roman
Russ Cochran	1985	personal work	Testament
S			
Sacrifice (1st version)	1968	paperback	Conan the Avenger
Sacrifice		revision	Frank Frazetta: Book Four
Salome (unused for "Salome's Last Dance")	1987	movie poster	Testament
Savage Pellucidar	1973	paperback	Savage Pellucidar
Savage World			
see **Young World**			
Sea Monster (1st version)	1966	comic book	Eerie #3
Sea Monster		revision	Fantastic Art of Frank Frazetta, Vol. 1
Sea Witch	1967	comic book	Eerie #7
Secret of My Success, The	1965	movie poster	The Secret of My Success
Secret People, The	1964	paperback	The Secret People
Self Portrait	1962	personal work	Frazetta #1
Serpent	1973	paperback	Ardor on Argos
Seven Romans	1980	comic book	Epic Illustrated #1
Shi	1995	comic book	Shi - Senryaku Collection
Silent Breeze			
see **Nude in Pond**			
Silver Warrior	1974	paperback	The Silver Warriors
Snake Bit (unused for Doubleday Book Club)	1972	promo item	The Frazetta Treasury (fanzine)
Snow Giants	1967	paperback	Conan of Cimmeria
Solar Invasion	1968	paperback	The Solar Invasion
Son of Tarzan, The	1962	paperback	The Son of Tarzan
Sorcerer, The	1966	comic book	Eerie #2

Painting title	Year painted	Intended for	First published appearance
Sorceress, The	1995	comic book	Verotika #3
Sound		advertisement	
Sound	1979	rough	Testament
Space 103 - Attack see Battlestar Galactica: Attack			
Space 104 - Scramble see Battlestar Galactica: Scramble			
Spiderman	1967	paperback	Nightwalk
Spirit of the Forest	1949	personal work	Testament
Stranded see Tomorrow Midnight			
Strange Creatures	1970	paperback	Strange Creatures from Time and Space
Sun Goddess	1970	magazine	Vampirella #7
Sunset (unused)	1972	promo item	Doubleday book club - Western Writers
Svengali	1980	letterhead	Frank Frazetta: The Living Legend
Swamp Demon (1st version)	1972	paperback	Witch of the Dark Gate
Swamp Demon		revision	Frank Frazetta: Book Five
Swamp God	1966	comic book	Creepy #5
Swordsmen in the Sky	1963	paperback	Swordsmen in the Sky
Swords of Mars	1966	dust jacket	Swords of Mars / Synthetic Men of Mars
T			
Tales from the Crypt	1965	paperback	Tales From the Crypt
Tanar of Pellucidar	1973	paperback	Tanar of Pellucidar
Tarzan and the Ant Men	1973	fan publication	Burroughs Bulletin #29
Tarzan and the City of Gold	1963	paperback	Tarzan and the City of Gold
Tarzan and the Jewels of Opar	1963	paperback	Tarzan and the Jewels of Opar
Tarzan and the Lion Man	1963	paperback	Tarzan and the Lion Men
Tarzan at the Earth's Core	1963	paperback	Tarzan at the Earth's Core
Tarzan the Invincible	1963	paperback	Tarzan the Invincible
Temptation	1987	personal work	The Rare Frazetta (poor reproduction)
Tempters, The	1951	personal work	
Terror in the Mist	1959	personal work	
Thor's Flight	1968	paperback	Thongor in the City of Magicians
Thuvia, Maid of Mars	1972	dust jacket	Thuvia, Maid of Mars / Chessmen of Mars
Torment AKA - **Man Impaled by Sculpture**	1975	promo item	Doubleday book club Mystery Guild
Torture Garden	1965	paperback	Torture Garden
To Catch a Crooked Girl	1964	paperback	To Catch a Crooked Girl
Tomorrow Midnight AKA - **Stranded**	1966	paperback	Tomorrow Midnight
Tree of Death	1973	dust jacket	Flashing Swords #2
Trial of Judas Wiley, The	1972	promo item	Doubleday book club - Western Writers
Tyrannosaurus Rex	1970	dust jacket	Orn
U			
Uncle Creepy	1964	promo item	Creepy Fan Club
V			
Vampirella (1st version)	1969	comic book	Vampirella
Vampirella (nude)		revision	Icon
Vampirella 1996	1996	comic book	Vampirella 25th Anniversary Special
Victorious		personal work	Legacy
W			
Warrior		personal work	Icon
Warrior With Ball and Chain	1973	dust jacket	Flashing Swords #2
What's New Pussycat? (A Sheet design)	1965	movie poster	What's New Pussycat?
What's New Pussycat? (B Sheet design)	1965	movie poster	What's New Pussycat?
White Gorillas	1966	paperback	Outlaw World

Painting title	Year painted	Intended for	First published appearance
Wild Ride (gift for Ellie Frazetta)	1989	personal work	Frank Frazetta: Book One
Wild Ride (preliminary)	1989	rough	Testament
Winged Terror	1966	comic book	Creepy #9
Winter of the Coup	1973	promo item	Doubleday book club - Western Writers
Withering (1st version)	1979	paperback	Withering
Withering (2nd version)		revision	Testament
Wolfman	1965	comic book	Creepy #4
Wolf Moon	1966	paperback	Phoenix Prime
Wolf Pack	1968	paperback	Atlan
Wolves Night	1996	art book	Frank Frazetta: Book One
Woman With a Scythe	1970	comic book	Vampirella #11
Y			
Young World AKA - **Savage World**	1969	magazine	Monster Mania #2
Yours, Mine and Ours AKA - **Family Portrait**	1968	movie poster	Yours, mine and Ours

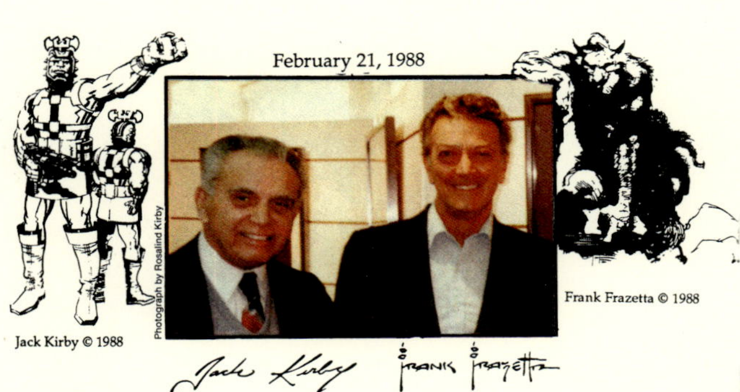

Jack Kirby © 1988

Frank Frazetta © 1988

The Meeting Of The Masters

By Michael Thibodeaux

As incredible as it may seem, after 40 years in the same field, Frank Frazetta and Jack Kirby had never made each other's acquaintance. November 14, 1987 will forever be a Red Letter Day in my calender because, at the L. Ron Hubbard Gallery in Hollywood, California, it happened: The Meeting Of The Masters, Frazetta and Kirby. The occasion: An awards presentation to Frank Frazetta in appreciation for his outstanding contributions to the Commercial Arts Field.

Frank Frazetta has won international recognition for the unique vitality of his paintings and black and white illustrations.

Frank Frazetta was born February 9, 1928. His formal training consisted of eight years at the Brooklyn Academy of Fine Arts. He continued to draw and paint for an enormous number of comics of all kinds, many of his own origination, as well as popular strips as "Li'l Abner, Buck Rogers Series, Playboy's "Li'l Annie Fannie", and Edger Rice Burroughs, "Tarzan".

Jack Kirby was born August 28, 1917 in the Lower Eastside of New York City. His training is from the school of Hard Knocks. He learned from anyone who had something to offer. Jack Kirby is best known as "The King Of Comics". Jack is Co-creator of almost every major character for Marvel Comics including Thor, The Fantastic Four, The Hulk, The Avengers, The X-Men, Captain America and that is literally just naming a few.

In the late afternoon I picked up Jack and Rosalind Kirby to escort them to this special event. As the final remnants of daylight diminished, we turned off the Hollywood Freeway onto Highland Avenue when it dawned on me how important this night was. I was actually going to meet the man, who in my opinion, is the BEST Fantasy, Sword and Sorcery Artist to ever grace this earth. How ironic it was that Jack Kirby was my connection in meeting the legendary Frank Frazetta.

The line crept slowly into the Gallery. Jack introduced himself to the doorman and we were quickly escorted up to the fourth floor. We were instant V.I.P.'s!

There were Movie Stars and other famous people roaming around, but the only one of any real importance to me was Frank Frazetta. It was like I was about to meet a second God (Jack being my first, of course).

28

Rosalind Kirby and I were talking to Mrs Simone Welch (a press agent for Author Services who was instrumental in bringing these two together).

I asked, "Where is Mr. Frazetta?"

Mrs Welch said, "See that crowd over by the piano?"

I replied with a depressing "Yes!"

She smiled and said, "He's in the middle of it".

Jack saw the agonizing expression on my face and said, "Don't worry Mike, We'll get to him eventually".

I shrugged my shoulders, "I'm sure there will be a crowd around him all night".

Jack took a second glance at me, grabbed my arm and said, "Let's go meet him before you die of anticipation!"

Jack and I had trouble getting through the crowd. Jack then told the hostess that he'd like to talk to Frank.

She delivered the message by saying, "Frank, a Mr. Kirby would like to speak with you", It was like the parting of the Red Sea. I will never forget that moment. The chills overwhelmed my body as I saw these two incredible giants clasp each others hands for the first time.

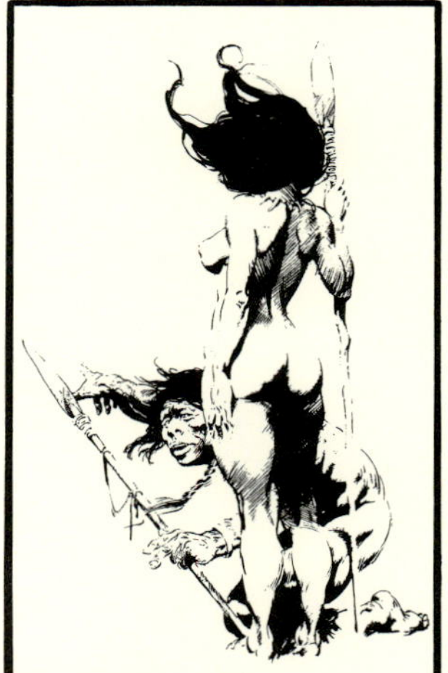

Frank Frazetta © 1988

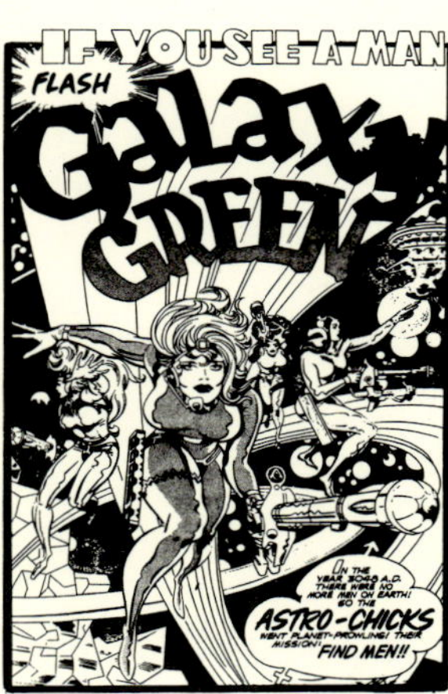

Jack Kirby © 1988

The first words spoken were from Frank saying,"Jack, it is an honor to meet you."

Jack came back with "The honor is mine Frank, I've always admired your work and am glad I finally had the opportunity to meet you".

"If you recall Jack, we did meet once before."

"Forgive me Frank, I don't remember!!"

"I didn't think you would, it was back in 1946 or possibly 1947 on the Brighton Beach Subway, I remember it quite clearly. We were coming out of Brooklyn near New Kirk Ave. I noticed you had a portfolio with Comic pages. Before I knew it, we were talking to one another. I also vaguely remember seeing original Artwork from Captain America".

Jack replied, "Are you sure it was me?"

"You were the short one, weren't you?" (Meaning the team of Joe Simon and Jack Kirby - Joe was a tall individual).

Jack abruptly stated, "With a Giant like Joe around, of course I was the shorter one!"

Although Jack could not recall this incident, both were able to establish they routinely took that train.

As their conversation continued, Frank said, "Jack, you are truly an inspiration to me".

29

ABOVE: LAST OF THE VIKING HEROES *Summer Special #1*
(Genisis West Comics May, 1988)

Appendix B

A chronological listing of Frazetta's comic book career

DATE	PUBLICATION
1944	
December 1944	Tally Ho
1946	
June-July 1946	Treasure Comics #7
Aug-Sept 1946	Treasure Comics #8
1947	
June 1947	Barnyard Comics #12 Goofy Comics #20
July 1947	Coo Coo Comics #34 Happy Comics #20
August 1947	Barnyard Comics #13 Goofy Comics #21
Aug-Sept 1947	Prize Comics #65
September 1947	Coo Coo Comics #35 Happy Comics #21
October 1947	Barnyard Comics #14 Goofy Comics #22
Oct-Nov 1947	Prize Comics #66
November 1947	Coo Coo Comics #36 Happy Comics #22
December 1947	Barnyard Comics #15 Goofy Comics #23
1948	
January 1948	Coo Coo Comics #37 Exciting Comics #59 Happy Comics #23
February 1948	Barnyard Comics #16 Goofy Comics #24
March 1948	Coo Coo Comics #38 Happy Comics #24 Monkeyshines Comics #19
April 1948	Barnyard Comics #17 Black Terror #22 Goofy Comics #25 Wonder Comics #17
May 1948	America's Best Comics #26 Coo Coo Comics #39 Happy Comics #25
June 1948	Barnyard Comics #18 Goofy Comics #26 Thrilling Comics #66
July 1948	Coo Coo Comics #40 Happy Comics #26
August 1948	Barnyard Comics #19 Goofy Comics #27 Manhunt #11 Thrilling Comics #67 Wonder Comics #19
September 1948	Coo Coo Comics #41 Happy Comics #27
October 1948	Barnyard Comics #20 Black Terror #24 Goofy Comics #28 Thrilling Comics #68 Wonder Comics #20
November 1948	Coo Coo Comics #42 Happy Comics #28
December 1948	Barnyard Comics #21 Goofy Comics #29 Thrilling Comics #69
Winter 1948-49	Circus Comics #1
1949	
1949	A-1 Comics #24
January 1949	Coo Coo Comics #43 Happy Comics #29
February 1949	Barnyard Comics #22 Goofy Comics #30 Thrilling Comics #70
March 1949	Coo Coo Comics #44 Happy Comics #30
April 1949	Barnyard Comics #23 Goofy Comics #31 Spunky #1 Thrilling Comics #71
May 1949	Coo Coo Comics #45 Happy Comics #31 Spunky #2

DATE	PUBLICATION
June 1949	Barnyard Comics #24 Goofy Comics #32 Thrilling Comics #72
June-July 1949	Outlaws #9
July 1949	Coo Coo Comics #46 Happy Comics #32
August 1949	Barnyard Comics #25 Goofy Comics #33 Thrilling Comics #73
Fall 1949	Joe College #1
September 1949	Boots and her Buddies #9 Coo Coo Comics #47 Happy Comics #33
October 1949	Barnyard Comics #26 Goofy Comics #34 Real Life Comics #50 Western Fighters #11
Oct-Nov 1949	Durango Kid #1
November 1949	Buster Bunny #1 Coo Coo Comics #48 Happy Comics #34 Sniffy the Pup #5
December 1949	Buster Bunny #2 Goofy Comics #35 Supermouse #1
Dec-Jan 1950	All Star Comics #50 Durango Kid #2

1950

DATE	PUBLICATION
1950	A-1 Comics #29
January 1950	Coo Coo Comics #49 Happy Comics #35 Jimmy Wakely #3 Leroy #2 Li'l Abner and the creatures From Drop Outer Space
February 1950	Supermouse #2
Spring 1950	John Wayne Adventure. Comics #2
Feb-Mar 1950	Durango Kid #3 Gang Busters #14
March 1950	Adventure Comics #150 Coo Coo Comics #50 Happy Comics #36 Jimmy Wakely #4 Western Hearts #2
April 1950	Adventure Comics #151 Barnyard Comics #29 Real Life Comics #52 Supermouse #3
Apr-May 1950	Durango Kid #4
May 1950	Happy Comics #37 Tim Holt #17
June 1950	Adventure Comics #153 Supermouse #4
Summer 1950	John Wayne Adventure. Comics #3
June-July 1950	Durango Kid #5 Romantic Confessions V.2 #9 Straight Arrow #3
July 1950	Jimmy Wakely #6
July-Aug 1950	Weird Fantasy #14
August 1950	Adventure Comics #155 Supermouse #5
Aug-Sept 1950	Durango Kid #6 Gang Busters #17
Fall 1950	John Wayne Adventure. Comics #4
September 1950	Jimmy Wakely #7
October 1950	Adventure Comics #157 Supermouse #6
Oct-Nov 1950	Durango Kid #7
Nov-Dec 1950	Tomahawk #2
December 1950	Adventure Comics #159
Dec-Jan 1951	Durango Kid #8

1951

DATE	PUBLICATION
1951	A-1 Comics #31 A-1 Comics #37 Chief Victorio's Apache Massacre
January 1951	Tim Holt #21
Jan-Feb 1951	Bobby Benson's B-bar-B #9
February 1951	Adventure Comics #161 Billy the Kid Adventure. Mag #3 Goofy Comics #42 Star Spangled Comics #113
Spring 1951	John Wayne Adventure. Comics #6
Feb-Mar 1951	Durango Kid #9
March 1951	Heroic Comics #65
April 1951	Adventure Comics #163 Movie Love #8
Apr-May 1951	Durango Kid #10 Mystery in Space #1
May 1951	Heroic Comics #66 Strange Worlds #3 Tim Holt #23

DATE	PUBLICATION
May-June 1951	Bobby Benson's B-bar-B #11
Summer 1951	John Wayne Adventure. Comics #7
June-July 1951	Durango Kid #11
July 1951	Heroic Comics #67
July-Aug 1951	Forbidden Worlds #1
August 1951	Billy the Kid Adventure. Mag #6 Movie Love #10
Aug-Sept 1951	Durango Kid #12
Fall 1951	John Wayne Adventure. Comics #8
Sept-Oct 1951	Bobby Benson's B-bar-B #13
Oct-Nov 1951	Durango Kid #13
November 1951	Buster Crabbe #1 Heroic Comics #67 Personal Love #12
Nov-Dec 1951	Forbidden Worlds #3
Dec-Jan 1952	Durango Kid #14

1952

DATE	PUBLICATION
1952	A-1 Comics #47
January 1952	Heroic Comics #70
February 1952	Straight Arrow #22
Feb-Mar 1952	Durango Kid #15
March 1952	Heroic Comics #71
Apr-May 1952	Durango Kid #16
May 1952	Buster Crabbe #4 Heroic Comics #72
July 1952	Buster Crabbe #5 Heroic Comics #73 Personal Love #16
August 1952	Real Clue Crime Stories Vol.7 #6
September 1952	Heroic Comics #75 Personal Love #17 Real Life Comics #59
October 1952	Movie Love #17

1953

DATE	PUBLICATION
1953	Danger is our Business #1 Famous Funnies #198
Spring 1953 #18	John Wayne Adventure. Comics
March 1953	Heroic Comics #81
May 1953	Heroic Comics #83
May-June 1953	Weird Science #19
June 1953	Lovers' Lane #20
June-July 1953	Crime Suspenstories #17
July-Aug 1953	Weird Fantasy #20 Weird Science #20
August 1953	Heroic Comics #86
September 1953	Heroic Comics #87
Sept-Oct 1953	Weird Fantasy #21 Weird Science #21
November 1953	Personal Love #24
Nov-Dec 1953	Weird Science #22
December 1953	Famous Funnies #209

1954

DATE	PUBLICATION
January 1954	Personal Love #24
February 1954	Famous Funnies #210
March 1954	Shock Suspenstories #13
April 1954	Famous Funnies #211 Masked Ranger #1
June 1954	Famous Funnies #212 Personal Love #27
July 1954	Beware #10
August 1954	Famous Funnies #213 Personal Love #28
October 1954	Famous Funnies #214
December 1954	Famous Funnies #215
	Heroic Comics #94

1955

DATE	PUBLICATION
February 1955	Famous Funnies #216
April 1955	Personal Love #32
May-June 1955	Weird Science Fantasy #29

AND BEYOND

DATE	PUBLICATION
Mar-May 1961	The Twilight Zone #1
Feb-Apr 1962	The Frogmen #1
May-July 1962	The Frogmen #2
September 1962	The Frogmen #3

DATE	PUBLICATION
1964	Creepy #1
1965	Creepy #2 Creepy #3 Creepy #4
October 1965	Blazing Combat #1 Creepy #5
December 1965	Creepy #6
January 1966	Blazing Combat #2
February 1966	Creepy #7
March 1966	Eerie #2
April 1966	Blazing Combat #3
May 1966	Eerie #3
June 1966	Creepy #9
July 1966	Blazing Combat #4 Eerie #4
August 1966	Creepy #10
September 1966	Eerie #5
October 1966	Creepy #11
January 1967	Eerie #7
March 1967	Eerie #8
June 1967	Creepy #15
August 1967	Creepy #16
October 1967	Creepy #17
September 1969	Eerie #23 Vampirella #1
January 1970	Vampirella #5
March 1970	Vampirella #7
April 1970	Creepy #32
June 1970	Vampirella #11
Spring 1980	Epic Illustrated #1
Summer 1988	Last of the Viking Heroes
Nov-Dec 1994	Penthouse Comix #4
1995	Shi - Senryaku Collected Ed.
March 1995	Jaguar God #1 Satanika #0
May 1995	Verotika #3
October 1995	Jaguar God #2

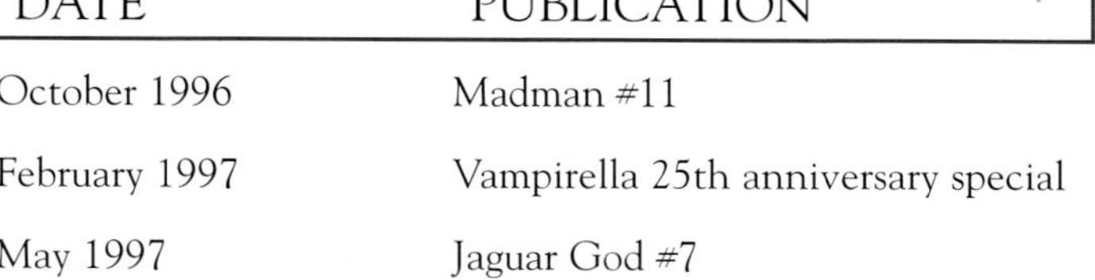

DATE	PUBLICATION
October 1996	Madman #11
February 1997	Vampirella 25th anniversary special
May 1997	Jaguar God #7

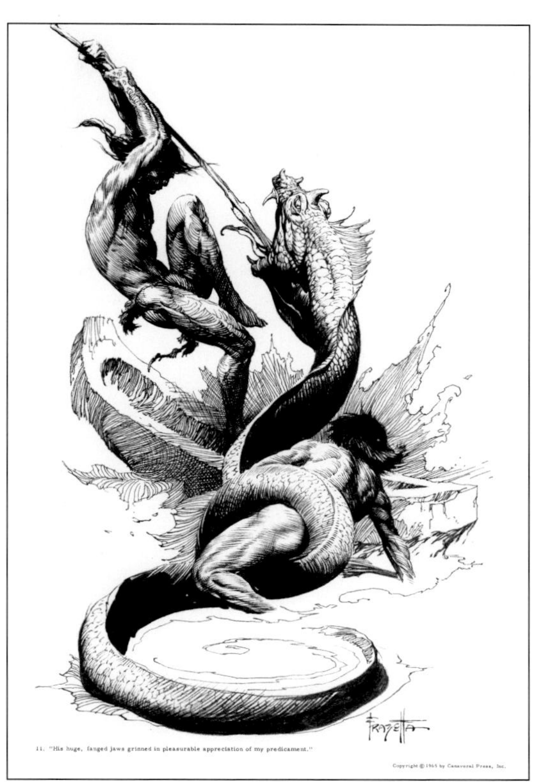

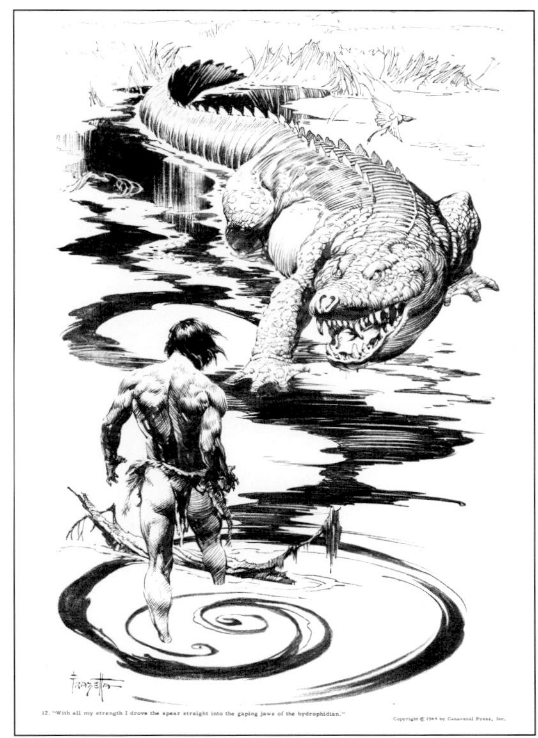

Plates from the Burroughs Artist Portfolio
Opar Press (1973)

Acknowledgements

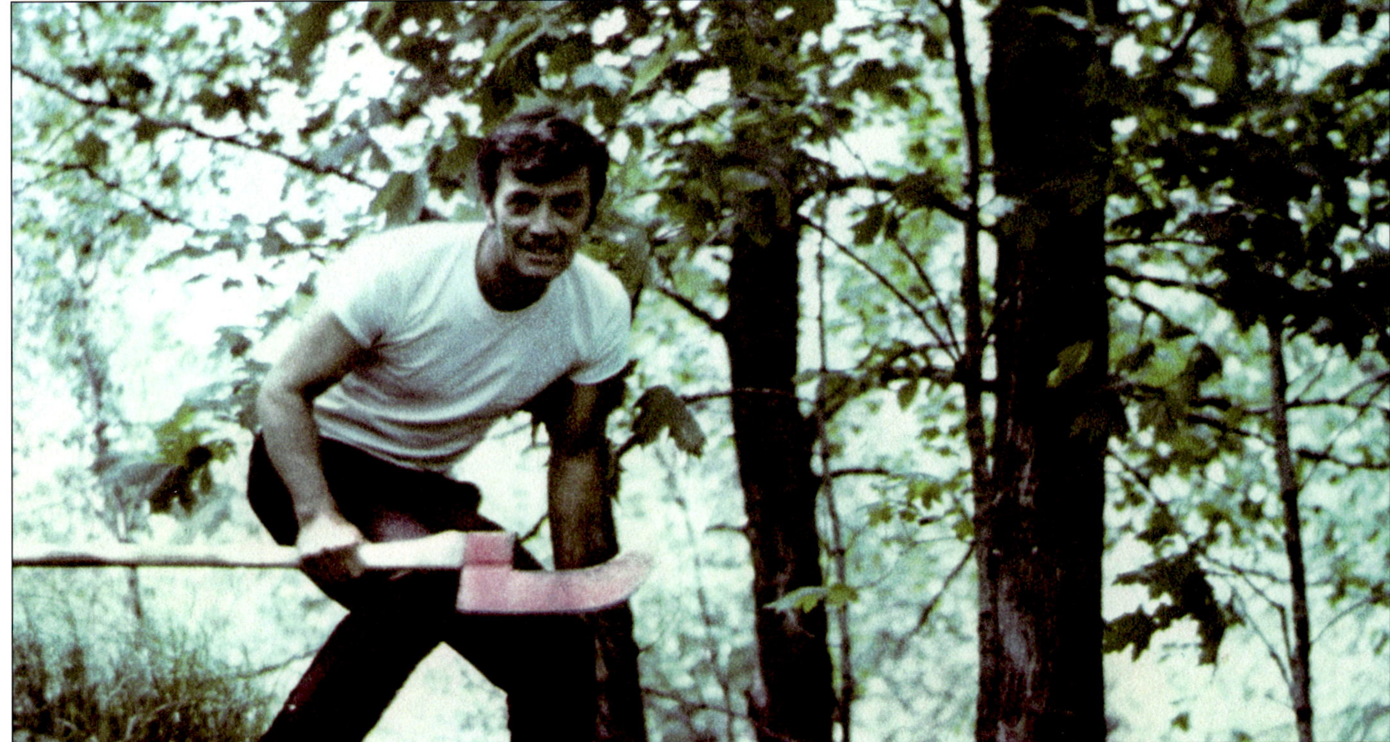

Photo from Frazetta-Fairfax promotional material.

This was a project that at first, was thought by many, for numerous reasons, would never be accomplished. That was a lifetime ago, and looking back on this, I'm glad I wasn't alone in its creation.

A project this size would never have been completed by just one person. My name is on the cover only because of playing semi-conductor to a grand symphony of very talented and altruistic individuals, and so I'd like to express my most sincere thanks to the following:

First and foremost, the Frazetta family. The respect I hold for you all will hopefully show in the contents of this book. It is, and has always been, a labor of love. And I'm sure I speak for all of us when I say thank you for all you've done.

To Dave Winiewicz. His sheer knowledge of Frank Frazetta stems from his respect for the artist, his personal insight comes from their lifelong friendship. Dave seems always eager to speak volumes of kindness based on both his knowledge and insight. His input to this volume is invaluable.

Andrew Steven is that rare breed of Frazetta collector who seems to collect not for himself, but for the benefit of others. His collection is immense, outshone only by his knowledge, his kindness and his altruistic nature. His enduring friendship has helped to keep this project going, even after some of us wanted to walk away.

A big thanks to J. David Spurlock at Vanguard for publishing the book and also to Dean Motter for his countless hours of hard work as book designer and fixer of many things.

And of course, there are those who tossed me a bone, sometimes out of generosity, oftentimes out of sheer pity.

Dan Busha,
James Collins,
Michael Goldman,
John Hopkins,
Kristen Perry,
Paul D. Shiple,
Wes "*Where's my name?*" Tillander

I know, I've failed to mention so many who've been there to share support, stories and precious information. These are the fans, the dealers and the professionals nationwide. You guys need to know that without your constant enthusiasm, this book never would have had the motivation to continue (let alone conclude.) Thank you all, so much.

— *James A. Bond*